CONTRIBUTORS

BARBARA HULTS, the author of a travel guidebook to Italy, has studied Italian civilization in Rome and has contributed articles to *Art & Antiques* and other magazines. She has also written *Balloon,* a newsletter for travel fanatics. She travels in Italy two months a year.

DWIGHT V. GAST has divided his time between New York and Italy since 1979. He studied art history in Florence and frequently worked in Rome as an editor at *Italy Italy* magazine. He contributes articles on travel and the arts in Italy to *Art in America, Travel & Leisure,* and other books and magazines.

JOANNE HAHN has lived and studied in Italy and returns there regularly. A contributor to several magazines, she is coauthor of a travel guidebook to Italy.

PAOLO LANAPOPPI was born in Italy, studied in Venice and Padua, and currently lives in Venice. He frequently contributes articles to *Travel & Leisure* and other major magazines. For 12 years he was professor of Italian literature and civilization at Cornell, Vassar, and other universities in the United States.

PETER TODD MITCHELL studied Italian art and architecture at Yale University and lived in Florence, Venice, and Rome before becoming a contributing editor at *Gourmet* magazine. He died in Spain as this book was being prepared for press; he will be missed.

ANNE MARSHALL ZWACK, raised in Cambridge, England, and educated in Belgium, divides her time between Florence and Austria. She writes for many publications, among them *Gourmet* magazine and the travel section of *The New York Times*.

D0913392

THE PENGUIN TRAVEL GUIDES

AUSTRALIA

CANADA

THE CARIBBEAN

ENGLAND & WALES

FRANCE

IRELAND

ITALY

NEW YORK CITY

THE PENGUIN GUIDE TO ITALY 1989

ALAN TUCKER
General Editor

PENGUIN BOOKS

PENGUIN BOOKS

Published by the Penguin Group
Viking Penguin Inc., 40 West 23rd Street,
New York, New York 10010, U.S.A.
Penguin Books Ltd, 27 Wright's Lane,
London W8 5TZ, England
Penguin Books Australia Ltd,
Ringwood, Victoria, Australia
Penguin Books Canada Ltd, 2801 John Street,
Markham, Ontario, Canada L3R 1B4
Penguin Books (N.Z.) Ltd, 182-190 Wairau Road,
Auckland 10, New Zealand

Penguin Books Ltd, Registered Offices:
Harmondsworth, Middlesex, England

First published in Penguin Books 1989
Published simultaneously in Canada

1 3 5 7 9 10 8 6 4 2

Copyright © Viking Penguin Inc., 1989
All rights reserved

ISBN 0 14 019.903 9
ISSN 0897-6848

Printed in the United States of America by
R. R. Donnelley & Sons Company,
Harrisonburg, Virginia

Set in ITC Garamond Light
Designed by Beth Tondreau Design
Maps by Nina Wallace
Illustrations by Bill Russell
Editorial Services by Stephen Brewer Associates

THIS GUIDEBOOK

The Penguin Travel Guides are designed for people who are experienced travellers in search of exceptional information that will help them sharpen and deepen their enjoyment of the trips they take.

Where, for example, are the interesting, isolated, fun, charming, or romantic places within your budget to stay? The hotels described by our writers (each of whom is an experienced travel writer who either lives in or regularly tours the city or region of Italy he or she covers) are some of the special places, in all price ranges except for the lowest—not the run-of-the-mill, heavily marketed places on every travel agent's CRT display and in advertised airline and travel-agency packages. We indicate the approximate price level of each accommodation in our descriptions of it (no indication means it is moderate), and at the end of every chapter we supply contact information so that you can get precise, up-to-the-minute rates and make reservations.

The Penguin Guide to Italy 1989 highlights the more rewarding parts of the country so that you can quickly and efficiently home in on a good itinerary.

Of course, the guides do far more than just help you choose a hotel and plan your trip. *The Penguin Guide to Italy 1989* is designed for use *in* Italy. Our Penguin Italy writers tell you what you really need to know, what you can't find out so easily on your own. They identify and describe the truly out-of-the-ordinary restaurants, shops, activities, and sights, and tell you the best way to "do" your destination.

Our writers are highly selective. They bring out the significance of the places they cover, capturing the personality and the underlying cultural and historical resonances of a city or region—making clear its special appeal. For exhaustive detailed coverage of cultural attractions, we suggest that you also use a supplementary reference-type guidebook, such as a Michelin Green Guide, along with the Penguin Guide.

The Penguin Guide to Italy 1989 is full of reliable and timely information, revised each year. We would like to know if you think we've left out some very special place.

ALAN TUCKER
General Editor
Penguin Travel Guides

40 West 23rd Street
New York, New York 10010
or
27 Wright's Lane
London   W8 5TZ

CONTENTS

MAPS

THE
PENGUIN
GUIDE
TO
ITALY
1989

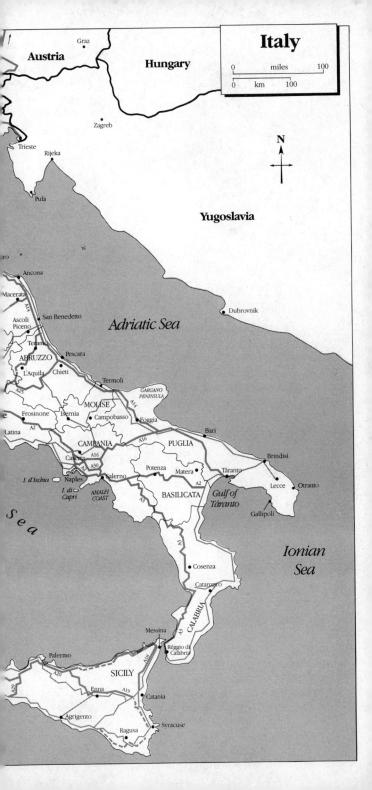

OVERVIEW

By Barbara Hults

Barbara Hults has lived, studied, and worked in Rome. Formerly the editor of Balloon, *a travel newsletter, she is the author of a travel guidebook on Italy and has written a series of walking-tour tapes on several Italian cities.*

Italy is an addiction.

The 19th-century English traveller was well aware of its power. Shelley, Keats, and Byron succumbed, and Browning cried that on his heart "was graven Italy." Perhaps there should be a sign at Rome's gates or Venice's lagoon entrances advising visitors to abandon all hope of ever wanting to go anywhere else. Those who fall victim are condemned, like the ancient mariner, to collar other travellers who have known its pleasures: Are the azaleas in bloom on the Spanish Steps in Rome yet? Does the old man still cane chairs in the piazza every afternoon? Did you happen to see the dawn in Venice? Was it that blend of scarlet and shell pink? Did you taste the jasmine ice cream in Sicily?

We have no intention of diluting the charm's potency. In fact, we'll shamelessly strengthen it. *Caveat lector.*

Italy, we all know, is shaped like a delicate boot, with Sicily just off the toe and Sardinia north of Sicily. France, Switzerland, and Austria provide the northern political boundaries. The Alps turn into the Apennines and follow the western part of the peninsula down its length. The eastern flatland ends in the marshy lagoons of Venice to the north, and beaches run down both coasts—with the best following Sardinia's island shoreline. Lakes dot the north above Milan: Como, Orta, Maggiore, and Garda.

The far northwest coast ends at the French border in an arc of coast called the Italian Riviera.

Along their southwest boundaries, the north-central plains of Emilia-Romagna give over abruptly to the mountains of Tuscany, with Florence near its center. Umbria, between Tuscany and Rome's region of Latium, follows ancient hills and valleys, and the provinces of Abruzzo and Molise, together familiarly called the Abruzzi, stretch from east of Rome to the Adriatic, rising at the center-point to the Gran Sasso peak, the highest peak of the Apennines. In the center of Latium, on the west coast near the Tyrrhenian Sea, is Rome, the Eternal City, to which all roads have led for two thousand years.

In recent years the south has arisen (to a degree) from its former poverty—though unemployment is still higher there than anywhere else in Italy. Campania follows the beautiful rocky coast of Amalfi on the west side of Italy down to the toe of the boot, to Calàbria's territory of mountains and lovely sea views. Eastward, the boot's instep is Basilicata, often neglected by travellers, partly because tourist facilities in its mountains and coastal villages are few. Its vineyards and olive groves, however, are beloved by those who take the time to know them. The high heel and spur of the boot are Apulia (or Puglia), the most industrially developed of the southern regions. Dramatic mountains cover its mystical northern Gargano peninsula; in the south, the stunning rocky eastern coasts, lined with lovely, white sandy beaches along the inner heel south of Táranto, are bordered inland with green hills. Near Alberobello are the famous *trulli*, the curious, conical stone houses.

The island off the toe, Sicily, has a mountainous center yielding to plains, encircled with small cove beaches along the coast. The other major island, Sardinia, west of the mainland, is ruggedly mountainous at the center, while its coasts are rimmed with white-sand beaches that are admired around the world.

Italy's geographical variety is only part of its interest, however. Add to that the different historical destinies of its regions and you have a beginning of the myriad permutations in the country. Italy's history is among the most complicated of all of Europe's history, for rare is the conquering foot that did not see something of value here, whether in natural resources or enticing plunder.

"Ancient Italy" traditionally begins about 20,000 B.C., although areas throughout the peninsula and Sicily were inhabited long before then. Among many central Italian tribes, the Etruscans—whose origins are not determined—emerged victorious.

Greek and Phoenician traders were then establishing trading ports in southern Italy, and soon colonies as well. Rome was traditionally founded in 753 B.C. by Romulus and Remus, and this date, or at least that century, seems accurate, according to recent excavations.

The city's power grew, and in 27 B.C., under Augustus, Rome finally became a full-fledged empire that ultimately stretched as far as England through North Africa and east to Syria. Invasions of barbarians from the north began about the time of Marcus Aurelius, and the empire was on the wane. When Constantine (whose Edict of Milan had ended persecution of the Christians) moved the capital to Constantinople, the handwriting on the wall was etched in stone.

During the Middle Ages the Ostrogoths ruled from Ravenna while the papacy grew in influence, laying the groundwork for the Papal States that would follow. This was largely the work of Pope Gregory the Great (590–604), whose strength of purpose helped the papacy emerge from the muddle of the Middle Ages as a major power. In the year 800 the pope crowned Charlemagne Holy Roman Emperor, after which papal power increased as its troubles multiplied. After Frederick Barbarossa was crowned emperor in 1155, war broke out among his supporters, the Ghibellines, and the pope's backers, the Guelphs. During this period in the south the Normans had established a successful kingdom in southern Italy and especially Sicily.

Renaissance princes and dukes struggled in the city states that had evolved, but foreign domination soon grew and lasted for centuries as France, Austria, and Spain held the reins. The Spanish Hapsburgs were a dominating force in Italy in post-Renaissance years, until the War of Spanish Succession (1701–1713) ended with Austria in control. Napoléon briefly annexed large portions of Italy, breaking the Austrian hold and moving Italy forward as a modern state. After the Congress of Vienna in 1815, the years were filled with riots, protests, and finally revolution as Mazzini, the great political thinker, joined forces with the man of action, Garibaldi, and with the brilliant Cavour, who would forge the new republic.

In 1860 the revolution began, and by 1870 Italy was an independent republic with a king. After the wars of the

20th century the king's popularity diminished, and the last king, Umberto II, would die in Portugal in exile.

Although Italy's governments changes frequently, and although terrorism, national strikes, and inflation have characterized recent years, Italy's economic status continues to rise and the nation now ranks fifth in Europe. This fact surprises no one as much as it does the Italians, who complain constantly of their tumultuous government. How could it happen? If you ask, you'll probably be greeted by a shrug and a smile of "Who knows? We must be doing something right."

Our discussion of Italy's attractions begins in the north. **Lago di Como** glistens like a watercolor in spring, while lesser-known **Lago d'Orta** and its town of San Giulio are so appealing that you may not want to move anywhere else at all. **Lago Maggiore** and its principal town of Stresa—from which the Isola Bella is an easy boat excursion away—and **Lago di Garda** farther east, are both quiet places, provided you don't choose to travel here in the high seasons. You may want to stay at the lakes when visiting Milan, allowing yourself a city to explore by day and an expanse of blue to soften the night.

In the far northwest is the mountainous region of Val d'Aosta, beloved of skiers and hikers. To its south is **Piedmont**, the region of the Nebbiolo grape, source of the Barolo and Barbaresco vintages—both of which have caused tasters to question France's primacy in wines. Piedmont's tables, laden with gnocchi, *fonduta* (fondue), *bollito misto* with *salsa verde* (boiled meat with a parsley-based sauce), and other passions of the gastronomic heart, lure many a hungry traveller.

Turin, the often neglected capital of the region, is not industrialized at all at its center, as is often believed. Instead, this former capital of Italy stretches out in a handsome pattern of parks and palaces, arcades and notable museums—its Museo Egizio (Egyptian museum) has few rivals. West of Turin, Sestriere and other resorts cater to skiers.

Liguria begins south of Piedmont along the Mediterranean, at the border of the French Riviera. Along the Italian Riviera we've singled out Portofino, which is well travelled, but we spend time also in Cinqueterre, where five little pastel-colored hamlets face the sea. Shelley lived here at Lerici, as did Byron (Shelley drowned offshore). At Genoa preparations are already under way for the gala of 1992, marking the five-hundredth year since native son Christopher Columbus sailed west looking for India.

The north-central region, **Lombardy**, is the richest in Italy, in finance, industry, and agriculture. There you will find **Milan**, the sleek capital of Italian design and finance, proud of its accomplishments that have given the "made in Italy" label precedence in the best of boutiques. The city's monuments to the arts—the Brera painting collections and the world-famous La Scala opera house in particular—keep the city high on artistic itineraries, and restaurants like Gualtiero Marchesi keep gourmands stylishly thin with *ravioli aperti* (open-topped ravioli) and scallopine with sweet-and-sour sauce. Go to Milan in August when everyone is gone and the vast city is quiet and pretty as a country town; many museums and restaurants stay open for summer these days—for the convenience of visitors.

East of Lombardy, the Dolomite mountains and green pastures of **Trentino–Alto Adige** betray the nearness of Austria. The towns and hamlets of this region are relatively undiscovered, by North American travellers in particular, who have many treats in store.

To the northeast is the **Veneto**, which claims the legendary **Venice** as one of its cities. The Veneto's plains are elegantly arrayed with Palladian villas, and the idyllic town of Asolo is a nice place to return to after a hard day's touring. Venice, the impossibly beautiful, is purely impossible when tourist crowds overrun its legendary canals. It's best to see this romantic city on breezy spring mornings when the wind whips the waves to whitecaps, jostling the gondolas at their moorings, or on winter days beneath a pearl gray sky.

A road we've not taken in this guidebook is the one east from Venice to the beautiful castle of Miramare, where Maximilian and Carlota lived—he who was soon afterward shot by a firing squad in Mexico and she who went mad—and on to Trieste, where James Joyce taught English and wrote his volumes in exile.

The north-central plain of Emilia-Romagna attracts lovers of food: truffles and porcini mushrooms, tortellini Bolognese and *zampone* (pig's foot) Modenese. Parma has French allure, with Parma ham and Parmigiano cheese thrown in for gastronomes; Bologna is a mixture of Medieval shadows and modern university life; Ferrara has splendid castles; and Ravenna shines with the soft gold of Byzantine mosaics.

Florence and its well-loved region **Tuscany** still represent the Renaissance, an age of inspired artists of indomitable spirit. Florence's incomparable wealth of aesthetic treasures is reassuringly unchanged, and now a car-free zone protects the visitor from the fumes of the traffic that has so plagued the city during recent years. Tuscany is golden fields and black-green cypresses defining hillside boundaries, but there is also a Tuscan coastline two hundred miles long, where the Argentario peninsula leads to Porto Ercole's expensive, glamorous coast and islands as well: Giannutri, whose sea depths reveal Roman galleons, and Elba ("Lucky Napoléon," wrote Dylan Thomas). Tuscany's Chianti is as pleasurable to see in the growing as it is to drink, and at Greve, just as an example, you'll taste the year's vintage accompanied by sausage cured on the ashes of a wood fire. You may want to stay on an estate and sample the land's bounty at close quarters.

Umbria's hills and monasteries of frescoed walls still evoke the region's mystical past. The town of Assisi is still enticing, despite the endless pilgrimages that march through its tiny, steep streets. Game and venison are the menu choices here, with wine from Orvieto, the town whose striped duomo guards the mystery of Corpus Christi and looks out across those soft Umbrian hills.

Latium (see the section on day trips from Rome) is a place where Etruscan tombs and ancient Roman apartment houses are silhouetted against the sea, and where shepherds, oblivious to approaching Alitalia flights, still lead their flocks along the road to the airport.

Rome, the seductive, infuriating colossus, smugly aware that everyone will go there sooner or later, makes few adjustments to visitors. Here you participate in Roman life; you do as the Romans do and you find it exhilarating. Rome provides visitors with layer upon layer of history—turning a corner may call up a new age altogether. You'll find the ghosts of Roman emperors and Renaissance popes, lavish Baroque churches, prisons and palaces, piazzas unchanged from the Middle Ages, arbors to dine under, and the age-old Tiber winding calmly past it all. Each age makes its presence known in Rome, bizarrely juxtaposed as in a Fellini circus. An unexpected bonus this year is the unveiling of the many handsomely restored monuments, Trajan's Column among them, that have been covered for years while work has been in progress.

The **Abruzzi**, a land of wolves and witches and the

highest mountains of the Apennines, is an eagle's nest a few hours from Rome, and almost unknown to North Americans. Frederick II found this region to his liking and enriched its cooking with his Eastern flair—red-hot pepper is used with Moroccan abandon. The pear-shaped scamorza cheese of Abruzzo is cooked on a skewer, and almond sweets are a regional favorite.

The Abruzzi towns of L'Aquila and Sulmona are reached on roads that glide through a world of lush valleys, rushing streams, and Medieval towns perched on terraced hills. The ski trails here are superb, and a national park protects chamois, fox, and bear. Its towns are so distant in origin that they predate Rome; the Samnites built them when Greece knew its golden age.

Campania, balm to body and soul, is known mainly for its splendid, rocky Amalfi coast and Capri's isle, for the ancient cities of Pompeii, Herculaneum, and Paestum, and, of course, for **Naples**—like the theater, a beloved invalid, its attraction is its wide heart and open arms. Neapolitan cooking comes as a wonderful surprise to those who think southern Italy is a poor cousin gastronomically.

In **Calàbria**, stark towns overlook mountain peaks and the sea, with its dramatic beaches and marinas. Cosenza's Medieval quarter encloses a bright cultural life of music, literature, and a brand-new university. A trip from town to town in this rural, mountainous region is an introduction to yet another Italy and, more than anywhere else on the peninsula, provides a look at an Italy fast disappearing as the tape decks and television bring even the remotest part of the Calàbria in contact with the world beyond.

Sicily, the mystery that has finally opened to the world, reveals the brilliance of Arab-Norman cathedrals, the glory of Greek temples, elegant, restrained Baroque palaces, and the incomparably beautiful resort of Taormina, high on a terraced hill that looks out to the beaches and sea and up to Mount Etna. Sicily's sophisticated cooking—more Arab in origin toward the island's west, more Greek to the east—takes advantage of the endless varieties of fish that fill the tropically blue seas around the island, and its almond desserts would please the sweetest teeth in Araby.

Apulia is a newcomer to travellers' itineraries. Attractions here include white beaches on the western coast, inside the heel of the boot; whimsical *trulli,* conical stone dwellings that have enlivened the landscape for millennia on southern hills amid almond blossoms in spring; the easy sophistication of the southwestern coast; the new hostelries created from old farmhouses that were once fortified for enemy onslaughts; and Lecce's Baroque elaborations. These come as gentle surprises. Don't neglect the windswept cliffs of the Gargano peninsula, mystical with its saints, dramatic with its views of caves and crashing surf. Along the shore are grottoes open to explorers; the catch of the day is always different. Apulia's cheeses—*ricotta forte* is the spicy-food lover's delight— and its wines rank among the finest. For a holiday of sailing, relaxing on the beach, and sightseeing, Apulia is enchanting.

Between Apulia and Calàbria lies **Basilicata**, to which we have devoted little time, because its accommodations are so few. But it has its rewards: mountains and streams, white beaches, and especially the city of Matera, seems like a camouflaged, almost abandoned village molded into the mountains. Metapontum, on the coast, is filled with the excavated ruins of a once-thriving Greek colony.

There is enough variety and pleasure in each of these regions to keep you coming back to Italy every year, as we think our description of each will prove. Read on.

USEFUL FACTS

When to Go
Spring and fall are the ideal months, of course—for climate, for flowers, and for lighter tourism. That said, both summer and winter have much to offer as well. Summer is a cavalcade of tourists and winter is often drizzly. But summer has the obvious advantages of beaches and water sports, and the unexpected discovery of cities when all the cars have gone. August is a wasteland, for all of Europe flees the cities, but that is when, ironically, they are at their most beautiful. Anna Magnani, asked about Rome, said she felt the old Rome only in August, when she could walk through the medievally dark streets that surround the Pantheon and hear the echo of her own footsteps. Trattorias are unrushed then, and life is slow. The downside of summer is the same as the upside: Everyone *has* left the cities, leaving many restaurants and shops closed, and those that remain open are filled with non-Italian faces for the most part. Museums, however, have recently realized that summer days are among their best attended, and they often stay open through August. Winter too has advantages, especially cultural: the opera,

the theater, concert halls, and near-empty museums. Because there are fewer tourists, there are fewer lines to wait in, restaurants are on their best behavior (in summer they sometimes think no one will know the difference if they take short cuts with the sauce), and the weather is often lovely—although showers or even heavy rain are common in the north, and even in Sicily.

Entry Documents

Just a passport is necessary, or an identity card for citizens of the European Economic Community. Motorists may need an international driver's license if they rent a car and a civil-liability insurance policy.

Arrival at Major Gateways by Air

From North America, flights touch down at Milan and Rome. Rome's Leonardo da Vinci Airport at Fiumicino is an advantage to travellers who wish to continue on another flight; at Milan you frequently have to travel to Linate, the domestic airport, which entails several hours of in-transit time, although Malpensa, the international airport, now initiates more domestic flights than it used to. Most flights from North America arrive in Italy during the morning, usually about 8:00 or 9:00 o'clock. A good travel agent will work out the most convenient routing, by plane or train.

Flights from the United Kingdom and from other European countries land at many other Italian airports as well, such as Venice, Turin, Pisa (for Florence), Bologna, or Catania (Sicily).

In both Milan and Rome, airport buses leave from the train stations. Airport buses run into the city at regular intervals: to via Giolitti at Stazione Termini in Rome, and to viale Luigi Sturzo near Stazione Porta Garibaldi in Milan. From these stations you can get a train, taxi, or public transportation—bus or Metropolitana (subway)— to your destination. The trip from the airport into town by taxi in Rome costs about 50,000 lire, and in Milan, about 90,000 lire. If you are travelling with a lot of luggage and the weather is bad or it is a holiday, you are better off taking a cab from the airport instead of waiting to find one at the train station, where there may be long lines. Normally, however, taxis wait in line at the railroad stations. They often charge a flat rate—to any hotel, even if it is around the corner—and a variety of supplements, for baggage, extra passengers, and even for riding at night.

Deluxe and first-class hotels will have a car meet you for about the same price if you so arrange with your travel agent.

Before leaving on the trip, investigate with your travel agent the cost of fly-drive programs, which are often less expensive (don't ask for the smallest car unless you're under four feet tall); and also special promotional offers and independent packages, such as Alitalia's Italtours and CIT offer, which include a choice of hotels without the disadvantages of group travel.

Many charter-flight organizations at present use regularly scheduled airlines, and the reserved seats can be arranged in advance. You'll probably be the one in the center if the plane is crowded, however, because the higher-paying passengers will of course get the more desirable aisle or window seats.

Around Italy by Train

Italy's rail service is excellent, and improving. The Milan-Rome express now flashes from point to point in four hours, and Florence to Rome requires only two hours, station to station.

Before leaving on the trip, check into the numerous train passes available, each with different advantages. For example, Italy's Unlimited Rail Pass, for U.S. $204, allows first-class travel (U.S. $130 for second) for 15 days, with unlimited mileage. With this pass, no supplement is charged for faster trains, for reservations, or for InterCity (ITT) trains (such as the Rome-Florence express). If you are travelling elsewhere in Europe, the Eurailpass is also available. Apart from the passes discussed above, which should be purchased before departure if possible (some *must* be bought in North America), youth, senior, and family passes are also sold at special rates.

Almost every city you will want to visit, large or small, has train service. For those that don't, bus connections are generally available though probably less frequent. If you are travelling any distance, ask about the InterCity trains, which are nonstop, at least between important cities on a given route. They run from Sicily to Venice or Genoa. Always reserve a seat if possible, especially on InterCity trains. They are heavily used by Italians as well as foreigners, midweek and midday as well as peak seasons. The new four-hour Rome-Milan train, the InterCity "Nonstop," *must* be reserved, as must several others. Even if it's not required, do it to avoid having to sit on your luggage in the aisle. It's worth the extra charge (unless you buy the special passes discussed above). Sleeping cars are available on long-distance trains and require supplements and reservations.

For information, ask your travel agent, or write to the Italian State Railways. (New York: 666 Fifth Avenue, 6th Floor, New York, New York 10103; Chicago: 500 North Michigan Avenue, Suite 1310, Chicago, Illinois 60611; Los Angeles: 6033 West Century Boulevard, Suite 1090, Los Angeles, California 90045; Montreal: 2055 Peel Street, Montreal H3A 1V4 P.Q.; Toronto: 13 Balmuto Street, Toronto, Ontario MAY 1W4.

Around Italy by Air

Italy's domestic airlines are often attractively priced for weekend packages under the Nastro Verde (Green Ribbon) plan: You must leave and return on specific days and hours, which are different for each city but generally cover the weekend period. These can be purchased only in Italy, however, at any travel agent or Alitalia office. (All domestic airlines are owned by Alitalia.)

If making plans for railroad or air travel, make sure no strike (*sciopero*) is planned for your day of departure. Strikes are announced in the newspaper, and your hotel *portiere* should be able to forewarn you if you explain your plans.

Around Italy by Bus

Although bus travel has fallen into disuse in this speedy age, Europabus maintains a fleet of express buses that cover long distances. Check the phone directory or travel agents in major cities. Each region has bus companies that vary from very comfortable, and frequently faster than local trains, to the sardine-can variety. From Rome to L'Aquila (in the Abruzzi), for example, bus travel is faster as it sometimes is from Palermo to Taormina. Travel agents and tourist offices in Italy are your best sources of information.

By Ferry and Hydrofoil

The islands of Sicily and Sardinia and smaller islands along the coasts are connected to the mainland by car ferry and sometimes by hydrofoil, especially in summer. The Tirrenia line is the largest of the long-distance lines (Naples–Palermo, Rome/Civitavecchia—Cagliari, etc.), and can be reached in North America through Extra

Value Travel, Fountain Building, 689 South Collier Boulevard, Marco Island, Florida 33937 (Tel: 813-394-3384), or through a travel agent. Always reserve and go first class on the overnight runs. (In summer the deck may be hidden under backpacks, and an important soccer match will sell out the boat in a flash at any time during the season.)

Smaller islands, such as Capri and the Aeolians, are booked at the departure cities, as discussed in the Getting Around sections of the regions in which they are located.

Renting a Car and Driving

Although you'll want a car in the countryside to follow your inclinations to turreted hill towns and sea resorts, driving in any of the major cities is far more pain than pleasure. Congestion, speedway-style driving (Rome), parking, and auto theft in some cities are a few of the reasons you will be happier parking at the hotel or a good lot, and walking or taking taxis or public transport.

You will need a valid license from your own country accompanied by a translation into Italian. The major rental car companies in Italy are Maiellano, Hertz, Avis, Budget, National (called Europcar in Europe), or Dollar Rent a Car (affiliated with InterRent). As mentioned above, the smallest compact is too small, so opt for at least the next largest. You may request an automatic (usually more than double the standard price, as is air-conditioning), but learn a bit about shifting gears on a nonautomatic just in case. Car rentals are subject to an 18 percent IVA, higher for luxury cars. Car rentals are also provided on the railroad's Treno+Auto Plan, where you pick up the car at the station.

Ask about car-leasing if you plan to stay a long time, although this type of arrangement is not yet well developed in Italy. Arrangement for long-term rental or leasing can be made in North America through rental-car companies or Auto-Europe in Camden, Maine; Tel: (800) 223-5555. Negotiate the contract before you set out. You must be gone three weeks or more, and the price will be lower than you would pay for a regular rental. There is a wide range of cars. You pay 25 percent before leaving and 75 percent in the currency of the country in which you pick up the car. The rate is guaranteed.

Insurance for all vehicles is compulsory in Italy. A Green Card (*Carta Verde*) or Frontier Insurance, valid for 15, 30, or 45 days, should be issued to cover your car.

Access America provides a health and theft policy that includes collision damage.

Telephoning

The international telephone country code for Italy is 39. When telephoning from outside Italy, omit the zero from the local area codes.

Local Time

Italy is six hours ahead of Eastern Standard Time, one hour ahead of Greenwich Mean Time, and nine hours behind Sydney. During the changeover to Daylight Saving Time there are a few days when Italy is an extra hour ahead or behind, so double check relevant hours near that period.

Currency

The monetary unit is the Italian *lira,* plural *lire,* written Ł. Notes are issued in denominations of 1,000; 2,000; 5,000; 10,000; 20,000; 50,000; and 100,000 lire. Coins are 10 (rare), 20 (rare), 50, 100, 200, and 500 lire. The exchange rate is subject to daily change; check with banks and daily newspapers for the current rates. Travellers checks are changed in banks at (usually) better rates than elsewhere. American Express offices in Rome, Milan, and Venice cash personal checks for members carrying their cards; the office in Rome also accepts mail for card holders. Few hotels will accept a personal check, and some do not accept credit cards. Be sure that the hotel or restaurant you choose accepts the card you have if you want to use it. The Banco d'America e d'Italia gives Visa cash advances. MasterCard advances are made in banks with Eurocard stickers on the door. Eurocard is equivalent to MasterCard for other purposes as well.

Business Hours

Learning Italian business hours would require a separate university course. They vary from region to region, with the north adhering in general to more European hours and the warmer south keeping the siesta tradition of closing for most of the afternoon and reopening in the evening. "Normal" business hours would see the shops open from 9:00 A.M. to 1:00 P.M. and 4:00 P.M. to 8:00 P.M. Many shops are closed Monday mornings. Banks are open usually from 8:30 A.M. to 1:30 P.M. and from 3:00 or 3:30 P.M. to 4:00 or 4:30 P.M., but individual differences require that you double check. Exchanges (*cambio*) keep store hours. Local post offices are open from 8:00 A.M. to 2:00 P.M., and the central office is usually open late in the evening in large cities. Barbers open from 8:00 A.M. to 1:00 P.M. and 4:00 P.M. to 8:00 P.M., and are closed Sunday afternoons and Mondays. Women's hairdressers are open 8:00 A.M. to 8:00 P.M., but most close all day Sunday and Monday.

Museum and Church Hours. State museums are open mornings all week and the weekend but close on Monday. Double check the specific museum you want to visit before setting out. In Rome, for example, the Forum is closed Tuesdays instead. Churches that are open to the public at specific hours are usually open mornings only, although some open afternoons as well. The dress code for churches is: no bare shoulders or bare legs, for men or women. Many churches require a 100 or 200 lire coin in the light box to illuminate certain dark chapels or paintings. Keep a supply, preferably in a tube such as the ones used for camera film; Italian coins are large and heavy.

Holidays

Offices and shops in Italy are closed on the following dates: January 1 (New Year's Day); January 6 (Epiphany); Easter Monday; April 25 (Liberation Day); May 1 (Labor Day); August 15 (Assumption of the Virgin); November 1 (All Saints Day); December 8 (Day of Immaculate Conception); December 25 (Christmas Day); December 26 (Santo Stefano).

Offices and shops are also closed in the following cities on the local feast days honoring their patron saints: Venice (April 25—St. Mark); Florence (June 24—St. John the Baptist); Genoa (June 24—St. John the Baptist); Turin (June 24—St. John the Baptist); Rome (June 29—Sts. Peter and Paul); Palermo (July 15—Santa Rosalia); Naples (September 19—St. Gennaro); Bologna (October 4—St. Petronio); Cagliari (October 30—St. Saturnino); Trieste (November 3—San Giusto); Bari (December 6—St. Nicola); and Milan (December 7—St. Ambrose).

Note: beware of *ponte* (bridge) weekends—the three-day weekends that include a holiday, when banking and other services will be closed. Remember that on Labor Day, May 1, absolutely *everything* in Rome and many other cities closes. This means the bus and subway as well, and taxis are far from plentiful. Few restaurants are open, but hotel restaurants and a few others will keep you from starving.

When banks are closed, you can change money in an emergency at the airport or railroad station or, with a service charge, at your hotel.

Day Hotels

Many services are offered by day hotels (*alberghi diurnali*), which are generally located near the main railroad stations. They are handy for day-trippers, providing baths, showers, barbers, hairdressers, shoeshines, dry-cleaning, telephone, baggage checking, writing rooms, and private rooms for brief rest periods (overnight stays are not permitted). Railroad stations are usually not in the safest areas in town, and you must be aware of your neighbors when in the vicinity.

Safety

A great many problems are easily solved by purchasing or making a money belt or undercover silk or cotton disco-bag-style pouch. An underarm-holster style (underneath shirts or dresses) works well for some. Carry enough cash for the day, and a credit card. Small towns are far safer (from thieves) than cities; and northern cities, with the exception of Milan and Turin, are safer than those in the south, including Rome, where thievery is a major problem at present.

If you *must* transport valuables, do so in a plain plastic shopping bag, or one from Upim or Standa, Italy's five-and-dimes. Cameras are easily cut off if you wear them around your neck. Pickpockets thrive in buses and other crowded areas. Gypsy children (with parental supervision) are among the most obvious; don't read any cardboard signs they put in front of you or your wallet will magically disappear. They normally work the railroad station areas, among others. Vespa thieves, boys or girls, grab shoulder bags. The final word: Don't leave your valuables unguarded, even in St. Peter's.

Receipts

All restaurants are required by Italian tax law to issue a *ricevuta fiscale,* a computerized cash-register receipt that you must carry with you upon leaving. You can be fined if you don't have it.

Country Living

A delightful way to see Italy is through the Agroturist organization, which arranges for stays in country houses that range from beautifully groomed villas and ancient castles to rough-and-ready farms. At present some Agro-turist offices are not set up for English-speaking people, but if you can communicate in Italian, do write or call them. The main office in Rome is located at Corso Vittorio Emanuele 101, 00186 Rome; Tel: (if you are calling from Italy), (06) 651-23-42. Many individual provincial offices are also organized. For Tuscany, the office is in Florence, on via del Proconsolo 13; Tel: (55) 28-78-38. Emilia Romagna's office is in Bologna, via Lame 15; Tel: (051) 23-33-21. Umbria's is in Perugia; write: Segreteria c/o Dr. Piero Borghi, via Tuderte 13; Tel: (075) 301-74. Other addresses can be obtained from the Italian Tourist Office or the main Agroturist office.

Longer Visits

If you are staying in one city a week or longer, your best bet may be a *residence,* a hotel apartment that enables you to have your own living room and kitchen, usually for less than the price of a hotel room for that period. In Rome the **Palazzo Velabro** on via Velabro is elegant and well located, near the piazza Bocca della Verità; the **Mayfair Residence**, via Sicilia 183, is also excellent, in a modern setting near the via Veneto and the Villa Borghese. Many hotels in other cities have suites that are rented on a weekly or monthly basis as well. Contact the Italian State Tourist Office or local tourist authorities for a list of residences.

Information

A good source of information is the booklet "General Information for Travelers in Italy," published annually by the Italian State Tourist Office. Major offices are located at: 630 Fifth Avenue, New York, New York 10111, Tel: (212) 245-4822; and 3 place Ville Marie, 56 Plaza, Montreal, Quebec H3B 2E3, Tel: (514) 866-7667.

BIBLIOGRAPHY

JAMES S. ACKERMAN, *Palladio.* A scholarly introduction to the most imitated architect in the world.

SIR HAROLD ACTON, *The Bourbons of Naples.* A witty biography of an extraordinary time.

MICHAEL ADAMS, *Umbria*. One of the best books about the region.

CORRADO ALVARO, *Revolt in Aspromonte*. One of the few books available in English by this prolific writer; discusses problems in the Italian south during the mid-20th century.

BURTON ANDERSON, *Vino: The Wines and Winemakers of Italy*. Even though it was published in 1980, it is still the best book on its subject—and with interesting asides on food, too—covering all 20 regions of the country.

VERNON BARTLETT, *Introduction to Italy*. An amusing and unusually comprehensive overview of the country's history from ancient times to the present day.

LUIGI BARZINI, *The Italians*. The late Dr. Barzini explains his countrymen to the West, with wit and knowledge based on deep affection.

JAMES BECK, *Italian Renaissance Painting*. A comprehensive and readable survey of one of the most important aspects of Western civilization.

EVE BOORSOOK, *Companion Guide to Florence*. An excellent, detailed guide to the city.

JACOB BURCKHARDT, *Civilization of the Renaissance in Italy*. The classic work on that period.

BALDASSARE CASTIGLIONE, *The Book of the Courtier*. An eyewitness account of one of the smaller ducal courts of the Renaissance and a penetrating excursion into Renaissance thought.

EDWARD CHANEY, *Florence: A Traveller's Companion*. Sites in the Tuscan capital as seen by writers throughout the centuries.

ELEANOR CLARK, *Rome and a Villa*. A novelist's portrait of the capital.

TOBY COLE, ED., *Florence: A Traveler's Anthology* and *Venice: A Portable Reader*. Both are compilations of literary depictions.

F. MARION CRAWFORD, *The Rulers of the South*. A two-volume history of southern Italy and Sicily.

VINCENT CRONIN, *The Golden Honeycomb*. A tour of Sicily that uncovers ancient myths and present pleasures.

CHARLES DICKENS, *Pictures from Italy*. Evocative portraits of scenes encountered.

DANILO DOLCI, *Sicilian Lives*. Sicily experienced through individual life stories.

NORMAN DOUGLAS, *Old Calabria*. Historical and personal accounts of life in the south; many still hit home three-quarters of a century after publication.

———, *Siren Land*. The ancient siren myth is related as it touches the Campanian coast.

———, *South Wind*. Once a cult book, it offers readers an escape to Capri, disguised as Nepenthe.

UMBERTO ECO, *The Name of the Rose*. An intriguing novel about the Avignon papacy.

M. I. FINLEY, DENIS MACK SMITH, and CHRISTOPHER DUGGAN, *A History of Sicily*. A brilliant three-volume history compacted into one volume.

E. M. FORSTER, *A Room with a View*. Florence as a setting for personal revelations.

JOHANN WOLFGANG VON GOETHE, *Italian Journey*. One of the most important Italian journals of its time.

ROBERT GRAVES, *I, Claudius*. An imagined autobiography by the classical poet and translator.

FERDINAND GREGOROVIUS, *Lucrezia Borgia*. A biography of Lucrezia, her family, and the Renaissance. Indispensable.

JULIEN GREEN, *God's Fool: The Life and Times of St. Francis of Assisi*. A loving and sensitive account of the saint and his contemporaries.

PETER GUNN, *A Concise History of Italy*. True to its title.

AUGUSTUS HARE, *Augustus Hare in Italy*. A compilation of the author's travel writings in turn-of-the-century Italy.

HOWARD HIBBARD, *Bernini* and *Michelangelo*. Biographies of the artists by one of the most respected art historians.

PAUL HOFMANN, *O Vatican! A Slightly Wicked View of the Holy See*. An insider's appreciation.

———, *Rome: The Sweet Tempestuous Life*. Sketches of all aspects of life in the Eternal City.

HOMER, *The Iliad*. Read the Sicilian and southern coast sections, especially regarding the Cyclops, the Sirens, and other myths.

HENRY JAMES, *Italian Hours*. His love affair with Italy. "At last—for the first time—I live!" he wrote.

D. H. LAWRENCE, *Sea and Sardinia, Etruscan Places,* and *Twilight in Italy*. All travel journals written with the Lawrence-ian passion.

GIUSEPPE TOMASI DI LAMPEDUSA, *The Leopard*. The sensuous and evocative story of a Sicilian prince facing the next generation of rulers: "We were the leopards ... those who take our place will be little jackals."

CARLO LEVI, *Christ Stopped at Eboli*. Life in southern Italy during the Second World War.

GIULIO LORENZETTI, *Venice and Its Lagoon*. The wonderfully detailed guide in translation; the bible of Venetian art historians.

GEORGINA MASSON, *Rome*. One of the best guides to Rome, divided by neighborhoods.

————, *Frederick II of Hohenstaufen*. A fine biography worth searching for.

————, *Italian Villas and Palaces*. A picture book full of good information.

MARY MCCARTHY, *The Stones of Florence* and *Venice Observed*. Books that lose nothing through time. Essential.

ALBERTO MORAVIA, *The Woman of Rome*. A novel of a prostitute under Fascism.

JAN MORRIS, *The Venetian Empire*. An expanded look at Venice.

————, *The World of Venice*. Amusing and insightful impressions by one of the best writers on travel.

H. V. MORTON, *A Traveler in Italy; A Traveler in Southern Italy;* and *A Traveler in Rome*. All three are filled with the lore and musings of the beloved tale-teller.

JOHN JULIUS NORWICH, *The Normans in the South* and *The Kingdom in the Sun*. Delightfully written accounts of Norman Italy.

————, *A History of Venice*. An exhaustive study of La Serenissima.

————, *The Italians: History, Art and the Genius of a People*. A comprehensive cultural history.

IRIS ORIGO, *The Merchant of Prato*. Essential reading about the birth of modern mercantilism whether or not you go to Prato.

GEORGE PILLEMENT, *Unknown Italy*. Up-to-date and off the beaten track, with a focus on architecture.

PINDAR, *The Odes*. Those on Sicily's Olympic heroes are especially interesting.

PLINY THE YOUNGER, *Letters*. Those that deal with his uncle's death at Vesuvius are riveting.

WAVERLEY ROOT, *The Food of Italy*. Anecdotes and a pleasurable introduction to the country's food and wine.

STEVEN RUNCIMAN, *The Sicilian Vespers*. The revolt as it relates to European history, written with immediacy and clarity.

JOHN RUSKIN, *The Stones of Venice*. The classic apprisal of the city's art history.

KATE SIMON, *Italy, the Places in Between* and *Rome Places and Pleasures*. Both are full of insightful observations.

D. MACK SMITH, *Cavour and Garibaldi 1860*. The definitive English-language study of the Risorgimento.

WILLIAM JAY SMITH AND DANA GIOIA, EDS., *Poems From Italy*. Almost eight hundred years of Italian poetry in parallel text form.

IRVING STONE, *The Agony and the Ecstasy*. An evocative if fictionalized portrait of the Renaissance artist.

SUETONIUS, *The Twelve Caesars*. He told what he knew and didn't know with great candor.

ITALO SVEVO, *A Life (Trieste)*. An antihero in turn-of-the-century Trieste.

GIORGIO VASARI, *The Lives of the Artists*. The life and times of the Renaissance masters; gives a sense of how they were judged by their peers.

HORACE WALPOLE, *The Castle of Otranto*. This forerunner of the gothic novel gives an amusing idea of how exotic Apulia was viewed in the late 18th century.

JOHN WHITE, *Art and Architecture in Italy: 1250–1400*. A thorough study of the period that immediately preceded the Renaissance.

RUDOLPH WITTKOWER, *Art and Architecture in Italy, 1600–1750*. The noted Baroque historian's scholarly examination of the period.

A. G. WOODHEAD, *The Greeks in the West*. A concise, highly readable introduction to Greek expansion in Magna Graecia.

LIGURIA
THE ITALIAN RIVIERA

By Anne Marshall Zwack

Anne Marshall Zwack, who has a home in Florence, writes for Gourmet *magazine and for the Travel Section of* The New York Times.

Liguria is a boomerang-shaped strip of land along the northwest coast of Italy that begins at the east where Tuscany leaves off and curves round the top of the boot toward the French Côte d'Azur at the west. One of the smallest regions of Italy, it is also one of the oldest, the Ligurians having been among the earliest primitive inhabitants of Italy.

Shielded from northern winds by the Alps and then the Apennines, Liguria has one of the mildest climates in Europe, an eternal spring where bright blossoms and bushes flower all year round. In the 19th century, sufferers from the *mal sottile* would come to winter along the Riviera.

Liguria has *two* Rivieras, the **Riviera di Ponente** at the west, between the French border and Genoa, and the more spectacular **Riviera di Levante** continuing eastward from Genoa, where we find Genoa itself, Portofino, the Cinque Terre, Lerici and Tellaro, and Ameglia. Although the Riviera di Ponente has its share of beauty and interest, the Riviera di Levante takes most of the prizes and is the more likely venue for visitors descending on Liguria.

MAJOR INTEREST

Genoa
Palazzi and churches
Street life

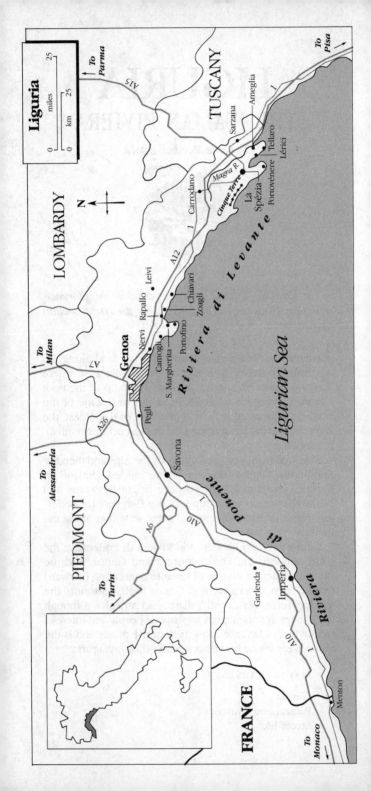

Riviera di Levante
Drive along coast from Chiavari to Zoagli and
   Portofino
Camogli and other picturesque fishing villages
Ca' Peo restaurant above Chiavari
The Cinque Terre
Tellaro
Lerici, especially at night
Locanda dell'Angelo in Ameglia

Since time immemorial, life for the Ligurians has been a struggle. Dependent on the sea for their livelihood, these peace-loving people were a constant prey to pirates. To grow vines and olives and basic crops, the Ligurians literally had to carry the soil by boat or on their backs and stick it to the rock face, creating a style of terrace agriculture unique in Europe and found elsewhere only in parts of China and Peru. Everything Ligurians have achieved has been with Winston Churchill's "blood, sweat and tears," and Ligurians prize hard work and thrift above all other virtues. Even today, it seems as if work is in progress on every inch of the landscape, littered as it is with ladders and tools, as though these tireless laborers planned to return to work at any moment. Unfortunately, particularly on the Riviera di Ponente, much of the Ligurians' hard-earned money seems to have been invested in *villette,* little bungalows that no amount of cascading bougainvillea can redeem. On the other hand, the coast road along the Riviera di Levante from Chiavari through Zoagli, Rapallo, and Santa Margherita toward Portofino is one of Italy's more memorable drives, past languidly elegant turn-of-the-century villas and imposing hotels swathed in luxuriant creepers and flanked by lolling palm trees and pines.

GENOA

"This is by no means a city that would strike an Englishman as being agreeable to *dwell* in. We cannot help acknowledging the grandeur for which it has been so reputed; but at the same time there are, mingled in the display of magnificence by which we are surrounded, some circumstances which render the general effect of the city far more dismal than delightful." So wrote J. P. Cobbett in 1830, and it remains true today.

Genoa, the capital of Liguria and its largest city, stayed black and white when the rest of the world went Technicolor. Parts of it, like the shoeshine booth off the piazza de Ferrari, seem left over from a Thirties or Forties movie, and there are still wartime OFF LIMITS signs on alley corners.

The Genoese are a busy people, hardworking and serious. Genoa, said Tobias Smollett, has the "face of business." The Genoese also have a reputation for craftiness, and an old saying claims that it would take six Christians to cheat a Jew, six Jews to cheat a Genoese, but a Genoese Jew is a match for the devil himself. The Genoese intend this, of course, as a supreme compliment to the Jews. Jokes abound about the parsimoniousness of the Genoese, who, it is said, cannot sleep at night for fear that the light has not gone out in the refrigerator. Nobody enjoys these jokes more than the Genoese themselves, for whom thrift *is* the cardinal virtue.

The City

Genoa is, and always has been, a city of the sea. Christopher Columbus was born here between 1450 and 1451, the most famous of a long line of Genoese navigators. (Normally his house can be visited, but it is currently being restored in honor of the "Columbiade" in 1992.) Byron called Genoa the untidiest port in the world, and like all ports it is a mixture of squalor and splendor. Acclaimed by Petrarch as "*la superba,*" Genoa has been known as "the proud" ever since, a city of formidable *palazzi,* the "heaviest, highest, broadest, darkest, solidest houses one can imagine," according to Mark Twain, who maintained that "you can go up three flights of stairs before you begin to come upon signs of occupancy." In the narrow streets, these palazzi are sometimes so close together that in more turbulent times fighting would be carried on from window to window and roof to roof. Behind the monumental façades of the Palazzo Doria Pamphili in piazza del Principe and the Palazzo Carrega Cataldi, the Palazzo Doria Tursi, and the Palazzo Rosso, all on via Garibaldi, there are riotously opulent interiors, a blaze of stucco and frescoes and gilt. Today these are public offices, but you can visit them, business permitting, upon request. Palazzo Rosso and the Palazzo Bianco opposite are the two main art museums, housing paintings by Van Dyck, Titian, Veronese, Rubens, Cranach, and

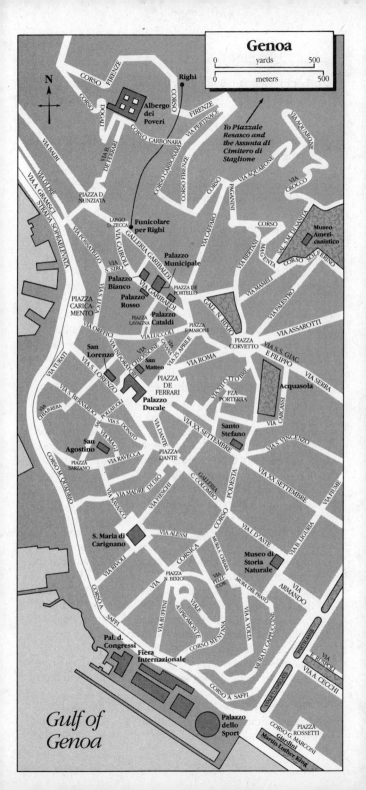

Zurbarán. Genoa is known as the city of the *seicento,* or 1600s; Rubens and Van Dyck heavily influenced the Genoese school.

Both Dumas and Flaubert called Genoa the "city of marble." Genoa's palazzi are covered in marble at least as far as the second floor; any more would have been considered ostentatious by the sober Genoese. Only leading citizens such as the Dorias had their palazzi made entirely in marble, in recognition of services rendered to their native city. The churches, on the other hand, have façades covered in white marble and black slate, striped horizontally like most basilicas and churches along the Tyrrhenian coast—a stylistic legacy of the Saracens, who plagued the Ligurians for centuries. There is the **Cathedral of San Lorenzo,** built between the 10th and 14th centuries in Romanesque/Gothic, where the dish in which Saint John the Baptist's head was presented to Salome is preserved. However, **San Siro,** in via San Siro, was the first cathedral of Genoa and, like most Genoese churches, is more remarkable for its architecture than for the art treasures it contains. Restored in the 16th and 17th centuries, the façade is Neoclassic, while the interior is splendid Genoese Baroque. With its fine Gothic doors and rose window, **Santo Stefano,** built in the 12th and 13th centuries on the via XX Settembre, is where Christopher Columbus was baptized. One church that is undoubtedly rich in Genoese seicento art is **Santissima Annunziata,** in the piazza della Nunziata, while among the most enchanting corners of old Genoa is the **piazza San Matteo,** with its Romanesque/Gothic **Church of San Matteo** and adjoining cloister, which dates back to 1308. The greatest of all the Dorias, Andrea, is buried in this church, and next door are the Case dei Doria, the Dorias' houses, not to be confused with their imposing Palazzo Doria Pamphili in the piazza del Principe.

Besides such magnificence there are, as Dylan Thomas observed, "heat and colors and dirt and noise and loud wicked alleys with all the washing of the world hanging from the high windows." From the main shopping street— the via XX Settembre—and the central piazza de Ferrari, corkscrew-shaped streets wriggle down the hillsides to the port. It is, as Henry James said, "the crookedest and most incoherent of cities."

This seamier aspect of Genoa, in spite of the palaces, is the most fascinating side of the city: the squalor rather than the splendor. There is the casbah atmosphere of the port itself, with its street stalls and palm readers, the **antiques stores** in the old streets between piazza Fontane Marose and piazza della Zecca, the **flea market** in piazza Lavagna, the back-street bakeries selling *torte e farinata,* the typical, flat, pizza-shaped pies made of chick-pea flour, which should be eaten hot from the oven. (Genoa, in common with the rest of Liguria, has its characteristic *focaccia,* a flat, dimpled bread—though not as flat and crisp as the Florentine *schiacciata*—baked with oil.)

Then there are the tortuous alleyways, or *caruggi,* with, high up on every corner, a *Madonnetta,* a statue of the Madonna. These *Madonnette* (Little Madonnas) were erected by the various artisan guilds or by sailors who left the port of Genoa to sail around the world. Indeed, many of them—the most remarkable being those from the 18th century—look like simple Genoese women, complete with apron.

For the best view of the city and the port, take the funicular railway from largo della Zecca to **Monte Righi**. An unusual landmark is the cemetery of Staglieno, where every tomb is adorned with the most outrageous 19th-century monuments in a conglomeration of styles.

There is no "great" hotel in Genoa. The only luxury hotel is the **Colombia**, furnished in that stilted glitz once considered *de rigueur* by luxury hotels. A perfectly adequate and centrally located little hotel is the inexpensive **Metropoli**.

Although there are no outstanding restaurants in Genoa, the general standard is high, as menus are based on fish fresh from the Ligurian Sea. An unusual antipasto is the *gianchetti,* tiny, newborn fish steamed and served with the local olive oil and lemon. Besides *pesto* (the local sauce made of basil, garlic, Parmesan cheese, and oil and ground to a paste), typical fare includes the *torta pasqualina,* an Easter pie (which is eaten all year round) filled with beet greens or artichokes. As an alternative to fish there is *cima,* veal stuffed with vegetables and egg, and the traditional cake, the *pandolce,* or Genoa cake, as it is sometimes known in the United States.

The best restaurant in Genoa is **Le Fate** on via Ruspoli, where only the best will do, whether it is the olive oil, the choice of Scotch, or the different daily home-baked breads. Le Fate is correspondingly expensive, and it takes no credit cards.

A much simpler, down-to-earth trattoria is **Osvaldo**, on via Dellacasa in a picturesque corner of Boccadasse, an inlet in the Gulf of Genoa west of the city. It serves typical local dishes the way they are meant to taste, in a very authentic atmosphere. Osvaldo has very few tables and is not as expensive as Le Fate—but it is not cheap.

One of the main reasons people come to Genoa is for the Fiera, a vast exhibition area on the sea that hosts a number of trade fairs, the most famous of which is the Salone Nautico, from October 22 through November 1 every year. Every four years there is the Euroflora, when the stands of the Fiera overflow with plants and flowers. In July there is an outdoor ballet festival in the **Parco di Nervi,** a complex of four palatial country villas just east of Genoa. Information can be obtained from the Teatro Comunale dell'Opera; Tel: (010) 553-10-05. Another beautiful villa is the **Pallavicini** at Pegli, west of Genoa and easily reached by train or bus, where in spring (usually April) the botanical gardens are opened for a month; the gardens feature a collection of, among other things, carnivorous plants.

West from Genoa

If your itinerary takes you from Genoa west to the Riviera di Ponente on your way to France, an ideal stopover is at the **Golf Hotel Meridiana**, an enchanting hotel in Garlenda near Savona, in the middle of an 18-hole golf course. The hotel, which also has a very good restaurant, **Il Rosmarino**, is not outrageously expensive.

THE RIVIERA DI LEVANTE
Portofino

The Greeks called the Ligurians dolphins because of their familiarity and dexterity with the sea: Portofino means port of dolphins. The town was renowned throughout antiquity and today is famous as a jet-set haven. Whereas nearby Santa Margherita and Rapallo have definitely seen better days, Portofino still has the power of enchantment that captivated the first English tourists during the last century. Because Portofino's horseshoe-shaped inlet, a few miles east of Genoa, is so tiny, few boats can moor at its jetties. For that reason, and because the town's boutiques and bars are so exclusive and expensive, mass tourism has never been a major threat here.

Despite the unique setting, none of the restaurants on

the seafront is particularly remarkable. It is best to scout out the cheapest, since a plate of pasta with *pesto* tastes much the same everywhere along the coast. The most common kinds of pasta are lasagne, but without the meat filling and cheese sauce, and *trenette*. The pasta will be cooked together with potatoes if it is the Ligurian "real thing."

The **Hotel Splendido** in Portofino is indeed splendid, especially since it has been bought and relaunched by the same chain that relaunched the Orient Express. Stout colonnades support rampant vines that shade a vast terrace on a hill dominating the bay; those who cannot afford the pampered luxury of a room here can at least enjoy a long-drawn-out drink with a view on the terrace.

The local beaches, such as Paraggi, tend to be overcrowded in summer, but during the tourist season a regular public boat service can take you around the castle on the headland overlooking the port to swim in the little **Bay of San Fruttuoso**, with its ancient abbey and the tombs of the Dorias. Andrea Doria was the most glorious of Genoa's seafaring heroes, the *Re del Mare,* or King of the Sea, who fought with the Spaniards against Barbarossa and under whose rule 16th-century Genoa, like Britannia, ruled the waves. Alternatively, the next stop is **Camogli**, a tiny, picturesque fishing village where you might eat at any one of the simple little trattorias on the port.

Chiavari

A more adventurous place to stay, about 20 minutes east along the coast from Portofino, is **Ca' Peo**. This restaurant with rooms is perched on a hilltop above Chiavari on a seemingly endless drive heavenward to a tiny place called Leivi. Ca' Peo is local dialect for Casa di Pietro (Peter's House), because there have been Peos in the owner's family for generations, tending the olives that grow on the slopes below the restaurant. (Ligurian olive oil is much lighter and less dense, not green like Tuscan olive oil, but a transparent golden color; it is ideal for the fish recipes typical of local cuisine.) Franco and Melly Solari, like true Ligurians, have worked very hard to earn for their sunny, French-style country restaurant the grandiloquent accolade of the "Girardet of Liguria" from France's *Le Figaro.* The food is indeed superb, from the opening terrine of *porcini* mushrooms, through the *tortelli* (pasta filled with eggplant and goat's cheese) and the Genoese *tomaxelle* (veal rolled around sweetbreads and home-grown herbs), to the flambéed chestnut ice cream. Franco is a connoisseur of the wines of Liguria, some of which, like the Pigato and Rossese, are practically un-known even in the rest of Italy.

The Solaris are still working on the rooms, which, unlike the cuisine, are not yet perfect; handles still drop off, and some of the taste in decoration is dubious, but the windows do look out on a sweeping vista of the Riviera, from the Cinque Terre to Portofino. Ca' Peo is expensive but worth every lira.

The Cinque Terre

The Cinque Terre (Five Lands) are five little hamlets clinging to a rock face perched above a splendid sea. From the Autostrada exit at Carrodano, 16 km (10 miles) from La Spezia toward Genoa, a small road winds down through woodland for about 40 minutes toward **Monterosso al Mare**, the most populous and touristy of the five, from where you can take a local railway that stops every few minutes, first at **Vernazza**, then at **Corniglia**, **Manarola**, and **Riomaggiore**. Difficulty of access has kept this unique, short stretch of coastline safe from tourist buses, and the people of the Cinque Terre for the most part live their lives—oblivious of tourists—the way they have for centuries, fishing from the little wooden boats moored in the tiny ports and tending their pocket-handkerchief-sized vineyards that stepladder down the hillsides to the sea. The wines of the Cinque Terre are famous, especially their sweet dessert wine, Schiacchetrà (pronounced "sharketrà"), made from grapes left to ripen in the Riviera sun after the harvest.

The most fascinating of the Cinque Terre are Manarola and Vernazza. Both are small fishing villages. The port of **Manarola** is large enough for only two or three boats at the same time, so that the others have to be hauled up with winches every evening when the fishermen come in with their catch. In the old days, anyone sailing past Manarola had to pay a toll, and shirkers would be swiftly apprehended by little sailboats darting out of the tiny port in hot pursuit. All the Cinque Terre were frequently raided by the Saracens; the Porta Rossa (Red Gate) in Manarola is named to commemorate the blood shed during one of these incursions.

Vernazza is a cluster of pastel-colored houses around a *piazzetta,* where artists set up their easels in summer, and a Romanesque church, with waves lapping around its rock foundations. All the Cinque Terre are linked by paths; walks between one village and the other are relatively strenuous but rewarding. Between Corniglia and Vernazza the path leads past Guvano, a nudist beach; the walk between Riomaggiore and Manarola is truly magical, aptly named the via dell'Amore (Way of Love).

For centuries the local diet here has been governed by the fact that olive oil was the only available kind of fat, since keeping a cow was largely impracticable, and by the abundance of fish. Anchovies would be salted to eat in winter, and meat was on the table only at Christmas and Easter. For other essentials the inhabitants relied on weekly boatloads of supplies from La Spezia. Today the Cinque Terre abound in unpretentious trattorias such as **Aristide** at Manarola; Aristide overwhelms you with antipasti and is known for *zuppa dei datteri,* or date-clam soup.

There are no hotels in the Cinque Terre. However, everything in Liguria is relatively close, and the best place to stay in the area, Tellaro (southeast of La Spezia), is not inconvenient.

Tellaro

"When I go to Tellaro to collect the post I expect every time to meet Jesus talking to his disciples, while I am walking along halfway up the hill, underneath the shining gray trees." The road D. H. Lawrence took to Tellaro is no longer the same, but Tellaro itself must be substantially unchanged. An unspoiled little fishing village, Tellaro is very like its counterparts in Greece—the way blue vistas of the sea suddenly appear around unexpected, wind-swept corners of low, old stone cottages in narrow alleyways meandering down to the tiny port. The diminutive church stands like King Canute, bravely repulsing the waves, which in winter pound mercilessly against the rocks. Lawrence retells the legend of the octopus of Tellaro, which, during a Saracen raid, managed to pull the ropes of the church bells with its tentacles and alert the sleeping populace. Despite the occasional boutique and a couple of bars, Tellaro lives its life impervious to tourists, who have not yet found their way en masse to this little fishing haven.

The **Ristorante Miranda** in Tellaro, a small, family-run restaurant with inexpensive rooms, serves "nouvelle Ligurian" menus based on the daily catch of the local fishermen. Be warned: Fresh fish, as opposed to frozen, is expensive here and everywhere else in Italy. Closed Mondays and from mid-November until the end of February, the Miranda accepts no credit cards.

Lerici

The **Gulf of La Spezia** is also known as the Gulf of Poets because, besides D. H. Lawrence, both Shelley and Byron lived here, as have artists such as William Turner and Arnold Böcklin. This is, however, La Spezia's only claim to poetry; today it is a dusty and industrious seaside town.

Baroness Orczy wrote *The Scarlet Pimpernel* while staying in Lerici at the eastern end of the gulf, and Mary Shelley was inspired by the dark outline of Lerici Castle to write *Frankenstein*. There are more tourists in Lerici now than there were in Shelley's day, and his house at Santerenzio could no longer be described as "a lonely house close by the seaside surrounded by the soft and sublime scenery of the bay of Lerici." Shelley complained about the contrast between "the two Italies," the one exemplifying the magnificence of the landscape, the other the odious ways of contemporary Italians, some of whom, he wrote in disgust, actually ate "garlick"! Shelley drowned while returning to Lerici by boat from Livorno, in Tuscany, and was cremated by his friend Edward Trelawney on the beach. Byron, who was present, requested the skull as a memento, but Trelawney, remembering that Byron had formerly used a skull as a drinking cup, was "determined Shelley's should not be so profaned."

Lerici can still be magical at night, with the lights of the port shaking out snakes of light in the oily water and the castle looming menacingly on the headland. It is a fun place to visit for a drink after dinner at one of the bars on the port, to people-watch the vociferous Italian families whose children never seem to go to bed, and to browse in the typical seaside boutiques for exotic shells and banal tee-shirts.

During the season, public boats take tourists on worthwhile trips from Lerici to the Cinque Terre and Portovenere, another little fishing village, smaller than Lerici but larger than Tellaro, with more boutiques and picturesque trattorias on the sea, serving local fish.

Ameglia

A Medieval hamlet perched above the Bocca di Magra not far from Lerici where the River Magra enters the sea, Ameglia was mentioned by Dante, who paused here on his way to Paris in order, he said, to find peace (*"Io vo cercando pace"*). Ameglia is most famous for the restaurant **La Locanda dell'Angelo.**

Angelo Paracucchi was among the first Italian chefs to be awarded Michelin stars. His beautiful restaurant was designed by Vico Magistretti, one of the most important designers in Italy today. A large personality and a showman, Paracucchi has since fallen into the trap that has attracted many famous chefs: He now spends more time travelling and promoting than cooking in his kitchen, to the detriment of the cuisine. If you happen by on a day when he is in Ameglia and in top form, however, this restaurant—with its *nouvelle* menu and fine selection of wines—is still worth the detour, albeit an expensive one. La Locanda also has 37 rooms for the perfect gastronomic weekend. To get there, exit from the Autostrada at Sarzana. (Just to the south down the Autostrada are Viareggio, Pisa, and Tuscany.)

GETTING AROUND

You can reach most of Genoa's outlying sights by public transportation: the Parco di Nervi by bus number 17 from the piazza de Ferrari; the Pallavicini at Pegli by bus number 2, 3, 4, or 5 from the piazza Caricamento or by train from Genoa's two train stations, the Principe and the Brignole; the cemetery at Staglieno by bus number 34 from the piazza Corvetto.

Coastal towns along the Riviera di Levante are easily reached from Genoa on Autostrada A 12, from which there are exits for Portofino and other towns. However, no one visiting this part of the world should miss the opportunity to pick up the coast road at Chiavari and follow it to Zoagli.

ACCOMMODATIONS REFERENCE

▶ **Ristorante Locanda dell'Angelo.** Viale XXV Aprile, 19031 **Ameglia.** Tel: (0187) 643-91.

▶ **Ristorante e Hotel Ca' Peo.** Via Caduti per la Patria 80, 16040 **Lievi.** Tel: (0185) 31-90-90.

▶ **Hotel Colombia.** Via Balbi 40, 16126 **Genoa.** Tel: (010) 26-18-41; Telex: 270423.

▶ **Golf Hotel Meridiana**. Via ai Castelli 11, 17033 **Garlenda**. Tel: (0182) 58-02-71; Telex: 272123.

▶ **Hotel Metropoli**. Piazza Fontane Marose, 16123 **Genoa**. Tel: (010) 20-15-38.

▶ **Ristorante e Hotel Miranda**. Via Fiascherino 92, 19030 **Tellaro**. Tel: (0187) 96-81-30.

▶ **Hotel Splendido**. Viale Baratta 13, 16034 **Portofino**. Tel: (0185) 26-95-51; Telex: 281057.

PIEDMONT AND TURIN

By Peter Todd Mitchell

Peter Todd Mitchell lived in Florence, Venice, Rome, and on Ischia. He studied Italian Byzantine and Renaissance art and architecture at Yale University, and most recently was a contributing editor at Gourmet *magazine. For his work at* Gourmet *he returned to Italy frequently until his death just before this book went to press.*

Piedmont or Piemonte: Italy's most northern province derives its name quite simply from *ai piedi del monte* (at the foot of the mountains). From almost every vantage point in the Piedmont you can see the snow-peaked barrier of the Alps. The vivid green of the Piedmont fields and orchards makes a starker contrast with the snows beyond than you would find in, say, Switzerland, because the region basks in a southern sun. It was this verdant prospect that whetted the appetites of the barbarian hordes who laid waste to Imperial Rome, and it lured the armies of the north that were later to descend in the Middle Ages and the Renaissance.

The rolling hills of the Langhe and Monferrato regions on the eastern side of the province are still studded with castles and abbeys, but they now also produce some of the best wines in Italy. The once fearsome mountains have long since opened up to well-known ski resorts—in **Sestriere**, west of Turin near the French border, and a dozen other places—and for nature lovers they hold the flora and fauna of the **Parco Nazionale Gran Paradiso** in the Val d'Aosta.

41

Piedmont is a province rich in every way, and its beauties include the sheltered tranquillity of its lakes, which range from the intimate beauty of Orta to the splendid expanse of Lago Maggiore. But the province is especially rich for lovers of Baroque architecture, fine paintings, and good food, all of which is available at Turin, its capital.

MAJOR INTEREST

Lago d'Orta
Food and wine
Sestriere ski resort
Parco Nazionale Gran Paradiso

Turin
Piazza San Carlo (cafés, Baroque churches)
Via Roma (shopping)
Galleria Sabauda (major art museum)
Museo Egizio (Egyptian Museum)
Museo Civico d'Arte Antica (Civic Museum of
    Ancient Art)
Cappella della Santa Sindone (Shroud of Turin)
Museo dell'Automobile
Museo del Risorgimento
Portanuova neighborhood (cafés and trattorias)

Environs of Turin
Baroque palace of Stupinigi
Baroque Basilica di Superga (Pantheon of the
    Savoys)

The Food and Wine
of Piedmont

The wines of Piedmont, particularly the reds, are considered superior, and the food isn't far behind. The Piedmontese are less than pleased when it is suggested that this excellence might be due to a proximity to the French border, but there might be a hint of truth in the assumption. François I was drinking wine from French vineyards in the 16th century, and the Nebbiolo grapes, which farther south produce Barolo and Barbaresco, begin right at the frontier in the French-speaking enclave of the Val d'Aosta. The hills of the southeast also produce the white truffles that play so large a part in Piedmontese cuisine.

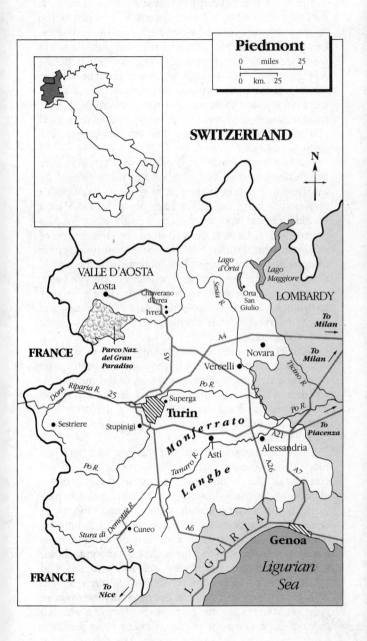

The most common of the region's wines, Barbera, is modest in price but is hearty company for much of the country cuisine. From the vineyards around Asti come the best of the whites. For decades Italians all over the world have been celebrating special occasions with bubbling Asti-Spumanti, but—though the town remains a wine capital—tastes have changed. For younger generations drier whites are in favor, and the growers here have produced one: Gavi, which is pale, dry, and, when served chilled, delicious. It appears in most restaurants—and is a name to remember.

The cooking of Piedmont goes well with its wines, both the dishes inherited from France and those offered by local Italian tradition. In the first category are the varieties of fondue—here, called *fonduta,* made with the local Fontina cheese and often served with white truffles grated over it. Or *sivé,* derived from the French civet of rabbit or game. From the Piedmontese countryside come minestrones of fresh vegetables; polenta, which is served with many main courses; and the region's favorite pasta, *agnolotti*—a large form of ravioli. Gnocchi are another favorite; so is the *bollito misto* of boiled meats and chicken served all over northern Italy, with *salsa verde* and other condiments.

Wine is often used in the cooking: red, for example, with braised veal, and white in the savory risottos. The desserts are often laced with the nuts of the mountains, whether in tarts or *amaretti,* and often use the apples and pears from the local orchards. Many of the cakes and pastries are examples of the Austrian and Swiss bitter-chocolate tradition.

There is no reason to wait for this fine fare until you reach Turin; on every road leading to the capital there are restaurants that would merit a detour if they weren't already in the path. Coming from Chamonix you pass through the ancient Roman town of Aosta, and in its center is the superb **Cavallo Bianco**, at via Aubert 15, where the wines are Valdostana and the cuisine is an excellent introduction to what is ahead. A random choice might include *agnolotti* stuffed with foie gras and wild mushrooms, or tournedos cooked in red *pinot,* served with gnocchi made of polenta. For those driving up from Nice on route S 20 the particularly charming arcaded town of Cuneo near the border offers two fine possibilities. One is the thoroughly Italian **Tre Citroni**—with *fondutas,* risottos, and fresh salmon—at via Bonelli 2. The other is the more Provençal **Le Plat d'Etain**, at corso Giolitti 18. If you enter from Parma and the east, you will come through **Asti**, a Medieval town famed not only for its wines but for its poet, Vittorio Alfieri; Asti will welcome you at the **Gener Neuv**, lungo Tanaro 4, with an avalanche of antipasto, fresh trout, and rabbit brewed in Barbaresco. The entrances from the northeast pass the Lakes, which have a world of restaurants all their own (covered in the Lake Country chapter).

TURIN

Many who have never visited Turin look upon it with apprehension because of its reputation as one of Italy's two industrial centers, which indeed it is. What has not been emphasized often enough is that the factories, Fiat and Pirelli among them, are far enough from the center of town to leave undisturbed one of the most sumptuous Baroque cities to be found anywhere. The heart of the old town has not changed all that much since the 18th century, when Charles de Brosses called it the "most beautiful city in Italy—if not in Europe—thanks to the planning of its streets and the proportion of its buildings."

The Torinese become irritated with the tired accusation that their town is the "most Italian city of France," but the fact remains that Turin was once the capital of the Ducal House of Savoy, and that the Savoy territories included much of present-day France—not just Savoy, but Nice and the Côte d'Azur as well. Much of Turin was built during the long reign of Louis XIV (whose Continental dominance in matters of taste was bound to have a heavy effect upon the city's appearance). As with the building of St. Petersburg, leading architects were called in from outside, and many of them had been influenced by the capitals where they had worked previously. The Baroque was a very viable regal style, used from Naples to Stockholm, so it is natural that in the border state of Piedmont we should find echoes of Fischer von Erlach in Vienna; the brothers Assam in Munich; and Mansart in France. One of the pleasures of Turin is the quest that takes place within your own memory for the exact places of which it is reminiscent.

The most notable building done in Turin in the 17th

and 18th centuries was at the hands of three very imaginative architects. The most Francophile of the three was the
Count of Castellamonte, to whom we owe the royal palace, the **Castello Valentino** (which would be at home in
the Ile de France), and the design of the most popular
public square, the piazza San Carlo, in the center of the
city on the via Roma. The Castello Valentino is located in
the extraordinarily beautiful Parco del Valentino on the
banks of the Po south of the Duomo. Another attraction in
the park is the Borgo Medioevale, with authentic recon-
structions of Medieval Piedmont buildings.

During his long life (1550–1640) the count had much
to do with the planning of the capital (which of course
involved the destruction of most of Medieval Turin), and
its streets are as rectilinear and clear-cut as those of the
bastides of Périgord or of Richelieu in the Val de Loire.
The scale of construction was to become even grander
after the arrival of the Sicilian Filippo Juvarra, an architect
of the Rococo who had been assistant to Carlos Fontana
in Rome. He was called to Turin in 1714, barely a year
after the ruling house had graduated from ducal to royal.
Juvarra, who earlier in his career had devoted much time
to theatrical design, knew just how to celebrate this aug-
mentation: with the Palazzo Madama, which cleverly
masked a façade of the Medieval Castello on the enormous piazza Castello; with the **Basilica of Superga**, just
above Turin, the so-called Pantheon of the House of
Savoy; with the churches on the piazza San Carlo; and
best of all, at **Stupinigi**. Here, on the outskirts of Turin, he
was called upon to design a royal hunting lodge, and the
resulting palace serves to remind us that Versailles was
born the same way. The *palazzina* at Stupinigi is one of
the most dynamic concepts in Baroque art: a domed,
centrifugal pavilion with the wings jutting out like the
arms of a windmill.

The most original of the three architects was a monk
from Modena, Guarino Guarini, who arrived in 1666. In
a class with Bramante and Bernini, he has been hailed as
the most adventurous architect of his period. His extraordinary church cupolas distinctively mark the silhouette
of the center of town, while the wavelike contours and
geometrically patterned courts of his **Palazzo Carignano**
make it far and away the most remarkable of Turin's
royal residences. (The palace now houses the Museo del
Risorgimento.)

Turin on Foot

The architectural district of Turin can be easily explored on foot, and it is with delight that the walker discovers how very well the concepts of its original planners have worked out. You will find it no wonder that it was Napoléon's favorite Italian city; his love of law and order in civic planning was shown clearly enough by what he did to the piazza San Marco in Venice. But here that order is tempered to serve the convenience and leisure of the citizens. In cool weather the cafés on the **piazza San Carlo** offer relaxing interiors typical of the time of Stendhal; but in warm weather they spill out onto the square and turn it into a gracious, open-air salon. Cars are few, as many of the streets are pedestrian; the graceful arches that enclose the old quarter frame views of the hills and mountains beyond, while giving a perspective within that is worthy of De Chirico. The main streets for elegant shopping, such as the **via Roma**, are arcaded, so you can stroll at your leisure and linger in front of the windows that feature names that are often familiar enough: Gucci, Armani, Ferragamo, and the usual lot. This neighborhood offers two things in convenient tandem for most visitors: museums and restaurants.

Of the former, two of the most notable are contained in the huge 17th-century Palazzo dell'Accademia delle Scienze on the piazza San Carlo. The **Galleria Sabauda** is one of the finest art galleries in Italy, its collections having been built around those of the House of Savoy—from which it gets its name—and later much expanded. Its Renaissance Italian paintings are, as you would suspect, of high quality—from Fra Angelico to Botticelli. But so are its Flemish primitives: Memling, van der Weyden, and a gem of a Van Eyck of Saint Francis. The later Flemish pictures—Rubens and the well-known series of Van Dyck portraits of the family of England's Charles I—are here largely because of the court connections of Christine of France, daughter of Henri IV and wife of Vittorio Amadeo II. The Sabauda has been totally modernized within; the lighting is excellent, and soon the 18th-century rooms—Guardi, Tiepolo, and Bellotto—will be reopened.

Also recently reinstalled, and downstairs from the Sabauda, is the **Museo Egizio** (Egyptian Museum), second only to that in Cairo. It is here thanks to a series of

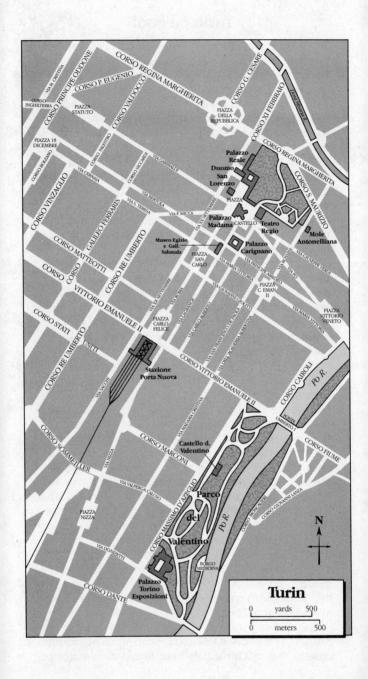

Turin

| 0 | yards | 500 |
| 0 | meters | 500 |

circumstances that began with the fervid collecting that followed Napoléon's Egyptian campaigns. Later, in 1824, King Carlo Felice managed to obtain the priceless finds of a Piedmontese, Bernardino Drovetti, who was adviser to the Egyptian ruler Mohammed Ali and so was allowed to take out whatever he wished. By 1900 archaeologists from Turin were firmly established in Egypt and Nubia, and two of them—Ernesto Schiaparelli and Giulio Farina—completed this collection, which includes tombs, small temples, papyruses, murals, and some wooden sculptures that are a miracle of preservation.

Painting is by no means confined to the Sabauda. The picture that is perhaps the most precious of all—a small portrait of a man in red by Antonello da Messina—is in the **Museo Civico d'Arte Antica**, along with a fine gathering of Tuscan and Piedmontese primitives. The Civico is installed in Turin's former Medieval Castello on the piazza Castello. When Christine of France retired to the fortress as a widow it became known as the **Palazzo Madama**. To enter it you pass through Juvarra's façade and beneath his magnificent staircase. The museum's interior remains that of the Castello, however, and the result is somewhere between the Cluny Museum in Paris and the Isabella Stewart Gardner Museum in Boston: Medieval furnishings, sculpture, and woodwork, much of it collected by the prominent Torinese Azeglio family. More paintings are to be found in the **Palazzo Reale** on the same square. A guided visit is required for the royal palace, which contains a huge collection of armor and some splendid 18th-century Chinoiserie rooms—for lovers of Rococo.

Almost part of the Palazzo Reale is the **Duomo**, the cathedral of Turin, which you enter via its Renaissance front, and which you should visit because it contains in its depths Guarini's fantastic **Cappella della Santa Sindone**, a chapel built to house the so-called **Shroud of Turin**, the treasured cloth that enfolded Christ when he was taken from the Cross and that bears his image. There are even X-ray photos, the tip of the iceberg of investigation (which continues to this day) on the veracity of this relic that remains the personal property of the House of Savoy. The altar shelters the shroud beneath a blaze of Baroque gold; the chapel itself, lined in black marble, is surmounted by Guarini's geometric star-burst of a cupola. Another such cupola can be found around the corner at **San Lorenzo**—probably his most perfect church. Turin's most unusual building—and some say its ugliest—is the **Mole Antonelliana**, with its ziggurat-like roof, near the Po on the via Montebello. Built as a synagogue a little more than a hundred years ago, it now provides a fine lookout from the terrace beneath its granite spire.

Luckily for your feet, this monumental section of Turin is replete with cafés and restaurants. The opera house—Il Teatro Regio—demands them, as do the feet. Near the Regio, at piazza Castello 29, is the most famous of Turin's vintage cafés: **Baratti**, with an entrance from a glass-covered arcade that could have been sent down from 1900 Vienna. The pastries served with its cappuccinos could have been sent from Vienna too, and the café's interior, sparkling with mirrors, painted glass, and chandeliers, has been carefully kept within its period. Turin produces most of Italy's aperitifs: the vermouths—Martini and Cinzano—and Carpano. But as elsewhere in the north there are many who prefer a cold glass of sparkling white wine, a *frizzante*.

With regard to their restaurants, the Torinese show all the enthusiasm—and fickleness—of their French neighbors. The very best places are by no means the most expensive, while some of the staid and starred have become slack in service and negligent in cuisine, and well replaced by newer favorites. One of the liveliest of the new candidates is the **Montecarlo**, via San Francesco da Paola 37, within a stone's throw of the via Carlo Alberto and the Sabauda. At lunchtime its bright, arcaded interior is thronged with a clientele partaking of Piedmontese cuisine treated with a light touch: risotto parmigiano; civet with polenta; *fonduta;* or brains *al burro fuco* (*au beurre noir*). To start, have a delectable spinach mousse, and for dessert, a coffee *zabayon*. For wine you might consider a chilled white Gavi San Pietro; but the sommelier has a particularly wide choice here, and to all intents and purposes runs the restaurant—a job for which he happily exchanged his high position at Fiat.

Some of Turin's more venerable restaurants *have* kept their standards, and, cuisine apart, their interiors are a treat. Situated in a town that has done wonders to retain its turn-of-the-century heritage, they offer the same elegance that patrons of that period expected. One, the **Due Lampioni da Carlo**, is right on the via Carlo Alberto, at number 45. Another, the **Vecchia Lanterna**, is at corso Re Umberto 21, not far from the main train station.

The Porta Nuova

Very convenient and different in decor are the trattorias. Not that they are rowdy or rustic by any means; their largely young clientele are stylishly dressed, the service is efficient, and the pasta and house wines are dependable. One of the best is the **Vittoria** (via Carlo Alberto 34). All these places are not only near the museums, they are also in the district of the Stazione Porta Nuova.

In many cities the neighborhoods surrounding central railroad stations are polluted and shabby, if not dangerous. In Turin the opposite is true. The station's 1868 façade has been left intact and is visible all the way down the via Roma, which terminates at the Palazzo Reale at the other end. The arcaded piazza Carlo Felice, with its well-tended garden, is the first thing voyagers by train will see; and the square also happens to harbor some of the better and older hotels: in particular the **Jolly Hotel Ligure** (at number 85), which has been brought up to date in comfort without being gutted visually. Another renovated hotel of the old school is the **Sitea** (via Carlo Alberto 35): spacious, tranquil—and in the midst of the sights. Two more modest havens are the **Roma e Rocca Cavour**, right on piazza Carlo Felice, and the **Bramante**, nearby at via Genova 2.

As the via Roma runs from the Porta Nuova to the palazzo it passes through a gambit of styles. The bazaar of cafés and street vendors of Carlo Felice are soon exchanged for the cool elegance of some of the most expensive shops to be found anywhere, and for the first few blocks of the avenue they are ensconced under Mussolini's marble arches, which are supported by monolithic columns. The arches terminate in the small piazza San Carlo, with fountains and statues that a few years ago would have been excoriated as symbols of a dictatorial style. Now that both the 1930s and Art Deco are being reassessed, they might be viewed in a different light—particularly when they are compared to some of the postwar eyesores, which would certainly include the appalling mess of an office building opposite the Duomo. Whereas in Germany many of the artists and designers left with the ascension of Hitler, here in the 1930s they stayed on and worked. They were often even subsidized by the government, which handed out money in many fields: to Elsa Schiaparelli, when she started to make sweaters; to Venini in Venice, to bring glassware into the 20th century; and to every branch of industrial design, for which Turin was to become a center.

Turin's many annual fairs, including the widely attended auto show, are to be avoided at all costs because of their effect on hotel space, but a permanent museum like the **Museo dell'Automobile**—which to lovers of art and history might sound like a festival of boredom—displays the degree of originality that the Italians had long before Nervi. A family like the Bugatti were artists in many areas. The Museo, which is just south of the Parco del Valentino at corso Unità d'Italia 10, even got its hands on the Isotta Fraschini used by Gloria Swanson in the film *Sunset Boulevard*.

Museo del Risorgimento

Of all the museums in Turin, the one that surprises the visitor most with its excellence is the Museo del Risorgimento, fittingly located in Guarini's Palazzo Carignano, which saw the birth both of Italy's first king from the House of Savoy, Vittorio Emanuele II, and of its first parliament. From its title you would gather that the museum deals with the movement that led to the unification of Italy; but in reality it goes far beyond that and emerges as a matchless résumé, in documents, letters, reconstructed rooms, and paintings (some of them very well known), of the country's entire history from the year 1709 on. The year 1709 was the date of the Battle of Torino, when Eugène of Savoy Carignano defeated the French troops of Louis XIV in the War of the Spanish Succession—the beginning of the end of foreign rule on the peninsula.

The victorious Eugène's House of Savoy was to remain in power until 1946, when by plebiscite the royal family was voted into exile (whether or not the ballot boxes were stuffed by the ever-energetic Communist Party depends on which Italian you are talking to, and where). Only recently has Maria Pia, the widow of King Umberto II, been allowed to return to her native land in these her final years. Permission for entry has been denied, however, to her grandson, Emanuele Filiberto. Evidently the presence of a 15-year-old child might menace the notoriously questionable stability of the Italian government. Maybe some day the prince will be allowed to see the very handsome town so largely built by his own family.

AROUND TURIN

The **Parco Nazionale Gran Paradiso**, once the preserve of
the Savoys, stretches from near Ivrea, 50 km (30 miles)
north of Turin, across the regional border into Val d'Aosta
and west into France. Chamois and ibex occasionally
sprint past the hiker in the brilliant Alpine scenery, and a
choice array of flowers brightens the meadows. Ivrea's
14th-century turreted castle blends surprisingly well with
what Olivetti hath wrought, making this a company town
from 1908 to emulate. Called Ivrea *"la bella,"* the town
retains its ancient charm, most evident in February during
the pre-Lenten carnival. Like Sestriere, Ivrea is reached
quickly by train from Turin. The **Castello San Giuseppe** at
nearby Chiaverano d'Ivrea is a convent that Napoléon
transformed into a fort. It has since joined the private
sector as a villa-hotel where Eleanora Duse relaxed in the
gardens of orange trees, cedars, and magnolias. The rooms
at the far ends of the wings have the best views. In Ivrea, the
Moro and the **Eden** are inexpensive hotels, convenient to
the nondriver who wants to hike.

Sestriere, west of Turin on the French border, is part of
a skiing network that encompasses hundreds of slopes.
Snow machines ensure a white terrain, and an assortment
of cable cars and ski lifts provide ascent and wonderful
views. Hotels range from the scenic **Grand Hotel Sestriere**
and the **Principi di Piemonte**, each in its own park,
to less extravagant rooms with views at the **Sud-Ovest**. To
soothe the wind-burned palette, the **Last Tango Grill**, via
La Gleisa 12, skewers snails in Cognac, whirls taglione in
lemon sauce, and roasts lamb. An alpine cheese and herb
pie is the thing for a lighter snack.

GETTING AROUND
From Milan and Rome, train connections are frequent to
Turin, and from Turin to Asti. From these two cities, bus
service is good to smaller towns in the region. Turin is
also linked by air to Rome and Milan, and to other Italian
airports, as well as directly to many principal European
cities, including London, Paris, and Frankfurt.

ACCOMMODATIONS REFERENCE
▶ **Bramante-Continental**. Via Genova 2, 10126 **Turin**.
Tel: (011) 69-79-97.
▶ **Castello San Giuseppe**. 10010 **Chiaverano d'Ivrea**.
Tel: (0125) 42-43-70.

▶ **Eden.** Corso Massimo D'Azeglio 67, 10015 **Ivrea**. Tel: (0125) 42-47-41.

▶ **Jolly Hotel Ligure.** Piazza Carlo Felice 85, 10123 **Turin**. Tel: (011) 556-41; in U.S., (212) 557-1116; Telex: 220167.

▶ **Moro.** Corso Massimo D'Azeglio 43, 10015 **Ivrea**. Tel: (0125) 401-70.

▶ **Principi di Piemonte.** Via Sauze, 10058 **Sestriere**. Tel: (0122) 79-41.

▶ **Roma e Rocca Cavour.** Piazza Carlo Felice 60, 10123 **Turin**. Tel: (011) 51-81-37.

▶ **Villa Sassi.** Strada al Traforo del Pino 47, 10132 **Turin**. Tel: (011) 89-05-56. In a private park amid Piedmont hills only a few minutes from central Turin. The 12 rooms are furnished with period pieces.

▶ **Grand Hotel Sestriere.** Via Assietta 1, 10058 **Sestriere**. Tel: (0122) 764-76.

▶ **Grand Hotel Sitea.** Via Carlo Alberto 35, 10123 **Turin**. Tel: (011) 557-01-71; Telex: 220229.

▶ **Sud-Ovest.** Via Monterotto 17, 10058 **Sestriere**. Tel: (0122) 773-93.

LAKE COUNTRY

*By Peter Todd Mitchell
and
Joanne Hahn*

The Lakes of Northern Italy are so varied in character that it is tempting to say that the only things they have in common are the backdrop of the Alps and a certain similarity in luxuriant flora. They are crisscrossed by borders—not only of provinces but also of countries—and each has its own enthusiastic partisans, including the many writers who have visited them in the past. Before the days of air travel, the Lakes were often the first part of Italy that many travellers would see; the ardor that they engendered in those arriving from the fog and rain of northern climes was often kindled as much by the sun-drenched wonder of being in Italy at all as by the Lakes' unique beauty.

MAJOR INTEREST

Scenic beauty

Lago d'Orta
Island and church of San Giulio
Baroque chapels at Sacro Monte

Lago Maggiore
Gardens and Villa of Isola Bella
Gardens of Villa Táranto in Pallanza

Lago di Como
Duomo in Como
Basilica of Sant'Abbondio

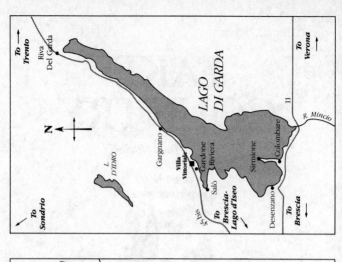

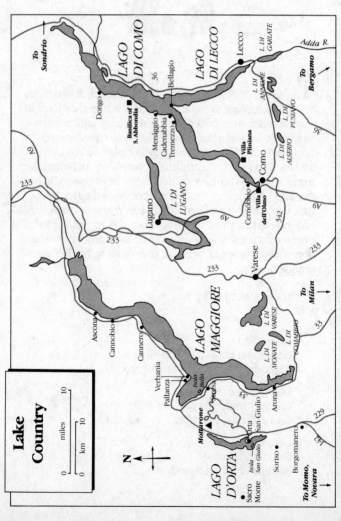

Como's Piazza del Duomo and Gothic town hall
Villa dell'Olmo
Villa d'Este in Cernóbbio
Villa Carlotta in Tremezzo
Villa Melzi in Bellágio
Boat ride from Bellágio to Cadenábbia

Lago d'Iseo
Monte Isola

Lago di Garda
Roman villa and grottoes of Catullus on scenic
     point
Castle of the Scaligers
Villa Vittoriale, D'Annunzio's home
The scenic drive from Salò to Riva along the
     Gardone Riviera

The Food of the Lake District

Meat and game dishes and, of course, lake fish dominate
the local cuisine. Fresh trout and perch are popular fish
here, and find their way into the varied *ravioli ripieni di
pesce del lago,* or are served grilled. In the area of
Brescia and Bergamo, once under Venetian rule, the delicate *osei,* tiny songbirds, are wrapped in pancetta (an
Italian bacon) and spit-roasted, served on a slab of
polenta, dribbled with cooking juices. Other delicacies
are *agoni,* a local type of shad, and *tinca,* a delicate,
sweet whitefish.

Polenta, a derivative of the Roman dish *puls,* which
during the days of the Empire was made with a variety of
grains, is today made with cornmeal. It is served in many
ways, most typically either creamy or in a slab, baked or
pan fried.

Agrodolce, a sweet-and-sour sauce, is found on many
menus and is served in a number of dishes, such as
stracotto con cipolline, tender braised beef and small
onions that have been marinated in the sauce.

Near Lago di Varese, just west of Como, the popular
Lombardy dish risotto takes on an exotic accent when
eels cooked in a spicy sauce are added. Northeast, in the
area of Sondrio in the beautiful Valtellina valley, you find
pizzocher, hearty buckwheat noodles that are usually
combined with potatoes, leeks, and cabbage, and *polenta
taragna,* a buckwheat and cornmeal combination. The
area also produces rich sausages and salamis, such as the

mortadella di fegato, a velvety bologna-type salami including liver; this mortadella goes remarkably well with
the regional beers that are made from the purest
mountain-stream waters.

LAGO D'ORTA

There are some who elect as their favorite of all the Lakes
one that is not only small, but that also has remained
unknown to the majority of today's voyagers. Orta is
wholly within the frontiers of Piedmont, and just to the
west of Lago Maggiore, though nowhere near comparable to Maggiore in size. It is for this very reason—its
intimacy—that the lake has elicited such feelings of
warmth from visitors as diverse as Balzac ("Studied grandeur is far away; the proportion returns to the human,"
he wrote of it) and Nietzsche, who found it one of the
most evocative places he had ever seen. Most of Orta's
devotees have stayed in **Orta San Giulio**, the little town
set at the end of a small peninsula that juts into the
eastern side of the lake and faces an island across the way
that, along with its church of San Giulio and its palace of
the archbishops of Novara, seems to be floating on the
lake. Both the island and the town have been meticulously kept within the styles of the periods in which they
were built, from Medieval to Baroque. Boats to the island
spin back and forth throughout the day, and it is well
worth making the trip just for the sake of seeing the
Romanesque church dedicated to Saint Julius, who slew
the island's dragon.

However, the tree-lined main square of San Giulio
itself, which looks out onto the lake and its points of
embarkation, is so well provided with shaded cafés and
restaurants that it is hardly conducive to moving anywhere at all. The square is dominated at its far end by a
frescoed town hall of the 16th century, which is supported by colonnades and surveys the market and the
goings-on below. Streets lined with palaces with beautiful
loggias, all within the appealing scale of the town, radiate
from the square, some of them leading to the churches
and sanctuaries that top the surrounding hills.

The most famous of these sanctuaries is the **Sacro
Monte**, where 20 Baroque chapels harbor painted terra-
cotta figures depicting scenes from the life of Saint Francis, with murals rather in the style of Neapolitan *presepi* as

background. Another place of pilgrimage on the Sacro Monte is of quite a different sort: the **Ristorante Sacro Monte**, installed in a 17th-century villa, is the best around, serving among its specialties prosciutto from Val Vigezzo, curried chicken with risotto, and a large selection of local wines (the more usual of which around here are of course those of Piedmont: Barolo and Barbera for red, Gavi for white).

The road to Orta from Novara and the south is paved with good restaurants: for example, the **Macallè**, at Momo, and the **Pinocchio**, at Borgomanero (via Matteotti 147). **Al Sorriso**, at Soriso (about 5 km/3 miles southwest of the lake), is elegant both in decor and in cuisine and would be a good choice for a dinner excursion. When you settle in at Orta it is preferable, because of these and other opportunities for eating around and taking trips, to avoid any sort of pension arrangement that might tie you down.

The hotels in Orta are by no means grandiose; Stresa is right over the hills, and its hotels are more than capable of catering to opulent tastes. Here at Orta, the **Orta** is right on the main piazza, with its restaurant on a terrace overlooking the lake, while the **San Rocco**, a remodelled 17th-century convent, and the **Bussola** are surrounded by their own gardens and are also lakeside and slightly out of town. None is very large, so reserve well in advance.

Of all the drives in the Lake District the most spectacular must be the one from Orta to Lago Maggiore, over the narrow ridge of mountains called the Mottarone. From the summit of the ridge you can see both lakes, the Alps, and the Po valley. In the winter there is skiing on the Mottarone, and all year round there are rustic lodges where travellers can break their journey.

STRESA AND LAGO MAGGIORE

There is nothing rustic about Stresa, the touristic capital of Lago Maggiore. It is on the main Paris–Milan rail line, and so convenient a stop that it attracts multitudes who descend from trains that have barely just passed the Swiss border. Its most renowned hotel, **Des Iles Borromées**, has been taken over by the Ciga chain, and they have wisely kept it visually within its original period. Its spacious rooms overlook well-tended gardens, and its neighbor, the **Regina Palace**, keeps it good company. You could deduce from their very size that these hostelries have hosted many an international conference, and indeed they have. Some of the meetings are foreboding in the very names of those who have attended them: for example, the Stresa Conference of 1935, with Mussolini, Laval, and Ramsey Macdonald. In more recent times the quite serious September music festivals have been held here, with concerts taking advantage of every possible site.

In the town itself there is a choice of lodgings that run to more reasonable rates around the piazza Imbarcadero; of these, the **Milan au Lac** is the most inviting. Also in town is the best restaurant around (apart from the stately dining room of Des Iles Borromées, with its high French windows, sparkling tableware, and everything to match): **Emiliano**, at corso Italia 48, right on the waterfront and specializing in fish, which it uses in highly imaginative ways—with pasta, in summer salads, and in risottos. Emiliano, being small and select, may be hard to get into, but Stresa is a large resort and is packed with every kind of trattoria and café. At **La Piemontese**, via Mazzini 25, accents of red and wood paneling make for a cozy setting. The service can be a bit crisp, but the food redeems all. The specialties include large ravioli, sometimes called *casonsei,* bathed in a creamy porcini mushroom sauce, and grilled veal chops. Fresh fruit and the runny, slightly sharp Stracchino cheese (Gorgonzola) top off a meal here nicely.

Far and away the best means of seeing Maggiore is by boat; the villas on the lake have high walls, so to see their gardens from the descending hillsides is often difficult, while on the other hand many face openly onto the lake itself. Boats leave frequently from the Imbarcadero. Excursions by water to well-known gardens can often be combined with lunching well in their vicinity. The only case where you would be advised not to combine food with a feast for the eyes would be that of **Isola Bella**, where any sort of visit is best timed instead for an off-hour, when the deluge of tourists can be avoided.

The Isola is the best-known sight on the lake, and was already so in the 18th century when the French scholar Charles de Brosses said that it looked as if it had been dropped from the Hesperides. It looks much more so now, for the centuries since Count Carlo Borromeo started it in 1630 have added a riot of verdure to the originally rather bare series of terraces and parterres designed by the Crivellis. No money was to be spared on Isola Bella, or time; its gardens took 40 years in their construction. Relays of architects, including Carlo Fontana of Rome, were called in to complete this marble gallery, which is the sort of thing Emperor Hadrian might have thought up. The villa at the far end can be visited, and has some very fine Baroque paintings, murals, furniture, and a substructure of grottoes, encrusted with shells, that are worthy of Arcimboldo.

An ideal excursion from Stresa combining sights and a good table would be a boat trip to the gardens of the **Villa Táranto** at Pallanza, just outside of Verbania and clearly visible from Stresa's shore. The terraces beneath the 18th-century villa abound in exotic and rare tropical plants. Also at Pallanza are two superior restaurants: **Il Torchio**, via Manzoni 20, and the **Milano**, with a fine choice of homemade pasta, at corso Zanitello 2.

The northern shores of Maggiore shelter the Medieval towns of Cannóbio and Cannero on the Stresa side; but a step too far and you are in Switzerland near the resort town of Ascona. From Cannero a ten-minute boat ride will take you to the **Castello di Cannero**, a rocky island with the ruins of two Medieval castles.

LAGO DI COMO

Of all the Lakes, Como comes to us as the most heavily romantic. Even its structure—three quite different basins, each seeming a lake in itself—lends itself to an emotional turn of mind. Its steep hills cascade down to a finale of villas and gardens reflected in particularly azure water, and the sentinel Alps hover closely behind. The very names of its tiny ports evoke nostalgia in those who have known them even for brief periods: Cadenábbia, Bellágio, Menággio. Castles and convents were built on its shores in the Middle Ages, and villas in the Renaissance; but when the Romantics of the 19th century arrived it was love at first sight, a magnificent love that was to make the lake famous all over the world. Franz Liszt was so enraptured by the lake that when his daughter was born there he named her Cosma; later, as Cosima, she was to marry Richard Wagner. Lord Byron stayed at the Villa Pliniana, where Rossini was to write one of the first passionate operas of the 19th century, *Tancredi;* later, at the Villa Margherita, Verdi was to compose most of *La Traviata*. Poets by the dozen were to laud the lake, but it was a writer of prose who sets it before us most vividly; Stendhal chose Como for many of the opening episodes of his novel, *The Charterhouse at Parma,* and depicted the younger days of his hero, Fabrizio, on its shores.

The Napoleonic years were glorious ones for building on Como, as we shall see, and the Emperor and his son-in-law, Eugène de Beauharnais, were constant visitors. It was not until the middle of the century, however, that hotels were to open and fill with Russian grand dukes and the wealthy from all over Europe. Their comings and goings were well described in a novel of our own time, written anonymously, entitled *Madame Solario.* (The work has since been republished under the author's real name—Gladys Huntington.) The eponymous heroine, with her friends of rank and fashion, would glide back and forth by boat for luncheons and parties in very much the same places that we still visit. In the town of Como there is a disused ramp descending from the Stazione Nord to an embarkation dock. There, surely, in the days when it was par for the course for an English milady to travel with 20 trunks, these sorts of visitors arrived and were wafted by boat to their hotels.

Como the Town

The town of Como is situated at the Lake's southern end and is all too often bypassed or rushed through on the way to the more natural settings to be found on farther shores. This is a shame, as Como is an active, charming city full of things to see, and with restaurants and hotels of every sort. It has a hidden advantage in its railroad station, the Nord, which has trains leaving every hour for the 40-minute trip to the Stazione Nord in the center of Milan, almost adjacent to the Castello Sforzesco. This means that for those who wish to see Milan without paying the steep prices of its ever-packed hotels, and who don't mind returning in the evening to a quieter place where there is fresh air, Como can be a convenient alternative. Of its hotels the most appealing is the **Metropole Suisse**, facing the lake on the main square, the piazza Cavour. Other smaller ones are scattered through the town: the **Posta** and the **Tre Re**, to name a couple.

The town, first Roman, then a Longobard capital, is very old indeed. From its early Medieval period comes the impressive Romanesque **Basilica of Sant'Abbondio**, with its frescoed interior, on the outskirts of town. The piazza

San Fidele, the vivacious and ancient center of city life, is surrounded by Medieval houses. The Church of San Fedele, on the piazza, has unusual carvings on its portals and some fine Renaissance paintings within. The pride of Como is its Duomo, built over centuries but always with the workmanship of the sculptors and masons known as the Comancini, who were based here but branched out to work throughout Lombardy and Emilia-Romagna. Its highly original façade is divided by four marble pilasters, filled with statues that include two of those senior citizens of Roman Como, the Plinys. The interior is a veritable museum of tapestries, sculpture, and altar paintings (including a fine Luini), and the dome was designed by the same Juvarra who helped build 18th-century Turin. Alongside the cathedral is the striped façade of the Broletto, the municipal palace, which is set above the square on arcades. The square itself is lined with inviting cafés. The small streets of the old town are dotted with trattorias, some of them very good. The best known is del Gesumin at via 5 Giornate 44, while Fiorino, very near the Duomo at piazza Grimaldi 8, is popular and convenient.

As a capital of silk-making, Como has outlets for silk fabrics and ties and scarves. Centro della Seta has two outlets in Como at via Volta 64 and via Bellinzona 3. Along the principal shopping street, via Vittorio, Emanuele A. Picci (among others) sells scarves and such; on nearby via Ballarini, Rainoldi sells silk fabrics.

The Shores of Como

Within walking distance of the town of Como is the first of the large villas on the western shore of the lake: the Villa dell'Olmo, now a communal cultural center and open to all. Begun by the Odescalchi family in the 17th century, the villa changed styles toward the end of the 18th; its present Neoclassical façade was ready in 1797 to witness the arrival of Napoléon and Josephine as guests. Its terraces, with a striking view of the town, are used for concerts during the autumn music festival.

Not so accessible is the Villa d'Este at Cernóbbio, a bit up the coast; you will have to show identification (passport) at the gates of what has been one of Europe's most luxurious hotels since 1873. The hotel has two restaurants, one in the grand style as part of the main building, the other a well-designed modern grill near the sporting facilities. There are two large pools, one outside on the lake and the other indoors. The lobbies, well kept and full of treasures from the villa's past, retain the feeling of affluence left by the former owners—brought up to date by shops for jewels and antiques. This is a villa that seems always to have demanded wealth; it was begun by the hugely rich Cardinal Tolomeo Gallio in the 16th century and refurbished in the late 18th by the Marchesa Calderera, who cleverly married one of Napoléon's ministers. It was she who added the Gothic Revival buildings that now serve as an annex to the hotel. The most famous occupant was to follow: Caroline of Brunswick retired here after the scandalous trial for adultery and sedition brought on by her husband, George IV of England. While continuing her riotous way of life, she decided that she was obscurely related to the Este family and changed the villa's name to suit her whim. Later in the 19th century, another resident, the Russian Empress Maria Fedorovna, was to bring to it a final social fling—before its doors opened to a wider public.

About 35 km (20 miles) north, at Tremezzo, looms the **Villa Carlotta**, probably the most famous one on the entire lake, due largely to its remarkable gardens. The villa itself has remained faithful to the period of Bonaparte, with a collection of Neoclassic paintings and sculpture by Canova and Thorvaldsen, all well set off by the Pompeiian ceilings and the Empire furniture. The villa was built largely by Giovanni Sommariva, who made a fortune supplying the Emperor's armies; the "C" over the door stands for his Clerici wife. The "Carlotta" was to come later with the arrival of a new owner, Carlotta of Nassau, sister to the kaiser and married to a Saxe-Meiningen, from whom the Italian government confiscated the villa on the outbreak of World War I. It was the German owners, however, who transformed the gardens, making them larger and less formal, adding the paths that in the spring blaze with azaleas and rhododendrons, and creating the sudden, operatic vistas of fern forest and jungle. Como is hardly on the same latitude as Palermo, yet there seems to be something in its climate that preserves a flora worthy of the Amazon.

The boat ride from Cadenábbia, just north of the Carlotta, to Bellágio, which is right across the lake, is breathtaking. Because in the 19th century this one-and-a-half-mile span was admired almost as if it were the Grand Canal in Venice, hotels sprang up on both sides. On the Carlotta side a good one is still the **Grand Hotel Tre-**

mezzo Palace, where palm trees and other tropical vegetation spill onto the grounds, though a room with a lake view (all have balconies) is probably advisable. There is fine swimming in the pool and in the lake, tennis and golf are available, and right next to the villa is a very nice café called **Timon**. At Bellágio the **Grand Hotel Villa Serbelloni**, with its fine gardens, presides over a multitude of smaller establishments. Those more modest quarters can be very useful all over the Lakes when the larger ones close down after a "season" that is nowhere near as long as it is in France or Spain. On the other hand, because Italian vacationers flood the region in July and August, you should plan a visit in spring or fall.

The gardens of the Villa Serbelloni cover much of Bellágio's point, and have an unsurpassed view of Como's every branch. To the south along the road they join the gardens of the **Villa Melzi**, which was constructed by Francesco Melzi d'Eryl, vice president of Bonaparte's Northern Italian Republic and a personal friend of the then-consul. Its manicured lawns, with its sphinxes and fountains, will remind you of Malmaison, except that here the urns are original Etruscan ones (Melzi was an avid collector). There is a perfect Neoclassical chapel, and a pavilion with mementoes of Napoléon. The villa itself, however, is closed to the public, as it still belongs to the Gallarati Scotti, a Lombard family of diplomats and writers who graciously allow visitors onto their grounds. We can be happy to see it in private hands; a lake with villas occupied only by the ghosts of tenants past would be a sad one indeed.

LAGO D'ISEO

Less well known, and therefore less commercial than the other lakes of Lombardy, Iseo, roughly halfway east of Milan toward Lago di Garda, is surrounded by quaint villages, olive trees, and rugged mountains. Its waters brim with trout, eel, and other fish, and flocks of wild ducks swoop over the lake to enjoy the extremely gentle climate, which some say is milder than Como's.

From the towns of Iseo and Sulzano, boats leave daily to **Monte Isola**, a small, lush island in the center of the lake, covered with olive and chestnut trees, and—delightfully—free of cars. The ferry lands there at Peschiera Maraglio; nearby along the quay is the flower-bedecked **Trattoria del**

Pesce Archetti, a simple, comfortable place bustling with local patrons. The restaurant is run by the Archetti sisters, who with their exceptional seafood dishes do more than justice to the fresh lake fish. Their *antipasto del lago,* a medley of little *lavarello* fish that are served with a sweet-and-sour sauce and home-cured lake sardines are a perfect prelude to the *pesce in carpione,* small fish fillets of either trout or whitefish that are lightly coated and fried and marinated in a spicy sauce of onion, garlic, bell pepper, wine, and herbs.

The island is a romantic place to spend the night, and a stay there affords the traveller a romantic escape from congested roads. The **Hotel La Foresta** has ten rooms for those who can enjoy a relaxed and quiet atmosphere.

In the town of Borgonato, just 20 km (15 miles) south-east of Iseo in the wine-producing region of Franciacorta, the Fratelli Berlucchi, principal winegrowers of the area, offer a splendid tour of their wine cellars housed in an elegant 16th-century villa set on lush grounds. Visitors are welcome to taste their fine sparkling wines.

LAGO DI GARDA

The colors of Garda on the eastern side of Lombardy are the colors of the Adriatic: turquoise and opaline. Almost half of the lake lies in the Veneto just west of Verona, with the border of Lombardy just east of the **Peninsula of Sirmione**, a splinter of land jutting up from the south that is the lake's most popular resort. Visitors are greeted with a crenellated castle of the Scaligers, and beyond it the beaches and groves that lead to the so-called **Grotte di Catullo**. Archaeologists have found enough Roman remains there to demonstrate that Sirmione was just as popular then as it is now. Of hotels in Sirmione there are plenty. The **Grand Hotel Terme** is perhaps the most convenient, since it is right by the castle and has excellent food, a large swimming pool, and facilities for those who wish to take the cure.

Many travellers, however, stop at Sirmione just to have lunch while enroute from Milan to Venice. The menus here are laced with hints of Venetian cuisine: cod à la Gardiana is served with polenta, and *tiramisu,* that richest of all chocolate-and-cream desserts, begins to make an appearance. Bardolino, the best of the local reds, comes from its own town on the eastern shore of the lake, while the most refreshing of the whites, Lugana, is produced just south of Sirmione. One of the most attractive of the restaurants is in the town itself: **Grifone-da Luciano** is a minute by foot from the center, but it seems much farther when you are ensconced on its terrace with a sweeping view of the lake. Five km (3 miles) out of town is the **Vecchia Lugana**, in an 18th-century villa near the hamlet of Lugana where the white wine is produced. There diners are allowed to help themselves from such a tempting mosaic of antipasti that they hardly have room for the eggplant *pasticcio* or the wild-mushroom pie that can follow. Meats are roasted on a spit in the ancient fireplace here, and in summer months there is dining on a terrace overlooking the lake. Another good bet outside the city limits is the **Al Pozzo da Silvio** in Colombare at via Statale 15—the simplest of all, but for country food perhaps the best.

It is particularly important at Sirmione to have a few refuges of your own. Germans have been descending into Italy, for one reason or another, for centuries; it is natural that many should take their vacations in a country that is both near and warmer in climate. Sirmione is one of the resorts where they form the massive majority of visitors, so others might be well advised to either search out Italianate havens—or start reading the *Frankfurter Allgemeine*. Sirmione is in any case an ideal base for visiting Mantua, Verona, and, of course, the rest of the lake.

Leaving Sirmione for the scenic drives of the Gardone Riviera, travellers first pass through the small port of Desenzano, and soon, above Gardone, reach Garda's foremost villa to visit. It is by no means out of a distant past; **Il Vittoriale** was the home of the poet Gabriele D'Annunzio, who lived here from 1921 until his death in 1938. D'Annunzio was a man of action as well as a writer, and there are mementoes of his political past on the grounds of the villa: the patrol boat that he used in World War I and the tomb of the companions who joined him in his dashing and successful rally to retake Fiume. There are also souvenirs of his other past—that of being the Don Juan of his age. Though small in stature and unprepossessing in looks, he had a magnetic hold over women, though that hold was certainly enhanced by the sensuality of his poetry and the glamor of his warrior's life. His conquests read like Leporello's catalogue in *Don Giovanni,* with one important difference: there were no Zerlinas or chambermaids, just women of talent or of high birth—among them his own wife, the Duchess de Gallise. The affair most featured in the villa is the one he had with the celebrated actress Eleanora Duse, to whom he managed to give quite a few years of almost guaranteed unhappiness. But others are remembered here, too; and in the upper reaches of the villa there hide Turkish corners and exotic recesses. It is odd, though, to see so many art reproductions instead of originals in the home of a man who had so many artist friends (including a particularly devoted one, the American painter Romaine Brooks). For Italians, D'Annunzio is by no means merely a figure of the past; his life was long, his talent was varied, and he produced work in many media. His plays are performed in the outdoor theater at the Vittoriale; the most famous, thanks largely to Duse, is *La Citta Morta*.

Farther up this coast at Gargnano is the last home of the leader to whom the poet was to give early support: Benito Mussolini. After the victory at Fiume, Mussolini was quite happy to pursue an independent course and leave D'Annunzio comfortably on Garda—far from Rome and far from possible embarrassment to Fascist policies.

The Duce's final years on the Lakes ended badly for him. The capital of his Fascist Republic (1943–1945) was on Garda, at Salò, as was his residence, the Villa Feltrinelli at Gargnano. When, with his mistress, Clara Petacci, he tried to escape to Switzerland by way of Como, his Varennes was at Dongo on the north shore of that lake, where they were recognized by partisans and brought to a quick and grisly death.

The north shore of Garda brings one magnificent view after another; from the heights of the Sanctuario della Madonna di Monte Castello to the cool promenades of Riva del Garda, at its northern end in the Alto Adige, and on the way to Trento and then Bolzano. Along the lakeshore, delightfully terraced lemon and lime groves are made more brilliant by the surrounding mountains—with a hint of Switzerland to the north.

GETTING AROUND

The major cities on each lake—Como, Stresa, Desenzano, and Orta Miasino—are accessible by train directly from Milan. The towns along the lakes are linked by regular bus service, and ferries and hydrofoils ply the lakes connecting the mainland to the islands and one town to the other.

ACCOMMODATIONS REFERENCE

This listing includes those hotels mentioned in this chapter, as well as other especially pleasant accommodations on the Northern Lakes.

Bellágio, Lago di Como

(Telephone area code, 031; postal code, 22021.)

▶ **Grand Hotel Villa Serbelloni.** Tel: 95-02-16; Telex: 380330; in U.S., (212) 477-1600 or (800) 366-1510.

▶ **Hotel du Lac.** Piazza Mazzini. Tel: 95-03-20. This century-old villa has been carefully managed and maintains its simple elegance and gracious touches—like the one lovely rooftop garden and glassed-enclosed terrace restaurant. Very reasonable rates.

▶ **Hotel Florence.** Piazza Mazzini. Tel: 95-03-42. This charming and moderately priced 19th-century villa—run by the Ketzlar family for more than 150 years—has 40 pleasant rooms, some with bath and shower. Tree-domed lakeside dining here—surrounded by scenes of spectacular nature—features superb grilled fish and pasta and attentive service by white-jacketed waiters who hover over impeccably set tables.

Como, Lago di Como

(Telephone area code, 031; postal code, 22100.)

▶ **Metropole Suisse.** Piazza Cavour 19. Tel: 26-94-44.

▶ **Posta.** Via Garibaldi 2. Tel: 26-60-12.

▶ **Grand Hotel Tremezzo Palace** (in Tremezzo, on the lake across from Bellágio). Via Regina 8, 22019 **Tremezzo**. Tel: (344) 40-446; Telex: 320810 PALTRE 1; Fax: 344/40201.

▶ **Tre Re.** Via Boldoni 20. Tel: 26-53-74.

▶ **Villa D'Este** (in Cernóbbio, outside of Como on the lake). Via Regina 40, 22012 Cernóbbio. Tel: 51-14-71; Telex: 380025; in U.S., (212) 838-3110 or (800) 223-6800.

Monte Isola, Lago d'Iseo

(Telephone area code, 030; postal code, 25050.)

▶ **Hotel La Foresta.** Peschiera Maraglio. Tel: 98-82-10.

Orta San Giulio, Lago d'Orta

(Telephone area code, 0322; postal code, 28016.)

▶ **La Bussola.** Tel: 90-198.

▶ **Orta.** Tel: 90-253.

▶ **San Rocco.** Tel: 90-222; in U.S., (201) 273-7373 or (800) 631-7373.

Sirmione, Lago di Garda

(Telephone area code, 030; postal code, 25019.)

▶ **Grand Hotel Terme.** Viale Marconi 1. Tel: 91-62-61.

▶ **Hotel Sirmione.** Piazza Castello. Tel: 91-63-31. This lovely, ochre-toned building stands at the edge of the water amid flower gardens. The smallish rooms, most with private balconies, are reasonably priced.

Stresa, Lago Maggiore

(Telephone area code, 0323; postal code, 28049.)

▶ **Albergo Italia E Svizzera.** Piazza Imbarcadero. Tel: 39-540. Simple, comfortable, and moderately priced rooms, all with bath and shower, and some with a lake view. The restaurant is good.

▶ **Des Iles Borromées.** Lungolago Umberto 1. Tel: 30-431; Telex: 200377; in U.S., (212) 935-9540 or (800) 221-2340.

▶ **Milan au Lac.** Piazza Imbarcadero. Tel: 31-190.

▶ **Regina Palace.** Lungolago Umberto 1. Tel: 30-171; Telex: 200381; in U.S., (212) 725-5880 or (800) 223-5695.

▶ **Speranza au Lac.** Piazza Imbarcadero. Tel: 31-178. An agreeable modern hotel facing the lake, with spacious, attractive, and reasonably priced rooms, within walking distance to major sights. Some rooms have balconies and a lake view.

MILAN AND LOMBARDY

By Peter Todd Mitchell

Lombardy remains the richest of Italy's provinces, in industry, finance, and agriculture. At times these elements all work together: The fields of Brianza grow mulberry trees, and the town of Como purveys the finished product, silk. Lombardy's herds of livestock produce the best milk and butter in the country, and the towns on the edge of the plains where the animals graze manufacture some of the best cheeses: Gorgonzola and Bel Paese.

Lombardy is sometimes thought of as a province of flat terrain and factory towns, but, luckily for the Milanese, the variety of the region's scenery offers some quick escape routes: In less than an hour from the capital you can be by the azure waters of Lago di Como, or in the green hills of the Valtelline wine country above the old town of Bergamo. (We cover Como and the other lakes of Lombardy in a separate chapter, "Lake Country.")

The agricultural prosperity of the region dates from what should have been a disaster: the destruction of Milan by the German emperor Barbarossa in the 12th century. Not only did the citizens rebuild their capital, but they drained the marshes of the surrounding country, created canals for transportation, and set up an irrigation system to water their crops (of which rice was soon to become the most important). It is difficult for us, entangled in a maze of modern roads, to imagine that more aquatic Lombardy when sails could be seen drifting by the poplar trees, when Prospero's ship could arrive at the port of Milan, and when Beatrice d'Este could disembark with her ladies-in-waiting from a gilded barge at Pavia when she arrived from Ferrara for her wedding with Ludovico Sforza. Later, Leonardo invented locks that made the river Po navigable, and the Po remains one of the rivers that help define Lombardy's borders (in its case, the southern). The Ticino, which issues from Lago Maggiore and the glaciers of the north, forms part of the frontier with Piedmont; while on the east the Mincio drifts lazily down from the Lago di Garda, edging by the Veneto before reaching Mantua. Every now and then you can catch a view of ilex and crumbling farms reflected in the water and be reminded of the Lombardy that was: where Virgil was born; where Manzoni was inspired to write his novel devoted to this land, *I Promessi Sposi.* Lombardy was even to inspire a later, American, writer; one of Edith Wharton's first successes was *A Valley of Decision,* set here.

The name Lombardy hails from the rough-going Nordic tribe of the Longobards, who swept down in the sixth century. They had been preceded in Milan by the Romans of the late Empire, who made it their capital for almost a hundred years before moving on to Ravenna. The region was to prosper under communal government in the Middle Ages, and continued to prosper even after it fell to the Viscontis in 1277 and to the Sforzas during the Renaissance. These two families commissioned most of the art and architecture that you will want to see here, and it was they who created Milan's Golden Age.

Nothing but scorn has been poured onto the occupying forces of the centuries that followed, but the fact remains that the Lombard farmer was by no means on the losing end during those times of foreign rule. The Spanish, by sheer force, brought an end to the days when the warlords and their *condottieri* systematically ravaged the crops of the peasants; while later the Austrians introduced new tax laws that greatly aided the small landowners. The French under Napoléon tore down the customs houses and did away with the economic frontiers that had slowed down commerce for centuries, laying the foundation for the prosperity we see today.

Of course, this same economic boom has left its mark on the countryside, but whatever their outskirts have ceded to industry, Pavia, Cremona, Bergamo, and other old towns have been kept intact with an iron fist; others,

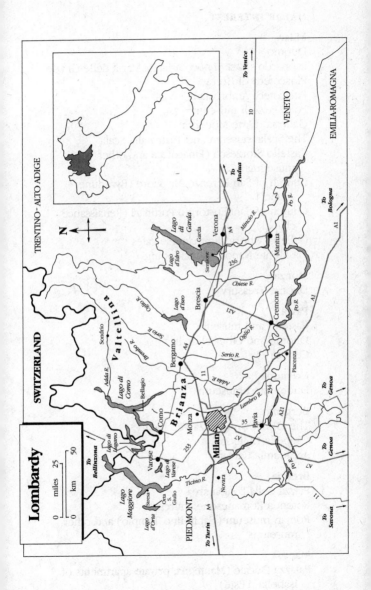

like Mantua, seem to have stayed adrift in their splendid past, quite apart from *any* current stream.

MAJOR INTEREST

Milan
Duomo
Leonardo's *Last Supper* at Santa Maria delle Grazie
Pinacoteca di Brera
Pinacoteca Ambrosiana
Poldi-Pezzoli museum
Galleria d'Arte Moderna
The Scala museum and Teatro alla Scala
Castello Sforzesco (Pinacoteca and other
    museums)
Church of San Lorenzo Maggiore (Byzantine
    chapel)
Church of Sant'Eustorgio Portinari (Renaissance
    chapel)
Galleria Vittorio Emmanuele cafés
Via Monte Napoleone shopping

Monza
Duomo Treasury

Pavia
Castello and museum
Duomo and other churches
Certosa

Cremona
Duomo and museums

Bergamo
The Old Town (piazza Vecchio)
Cappella Colleoni
Accademia Carrara

Brescia
Piazza della Loggia area
Rotonda Romanesque church
Roman museum (Capitolino Tempio) and other
    museums

Mantua
Palazza Ducale (Mantegna, private apartments of
    Isabella d'Este)
Palazzo del Té
Alberti's church of Sant'Andrea
The Palaces at Sabbioneta

Food and Wine
of Lombardy

The quality of the local agricultural products makes the
excellence of Lombard cuisine a fairly sure thing—once
those products have fallen into the hands of Milanese
chefs, whose specialties have long dominated the province (apart from the once-Venetian enclaves of Garda,
Brescia, and Bergamo). Once again, too, the hated foreign rulers have left behind a few souvenirs, though in
most cases "interchange" would be the preferred word.
The Viscontis introduced rice, but the Spanish brought
saffron. The pastures of Lombardy produced butter, but
surely Gallic neighbors showed the Lombards how to use
it with a light touch, and Lombardy remains the only
Italian province where, as in France, butter is used instead of olive oil in cooking. Some specialties, such as
scallopine *alla milanese,* were snapped up by the Austrians (in that case by their General Radetzky, and the
Austrian result, by no means identical, was *Wiener Schnit-
zel*). In return, Viennese pastry cooks left behind them an
expertise that makes breakfast in any café a treat—along
with an addiction to *schlag,* the whipped cream that
Italians call *latte-miele.*

Many of the dishes produced here are so widely known
that we forget their origin is Milanese. Ossobuco is one
such: shank of veal with bone and marrow, simmered
long enough to remind you that the Milanese, like their
Germanic neighbors, prefer meat that is cooked through
(a far cry from the Florentine passion for raw slabs of
steak cast over charcoal). *Costoletta alla milanese,* veal
cutlet dipped in egg and bread crumbs before being fried
in butter, has become an international favorite, and so
have its variations: scallopine of veal cooked with capers
and chopped onion, or with lemon, or with sage. A third
meat dish encountered frequently is the *bollito misto*—
again, a matter of long cooking, with a basis of boiled
beef, capon, or chicken. The Modenese *zampone* (stuffed
pig's foot) is thrown in later, and the dish is served with a
salsa verde.

Bollito is very much a winter dish; and so, for many, is
minestrone, the hearty vegetable soup served with rice in
Milan; the vegetables vary with the season: carrots, squash,
zucchini, beans, or cabbage. For most visitors the preferred first course is risotto; and though *alla milanese*

can vary in its preparation, the basic ingredients remain the same: stock, chopped and browned onion, the cheese called *grana*—a young relation of Parmesan—saffron, and the patience to bring the rice to its final rich consistency. Because rice is Lombardy's staple food, it is natural to see it turn up in many other guises: with lentils, with mushrooms, with chopped leeks or celery, or *alla primavera,* using whatever spring vegetables the market might offer. It can be cooked with shrimp and saffron, or scooped out in the center and filled with diced veal kidneys (*rognoncini trifolati*). These dishes are usually served as separate first courses, not as an accompaniment; except, at times, risotto *alla milanese* is presented alongside ossobuco.

The favorite side dish of the region has always been polenta, which might look familiar to travellers from the southern United States, as it is a form of cornmeal mush—with many variants. Once boiled it can be served still retaining a semiliquid texture, or it can be sliced into squares and be presented with anything from codfish to liver and onions—going particularly well with sauces involving sage. As you head east to the former Venetian territories, headwaiters will urge it on you along with *uccelli,* small songbirds looking fairly unhappy, wrapped in bacon, and lying in state on a bier of polenta. Many Italians crave this delicacy, but if you don't, beware; it is often touted for its price, and there can also be a mind-bending scene like the one in the film *Gigi,* where the poor girl is taught how to eat *ortolans.* On the other hand, a dish definitely to search out is polenta *pasticciata,* a delicious combination of cheese, butter, and layers of polenta put into the oven until a crust forms on top. Gnocchi, found throughout Lombardy, can be treated in this same way.

Milan's gift to every Italian Christmas table, from Buenos Aires to Boston, is panettone, a light cake made of eggs, flour, and sugar, and studded with sultanas and the candied peels of citrus fruit. Invented very quietly in the 15th century, it has gone very public thanks to Motta and Alemagna, who export it all over the world. Less exportable is the fresh, soft cream cheese called *mascarpone,* which can be eaten as a dessert on its own, but which is best when it turns up in the heady combination known as *tiramisu,* where it is combined with soft sponge cake, chocolate, and lots and lots of alcohol.

The wines of Lombardy have never rivaled those of

Piedmont to its west or those of the Veneto and Trentino to the east; and now, with modern transport available to rush in the Barberas, Barolos, Soaves, and Valpolicellas from outside, the astute growers of the plain of the Po have turned many vineyards into rice fields. There are, however, a few exceptions. Where the river Adda descends from the Alps and passes through Sondrio on its way to empty into Lago di Como, its banks are terraced to produce three fine reds: Sassella, Grumello, and Inferno. From the southern shores of Lago di Garda comes a dry, white Lugana, made with Trebbiano grapes and excellent with trout and other freshwater fish.

MILAN

Any guidebook will tell you that Milan is Italy's economic capital and the country's second city in population, and that its citizens are organized, industrious, and punctual almost to the point of being Teutonic—in distinct contrast to their southern neighbors. Of more immediate interest to the general visitor is the fact that Milan is the most expensive city in Italy. This means that unless you are on an expense account, or have unlimited funds at your disposal, a visit to the city's many sights should be carefully planned so you waste as little time as possible (i.e., try not to be there on a Monday, when much of what you want to see is closed). Most of Milan's art and history is to be seen in a galaxy of museums and several churches; sift through a list of their contents beforehand, select, and set off. You will find that the area of interest to you is nowhere near as great as you would expect from a city of this size; most sights of interest are within walking distance of the Duomo.

Earliest Milan

Milan became important when it was made capital of the Western Empire in 305, and it remained one for a century. It was here in 312 that Constantine adopted Christianity as the Empire's official religion, and it was here that the early Church fathers were to shape doctrines for a creed that was to become far more rigorous than many early converts had suspected. Saint Ambrose, bishop of Milan, had the pagan temples closed, and the worship of pagan gods was outlawed. He governed Church affairs for

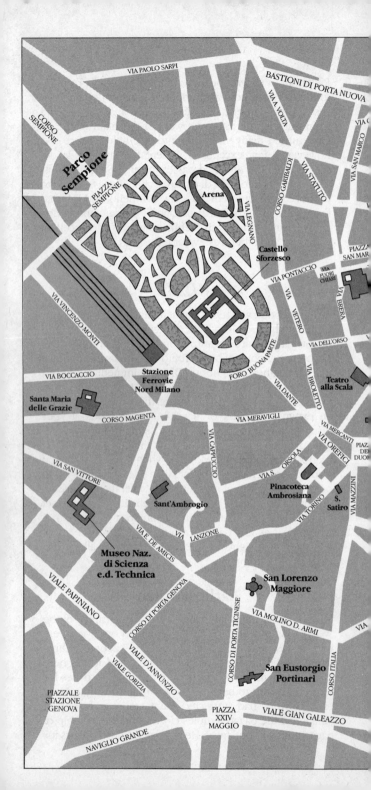

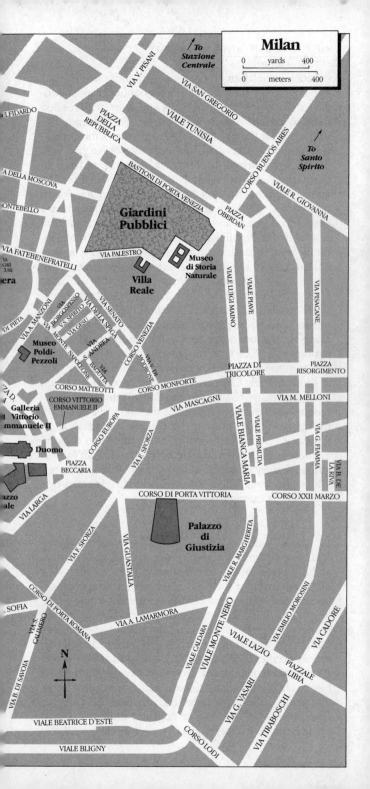

decades, buried four Roman emperors, introduced hymns into church services, and founded a basilica (Sant'Ambrogio). In it he was to baptize Saint Augustine, who resided in Milan for four years with his mother, Saint Monica. The **Church of Sant'Ambrogio** is still here, west of the Duomo and reached by the via Torino, and well worth a visit: with its handsome atrium, its portico by Bramante, and its gold Carolingian altar (the last is a reminder that later the Franks were to arrive and their king, Charlemagne, was to be crowned in Milan with the Iron Crown of the Lombard kings). The piazza and complex of Sant'Ambrogio form an island of tranquillity near the town's center; its Romanesque and Byzantine treasures spill over into a little museum above the Bramante rectory. In the same neighborhood there are more remains of the Milan of Saint Augustine—amazing for a city that has been both extensively bombed and extensively modernized. The **Church of San Lorenzo Maggiore**, reached from Sant'Ambrogio along via Edmondo des Amicis, is reminiscent in its Syrian design of San Vitale in Ravenna; and its Cappella di San Aquilino is adorned with mosaics and sculpture akin to those of early Christian Rome. San Lorenzo is fronted by 16 impressive columns from a Roman temple. A subterranean canal surfaces alongside the church: a small remaining testimony of a city that still had a Venetian air in the early 19th century. Farther along the corso di Porta Ticinese is Milan's second Medieval church, **Sant'Eustorgio**, a treasury of late Gothic and early Renaissance art. With its Portinari chapel it is considered to be Lombardy's most perfect example of the Tuscan style.

The Duomo

The Visconti family came to power in the 13th century as archbishops of Milan, but they were a far cry from Saint Ambrose. Even for their time they were, with few exceptions, a vile breed of rulers; but—at the same time—they were great builders and scholars. They were to lay the foundations both of the Duomo and of the present Castello Sforzesco, which still stand near each other in the very center of Milan. By 1387, when Galeazzo Visconti III commissioned the Duomo as a votive offering toward having a male heir, the Viscontis had indeed come up in the world: Galeazzo's sister had married the Duke of Clarence, son of the King of England, while his brutish uncle Bernabò had been able to force two abbots delivering an unwelcome letter from the Pope to eat it. Decades later, Galeazzo's grandeur brought disaster onto Italy. Because his first wife was a Valois, the French were given a claim to Milan's dukedom when their daughter married into the House of Orléans, and they were to pursue it with a vengeance. As for the cathedral, Galeazzo's prayer was answered. His church, dedicated to the Virgin, became one of the largest in Christendom. His granddaughter Bianca was to marry Francesco Sforza, one of the most popular and decent of the condottieri, and who was acclaimed Duke when he entered Milan in 1450.

The atmosphere within the cathedral is one of such immense calm that its origins are soon forgotten amid the forest of columns and the reflections of stained glass. Saint Carlo Borromeo, born to one of Milan's noble families and destined to become the town's patron saint, cleared away much of the bric-a-brac in the Duomo's interior in the 16th century, and so you will encounter an overall feeling of vast space. There are still treasures to track down, however, from a huge, French Gothic candelabrum to the tomb of Gian Giacomo Medici, in the right transept. Borromeo is buried in the crypt, in a tomb donated by Philip II of Spain. His detractors say that he destroyed far too much of Medieval Milan, but one of his main claims to fame was his valor in fighting the plague, and there might have been an element of sanitation in his alterations. To get an idea of the armies of artists who worked on the Duomo for centuries, go to the roof and see the old town and the distant mountains through the legions of statues and pinnacles left behind by sculptors who came from all over Europe. This promenade was of course a "natural" for 19th-century visitors, particularly after Alfred, Lord Tennyson, penned his impressions of first seeing the Alps from it.

Castello Sforzesco

When we visit the Castello Sforzesco, which is directly up the via Dante from the Duomo, the Viscontis and the Sforzas move over from the Duomo with us, since the castle, built by the Viscontis and then destroyed by a populace who loathed them, was promptly reconstructed by Francesco Sforza when he came to power. The Castello was an arsenal of military might used to dominate Milan and its surroundings, and one used not only by the dukes, but later, too, by the Spanish, who turned it into an impregnable fortress during the 200 years after Charles V took the city; and it was to the Castello that the Austrians retreated in the 19th century during the five days of heroic revolt on the part of the Milanese (all over Lombardy you find squares and streets called *Cinque Giorni*).

The castle hardly brought good luck to the Sforzas. Francesco's son Galeazzo Maria had inherited the best qualities of his Visconti mother and his Sforza father and began a brilliant reign that showed signs of rivalling that of Lorenzo de Medici in Florence. Then, after ten years of rule, he was murdered by three idiotic students who thought that they were reenacting the assassination of Caesar. This murder did for Italy about as much good as the shooting at Sarajevo was later to do for Europe. Galeazzo's heir, still a child, was to be raised by his uncle, Ludovico Il Moro, who became Duke after the mysterious death of his ward. It was Ludovico who called in the French—and thereby signed the death warrant of the Renaissance in Italy.

But before that there had been a golden age, however brief, and this castle has many a reminder of it, in the frescoes of Bramante and in the bowered room supposedly designed by Leonardo. Both of them worked for Ludovico Il Moro and his delightful young wife, Beatrice d'Este; and like all court artists they were expected to design costumes and decorations for the endless masques and balls that echoed through the Castello's chambers. Milan had never been so rich; when Beatrice's sister, Isabella, came up from Mantua she was amazed by the carriages of the wealthy and by the paved streets. Centuries later the cleanliness of Milan was still to be a matter of wonder; to Stendhal, for one, whose pre-Haussmann Paris was often little better than an open sewer. Isabella d'Este visited the Castello during the happy days before her sister's tragic death at the age of 22, a loss from which Il Moro was never to recover. His luck was to descend from then on, and at the end of his life he spent years in a wretched dungeon in the castle of Loches on the Loire, after having been deposed by the French King Louis XII.

Apart from the refurbished rooms where this couple once lived and played, the Castello is divided into several museums: the **Pinacoteca** with some superb Mantegnas and Bellinis, being one. The sculpture collection will come as a surprise to many, since its masterpieces include the last work of Michelangelo—the very moving Rondanini *Pietà*—and also a head, said to be of the

Empress Theodora, that is one of the finest Byzantine portraits extant. There are sections devoted to reconstructed frescoes from outlying castles, and others for furniture and ceramics of the Renaissance, as well as tapestries, among them the series by Bramantino devoted to the months of the year. One of Europe's largest collections of ancient musical instruments is also here. The *musei* of the Castello were Italy's first venture into "modern museum design": paintings without frames, lots of plate glass, and abrupt functional stairways. Some like it, some do not; but there is an emphasis on light—and the collections are not to be missed.

Also of Interest in Milan

The creative activity during the reign of Ludovico Il Moro was so frenzied that it was as if the artists— Leonardo and Bramante in particular—knew that a deluge was due. Near the Castello is the **Church of Santa Maria delle Grazie**, with a marvel of an interior commissioned by Ludovico from Bramante to receive the tombs of the Sforzas in a setting with which Milan could enter the new times—the Renaissance—and forget, if only for a while, its huge anachronism of a Gothic cathedral. Leonardo, who had scant time between creating designs for pageants and designs for war, managed somehow to paint his **Last Supper** in the refectory of the Carthusian monastery of Santa Maria. Now cleaned of all its later alterations, the fresco looks better than it probably has for centuries. Not far from the church is the **Museo Nazionale della Scienza e della Tecnica Leonardo da Vinci** (via San Vittore 21), where, on the second floor, Leonardo's sketches for airplanes, submarines, and machine guns have been brought to life in reconstruction (his letter of introduction to Ludovico described him as an "engineer"). Not reconstructed, unfortunately, was his only masterpiece of sculpture: an uncast clay equestrian statue—larger than life—of Francesco Sforza that was once in the Castello and later used for target practice by bored French soldiers. Yet the king of France, François I, was to be Leonardo's final host, at Amboise on the Loire, and Leonardo's most noted paintings reside in the Louvre.

Bramante managed another jewel of a church, **San Satiro,** and it is easy to visit because it is so near what is for many Milan's most enticing gallery of paintings: the **Pinacoteca Ambrosiana**. This gallery, housed in the same building as the famous library, was founded by Cardinal Borromeo in 1609. Its collections are replete with souvenirs of the Sforza Renaissance: the De Predis profile of a girl now thought to be a daughter of Ludovico, and Leonardo's musing head of a musician. (His *Codice Atlantico,* which comprises most of his scientific sketches, is in the adjoining Biblioteca.) The miracle of the Ambrosiana is the full-scale Raphael working cartoon for his *School of Athens* in the Vatican. The master drawing is dramatically shown in its own room, giving no hint that it was once rolled up and hauled off to Paris by Napoléon (and later—astonishingly—returned). The Pinacoteca also has a perfect Caravaggio still life, a Titian *Adoration* commissioned by Henri II and Diane de Poitiers, and Cardinal Borromeo's collection of Jan Breughel. It is a museum of an ideal size and contains little that is short of being a masterpiece.

The **Biblioteca Ambrosiana** adds a few romantic notes: Petrarch's copy of Virgil, with his own annotations on Laura in the margin, and the letters exchanged between Lucrezia Borgia and the poet Cardinal Pietro Bembo. Byron read these here (they have just been translated into English and published); he also stole a strand of Lucrezia's golden hair, a lock of which is now shown in a glass case upstairs.

Near the Ambrosiana is the **piazza Mercanti**, the only Medieval square of the city to have survived. And on it— ideally placed for the hungry and the footsore—is the **Ristorante Al Mercante**, excellent for the quality of its pasta and house wines, and with a tempting display of antipasti and *ripieni* (stuffed vegetables) for starters. The Mercante has been here for years, but the interior has recently been redecorated (well); in warm weather you can lunch under the arcades outside.

A stone's throw away is the piazza del Duomo and the **Galleria Vittorio Emmanuele**, with its many cafés, **Zucca's**, with its 1900 decor, being the most pleasant, where you can have an aperitif and watch the crowds; or dine elegantly at **Savini** on Milanese specialties—risottos, *costolettas*—and rich desserts. Window shoppers have a field day in the Galleria: Ricordi for records, Rizzoli for books, and not far away the newly revamped Rinascente department store, with just about everything. For Italian design at its best you should take a look downstairs at the kitchenwares. Those who have come to Milan for food, however, will jump into a cab and head for

Gualtiero Marchesi (via Bonvesin de la Riva 9), where Lombard food has been treated to a dash of *nouvelle cuisine* (*ravioli aperto;* veal scallopine with sweet-and-sour sauce); or for the very attractive **Scaletta** (piazzale Stazione Genova 3) to sample their sweetbreads in cream or their rabbit with *peperonata.*

The second of Milan's small but memorable museums for painting is the **Museo Poldi-Pezzoli**, at number 12 on the via Manzoni, which is one of the busiest thoroughfares in town. Founded by a wealthy collector, Gian Giacomo Poldi-Pezzoli, it echoes his personal taste with much the same results that we find in the Frick Collection in New York. The paintings are set off with antique furniture, brocaded walls, and Renaissance bronzes, and the pictures include a Pollaiuolo profile of a girl that is so often reproduced that we feel we know her, as well as superior Botticellis and Bellinis and a moody Guardi of a gondola drifting on a gray lagoon.

The luxurious setting of this museum is echoed close by on the **via Monte Napoleone**, a shopping street that is renowned for its elegance all over Europe. Built in Milan's splendid Napoleonic period, it now harbors such jewelers as Buccellati and Calderoni, antique stores, and above all the home bases of those Italian designers who have become household words for those who can and those who can't afford their wares: Gucci, Valentino, Ferragamo, and Mila Schön. Armani, Fendi, and the rest are to be found on the adjacent via della Spiga and the via St. Andrea.

Shoppers and lookers in this neighborhood all have their favorite luncheon spots: from the fashionable **Bice** at via Borgospesso 12 to the pizzeria called **Paper Moon** at via Bagutta 1. On that same street is the amusing trattoria called the **Bagutta**, which has paintings from many of its former clients on the wall. Those who like Italian painting of our century can find more in the grandiose setting of the **Galleria d'Arte Moderna**, housed in the Villa Reale, which is on the via Palestro facing the Giardini Publici on the northern end of the via Manzoni. De Chirico, Morandi, and Marini—all represented here— have long been favorites with the international public. (Tommaso Marinetti of Milan, by the way, was the author of the highly influential Futurist manifesto of 1909.) But now the earlier age of Boldini, De Nittis, and Fattori is coming into its own, and, as so often happens in Italy because of a misunderstanding of designation, those who think they are going to be confronted by a mass of Jackson Pollocks in a museum of *arte moderne* find themselves instead in a 19th-century world copied time and again by Visconti in his films. More and more, visitors do *not* complain. As for the **Villa Reale** itself, it is well worth seeing for its own sake; built in 1790 for the Counts of Belgioioso, it was the residence in Milan of Napoléon and his stepson, the viceroy Eugène de Beauharnais. Eugène was Josephine's son by her first marriage; Napoléon was devoted to him. He was an excellent administrator, and many of the reforms put through during his rule were to become, 50 years later, part and parcel of the New Italy. The French also brought into being a whole new class, hitherto unknown in Italy, of civil servants, educated and intelligent. They were to be sorely missed later, after the return of Austrian rule.

At the other end of the via Manzoni is the piazza once occupied by a church dedicated by Bernabò Visconti's Veronese wife, Regina della Scala. In the second half of the 18th century, the church was pulled down to make way for a theater devoted to opera. The theater adopted her name, made Milan the musical capital of the country, and kept the city's upper classes busy from then on—thanks to boxes with facilities for eating, drinking, and playing cards (not permissible during arias). For foreigners, **La Scala** was a social haven for seeing who was in town, while for the natives it was a convenient escape route from more formal domestic entertaining. Various salons were reserved for "members"—just as they are today at New York's Metropolitan—and the whole place naturally became a hotbed of intrigue, gossip, and amorous stratagems. One of the most enthusiastic foreign visitors to Milan, Henri Beyle (Stendhal), was quick to learn the local rules for marriage, for courtship, for love affairs. And none too soon, as he was to embark on a decade of passion for the enchanting *allumeuse* Gina Pietragrua, who was already surrounded by other suitors and was later to be a model for the Sanseverina. He also managed to be insulted by Lord Byron, who didn't know who Stendhal was and who was to live to regret it.

The theater was thoroughly reconstructed after a bomb hit in World War II, but it is the **Museo Teatrale**, which you enter from the piazza, that best gives us an idea of La Scala's past. Arranged with a judicious dose of nostalgia are souvenirs of singers, from Maria Malibran to Claudia Muzio and La Pasta. The composers are represented, too:

Bellini, Donizetti, and above all Verdi, who is given two rooms of priceless documentation. There are rare portraits of both his wives, Margherita Barezzi and Giuseppina Strepponi. There is also a portrait of our own era's heir to the temperament of a diva, Maria Callas (a postcard of her costs more, and sells more, than any other at the exit counter). Her fans should go next door and have an aperitif at **Biffi Scala**, where she was wont to retire with her coterie after the opera.

The greatest and largest gallery of painting in Milan is the **Brera**, on the via Brera within easy walking distance of La Scala. To counteract its size, many masterpieces, such as della Francesca's Montefeltro Madonna or Mantegna's *Christ Deposed,* are shown in areas intimate enough to display them at their best. To see the Brera's placing of Raphael's *Wedding of the Virgin* should give other museums an idea for improvement. The collections of the Brera can take a long time to survey; and there is a very sophisticated cafeteria on the museum's premises. There is also a new and restful restaurant, the **Stendhal,** nearby on the via San Marco. Not all that long ago the neighborhood of the Brera was the St-Germain-des-Prés of Milan, with students filling the bars and trattorias of the streets called Fiori Chiari and Fiori Oscuri. The area has now been engulfed by trendy boutiques; where you could once have a reasonably priced meal or drink, you will instead be offered something like gold-lamé beach pajamas.

Hotels in Milan are just as highly priced as you would expect, but of these the **Principe di Savoia** is properly luxurious; if you want to get into one that is small, comfortable, and central, such as the **Manzoni** (via Santo Spirito 20), you will have to book long ahead. Since taxis are highly priced too, it is wise to stay toward the city's center—doubly so, as the modern stretch of town, from the piazza della Repubblica to the Stazione Centrale, might seem impersonal (though it is being refurbished). This neighborhood seems slightly worn at the edges since the days when the Pirelli tower astonished Europe. Here, so far, is lacking the very human structure of Minneapolis on the one hand, and the grandeur of the new Chicago on the other. In the meantime, seek lodgings in the old town; in congenial hostels such as the **Casa Svizzera** (via San Raffaele 3) or the **Centro** (via Broletto 46).

Another solution is to stay out of town—in Como, Monza, or Bergamo—and commute. (For Como, see the

Lake Country chapter; see Monza and Bergamo below.) If Milan has in so many instances engulfed the small piazzas and tree-lined streets that made for its charm in the 19th century, you can catch a glimmer of its former attraction in these old towns surrounding it that are barely an hour away.

LOMBARDY OUTSIDE MILAN

The most obvious retreats to offer beauty and quiet near Milan are the lakes—Como and Garda in particular—and they can be used for excursions to some of Lombardy's historic towns quite easily. (Sirmione on Garda is less than 50 km/30 miles from Mantua, for example.) There are, however, a welter of old towns in every direction from Milan, each of special interest, and all with facilities for lunching (on a day trip) or for spending the night.

Monza

The least expected attraction happens to be the nearest to Milan (north-northeast on the way to Bergamo): Monza, known to most for its auto races, is actually a city that can take you back to the sixth century, when the Longobards were devastating the countryside. Their leader, Authuri, took time out to go to Bavaria and court a flaxen-haired princess of whose beauty he had heard. Theodolinda became his queen, and calmed him down for the one remaining year of his life. As an early widow she was asked to choose another man to help her rule, and with unseemly alacrity she elected the best-looking warrior around (Agelulf, from Piedmont). Together they ruled for 20 years.

Pope Gregory was grateful to the northern princess on several counts, and among the gifts he sent here we see in the cathedral of Monza the most famous of all: the Iron Crown of Lombardy. Marvelously constructed around what is said to be a nail from the true cross, it was later used in the coronations of Italy's kings and rulers—44 emperors in all, from Barbarossa to Napoléon. The latter had the crown brought in an elaborate procession from Monza to the cathedral in Milan when he became King of Italy in 1805; he even had the façade of the Duomo completed (finally) for the event. Monza's treasury harbors much more, however, that is interesting: crosses and reliquaries in ivory and gold; other Byzantine articles; and Theodolinda's gilded set of chickens at play. Monza's Duomo, designed by Matteo da Campione, has a handsome striated façade that presides over a quiet square, which seems far indeed from Milan and which boasts an excellent restaurant, the **Corona Ferrea**, with a full view of the church.

Monza's history by no means ended with the Middle Ages; its **Villa Reale** served as country residence to Eugène de Beauharnais, and it was he who landscaped the vast park in the romantic manner called *à l'Anglaise* (if it looks familiar, it is because it was used extensively in the film *The Garden of the Finzi-Continis*). Another less fortunate resident of the villa was King Umberto I, who in 1900 was shot in Monza by an anarchist. Now the Reale is a museum of Neoclassical painting and furnishings.

Pavia

Pavia, 38 km (22 miles) south of Milan, was a Longobard capital that once rivaled the now much more important city. Its Castello served as a secondary residence both to the Visconti and to the Sforza, and its university, once considered second to none, was attended by a variety of students including Petrarch, Columbus, and the Venetian playwright Goldoni. Its physics department was to light up the world by graduating Volta—whose electrical experiments we can still see here. The Visconti had much to do with enlarging the university in the 14th century; and Stendhal was delighted to find that its main benefactor had been the same Galeazzo II, evidently a real charmer, who had experiments made to enable his victims to be tortured for 41 days before they died. Those who weren't destined for this end apparently had the right to a good education, and soon the schools and courts of Pavia were rising on every side. Its Duomo—both Bramante and Leonardo were among its architects—is one of the best examples of Lombard Renaissance; its dome, the third largest in Italy, dominates the town's center. Also to be seen in Pavia is the Romanesque **Church of San Michele** (south of the center near the river off corso Garibaldi), with a remarkable façade, and **San Pietro in Ciel d'Oro** (north of the center near the Castello), with its main altar and the extraordinary *arca* of Saint Augustine. The *arca* is the tomb of the saint, whose remains took centuries to travel from Hippo to Sardinia and then to here.

One of the wonders of Pavia is the Old Town itself and the care with which it has been preserved. In the area around **San Michele**, completely cut off from traffic of any sort, there are courtyards and streets, green with plants and grass, that resemble the Italian scenes painted by Hubert Robert in the 18th century.

Pavia's **Castello** is a museum, and a good one, for paintings, sculpture, and the elaborate arcaded courtyard where Ludovico Il Moro and Beatrice d'Este were to spend some of their happiest years. Many say that if he had married her hard-willed sister, already the Marchioness of Mantua, the French armies never would have flooded down. But he didn't and they did, and the Castello library, accumulated by the Viscontis, is now part of the Bibliothèque Nationale in Paris, while several of the towers were destroyed by the Maréchal de Lautrec. Soon, in 1525, François I was to be taken prisoner at the Battle of Pavia by Charles V, and the French adventure was to give way to centuries of Spanish occupation.

Too many visitors to Pavia skip the town and rush to the Certosa, the famous monastery that the Viscontis founded in its northern outskirts in 1396, to see the Pantheon of the Visconti and the Sforza. This by no means indicates that the Certosa is an easy visit. It closes in the morning at 11:30, which means that visitors inside are given warning signs by 11:00. The traffic from almost any direction is formidable, thanks to Milan's proximity, so unless you are willing to arise very early, an afternoon visit is more convenient—particularly since there happens to be a lucky choice of restaurants right in the vicinity. One, the **Chalet della Certosa**, is right outside the gates of the monastery; another, **Al Cassinino**, considered one of Lombardy's best, is just a couple of miles before the Certosa on the Milan-Genoa road. In the town of Pavia itself is the **Bixio**, opposite the Castello, and **Ferrari-da Tino**, animated and reliable, at via dei Mille 111, right across the covered bridge.

The **Certosa** remains, along with Milan's Duomo, a testament to the building mania of the Viscontis. Its façade, like a huge intaglio of colored marbles, is enlivened by large circular medallions based on Roman coins, and resembles the architecture in the backgrounds of Mantegna's paintings. The interior is a veritable museum of frescoes (many dedicated to the religious gestures of the founding family); of paintings, from Perugino to Luini; and above all of sculpture, most of it adorning tombs. The

finest is on those of Gian Galeazzo Visconti and Ludovico
Il Moro and his Beatrice. The latter tomb was formerly in
Milan's Dominican church of Santa Maria delle Grazie,
which Il Moro had conceived as a Sforza mausoleum. The
monks there took it upon themselves to sell the tomb,
and the Certosa bought it. (It was these same Dominicans
who were so reluctant to pay Leonardo for his *Last Supper*. If they could have dislodged it, they probably would
have sold that, too, since money seems to have been high
on their bill of fare.)

Cremona

Like Pavia, Cremona is on the river Po (farther east), and it
shares with it the honor of being one of Lombardy's most
monumental architectural cities—its **piazza del Comune**
being, along with that of Siena, one of the finest in Italy.
The piazza is faced on one side by a Gothic arcaded
Palazzo Communale; on another by an octagonal Romanesque Baptistery; and is fronted by the magnificent façade
of the **Duomo**, which is Romanesque, with a gigantic rose
window. Alongside is Italy's tallest campanile, the **Torrazo**, built in the 13th century but with later additions,
such as its enormous clock. The cathedral's interior is
literally covered with late Renaissance frescoes, and very
good ones, in particular those by Pordenone and Boccaccino. Try to go in the morning, when the light is good.

For that matter, with its lively markets, Cremona is a
morning town anyway. And later in the day you will find
that the first-rate **Pinacoteca** in the Museo Civico has no
electric light at all, so that to see its Cremonese masters,
its Magnascos, and a superb Veronese deposition, you
have to come equipped with your own source of illumination. It is a good lesson in what Goethe and other travellers on the Grand Tour must have gone through to perceive the masterpieces about which they wrote so well.

The very name of Cremona brings to most minds another art: music. Two famous composers were born here
centuries apart: Claudio Monteverdi, who did much to
launch opera as a form (in Mantua), and Amilcare Ponchielli, who later livened it up with *La Gioconda*. But it was
the manufacture of one type of musical instrument that
made the town famous. Around 1530 Andrea Amati created
the violin, and a new sensitivity was to enter musical
composition. Amati also founded a school for making the
instruments, and later such great craftsmen as Guarnieri

and Stradivari were to perfect his invention. Stradivari made about 16 violins a year; but since he lived to be 93, they added up. About 600 are extant—turning up often in surprising ways, and selling for a lot more than the already hefty price that Stradivari charged. A couple can be seen on show in the **Palazzo Comunale**; but most of the documentation of value, and more violins, are in the **Museo Stradiveriano**, in the same Museo Civico that houses the Pinacoteca (via Dati 4).

You can lunch well in Cremona: at the **Trattoria Cerri** on the piazza Giovanni XXIII, and near the cathedral at the **Ceresole**—which is so exceptionally good that it is best to reserve (via Ceresole 4; Tel: 233-22).

Bergamo

Northeast and east of Milan, Bergamo and Brescia are two Lombard towns that share a Venetian past, as they were both ruled by La Serenissima from 1428 until Napoléon's advent. But, diet apart, that is about all they share, since in character they are different indeed. Neither should be missed by visitors to Lombardy.

When we think of Bergamo we usually mean the *Città Alta;* the **Upper Old Town**, girded by green, and jutting out on its Venetian bastions from the hills of the Valtelline, which rise sharply from the plain below. So bucolic in spirit that you would scarcely guess that it is only 50 km (30 miles) east of Milan, Bergamo is a blessing to the inhabitants of that larger city; when they can, they drive up the steeply winding road, passing beneath hanging gardens and pergolas, to reach the cool, ancient city. Exhaust fumes are left behind at the gates, and inside is a chessboard of piazzas and fountains, cafés, palaces, and restaurants. This Upper Town is studded with monuments left by centuries of Venetian rule, centered around the **piazza Vecchia**, with its fountain of stone lions and its arcaded Palazzo della Ragione. It is easy to believe that the composer Gaetano Donizetti was born here, as one vista gives onto another with the rapidity of scenes in an opera. A step through the arches of the Palazzo della Ragione, and you are faced with the resplendent façades of the **Church of Santa Maria Maggiore**, its baptistery, and the **Cappella Colleoni**. Colleoni was the same successful condottiere seen by so many in Venice, thanks to Verrocchio's equestrian bronze. In gratitude for the soldier's services, the

Venetians gave him the Bergamasque region to govern. Here he sits astride a gilded horse of wood, and in his elaborate mausoleum he lies near his favorite daughter, Medea, beneath a ceiling frescoed by Tiepolo.

The interior of Santa Maria Maggiore was heavily refurbished in the late Renaissance, hung with tapestries and its choir encased in wooden intarsia designed by Lorenzo. This painter was Bergamasque by adoption; thanks to a prevailing surrealist mood in much of his work, he has come very much into favor. For those interested, the churches of lower Bergamo are replete with his paintings.

Not far from Santa Maria is the **Museo Donizettiano**, dedicated to that composer, and exhibiting his pianos, manuscripts, and various souvenirs. His birthplace—far from grand (he always said he was born in a cellar)—is in the borgo Canale. Bergamo also gave birth to the commedia dell'arte, which influenced much opera of the 18th century. Gian Carlo Menotti considered having his music festival here before he fell upon Spoleto; considering the nearness of Milan and the enthusiasm of its public, it wouldn't have been a bad idea.

The charm of Bergamo's Upper Town should not tempt you to skip the **Accademia Carrara**, one of Italy's finest painting museums, whose quality announces itself right away with Pisanello's portrait of Lionello D'Este; Botticelli's of Giuliano de Medici; and one of a sulky, dark head—said to be Cesare Borgia—against a Giorgionesque background. This gallery, at the far east side of the Upper Town, can actually be reached on foot, descending via the church of Sant'Agostino; its Bellinis, Guardis, Titians, Mantegnas, and Tiepolos are worth that short walk. If the paintings shown are of a rare excellence, it is no accident. The Accademia was founded by Count Carrara, and on the brochure's list of later donors there appears a raft of names. The one that should be noted is that of a Senator Morelli, who was one of the first Italian collectors to devote himself to the correct attribution and classification of Italian paintings. It was thanks to the reputation of the senator that a young, penniless, and very serious student, Bernard Berenson, would come here at the very start of his career, to make sure that "every Lotto is a Lotto," and from then on change the face of connoisseurship on two continents. Ironically, these classifications had been started by the French under Napoléon—whose soldiers, out of ennui, had destroyed so much (when a Bolognese aristocrat complained to Stendhal about a family canvas slashed to ribbons by French bayonets, he was cooled down with "If it hadn't been for us, you never would have heard of Montesquieu!"). The fact remains that the monks and priests of Italy had small idea of who had produced the masterpieces that they guarded, and when hundreds of their churches and monasteries were deconsecrated, Bonaparte called in an army of experts to clean, classify, and—all too often—take away. Even the dates of the founding of most Italian museums make a case: that of the Carrara (1795) is typical.

Bergamo is on the edge of Brianza, which produces the region's best cheese and meat, and at the foot of the Valtelline, with their vineyards, so the cuisine here is of high order. There are starred restaurants in the Lower Town; **Dell'Angelo**, near the Carrara; and **Lio Pellegrini**, right across from it. But the appeal of dining on the piazzas and in the courtyards of the Upper Town is difficult to resist. There the most obvious is the **Taverna del Colleoni**, facing the lion fountain on the piazza Vecchia, with its local versions of tortellini or crêpes stuffed with the wild mushrooms that come down from the hills around the spa of San Pellegrino. A view both of the *Città Alta* and the Valtelline hills can be accompanied by imaginative cooking at the **Gourmet**, via San Vigilio 1. In the evening you can also opt for more rustic spots, where the younger generation goes. At the **Trattoria del Teatro**, on the piazza Mascheroni, you can count on lots of polenta and local wine. The **Agnello d'Oro** has the double qualification of good food and of being the best hotel in the Upper Town (20 rooms only, so reserve ahead).

Brescia

Brescia, east of Bergamo on the way to Verona, is Lombardy's other "Venetian city," and from a distance the natural reaction to its belt of industry is to step on the accelerator or stay on the train. The manufacture of arms was already making Brescia one of the richest cities of the Renaissance. Once you pass through the suburbs, however, you emerge into a town of fountains, palaces, Medieval churches, and Roman temples. The **via dei Musei** harbors the ruins of the former forum; and the **Tempio Capitolino** has been turned into a Museo Romano, a museum for ancient finds, which include the oft-reproduced bronze *Victory of Brescia*. The **Museo dell'Età Cristiana** deals with the Byzantine, and is adjacent to the

Romanesque church of San Salvatore. Later art is well shown in the **Pinacoteca Tosio Martinengo**, on via Francesco Crispi, a surprisingly high caliber collection of the School of Brescia—Moretto and Foppa—as well as Raphaels, Lottos, and even Clouets.

This town is not divided, like Bergamo, into upper and lower sections, nor does it particularly cater to tourists, being very well off on its own. But the crowded central section is remarkable for its array of Medieval buildings; the piazza della Loggia; the Romanesque Rotonda; and the Medieval *Broletto,* or town hall. They are all within easy call of one another, and if they were in France would be considered something to rival the palaces of Avignon. As it is, travellers dash by in a rush to get to Venice, while instead they could lunch here in a palace—**La Sosta**, at via San Martino della Battaglia 20—and see a city that we're very lucky to have.

Mantua

It is by a hair's breadth that Mantua (Italian, Mantova) is part of Lombardy at all, thanks to a technical boundary and the meanderings of two rivers. Mantua lies within a triangle formed by three cities, Parma, Verona, and Padua (Italian, Padova)—none of them Lombard towns, though it can be visited easily from each. The city's history has been very much its own; this celebrated capital of the Gonzagas was for centuries an independent dukedom known to every court in Europe, and with a palace second in size only to the Vatican.

In the arts its list of celebrities begins with a native son: the poet Virgil, who was born just outside, but who considered Mantua his town, to which his fame was to add luster. Its broad, reflective river, the Mincio, flows through his *Bucolics.* As Gilbert Highet notes in *Poets in a Landscape,* there is a certain sadness in Virgil's every description of this country. Centuries later this despondency was echoed by Aldous Huxley in *Along the Road:* "I have seen great cities dead or in decay—but over none, it seemed to me, did there brood so profound a melancholy as over Mantua."

That was written in the 1930s, before the Palazzo Ducale had been restored and when it was still a shadow of its former self: "For wherever the Gonzagas lived, they left behind them the same pathetic emptiness, the same pregnant desolation, the same echoes, the same ghosts of splendor." This for the family that nonetheless brought to Mantua the painter Andrea Mantegna, the architect Leon Battista Alberti, and the court composer Claudio Monteverdi. Nor, thanks to their marriages with the great houses of their day—the Sforza, the Montefeltro, and the Medici among them—were the Gonzagas isolated. The marriage in 1490 of Isabella d'Este to Francesco Gonzaga brought one of the most brilliant women of her time to Mantua, and she was to be followed by much that was best in the humanist Italy of her day: poets, philosophers, and writers such as Castiglione. By way of these shrewd marriages and clever politics the Gonzagas made a miraculous leap from their peasant origins and especially beginning with the year 1328, when they took Mantua from its ruling family, the Bonacolsi. That battle was the beginning of their success, but the truth is that it was their benevolent and stable government that kept them in power—the dead opposite of the rule of the aristocratic Visconti in Milan. The Gonzagas never had the money of the Medici, but by their contacts they were able to hire the best artists of their day and to receive luminaries, who included Emperor Charles V (who made them dukes in 1530), Henri III of France, and Pope Pius II. The arrival of the Hapsburgs and the Spanish was by no means a tragedy for them; they made more marriages that consolidated their position in international politics—and all of this with looks often unfortunate, and many of them with a recurrent back ailment (which the family inherited from the Malatestas, a clan of powerful overlords with whom they intermarried).

It is not, however, for the Gonzagas' politics that you go to Mantua. It is to see their ducal palace, or *reggia,* and its satellite palaces both in Mantua and in the nearby village of Sabbioneta. The entrance to the **Palazzo Ducale**, Gothic and crenellated, is on the rectangular piazza Sordello (near the water at the northeastern end of the city) and gives small hint of the splendors within: the Baroque halls; the wide, winding stairways; the elaborate quarters for the court dwarfs; and the later additions, Empire and Rococo, made when the Austrians came. It is the Medieval part of the Castello, however, that contains the most of interest. Designed by the same architect who built the castle at Ferrara, it is mirrored in the lagoons formed by the Mincio.

When an inventory of the Gonzaga holdings was made in 1627, it was found that there were 2,000 paintings in the Castello alone, their villas and pavilions apart. Most of these were later sold or looted, but not the most priceless of all—because it was painted on the walls of a room, and could not be moved. Andrea Mantegna took nine years to paint the **Camera degli Sposi** for Ludovico Gonzaga, initially to celebrate the fact that one of Ludovico's sons had been made a cardinal. By the time the fresco was finished it included new figures, such as the King of Denmark and Emperor Frederick III, who had visited Mantua during Mantegna's meticulous travail. It remains our finest view of a Renaissance court at work, crowned by a circular trompe l'oeil from which spectators stare down at the viewer. Mantegna painted three series of frescoes in his lifetime: one in the Belvedere of the Vatican that is completely lost; the second—a work of ten years of his youth—was in the Ovetari chapel of Padua's church of the Eremitani, which was leveled by a direct hit by an Allied bomb in World War II. This leaves the Camera as the sole survivor of the master's fresco work.

The Gonzagas had gone to great trouble to lure Mantegna to Mantua. He already had commissions elsewhere, and his marriage to Giovanni Bellini's sister gave him connections aplenty. But come he did, and he settled here for the rest of his life, which was fortunate for him and for us. He thus avoided the wasteful wanderings of Leonardo, and he had none of that artist's ambitions to design planes, submarines, or whatever. Creations for court masques apart, he could devote his time to one occupation: painting. Vasari depicts him as the most gentle and affable of men, but Vasari was often wrong, and others make it clear just how disagreeable Mantegna was: litigious, tight-fisted, and constantly engaged in feuds ("He is so hostile and unpleasant that he never had a neighbor with whom he hasn't gone to law," wrote a Mantuan to the Gonzagas). Born the son of a carpenter and adopted by a certain Paduan painter, promoter, and antique dealer called Squarcione (with whom he had his first feud), Mantegna soon developed the love of Classical art which he was to retain throughout his career. Luckily he was snobbish, so when the Gonzaga coffers were low, they could pay him in lands and titles.

Some of his most famous paintings were done for the *studiolo,* or little study, of the most celebrated occupant of that part of the palace known as the Castello. Hardly had Isabella d'Este arrived in Mantua when she started to plan the decoration of this room, and for it Mantegna painted his famous *Parnassus*. This and his other works that adorned it, as well as its Perugino and Correggios, are in the Louvre—and the Mantuans want them back. In later life Isabella moved her private apartments downstairs, where we see them still, marquetry, marble doors, and ceilings intact. This series of salons was the magnet for intelligent visitors to the Castello during her lifetime, which was a fairly long one. She arrived in 1490 at the age of 16 and died in 1539, which gave her 50 years to devote to her collections of antiquities and paintings, dealing with everyone from Leonardo to Michelangelo. She was a difficult patron, demanding the best artists and dictatorial in her orders. Nor, in spite of her own income, did she have all that much money; one reason that she so disliked her sister-in-law, Lucrezia Borgia, was the fact that the latter was very rich. She had little in common with her husband, who was a warrior; but she was devoted to her son Federico, who turned out to be one of the most avid collectors in Italy: a friend to Titian and capable of buying 120 Flemish landscapes as a lot.

When he was young, Federico had been held prisoner in Rome—on a very grand scale—by Pope Julius II, and had met all the artists of note there. Among them was Raphael's pupil, Giulio Romano, who was finally induced to come to Mantua, where at great expense he redesigned much of the town, the Palazzo Ducale, the Duomo, his own house, and Federico's **Palazzo del Té**, which you can reach by following the via Roma (it changes its name several times) south through the city from the piazza delle Erbe. This palazzo, a former stable, was rushed to completion to receive Charles V; and on its walls were celebrated all of the Gonzagas' favorite things: horses, astrology, pornography, and mythology. Many of Federico's paintings were in the Té too, and when, by 1627, the Gonzaga debts had become as large as their collections, Duke Vicenzo decided that something had to be done.

It was known that Charles I of England was an enthusiastic buyer of pictures; with the mediation of a fellow art lover, Lady Arundel, it was arranged to sell the best part of the Gonzaga paintings to the English King. The sum asked was enormous: 5 percent of the exchequer. The Stuart ruler, having dissolved Parliament, already had financial problems. By the time the paintings arrived—and it took a decade—the purchase seemed to the English a folly just as the sale had seemed to the Italians a scandal. When the English Civil War broke out, the Puritans gave short shrift to art of any sort, and this incomparable collection, which would have made London the equal to Paris and Madrid in masterpieces, was put up for auction by Cromwell. Now many of them can be seen in the Prado and the Louvre (the royal families of France and Spain were quick to send agents). Some have lauded Cromwell for holding back the Mantegna series of the *Triumphs of Caesar,* which have now been cleaned and can be seen in Hampton Court Palace. He probably liked them for their military subject matter—small recompense for the disposal of a priceless legacy.

Near the gates of the Té, which is on the inland edge of Mantua beyond the Porta Pusteria, is the house of Mantegna, which, with its oval courtyard, he himself designed. Across the way is the small church of San Sebastiano, created by the architect Gian Battista Alberti. This was by no means his only church in Mantua, as it was to his designs that the largest in town, **Sant'Andrea**, was built. Again Vasari gets a great deal wrong, giving Alberti credit for being "admirable," but hinting that his fame came from the fact that he was an author, widely read, who used his books for self-promotion. Now we know better. Alberti was a writer and a master mathematician as well. He also knew a great many important people; his work for the Malatestas on their *tempio* in Rimini brought him early fame. The Rucellai family in Florence procured his assistance on everything from their own palace to the façade of Santa Maria Novella. It was in Florence that Ludovico Gonzaga commissioned him to do a chapel in the Annunziata, and subsequently brought him to Mantua.

For most of today's architects Alberti was far and away the most interesting practitioner in the Renaissance. The miraculous lightness and simplicity of his work has taken centuries to come back into its own. Many would trade just one of his arches, seemingly floating in space, for the whole ornate façade of the Certosa in Pavia. And Sant' Andrea here in Mantua remains perhaps his purest creation, since bombs have laid waste to so much of the *tempio.* It is worth sitting in the café on the piazza Sant' Andrea across from the church to appreciate an approach to architecture that has had such influence—influence always acknowledged, as by Philip Johnson. Those who can't visit Mantua immediately might go to Madison Avenue and 55th Street in New York City to see, on the AT&T building, how far the façade of Sant'Andrea has come.

The piazza delle Erbe, with its market stalls, is near Alberti's church, but by the time you get here you will have trekked through miles of palace corridors, and a restaurant is the first thing that you will want to see. One of the most beautiful in Italy is **Il Cigno**, occupying yet another palace—this one on the piazza d'Arco—and serving the finest food around: pigeon cooked in black grapes; duck in liver and orange sauce (the menu might have appealed to the Gonzagas). The interior, with its patios, paintings, and charmingly arranged fruit and flowers, certainly would. More humble—but still in a remarkable setting—is the **Aquila Nigra**—(vicolo Bonacolsi 4), set in a former 14th-century convent, its frescoes and arched rooms intact. There are trattorias aplenty near the Palazzo Ducale, but it just might be that you want to get away from tourist mobs, and both of these havens will guarantee coolness and calm.

Staying over in Mantua is not a bad idea; there are lots of walks to take, and when evening falls almost all the other visitors go away. Those who want to spend the night in Mantua have the hotels **Rechigi** and **San Lorenzo**—central and well-appointed—and the more modest **Dante**.

Those with the energy for more palaces will drive on to **Sabbioneta**, on the Parma road: a whole little town of them, created by Vespasiano Gonzaga. It has come a long way since Huxley and his Bloomsbury friends found Sabbioneta an abandoned wreck. Now the Palazzo Ducale on the piazza has been repaired, and so has the festive garden palace, alive with mirrors and frescoes. Concerts are held once more in the Teatro Olimpico (which was a cinema when visited by Vita Sackville-West), and antique shops line the piazza Castello.

GETTING AROUND

Milan's national airport is Linate, 7 km (4 miles) east of the city, and its international airport is Malpensa, 50 km (30 miles) to the northwest. Buses connect them and run from the airports to the center of town. Buses leave for Linate from the Porta Garibaldi station and for Malpensa from the main station, Stazione Centrale. A taxi costs about 60,000 lire to the center from Malpensa.

Lombardy is extremely well linked by train. Milan is a major rail hub, with good service to and from virtually all of Europe. Bus service to smaller towns is also good, with the usual restrictions of time that bus schedules to small towns impose. Roads are well marked and well maintained.

ACCOMMODATIONS REFERENCE

▶ **Agnello d'Oro.** Via Gombito 22, 24100 **Bergamo.** Tel: (035) 24-98-83.

▶ **Antica Locanda Solferino.** Via Castelfidaro 2, 20121 **Milan.** Tel: (02) 657-0129. The 11 relatively inexpensive rooms are usually booked well in advance; the on-premises restaurant is excellent.

▶ **Ariosto.** Via Ariosto 22, 20145 **Milan.** Tel: (02) 49-09-95. A lovely garden and 53 moderately priced rooms, near the church of Santa Maria della Grazie.

▶ **Casa Svizzera.** Via San Raffaele 3, 20121 **Milan.** Tel: (02) 869-22-46; Telex: 316064.

▶ **Centro.** Via Broletto 46, 20121 **Milan.** Tel: (02) 87-52-32; Telex: 332632.

▶ **Dante.** Via Corrado 54, 46100 **Mantua.** Tel: (0376) 32-64-25.

▶ **Gourmet.** San Vigilio 1, 24100 **Bergamo.** Tel: (035) 25-61-10.

▶ **Manzoni.** Via Spirito 20, 20121 **Milan.** Tel: (02) 70-57-00.

▶ **Principe di Savoia.** Piazza della Repubblica 17, 20124 **Milan.** Tel: (02) 6230; Telex: 310052.

▶ **Rechigi.** Via Calvi 30, 46100 **Mantua.** Tel: (0376) 32-07-81.

▶ **San Lorenzo.** Piazza Concordia 14, 46100 **Mantua.** Tel: (0376) 32-71-53.

▶ **Villa del Sogno.** Corso Zanardelli 107, 25080 **Fasano** (33 km/20 miles from Brescia). Tel: (0365) 202-28. Delightful, moderately priced accommodations in a villa on Lago di Garda.

VENICE

By Paolo Lanapoppi

Paolo Lanapoppi, born and educated in Venice, was a professor of Italian literature and civilization at Cornell University, the City University of New York, and Vassar College for many years. He is now back in Venice as a travel writer for Travel & Leisure *and other magazines, and is working on a biography of Mozart's librettist Lorenzo Da Ponte.*

The unique nature of Venice as a city has been acknowledged and exalted since the very beginning of its existence. People were amazed: They had seen harbors and riverfronts and even small islands included in settlements, but a city rising in the middle of a lagoon, with water flowing between streets and squares, intruding in front of homes, churches, and shops—this seemed as weird a thousand years ago as it seems today.

It would be wrong to believe that Venetians added to or took from the lagoon islands. The layout of the city was there from the very beginning: There was a large lagoon, well protected from the open sea, and in the middle of it the tides had dug dozens of small canals between the barely emerging islands. It was on top of those islands that the Venetians built their city. Even in the worst of storms the waves never rose higher than a couple of feet, while most of the time the water flowed quiet and clean (even in the beginning of our century, Marcel Proust marveled over the "splendid blue of the water").

One of those canals, the largest and deepest of all, ran through the clusters of islands as though it had been designed to touch on as many of them as possible. With its large, lazy curves it took two and a half miles to cover a

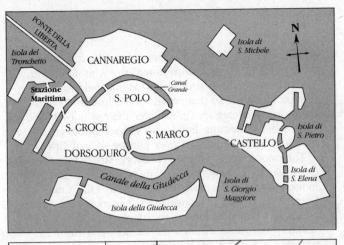

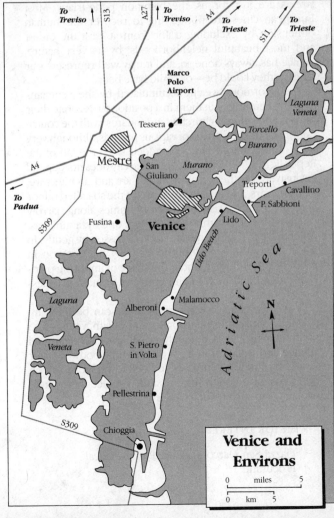

Venice and Environs

straight distance of three-quarters of a mile. It was deep enough for the largest ships to navigate without danger. The richest merchants soon began to build their headquarters on its banks, so that vessels could load and unload their precious cargoes right under their windows. The canal's banks became lined with elegant buildings that made its name famous all over Europe—Canal Grande.

This double communication network (streets for pedestrians, canals for passengers and merchandise) is as much in use today as in the early years of the city's life. Crates of Coca Cola as well as construction materials and other goods are patiently loaded into large motorboats and skillfully navigated through the canals. As a result, the streets are just for us, the common pedestrians. Most European cities are now trying to recover this human dimension by excluding traffic from at least the oldest and most beautiful neighborhoods; by its very nature, Venice has always done so, and it may well represent our cities as they could be—or could have been.

The enormous wealth accumulated by the Venetians over the centuries put them in a position to decorate their houses and palaces, churches and squares, with the contributions of the best artists of various periods, although very little of importance has been added since the fall of the Republic in 1797. Yet the charm of the city does not depend exclusively on the major works of art and architecture. Many visitors, and most natives, prefer the so-called minor Venice, which consists of two-story homes along narrow canals with just a Gothic window here or a Byzantine bas-relief there to capture the attention of passersby gently. In these labyrinthine neighborhoods daily life goes on in relaxed, colorful ways, under the shade of imposing patrician palazzi and next to churches that contain priceless works of art.

So Venice is a place where a visitor can be duly impressed by magnificence, power, and wealth, yet it is also a city in which it is uniquely possible to stroll in total silence and isolation in front of a friendly body of water dotted by far-away cypresses and bell towers, or to sit on the steps of a lonely bridge and, yes, let a streak of romanticism surface for a while.

MAJOR INTEREST

Piazza San Marco: Basilica, Palazzo Ducale
Procuratie

The Canal Grande
The Gallerie dell'Accademia
Scuola Grande di San Rocco (Tintoretto)
Scuola Grande di San Giorgio degli Schiavoni
   (Carpaccio)
Ca' Rezzonico (Museum of the Venetian 18th
   Century)
Ca' d'Oro–Galleria Franchetti (Gothic palace and
   art collection)
Peggy Guggenheim Collection (contemporary art)
Island of Torcello (Veneto-Byzantine art)
Island of Murano (glass factories and the glass
   museum)
Island of Burano (lace)
Island of Lido (beaches)

From the fifth century on, Venice was built with an enormous display of military courage and business skill. The wars, first to conquer a vast empire, then to defend it (mostly against the Turks), were relentless and bloody; Venetians have been at war against every power in Europe—and on at least one occasion against a coalition of all of them. Meanwhile, business was thriving, but the competition never let up; Venetians are credited with inventing banks, income tax, and modern bookkeeping.

Have any of those qualities of persistence and competitiveness survived in the descendants of the city's fathers? To paraphrase a Venetian saying, too much water has flowed under the bridges since those glorious times. The character of contemporary Venetians has probably been shaped much more by the sad events that followed the loss of independence: French domination (1797–1815), Austrian domination (1815–1866), and finally reunion with the new Kingdom of Italy as just one province among many. To find early features still recognizable today, you can turn no farther back than the comedies written by Carlo Goldoni in the second half of the 18th century, in which there are no heroic figures, just a smiling wisdom tinged with cynicism, a constant self-irony, a resigned acceptance of the world's ways.

This could also be called superior detachment, and it is in a way a civilized attitude. Venetians are fiercely but cynically attached to their past. They crowd the weekly lectures on Venetian art and history at Università Popolare, Ateneo Veneto, Venezia Viva, and many other cultural clubs; many of them know, or think they know, their

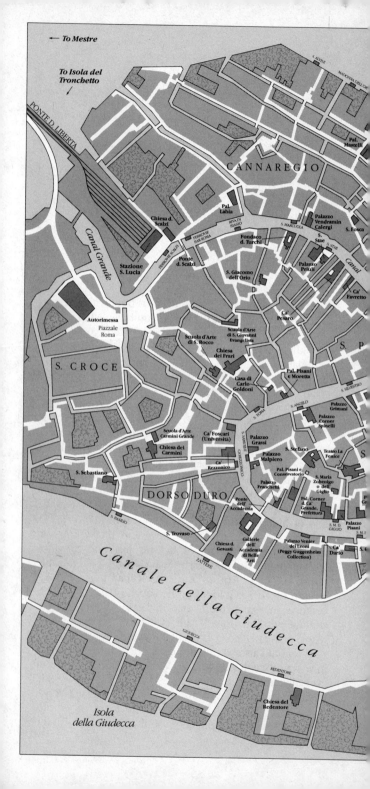

city stone by stone. But they remain ill at ease with the glorious past, as it clashes against a reality made of down-to-earth, unresolved problems; like the ruined offspring of ancient nobility, they have only a few old albums to show. The pendulum of history has swung hard for Venetians; their smile as they display the ancient glory, and present-day banality is the only protection they can afford—together with a subtle innuendo: Don't worry, they seem to be saying, it will swing for you too.

In the past thirty years the tourist boom has created a new breed of Venetians. They are the merchants and shopkeepers, often lured into Venice from the mainland, often not cultivated at all, and ready to exploit the thriving tourist trade. Cafés and restaurants, hotels and clothing shops are often run by this not-so-pleasant crowd. They make you think with regret of the courteous, even quixotic attitude of an antique dealer quoted by Mary McCarthy in her 1961 book on Venice: " 'Eighteenth century?' she had asked him hopefully about a set of china on display. 'No, nineteenth,' he answered with firmness, showing off his expertise and losing the sale."

SAN MARCO

Entrance into Venice was carefully planned by the founding fathers of the city. It was, of course, by water (the bridge over the lagoon was built in the 19th century, a controversial idea and a heavy price to pay for modern comfort), and not from the mainland side, but from the open sea. On those waters, beyond the frail, damlike islands of Lido and Pellestrina, the glory and wealth of the Republic had their bases: the eastern coasts of the Adriatic, the Peloponnesus, Cyprus and Crete, plus countless harbors in the eastern Mediterranean—all under Venetian domination. From those exotic centers, ships would sail up the Adriatic to the narrow entrance of the Venetian lagoon; they would then raise their best flags, dress their sailors and officers in their most splendid uniforms, and be allowed through the narrow, heavily protected channel into the waters of the mother city.

Century after century careful touches were added to the naturally grandiose stage setting. It was a matter of image, the importance of which had been discovered by this republic of merchants long before the advent of our public-relations wizards. As you sail in from the Lido (it can be done today by water bus), Venice's skyline is exactly what the ancient rulers wanted it to be. The lagoon waters are always quiet; often a slight mist veils the distant domes and bell towers, and the city seems to materialize out of the water, revealing one wondrous building after another. In the morning the sun rises beyond the visitor's shoulders and is caught and reflected by patches of gold finish: the angel on top of the Campanile di San Marco, the huge globe over the ancient Dogana di Mare (customhouse). In the evening it sets right in front, beyond the Baroque domes of La Salute and the Byzantine profile of the basilica di San Marco.

Landing must be on the **Molo**, the ancient waterfront built for this purpose just off the piazza San Marco. The visitor is welcomed by two huge columns standing near the water: On top of the first is a statue of Saint Theodore, the ancient patron of the city who was dethroned by Saint Mark, while on the second is a puzzling animal with wings, a chimera, looted by Venetian sailors on some Eastern shore and still mysterious to scholars (Etruscan? Persian? Chinese?). The two immense granite columns are booty of war as well—they were carried in by boat in 1170—and are just the first among countless precious objects shipped into the lagoon by the victorious fleet of the Republic—reminders that beyond the wealth, the power, and the beauty there lay war and conquest, cruel battles, and constant risk of life.

This landing area is called **the piazzetta** (the small square). It seems magnificent enough, with the Palazzo Ducale on the right and the Renaissance building of the Libreria Marciàna on the left; but as you walk through it, in the direction of the basilica with its gray-tiled domes, you see that the surprises are far from over. After the powerful shape of the campanile (bell tower), the view opens onto the piazza San Marco proper.

Piazza San Marco

Venetians often quote Napoléon as calling the piazza "the most elegant living room in Europe." He may indeed have said it, but the phrase is also attributed to Goethe, Byron, even Wagner, and is probably reinvented every year by dozens of tourists. It is pretty much impossible to say anything about Venice that hasn't been said by someone else; and the worst of it, as noted by Mary McCarthy in her book on Venice, is that nearly all these clichés (stage setting, etc.) are true.

But the piazza is indeed a living room. It may be less so during the tourist frenzy of the summer days, when the crowd is such that all perspectives get twisted, yet even in the summer it is enough to walk here after ten at night to find yourself in total agreement with Napoléon and company. This is, if anything, the prototype of stage settings, the Platonic Ideal of them all.

A reference to Plato is not as arbitrary as it may seem. When the merchant fathers of the city decided that it was time to redesign the piazza in the most impressive way possible, they turned to the most acclaimed architects of their times. It was the height of the Italian Renaissance: The writings of Vitruvius had just been rediscovered and printed (in Venice, of course); Neoplatonic ideas had become fashionable among writers and figurative artists; the Venetian erudite Pietro Bembo had just written, in the quiet hills of Asolo, his treatise on love, inspired by Plato; Latin and Greek civilization were the objects of endless study and painstaking philological attention. The general feeling was that a barbaric era was over and a new, refined civilization was just being born. The restructuring of the piazza became the subject of heated discussions in the parliament and the senate; we can say that no stone was laid without the patrician government studying it carefully from all angles.

The appointed architect was Jacopo Sansovino (1486–1570), a Tuscan who had worked in Rome with Michelangelo and Bramante. He was a great architect but also, in those difficult times, a cunning promoter of himself: For many decades until his death he was able to keep such rivals as Andrea Palladio out of the official commissions, so that Palladio had to limit himself to private villas on the mainland or at most ecclesiastical monuments in Venice (the church of San Giorgio Maggiore, for instance, which looks at Sansovino's piazzetta from across the Bacino di San Marco). Sansovino, Titian, and the Tuscan poet Pietro Aretino were a formidable trio in Venice at that time, close friends and undefeatable allies in obtaining or assigning every public project.

The piazza is probably at its best at night, when the ancient silence is not disturbed by too many tourists. Yet even in the middle of a summer day it remains an enchanted space. The wonder and admiration in the eyes of the colorful crowds; the relaxing, old-fashioned music

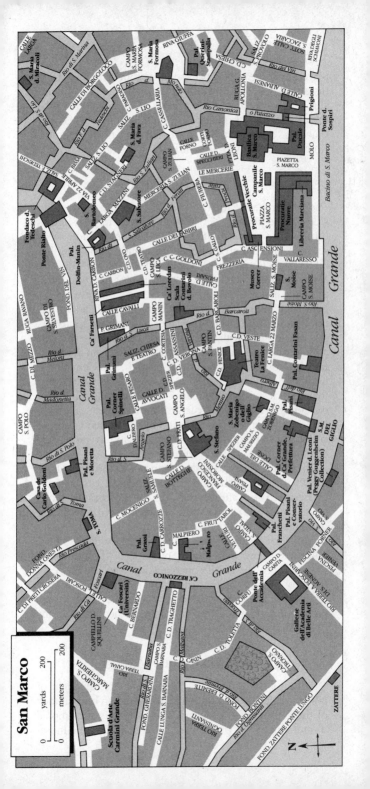

played by three expert bands for the tourists sitting at the historic cafés; and, naturally, the total oblivion of the automotive world of the forsaken mainland, all contribute to a feeling of quiet ease. You almost forget that this space was designed to be the center of an efficient administration and the visible symbol of its wealth and power.

The Procuratie

The Procuratie are the two parallel buildings on the long sides of the piazza. They housed the government offices during the time of the Republic. (The *procuratori* were six magistrates high in the administration.) The building on the right (Procuratie Vecchie) was designed in 1500 by Mauro Codussi, one of the first architects to introduce the new Renaissance style in Gothic Venice; the one on the left (campanile side) is the work of Sansovino, and of his pupil Scamozzi (1586). The latter is definitely more imposing, in line with the grandiose ambitions of both architect and government. The side across from the basilica used to be closed by a small church, San Geminiano, until the French conquest. Napoléon's architects were invited to leave a visible mark of their presence, and they conceived the present structure, appropriately called Ala Napoleonica and today occupied by the **Museo Correr**, a collection of paintings and objects related to the history of Venice.

Three world-famous cafés open under the porticos of the Procuratie, each with tables outdoors and a small orchestra. The **Caffè Florian**, on the Procuratie Nuove (campanile side) is the oldest café in town and is still decorated in the original 18th-century style. A pleasant surprise for visitors who don't particularly like "O Sole Mio" and "Love Is a Many-Splendored Thing": inside Florian there is a small counter where you can sit, relax from too much walking, and enjoy refreshments at perfectly affordable prices (look for the counter, though; the prices jump dramatically if you sit in the lacquered rooms behind the windows).

Basilica di San Marco

"Nothing is sweeter to the human eye than the sight of gold," wrote Lorenzo Da Ponte, the Venetian-born author of three librettos for Mozart. The basilica is a triumphal monument to this precious metal. It shines on the mosaics of the façade, it reflects the sun from the four horses over the main door, it gleams mysteriously in the darkness of walls and domes inside. A strange atmosphere of mysticism and wealth receives visitors as they walk toward the central altar. It is a feeling totally different from that of any cathedral in the West.

Saint Mark, the apostle and evangelist, was said to have landed on the Venetian lagoon during his preaching years and to have converted the mainland communities, then under Roman domination. Venice had not been founded yet—its beginnings are set in the fifth century A.D. But when it later emerged as an international power, it needed a visible token of authority. The opportunity was offered in 828, when two Venetian sailors doing business in Egypt discovered that the saint's body was buried in Moslem Alexandria. They stole it, hiding the relic under a mass of salted pork (a taboo for the Arabs). On the right pillar next to the main altar, the scene is depicted vividly in mosaic: Against a huge sky of gold, the small vessel navigates with the precious body, while a caption reads, "*Kefir, kefir vociferantur*" ("Pork, pork they yell").

Over this relic the church grew in different stages. It was not the cathedral of Venice—that was San Pietro di Castello. It was at first only Saint Mark's sanctuary and the private chapel of the *dogi,* although it soon became the center of all important religious ceremonies. The present structure dates from the 12th century, and it is a strange mixture of different architectural styles, mostly Byzantine, Romanesque, and Gothic. The splendid floor, all in marble mosaics, was raised in the 12th century over the original level, to avoid submersion in case of flood. But nowadays that floor is again the lowest point in the whole city, and the first to be covered by high tides. This happens regularly many times a year, especially in November–December and February–March.

The basilica seems designed to embody, more than the Republic's religious feelings, its economic and military power. The four superb horses on the façade are booty of war, taken from Constantinople after the Fourth Crusade (they have been recently replaced with copies; the originals can be visited in a room off the basilica's main entrance). Most of the countless capitals, statues, bas-reliefs, and columns that adorn the basilica inside and out were carried over after victorious expeditions to the East—a rather weird way to pay homage to God. Among the large mosaics over the doors, only the central one represents a traditional religious scene (a 19th-century *Christ in Glory*), while the other four describe once again the legendary abduction of Saint Mark's body, the most interesting one being the first to the left (*Transportation of the Body,* 1260–1270), in which the basilica appears as it was at that time.

The floor plan has the shape of a Greek cross (all four arms equal in length), with one dome at the center and one in the middle of each arm. The domes, originally low in profile as in Constantinople's Hagia Sophia, were covered with higher structures in the 13th century. The interior mosaics, covering the top part of the church almost wall to wall, date from the 11th to the 16th centuries and anticipate the Venetian taste for rich, colorful decorations, while showing almost step by step the birth and development of a figurative style that originated in Byzantium and slowly acquired Romanesque, Gothic, and finally purely Venetian accents.

Some details of particular interest:

- Mosaics illustrating the Creation of Adam and Eve and other events from the book of Genesis in the entrance portico (13th century)
- Catwalks on inside galleries, which provide a closer look at the mosaics
- Iconostasis (separation between public space and altar), with 14th-century statues
- Pala d'Oro, an immense gold-plated altarpiece decorated on both sides, dating from the 10th to the 14th centuries
- Museo San Marco (same admission ticket as Pala d'Oro), in large part composed of precious objects carried over from Byzantium
- For the visitor with extra time (a few hours or a few days), a close inspection of the mosaics with the help of a detailed description may turn out to be a memorable experience.

Early Venice and the Rise of the Republic

The unmistakable, fascinating Oriental look of the city is due to its geographically unlikely ties with Byzantium, capital of the eastern half of the Roman Empire. For many centuries after its founding, Venice seemed to ignore its immediate neighbors in Italy and Europe; its commercial, political, and military life was oriented toward the East, with resulting enormous influence on the arts.

From the time of its founding, Venice was a republic. Its citizens were as proud of their constitution as today's United States citizens are of their own. Even the founding of the city is credited not to one hero, as in most other cases, but to a group of equals. Their descendants, with proper and careful additions of new blood from time to time, continued to run it collegially for 1,300 years.

Official historians used to set the origin of Venice at the time of Attila, the cruel king of the Huns, who invaded Italy in A.D. 412, causing the population of the mainland to seek refuge in the lagoon islands. It has now been ascertained that at the time of the barbaric invasions a lagoon community was already established and functional; this is abundantly confirmed by archaeological material. The passage of invading populations just increased the importance of the existing community, both as a refuge and as a strategic hold for what was left of the Roman Empire.

With the collapse of Rome (A.D. 476), a few territories on the eastern coast of Italy, unconquered by the barbarians, remained attached to the Eastern Empire, which had its capital in Byzantium (Constantinople). Like Ravenna, the Venetian lagoon was one of these areas, and by the sixth century its inhabitants formed a strong and well-organized community. Untouched by the passage of the barbarians, they were formally under the protection and rule of Byzantium, and when Emperor Justinian decided to wage war against the Goths, who had conquered almost all the rest of Italy, they were in a position to offer very substantial help.

Cassiodorus, a scholar and prime minister at the service of the Goths, had words of high praise for the lagoon people: In a letter to their chieftains (537), he described in flattering terms their homes surrounded by water and their agile, maneuverable boats. In 551 those boats and the organization behind them were able to transport a Byzantine army of 25,000, so as to avoid the Gothic armies that were ready to ambush them in the mainland.

Northern Italy was then conquered by the Lombards (seventh century), and yet again by Charlemagne, king of the Franks (end of the eighth century). In those war-ridden times the lagoon community was able to survive brilliantly by leaning mostly (but by no means exclusively) toward the Byzantine side. In 812 Pepin, the son of

Charlemagne, officially acknowledged Byzantium's rule over the lagoon (and over southern Italy), in exchange for acceptance of his title of Holy Roman emperor.

Until that time the chief islands of today's Venice, although even then partly settled, were of little importance. The political and military center of the area was the island of **Torcello** (evidently a fortified town, as the name, derived from *torre* or *tour,* seems to indicate). And in Torcello the lagoon civilization of that period has left a few splendid monuments (discussed below).

The wealth of Venice was mostly from commerce. Production of goods was limited to local needs and was often insufficient—with the important exception of salt, easily extracted from the lagoon and exported in great quantities (the beginnings of Rome were also tied to the commerce of salt). Having thus established a commercial network, the Venetians started to deal in other products, gradually expanding their range from the northern lagoon to the whole Adriatic Sea. In the ninth and tenth centuries they were already importing grain, oil, and wine from Apulia, to redistribute them in the northern Italian markets; soon they secured landing facilities for their commercial fleet in a number of strategic spots on both sides of the Adriatic Sea. A sign of their success is the marriage of a doge's son to a Byzantine princess around the year 1000, and of a doge to the Eastern emperor's sister 70 years later.

By the 12th century the importance of the lagoon community was widely acknowledged by Europeans. One episode, later exalted by state artists to the level of myth, underlined this in 1177: the meeting in Venice, due to the diplomacy of its rulers, of the two great rivals in the fight for European supremacy, Pope Alexander III and the Holy Roman Emperor Frederick I, called the Barbarossa (red-bearded). The reconciliation took place with a memorable ceremony in the piazza San Marco, which had been enlarged by filling a canal that was flowing in front of the basilica (the first of many such fillings that were to substantially modify the geography of the city).

A few years later the military and economic power of the community emerged in full strength with the Fourth Crusade (1202–1204): Venice obtained the contract for the transportation of all troops and materials to the Holy Land (4,500 horsemen, 9,000 squires, 20,000 infantrymen), and when the crusaders proved unable to pay the amount agreed upon, Doge Enrico Dandolo proposed that they work for Venice instead: There just happened to be a few coastal towns that didn't seem to like the Venetian domination very much and needed to be taught a lesson. As these towns were situated just on the way to Jerusalem, the whole operation would require only a slight detour for the Christian armies. The crusaders agreed, but when the deed was accomplished the Venetians found other pretexts to keep these debtors busy in their favor and the whole enterprise turned into a war of conquest, climaxing with the siege and occupation of Byzantium itself.

Thus the old vassals conquered their former lords. The doge refused the title of emperor for himself or for other Venetians; the democratic tradition was already extremely strong in Venice, and primacy of one single family would not have been tolerated. He knew he had to answer to a group of solid, realistic merchants who were running the city's political life with an eye, or both eyes, to profit and security. In the final settlement with the crusaders, Venice obtained more than it had originally hoped for: large quarters in Byzantium, plus a maritime empire of cities and harbors on the eastern Adriatic and Greek coasts, enabling the city to secure its commercial ventures for centuries to come.

Palazzo Ducale

Next to the basilica, along the eastern side of the piazzetta and cornering on the waterfront, the Palazzo Ducale is a miracle of Gothic engineering and one of the most famous buildings in the world. It typifies a constant feature of Venetian architecture: the predominance of open spaces on the façades, especially in the low floors. This confers to Venetian palazzi their peculiar quality of lightness, emphasized in turn by the water environment and strongly contrasting with the stern, fortresslike aspect of so many buildings of the Florentine Renaissance.

The origin of this style lies not so much in an aesthetic principle as in a set of circumstances. Only a rich Venetian, of course, could afford to build himself a palazzo, no matter how small; and every rich man in Venice owed his fortune to the sea trade. So the palazzi had to stand in front of a canal, possibly the Canal Grande, which was the largest of all; on the first floor the palazzo had to have space for the loading and unloading of merchandise from the owner's ships when they came in from their journeys. Hence the large first-floor porticoes, through which goods could be moved with relative ease. On the second floor, which housed the residence of the owner and was known as the *piano nobile,* a large balcony offered the double advantage of letting in floods of light and allowing constant surveillance of the operations.

A final element that made all this possible was the exceptional lack of family feuds within the Republic. While all other Italian cities were torn by civil wars between Guelphs and Ghibellines, the Venetian merchants were quietly counting their money; thanks to their much-admired constitution, nobody needed to fortify his residence against armed attacks by the neighbors.

Inside the Palazzo Ducale were the doge's apartments, the patrician parliament, and the government offices. It also included several prisons with different degrees of security, among them the famous *piombi* (the term refers to the lead-covered roof over the cells) from which Casanova escaped in 1756.

On the entrance next to the basilica, the **Porta della Carta** (1438–1443), once painted in blue and gold, is a masterwork of late Gothic architecture by Giovanni and Bartolomeo Bon, a father and son who adorned many palazzi and churches of Venice. The doge kneeling in front of the great lion is Francesco Foscari (1423–1457), one of the greatest rulers of Venice and the promoter of a new policy of expansion on the mainland. His predecessor, Tommaso Mocenigo, had warned the government against electing Francesco to succeed him. In a lucid and historically precious document he had listed the possessions of Venice, including ships, cash, and colonies, begging the patricians not to abandon the old ways in favor of involvment with European politics. But Fóscari was elected, and some Venetians still believe that the deep roots of the Republic's decline are to be found in his leadership.

In the courtyard, the façade facing the entrance is by Antonio Rizzo (1490), while the other three façades were rebuilt in the early 17th century by the amazing Bartolomeo Manopola, a carpenter and engineer who was able to support the building on wooden beams while replacing the columns.

The most impressive feature of this impressive building is the **Sala del Maggior Consiglio**, built in 1340 to be the largest hall in Europe without inside support, and redecorated after a fire in 1577. An entire wall is occupied by Tintoretto's interpretation of Paradise, while one of the ovals on the ceiling contains the *Apotheosis of Venice,* one of Veronese's most acclaimed works. The standard tour of the palazzo includes a great number of halls, corridors, and stairs decorated with the most magnificent materials available and with paintings, mostly by Mannerists. The 1577 fire destroyed many works of art (remnants of Guariento's *Coronation of the Virgin,* which occupied the place of Tintoretto's *Paradise,* are conserved in the sala dell'Armamento), so that only a famous *Winged Lion of Saint Mark's* by Carpaccio and a Pietà by Giovanni Bellini are left from the preceding period (they are in two rooms opening on the loggia off the sala del Maggior Consiglio). A ceiling by Veronese is in the sala del Consiglio dei Dieci.

The Merchant Patricians

The constitution of Venice was pretty much the backbone of the city's stability and success. It was studied and envied by political theorists (Machiavelli among them) for centuries, and it lasted unmodified until the fall of the Republic in 1797. (In the last one hundred years before the fall, however, it was probably one of the main causes of the weakness that led to the end. The times had changed, but the patricians were unable to adjust.) The state was a democratic oligarchy, in the sense that within the ruling group democracy was jealously preserved, while the rest of the population was totally excluded from the political scene.

This ruling group, originally rather fluid, was defined precisely in 1297: All the families that were in it were allowed to stay, and no one else could join. They called themselves patricians (this was the only title of nobility allowed), and they formed the Maggior Consiglio (Greater Assembly), which met in the great hall at the Palazzo Ducale. The patricians formed 3 to 4 percent of the population; all the patrician males over 25 years of age sat in the Maggior Consiglio, for a total of 900 to 1,200 members. After the constitution of 1297, new families were allowed to enter the group only on rare occasions, mostly when a serious war was swallowing up the Republic's funds and new money was needed. The richest among the nonpatricians could then contribute to the war effort and be made patricians; this ensured a constant filling of the gap between ancient nobility and emerging bourgeoisie. The Maggior Consiglio elected from its own body the doge, the doge's counselors, including the later infamous Consiglio dei Dieci (Council of Ten), the senate, the judges, and all other magistrates.

To prevent consolidation of power in a few hands, all periods of office were extremely short, ranging from six months to three years—only the doge was elected for life—and very few implied a salary. Civil service was considered a duty and an honor, and each family consigned at least one male member to a political career, supporting him with family funds (some posts, like the ambassadorships, required enormous expenditures).

Another 3 to 5 percent of the population enjoyed the title of *cittandini* (citizens). They had access to the bar and to the technical jobs in the administration and constituted a solid, expert, and faithful bureaucracy at the patricians' service.

The rest were the *popolani*. They had no political rights, but they were grouped in professional associations or corporations called *scuole* (schools), of which about 200 existed in town. As sponsors of buildings and paintings, the scuole are responsible for some of the greatest artworks in Venice; some of Carpaccio's and Tintoretto's best work was done on commission from them.

The government—that is, the patrician merchants themselves—used public funds to organize all important commercial expeditions and provide them with military protection. It was the Republic that built the ships in the huge Arsenale and rented them out to groups of patricians. The itineraries of the major yearly convoys were publicly established: They included Constantinople, Palestine, and Egypt on the east, and Gibraltar, France, and England on the west. Venice's organization was in effect an extremely smart corporation of merchants having at its disposal the resources of a whole state. When commercial success required the waging of wars, the state would provide funds and men; all aspects of the state's life, from education to justice to religion, were subordinate to the corporation's needs and especially to the final figures on its balance books—a real dream for some of our modern business conglomerates.

The Piazzetta

The area between the piazza San Marco and the lagoon goes by the name of the Piazzetta. Here the patricians—

and only the patricians—could walk back and forth as they fixed alliances and discussed bills of law. They moved to the side that was in the sun or in the shade according to the time of year, and here the family members coming of age were officially introduced to the group, often with sumptuous ceremonies. It was Sansovino who redesigned all the architectural volumes, here as well as in the piazza. The side opposite the palazzo was rebuilt by Sansovino to host a precious collection of manuscripts bequeathed by Petrarch and later by Bessarion (1468); it still contains them and, as the **Libreria Marciana,** is today one of five national libraries in Italy. It is crowded with college students, while scholars from all over the world occupy the pleasant consultation rooms overlooking the back garden.

Today's Venice is a paradise for the historian and the art student. Besides the Marciana, they can work with great ease in the library of the **Museo Correr,** also in the piazza San Marco; in the **Palazzo Querini-Stampalia,** with its squeaking wood floors and large 17th-century canvases; amid Renaissance cloisters in the splendid art library of the **Fondazione Giorgio Cini** (see the section on the island of San Giorgio), aided by courteous assistants; in the music and opera library of the same foundation; in the theatrical studies library of the **Casa Goldoni;** in the uniquely rich **State Archives,** run with old-fashioned class by a descendant of Venice's Tiepolo; and in a number of smaller centers, including one for **Jewish Studies** just off the campo del Ghetto. Definitely not bad for a city of around 75,000.

Other Elements of the Piazza

The **Campanile** (bell tower) took its present shape in 1514. It collapsed in 1902 but was rebuilt exactly as it had been. The view from the top (open 9:30 A.M. to sunset, ascent by elevator) includes the whole city plus large stretches of the lagoon. The loggia at its base (loggetta) was built by Sansovino and includes four bronze statues and a terra-cotta group by him. The **Torre dell'Orologio** (clock tower) at the beginning of Procuratie Vecchie was designed by Mauro Codussi in 1496, and it is crowned by two large bronze Moors animated by a mechanism that makes them strike the hours on a bell (1497; visits 9:00 A.M. to noon and 3:00 to 5:00 P.M., Sundays 9:00 A.M. to noon only; closed on Mondays).

THE SESTIERI

Since time immemorial Venice has been divided into six districts called *sestieri,* three on each bank of the Canal Grande. The comb-shaped, six-tooth decoration on the front of all gondolas is supposed to refer to that division, while the lonely tooth on the comb's back stands for the separate island of Giudecca. The division into sestieri is still very much alive; all street numbers refer to the sestiere, starting with "1" in a more or less arbitrary location and winding through streets and squares to cover the whole sestiere. A house number in the thousands is therefore very common, and only the mail carrier knows where the corresponding door is to be found. The six sestieri are *San Marco, Castello,* and *Cannaregio* on the east bank of the Canal Grande and *San Polo, Santa Croce,* and *Dorsoduro* on the west bank.

Sestiere di San Marco

Strictly speaking, there is no difference between rich and poor neighborhoods in Venice. The patricians had their homes on the Canal Grande, which winds through the city, touching all neighborhoods. When that space was filled, other palazzi rose on important canals or around the major squares scattered throughout the city. Until recent times, the San Marco–Rialto bridge area was considered a very desirable place to live because it is central and monumental and because it contains the most offices and fancy shops. But today more and more Venetians prefer to live in other sestieri, away from the intense tourist traffic that often clogs the tiny streets in the center. Also, essential shops such as groceries and bakeries have tended to move out of San Marco because of the high rents, which only mask and souvenir shops now seem able to afford (Manhattanites and Central Londoners are familiar with this phenomenon).

Mercerie. The main shopping alley is still called the **Mercerie**. It starts right under Codussi's Torre dell'Orologio in the piazza San Marco and winds lazily to meet the Canal Grande at the ponte di Rialto. Most of the houses in this part of town are 400 or 500 years old, and they have always been used as a display area by the Venice merchants. In the same little rooms where Oriental damasks and rare spices used to be sold, fancy modern windows today exhibit the best products of contemporary crafts, particularly in clothing: From Missoni to Armani to Krizia and Versace, all the great brand names are represented in Venice.

San Salvatore. Right off the end of the Mercerie, the splendid **Church of San Salvatore**, its façade currently under restoration, is one of the first Renaissance buildings in Venice. It was planned and built in 1506 by architect Giorgio Spavento with a strictly mathematical scheme, based on a square of 15 by 15 feet, marked by a column on each corner and repeated vertically as well. It is a Neoplatonic attempt to achieve perfect proportions (Sansovino was to try the same effect on San Francesco della Vigna in Castello), and it remains a bit cold and distant, like most attempts to transpose metaphysics into objects (Brunelleschi did better in Florence).

Certainly not cold, on the other hand, is the *Annunciation* by Titian, behind the main altar: It is one of the last works by the great master (1566), and one in which he seemed to jump way ahead of his time in search of a technique that could be called impressionistic (or was he, as some historians suspect, too old to paint with his customary precision?). *"Titianus fecit fecit,"* he wrote on this painting, as though he intended to underline that what he had done, he had done intentionally.

Ponte di Rialto. The **ponte di Rialto**, which replaced a previous wooden drawbridge, was built in 1592 by Antonio da Ponte, the winner of a competition in which a project by Palladio had been rejected. Notice a sculpted Annunciation at each end of the bridge on the south side. The view from the top is magnificent. The whole area down the bridge across from St. Mark's on the San Polo side was reconstructed in the feverish second half of the 16th century, when the government of Venice was determined to dress up the city in the best Renaissance clothes available.

Santa Maria della Fava. Calle dei Stagneri, a tiny street parallel to the Merceria and just before campo San Bartolomeo (a "campo" in Venice means a square) leads to a secluded church that hides two masterworks of 18th-century Venice. **Santa Maria della Fava** is the name of the church (there used to be a pastry shop nearby where sweet beans, called *fave,* were sold), and the two paintings are *The Virgin with Saint Filippo Neri* by Piazzetta (1727) and *Saint Anne with the Virgin and Saint Joachim* by Tiepolo (1732). They both are among the best works by their authors, Tiepolo in his young years receiving Piazzetta's lessons and preparing to transform them into his own great visions.

San Moisè to Santo Stefano. From the piazza San Marco, the exit under the Ala Napoleonica (and the Museo Correr) leads to one of the busiest tourist circuits in town. Some of the best hotels of Venice are located in this neighborhood, close to the most monumental part of town. A street to the left, a few steps after the piazza's portico (calle Vallaresso), leads to **Harry's Bar** on the Canal Grande across from the **Hotel Monaco**. Both places offer a welcome pause to the art viewer. Farther ahead, the modern façade of Hotel Bauer Grünwald stands in embarrassed proximity to one of the weirdest products of the Venetian Baroque, the church of San Moisè.

San Moisè. As it was late in welcoming the Renaissance, so Venice only discovered the Baroque style when it had already triumphed in Rome and in quite a few other European capitals. The Venetians retained especially the impressive, spectacular aspects of the new style, purposely excluding the psychological unease so sharply present in the works of many Baroque artists elsewhere. The main Venetian architect of this period was Baldassarre Longhena (1598–1682; see his church of La Salute). In Venice, the architects of the Baroque churches often abandoned all pretense of mysticism (of which there was very little tradition anyway); they intended to create spectacular settings that often looked like theater props rather than religious monuments.

The **Church of San Moisè** represents this trend at its climactic point. It was built in 1668 by Alessandro Tremignon, one of Longhena's rivals. (Longhena answered with the even more delirious façade of the Ospedaletto, in Castello.) Rather than religious symbols, this façade collects all kinds of decorative motifs; and rather than images of saints, it exhibits at its center the bust of the merchant/financier Vincenzo Fini, with those of two of his relatives over the side doors. This is a peculiarity of many Venetian churches, as is the habit of calling them with the names of Old Testament prophets. (Thirty-five churches are also named after different appellations of the Virgin Mary.)

Santa Maria del Giglio. Leaving San Moisè, cross two small bridges to reach the **Church of Santa Maria del Giglio**, the façade of which was redone by Giuseppe Sardi (1683) and paid for with 30,000 ducats kindly offered by the Barbaro family. As a result, Captain Antonio Barbaro stands at the center, between the statues of Honor and Virtue, while four of his relatives look down at the passersby from huge niches at his sides. The plans of fortresses they had commanded are sculpted in bas-relief at the bottom of the façade. Walk west from the front of the church across the canal to the campo San Maurizio. After this campo, the next bridge offers a curious sight: Parallel to it, on the right-hand side, another bridge crosses the same canal. But it is not for pedestrians: It supports part of a gigantic church. Unwilling to limit the size of their ambitions just because of a canal, the friars of Santo Stefano simply ignored it and extended the church over it in the 15th century. Three large canvases by Tintoretto are preserved in the sacristy of the church.

Campo Santo Stefano. This campo, one of the largest in Venice, is a busy but friendly crossroads. On the corner opposite the church's entrance, the **Caffè Paolin** is an important institution in town. Young and old Venetians meet there every evening before dinnertime and on Sunday morning before lunch. They are grateful that, unlike the café across the square, Paolin has so far resisted the temptation to sell pizzas and salads at astronomical prices or to buy bright-colored umbrellas for shade. It is still a café for residents, and it serves delicious ice cream as well as (of course) "spritz"—white wine and seltzer with a touch of bitter and a lemon peel. Only after a few months of sharing spritzes does a Venetian's heart open up to friendship.

The Venice Conservatory. On the south end of campo Santo Stefano (the side toward the Canal Grande), a wide passageway opens into campiello Pisani. The large building dominating the campiello is the conservatory of music in the **Palazzo Pisani**, built by Bartolomeo Manopola in the 17th century. In recent times it has been directed by known musicians such as Ermanno Wolf Ferrari and Francesco Malipiero. The musical traditions of Venice go back to the early Middle Ages, and the city soon reached European fame, especially for the writing and performing of operas (a dozen opera theaters were active in the 18th century). The word "conservatory" actually originated in Naples, where it meant a place for the survival and education of abandoned children; these children were then prepared for musical careers. Venice had four such centers, called Ospitali, very famous in Europe for the quality of their musical performances. Among the great composers who worked in Venice are Adriaen Willaert, who moved here from his native Flanders and stayed until his death in 1562; Andrea and Giovanni Gabrieli (both Venetians, late 16th century); Claudio Monteverdi (from Cremona, but in Venice from 1613 to 1643); and Antonio Vivaldi (1675–1741). One of Italy's foremost contemporary composers, Luigi Nono, is a Venetian and lives near La Salute.

Ponte dell'Accademia. Campo Santo Stefano is a crossroads because it is near the **ponte dell'Accademia**, one of three bridges on the Canal Grande. The wooden bridge was built in 1932 as a temporary structure to replace a hideous iron thing erected in 1854. But such is the feeling of awe for the city's appearance that no administration so far has dared approve of a replacement. When the bridge became unsafe in 1986 the administration decided just to reinforce it, leaving it as it was.

Palazzo Grassi. Near ponte dell'Accademia, in the area called San Samuele, Mr. Agnelli has played one of the most important cards in Fiat's image-building. He bought an impressive 18th-century palazzo on the Canal Grande, had it restored (one of the two architects was Tonci Foscari, descendant of Doge Francesco Foscari, and the other was Gae Aulenti, who also remodeled the Gare d'Orsay in Paris), and turned it into a center for cultural events. Immediately after its opening in 1985 with a show on Futurism, **Palazzo Grassi** became a preferred rendezvous for visitors to Venice. Its exhibits attract over 2,000 people a day, more than any other museum in Venice.

The San Samuele Area. The area around Palazzo Grassi is a very interesting hunting ground for shoppers in search of authentic Venetian artisans. Within a couple of hundred yards, from calle delle Botteghe (campo Santo Stefano, corner of Paolin) to the palazzo, there are some of the best wood-carvers in town (gilded frames, mirrors), an old-fashioned maker of marbled paper, a wood sculptor who delights passersby with his works representing clothes (jackets, tablecloths, laundry hanging on a line—you feel like touching it for dryness), and, among other people, an aristocratic lady who hand-paints velvets in the manner of Fortuny—she has a shop on calle delle Botteghe, but she also receives visitors in her nearby workshop.

Campo Sant'Angelo. A calle along Santo Stefano's façade (calle dei Frati) leads to spacious, graceful **campo**

Sant'Angelo. This offers a good opportunity to stop and muse about the freshwater supplies in ancient Venice.

Venice's urban structure is made of small neighborhood units centered around large or small squares. In the middle of each campo or campiello one or more cisterns used to supply fresh water to the neighborhood. Since there is no fresh water available at reasonable depths, Venice's early inhabitants had to content themselves with rainwater. To that purpose, large cisterns 10 to 15 feet deep were dug in the middle of each campo, and filled with river sand to act as a filter. A brick pipe at the center allowed water to be collected with buckets and pulleys. The visible part of the pipe (*vera da pozzo*) was often carved by the best craftsmen and was sometimes covered with bronze (as in the courtyard of the Palazzo Ducale). It is easy to recognize the square or rectangular shape of the cistern in every campo; it is marked by the inclination of the pavement in order to convey the rain water to special holes at the four corners (*gattoli*).

All patrician houses had their own private wells in the inner courtyard. The drinking water, however, rarely came from the wells. It was carried into the city by special boats and sold door-to-door. On the other hand, the wells could also serve other purposes: In 1716 one of those in campo Sant'Angelo yielded the body of a murdered lady.

La Fenice. Two narrow calli on the south side of campo Sant'Angelo lead to the nearby campo San Fantin, where the **Teatro La Fenice** has its main entrance. The sober Neoclassical façade of this theater, built in 1792, conceals one of the most elegant performing halls in the world. The Republic was enjoying its last years of independence when this ambitious project was realized by a group of patricians; the wealth and refinement of the decoration created an island of oblivion, a perfect place to savor the last pleasures offered by a dying century. The original interior was destroyed by fire in 1836 and immediately reconstructed—thus the theater lived up to its name (*fenice* means phoenix).

Scala del Bovolo. This is a curiosity much admired in this neighborhood (see the sign on campo Manin): an elegant staircase built in 1499 to permit external access to the top floors of the Palazzo Contarini del Bovolo (*bovolo* means snail in Venetian dialect, and the spiral shape of the staircase is clearly reminiscent of a snail shell and also of the Tower of Pisa).

Campo San Luca. Near La Fenice, campo San Luca is a meeting point for real-estate middlemen, lawyers, and business consultants, all attracted by the delicious pastries and spritzes of **Rosa Salva Café**. The modern building on the campo—headquarters of a bank—bears a sign near the southeast corner reminding passersby that here were the printing presses of Aldo Manuzio, one of the first and greatest printers of all times. During his lifetime and for centuries afterward, Venice was one of the most important printing centers in Europe. An unusually wide street (calle del Teatro) leads from this campo to the Rialto through the ponte del Lovo. But just before the bridge, a very tiny calle on the left cuts through the buildings to the Canal Grande, in one of the few points where it is possible to walk along its banks. Two handsome Byzantine palazzi adorn the canal at this level: Ca' Farsetti and Ca' Loredan, both of which now house city offices.

Ca' Farsetti and Ca' Loredan. Byzantine-style palazzi are among the most charming in Venice, and not only because they are the oldest. Even in their wealth they keep a quality of simplicity and friendliness that is often absent from the architectural modes of the High Renaissance. The **Ca' Farsetti** and **Ca' Loredan**, two of the most striking specimens of this kind, offer a good opportunity to identify the main features of this style: The arches are frequent, often relatively narrow, and characteristically elongated at the base; between the arches are often inserted round decorations in carved stone representing stylized animals (*patere;* some splendid specimens are in the Basilica di San Marco, others on the façade of the Ca' da Mosto on the Canal Grande). A top floor has unfortunately been added to the Ca' Farsetti and Ca' Loredan, modifying their original elegance.

Byzantine-style buildings of minor size and importance are scattered throughout the whole town, and it is always a pleasant, endearing surprise to discover Byzantine details on a campo or a calle incorporated in later restoration or remodeling.

The Venetian Gothic. A look at the Canal Grande from the top of the ponte di Rialto is an unforgettable experience, both for visitors—who seem unable to get away from the bridge's rails—and for Venetian housewives busily walking toward the vegetable and fish markets on the other side of the canal (they pretend they don't look, but they know very well how privileged they are). The parade of façades on the canal's banks includes pretty much all the periods of Venice's history, with a slight predominance of Gothic elements (see the *vaporetto* tour of the canal, below).

The Gothic period—from the 13th to the 15th century—can well be called the first great building season in Venice. But the label of Gothic must be applied with particular care, since the Venetian version of that style has very little in common with the stern, often somber buildings that embodied the ideal of Medieval mysticism (or, in so much neo-Gothic, of 19th-century erudite aloofness). The first master builders to introduce the Gothic style in Venice arrived a long time after the great cathedrals had been conceived across the Alps, and by that time the style had evolved away from its original asceticism. The lagoon environment, the preexisting Byzantine look of the city, and the practical requirements imposed by the merchant patrons all further contributed to the creation of a very specific variety of Gothic in Venice. Even the two huge churches that most imposingly represent it here (Frari and San Zanipolo; see below) have kept nothing of the northern austerity.

Venetian Gothic immediately spread through the whole city, marking every corner of it with its unmistakable grace. The Byzantine principle of lightness of the façades was respected and at times carried to surprising extremes, while the pointed arch soon became a pretext for decoration, with effects approaching the look of embroidered stone. This process is documented in dozens of buildings along the Canal Grande.

The typical Gothic palazzo would have a waterfront with a portico for the usual loading purposes; on top of it there would be one or sometimes two floors for the owner's use. The large room just behind the Gothic balcony was normally a reception room, with doors leading to the offices and living quarters; very soon there also appeared an inner courtyard, often artistically planned to include a well and an open staircase.

Unaware, or rather, uninterested, in the building revolution brought forward by Renaissance architects in central Italy, the Venetians kept using their peculiar kind of Gothic until the end of the 15th century. Then the Renaissance exploded here too, in a conscious project of urban renovation (*renovatio urbis,* it was called) that was to serve as an exterior sign of the Republic's wealth and power—and found in Sansovino its greatest achiever.

Sestiere di Castello

This ancient and industrious sestiere has a totally different atmosphere from the San Marco–Rialto area to its west. The majority of the one-day tourists never walk its narrow streets, and very few of the national or international firms with offices in Venice choose this area—mostly because of its relative distance from the garages and the railway station.

Thus for the visitor Castello offers a new, unsuspected, and totally charming image of Venice. You can easily start from the piazza San Marco and walk east along riva degli Schiavoni toward the large garden that can be seen in the distance in the direction of Lido. Every two years the garden turns into one of the most important art centers in the world, when it hosts the **Biennale Internazionale d'Arte**—an exhibit of contemporary art in special pavilions built and decorated by the participating countries.

Ponte dei Sospiri and the Church of San Zaccaria. The first bridge after Palazzo Ducale is the site of constant bottlenecks because of the view it offers of the famous **ponte dei Sospiri** (Bridge of Sighs), a passageway built in 1600 to join Palazzo Ducale with the newly built prisons across the canal. After the next bridge, a portico leads to campo San Zaccaria. We are still in the monumental area of Venice; the **Church of San Zaccaria**, built over a preexisting shrine at the end of the 15th century, is one of the most important religious buildings in town.

The author of the façade is Mauro Codussi (1440–1504), an inspired architect who had moved to Venice from Bergamo, a city conquered by Venice in the 15th century. His work coincides with the abandonment of the old-fashioned Gothic style in favor of the new Renaissance principles inspired by Roman antiquity.

Codussi's first exploit had been the delicious church at the island of San Michele (today the city's cemetery, near Murano), where he had experimented: His typical façade was crowned there by a central arch flanked by two half-arches corresponding to the inside naves. This principle, subsequently widely imitated in Venice, confers to Codussi's churches a grace that harmonizes with the Gothic environment (Venice is a city of curves, Florence of straight lines; or, as has been said so often, Venice is a feminine city, Florence a masculine one). The other great work by Codussi is the **Palazzo Vendramin Calergi** on the Canal Grande, which was the last

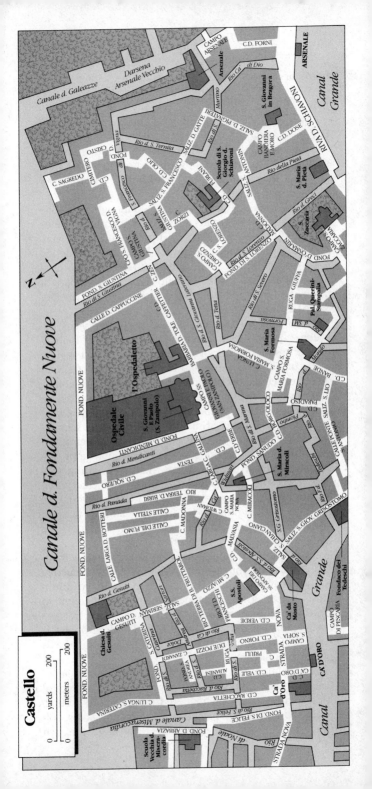

home of Richard Wagner and today is the **Winter Casino** of Venice (in the summer, the Casino moves to the **Lido**).

Inside San Zaccaria a splendid painting by Giovanni Bellini—*Madonna with Child and Saints,* 1505, on the second altar to the left—bears witness to the enormous ground covered by this Venetian master in abandoning previous Byzantine and Gothic techniques. A group of frescoes in the vault of the chapel of Saint Tarasius, attributed to Andrea del Castagno (1442), is thought to be one of the first examples of Renaissance art to arrive in Venice and to influence the Gothic- or Byzantine-oriented painters of that time. San Zaccaria was a crossroads of painting experiences: Paolo Uccello seems to have worked there in the same period, while Antonio Vivarini was working at three old-fashioned polyptychs in the same chapel of Saint Tarasius (1443).

Early Venetian Painting. In the fascinating years between 1450 and 1500 Venetian painters laid the foundations of an original school that was to climax with the great works of Titian, Veronese, and Tintoretto. Venice's **Gallerie dell'Accademia** contains in its first rooms a large collection of works by Byzantine- and Gothic-oriented masters, particularly Paolo and Lorenzo Veneziano, Michele Giambono, and Antonio Vivarini. These early masters seem to ignore not only the great lessons of Giotto, who painted in Padua in 1304–1306, but also those of Filippo Lippi, Donatello, and Paolo Uccello, who worked in Padua a century later. It was the Bellini family that opened Venetian painting to the Renaissance—first Jacopo Bellini, who kept close contacts with Padua (in 1433 his daughter married Andrea Mantegna), and then Jacopo's son Giovanni, one of the greatest painters in Venetian history.

With Giovanni Bellini (1430–1516) and his contemporary Cima da Conegliano (1459–1518), the Venetian School acquired the characteristics that were to distinguish it from the Florentine-Roman style: attention to color more than to line, to emotions more than to abstractions—little metaphysics and a lot of earthly interests, including the celebration of the families and deeds of Venetian history.

This attitude reflects the practical mind of the Venetians. It is also embodied in the parallel development of local architecture, which steered clear of pure abstractions and aimed at a balanced play between color, volume, and the lagoon environment. (Most of the rich palazzi used to be painted externally, sometimes by the best artists available; Giorgione and Titian, for example, decorated the **Fondaco dei Tedeschi** near the Rialto.)

San Giovanni in Bragora. To see a fine work by Cima da Conegliano, it is necessary to take only a small detour. After walking back from the church of San Zaccaria to riva degli Schiavoni, take the street immediately after the church of La Pietà (see below) to enter campo San Giovanni in Bragora (also called campo Bandiera e Moro). On this very pleasant campo, where a charming Gothic building contains a small pensione (see the Accommodations section, below), the **Church of San Giovanni**— where Vivaldi was baptized—is decorated by one of the best paintings by Cima, the *Baptism of Christ* (1495), located over the main altar. For the first time in Venetian painting, Cima opened up the space behind the figures, letting more and more of his native landscape fill the background. (Other masterworks by Cima are at the Madonna dell'Orto and at Carmini.)

La Pietà. Back on the riva degli Schiavoni, it is well worth entering the **Church of La Pietà**—a fine specimen of 18th-century architecture. It was built to serve mainly as a concert hall for the famous musical girls of the nearby center for abandoned children—one of four similar institutions that taught music to the youth and were famous in Europe for the quality of their performances. **Antonio Vivaldi** composed and taught here, although he never saw the completed church, because he died—lonesome and poor in far-away Vienna—a few years before its consecration in 1760. Tiepolo painted the splendid ceiling (1755), and the whole church has an unusual oval plan, for acoustic reasons—another example of the Venetian primacy of spectacle over religion. The church was accurately restored in 1986 by the Venice Committee of the World Monuments Fund.

The Arsenale and Minor Architecture in Castello. It may be time to leave the crowded streets of the tourist circuits and enter the labyrinths of the so-called minor Venice. From campo San Giovanni in Bragora it is not difficult—with the help of a map and by asking directions—to find your way through the back streets to the Arsenale, which is marked by a long-crenellated wall and a triumphal door with two towers and four splendid lions.

The **Arsenale** was the large compound where Venice's ships were built—up to 16,000 persons could be employed at the same time, producing a ship a day in times of need. The enclosed area is about one-sixth of Venice's total surface, and it was the working heart of the Republic; its employees were treated with respect. The Republic established the length of the working day, and it provided the workers with social assistance and housing (many of the homes in this area, some of which are four and five centuries old, were built for them).

The Arsenale's monumental entrance at the campo is the first Renaissance structure in Venice, built in 1460 and renovated after a great naval victory against the Turks (the Battle of Lepanto, 1571). The four lions were all taken from the East: The one standing alone at the left used to guard the entrance of Athens's Piraeus, and it carries a curious runic inscription dating from 1040 on its back (it had been given by an emperor to a group of Scandinavian sailors), while the one with the elongated body comes from Delos and goes back to the sixth century B.C.—a detail rather unimportant to the neighborhood children, who love to play on top of its comfortable back.

Today the Arsenale is semi-abandoned, although it is frequently the subject of heated discussion about its possible uses. Among the current proposals are a world's fair in the year 2000, a luxury marina, a university campus, and a new home for the Biennale.

From the campo dell'Arsenale it is easy to find the wide **via Garibaldi**, planned by the French conquerors after 1797 according to a rather un-Venetian concept of what a boulevard should be. From via Garibaldi, a 15-minute walk through the depths of the sestiere leads to the **Church of San Pietro di Castello**, one of the first churches in Venice and the city's cathedral until 1807. Most of the unpretentious homes in this neighborhood date back to the 14th, 15th, and 16th centuries; life here is quiet and pleasant, still centering around campi where everybody knows all his or her neighbors—down to the color of their bed sheets hanging out to dry as soon as a bit of sun appears in the sky.

On the way back from the former cathedral, a welcome rest can be enjoyed at informal cafés either in **campo Ruga** (where there is also a restaurant, inexpensive and delightfully secluded) or in **campo dell'Arsenale**, right in front of the monumental door. These are quiet places; at the Arsenale too you can choose between a café and a restaurant (**Da Paolo**; see below in the Dining section), both with outdoor tables.

You cannot leave this neighborhood without a visit to

the Carpaccio works exhibited at the small **Scuola di San Giorgio degli Schiavoni**, five minutes from the Arsenale.

Scuola di San Giorgio degli Schiavoni. The 15th century marks, as was said above, the entrance of Renaissance art into the Venetian scene, but it also marks the beginning of a great tradition of social and civil paintings. In this community of merchants and diplomats, proud of their success and working hard to keep it going, the sense of the urban and social structure was as strong as the religious spirit in other places, often to the point of eclipsing it. Not only the state but more and more frequently the trade associations began to commission buildings and paintings, and Carpaccio's work for the Scuola degli Schiavoni (1502–1508) is one of the first and more delightful cases of these new, more earthly interests (Schiavoni means Dalmatians, and Carpaccio was born in Dalmatia, although to a Venetian family). The subject of such paintings might well be religious, but the real intention was often transparently the glorification of the patrons.

In Carpaccio's paintings, with their enchanted attention to colorful detail, we can easily read the end of religious domination over the figurative arts, at least as far as Italy was concerned.

Santa Maria Formosa. Another 15 minutes of labyrinthine wanderings will take you to the large and beautiful **campo Santa Maria Formosa.** (*Formosa* means shapely, and the word has a connotation of plumpness. Such was the image of the Virgin Mary that appeared to a bishop in the seventh century, ordering him to build a shrine here in her honor.) The façades (on the campo and on the canal) are embellished with the usual busts of the financing patricians. The remodeling of the church's interior was planned by Codussi. The buildings of the campo are a fruitful exercise field for the student of Venetian architecture: Down one of three parallel bridges behind the church is Ca' Malipiero (early 16th century, at number 5250), while on the campo, Palazzo Vitturi (Number 5246) is a nice example of passage between Byzantine and Gothic styles, and Palazzo Priuli (number 5866) is full Renaissance (1580).

Calle del Paradiso. A few steps along the other canal bordering on the campo are ponte del Paradiso and **calle del Paradiso.** This street is one of the best preserved specimens of low-income housing from the 14th century. Gothic arches mark its entrance on both sides, and the purpose of those handsome wood beams over the ground floor (*barbacani*) was to enlarge the apartments without taking too much room from pedestrians, while offering the shops that line both sides of the calle a bit of shelter from the rain. This may be a good opportunity to devote a few words to building techniques in this unique city.

The Building of a Lagoon City. It is often thought that Venice is built on piles stuck in the ground under the water, but that is not so. The reason many buildings rise straight up from the canals is that their façades were made to coincide with the borders of the preexisting islands on which they were standing. In some cases a passageway was left along the water; it was then reinforced and paved and took the name of *fondamenta* (as opposed to *calle,* which is a street *between* buildings). The sandy bottom of the islands was often not strong enough to support construction, especially in the case of churches or heavy palazzi. Therefore a special technique was required for laying and strengthening foundations in Venice.

1. The sandy bottom of the island was dug out for 3 to 6 feet.

2. Short, thick wooden poles were hammered in until they reached the next geological layer, which consists of clay mixed with sand. This layer is called *caranto* in Venice. It is stronger than the surface layer and here the Venetians were unexpectedly lucky: Rather than rotting the wood, it starts a process of mineralization that strengthens the poles forever.

3. On top of the poles a double raft of pine wood was laid, thus creating the first flat surface.

4. Over the pine raft were laid the large blocks of stone (imported from across the Adriatic and called *pietra d'Istria*) that would support the building's walls.

The number and disposition of wood poles varied with the nature of the ground and the weight of the building.

Sand and caranto are not as solid as rock—they move and adjust quite a lot—so the buildings had to remain elastic. This was achieved with extensive use of wood in key places. Being experienced boatbuilders, the Venetian carpenters transferred to the land the skills they had acquired at sea, so that quite a few fascinating analogies can be found here between land buildings and ships, particularly in the roofs, which are often compared to upside-down hulls. Inside the brick walls the builders often inserted horizontal strips of wood, called *reme* (oars), that would alternate with layers of brick, permitting horizontal adjustment; wood lintels are still often seen over stone pillars, especially in shop entrances. This is the case with the ancient shops along both sides of calle del Paradiso.

The result of these building techniques and the softness of the ground is that very rarely are straight lines or 90-degree angles seen in Venice. Inside homes, floors often lean heavily downward or upward, while walls and partitions have variously adjusted to the passage of the centuries. Most buildings shake heavily throughout if you take a little jump in a room; this is considered—and probably is—a good sign, since elasticity is a must to avoid collapse. The same principle, in a way, applied to the home and foreign policy of the Venetian state.

Campo Santi Giovanni e Paolo. From campo Santa Maria Formosa, on the side opposite the Paradiso, a small calle leads to another must in Castello, the glorious **campo Santi Giovanni e Paolo** (also called San Zanipolo; just follow the signs for the *ospedale*). Here are at least three landmarks worthy of an attentive visit, so you might as well start with cappuccino and pastry at one of the oldest and least pretentious cafés in town, the *pasticceria* at number 6779, across the side of the church. Its interior is exactly as it was a hundred or so years ago, and it seems that the owners have also remained the same: a mustachioed old man and his wife, the only ones in town to make a once-famous green pastry.

Thus encouraged, take a long look at the splendid monument in the middle of the canal-flanked square: The superb horse rider is Bartolomeo Colleoni, a mercenary captain who bequeathed a fortune in order to have a monument built in the piazza San Marco. The city fathers proceeded to pocket the money and place the statue in a less conspicuous setting, but they were considerate enough to entrust the commission to the great sculptor Verrocchio (1488), who created this masterwork, considered by many to be the best equestrian monument in the world.

Scuola Grande di San Marco. The marbled façade bordering on the canal, now the entrance to the compound of the city hospital, is by Mauro Codussi, while the delicious trompe l'oeil in marble is by Tullio Lombardo. The building had been commissioned by one of the richest charitable associations in town, the Scuola Grande di San Marco, and was later united to a nearby monastery to form the city hospital. Entrance into the hospital is free, and it may be interesting for the visitor to go and have a look at how medicine is practiced in this strange city: Two Renaissance cloisters are included in the compound, together with at least a couple of churches, a library and staircase by Longhena (1664), and countless other memorabilia; all this in the middle of noisy, sometimes frantic activity, not much cleanliness (dozens of cats wander around), and patients' relatives trying to find their difficult way in the labyrinth of alleys. Across a small body of water, the cypresses of the cemetery island of San Michele comment silently on the scene.

Church of Santi Giovanni e Paolo. The gigantic construction dominating the campo is the **Church of Santi Giovanni e Paolo**, built by the Dominican friars in open competition with the Franciscans, who in the same years were planning the equally gigantic church of Frari in the sestiere of Santa Croce. Both churches date from the 14th century, and both are Gothic in style. But this is Gothic without the forest of pinnacles and gargoyles so frequent in the northern Gothic style (and abundantly present, for instance, in the duomo of Milan). The façades and outside walls of both churches are made of uncovered brick, as though the builders wanted to emphasize their distaste for the delirious aestheticism of the great northern masters.

The interior contains an accumulation of priceless art treasures. You should see at least the funerary monument to Doge Pietro Mocenigo on the interior façade, to the right of the door (by Pietro Lombardo, 1476); an early polyptych by Giovanni Bellini on the second altar, right nave; the magnificent *Glory of Saint Dominic,* painted by Piazzetta in 1727 (San Domenico chapel, last chapel on right before transept); Lorenzo Lotto's *Saint Antonino Pieruzzi* (right wing of transept; this 1542 painting is one of the very few Lottos in Venice, where Titian unjustly eclipsed the glory of this rival); and the Veronese paintings in the ceiling of the Rosary Chapel off the left wing of the transept.

Santa Maria dei Miracoli. An extra walk of three hundred yards from the bridge opposite the church's façade is well rewarded by a look at the fascinating little **Church of Santa Maria dei Miracoli**. Inlaid with marble and flanking a canal on one side, this jewel of the Venetian Renaissance (technically in the sestiere of Cannaregio) was built in the 1480s, and it is a favorite wedding site for Venetians and foreigners alike. (On the opposite end of the wedding spectrum is the grandiose setting of La Salute.)

Getting married in Venice is not as hard as it may seem. Dozens of foreigners get married every year at Venice's City Hall or in the Venetian churches. Among the pleasures involved is of course the gondola ride to the party after the ceremony. Gondoliers have special uniforms—and correspondingly special rates—for such occasions. Two gondoliers, usually dressed in white and gold, row on each gondola, amid the smiles and applause of the crowds standing on streets and bridges.

Sestiere di Cannaregio

Cannaregio is also a not-so-touristic sestiere, and it offers quite a few pleasant surprises to the visitor looking for a genuinely local atmosphere. It includes all the northern part of Venice, on the left bank of the Canal Grande coming from the station. It is run lengthwise (parallel to the Canal Grande) by three long canals, each flanked by streets and lined with unpretentious homes. Very few tourists venture to walk along these canals, which are among the most handsome and romantic in town.

The Ca' d'Oro. A tour of Cannaregio may well start with this extraordinary palazzo, recently restored by the city administration and site of a pleasant museum (public boat number 1, first stop after Rialto, or a short walk from ponte di Rialto).

The **Ca' d'Oro** (c. 1450) is the most splendid achievement of the Venetian Gothic period. Its elegant façade, almost an embroidery in stone, used to be covered in brilliant colors, with gold trimmings that gave the building its name (House of Gold). The best view of the façade is from the opposite bank of the canal, reachable by public gondola from the nearby campo Santa Sofia. The crossing costs 300 lire and is much used by Venetians going to shop at the fish and vegetable markets visible on the other bank. Both the crossing and an early morning browse in the colorful markets are highly recommended.

The museum has recently been redecorated with great taste. It would be worth a visit just for the view from the Gothic loggia at the *piano nobile,* but it also includes astonishing sculptures from the Veneto-Byzantine period, a delightful room devoted to early Tuscan painters, a famous *Saint Sebastian* by Mantegna, a Titian, a Van Dyck, and a collection of bronzes and medals of the Renaissance. The narrow calle along the Ca' d'Oro side leads to a street that is rather unusual for Venice. It is, extraordi-

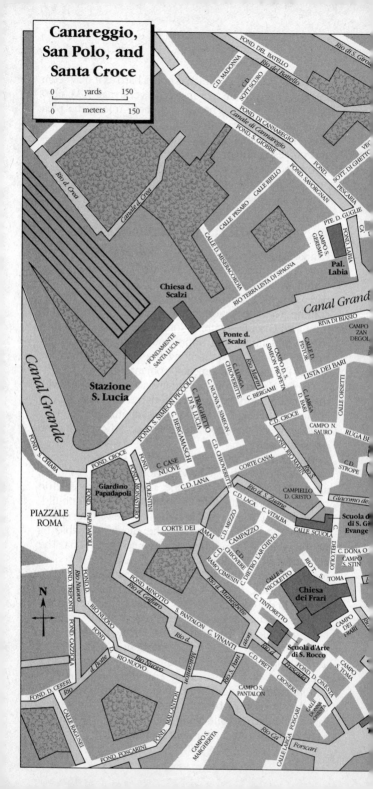

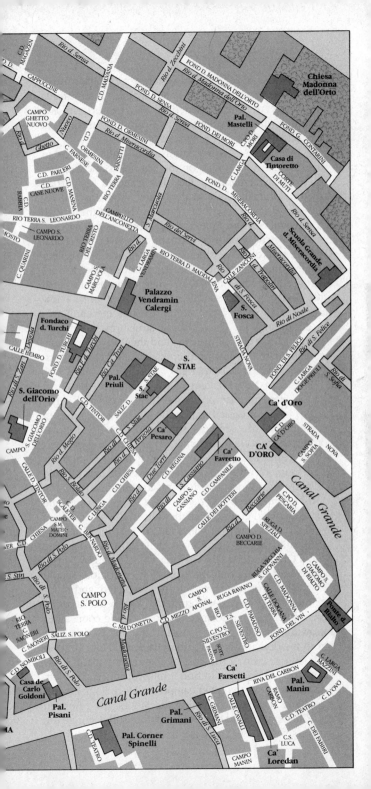

narily, almost wide and almost straight, similar in this respect only to Castello's via Garibaldi. Called **strada Nuova**, the street was opened in 1872 to perform as a quasi-direct link between the city's commercial center at Rialto and the then new railway station.

In 1846 the Austrian administration built (a first in Venice's history) a bridge on the lagoon, connecting the city to the mainland—a fact that changed the urban structure dramatically and that many Venetians still regret (more or less serious plans to destroy the bridge are introduced from time to time). This was followed by the construction of two extra bridges over the Canal Grande: ponte dell'Accademia in 1854, and Scalzi, near the new train station, in 1858. They were made of iron, like the future Eiffel Tower, and they cut across the canal with perfectly level spans (no arches but only a few steps at each end). Later administrations mercifully replaced them with less clashing structures; soon they became a vital part of the city, and they played a fundamental role in the new predominance of foot transportation over water transportation.

The strada Nuova runs roughly parallel to the Canal Grande from the station to the Rialto area, and it has proved to be of capital importance in our own times to accommodate the endless streams of one-day tourists coming in from the mainland. It is certainly the quickest way to reach the city's center, and it is not without its interesting, very Venetian stretches; but for less hurried and more knowledgeable visitors it is not the best itinerary.

Misericordia and Rio della Sensa. Cross through the busy strada and enter one of the calli on the other side of the Ca' d'Oro, and you will soon be in front of a huge brick building on the Canale della Misericordia. The **Scuola Grande della Misericordia** was planned by Sansovino to host one of the largest and most ambitious scuole in Venice; construction was never completed, and today the interesting interior is occupied by a basketball association, which has transformed it into a playing court. After following the side of the scuola to the first bridge, turn left to the deliciously quiet **rio della Sensa**. Following rio della Sensa, even at the cost of abandoning it for a few yards at corte dei Muti to find it immediately at your left, you will run into the quiet **campo dei Mori**: Four Eastern merchants, traditionally called the Moors, lived here in the 12th century, and their weird statues still decorate the campo's walls (only three are in the campo; the fourth is on the nearby *fondamenta* at number 3399 and next door to the house where Tintoretto used to live). The Moors—or their descendants—lived in Palazzo Mastelli on the canal on the other side of the campo (rio della Madonna dell'Orto), and they decorated the palazzo's façade with an amusing stone panel representing the source of their wealth: a camel well burdened with merchandise. But along this canal a great masterwork awaits the visitor: the **Church of the Madonna dell'Orto.**

Madonna dell'Orto. The great Gothic façade, adorned with a double row of niches, was built in the 15th century. The church is very handsome in itself, but it also contains some extraordinary paintings: One of the best works of Cima da Conegliano is on an altar on the right side near the entrance (*Saint John the Baptist,* with a delightful landscape), and a Madonna and Child by Giovanni Bellini, one of the most intense and delicate painted by the master, is on the other side of the nave.

The glories of this church, however, are the huge canvases by Tintoretto that adorn the main apse and one altar at its right. The latter is the *Presentation of the Virgin Mary;* on the left side of the apse, Tintoretto painted the *Adoration of the Golden Calf,* and on the side opposite, a *Last Judgment.*

Fondamenta degli Ormesini. There are two reasons to reach this *fondamenta* (second canal parallel to Madonna dell'Orto, on the south side) at sunset time: One is the golden light that fills the street—with its small rowboats tied at the canal's banks—when the sky turns red at its far end, and the other is that there are two good restaurants along it. The first is an old wine shop, informal and inexpensive but genuine in quality (**All'Antica Mola**—see the name on the lantern outside); the other, far ahead after the iron bridge, has no name outside but is called **Il Bacco.** It offers a more refined cuisine, and the decor is the prototype for many Venetian imitations: wooden tables, no linen, but clean and efficient. Both places are—as of this writing—unknown to tourists, and both are affordable in price.

The Ghetto. Just down that iron bridge, the spacious, paradoxically merry **campo del Ghetto** is the center of the tiny island (the contours are clearly visible) to which the Jewish community was relegated in 1516. This campo was called Ghetto before their arrival, and it is the unfortunate location that gave its name to all the ghettos in the world. Because they were obliged to stay within the island, the inhabitants could only build up, not out, and the buildings here are among the highest in Venice, reaching up to seven stories; their ceilings are unusually low. Three synagogues, one of them by La Salute's Longhena, bear witness to the high level of artistic refinement of this community. In the campo del Ghetto, the Jewish residents of Venice were obliged to keep their three pawnshops open for the population in need of cash (which often included ruined members of noble families). The rate of interest was fixed by the city government (5 percent) and was totally insufficient to cover expenses. All of the Jewish communities of the mainland, and often those abroad as well, had to contribute financially to the operation—a condition for keeping the Jews in Venice—until the community was forced to declare bankruptcy in 1735. It then turned out that the Jews owed a great deal of money to the nobility of Venice. Contemporary historians agree that with the institution of these pawnshops the shrewd city fathers had found a way to make some money, exploiting the foreign community and letting the blame for moneylending fall entirely on someone else.

Fondamenta Nuove. This long stretch of lagoon-side walk north of the hospital was built in the 16th century to define and strengthen the northern border of the city. The **fondamenta Nuove** is very quiet, except for the small area where the public boats for Murano, Torcello, and other islands land and depart. It offers a wide view over the lagoon and the mainland, and on clear winter days the snow-capped mountains of the Veneto are perfectly visible. A walk on the fondamente can be a very romantic experience, particularly at sunset or at night, when the street is totally silent. The church of Gesuiti, easily identifiable because of its monumental Baroque façade, is famous for its marbled interior and contains a great Titian, *The Martyrdom of Saint Lawrence.*

The association of Cannaregio hotel keepers has sponsored the publication of a small but detailed and intelligent guidebook to this sestiere; it is distributed free of charge to the guests of Cannaregio hotels.

The Sestieri di San Polo and Santa Croce

These two neighboring sestieri occupy the territory behind the right bank of the Canal Grande, from Piazzale

Roma (parking lots) to the large curve before ponte dell'Accademia. They include some of the most charming canals and streets in Venice. A tour should start at ponte di Rialto with a walk through the vegetable market just down its steps. Farther along, the retail fish market is very active every morning in this city where fish has always been the basic staple in any menu.

Unfortunately the lagoon is partly polluted, while the northern Adriatic has been heavily overfished and yields almost no fish anymore. Today, 80 percent of the fish marketed in Venice comes from other parts of Italy (mostly Sicily) or from abroad. Local species are limited to clams and mussels; a kind of bass called *cefalo;* very small quantities of *orate* (a delicious snapper) and *branzini* (sea bass) that sell at astronomical prices; and, in season, squid and cuttlefish. See the Dining section below for more details.

Campo San Polo. The usual labyrinth of small *calli,* very busy with Venetians mostly shopping for food, takes you to the large and pleasant campo San Polo, a preferred playground for children and gossiping mothers at all times of the year. One of the possible ways to reach it is through campo Santa Maria Mater Domini, with its beautiful 13th- and 14th-century homes, both Byzantine and Gothic. From campo San Polo it is only a short walk to the **Church of Frari**.

Frari and 16th-Century Venetian Painting. The name "Frari" means friars, and this enormous church is the Franciscan response to the Dominican Santi Giovanni e Paolo. It was built in the 14th century over an existing shrine of more moderate size, which was kept functioning while the architects were surrounding it with the new structure. Like its rival church, the Frari is a whole world in itself and would take days to explore, so it is necessary to be selective.

The greatest masterworks here are two paintings by Titian. Over the main altar his *Assumption* (1518) marks the first high point in a long and glorious career. Titian seems to have understood and magnified a concept of art that can be called typically Venetian: great emphasis on color; open exaltation of life as a positive, exciting adventure; and faith in the basic soundness of the social environment. The same elements can be found in the work of Paolo Veronese (1530–1588), although in his paintings we detect less of the sense of exciting discovery and more of a feeling of official, somehow artificial celebration.

The severe world of the Counter-Reformation also seems infinitely distant, for example, from Veronese's rich, formally stunning canvases, in which all the tricks of perspective and color are obviously meant to contribute to the delight of the wealthy sponsors and to the awe of the *popolani* admitted to glance at such sumptuous environments. Jacopo Tintoretto (1518–1594), a contemporary of Veronese, carried these effects to unsurpassable extremes in Venice, creating complex, intense, and often gigantic canvases in which he plays with light and surfaces with a strong foreboding of the new restlessness that was to characterize the European arts in the 17th century.

On the left-side altar, before the transept, is another great work by Titian, the *Madonna Pesaro.* The two columns in the painting may be a perspective continuation of the church's columns as you approach the painting from the main door.

Titian is buried in this church; the monument was sculpted in 1836 and is located on the right aisle next to the door. On the sacristy's altar (off the right wing of the transept) is a splendid *Madonna and Child* by Bellini (1488). Two small chapels away there is a wood *Baptist* by Donatello (1453). Finally, have a look at the monument to Antonio Canova (left nave, toward the back), realized in 1827 by followers of the great Neoclassical sculptor from plans he had prepared for a monument to Titian.

Scuola di San Rocco and Tintoretto. A few steps away from the church's back, the members of the wealthy Scuola di San Rocco—one of many charitable associations—had a sumptuous Renaissance building, also known as the **Scuola di San Rocco**, erected for their meetings. They decided to commit the decoration of the interior to Tintoretto, who painted some of his best canvases for this purpose. Among the most successful are the *Crucifixion, Christ before Pilate,* and *Christ Carrying the Cross.*

San Giovanni Evangelista and Rio Marin. A left turn down the bridge in front of the Frari façade will bring you to the nearby compound of the **Scuola Grande di San Giovanni Evangelista.** The very long building at the left contains the immense State Archives, a wonderful mine of documents related to Venice's government and history. A few steps after the archives, the 1481 scuola deserves a look, at least at the outside, which was designed to impress the passersby.

The interior shines with a splendid staircase by Codussi; the paintings that once decorated the hall—a great cycle by Gentile Bellini and Carpaccio narrating the Miracles of the True Cross—are now in the Gallerie dell' Accademia. The scuola was believed to own a piece of wood from Christ's cross. The delightful canal near the scuola is called **rio Marin**. Here Henry James set the scene for *The Aspern Papers,* one of his many novels having to do with Venice. At the beginning of the rio, a recently redecorated restaurant—**Caffè Orientale**—is one of the best in Venice. It has a small terrace on the rio, and an early reservation may obtain you one of those coveted tables (see Dining, below).

San Giacomo dell'Orio. Across the rio Marin and down a calle or two, you reach a very old center of Venetian life, the **Church of San Giacomo dell'Orio**. The area is still quiet and not well known to tourists. The church has at least three entrances because of modifications made during the 1,100 years of its existence. In the stunning interior, the play of wood beams that support the vault is one of many examples of shipbuilding carpentry transferred to land construction. A particularly fascinating sight is the large painted crucifix by Paolo Veneziano (c. 1350), restored in 1988.

Campo San Zan Degolá. This name is the Venetian rendering of San Giovanni Decollato (Saint John the Beheaded). It is definitely worth taking the short walk from San Giacomo dell'Orio to this quiet, enchanted campo, with its 11th-century church (remodeled more than once) and its unpretentious old homes creating one of those vital environments that make Venice one among the most human cities in the world.

Sestiere di Dorsoduro

This is one of the largest sestieri and definitely one of the most charming. It occupies the southern and western part of town on the west bank of the Canal Grande, from Piazzale Roma all the way to La Salute, with a long stretch on the Canal Grande itself.

La Salute and Venetian Painting in the 17th Century. The extraordinary **Church of La Salute**, a small distance across the water from the San Marco area, was built between 1632 and 1682. By that time architectural thinking had progressed to consider buildings not only for themselves, but in relation to the space they were destined to occupy. The Baroque feeling for scenographic setting plays an important role in the conception of this gigantic church, which enclosed the privileged space between the San Marco center and the opening of the Canal Grande. It was in this body of water that trading ships would stop and be moored, waiting for customs or for more journeys, as Canaletto's paintings abundantly confirm. For someone coming in from the Lido and the open sea, La Salute is the most visible sign of Venice's exciting presence, defining, together with the high Campanile di San Marco, on the other side, the Canal Grande entrance.

The church was built as a thanksgiving to the Virgin Mary after a terrible plague in 1630. That event is still celebrated by Venetians with astonishing devotion every November 21; they take advantage of a temporary bridge built over the Canal Grande to allow access from the piazza San Marco. The November fogs, the lack of tourists at that time of the year, and the presence of children, candle vendors, and simple food stands: All these make the Festa della Salute the most intimate and cherished among Venetian traditions.

Inside La Salute, three altarpieces by Luca Giordano offer a good idea of Venetian painting in the 17th century (the first three altars at the right of the main door).

The great masters of the Venetian Renaissance and Mannerism were not followed by personalities of comparable impact. Jacopo Palma il Giovane (1544–1628), for example, was a virtuoso of the brush but hardly an original painter. He was, however, greatly appreciated here, and he left canvases in just about every important building, including the Palazzo Ducale.

Most of the successful painters of the 16th century came to Venice from other centers. Today these painters do not attract more than a local interest, but their work should not be underestimated, as they introduced to Venice the great lessons of Caravaggio, Rubens, and other European masters. Their new concept of space, their Counter-Reformation solemnity, their compositions that sometimes are somber or even gloomy and sometimes shine with color, exercise a fascination of their own. And this period of research into color and perspective prepares the ground for the explosion of another golden period of Venetian painting in the 18th century.

The queen of the gigantic La Salute is a small image of the Virgin Mary carried over from Crete in 1672, a Greek-Byzantine icon identified by the population with the Vir-

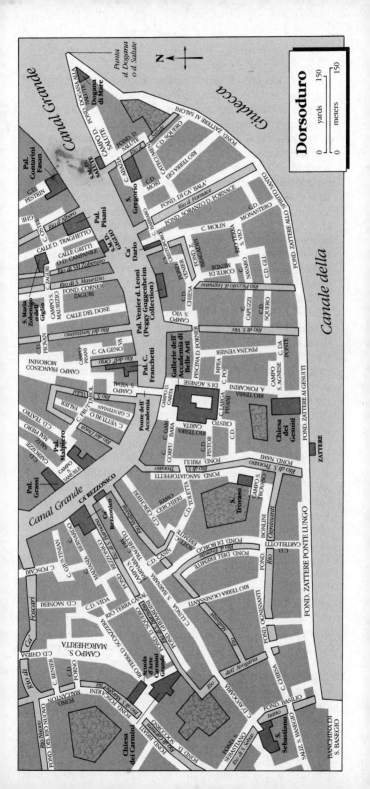

gin of Good Health (good health being the meaning of the word *salute*). The most interesting paintings are in the sacristy (left of the main altar): canvases and ceiling by Titian, and the *Marriage of Cana* by Tintoretto.

Punta della Dogana. Down the steps of the church and to the right, the extreme tip of Dorsoduro forms a triangle where the Republic used to have its customs offices. The promenade around the tip—a superb and crowded lovers' lane until very recent times (nowadays the young can take their friends home)—is part of Le Zattere, a long bank along the Canale della Giudecca, about which more will be said very soon. But, for the moment, cross the bridge at the church's side and enter the enchanted atmosphere of the **San Gregorio** neighborhood.

San Gregorio. The area between La Salute and the Gallerie dell'Accademia has all the best characteristics of Venice: quiet; dotted with beautiful canals and frequent gardens; handsome and romantic. It is a preferred residential area for foreign expatriates, particularly Americans. Here used to be the American consulate, later closed in an attempt to cut government expenses and taken over by Wake Forest University of North Carolina for its Venice program, and here was the home of American art patron Peggy Guggenheim, now a museum of contemporary art.

The palazzo housing the **Peggy Guggenheim Collection** has one side on the Canal Grande. It was begun in 1749 and never completed: Only the ground floor is now standing—a strange yet pleasing sight from the canal— surrounded by a large garden. The collection includes works by masters contemporary to Peggy Guggenheim and often intimate with her: Magritte, Picasso, Ernst, de Chirico, and Duchamp are represented, together with Jackson Pollock and a large selection from the Abstract Expressionist school.

Another, totally different art gallery awaits the visitor a couple of hundred yards away, at the foot of ponte dell'Accademia. On your way you can sit for cappuccino at the outdoor tables of the café just down the bridge— the next gallery has no cafeteria—and prepare for a couple of hours of immersion in Venetian paintings, from the beginnings to the 19th century.

Gallerie dell'Accademia. The grounds of the **Gallerie dell'Accademia** used to be occupied by a monastery and church—and of course by a scuola. Inside the monastery (now a school of painting) a cloister and staircase by

Palladio can be visited with permission from the headmaster's office.

Among the countless masterworks included in the Gallerie dell'Accademia itself, even a rigorous selection would have to mention the early masters such as Paolo and Lorenzo Veneziano and, of course, Giovanni Bellini. Rooms 20 and 21 contain works painted for the scuole in the 15th century, among which are Carpaccio's *Cycle of Saint Ursula* (1475–1495) and a famous *Procession of the Corpus Domini* by Gentile Bellini, one of the first paintings in which the interest and pride in social aspects of life seem to overwhelm the religious inspiration.

Giorgione's *Tempest* and *Old Woman* are concrete evidence of the new humanistic world to which the young master was introducing a delighted audience. A *Portrait of a Young Man* by Lorenzo Lotto (1525; Room 7) is one of very few works to be seen in Venice by this Venetian genius who, eclipsed by Titian, had to look for recognition elsewhere.

The best Veronese in the gallery is the famous *Dinner at the House of Levy* (1573). It was supposed to be a Last Supper, and was to have adorned the dining room of the Dominican friars at Santi Giovanni e Paolo, but the picture's obvious delight in frivolous details provoked an intervention by the Inquisition. Veronese's brilliant solution to the problem was to change the title of the incriminating work. Tintoretto is abundantly and gigantically represented in Rooms 10 and 11: His work is delirious and stirring.

In Room 17 is the only Canaletto to be seen in Venice. This famous painter of cityscapes worked almost exclusively for foreign customers—particularly English—and most of his works have remained abroad. A good selection of 18th-century works by Longhi and Guardi is shown in Room 17, together with seven pastel portraits by Rosalba Carriera, a painter who had become justly famous in 18th-century Europe for her mastery of this difficult medium. Over the door of the last room (24) there is a *Presentation of the Virgin* painted by Titian in 1538 to fit exactly in that spot, to which the canvas adapts to perfection.

Le Zattere. Such an intense exposure to art—without a lounge room or a cafeteria—deserves to be followed by at least a relaxing walk and a rest at a pleasant canal-side café. The **fondamenta delle Zattere**, just across the short width of Dorsoduro and along the Canale della Giudecca, offers exactly what the tired visitor needs. Le Zattere is a preferred walk for Venetians of all classes, sexes, and ages. In the warm spring days it is crowded during the first hours of the afternoon: Its southern exposure makes it sunny all day long. In summer, Venetians come here after sunset to meet friends and to eat relatively inexpensive pizza in one of three restaurants with tables on terraces over the canal.

La Giudecca. The **island of Giudecca**, right in front of Le Zattere, has both suffered and gained because of its separation from the rest of the city, to which it is connected during the day by vaporetti (lines 5 and 8) but at night only by an infrequent ferry, leaving the Zattere in front of the Gesuati church. Its inhabitants may suffer some discomfort if they miss the night ferry in the bitter winter nights (after midnight there is only one crossover every hour), but the island rewards them by remaining quiet and ancient, modest and charming. Signor Cipriani, the owner of the Harry's Bar restaurant near San Marco, recently took over an abandoned storefront on the western tip of the island along the canal and turned it into the very successful **Harry's Dolci**, where he offers international cuisine at reasonable prices under elegant canvases. In his own time, Andrea Palladio also did his best to embellish the island; it was he who built the splendid **Church of the Redentore** (like La Salute, built in thanksgiving after a plague), which is still the center of devoted pilgrimage—and fireworks—on the third Sunday of July every year.

Gesuati. Across at Le Zattere again, the large church at the corner of Le Zattere and rio terrà Foscarini (the wide, tree-lined alley that runs between the Gallerie dell'Accademia and Le Zattere) is properly named Santa Maria del Rosario, but it still goes under the name of **Gesuati**, a monastic order suppressed in 1688 and of course different from the more lasting Gesuiti (Jesuits). The church, however, actually has nothing to do with those other monks; it was built by the architect Massari on commission from the Dominicans in 1743. Its façade seems elegant to some, rather heavy to others, but it still basically represents a variation on Palladio.

It may be noted that here and elsewhere the canal bank is landscaped with steps built in proportion to the church; access by boat was still the rule in the 18th century. Inside, the church contains a feast of paintings by another fashionable artist of those years and a frequent collaborator of

Massari's, Giambattista Tiepolo, who painted the ceiling and an altarpiece (first on the right), while Piazzetta contributed one of his best canvases, *Saint Vincent Ferraris.*

A Squero and the Rio di Borgo. On the way to the next museum—there are two more to come—take the first right turn after the church of the Gesuati, along the canal called rio di San Trovaso. A few steps farther, across the canal and near the church of San Trovaso, is the workshop of one of the oldest **gondola builders** in town, dating back to the 17th century (these workshops are called *squeri* in Venetian dialect); it is one of only two that have survived. The wood-topped houses behind the ramp are characteristic of the mountain area of the Cadore, where the wood for the gondolas used to come from. The whole workshop is a national landmark.

Behind the church of San Trovaso (17th century) is one of the most charming canals in Venice, the **rio di Borgo**, flanked by a street called fondamenta di Borgo but known as fondamenta delle Eremite. On this street is the entrance to **Montin's,** one of the most popular restaurants in town, which features a pleasant garden.

Ca' Rezzonico and 18th-Century Venice. Through calle Lunga and campo San Barnaba it is easy to reach the entrance of **Ca' Rezzonico,** a 17th-century palazzo with an impressive façade on the Canal Grande. The construction of this palazzo was begun in 1667 by Longhena (of La Salute) and completed in the 1750s by Massari (of Gesuati and La Pietà). Today it houses the **Museo del Settecento Veneziano,** a delightful experience and a good place to stop and muse about this extraordinary period in Venice's history.

Venice's independence came to an end in the year 1797 under the blows of the very young Napoléon. It was an anticlimactic end, without even the appearance of a fight, and it poses a puzzling problem to historians: What were the causes of the decline and final collapse of this wealthy and civilized republic? All the superficial answers fail to withstand factual analysis. In the 18th century Venice was still the capital of a flourishing state where commerce, although deprived of its ancient splendor, was nonetheless active and profitable; in addition, the ruling class had been able to adapt to the new European reality, investing in land the large fortunes accumulated at sea and often increasing the profitability of their land possessions by applying the managerial spirit that was their tradition.

A fascinating theory suggests that the main cause of

Venice's collapse was psychological. The new generations of patricians were managing a state and a wealth
they had inherited, not created; they may not have had
the energy and the motivation to run public life anymore. It may well be that when young Napoléon ignored the declared neutrality of Venice and invaded its
territory in pursuit of the Austrian armies, and when he
finally ordered—by messenger—the end of the glorious
Republic, some of them felt relieved to lose their responsibilities. Without even considering resistance, the patrician government voted itself, the doge, and the whole
administration out of office.

Whatever else may have been missing in Venice during
the preceding 100 years, the desire to enjoy art and life was
certainly still there. The process of beautification of the city
had continued unimpaired: Some 49 new churches and
convents were built, a large number of façades were
redone in the fashionable modern style, and new bridges
and streets were opened. Festivities and celebrations became more frequent and more elaborate; all year round,
four musical centers were offering the best concerts to be
heard in Europe (see La Pietà), while a good dozen
theaters were active during the century—at least eight of
them of first quality—and performing more new operas
than anywhere else in Europe. It was in this environment
that some of the best librettists learned their trade, which
they exported abroad: Da Ponte, author of three libretti for
Mozart; Mazzolà, an author preferred by Salieri; Bertati,
author of Cimarosa's *Matrimonio Segreto*. In a way, Venice
still lives off the memory of its glorious 18th century; the
recent resurrection of the Carnival is one of many signs of
Venetians' attachment to this period—and their willing-
ness to exploit it for the attraction of tourists.

In this artistically active environment a new golden
season opened up for painting. The traditional Venetian
values of light, color, and space found a new expression
in the works of Piazzetta and Tiepolo. Many churches and
palazzi in Venice host the latter's frescoes and canvases,
rich in light and open spaces, spectacular and magical.
Lovers of Tiepolo should see, besides the ones already
mentioned, the churches of Santi Apostoli, San Stae, and
Scalzi, and the frescoes in the sumptuous reception hall
of Palazzo Labia in Cannaregio, the Scuola Grande dei
Carmini, and Ca' Rezzonico.

Together with the Piazzetta and Tiepolo schools, another manner of painting flourished in this period that

was more rational in a way, more attuned to the new scientific ideals of the Enlightenment: the painting of *vedute,* or cityscapes. The famous name in this field is Canaletto.

Another school is represented by the Longhi and Guardi families, who painted mostly scenes of Venetian life, very far from the triumphal views of Tiepolo or the impassive, rational look of Canaletto: more intimate, enclosed scenes in the Longhis, more airy scenes in the Guardis. The latter propose a Venice still theatrical but somehow sentimental, perhaps already tinted with nostalgia. The shadows of the 19th century seem to be lurking near to these painters' horizon.

The Interior of the Ca' Rezzonico. The furniture and decorations of most of these rooms are not necessarily the original ones, but they were transported here in order to reconstruct as closely as possible the atmosphere of an 18th-century palazzo. Among the artworks are ceilings by Tiepolo, some disquieting frescoes by his son Giandomenico, pastels by Rosalba Carriera, astonishing furnishings by Brustolon, a large collection of Longhi paintings, and in the Sala del Ridotto two of the best Guardi paintings (the *Nun's Parlor* and the *Ridotto*).

Rio Terrà dei Pugni. From the rio di San Barnaba, the canal flowing along the side of the Ca' Rezzonico, the third street on the right is the spacious rio terrà dei Pugni, leading to the charming campo Santa Margherita. On this *rio terrà* (a filled-up canal) is one of the first and best mask shops in Venice, Il Mondonovo, where Carnival masks are fashioned with imagination but also with rare historical accuracy.

Campo Santa Margherita. This large and pleasant square is a preferred rendezvous for Venetians, especially in the warm weather, when its three restaurants enlarge their outdoor space as much as allowed by the city regulations—and possibly more. They serve pizza, of course, but other food as well. They may not be the best in town, but they are reasonable in price and the setting is so pleasant that no one cares about gastronomic perfection. The campo Santa Margherita is a real anthology of old building styles, and a closer look can give an idea of the age of many other houses scattered over the city. The two houses at numbers 2920–2935 were built in the 14th century over preexisting structures: Notice the Gothic windows, the wood lintels over the shops' doors, and the arch over the main portal (Byzantine, 12th or 13th century). The two Gothic houses at numbers 2954–2962 belong to the 14th century. More recent are the small palazzi at numbers 3034–3035 and 3042–3043 (both from the 18th century, as are numbers 3429–3430 on the other side of the campo).

Scuola Grande dei Carmini. The **Scuola Grande dei Carmini** is near the church of the Carmini, off the west side of the campo. The scuola was built in 1663, and it is worth a visit because of the splendid ceiling in the main salon, decorated with nine canvases by Tiepolo (1744; they are considered among his best works). A smaller room also contains a *Judith and Holofernes* by Piazzetta.

Carmini. The 14th-century **Church of the Carmini** has been redecorated several times, especially in the 17th century. It contains two exceptional masterworks: an *Adoration of the Shepherds* by Cima da Conegliano (c. 1500) and one of the few Lorenzo Lottos to be seen in Venice, *Saint Nicholas of Bari.*

San Sebastiano. Near the church of the Carmini and after the peaceful fondamenta del Soccorso, the fourth bridge at the right leads to a university building (door by Carlo Scarpa, a leader of 20th-century Venetian architects), and to the **Church of San Sebastiano** (1505–1548), famous for its Veronese paintings. It was through his work here that the young painter from Verona conquered Venice's admiration, and it is here that he is buried. A visit should start with the ceiling of the sacristy and continue with that of the church and the friezes high up on the walls (best seen from the choir). Next come the main altarpiece, a grandiose *Virgin in Glory,* the organ's doors, and the main chapel with two large canvases representing scenes from the life of Saint Sebastian.

A VAPORETTO RIDE ALONG THE CANAL GRANDE

This princely waterway is the glory of Venice and one of the major glories of the world. No matter how many times you have seen parts of the Canal Grande reproduced in works of art or in postcards, it is hard to avoid a surge of genuine emotion when riding through it or looking at it from ponte dell'Accademia or ponte di Rialto. All of its palazzi can be reached on foot by back

streets, and many have been discussed above in the appropriate sestiere; still, a view from the water is immensely
rewarding and an absolute must.

This brief overview starts from the entrance at Piazzale
Roma (parking lots). It is a good idea to save this ride for
the end of the day (sunset, as well as dawn, is a perfect
time) after reaching the boat stop on foot through the
sestieri.

With a bit of luck and planning you should be able to
install yourself in one of the few front seats of the *vaporetto* (public boat) to be able to enjoy the sights oblivious to the crowds stepping in and out at each landing.
This is how to do it: Go to Piazzale Roma and look for the
pontoon of vaporetto number 1. This is the beginning of
the line, so the vaporetto starts without passengers. If a
line has already formed, let the people embark and position yourself for the next boat; there is one every ten
minutes. Whether you sit on the right or left side doesn't
make much difference. (All this advice is necessary because the administration of Venice hasn't been able to
come up with a tourist line as yet, so Venetians and
visitors mingle suffocatingly in the same spaces). Vaporetto number 34, coming in from the parking lot called
Tronchetto, also runs through the Canal Grande. But the
best places are usually taken by the time it lands at
piazzale Roma.

After the stop at the railway station, the **Church of the
Scalzi** appears on the left, just before the bridge (1670,
façade by Sardi; it contains three frescoes by Tiepolo).

Just after the San Marcuola boat stop, **Palazzo Vendramin Calergi**, on the left, is a masterwork by Codussi and
the first sizable Renaissance building to appear in Venice
(early 16th century).

Almost directly across from it is the **Fondaco dei
Turchi** (Turks' Warehouse), one of the oldest buildings
on the canal, built by the Pesaro family and then assigned
to the Turkish community for trading. Notice the Byzantine arches and the round *patere* between them.

Behind the San Stae landing, the **Church of San Stae**
(façade dates from early 18th century) includes paintings
by Piazzetta and Tiepolo.

On the right, the second building after San Stae is the
imposing **Ca' Pesaro** (Longhena, 17th century), which
now houses a gallery of modern art and a museum of
Oriental art.

On the opposite side, the **Ca' d'Oro** appears just before the landing of the same name (see the Cannaregio section).

Across from Ca' d'Oro is the portico of the fish market (*pescheria*), built in 1907 in a weird mixture of Gothic-style first floor and Renaissance roof.

At the curve of the canal, the Ca' da Mosto (left side), in need of restoration, is also one of the oldest Byzantine palazzi in Venice (13th century).

On the same side, just before ponte di Rialto, is the **Fondaco dei Tedeschi** (1505), a warehouse used by the German community. Its façade used to be adorned with frescoes by Giorgione and Titian, but these paintings are now lost except for a few fragments conserved in the Ca' d'Oro.

After ponte di Rialto, on the left side, is Palazzo Manin, built by Sansovino in 1538. Still on the left are the **Ca' Farsetti** and **Ca' Loredan**, in the 13th-century Byzantine style (see the San Marco section).

Palazzo Grimani, also on the left, was built in 1557 by Michele Sanmicheli to closely resemble Rome's Arch of Constantine. Again on the left, just before the Sant'Angelo landing, is another majestic Renaissance home: **Palazzo Corner-Spinelli** (1490), probably designed by Codussi.

On the right bank, before the San Tomà landing, is **Palazzo Pisani Moretta**, with a particularly successful Gothic façade (15th century).

At the bend in the canal, on the right, is **Ca' Foscari** (15th century), today the administrative center of the University of Venice. Still on the right, just before the next landing, **Ca' Rezzonico**, with a façade by Longhena (1667), contains the Museo del Settecento Veneziano (see Dorsoduro).

Across the canal from Ca' Rezzonico, **Palazzo Grassi** (Massari, 18th century), lavishly restored by Fiat, hosts special exhibits.

On the left side, just after ponte dell'Accademia, is **Palazzo Franchetti**, built in the 15th century but somewhat spoiled by a 19th-century restoration. Still on the left, the huge Renaissance building is **Palazzo Corner** (Sansovino, 1545), the tallest on the canal. It is said that the immensely rich Corner family prevented the Venier family from completing the building across the way, of which only the first floor was erected. The administration of the Venice Provincia (a *provincia* is a large district centering around a capital city, in this case Venice) has its offices here.

Right across, the unlucky Veniers planned an equally enormous home in 1749 (**Ca' Venier dei Leoni**). The unfinished building, full of a strange charm, was the house of Peggy Guggenheim and is now a museum, the **Peggy Guggenheim Collection** (see Dorsoduro). Still on the right side, the elegant, dangerously leaning palazzo on the canal after Ca' Venier is **Ca' Dario**, a delicious building of 1488 recently acquired by the emerging Italian tycoon Raul Gardini, owner of Montedison.

On the left side, just after the landing called Santa Maria del Giglio, is the 14th-century **Palazzo Gritti**, now a luxury hotel in the CIGA chain owned by the Aga Khan.

Two buildings after the Gritti, still on the left, is a smaller palazzo that is supposed to have been the house of Desdemona. In 1987 it was bought and restored by a private entrepreneur, who converted it into a luxury co-op. Notice the elegant stone carvings on the balconies.

On the right side, just before the Bacino di San Marco (the water basin in front of San Marco), the **Church of La Salute** (see Dorsoduro) is followed by the ancient Dogana di Mare (customhouse, low building on the very tip), surmounted by a large gilded globe with a statue representing Fortune.

THE LAGOON ISLANDS
San Giorgio Maggiore

Like La Giudecca (see Dorsoduro), from which it is separated by a small canal, this island is effectively part of downtown Venice. It sits right in front of the San Marco area, and it marks the entrance to the Canal Grande with the handsome façade and campanile of the **Church of San Giorgio Maggiore**

A Benedictine center since the tenth century, this small island was landscaped and rebuilt in its entirety by Andrea Palladio, who could apply here the grandiose ideas he developed in his mainland villas. San Giorgio Maggiore is therefore a kind of *revanche* by this architect, whose plans for secular buildings in Venice had been systematically rejected as long as his rival Sansovino was still alive and in charge of the building committees. Sansovino died in 1570, Palladio in 1580; after Palladio's death, other architects completed the realization of his project by 1610, possibly modifying a few details. Longhena added a sumptuous staircase to the first of two cloisters in the Benedictine monastery next to the church and built a handsome library.

The church, still used for worship, represents one of Palladio's greatest achievements: Here the architect could apply his principles concerning the relationship between architecture and environment, conceiving the structure so as to inscribe it in the lagoon's space with a perfect sense of harmony. The façade, on the other hand, seems to embody Palladio's ideals of geometric perfection, painstakingly distilled from a lifelong study of Roman antiquity.

Two paintings by Tintoretto are the highlights of the interior: a *Last Supper* at the chancel's right wall and a *Deposition* in the so-called Deposition Chapel (1594; perhaps the last work by Tintoretto).

In 1951 the wealthy Count Vittorio Cini restored the island and its structures and transformed the monastery into the home of the **Fondazione Giorgio Cini**, one of the most prominent cultural centers in Italy. High-level symposiums are constantly organized on its premises, and in 1982 the summit of the seven leading heads of state of the Western world was held here.

Palladio's two cloisters, now included in the foundation's grounds, can be visited by asking permission of the doorman (the entrance is clearly marked on the building at the right of the boat stop). The upstairs library is open to the public. With its beautiful windows, large collection of art-history books, and kind personnel, it is an invitation to abandon all other activity and turn to scholarship forever.

Murano

The public boat for Murano reaches the island in less than ten minutes from fondamente Nuove (Cannaregio). But Murano is also linked to Venice by the regular boat line number 5, the one that circles around the city and touches on the most important areas (station, garages, San Marco; a boat every 15 minutes).

Traditionally a center for the production of glass, Murano has greatly profited from the tourist boom, to the point of turning into a kind of bazaar. Serious, competent glass producers are side by side with improvised shops aiming at the exploitation of visitors. The rumor in Venice is that Murano prices are much higher than those downtown for the same items, so fruitful shopping in this island takes a bit of care and perhaps a lot of bargaining. A visit to the **Museo Vetrario** (Glass Museum; fondamenta Giustinian, not far from the first boat stop on Murano) may help you get your bearings; the most solid shops are **Barovier e Toso** (on the main shopping street just off the boat, number 28), **Venini** (at nearby number 50, but with a shop at San Marco in Venice), and **Nason e Moretti** (number 54 of same street). But a visit to Murano is pleasant also because of the lagoon ride and because of the beauty of the island itself. A real must is the **Church of Santa Maria e Donato**, a 12th-century building with a splendid apse facing a canal and with a mosaic floor dating back to 1140.

Burano

The boat to Burano leaves from fondamente Nuove approximately every hour; after Burano it continues to nearby Torcello, so that the two islands are best visited in the same day (the boat ride takes 45 minutes).

Burano is a friendly and pleasant island, famous for the vivid colors on the walls of its homes. It is a traditional center for the manufacture of lace. Unfortunately, the laborious hand production generates astronomical prices, so that most of the items sold today on the island are machine made in the Far East. However, the **Scuola dei Merletti** (Lacemaking School) on the piazza Galuppi (the main square), open to visitors, keeps the tradition alive, and has a shop where the real thing is still sold. The largest assortment, however, is at the **Jesurum Workshop**, not in Burano but in downtown Venice (ponte della Canonica, behind the Basilica di San Marco).

Torcello

Before moving to the Rialto and San Marco area, the center of the lagoon population was on this island, today almost deserted and full of unforgettable charm. It hosts three restaurants, all with a few rooms for accommodations for peace-seeking, romantic visitors, and the houses of a half-dozen families. The great surprise is the well-preserved religious center of the old settlement: On a secluded, grassy little square along the water there rise the **Baptistery, Cathedral, and Church of Santa Fosca**. A visit to these monuments, still surrounded as they are by the friendly, almost untouched lagoon, gives an idea of life as it must have been at the beginning of Venice's history. It is a place for silence, meditation, and appreciation of ancient beauty.

The old cathedral (seventh century) was reconstructed in the 11th and 12th centuries; as it stands now, it is reminiscent of the great Byzantine churches of Ravenna, both in the basilica plan and in the rich mosaic decoration of the interior. It was a style particularly suited to the water environment, inviting the sun's reflections in the large windows and in the rich chromatic plays of the mosaic. It has been compared to a great ship, a Noah's ark surviving a great flood with its exquisite art products (Ruskin). Most remarkable are the mosaics with the blue-clad Mother of God on a gold background in the main apse and the great mosaic of the Last Judgment on the entrance wall (12th–13th century). The oldest mosaics (7th century) are in the right-hand apse. Of great interest and beauty also are the Byzantine-style bas-reliefs (10th and 11th centuries).

The Lido

See the beach section of the Veneto chapter for a description of this pleasant resort, comfortably located 15 minutes from the piazza San Marco, and of the close-by island of **Pellestrina**. In the Getting Around section, below, we discuss the pros and cons of establishing your headquarters on the Lido.

GETTING AROUND

When to Go

July and August tend to bring crowds of tourists and are sometimes hot and damp (and the south wind, called *scirocco,* can be a real nuisance). September usually offers splendid weather. It is also, unfortunately, the busiest month in the tourist season. The most crowded days are those between August 20 and September 10 (Film Festival, Historic Regatta—the latter held on the first Sunday of the month). October is usually a very good month, with local life returning to normal after the tourist invasion and with the first thin fogs making the city especially romantic. In November and early December the temperature is mild and the city wonderfully intimate; the tide-related flooding called *acqua alta* is frequent. The Christmas weeks, lasting until January 6, are very busy in Venice, and so are the frantic but amusing Carnival weeks. Carnival climaxes on the seven days preceding Ash Wednesday; piazza San Marco is thick with people from all over Europe, often wearing costumes of astonishing sophistication and cost. Hotel reservations are necessary months in advance for this period. Spring is mild, and the skies over the lagoon are delightfully clear. May is probably the second best month after September so far as climate is concerned, and Venice is not at all crowded at this time. In June the first thick vanguards of tourists appear all over town.

Arriving

By Car. The main car terminal in Venice is called **Piazzale Roma**. It opens just across the 3-mile-long bridge over the lagoon, and it is the absolutely last point where cars are allowed. Unfortunately, its two covered parking lots are usually almost totally filled by residents' cars, and only in the off-off-season is there a chance to find available space. So the city administration built an artificial island nearby, called **Tronchetto**, devoted exclusively to parking space. At Tronchetto you can leave your car (uncovered parking only) and catch public transportation (line number 34) to your hotel. People with a lot of luggage may call their hotel from the boat stop as they get off, and the hotel will arrange for a porter. At Tronchetto, shamefully allowed by the city administration to turn into a madhouse of people offering all kinds of dubious services to tourists, it is a good policy to ignore all solicitors, no matter how official their caps and uniforms may look.

The city has built two other parking places, one on the mainland and one just before the lagoon bridge: **San Giuliano** for traffic coming from the east and the north, and **Fusina** for traffic coming from the west and south (also uncovered). They are rarely full, and they are very well connected to Venice by public boat service. Entrance into Venice actually *should* be by water: The short ride across the lagoon prepares the visitor for the new environment, and the view is much more exciting than at gloomy Piazzale Roma. From San Giuliano the boat goes to **fondamenta Nuove**; from Fusina it stops at **Le Zattere** and **San Marco**, where it is easy to find both porters and other boat lines to pretty much anywhere. Both lots are guarded day and night and are much less confusing than Tronchetto. If you have a rental car it may be a good idea to look for your company's offices at Piazzale Roma (all major car-rental outfits have counters there) and discuss with them the best way to take care of your car during your visit.

An interesting solution is also offered by the **Lido**, the very thin island that separates the lagoon from the open sea. It is open to car traffic, so that you can park right at the hotel door if you are staying on the Lido. The island affords a few miles of wide, sandy beaches and some of the best hotels in the world, plus a large number of less expensive places. (See Accommodations below, and see the beach section in the Veneto chapter for more information on the Lido.) There is frequent public boat service from the Lido to the San Marco area; the splendid ride through the lagoon basin takes only ten minutes. To reach the Lido by car, just cross the lagoon bridge and look for signs for the Ferry-Boat (as it is called in Italian, too): It leaves from Tronchetto every hour and a half.

By Train. At the Venice station it is easy to find porters, currency exchange, and all the services offered by a modern terminal. Just outside the building is the beginning of the Canal Grande, with boat stops for all the main lines.

By Air. A bus service meets every flight and connects the airport with **Piazzale Roma** in 25 minutes; tickets are 4,000 lire. Porters and boats are easily available at Piazzale Roma. A worthwhile luxury is the water taxi from the airport: It is rather expensive (60,000 lire plus a few extra for luggage), but it takes the exhausted traveller right to the hotel door, and again it enters the city the right way, from the water surrounding it and most likely through a stretch of the Canal Grande. Most Venetians, however, use the boat service run by Cooperativa San Marco. Boats are linked with most flights and land right at the **piazza San Marco** after a stop at the **Lido** (one-hour ride, 11,000 lire per person; look for the counter in the arrival hall; the sign reads "Cooperativa S. Marco—Water bus").

In Venice

Venice enjoys a double communication system: the canals and the streets. In spite of appearances, every house and palazzo can be reached on foot, and this is by far what Venetians prefer to do. Private boats, although dramatically increasing in number with the economic development, are exclusively for pleasure purposes. The city is far from immense, and very often the use of public transportation doesn't save any time, so people go on foot, except when they don't feel like walking or when they are carrying packages.

The most used lines, served by relatively large boats called **vaporetti**, run through the Canal Grande. They are line number 1, a local line stopping every few hundred yards, usually at alternate sides of the canal, and line number 34, which covers the same route skipping a few stops (the express line, so to speak). Each runs every ten minutes, offering a service that is fabulous in wintertime and overcrowded in the tourist season. They both ride all the way to the Lido, which is also independently served by a comfortable shuttle service from the piazza San Marco.

Line number 2, a direct link between Piazzale Roma and San Marco and the Lido, is better left to Venetians: It cuts through a side canal called rio Nuovo, not very interesting in terms of architecture, and it is so crowded in the summer that riders are totally unable to look around.

Traghetti. A help to pedestrians is offered by public gondolas in strategic spots on the Canal Grande, to avoid the detours necessary to reach one of the three bridges; for 300 lire the gondolas (these are called *traghetti*) ferry people back and forth. This service runs only during the day, and is particularly useful at the Rialto fish market (*pescheria*) as well as in San Tomà near the Frari church. These boats across the canal often make walking the quickest way between any two points in Venice.

The Gondolas. The other gondolas, finely polished and luxuriously cushioned, are used by Venetians only for marriages or rare ceremonies. Quite a few locals have never set foot in one of them: A 30-minute ride costs about 50,000 lire, and there is no reason to spend that when the public boats go much more quickly for much less. They are basically for the exclusive enjoyment of the tourists, and when so used they are worth the fee. A good idea, however, is to avoid taking them for just an aimless tour; gondolas are best used to go from one place to another, as, for instance, to ride back to the hotel after a day of visits, or to a nice restaurant for dinner.

Motorized Taxi Boats. They are numerous and quick, but again they are rather expensive: A short ride within the city starts at 30,000 lire during the day (at night there is an extra charge). Venetians use them only in times of dire need, but they may be very useful to the visitor who doesn't want to bother with suitcases and searching out addresses.

ACCOMMODATIONS

(The telephone area code for Venice is 041. When telephoning from outside the country, omit the zero in the city code.)

Preeminent among the luxury hotels of Venice are the Cipriani for its comfort and modernity and the Gritti for its atmosphere; they are both on a par with the best (and most expensive) hotels in the world. The **Hotel Cipriani** is quietly set on the island of **La Giudecca**, very close to San Giorgio Maggiore; its water taxis are always ready to take guests across the small body of water separating it from the San Marco area. Among its amenities are an exceptionally good restaurant and a swimming pool (a real eccentricity for Venice). All of the room windows open onto the lagoon, mostly on the back side of La Giudecca, where the view can be almost achingly beautiful, with the quiet water dotted by small islands and often veiled by a thin layer of mist.

Giudecca 10, 30123 Venezia. Tel: 520-77-44.

The **Gritti Palace Hotel** occupies a 15th-century Gothic palazzo, right on the Canal Grande and a short walk from San Marco. It is a preferred residence for successful intellectuals and artists; its halls are always quiet (no organized groups are accepted), and its terrace on the water, open for drinks and dining, is set in one of the most attractive stretches of the Canal Grande. For guests who really need a beach and/or a swimming pool, an hourly service connects the hotel to the great Excelsior on the Lido. (The Excelsior belongs to the same chain, CIGA, recently acquired by the Aga Khan.)

San Marco 2467, 30124 Venezia. Tel: 79-46-11.

The Monaco and Metropole are probably the best bets in the four-star category. **Hotel Monaco e Grand Canal** is also set on the Canal Grande, in a former patrician residence, and has kept a lot of ancient flavor. Its ground-floor lounge and piano bar, with large windows on the canal, are wonderfully quiet and often visited by Venetians or by a few smart tourists looking for a rest between walks. (Unless, of course, they prefer to stop for the original Bellini cocktail at **Harry's Bar,** just across the narrow calle from the Monaco. The atmosphere is more colorful at Harry's, more intimate at the Monaco.)

San Marco 1325, 30124 Venezia. Tel: 520-02-11.

The **Hotel Metropole**, on the riva degli Schiavoni near the piazza San Marco, is a modern and comfortable hotel with excellent professional service. Its front rooms open onto the Bacino di San Marco, with San Giorgio Maggiore and La Salute in full view; the southern exposure allows for enjoyment of sunrises on the Lido side and sunsets behind the domes of La Salute. All the rooms include a small safe for valuables, and most have at least one piece of antique furniture.

Castello 4148, 30122 Venezia. Tel: 520-50-44.

In a more affordable range, the relatively small **Pensione Accademia–Villa Maravegie** (26 rooms) offers all the comforts of a good hotel, plus a secluded canal-side garden for breakfast. The pensione is actually a small independent villa, surrounded by gardens on three sides and a canal on the fourth. The rooms are spacious and furnished with taste; the service is friendly and discreet. You have to reserve well in advance at this much-coveted place.

Dorsoduro 1058, 30123 Venezia. Tel: 523-78-46.

A lesser-known hotel is the **San Cassiano–Ca' Favretto** on the Canal Grande near San Stae. The building goes back to the 14th century, with traces of preceding Byzantine construction, and in the 19th century it was the residence of the Venetian painter Giacomo Favretto. The setting, relatively far from the San Marco area, is very Venetian and pleasantly off the main tourist paths, near the colorful fish and vegetable markets; the hotel's layout favors conversation with other guests.

Santa Croce 2232, 30125 Venezia. Tel: 524-17-33.

On the beautiful campo Bandiera e Moro, a few minutes from San Marco, is the small pensione **La Residenza** (17 rooms). Like the hotels that follow on this list, it is very affordable (around 70,000 lire for a double room with bath; when reserving, a private bath should be requested, since not all rooms have one). Its reception and breakfast hall is a nice example of Venetian Gothic, with a striking multiple window on the campo; rooms, doors, and walls have that old Venetian look—with its pros and cons (no use looking for a straight floor). La Residenza is perfect for people who prefer atmosphere over total comfort.

Castello 3608, 30122 Venezia. Tel: 528-53-15.

Restored to be more modern is the **Pensione La Calcina**, a former residence of John Ruskin, at Le Zattere, just behind the Gallerie dell'Accademia. For decades La Calcina has been the meeting point for those real lovers of Venice who cannot always afford the five-star hotels but who like a good degree of comfort in a friendly, almost family-like atmosphere. The pensione's location could hardly be better, on the sunny Zattere where Venetians stroll in the afternoon and evening, and a short walk from all the major points of interest.

Dorsoduro 780, 30123 Venezia. Tel: 522-70-45.

On the riva degli Schiavoni and near the Arsenale is the very interesting **Pensione Bucintoro**, run with very friendly care and inhabited by a seemingly endless stream of French painters. The reason? The pensione occupies a corner building with a breathtaking view over the Bacino di San Marco, and all the rooms enjoy that view. Among its other advantages is its proximity to the Lido (a quick swim may well be the best way to close a summer day), the colorful via Garibaldi, and the Biennale grounds.

Castello 2135/A, 30122 Venezia. Tel: 522-32-40.

Also on the riva degli Schiavoni, very close to the piazza San Marco and a few steps from the Bridge of Sighs, is the **Pensione Wildner**. A motherly, friendly lady runs it with love and pride. Two-thirds of the rooms have a splendid view over the Bacino di San Marco; weather permitting, breakfast and dining are out of doors, right on the riva.

Castello 4161, 30122 Venezia. Tel: 522-74-63.

Finally, a great bargain implying a tiny bit of sacrifice: **Locanda Montin** near the Gallerie dell'Accademia has seven charming rooms for what is probably the cheapest price in Venice (40,000 lire for two). The location is along a canal famous for its romantic look, and the **Restaurant Montin** is one of the best in town (American presidents have dined here, and the dining garden has been in quite a few movies). The drawback is the lack of private bathrooms (there are four bathrooms for the seven rooms). But the furniture is very pleasant and the Montin family runs the premises with a kindness and professionalism born of generations of experience in the restaurant business.

Dorsoduro 1147, 30123 Venezia. Tel: 522-71-51.

Other Accommodations in Venice

Pensione Seguso. Dorsoduro 779, 30123 Venezia. Tel: 522-23-40. Medium-priced, comfortable, centrally located at Le Zattere.

Hotel Al Sole. Santa Croce 136, 30125 Venezia. Tel: 523-21-44. Near the Piazzale Roma, recently renovated, moderately priced.

Alla Salute Da Cici. Dorsoduro 222, 30123 Venezia. Tel: 523-54-04. Very pleasantly located near La Salute; moderately priced.

Accommodations on the Lido

Hotel Des Bains, of the CIGA chain, is a magnificent building dating from 1901, in the best hotel tradition of those years. All decorations are Art Deco originals. The famous movie by Visconti, *Death in Venice,* was shot here.

Lungomare Marconi 17, 30126 Lido (Venezia). Tel: 78-88-00.

About one mile down the beach, the astonishing **Hotel Excelsior** (also a CIGA hotel) was built with Moorish touches in the same period. It is a rendezvous for the international movie crowd during the yearly **Film Festival** in September. Besides the beach, it has a swimming pool, and it is next door to **Casino of Venice**, one of four gambling houses allowed to operate in Italy.

Lungomare Marconi 41, 30126 Lido (Venezia). Tel: 526-02-01.

The Lido also hosts a large number of more affordable hotels and pensioni. Totally amusing is the tiled façade of **Hotel Hungaria**, right on the Gran Viale and a five-minute walk both from the seaside beach and from the lagoonside boat to San Marco (prices in the moderate range).

Gran Viale 28, 30126 Lido (Venezia). Tel: 526-12-12.

An Art Deco building (typical of the Lido) on central via Lepanto has been converted into the **Hotel Villa Otello**, with a pleasant garden and impeccable service (same price range).

Via Lepanto 12, 30126 Lido (Venezia). Tel: 526-00-48.

DINING

Recently a team of researchers in Venice's Marciàna Library unearthed 1,718 books related to cooking, dating from 1469 on. This great gourmet tradition, however, succumbed first to French predominance, then to the tourist trade in more recent times. Today the Venetian dishes still in use can be counted, as the saying goes, on the fingers of one hand.

There is also a problem with the availability of things to cook. Venice's cuisine is based on fish, but the lagoon is partly polluted, and the Adriatic Sea doesn't yield much fish anymore. The best species are only rarely caught, and they go at astronomical prices, so that only a few restaurants can afford to serve them. On the other hand, 80 percent of the fish traded in the busy Venice market is imported from Sicily or abroad. The best and most expensive local species are *branzino* (a kind of sea bass, known as *spigola* in other parts of Italy and as *loup de mer* in France) and *orata* (a snapper). Both are also farmed on the lagoon. A few sole are also caught by the Chioggia fishermen. This fish should be ordered only in the best restaurants to be sure it is really fresh.

Many less rare species are still caught in abundance, and it is to those that a money-wise visitor should stick. Actually, Venice's restaurants have developed great expertise in cooking the available seafood; the only problem is the lack of variety. Clams and mussels are tasty and wonderful with spaghetti (they are supposed to be served with the shells, to guarantee freshness); cuttlefish (*seppie*) is a gourmet dish when cooked the Venetian way and accompanied by polenta; a local kind of crayfish, called *canoce,* is served as an appetizer or again as a base for spaghetti sauce; eel is always fresh, and is either grilled or stewed with tomatoes (*anguilla in umido*); a local crab, *granceola,* is one of the best appetizers to be found anywhere in the world. Even the homely sardine has become the base of an excellent and curious dish, called *sardine in saor,* an inheritance from the time when the Venetian navy discovered that most proteins are well conserved in a bath of fried onions and vinegar.

Meat dishes are for the most part not regional, which doesn't mean that they are not prepared properly. At least one among the few meat restaurants in town seems to us particularly worthy of praise: Da Arturo (see below).

Sestiere di San Marco–Rialto

Excellent fish is served at the first-class **Do Forni**, a landmark of cuisine in Venice, as is the world-famous Harry's Bar. At Do Forni, a couple of hundred yards from piazza San Marco on the Merceria (San Marco 457; Tel: 523-77-29), it is common to see the political and commercial leaders of Venice, in an atmosphere full of local color (closed Thursdays); **Harry's Bar** (calle Vallaresso; Tel: 523-67-97; closed Mondays) has become a must for all important visitors, whether American movie stars or world-famous writers. Harry's Bar service is among the best in the world, and its second-floor windows in front of La Salute are a splendid extra treat.

The bar has now opened an extension called **Harry's Dolci** on the island of Giudecca; it is much more moderate in price and has very quickly become a favorite among Venetian society. Tel: 522-48-44; closed Sunday evenings and Mondays.

On the campo San Fantin, right along the façade of La Fenice, the restaurant **Al Teatro** has a blessed policy of staying open till late at night. This is where Venetians go for a meal after the Fenice performances. In the summer the restaurant takes over the handsome campo with its tables, and although a lot of its customers are tourists, many are also Venetians. The food is consistently good, the service very professional, and the prices in the upper-middle range. Tel: 523-72-14; closed Mondays.

Down a narrow street from La Fenice, **Da Arturo** on calle degli Assassini (Tel: 528-69-74) is probably the best meat restaurant in town. It has only seven tables, which allows for total attention from the owner (whose name is, unexpectedly, Ernesto). Ernesto serves excellent meats, imaginative salads, and very good wines (his Amarone is memorable). This is also one of the few restaurants where customers are welcome to order just a pasta and a salad without feeling pressed for an entrée: a detail that makes it, paradoxically, the best vegetarian restaurant in town (Ernesto has a knack for interesting vegetable dishes). The prices are rather on the upper side of the range. Closed Sundays.

Although technically in Cannaregio, the two restaurants that follow are mentioned in this section because of their proximity to the monument area. The **Fiaschetteria Toscana**, near the main post office at Rialto, has a wide and faithful clientele of lawyers, architects, and gourmets from the rest of the professional world. In spite of its name, it is one of the leading centers of Venetian cuisine, and it has a special reputation for wines. In the summer it takes over a small area in the front square; it fills up very quickly, so reservations are a must. Tel: 528-52-81; closed Tuesdays.

A few steps from the Fiaschetteria, the popular restaurant **Osteria Il Milion** is always crowded with young and not-so-young Venetians who are out for a good meal at affordable prices. The menu is handwritten, in Italian of course, on a pad that the owner will lend for a few minutes; the setting is totally unpretentious and gives a good idea of what in Italy is considered a pleasant family restaurant. The wines are good, and so is the service. This restaurant has started operating as such only in very recent times, so it hasn't entered the tourist circuit as yet. Tel: 522-93-02; closed Wednesdays.

Sestiere di Castello

A number of tourist restaurants line the beautiful riva degli Schiavoni east of San Marco. Among them is **Il Gabbiano**, one bridge after the church of La Pietà. Gabbiano has been recently renovated and is one of those few restaurants here that truly care about food quality. The service is very professional, and the setting is splendid. Tel: 522-39-88; closed Wednesdays.

In a tiny street between the Arsenale and campo Bandiera e Moro is **Corte Sconta**, one of the best fish restaurants in town; Tel: 522-70-24. In the summer the tables are set on a delightful inner courtyard, with an informal but refined style that puts everybody at ease. Here the tradition is to put aside the menu and let the two waitresses (the wife and sister-in-law of Claudio, the owner) run the whole show. They serve a long series of antipasti, with perfect timing and in increasing order of interest; then they introduce the three pasta dishes of the day, a taste of each, and for the few people who may feel up to it they have ready a whole array of entrées. The house wine is perfectly fine: Prosecco or Marzemino from the Veneto hills. (Marzemino is the wine that Don Giovanni drinks in the last act of Mozart's opera. No wonder, since the librettist was from a village near Venice.) Closed Sunday evenings and Mondays.

Another real find—this one on the unpretentious side—is a restaurant right on the campo dell'Arsenale, with tables outdoors in front of the great lions that guard the Arsenale's monumental entrance. It has no name, but it is known as "**Da Paolo**," the name of the owner. His young wife and charming daughter—a student of English—try their best as waitresses. The setting is extremely pleasant, and the whole neighborhood sits here for pizza or spaghetti on the warm summer nights. They all seem to be friends and relatives of each other, and not very shy in calling for service. The prices are affordable and the pasta is cooked to order; try spaghetti with clams or with *seppie,* or ask for the pasta of the day. Tel: 521-06-60; closed Mondays.

Sestieri di San Polo–Santa Croce

In San Polo, not far from the Frari church, on charming rio Marin, is the **Caffè Orientale**; Tel: 71-98-04. Sandro and Mario, the two brothers who own it, are Venetian to the core and have resurrected this name from a 19th-century establishment. Here the local fish reigns supreme: Sandro buys it directly from the fishermen every morning. He is very proud of his Art Deco furniture and will spend hours talking about tables and chairs, a second obsession of his—after, of course, recipes. The caffè has a tiny terrace over a canal, and you must call in advance to reserve a table on it: It makes for a quiet, intimate evening. Also, many people ask Sandro to call for a gondola at the end of their meals. The gondola picks them up right at the terrace—no better way to end a day of Venetian relaxation. Closed Mondays.

On a narrow street between campo San Polo and campo San Tomà is **Da Ignazio** (Tel: 523-48-52), very busy with local customers who like Ignazio's fish dishes and his pleasant garden. The atmosphere is friendly, the service professional. Closed Saturdays.

Restaurant **San Tomà**, also in San Polo, is set on the quiet and charming campo of the same name (outdoor tables). They serve pizza too, but they are very good with antipasti, pasta, and fish entrées. Tel: 523-88-19; closed Tuesdays.

On calle della Regina in Santa Croce, near the handsome campo Santa Maria Mater Domini, Mr. Dino Boscarato has recently opened **La Regina Cornaro**, an elegant, top-class restaurant. Mr. Boscarato is the owner of nationally famous All'Amelia in Mestre and the president of the European sommeliers. His chefs are real wizards, and the fish is the freshest available. Because it opened only in 1988, the restaurant is not crowded yet; with its elegant furniture and candlelit tables it makes for an especially charming evening. Tl: 524-14-02; closed Mondays.

Sestiere di Cannaregio

We mentioned Cannaregio's Fiaschetteria Toscana and Il Milion in the San Marco–Rialto section. After a visit to the Ghetto or to Madonna dell'Orto, two other restaurants in this neighborhood are to be recommended.

All'Antica Mola, on fondamenta degli Ormesini, is totally unpretentious, with family-style cooking and service. The *naïf* views of Venice on the walls bear witness to the simple yet somehow uncorrupted taste of the old owners (and take a look at the fresco in the back courtyard, though a mosquito problem makes it better to eat inside). Tel: 71-74-92; closed Saturdays.

Osteria Il Bacco, at fondamenta degli Ormesini down the iron bridge off the campo del Ghetto, is one of the best places for Venetian food in an informal yet pleasant setting. It was an old wine shop, remodeled with a reverence for tradition. Very few outsiders have discovered this little jewel, and one of the side pleasures is the walk back along the fondamenta degli Ormesini and fondamenta della Misericordia. Tel: 71-74-93; closed Tuesdays.

Sestiere di Dorsoduro

Two medium-priced restaurants in the Accademia area are held in very high esteem by Venetians. **Il Cantinone Storico** (Tel: 520-75-28) has a few tables along a canal between the Accademia and Le Zattere, and is famous for gnocchi as well as osso buco and meat dishes; closed Sundays. **Montin**, in the fondamenta delle Eremite near Le Zattere, is a real institution in town; its walls are crowded with the works of painters who patronize it, and there is a charming garden in the back. Many Venetians have held their marriage banquets here, and the atmosphere has a constant ring of festivity; it is not rare at all for otherwise stern university professors and business managers to show up with guitars and get lost in reminiscing with songs of the '50s and '60s. Giuliano Montin and his wife have known all these people since childhood, and this sort of thing is the real beauty of being a Venetian. Tourists, especially Americans, discovered this place years ago. They love it, and in the summer they fill up the large garden rather quickly, so you should reserve. Tel: 522-33-07; closed Tuesday evenings and Wednesdays.

Although it has no tables outdoors, restaurant **Donna Onesta**, at the foot of the bridge of the same name, is very well liked by Venetians for the excellent quality of the food and the affordable prices. Few foreign visitors ever set foot in this very pleasant restaurant; it may be that they see the locals drinking the traditional glass of wine at the counter and they think it too Venetian an affair. Fish appetizers and pasta are the things to order here. Tel: 522-95-86; closed Sundays.

In the summer evenings Venetians stream to romantic Le Zattere and stop for pizza or for an inexpensive meal in one of two restaurants that have wood terraces along the water of the Canale della Giudecca (**Da Gianni**, near the boat stop for Giudecca, or **Alle Zattere**, a few yards away toward La Salute). The quality of the food, while not haute cuisine, is definitely acceptable; and the setting is magnificent. Customers sit out in the open, catching every tiny breeze that may be around, seeing old friends at nearby tables, and watching the huge container ships that still cruise past on their way to or from the Venice harbor.

SHOPS AND SHOPPING
Clothes, jewelry, shoes, Murano glass, Burano lace, Carnival masks: Venice is really a shopper's paradise. The narrow passageway between San Marco and Rialto, appropriately called the Merceria (Merchandise Street), has been lined with all kinds of stores since the 14th century; today all the great brand names are abundantly represented, from Missoni to Armani to Krizia and Versace. Even Cartier has recently opened a luxurious extension on the Merceria. The other busy shopping area—also near San Marco—is Frezzeria, running from Harry's Bar to the La Fenice theater. Only the constant stream of visitors could keep so many shops alive in this city of a mere 75,000; thus foreign languages, especially English, are spoken everywhere, to the point where it becomes very difficult to practice your painfully learned Italian.

Murano Glass
You don't have to ride to Murano to find the best products of that island, or to find better prices. Actually, word has it that in most cases the Venice shops and glassmakers' furnaces are cheaper than those in Murano. For classic, traditional glass go to **Cenedese**, which occupies a whole palazzo on the Canal Grande near La Salute in Dorsoduro; quite a few antique pieces can be seen there, giving you a good idea of the history and evolution of the glass industry (there is also a furnace for demonstrations). For contemporary design, the most famous and praised among the large firms are **Venini**, with a shop on the piazzetta dei Leoncini in sestiere San Marco, across the left wall of the basilica, and **Barovier & Toso**, at campo San Moisè near San Marco. A very large assortment of works by the best glass masters is to be found at **Pauly's**, on the side of San Marco all the way across from the basilica. The salesmen are true and serious professionals, and they ship reliably all over the world.

Burano Lace
The best lace production of Burano can be seen in the large **Jesurum** store in Venice, near ponte della Canonica behind the Basilica di San Marco and a few yards from the Bridge of Sighs (ponte dei Sospiri).

Carnival Masks

Ever since the Venetian Carnival was resurrected by the city's tourist office at the end of the 1970s, shops of Carnival masks have been mushrooming in every neighborhood. The best are the ones in which advanced craftsmanship is coupled with a serious study of the old traditions; such is **Mondonovo**, a small and crowded shop run with great expertise by Guerrino Lovato between campo Santa Margherita and ponte dei Pugni in sestiere Dorsoduro. Lovato is very popular among Venetians for his knowledge of art history and for his contributions to frequent spectacles requiring the use of masks; it is not unusual to find him involved in heated discussions of the Commedia dell'Arte with actors and directors, amid the surrealistic decor of his often disquieting creations.

Jewelry

It is well known that the large majority of the jewelry exported from Italy is manufactured in Vicenza, a town on the Venetian mainland. Therefore the local stores are very numerous and always up-to-date in terms of style. Quite a few are on the Merceria, while some of the oldest and most reliable have their premises right on the piazza San Marco. Among those latter, Venetians seem to prefer **Missiaglia**, which has been at their service for many generations. Another good shop is **Codognato** on calle Ascensione.

Venetian Craftsmanship

Besides glass and lace, Venetian artisans used to excel in wood carving, textile printing, bookbinding, bronze casting, and many other fields. Some of these specialties have now been resurrected after a long period of neglect. More and more people are looking for handmade objects in spite of the necessarily high prices, and the offerings are increasing with the demand. A good area to explore for this purpose is the neighborhood of Santo Stefano–Palazzo Grassi. The stores that follow are concentrated there.

Marbled Paper. **Alberto Valese**, at 3135 salizzada San Samuele near Palazzo Grassi, prepares the paper on the small premises, and he doesn't mind if visitors watch him or his wife while they do it.

Legatoria Piazzesi, near campo San Maurizio, is an old institution in Venice. Formally a bookbindery, it has enlarged its scope to include a large variety of related items, from notebooks to calendars to picture frames. **Il Papiro** is a recently opened shop on the calle between San Maurizio and campo Santo Stefano, with a large variety of paper items, mostly imported from Florence.

Wood-Carvers. Variously called *indoradori* or *marangoni da soase,* these artisans still flourish in Venice. They offer gilded frames, lamps, and wood statues, mostly in 18th-century styles. A good one, with no known name, is in salizzada San Samuele at number 3337; another, called **Cavalier**, is on nearby campo Santo Stefano at number 2863/A.

Lino de Marchi, a few steps from Palazzo Grassi in sestiere San Marco, at number 3157/A, is halfway between an artisan and a sculptor. He produces delicately crafted wood sculptures that bear an astonishing resemblance to everyday objects. **Venice Design**, a gallery of contemporary design, on the same street, salizzada San Samuele, specializes in glass and metal objects by known designers. Besides the items in the windows, they keep some astonishing surprises in their safe.

Textile Printing

A tradition of textile printing was established in Venice by the painter and inventor Mariano Fortuny (1871–1949). His workshop is still producing textiles on Giudecca, and samples can be seen at **Trois**, in the via XXII Marzo near San Marco.

Marvelous velvets are still hand-printed in Venice with Fortuny's methods. A good assortment can be seen at **Cilla Gaggio**'s, in calle delle Botteghe just off the salizzada San Samuele at number 3451.

Books

While most good bookstores carry English-language publications on Venice, the largest choice is to be found at the **Libreria Sangiorgio**, in the via XXII Marzo near the piazza San Marco. There is also an English bookstore called **Il Libraio a San Barnaba**, a preferred rendezvous (in Dorsoduro, number 2835/A, near Santa Margherita) for the many English majors at the nearby university. In these places you will be sure to find such classics as Jan Morris's *Venice* and Mary McCarthy's *Venice Observed,* together with Toby Cole's collection, *Venice, A Portable Reader,* and M. Battilana's *English Writers and Venice,* and of course a few English-language copies of Giulio Lorenzetti's *Venice,* the unsurpassed guidebook, constantly updated since its first publication in 1926.

Specializing exclusively in the astonishingly abundant literary production about Venice is the **Libreria Filippi** in the calle (Sottoportego) della Bissa near the Rialto in sestiere San Marco. To the visitor who can read Italian this bookstore offers a wide range of works, from the most specialized academic contributions to superbly illustrated volumes on Venetian architecture. Particularly interesting are the catalogs, in many languages, of exhibits held in the city's museums.

THE VENETO

By Paolo Lanapoppi

Life is particularly sweet to the inhabitants of this privileged part of Italy. Within a two-hour drive they can move from some of the most impressive peaks in the Alps to a hundred miles of Mediterranean beaches; between those two areas gentle hills create a landscape known to the world through the paintings of Giorgione and Cima da Conegliano, in a countryside that is also home to some of the best wines—as well as some of the best cooking—in Italy. From the Romans to the Ostrogoths to the Renaissance and up to today, 20 centuries of civilization have left their artistic traces in every urban center, and in the last 40 years the local economy, previously depressed, has unexpectedly boomed, spreading prosperity and security through every level of society.

The Veneti take full advantage of this situation. They are hard workers, great managers, and proud professionals, but they love to enjoy their free time and would think nothing of driving an hour to try a new trattoria with a good reputation. They would then discuss the quality of its food and wines with astonishing energy. Because the Veneti are attached to family values and to the traditions of their land, they raise their children in old-fashioned ways, speak the local dialects in spite of the leveling effects of the centralized media, and know every corner of their region. Ever since they started to flock to vacations in Kenya, the Seychelles, and Thailand—like every good European—they have been comparing destinations, and they may not be wrong when they conclude that there are few—if any—corners of the world as worth visiting as the Veneto.

For visitors, the Veneto can be divided into three sections: the Plains, the southern area outside Venice that includes Treviso, Padua, Vicenza, and Verona; the Hill Belt, which includes the eastern shores of Lago di Garda, the thermal-water centers, Asolo, and the birthplaces of Giorgione and Cima da Conegliano; and the Mountain Belt, at the north of the Veneto, including Cortina d'Ampezzo and the Cadore.

MAJOR INTEREST

The Plains
Country villas, many by Andrea Palladio
Regional cooking
Old cities of Verona, Vicenza, Padua, and Treviso
Brenta Canal, lined with villas
Bibone and other coastal resorts

Hill Belt
Fine cuisine and wines
Lago di Garda
Abano and Recoaro thermal baths
Castlefranco
Asolo's scenic beauty

Mountain Belt
Skiing, hiking, scenery
Cortina and other resorts
The Cadore

THE PLAINS

The spaces between the major cities on the plains of the Veneto have now become a continuum of farms, dwellings, and small firms, so the whole area can be considered a huge—although untypical—urban settlement. Here the houses are scattered throughout the land and join in clusters only in correspondence with preexisting (often Medieval) towns and villages. All of the four major cities on the Veneto plains are rich in history past and present; almost all are built on a river of some sort and have large sections of green, making life in each more pleasant through constant contact with nature.

Verona

On the western side of the plains, Verona is the natural link between Venice and Milan and between the rest of Italy and many other European countries. Its province includes the eastern shore of Lago di Garda, which is dotted with Medieval citadels and world-famous vineyards and is very popular in the summer with German and Austrian tourists. The city itself is probably the most interesting among the district capitals of the Veneto due to its architecture, which ranges from the ancient Roman to the Medieval, the Renaissance, and the Baroque.

A walk down the streets of Verona's center, between the Medieval **piazza delle Erbe** and the Roman arena in piazza Bra, especially on a weekday morning, gives a good idea of the composite population living in the city and in the surrounding towns. A large percentage of café and restaurant customers are unmistakably farmers who have come downtown for business. They may still wear old-fashioned hats or be slightly uncomfortable in their business suits, but they run one of the most advanced agricultural communities in Italy; they are the modern and sophisticated heirs of the poor *contadini* of old times. Here in Verona they mix with lawyers, accountants, service managers, and the leaders of countless family businesses. The annual per capita income here is the highest in the Veneto.

All this activity takes place in the middle of an urban landscape crowded with Medieval and Renaissance masterworks. In the central piazza Bra, the **Roman Arena** is the ancient amphitheater, only slightly damaged through its almost 2,000 years. In July and August 20,000 persons still crowd it every evening to watch opera performances. Lombardic and Gothic kings made Verona their preferred residence—and of course left a few signs of their passage—but the most impressive buildings are probably the Medieval ones: The **Church of San Zeno** is Romanesque architecture at its purest (and includes a famous triptych by Mantegna); the piazza dei Signori was the former center of government, with its Palazzo della Ragione (1193), Palazzo del Governo (end of the 13th century), and beautiful Loggia del Consiglio (end of the 15th century). The great family of Della Scala—rulers of Verona between the time it was a republic and the conquest by Venice, protectors of Dante, and at a certain

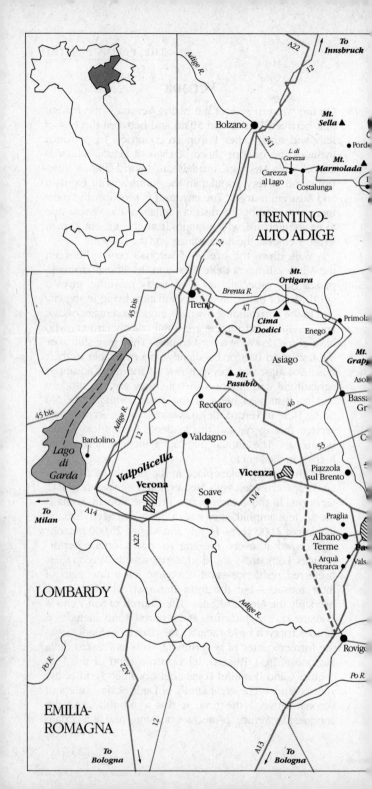

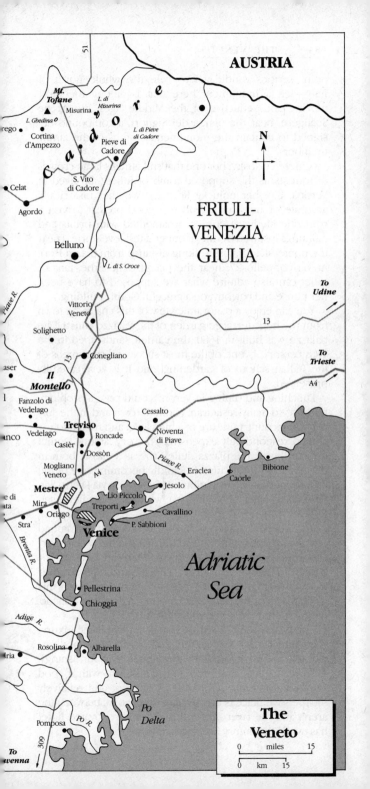

point serious candidates to rule the whole north of Italy—left a monument here that is among the most moving and seductive of the Middle Ages: the **Arche Scaligere**, near the piazza dei Signori, a compound designed to contain the monumental tombs of the family members.

A mere curiosity, but one that still attracts large crowds of tourists, is the supposed tomb of Juliet (she lived in Verona, like her unlucky Romeo). Whether historically accurate or not, the legend is a good pretext to visit a romantic Medieval corner ornamented with prints and paintings inspired by one of our greatest love stories (near the ponte Aleardi, just walking distance from piazza Bra). At via Cappello 27, near the piazza delle Erbe, fans of Juliet can also admire what are supposed to have been her house and balcony, on a graceful Gothic building.

You can enjoy a panoramic view of this charming town from the huge terraced garden of the **Palazzo Giusti**. The palazzo was built in 1580; the garden, landscaped in the 18th century, is one of the most successful specimens of the Italian school of gardening, and it is very carefully preserved.

Lunching and dining in Verona could pose a problem, because so many restaurants both in town and in the surrounding countryside are of a high level and reputation—and correspondingly expensive. The very famous **Dodici Apostoli**, near the piazza delle Erbe, is a classic both in decor and in local cuisine. Rapidly becoming one of the best restaurants in the nation is **Il Desco** (on via Dietro San Sebastiano near Juliet's house), where in a Medieval setting the traditional food of the area—fish from Lago di Garda, venison, mushrooms—is served with daring and often memorable innovations. Verona also has two restaurants specializing in fish: **Il Nuovo Marconi** (sea bass or pike from Lago di Garda; on via Fogge, around the corner from Il Desco) and **Arche** (near the Arche Scaligere); this is the place for *branzino al cartoccio,* a delicious concoction of sea bass wrapped with mollusks.

The best among the many hotels in town is the luxury-class **Due Torri**—very central, endowed with a good restaurant, and noteworthy for the quality of its furnishings. The **Accademia**, also very central and also with a good restaurant, is more affordable. A pleasant and relatively inexpensive place is the **Antica Porta Leona**, between the arena and the river Adige; this recently renovated hotel has two 17th-century fireplaces in its salon.

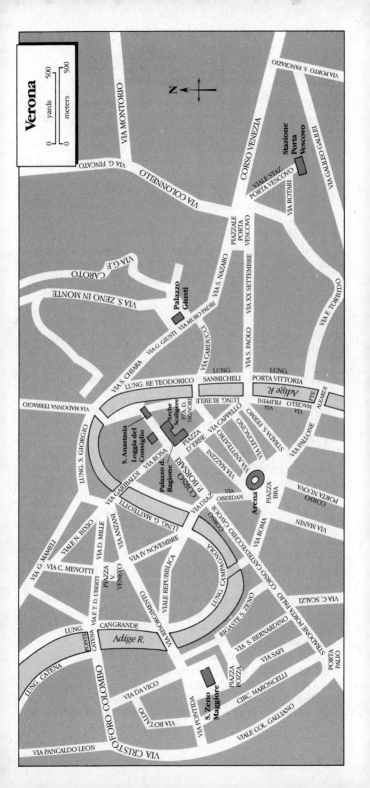

Vicenza

Like Verona, Vicenza, in the center of the Veneto, has recently emerged from a history of relatively poor agricultural economy to become one of the most affluent centers on the peninsula. The *modello Veneto,* a much-studied pattern of economic transformation, has achieved some of its most striking successes here. (For more on this, see the Hill Belt section that follows.) Among the protagonists of this transformation a very important place belongs to the countless goldsmiths, who fashion all kinds of jewels for the international markets. Three times a year (January, July, and September) these patient, imaginative heirs of Benvenuto Cellini hold their international fair, a dazzling event: 15,000 professional buyers from all over the world come to Vicenza to buy from 1,000 exhibitors. One afternoon per session the fair is open to the general public; no direct buying is allowed, though—only watching, admiring, and possibly writing down a few addresses for later visits.

Although a pleasant city in itself, with large green areas and three small, idyllic rivers, Vicenza owes its celebrity especially to Andrea Palladio, who moved to this city in early childhood from his native Padua and built some of his best palazzi here, as well as many villas in the surrounding countryside. These are the prototypes of hundreds of mansions and churches scattered throughout Europe (particularly England); Palladio was seen as having interpreted Roman antiquity in the best Italian Renaissance terms. These masterworks are all within walking distance—or, at worst, within a short taxi ride.

A real must is the **Teatro Olimpico**, the last work by Palladio (1580, the year of his death; construction was completed by Vincenzo Scamozzi, who built important structures in Venice). With the Olimpico, the great architect, following his familiar Vitruvius, tried to recreate a Roman classical space but, of course, modernized it to meet the architectural and theatrical standards of his times, adding 95 statues and a famous trompe l'oeil scene representing the five streets of Thebes.

Not far from the theater is the **piazza dei Signori**, where Palladio rebuilt, or rather covered up with his façades, the old Palazzo della Ragione, calling it the Basilica, and added the powerful Loggia Bernarda. This is a fine starting point for a half-hour walk to cover some of the best Palladian palazzi in town. Across the nearby main street of

Vicenza, appropriately called corso Andrea Palladio, is the famous **contrà Porti** (*contrà* is one of the local names for street). A few steps up the contrà, at number 11, is Palazzo Porto Barbaran, remodeled by Palladio in 1570 over an existing structure. At number 12 across the way a modern bank has taken over Palazzo Thiene (the eastern façade is by Palladio, 1558). At number 21, Palladio's Palazzo Iseppo Da Porto, unfinished, was deemed "unsurpassable" by Vasari. Many Gothic buildings line this beautiful and busy street. Along Palazzo Porto Barbaran is the contrà Reale, leading to corso A. Fogazzaro, where Palladio built Palazzo Valmarana Braga (number 16). Back on corso Palladio (closed to traffic on Sundays), you can walk 500 yards to Palazzo Chiericati, near the Teatro Olimpico and now the Museo Civico. (Palladio built it in the 1550s.)

It was not exclusively out of love for his adoptive city that Palladio spent so much energy here. The truth is that in the capital city of Venice, his rival Sansovino—in alliance with Titian and with the poet Pietro Aretino—enjoyed a monopoly over all civilian art. In Venice Palladio had to limit himself to religious buildings, and, moreover, he saw quite a few of his projects rejected by the city fathers.

A somewhat longer walk along the banks of the river Retrone leads to Palazzo Civena Trissino, one of the first works by Palladio and the one that made his reputation. The Trissinos were the discoverers of Palladio's talent when he was a young stonecutter in Padua; this 1540 building, now a private hospital, shows a clear kinship with the great Roman architecture of the time, particularly of Raffaello and Bramante.

Because of this Palladian feast, little attention is usually given to structures in and around Vicenza that otherwise would merit much more than a passing glance. Such is the Medieval compound of piazza dei Signori, piazza delle Biade, and piazza delle Erbe, with the daringly slim Torre di Piazza, and the nearby house of the navigator Antonio Pigafetta (a companion and lieutenant of Ferdinand Magellan), an astonishing mixture of Gothic, Renaissance and Spanish elements at number 5 via Pigafetta. Of great archaeological interest is the early Medieval **Church of Santi Felice e Fortunato**, with remnants of a fourth-century church, a km (half a mile) west of Porta Castello.

Fifteen minutes by car from the Medieval center, on top of a carefully landscaped hill, is the **Basilica of Monte**

Berico, rebuilt in Baroque style at the end of the 17th century. (You can also go on foot, through the 192 steps of the strada delle Scalette departing from Porta Monte, and then under the 150 arches of an amazing 18th-century portico. The portico is also visible from the car.) The basilica offers a splendid view of town and country-side, and it hosts a grandiose canvas by Veronese: the **Supper of Saint Gregory the Great** (painted in 1572). At 25 × 15 feet, the painting is one of the largest of its kind, and it is considered to be among Veronese's master-works. Its purpose was to adorn the dining hall of the Berico friars, and for many centuries it must have bright-ened up their disciplined meals, just like the controver-sial *Last Supper* Veronese painted in 1573 for the Domini-cans of Venice, a work whose interest in frivolous detail cost him a trial and a partial retraction.

On the slopes of Monte Berico, on the way from Vicenza to the basilica, is the 18th-century **Villa Valma-rana**, called "Dei Nani" because of the dwarfs sculpted on the garden walls. (To get there by car from the train station, cross the Retrone at Porta Lupia and drive up viale 10 Giugno to the panoramic Spianata del Cristo; a small road on the left leads to the villa after half a mile.) To the surprise and delight of the casual visitor, this villa con-tains one of the most fascinating cycles of frescoes in the entire Veneto, done by Gian Battista Tiepolo and his son, Gian Domenico. The father painted the Palazzina; the son, the nearby Foresteria. The Venetian 18th century is represented here at its highest: luminous, optimistic, and festive from Gian Battista; and touched by a feeling of imminent catastrophe from the intense, disquieting Gian Domenico (open 10:00 A.M. to noon and 4:00 to 6:00 P.M.; holidays, 10:00 A.M. to noon only).

A short walk from Villa Valmarana is another villa, per-haps the most celebrated among Palladio's masterworks: Villa Capra, known throughout the world by the name of **La Rotonda**. Only the outside of the building is open to visitors, and that only on Tuesdays, Thursdays, and Satur-days, 9:00 to noon and 3:00 to 5:00 P.M. Permission to visit the interior must be obtained from the Counts Valmarana at their Venice address: San Marco 3903, Tel: (041) 522-29-44 (there are Dorigny and Maganza frescoes, of limited interest). But no lover of Palladio is likely to want to miss this jewel of Renaissance architecture. Here the artist seems to have succeeded in his attempt—highly original for his times—to have the building merge with the landscape in a totally harmonious way. (He was able to achieve a similar result in the water and sky environment of Venice with the two churches of San Giorgio Maggiore and Redentore.) In accordance with its creator's aims, La Rotonda seems to represent physically the philosophical ideals of the late Renaissance: order and balance, elegance and harmony, even at the expense of other, perhaps equally positive, human characteristics, such as the tensions and emotional upheavals that were to resurface in the Baroque age.

Vicenza is abundantly served by good restaurants, although they are less princely than in nearby Verona. Here, too, the regional cuisine is the most popular: only fish at **Cinzia e Valerio** on the piazzetta Porta Padova near the old city walls; poultry and venison (and also the famous *baccala' alla Vicentina*) at the moderately priced **Tre Visi** near the piazza dei Signori; and a remodeled rustic setting, with the possibility of outdoor dining, at **Da Remo**, a little over a km (half a mile) outside the city walls at via Caimpenta 14 (exit through corso Padova, driving east toward Padua).

Padua

Very rich in Medieval and Renaissance art, Padua (Italian, Padova) has grown dramatically and somehow frantically in the past 40 years. The usual ring of crowded, ugly new developments surrounds this once very pleasant city between Vicenza and Venice, and in the historic center the traffic is definitely too heavy, making it rather hard for visitors to enjoy the many masterworks spread within the city limits.

In Medieval and early Renaissance times, Padua was the most active patron city of the arts in the whole Veneto. Giotto worked here early in the 14th century, leaving a series of extraordinary frescoes in the **Cappella degli Scrovegni** (Scrovegni Chapel) more than a century later, Paolo Uccello, Filippo Lippi, and Donatello were called to Padua (nothing has remained here of the works of the first two), influencing Squarcione and Mantegna, who in turn introduced the Venetian painters (such as Giovanni Bellini, who was Mantegna's brother-in-law) to the new approach that was to form the core of so much Venetian art.

Besides the Scrovegni Chapel (off corso Garibaldi, a short walk from the train station), a landmark in the history of European painting, you should see (on piazza Eremitani, 200 yards from the Scrovegni Chapel) the **Eremitani Church**, where Mantegna painted frescoes for one chapel in the 1450s. Unfortunately, World War II bombing destroyed a large part of the frescoes, leaving only two of them untouched (some of the others have been painstakingly restored).

Not far from the Eremitani is the ancient center of the **University of Padua**, the second oldest in Italy after Bologna, having been founded in 1222. Thousands of students still make the 20-minute walk daily from the station to the university, through corso Garibaldi, piazza Garibaldi, and piazza Cavour. The ancient portals of the university building, known in Padua as Il Bo' ("The Ox"), open on via 8 Febbraio, a hundred yards beyond the Caffè Pedrocchi. Here Dante, Petrarch, and Tasso studied; here for many years Galileo taught. The courtyards and stairs are decorated with the coats of arms of Italian and foreign families that sent their offspring here, and the atmosphere remains surprisingly close to that of a Medieval university. A university it still is, crowded with students, professors, and administrators. Following an old Italian tradition, the grounds *and* classes are open to the general public: Enrollment is required (upon payment of a very moderate administrative fee) only to pass examinations and to receive credits. The entire university system in Italy is supported by the state, and—to complete this paradise of educational democracy—enrollment is open to any candidate who possesses a high-school diploma. Professors, in turn, are treated extremely well: Tenure is pretty much automatic; the teaching load includes only three hours a week; courses start late in November and end at the beginning of May (with long recesses at Christmas and Easter, of course).

A visit to the **Basilica of Il Santo** (the saint is Anthony, protector of Padua) offers a good opportunity to see one of Donatello's masterworks, the equestrian monument to *condottiere* Gattamelata (1447) on the square in front of the church (a 20-minute walk from Il Bo', down via San Francesco and via del Santo). There are other works by Donatello inside, including a marble bas-relief of Christ's Deposition that is familiar to every student of art history.

A short and pleasant walk, protected from the city traffic, is offered by the stretch between Il Bo' and the two Medieval squares **piazza della Frutta** and **piazza delle Erbe**, where the modern city has managed to use ancient structures for their original purposes. The fruit and vegetable market in this area is as active and colorful today as it was in the 13th and 14th centuries.

The same area, usually crowded with students as well as professionals and businessmen meeting in the historic **Caffè Pedrocchi** (Neoclassical; 1831), also includes some of the best restaurants in a city justly famous for its cuisine: **Dotto** (via Squarcione 25), equally crowded for Italian-style business lunches—a good couple of hours—and for more leisurely dinners; and **El Toulà** (via Belle Arti 11), the most expensive restaurant in town. A bit out of the way—a short taxi ride from the center—there is the informal and very moderate **Da Giovanni** (at piazzale Stanga), with a composite clientele that includes all social classes and a widespread reputation for boiled and roasted meats. At **Padovanelle**, a hotel and restaurant only 6 km (4 miles) outside of the center of the city, well-to-do Paduans enjoy haute cuisine next door to an elegant horse-racing track, in pleasant countryside surroundings. Padovanelle is known for its antipasti table, a buffet with 30 or more appetizers; for its risotti; and for giving a ceramic dish as a souvenir to customers who order certain entrées.

Padua, like all the urban centers in the Veneto, is surrounded by an economically healthy and very active countryside outside its ring of modern development; and here, too, the good and great restaurants have steadily grown in number. Many people, when visiting Padua, prefer to stop for a good meal in the countryside, especially in the summer. Particularly beautiful is the Riviera del Brenta, a road connecting Padua to Venice along the Brenta Canal and a preferred vacation spot for the Venetian nobility since the 16th century. Some of the best patrician villas lie here, and along with them there are some of the best fish restaurants in the Veneto (see below).

Treviso

This delightful city a few miles north of Venice has managed to keep a rare idyllic atmosphere in spite of the extraordinary vitality of its economy. Treviso claims to have been the original inventor of the economic *modello Veneto* (discussed in the Hill Belt section).

Huge economic and social changes lie behind the success of the *modello Veneto*. Such transformations could not have taken place without long preparation. The people of Treviso are convinced that their present happy welfare has deep historical roots; this has always been a land where agriculture was mixed with commerce and with manufacturing. Even more than the other cities of the Veneto, Treviso has been a crossroad between north and south and between east and west since Roman (actually pre-Roman) times. It was from here that the founding fathers of Venice moved to the lagoon islands in the fifth century. To take an example from our own times, the textile boom represented by such firms as Benetton and Stefanel (both from Treviso) may simply be the consequence of growing silkworms and weaving and selling textiles for centuries—a typical combination of agriculture and industry.

The idyllic nature of Treviso is largely due to its quiet, romantic river (the Sile) and to the canals branching from it, their banks lined with poplar trees and weeping willows. Many homes have small or large gardens planted with flowers, especially roses. Naturally there is no lack of remarkable artistic monuments: The **Palazzo dei Trecento** and the **Palazzo del Podestà**, in the beautiful and very active piazza dei Signori, are Romanesque buildings of the early 13th century. The nearby **Duomo** is an interesting mixture of early Renaissance and 18th-century additions; the **Church of San Nicolò**, a km (half a mile) southwest of the Duomo, is an original architectural solution of tensions between Romanesque and Gothic. But the beauty of Treviso is best enjoyed by a stroll through its **Città Vecchia** (Old City), especially on the market days of Tuesday and Saturday. Make sure to allow some time for a meal in one of the many good restaurants; there is a wide choice of them in this sophisticated little town, from the exclusive **El Toulà** (via Collalto 6) to trattorie such as **Al Bersagliere** (via Barberia 21) and **Le Beccherie** (piazza Ancillotto 10), both in the middle price range and both crowded with demanding local customers.

As with the other cities in the Veneto, a surprising number of very good restaurants are also scattered in the prosperous Treviso countryside. They range from fish restaurants such as **Tajer d'Oro**, at Fossalta Maggiore, to places specializing in local venison (**Al Cacciatore**, at Roncade), to friendly, informal trattorie (a famous one is **Alle Guaiane**, at Noventa di Piave). An extraordinary place, both for the cooking standards and the old farmhouse setting, is **Osteria Pasina** at Dosson di Casier, where the owner/chef and the customers seem to be equally knowledgeable about the traditional cuisine of the Veneto. Finding these places is the easiest thing in the world: Everybody can give directions—often accompanied by a congratulatory smile—for miles around the lucky villages where they are located.

The Patrician Villas

After the Venetian Republic conquered mainland territories in the 15th century, it became fashionable among its patricians to spend two parts of the year, usually a month in the spring and one or two in the fall, at their country houses. Their homes (*villa* in Italian means "country residence") became more and more luxurious, competing with one another and even with the mansions of Venice. In many cases, it was the farmland and its revenues that made up for the decline of power overseas, so that the Venetian nobility transformed itself from merchants to landholders, transferring the entrepreneurial skills inherited from their fathers. By the 18th century many of the villas had become the real center of a family's wealth. The masters no longer went there to enjoy only a few months away from the city but more and more to supervise the production of crops. The long, porticoed wings on both sides of the main façades, therefore, had a precise practical function—as storage and processing centers, exactly as the ground floors of the Venice palazzi had been merchandise warehouses during the great trading years.

There are some 3,000 of these homes scattered in the Veneto, and at least 700 of them are of artistic interest. A large number of the latter are in serious decay and can often be found for sale at prices that seem very low—until the contractors give their astronomical restoration and maintenance estimates. The periods and styles vary from Gothic to Renaissance to Baroque to Neoclassical, but the most celebrated villas are those built by Palladio in the 16th century. Palladio was able to express his enthusiastic understanding of Roman antiquity, but not without a more or less conscious process of modernization that went right to the heart of the patrician taste: splendor without vulgar display of means, harmony of volumes in a solemn yet friendly context. A careful study of a building's impact on the surrounding landscape was another of Palladio's concerns, one that was to win for him the admiration of so many English architects.

We mentioned La Rotonda in the Vicenza section; other masterworks by Palladio are the **Villa Barbaro** at Maser, northwest of Treviso; the **Villa Emo Capodilista** at Fanzolo di Vedelago, west of Treviso near Castelfranco; the **Villa Foscari** (called "La Malcontenta"), halfway between Venice and Padua, at Mira; and the **Villa Badoer**, near Fratta Polesine in the Po Delta southwest of Venice.

Villa Barbaro (with frescoes by Veronese) can be visited on Tuesdays, Saturdays, and Sundays, 3:00 to 6:00 P.M. in summer, 2:00 to 5:00 P.M. in winter; Villa Emo Capodilista (be careful; there are other villas with the same name in the Veneto) on Saturdays, Sundays, and holidays, 3:00 to 6:00 P.M. or 2:00 to 5:00 P.M. in winter; La Malcontenta on Tuesdays, Saturdays, and the first Sunday of each month, 10:00 A.M. to 2:00 P.M. and 3:00 to 6:00 P.M. Villa Badoer has yet another schedule: In the summer it is open on Sundays, 10:00 A.M. to noon, Tuesdays and Thursdays, 9:00 A.M. to noon, and every day from 3:30 to 7:00 P.M. (in winter every day, 2:00 to 5:00 P.M.).

The city of Vicenza lists 56 villas of primary importance in its district, and Treviso and Padua can certainly boast at least as many. The best itinerary for a visit is probably by car or **boat ride along the Brenta Canal**, a tranquil, idyllic stream that flows from Padua to Venice. Many patricians had their villas around the Brenta, and the historic boat service up and down the river, called *Il Burchiello* from the name of the large boats that were used for many centuries, has now been resurrected for sightseeing. Originally pulled by horses from the riverbanks, the boat is today motorized, but it advances slowly and romantically in a landscape that is striking for its mixture of idyllic nature and great architecture (that is, once it sails past the industrial area of Porto Marghera). The Brenta banks were, after all, the Beverly Hills of the Venetian nobility: Foscaris, Contarinis, Veniers, Valmaranas, and many others had their villas built here. The memorable voyage lasts a whole day, with return by bus, and it includes stops with guided tours at La Malcontenta, Villa Querini, and Villa Pisani in Stra, plus lunch at a riverside restaurant. The service is offered from March 26 to October 30. Departures from piazza San Marco in Venice are on Tuesdays, Thursdays, Saturdays at 9:00 A.M., return at 7:45 P.M.; departures from Padua are on Wednesdays, Fridays, Sundays at 8:45 A.M., return at 7:15 P.M. Tickets include visits and meals at 98,000 lire per person. In Venice call CIT at (041) 528-5480, or buy your tickets at CIT's counter on piazza San Marco next door to

Caffè Florian; in Padua call Siamic at (049) 660-944 or go to their office on via Trieste 42. Most travel agents in both towns can also make reservations.

Although far from exhausting the architectural range of villas in the Veneto, this particular area will give you a good idea of their variety and beauty. All of them, of course, are also approachable by car. The most magnificent is definitely the 18th-century **Villa Pisani** at Stra', halfway between Padua and Venice, now a national museum. It includes a famous labyrinth-shaped garden and, more importantly, a series of splendid frescoes by Tiepolo (open 9:00 A.M. to 12:30 P.M. and 3:00 to 6:00 P.M.; on holidays, only in the morning except for the park; in winter, only mornings 9:00 A.M. to noon, holidays 9:00 A.M. to 1:00 P.M.).

A few miles north of Padua is another jewel, **Villa Contarini** at Piazzola Sul Brenta (17th century and grandiose; open 9:00 A.M. to 12:30 P.M. and 3:00 to 6:30 P.M. except on holidays).

The ride along the Brenta is a preferred itinerary for Venetians and Paduans in the warm spring days as well as in September and October, and this has encouraged the establishment of remarkably good restaurants, many of which specialize in fish from nearby Chioggia on the Adriatic: **Da Bepi Ciosoto**, near Villa Foscari; **Il Burchiello**, at Oriago, near Mestre; and **Margherita**, with a large garden, at Mira. Real connoisseurs in search of an exceptional gastronomic treat drive all the way to Mestre (just across the lagoon from Venice) and stop near the train station at a crossroad called La Giustizina, to enjoy a meal at busy, colorful **Dall'Amelia**, one of the best restaurants in Italy, run with great competence by Dino Boscarato, the president of the Italian sommeliers.

The Beaches

The beaches of the Veneto—there are almost 100 miles of them—were beautiful until the tourist trade transformed most of them into playgrounds for two-week vacationers from Central and Northern Europe. Only off-season or in a few secluded stretches is the old atmosphere conserved: a flat, gently curving coastline with mountains and hills on the far horizon, sand dunes dotted with wild bushes, frequent river mouths and lagoons.

Among the developed centers, **Bibione** at the far east has kept a large wood of umbrella pines right on the sea and can still offer some rest; Caorle, grown around a Medieval center with an 11th-century cathedral and bell tower, has lined its beaches with modern hotels and pensioni, deck chairs and umbrellas; Eraclea Mare has three miles of beach also occupied by hotels and campgrounds; and finally, Jesolo, the capital town and pride of this kind of summer resort, is infested with portable radios and pizza parlors, souvenir shops and immense campgrounds (some of them hold as many as 7,000 people).

Behind Jesolo, however, small local roads penetrate deeply into the islands of Venice's lagoon, still deserted even in summer and still inhabited by fishermen and farmers. Jesolo is worth a visit just for a ride on the road that abandons the coast at Cavallino to enter the lagoon territory and its villages of **Treporti** and **Lio Piccolo**. The latter has been recently acquired—school, church, and all—by an Austrian businessman who stated that he had no plans to exploit it touristically. It may well be so, but many Venetians are rushing to have another look at Lio Piccolo, in fear that it won't stay untouched for long.

An extra advantage of the Jesolo beaches is their proximity to Venice. From the tip of Punta Sabbioni—endowed with many parking facilities—public boats run back and forth all day to a landing at piazza San Marco. It is a pleasant half hour on the lagoon and a triumphal entry into Venice, much more exciting than the usual arrival by car from Mestre (see the Venice chapter).

The best beach in the Veneto is probably the **Lido** of Venice. Here the hotels are sparse and discreet, and at least two of them range among the best in the country. The part of the beach that is closer to the Lido's major street (Gran Viale) is curiously occupied by thousands of small cabins in neat rows that often leave only a few yards of space near the water. Some hotels, but mostly the city administration itself, own these cabins and rent them out by the day or by the month. The whole area is fenced, with occasional gate openings. There is no admission charge, and city guards patrol the area to make sure nobody undresses on the beach or sits on the sand next to a bundle of clothes. A suggestion to the visitor who wants to take a swim: Go to an area called Zona A, next door to the Hotel Des Bains. It is run by the city, and a small cabin can be rented for the day at an almost affordable price. Or read further, and go to Murazzi or Alberoni for a free swim in much cleaner water.

A walk of half a mile in a southern direction from the Gran Viale will take you to the last—and perhaps most impressive—of the beach hotels, the **Hotel Excelsior**. Now run by Aga Khan's CIGA, it was built at the turn of the century in an amusingly Oriental style and correspondingly voluptuous comfort. It stands a few steps from the summer Casino and the Palazzo del Cinema. During the International Film Festival in September, stars and important guests stay at the Excelsior and swim off its luxuriously serviced beach.

Just after the Excelsior, a long stretch of the seaside is formed by huge blocks of stone (*murazzi*) carefully laid to hold back the winter storms and prevent erosion. Venetians, especially the younger crowd, bathe at the so-called **Murazzi** in total relaxation; the area is never crowded. Farther ahead, after the village of Malamocco, the Lido ends with an area called **Alberoni** (ten minutes by bus from the Excelsior, 15 from downtown). This area is still undeveloped and is a preferred goal for young families and topless women (topless is accepted on all beaches, however).

The coast then continues with the long, thin island of **Pellestrina** (frequent ferry service from Alberoni). It, too, is undeveloped and striking, with its two villages of San Pietro in Volta and Pellestrina (each graced by a renowned, informal fish restaurant), with the Adriatic visible on one side and the lagoon on the other. Swimming is possible, although in most places it is not very comfortable because of the boulders reinforcing the shoreline (there is a small sand beach right in the village of Pellestrina).

The lagoon's southern boundary is occupied by the ancient fishing center of **Chioggia**. The village itself has managed to retain much of its old atmosphere: It is really like a miniature Venice, without the grandiose architecture of the capital city. Most inhabitants are still fishermen (for sardines) and clammers, or they are involved in related activities; and the town is busy with old-fashioned occupations: nets are fixed at people's doors, card games are played at cafés and restaurants, and the day's catch is sorted out and unloaded at the harbor.

The long beach of Chioggia—around a settlement called Sottomarina—has also been developed for tourists. Unfortunately, it will make you feel nostalgic for Jesolo, which probably was the model for Chioggia's local entrepreneurs.

South of Sottomarina, the coast breaks into small islands and marshes, most of them inaccessible by car but fascinating for their wild vegetation and fauna.

The Po Delta

Here, for a change, is an area that has been almost untouched by the recent economic boom in Veneto and has, therefore, kept its intense character as a natural sanctuary. This area stretches between two rivers, the Adige and the Po, down to the border with Emilia-Romagna, where both rivers divide into numerous branches before flowing into the Adriatic. The main feature of this silent, fascinating landscape is the water, slowly moving among very low strips of land inhabited by all sorts of rare birds; if it wasn't for the faint roar of a faraway motor from time to time, you would have the feeling of having travelled way back in time. There is undoubtedly a subtly melancholy character to this vast expanse of water and land; the air is often misty and silence reigns, interrupted only by the calls of seagulls and wild ducks.

Yet here, too, among wood huts still used by fishermen and hunters, among canals and embankments built during centuries of fights against floods, you have the unexpected and almost dreamlike vision of buildings of ancient beauty. Such is the **Benedictine Abbey of Pomposa**, with its early Medieval church and bell tower, rising in the middle of nowhere (50 km/30 miles south of Chioggia on route 309 and 10 km/6 miles past Mesola; Pomposa is technically in Emilia-Romagna).

This area, centering around the towns of Adria (east of Rovigo, the district capital) and Rosolina, on the Adriatic, has recently become very involved with a new Italian passion, so-called ecological tourism. Old-fashioned boats take awestruck city dwellers through lagoons, canals, and marshes, while the guides point out the scattered remnants of ancient fishing and hunting cultures. **Albarella**, a beautiful island off the coast south of Rosolina, has recently been developed into an exclusive resort, and it has become a paradise for wealthy lovers of boating, fishing (including deep-sea tuna fishing in the Adriatic), and bird watching, surrounded as it is by hundreds of small islands untouched by man. Among the island's well-equipped hotels are the **Golf**, with 22 rooms, and the less expensive, 45-room **Capo Nord**.

THE HILL BELT

Directly south of the high mountains, a series of gentle hills descends gradually into the southern plains of the Veneto. This belt runs from Lago di Garda in the west to the eastern boundary with Friuli, and it includes some of the best vineyards in Italy as well as a series of small urban areas with very long histories and, at the moment, promising futures. Starting from the east shore of Lago di Garda, you will encounter names such as Valpolicella, Bardolino, and Soave: all hill towns east of the lake and north of Verona made famous by the local wines. In the hills to the north of the road between Verona and Vicenza are also Valdagno, center of the Marzotto clothing factories, and the Liberty-style (as the Italians call Art Nouveau) town of **Recoaro**, a busy and elegant resort that owes its fortune to the abundant presence of thermal waters.

The province of Padova, down to the south, boasts another important thermal resort, **Abano Terme**. It is set in the hills called Colli Euganei, southwest of Padua, and visited every year by thousands of Italians for one or two weeks of cure in its warm waters (they emerge from underground at 190 °F, and they *do* work—for rheumatism and arthritis as well as respiratory and urinary diseases). Many hotels in Abano now include their own swimming pool fed by the thermal waters. The Colli Euganei are by themselves a small universe, with old monasteries (such as the one at Praglia), ceramic factories, and many patrician villas: A rare Baroque specimen is the **Villa Barbarigo** at Valsanzibio (the interior is not open to the public, but the park and exterior can be visited March 15 to October 31, 10:00 A.M. to noon and 2:00 to 7:00 P.M. Closed on Mondays, Sunday mornings, and the rest of the year). Literature and landscape lovers should not miss delicious **Arquà Petrarca**, where the father of the Italian love lyric spent the last years of his life in a totally idyllic surrounding. The interior of the house, supposedly untouched since Petrarch's death in 1374, is open to visitors; and there is a wonderful restaurant nearby, **La Montanella**, surrounded by a large garden. La Montanella is a perfect initiation to the cuisine of Padova: homemade pasta, duck, quail, deer, and extremely good wines produced by the owners, all at very moderate prices.

Grappa and Piave

Next in a northeasterly direction from Recoaro are the Grappa and the Piave, a mountain and a river equally dear to the Italian historic memory because of the fierce fights there against Austrian troops in World War I. (The Veneto has always been the gateway to Italy for populations invading or trying to invade from the east, from the barbarians who hastened the end of the Roman Empire to the Holy Roman Emperors during the Middle Ages. It took domination by a strong Venice to put an end to these invasions, which were immediately resumed after Venice's fall in 1797.) After a major Italian defeat in the first phase of World War I (the episode is described in Hemingway's *A Farewell to Arms*), Grappa and Piave became the absolute last defense line; beyond them, the Veneto plains and the rest of Italy lay flat and open to the foreign troops. This time, however, the defenses *did* hold; the Austrians were pushed back, at a tremendous price in human lives on both sides. The bodies of 25,000 soldiers, almost all unidentified, are buried in a huge cemetery at the top of Monte Grappa. The Veneti come often to visit this vast memorial and bring their children with them. Not many places in Italy can teach such a solemn lesson on the futility of war, and it may well be that the memories of this and of World War II play an important role in the Veneto approach to life.

The Veneto has given Italy some of its best writers of the past 30 years, from Dino Buzzati to Giuseppe Berto to Luigi Meneghello to the poet Andrea Zanzotto, and it is probably the area where the Italian love for life and beauty blends most harmoniously with a wisdom that sometimes manifests itself as a melancholy awareness of human frailty.

To this section of the Hill Belt, roughly north and northwest of Treviso, belong the landscapes that appear in the works of the first great Venetian painters, from Cima (born north of Treviso in the town of Conegliano, from which he took his name), to Giorgione, born in **Castelfranco**, west of Treviso. (Another great painter, Titian, was born in Pieve di Cadore in the Mountain Belt.) Some of the works of these painters have remained in their hometowns and can be seen there. The Treviso section of the hills is one of the most interesting parts of the Veneto due to its fine climate (the hill roads are jammed on summer weekends, when everybody drives up from the Plains in search of coolness), fabulous wines (this is the realm of the Prosecco), and countless specimens of minor architecture dating from as early as the 13th century.

It is here that the Venetian Republic assigned a territory to Caterina Cornaro at the end of the 15th century. The lady had inherited the kingdom of Cyprus from her husband. Because the island was of enormous strategic importance to Venice, it was decided that the new queen would graciously (although not necessarily with great enthusiasm) hand it over to her mother country in exchange for a dominion on the mainland. The chosen town was **Asolo**, where Caterina held a princely court until her death in 1510. Asolo, to the west-northwest of Treviso, is now famous for the beauty of its surroundings, for having been the residence of celebrities such as Robert Browning and Eleonora Duse, and in our own times for the splendid hotel **Villa Cipriani**, one of the best in the Veneto.

The hill area is also justly famous for its restaurants. At least a dozen of them are well worth the trip from Venice, Treviso, and even Milan, as is proven by the variety of the dialects spoken at the tables. Ranging in price from moderate to moderately expensive, these restaurants grew together with the now-flourishing local economy and are one of the rewards that this area offers to its successful entrepreneurs. Tables are usually for four or more, often for groups of more than ten; the head of the family or the boss of the small firm sits proudly at one end and unblinkingly pays the half-million-lire bill that a ten-person treat would probably cost.

The secret of the economic boom in this area is, as in the nearby plains, the smallness and specialization of the firms and their great ability for marketing and organization, which together constitute what is known as the economic *modello Veneto*. More than 50 percent of the Veneto products go to foreign buyers, from the European Community to the U.S. to the Middle and Far East, and are as varied in nature as eyeglass frames (in the Cadore), shoes and clothes, toys, and sporting goods. A special feature of the Veneto boom is that these firms do not concentrate in one single area but are, for the most part, evenly scattered through the territory so that they are almost unnoticed. Modern production has found a way here to coexist with the old agricultural background, so the fields are still plowed and the crops are still grown; most of the factory workers also moonlight as farmers.

In this context, it is not surprising that the local cuisine, based on very old traditions, has risen to formidable heights, so a visit to idyllic Conegliano or fortressed Castelfranco or to Bassano del Grappa (the seat of scores of ceramic factories) can easily become a pretext for a very memorable meal. Mushrooms, radicchio, home-raised poultry, venison, local vegetables, and great wines are the basic staples of the menus, while the settings can vary from elegant city dining, as in **Al Salisà** in downtown Conegliano, with antique furniture and elegant service, to a countryside patrician villa, such as **Tre Panoce**, on top of a hill near Conegliano, with a large landscaped garden. **Da Lino**, at Solighetto in the Montello area north of Conegliano, boasts an unusual example of high cuisine in a very large and often crowded restaurant, the decor of which is worth the trip just by itself. The unpretentious yet impeccable **Barbesin**, in downtown Castelfranco, serves radicchio, truffles, and all kinds of meats.

A sumptuous and elegant setting for Hill Belt visitors staying the night is also offered by the four-star hotel **Villa Corner della Regina** at Vedelago near Castelfranco. The hotel occupies a 16th-century villa, impeccably restored by its present owner, Count Dona' Dalle Rose of ancient Venetian nobility. The villa is surrounded by a huge garden, and it vies with Asolo's Villa Cipriani for primacy over the Hill Belt accommodations.

THE MOUNTAIN BELT

This is a long rectangle that runs from the Austrian border in northeast Veneto to the northeastern shores of Lago di Garda in the southwest. The most scenic part is definitely in the north, where a lucky series of geological circumstances created the mountains of the Dolomites, and human ingenuity created the jewel town known as Cortina d'Ampezzo. One of the striking things about the Dolomites (originally underwater coral reefs) is the abruptness with which they rise to their more than 10,000 feet from the pine-covered slopes at their bases; another is the rare gray-pink colors of the rocks.

The main Dolomite road, coming east from Bolzano in the Alto Adige through the hairpin bends of the Costalunga, Pordoi, and Falzarego passes to Cortina, gives a good foretaste of the pleasures awaiting mountain lovers. (Driving is not very easy in these mountain roads, which are, however, perfectly well serviced in summer and winter.) Alpine lakes such as Carezza and Misurina; snow-covered peaks such as Sella, Marmolada, and Tofane; deep gorges followed by high panoramic terraces: All these are the features of this landscape, which is dotted with typical Alpine buildings (stone or brick base, wood top and roof). Then the view opens onto the high Cortina valley (3,600 feet) and its glaciers—the site of one of the most exclusive mountain resorts in the world.

Cortina

Cortina has a very long touristic tradition, and it even hosted the Winter Olympics in 1956, but it has never yielded to the temptation of "land development." Because of super-strict regulations, only the richest can afford to buy a few square meters of land here, and only the well-off can afford even a weekend of skiing or summer sight-seeing. So Cortina has remained a small village, but one that nonetheless offers all the luxuries its demanding guests are used to: miles of ski runs at all levels of diffi-culty, funicular service to the peaks of Tofane (10,000 feet) and Faloria (7,000 feet), exclusive hotels such as **Cristallo** and **Miramonti**, and at least a half dozen high-quality restaurants, from **El Toulà** (father of what has become a small chain known for haute cuisine served in a carefully simple decor) to the more affordable **Meloncino al Lago**, specializing in local venison, poultry, and of course mush-rooms, all served on a terrace overlooking a lake. The Meloncino, in front of little Lago Ghedina, is also a very small hotel (six rooms in all), not terribly expensive for Cortina and certainly one of the most coveted by those regulars who prefer to be only a quarter of an hour away from the center of town and perfectly comfortable and pampered in the silence of the mountains.

The Cadore

This name refers to a large mountain area east and south of Cortina, basically the basin of the river Piave. We will also discuss the region to the southwest (technically Valle Zoldana and Valle Agordina), which is very similar to the Cadore in landscape and in geological nature.

The mountain peaks of these areas, all made of dolo-mite, are among the most impressive in the Alps. The valleys, covered with intensely green grass alternating with pine forests, shining with dew on summer mornings and white with snow in winter, are almost too postcard-perfect. At the top of the green slopes, where the rock emerges from the mountain base to aim straight at the sky, comfortable wooden huts receive the courageous trekkers. The huts are called *malghe* or *baite*—summer residences of cow farmers, who take their herds to graze the cleanest fields. Robust women sell cheese, butter, and milk; sleeping accommodations are often available (local trekking maps give all the details).

Yet the most fascinating finds in the Cadore are probably the villages. Most of their present sites have been inhabited since pre-Roman times, and the whole Cadore bears the signs of millennia of human presence, causing a curious feeling in visitors used to the wilderness of other mountain ranges. Even in these days of affluence—and winter tourism is booming—most villages maintain their ancient charm: They include the square with church and bell tower, the grade school, the post office, many steep little alleys, and a spontaneous architecture born of simple taste and long experience.

The usual itinerary for a basic acquaintance with Cadore is a drive of about 30 km (20 miles) from Cortina down the valley of the Boite (a mountain stream) and to Pieve di Cadore. The first sizable village is **San Vito di Cadore** (altitude 3,000 feet), with a 16th-century church (Madonna della Difesa), a pleasant little lake with a restaurant, and too many modern tourist facilities. The road then winds downhill, between the immense slopes of Monte Pelmo at the right and Monte Antelao at the left, to nearby **Borca di Cadore**, in a beautiful valley—a starting point for all kinds of mountain walks. An easy and rewarding one is to **Rifugio Venezia**, a mountain hotel with 60 beds at 6,000 feet, which you can reach in three hours.

Down through Vodo, Venas, and Valle (the latter with a well-preserved historic center and with archaeological evidence of Roman settlements), the road leads to the large village of **Pieve di Cadore**, the birthplace of Titian. The main square—piazza Tiziano, of course—has a 16th-century palazzo and a 15th-century tower. The not-so-documented birth house of Titian hosts a museum of memorabilia related to the great artist (no paintings, although a fresco on the façade of a nearby house is attributed to the boy Titian).

From Pieve di Cadore you can easily head toward Venice (three hours by Autostrada at Vittorio Veneto), using beautiful route 51. Mountain lovers, however, should not miss the memorable valleys Val Zoldana and Valle Agordina, which run parallel to the Boite valley (called Valle Ampezzana) to the southwest and are serviced by efficient although winding roads. In many places these valleys, slightly out of reach for hurried city skiers, have kept more of their original purity than the Ampezzo area.

Route 51 rides along the banks of the River Piave to **Belluno**, the capital city of the Mountain Belt (altitude 1,200 feet). Also a pre-Roman settlement, Belluno is now emerging from a long period of economic distress, and life is very active in the central piazza dei Martiri. The best architecture, though, is to be found in the nearby piazza del Duomo. The Duomo was built in the 16th century; the bell tower in the 18th. The Palazzo dei Rettori, at number 38, is an early Renaissance masterwork flanked by the 12th-century Civic Tower.

From Belluno, a 30-km (20-mile) stretch of route 51 leads to the Autostrada at Vittorio Veneto, running along the large and beautiful Lago di Santa Croce, on the shores of which numerous cafés and restaurants offer healthy mountain food and panoramic terraces at very affordable prices.

The cuisine of the Cadore district is an attraction almost as celebrated as its landscapes, and the locals are even more demanding than the many visitors. So it is not surprising that the area includes restaurants famous in the whole Veneto and beyond, from the pure, family cooking of **Alle Alpi** (in Cima Sappada, at the extreme northeastern corner of Veneto, near Austria) to the sophisticated yet very affordable meals served by Signora De Dea in her **Val Biois** (in Celat, between Agordo and Falcade, at the foot of the Marmolada and not far from beautiful Lago Alleghe southwest of Cortina—a good reason to visit the Valle Agordina).

Altopiano di Asiago

Another mountain area, farther south and west of the Dolomites and due north of Vicenza, is the Altopiano di Asiago, a large tableland at about 3,000 feet that is rich in gentle slopes and is ideal for skiing. In winter it is crowded with weekend visitors from Verona, Vicenza, and Treviso, and in the summer it is one of the preferred rendezvous for outdoor eating, away from the heat of the plains. During World War I this area, together with the neighboring territory to the east, was the object of fierce battles between Italians and Austrians, and it is still scattered with trenches and other mementos; the names of mountains such as Pasubio, Ortigara, and Cima Dodici have entered Italian folklore through songs and novels, and the battle sites are frequently visited by Italian families. Particularly panoramic is the road from Asiago northeast to Enego and Primolano: Large woods of pine trees give way to apple groves and vineyards as the road descends in hairpin curves toward the Brenta valley.

GETTING AROUND

In the Veneto, as in the rest of Italy, public transportation is omnipresent, and most of the time it is comfortable and cheap. Trains go almost everywhere, and bus services connect the stations to the downtown areas. However, while the use of trains is easy and highly recommended, a good knowledge of Italian and quite a bit of patience are prerequisites for a bus trip. So the best way to visit the main cities in the Veneto is by making your headquarters in one of them—Venice, for instance—and taking one-day trips by train, using taxis when required. Almost all the places mentioned in this book are connected to Venice by frequent train service.

Cars are a hindrance in cities such as Padua, Vicenza, Verona, and Treviso; their interesting neighborhoods are in the historic centers, never beyond the reach of reasonable walks. Padua is particularly difficult to tour by car because of the intense traffic and the one-way streets; it is definitely better to drop your car someplace (the train station is perfect) and continue on foot.

But such areas as the Hill Belt and particularly the Mountain Belt should be seen by car, especially in view of the fine restaurants and hotels scattered in the countryside. The roads are comfortable, and visitors will be surprised by how tame Veneto drivers have become compared to their old reputation of hair-raising irresponsibility. Car-rental agencies have outlets in all major centers, and the usual credit cards are accepted everywhere. Most companies have special convenient weekend rates.

A regular boat service connects Venice to Chioggia at the southern end of the lagoon, southeast of Padua, eliminating the long and unpleasant detour by road. The island of Pellestrina is also serviced by comfortable public transportation from Venice. Jesolo and the surrounding beaches can be reached from Venice by public boat with a bus connection from Punta Sabbioni. The Treporti–Lio Piccolo detour requires a car.

Horse Riding in the Veneto

The Italian National Association of Horse Riding (ANTE) has recently established conventions with more than a dozen stables and hotels in the Veneto to offer packages of a week or a weekend of room and board plus horse service (and instructors). The Veneto lends itself beautifully to this kind of vacation, and there are centers in the Mountain, Hill, and Plain belts. The prices vary. For information, write ANTE, via Montello 12, 36034 Malo (Vicenza).

ACCOMMODATIONS REFERENCE

▶ **Hotel Accademia.** Via Scala 12, 37121 **Verona.** Tel: (045) 59-62-22; Telex: 480874.

▶ **Hotel Antica Porta Leona.** Corticella Leoni 3, 37121 **Verona.** Tel: (045) 59-54-99.

▶ **Hotel Capo Nord.** Isola di Albarella, 45010 **Rosolina.** Tel: (0426) 671-39. Open May through September.

▶ **Villa Cipriani.** Via Canova 298, 31011 **Asolo.** Tel: (0423) 554-44; Telex: 411060.

▶ **Villa Condulmer.** Località Zerman, 31021 **Mogliano Veneto.** Tel: (041) 45-71-00. This splendid villa is surrounded by a large park.

▶ **Villa Corner della Regina.** Località Cavasagra, 31100 **Vedelago.** Tel: (0423) 48-14-81.

▶ **Hotel Cristallo.** Via Menardi 42, 32043 **Cortina d'Ampezzo.** Tel: (0436) 42-81; Telex: 440090.

▶ **Hotel Donatello.** Piazza del Santo, 35123 **Padua.** Tel: (049) 365-15. Rooms and a pleasant terrace overlook the piazza Santo.

▶ **Hotel Due Torri.** Piazza Sant'Anastasia 4, 37121 **Verona.** Tel: (045) 59-50-44; Telex: 480524.

▶ **Golf Hotel.** Isola di Arbarella, 45010 **Rosolina.** Tel: (0426) 670-78. Open April through October.

▶ **Locanda da Lino.** Via Brandolini 1, 31050 **Solighetto.** Tel: (0438) 821-50. A few comfortable rooms attached to this famous restaurant near Treviso.

▶ **Ristorante Hotel Meloncino al Lago.** Lago Ghedina, 32043 **Cortina d'Ampezzo.** Tel: (0436) 603-76.

▶ **Hotel Miramonti Majestic.** Località Pezziè 103, 32043 **Cortina d'Ampezzo.** Tel: (0436) 42-01; Telex: 440069.

▶ **Le Padovanelle.** 35020 **Ponte di Brenta.** Tel: (049) 62-56-22; Telex: 430454. These pleasant chalets, near Padua, are built around a garden; swimming pool and tennis courts.

▶ **Parc Hotel Victoria**. Corso Italia 1, 32043 **Cortina d'Ampezzo**. Tel: (0436) 32-46; Telex: 44004. An elegantly rustic hotel set in a beautiful garden; moderately priced— by the standards of expensive Cortina.

▶ **Relais El Toulà**. 31100 **Ponzano Veneto**. Tel: (0422) 96-90-23; Telex: 433029 Toula'I. Just 11 km (7 miles) from downtown Treviso, El Toulà is a perfect retreat: only ten rooms and one suite in a villa, perfect service, a first-class restaurant, outdoor swimming pool, and a large garden.

▶ **Rifugio Venezia**. **San Vito di Cadore** 32046 **Belluno**. Tel: (0436) 96-84. Open July 15 to September 15. Reservations recommended.

TRENTINO–ALTO ADIGE

By Paolo Lanapoppi

The great attractions of this Alpine region are its land-scapes and its climate. The area includes (at its west) the eastern part of the Alps, from the watershed down, and, in the east, a large section of the Dolomites, a mountain range different in origin and structure from the Alps. While the Alps, a much older chain, have been somewhat rounded by glaciers and atmospheric erosion, the Dolomites have emerged from the ocean relatively recently—they are really gigantic coral reefs—and because of this they often rise vertically from their green slopes.

The area has been inhabited since prehistoric times, and is rich in monuments dating from the Middle Ages, particularly castles and walled citadels. An important tourist trade, established in the 18th century, has been much developed in the past 40 years, during which winter tourism tied to skiing has come to surpass the area's traditional summer activity.

MAJOR INTEREST

Trentino
Madonna di Campiglio and the Dolomites of
   Brenta
Mountain lakes and streams

Alto Adige
Alpine and Dolomitic valleys
Merano
Bolzano

Medieval castles
Tirolese cooking

We start our coverage with the Trentino, the southern half of the area—bordered on the west and south by Lombardy and on the east and south by the Veneto—and then move up to Alto Adige, which borders Switzerland and Austria on its north and the Veneto (and of course the Trentino) on the south. The entire area is in effect divided up the middle by the Adige and Isarco river valleys, which form a continuous corridor from Verona at the south and run more or less north through the towns of Trento and Bolzano and up to the Passo di Brennero and Austria. (The Autostrada follows this corridor.)

To the west of this corridor the Alps dominate, and to the east, south of the Bressanone–San Candido line, the Dolomites.

THE TRENTINO

As in the Alto Adige to the north, the Trentino's territory is divided between mountains of Alpine and Dolomitic origin. The division runs along the Valli Giudicarie, parallel to Lago di Garda at the northwest, and is especially dramatic and beautiful at the world-famous mountain resort Madonna di Campiglio, with the Alpine Monte Adamello on the west and the Dolomitic Gruppo di Brenta on the east.

Unlike in Alto Adige, only Italian was spoken here during the long history of union with the Austrian empire (along with Alto Adige, the Trentino was annexed to Italy in 1918). Agriculture and especially the production of wine are still among the main sources of income in the area, although in the past 30 years clusters of small industries have been established in the Valle dell'Adige between Verona and Trento. As in the nearby Veneto, however, industrial workers usually have not given up their connection with the land and often moonlight as farmers. This area provides an interesting example of semi-industrial development that has spread affluence without disfiguring the environment. In other valleys, deeply cut between high mountains, a tradition of poverty has been rapidly overcome by the boom of the tourist trade, in both summer and winter. The Trentino, like the Alto Adige to the north, is dotted with hundreds of hotels and *pensioni* of all sizes and price ranges. It is surprising to see that efficiency and cleanliness are superb in pretty much every one of them, so the chances are very high, especially in the summer, that a visitor will find a pleasant hotel very close to any area. (Not so in winter, and especially not in the dramatic Christmas period.)

Trento

The main historic event in the life of this quiet, industrious urban center, a crossroads of the German and Italian worlds, was the Council of Trent, a meeting of Catholic bishops held between 1545 and 1563 to formulate a Catholic answer to the Reformation movement. Important and lasting changes were introduced in Catholic doctrine and discipline during the 18 years of passionate discussion here. The location had been recommended by a great scholar and humanist from Trento, Bishop Bernardo Clesio.

A fine panoramic view over the city can be enjoyed from the area called Verruca or Doss Trento, a short ride from the railway station west across the river Adige.

The city's center pivots around the **piazza del Duomo** and the **via Belenzani,** a handsome street lined with 15th- and 16th-century buildings where many of the Catholic prelates lived during the long council years. The Duomo has a 14th-century façade; other interesting buildings on the square are the Torre Civica (11th century), the Castelletto dei Vescovi (13th century, at the right of the apse), and the Palazzo Pretorio (13th century, next to the tower). Inside this palazzo, the **Museo Diocesano** includes precious wood sculptures and Renaissance tapestries (open 9:00 A.M. to noon and 2:00 P.M. to 7:00 P.M.; closed Wednesday afternoons).

A short walk from via Belenzani, through via Manci and via San Marco, is the **Castello del Buonconsiglio,** for many centuries the residence of the bishops of Trento. The Palazzo Magno, one of the buildings included within its walls, was greatly embellished by Bishop Clesio in an attempt to keep up with the great palaces that the noble cardinals were building for themselves all over Italy. The second floor includes an interesting **Archaeological Museum,** with artifacts from the prehistoric sites discovered in the Trentino; this material has invaded the bedroom, study, library, and wardrobe formerly used by the bishop. Other rooms are occupied by the **Museo del Risorgi-**

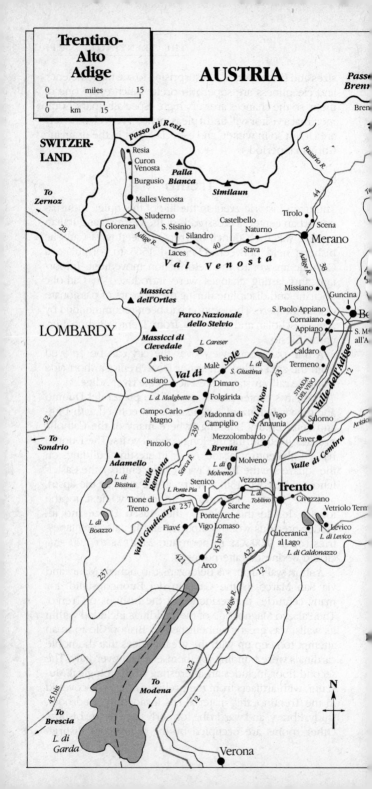

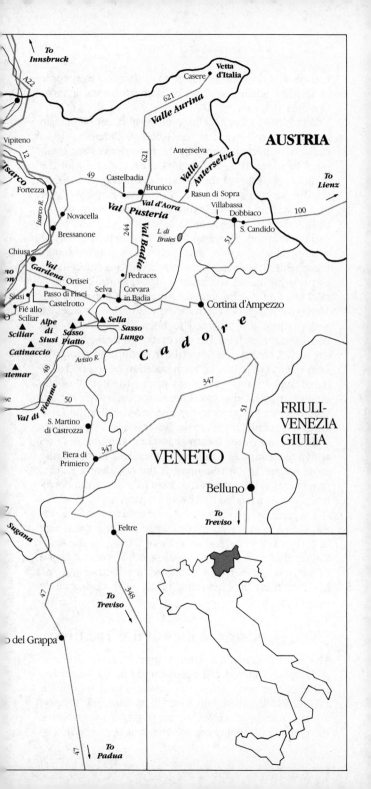

mento, with documents related to the fights of the people of Trentino against the Austrian domination and in favor of annexation to Italy.

Very close to the castello, on a small street off via San Marco, the restaurant at the **Hotel Accademia,** vicolo Colico 6, is justly honored by the most demanding gourmets in town. The menu varies every month, with the addition of dishes of the day as suggested by the season and by the chef's inspiration. With a bit of luck you may find *sguazet di capretto,* a dish based on kid meat, but the tagliolini are also memorable, as are the trout with herbs and the veal with asparagus. The wines are the best of this wine-producing region, and the prices are astonishingly reasonable. The restaurant is attached to a very nice hotel of the same name. A reputation for regional cooking is also enjoyed by the famous restaurant **Chiesa,** via San Marco 64, which is a bit more expensive than Accademia, and perhaps too crowded to keep the standards at a consistently high level; but you cannot go wrong by ordering such Trento specialties as the frog soup, the *strangola-preti* (a kind of pasta that is supposed to be so good as to have caused a few gluttonous priests to choke), or the cheese strudel. Other good restaurants, all rather reasonable in price, abound in this refined city: Try the **Orso Grigio,** via degli Orti 19, or the **Roma,** via San Simonino 6.

The **Grand Hotel Trento** is another comfortable hotel with a restaurant, **Al Caminetto**—excellent, but not in the same league as the restaurant at the Accademia. A nice, quiet hotel is **Villa Madruzzo,** 3 km (2 miles) from downtown and surrounded by a beautiful garden.

For people driving on the Autostrada as well as for those staying in Trento, a worthwhile detour is the village of Civezzano, 5 km (3 miles) east of Trento, for the **Maso Cantanghel.** In a marvelous setting, this restaurant is one of the best in the Trentino, although it is hard to find. Ask for directions at Civezzano, or call the restaurant at (0461) 85-87-14.

The Food and Wines of the Trentino

The famous Alto Adige knödel appears in the Trentino with slightly different ingredients, and with the Italianized name of *canederli.* Among the pastas, a local specialty is ravioli, usually filled with meat. Beef, hare, and venison are the main meat staples; a great tradition also concerns the cooking of trout (*trote alla trentina,* accompanied by mint, lemon, and raisins) and eel (roasted and then cooked in wine—a real delicacy).

In fact, this region, with its dozens of small and large lakes and countless mountain streams, is the best place in Italy for freshwater fishing. Four small mountain lakes (each less than a square mile in surface) that are excellent for fishing are: Lago di Malga Bissina; Lago di Malga Boazzo; Lago Careser; and Lago delle Malghette. Information and fishing permits can be obtained at Provincia di Trento, Servizio Foreste, Caccia e Pesca, Torri di Gardolo (Trento). (Torri di Gardolo is on the outskirts of Trento.)

Dozens of DOC wines (Denominazione di Origine Controllata) are produced in the hills of the Trentino. Cabernet and Merlot are the best-known red wines, while among the area's whites are Pinot, Riesling, and Traminer, nowadays sold all over Italy.

West of Trento:
The Dolomites of Brenta

The mountains of the Trentino are so consistently beautiful that ranking them on the basis of looks alone isn't feasible. However, an exploration of the area west and north of **Trento** will give you a good idea of the majesty of these landscapes. From Trento on route 45 *bis* it is easy to reach Toblino after a 20-km (12-mile) drive that passes through Vezzano. Little **Lago di Toblino** is delightful and romantic, with a Medieval castle that is one of the most charming in the Trentino, and that now hosts a wonderful restaurant, **Ristorante Castel Toblino**, specializing in regional food (mushrooms, venison, and trout). At **Sarche**, route 237 leads west to Ponte Arche and Tione di Trento along the river Sarca and the long, artificial Lago Ponte Pia. A good restaurant farther south of Sarche, at Arco, just before Lago di Garda, is the **Cantina Marchetti**, located in a 16th-century palazzo.

From Ponte Arche, a 16-km (10-mile) panoramic road runs south through the pleasant village of Vigo Lomaso, with a handsome Medieval church (San Lorenzo; 11th and 13th centuries), to the **Fiavè plateau**, with its Torbiera, a site where prehistoric settlements have been discovered and studied. Corn growing and animal farming are the main activities of these small centers, built in tight, picturesque clusters, with narrow streets and Medieval porticoes.

From Ponte Arche toward the north, route 421 runs through the village of **Stenico**, with one of the most ancient and best-preserved castles in the Trentino. Within the castle walls are Romanesque and Gothic buildings, with interesting 16th-century frescoes (ask the custodian for permission to visit). The quiet, pleasant, and reasonably priced **Hotel Flora** is a nice place to stay here. About 20 km (12 miles) after Stenico, a wide plateau opens up with beautiful **Lago di Molveno** at its center. A good restaurant at Molveno is **Al Caminetto**.

Farther west from Ponte Arche, at Tione, route 239 runs north through the **Val Rendena** (river Sarca). In the village of **Pinzolo**, it is customary to stop at the **Church of San Vigilio** to look at the outside frescoes representing the *danza macabra,* a memento mori painted in 1539. Val Rendena, a particularly green valley with small villages and much animal farming, is deeply cut between two mountain giants: the **Gruppo dell'Adamello** in the west and the **Gruppo di Brenta** in the east. A large part of this area is now a national park with an abundance of rivers and lakes and inhabited by many species of deer, a few bears and eagles, and the more common ermines and foxes. Pinzolo also affords one of the best restaurants in the Trentino, **Prima o Poi,** on the road to Campiglio, in the town of Le Pozze. It is a small restaurant run by lovers of food, and it offers the most refined versions of the local cuisine.

Madonna di Campiglio, to the north of Pinzolo, is a justly famous center for winter sports as well as summer residence. Here we are in fully Alpine landscape. The first hotel was built in this privileged valley in the year 1872; soon afterward Madonna di Campiglio became a fashionable resort for the European aristocracy and the high bourgeoisie. Since the 1930s ski facilities have been added and expanded, and today more than 40 miles of ski slopes of all levels of difficulty surround the area. Among the restaurants at Madonna di Campiglio, **La Genzianella** is probably the best; try their *gnoccone di verdura*—a vegetable and dumpling concoction—and the roasted meats.

Toward the **Valle di Sole**, through Folgárida and Dimaro—also well equipped for skiing—the road joins route 42 and continues toward **Malè**. The valley widens as it descends toward Lago di Santa Giustina, and the pine forests give more and more room to the fruit groves, which, together with tourism, are the main source of local income. **Ristorante Cusiano**, at Cusiano Valle di Sole, west of Dimaro, is a delightful adventure in genuine food at reasonable prices. At Malè a good restaurant is **La Segosta**, while visitors with enough time for a detour to the Parco Nazionale dello Stelvio (leaving route 42 northbound at Cusiano) will find excellent food at **Il Mulino**, near the town of Peio, in an old water mill remodeled to offer a most pleasant setting.

Following route 42 east of Malè through the Valle di Sole, you will come to **Lago di Santa Giustina**, the largest among dozens of artificial lakes that produce abundant electricity for Trentino as well as nearby Veneto. Oblong in shape, it is very pleasantly inserted in the green landscape of this gentle valley. From Lago di Santa Giustina route 43 leads back to Trento through the Valle di Non. About 11 km (7 miles) south of the lake it is well worth your time to take a short detour to the east to Vigo Anaunia and its hilltop *castello,* Thun, built in the 13th century and rebuilt in the 16th. This is really an entire walled compound of buildings, and is one of the most striking castles in the Trentino; it affords a splendid view over the Valle di Non (ask the custodian for visits). At Mezzolombardo, back at the Valle dell'Adige, north of Trento, **Ristorante Al Sole**, via Rotaliana 5, specializes in meats and in regional dishes at affordable prices.

East of Trento: Valle di Cembra and Valle di Fiemme

The river Avisio flows very deep in a canyonlike gorge inside the Valle di Cembra, which runs northeast from the Valle dell'Adige between Trento and Mezzolombardo. At the gorge's edge, about 600 feet above the riverbed, is a green plateau dotted with villages and fruit groves. The town of **Cavalese**, technically in the Valle di Fiemme, is a preferred resort for Venetians and other city dwellers of the Veneto. It is well serviced with ski slopes and summer trails winding gently through the surrounding pastures. The road (routes 48 and 50) then continues eastward and then down toward Feltre in the Veneto, with superbly scenic mountain passes leading through the towns of San Martino di Castrozza and Fiera di Primiero on the way.

At Faver, back in the middle of the Valle di Cembra, is an old *maso* that has been transformed into **All'Olivo**, an excellent restaurant with genuine, simple regional cooking. (For an explanation of *maso,* see the Alto Adige section below.)

East of Trento: The Valsugana

Running east from Trento, this rather narrow valley leads to the Veneto's Bassano del Grappa and to Venice. It contains, unfortunately, the best road connection between Trento and the Treviso-Venice area (route 47), so traffic can be a nuisance in spite of many attempts to enlarge the road. The main attractions of the valley are the beautiful **Lago di Caldonazzo** and **Lago di Levico**, much loved by Venetians looking for a few days of rest and clean air.

At Calceranica, along the Lago di Caldonazzo, the **Ristorante Concorde** has a very pleasant garden and terrace over the lake, and takes special pride in ancient recipes, but just its modern *gnocchetti verdi* (small green gnocchi, called spaetzel in the Alto Adige) would be sufficient to recommend it.

THE ALTO ADIGE

The name Alto Adige refers to the very large basin of the river Adige, which originates in the northwest corner of the region, flows down through its main settlements (Merano and Bolzano), and continues its southbound course through Trento and Verona before running into the Adriatic Sea just south of Venice. At 255 miles, the Adige is the second-longest river in Italy (the longest is the Po). Of course, only the valleys in this very mountainous area are settled; they are often different from one another in aspect, vegetation, and local customs, and some have even kept a language of their own, called Ladino, which is an independent offspring of ancient Latin.

Until the end of World War I, the Alto Adige, like the Trentino, had been part of the Austrian empire. When Italy turned out to be on the winning side of that war, it was agreed that she would annex both areas, thus making the political border coincide with the Alpine watershed. (The "liberation" of Trentino–Alto Adige was one of the main reasons Italy entered the war against Austria.) While the annexation did not create serious problems in the

Trentino to the south (traditionally Italian speaking), it did in the Alto Adige, where the population was decidedly Austrian in language, traditions, and loyalty.

The area had been part of the greater Tirol, centering on Innsbruck, and its proper historical name was—and still is—Südtirol. The nationalistic government of Mussolini worsened the situation considerably by injecting large groups of Italian-speaking newcomers in an effort to submerge the German-speaking locals. Italian settlements, however, took place mostly in the cities, leaving the mountains and valleys untouched. In 1921 a mere 10 percent of the inhabitants spoke primarily Italian, against 76 percent German.

Bolzano, the capital city, had only 10,000 inhabitants then. Today it has more than 100,000 inhabitants, a large majority of whom are Italian-speaking descendants of the "colonizers." After World War II the Italian government conferred a large degree of autonomy on Trentino–Alto Adige, but in spite of this the tension between the Italian- and German-speaking communities is still quite strong. Today the Italian-speaking population is about 35 percent of the total Alto Adige population of 500,000.

There are three main accesses to the Alto Adige from the north, in correspondence with deep cuts in the Alpine range. They are **Resia** at the west (Val Venosta), **Brennero** (Brenner Pass) at the center (Val d'Isarco), and **Dobbiaco** (Val Pusteria) at the far east. Each has a long Alpine valley running south of it, along which most of the Alto Adige settlements are to be found.

Together with tourism, farming is the principal source of revenue in this active and economically comfortable region. Farmers here usually live in homes separated from the villages and surrounded by their own land (whereas in southern Italy they tend to live in the villages, walking, or today driving, to the fields). These neat, well-kept homes are usually built of brick or stone and plastered and painted white, with a characteristic wood roof.

Inside, these homes invariably contain a *stube,* the ground-floor kitchen and living room, paneled in wood and endowed with a majestic ceramic stove that is the center of the family life. Together, the home and the land constitute a *maso* (in German, *Hof*), averaging about 60 acres. As it has been for centuries, this is still the amount of land considered sufficient to support a family. Under Italian law only one of a family's sons or daughters inherits the *maso,* and is obliged to compensate the others; this has contributed to the survival of a prosperous farming community in this part of Italy.

The Food and Wine of the Alto Adige

The gastronomic traditions of this region have kept a personality of their own and are distinctly different from those of the rest of Italy, as well as from those of nearby Trentino. Clearly belonging to Austria and the mountains, the cooking is centered around hearty, substantial dishes necessary to sustain a population of mountaineers. A staple, served in countless variations, is *knödel,* basically balls of bread to which pretty much anything can be added: flour, milk, and butter (Semmel Knödel), bacon and salami (Tirol Knödel), liver (Leber Knödel), even apricots (Marillen Knödel).

Among the meat dishes, a delicious specialty is *Speck,* smoked pork prepared with different spices according to recipes that vary with the area and often with the family. *Speck* is served as an appetizer or as an entrée, often accompanied by smoked sausages (*Kaminwurzen*) and horseradish. Pork, smoked or boiled, is also the base of *Bauernschmaus,* an entrée usually served with sauerkraut. A specialty of Val Pusteria are *Tirtlen,* large fried ravioli, while Merano contributes a snail soup, *Meraner Schneckensuppe,* and the Val Venosta a soup of rye bread, *Bauernbrotsuppe.*

Sauerkraut, red cabbage, potatoes, and mushrooms are the main vegetables. A real must to try here is the *Pfifferle,* a local mushroom fried with garlic and onion. Among the desserts, the king is the apple strudel, but there is also a delicious nut strudel and even a poppy strudel (*Mohnstrudel*); another favored dessert is *Schmarrn,* an omelet filled with prunes or cherries or apples—or with all of them.

The Alto Adige is also an important producer of wines, many of which are well known in Italy and abroad and almost all of which are protected by the official DOC system (Denominazione di Origine Controllata). Eighty percent of the production here is of red wines. Cabernet and Merlot, slightly lighter than Burgundies, are usually served with meats and are loved by the population of the nearby Veneto; Malvasia is great with *Speck,* while the Pinot Nero or Blauburgunder goes with venison. Among the white wines, the Pinot Grigio (Ruelander) has become a preferred aperitif all over Italy, while Sauvignon is a dry, slightly fruity wine ideal for trout. Gewürztraminer, full and round, goes equally well with fish and desserts.

Val Venosta

From 4,500 feet above sea level at the **Passo di Resia**, this valley, drained by the river Adige, reaches first south and then east to the handsome town of Merano. Most of the Alto Adige valleys are very deeply cut through the mountains, so their modest height above sea level doesn't give a good idea of the height of the surrounding peaks. At the south of the Val Venosta are the *massicci* (massifs) **Ortles** and **Cevedale**, massifs around 12,000 feet above sea level, while at the north the Palla Bianca and Similaun are over 11,000.

The Val Venosta is remarkably wide and green, with a dozen small centers in which you frequently encounter Medieval churches and castles (we follow the valley down and east to Merano). Five km (3 miles) out of Malles Venosta, near the village of Burgusio, is the 12th-century **Abbey of Monte Maria**, an imposing compound that was the highest above sea level of any Benedictine abbey in Europe. Although largely rebuilt in the 15th century, the abbey keeps some of the original features, among which is a fresco of 1180. Both the monastery and its chapel are open to visitors. Just below Malles is the village of **Glorenza**, still surrounded by its Medieval walls (rebuilt in the 16th century), which give a good idea of the appearance of a fortressed town in Medieval times.

Up above the town of Sluderno the **Castello di Coira**, from the 13th century, is the most interesting among the Val Venosta castles because of its excellent state of conservation and because of the precious objects it contains (open March to October, 10:30 A.M. to noon and 2:00 P.M. to 4:30 P.M.; closed on Mondays)—see the armor room in particular. The church of San Sisinio in the village of Sisinio also dates from the 13th century; the Coldrano castle near Silandro dates from the 16th century.

About 16 km (10 miles) down, the **Schloss Kastelbell** at Castelbello has been accurately restored to its 13th-century appearance and is open inside, though unfurnished. (Open June 15 to September 15, on Monday, Wednesday, Friday, and Saturday, 9:00 A.M. to 11:00 A.M.) Naturno also has its 13th-century castle, now turned into the **Hotel Burg Hochnaturns**, with a garden and very nice views.

At Stava, just outside of Naturno, is one of the best restaurants in the valley, the **Schnalserhof**, reasonably priced and rich in Alto Adige specialties. Another fine restaurant, specializing in venison, is **Stocker**, at Curon Venosta back up at the head of the valley near the Passo di Resia. At Malles both locals and visitors go to the informal and inexpensive **Al Moro**, a dining room connected with the **Hotel Plavina**. There are good hotels and guesthouses in every village of any size in the Val Venosta.

In this valley perhaps more than in others, the contrast between the luscious green of the lower part and the snow-covered peaks above is particularly striking. In the spring this territory offers a totally magical spectacle of flowering trees, since it is an area given mostly to the growing of pears, apricots, and especially apples—of which the Alto Adige is the largest single producer in Europe.

Merano

Close to Merano, to the town's west, the valley widens and a quantity of vineyards starts to appear next to the fruit groves. The gentle landscape of Merano has attracted tourists and vacationers since the 18th century: first the Austrian nobility, then the Viennese and European bourgeoisie. An important feature of this climate is the lack of humidity and the mildness of the temperature (it is the northernmost part of Europe where palm trees can grow). To its luxurious 19th-century hotels Merano has added a great number of recent accommodations, and it is now booming with winter as well as summer tourism because of the splendid skiing facilities installed on the slopes of the surrounding mountains.

The Medieval town, on the right bank of the river Passirio, centers around the Gothic via dei Portici. Near that street are the **Castello Principesco**, a castle built in 1470 and furnished mostly with original items (open 9:00 A.M. to noon and 2:30 P.M. to 4:30 P.M.; Saturday 10:30 A.M. to noon and 2:00 P.M. to 5:30 P.M.; closed on Sunday), and the **Duomo**, a Gothic building of the 15th century with a curiously crenellated façade. Along the river Passirio there are two pleasant walks, called Passeggiata d'Inverno and Passeggiata d'Estate (Winter Walk and Summer Walk); the first faces south, the second north.

The restaurant tradition in Merano is alive and well: At

via San Marco 26, the **Villa Mozart**, run by the internationally famous chef Andreas Hellrigl, is one of Italy's choice
hotels and, with a kitchen serving at least a dozen memorable specialties—including sturgeon, lamb, trout, and
deer—one of its choice restaurants as well. Unfortunately, it is not easy to obtain a table in this coveted
institution (reservations are necessary, and only parties of
four or more are accepted; Tel: 0473-306-30.). The best
way to enjoy the experience is to stay overnight at the
hotel, thus being assured access to the dining room,
which in the summer moves to the garden outdoors.
Andrea, via Galilei 44 (also owned by Mr. Hellrigl), and
Flora, via dei Portici 74, are also exceptionally good restaurants in this gastronomic paradise. The former is perfect in decor and service, while the latter is a bit less
formal but also more affordable, serving salmon, trout,
venison, and great pasta (a specialty in season is the
ravioli filled with Pfinfferle mushrooms).

In addition to restaurants, some of the region's best
lodging is to be found in and around Merano too. Among
the truly remarkable first-class hotels are the aforementioned Villa Mozart, the **Palace**, on the via Cavour, with a
large garden and swimming pool, and the **Castel Labers**,
several km (a couple of miles) out of town on the road to
Scena. It also has a swimming pool and a striking garden.
Another outlying hotel is the **Castel Freiberg**, a converted
14th-century castle 8 km (5 miles) south of Merano in the
town of Freiberg. The Medieval atmosphere is still strong
here, in spite of the modern conveniences, and the views
are incredible. Good walks are to be had in the surrounding hills.

About 3 km (2 miles) north of Merano and a short
distance from the village of **Tirolo** is the **Castel Tirolo**,
built in the 12th century by the counts of Venosta, who
later became the rulers of the entire region. It was in
1363 that their last descendant handed their possessions
over to the Hapsburgs of Austria, who were to rule until
1918 (in 1420 the capital was moved from Merano to
Innsbruck). Although still inhabited, the castle can be
visited from March 1 to October 31, 9:30 A.M. to noon and
2:00 P.M. to 5:00 P.M. (closed on Monday), and guided
tours are available every hour. The most interesting parts
are the Romanesque chapel, with 14th-century frescoes;
the main entrance door, with 12th-century sculptures;
and the Sala del Trono (throne room), which also affords
a magnificent view.

Main route 38 leads southeast out of Merano directly down to Bolzano.

Bolzano

This city lies in a deep but very wide valley at only 600 feet above sea level. Bolzano is located in the heart of Alto Adige on the north-south Isarco-Adige river corridor from the Passo di Brennero down through Trento to Verona. Since the early Middle Ages it has been an important crossroad for commerce between Italy and Germany and famous for its trade fairs. Originally ruled by the bishops of Trento, it was conquered in the 13th century by the Merano-based counts of Tirol, thus passing to the German-speaking side of the Alps. (It seems that originally the local language had been Italian—a rather academic point that is often made nowadays in the disputes between the Italian and German communities.) It remained under the Hapsburgs (with the usual Napoleonic exception) until 1918, when it was annexed to Italy. The Fascist government then tried to modify the ethnic balance in favor of the Italian element, which created a rather tense atmosphere still felt today by a large part of the population.

The city lies at the confluence of the Talvera and Isarco rivers, just a couple of miles before they join the Adige. The presence of these rivers and the green slopes of the surrounding mountains give Bolzano a particularly friendly aspect; in a successful encounter between man and nature, Bolzano has become a city where ecological balance with the environment is never lost.

Bolzano has a charming Medieval town center at the fork between the Talvera and Isarco rivers. It is striking, when walking along the old, well-preserved, basically Gothic **via dei Portici**, to compare it with the Gothic centers of other Italian cities, such as in Umbria or Tuscany; the feeling here is totally different—and clearly Nordic, with the pointed roofs, the characteristic balconies, even the way people dress and act. At the center of the Old Town is the **Duomo**, Gothic and accompanied by a handsome bell tower of the 13th century; a few steps away is the **Convento dei Dominecani**, a monastery that has a chapel with 14th-century frescoes influenced by Giotto, and a very pleasant 15th-century cloister.

Even more graceful and intimate is the cloister of the **Chiesa dei Francescani** across via dei Portici, a church worth a visit also because of the impressive **Altarpiece of the Cappella della Vergine** (c. 1500)—one of the best examples of Flamboyant Gothic to be found in the Alto Adige.

At the Franciscan church, via di Castel Roncolo leads after a km (half a mile) to **Castel Roncolo**, originally built in the 13th century and reconstructed in the 16th. It contains a unique series of nonreligious frescoes (14th and 15th centuries) representing knights and dames and scenes from popular romances of chivalry, such as the story of Tristan and Isolde. The style is Gothic, and the atmosphere is quite moving because of its mixture of stylized elegance and delicious naiveté. A visit to this well-preserved castle gives a good idea of life at a Tirolese court in the late Middle Ages (open 10:00 A.M. to noon and 3:00 P.M. to 7:00 P.M., closed Sunday and Monday).

The best restaurant in Bolzano is probably **Da Abramo**, piazza Gries 16, with very elegant Viennese decor (outdoor dining in the summer) and a varied menu oriented toward the cooking of the nearby Veneto. A very pleasant experience is also offered by the new restaurant at **Castel Mareccio**, very close to the city center and surrounded by vineyards. The restaurant is rather informal and popular with both the Italian and German communities, perhaps because of its intelligent menu, which includes international dishes as well as local specialties. **Rastbicher**, via Cadorna 11 (outdoor service in summer), and **Tabasco**, via Conciapelli 38, are two other popular restaurants in the middle price range.

This center of commerce and tourism is not lacking in good and very good hotels; you can also visit Bolzano while staying in one of the many secluded, idyllic hotels in the surrounding region. In town, the luxurious and centrally located **Park Hotel Laurino** has a splendid garden. The **Hotel Scala Stiegl** is also close to the center as well as to the cable car to the Altopiano del Renon, and boasts a garden too, where guests can dine in good weather. Both hotels are open all year.

Hotel Reichrieglerhof is just 3 km (2 miles) out of Bolzano in the village of Guncina, but it is very rural and very quiet, and has a nice garden with a swimming pool and a view over the city. Its 18 rooms, all with private baths, are reasonably priced. On the Strada del Vino (see below) about 10 km (6 miles) out of town is the **Schloss Korb**, a Medieval castle that has been perfectly restored. In the middle of vineyards and orchards, it has great views and a large garden that is endowed with two swimming pools (one indoor and one outdoor) and several tennis courts; open Easter through October.

The **Altopiano del Renon** is a green plateau overlooking Bolzano from the northeast, at 3,600 feet above sea level. It offers a splendid view of the surrounding Dolomites, notably the peaks of Latemar, Catenaccio, and Sciliar, and can be reached either by car—24 km (15 miles) starting from via Rencio at the eastern limit of the city—or by a comfortable cable car departing from via Renon, a 20-minute walk from the Duomo.

The Strada del Vino (Wine Route)

This pretty route follows a wide and gentle valley running south from Bolzano, slightly to the west of the parallel Valle dell'Adige leading to Trento. For unhurried visitors it is a worthwhile alternative to the Autostrada between Bolzano and Trento. It runs through Appiano and Caldaro and reaches the river Adige again at Salorno. The landscape along this route is one of gentle hills covered with uninterrupted vineyards and dotted with small villages that are famous in Italy for the wines that bear their names.

Wine shops and restaurants are, of course, abundant. Before Appiano, at Cornaiano, is the **Bellavista Markhof**, via Belvedere 7, a former Benedictine monastery specializing in venison and serving its own wines; at **Termeno** (Tramin in German, and the home of well-known Traminer wine), the **Traminerhof**, strada del Vino 33, offers the basic staples of any Alto Adige menu: smoked pork, sauerkraut, goulash, and knödel; and at San Michele all'Adige, **Da Silvio**, via Brennero 2, offers a very inexpensive fixed-price menu (*menù degustazione*) that includes appetizers, first and second courses, and dessert. The dishes at Da Silvio vary from the purely Alto Adige cooking (San Michele is technically in Trentino), and include homemade ravioli, risotto, and freshwater fish.

Val d'Isarco

This long north–south valley is the traditional route between Germany and Italy, via Innsbruck and the **Passo di Brennero**. An autostrada now runs the 89 km (55 miles) between the pass and Bolzano. The best way to enjoy the landscape, however, is probably to leave Bolzano on route 12, driving northeast through Siusi and then Castelrotto to the Passo di Pinei (on the other side of which are Ortisei and the Val Gardena). On the way to Siusi, the imposing mass of Mount Sciliar dominates the landscape on the right side. The town of **Siusi** is a famous ski resort, with slopes of all levels of difficulty at nearby Alpe di Siusi, 6,000 feet above sea level. But Alpe di Siusi is a marvelous place to visit in the summer too, when the plateau is covered with flowers and grass among the pinewoods. After Siusi, the road reaches Castelrotto and then winds through Passo di Pinei, where the splendid **Val Gardena** opens on the right-hand side. The best hotels in the Val d'Isarco are to be found in Bressanone, near Siusi, and in the Val Gardena.

In Val Gardena you are in fully Dolomitic territory, as is apparent from the vertical peaks of Mounts Sella, Sassolungo, and Sasso Piatto, all over 10,000 feet high. Ortisei and Selva are the main centers of this valley, a real skier's paradise and one of the most crowded resort areas in the Alto Adige.

Back through the Passo di Pinei and in the Val d'Isarco heading northeast, you reach Chiusa and the impressive plateau of the town of **Bressanone**, a very old and tranquil urban center where the Tirol bishops had their residence. The **Duomo** (13th century, but remodeled in the 18th) and its handsome 14th-century cloister, together with the nearby **Palazzo dei Principi Vescovi** (early 17th century) are the main monuments to visit, but the town itself is very pleasant and one of the most attractive centers in the Alto Adige. Be sure to see the via dei Portici Maggiori near the Duomo. Near Bressanone is the **Abbey of Novacella**, a center of Augustinian monks that was continuously enlarged and embellished from the 15th to the 18th century (guided visits every day, 10:00 A.M. to 11:00 A.M. and 2:00 P.M. to 3:00 P.M.).

Bressanone also enjoys an excellent reputation for cuisine, and one of its restaurants, at the **Hotel Elefante**, is among the best and most elegant in the Alto Adige—while remaining in an affordable price range. The rooms in this 16th-century building, furnished with antiques, are lovely. More informal but definitely very good are **Fink**, via dei Portici Minori 4 (the soups are a must), and **Oste Scuro**, vicolo Duomo 3, specializing in venison and mushrooms.

The road northeast up the valley to the Passo di Brennero then runs through Fortezza to reach **Vipiteno**, less than 16 km (10 miles) from the Austrian border, also an important ski resort and a center for short walks on the valley's slopes. The **Hotel Krone** in the Old Town, formerly a monastery, has a handsome garden and an excellent restaurant, serving all the Tirolese specialties and more.

Thirty-two km (20 miles) east of Bressanone a southward road enters the splendid **Val Badia**, connected to the Val Gardena at Corvara, another 32 km (20 miles) down. This narrow valley, surrounded by imposing Dolomitic peaks and one of the preferred ski resorts of the Alto Adige, opens up at Pedraces.

Val Pusteria

Val Pusteria, in the northeast corner of Alto Adige, is one of the few Alto Adige valleys that run east to west rather than north to south; it connects Bressanone with the Alpine pass of **Dobbiaco**, and Lienz in Austria. The northern side of this handsome valley is of course exposed to the south, and so lends itself beautifully to fruit farming and wine making. It is dotted with small villages and isolated *masi*, where visitors are often welcome to buy the local produce and sometimes to spend the night for a small fee (see Accommodations Reference).

This valley is, or rather was, one of the contact points between the European and the African continents (it seems that geologically speaking all of peninsular Italy belongs to the African side). The African mass is still quietly pushing northward, penetrating below the Alpine crust (hence the frequent earthquakes in Friuli as well as in southern Italy). The visual counterpart of this state of things is the obvious contrast between the rounded mountains north of this valley and the vertical and pointed Dolomites, made largely of primeval corals, on the south side.

Brunico, northeast of Bolzano and, nearer, Bressanone, is the main center of the Val Pusteria. It has a 13th-century castle still surrounded by walls (no entrance), and it is at the center of pleasant walks on the gentle slopes that surround it. One of its restaurants, **Andreas Hofer**, is well known for its Tirolese specialties.

The long **Valle Aurina** runs north and east toward Vetta d'Italia, the northernmost point in Italy. As the road has no exit, the top part of the valley has remained a bit secluded, and is one of the most picturesque parts of the Alto Adige.

East along the Val Pusteria from Brunico toward Dobbiaco, at **Valdaora** a road to the left leads to the **Valle d'Anterselva**. There is a refined restaurant with 15th-century decor at Rasun di Sopra in this valley: **Ansitz Heufler**, offering the best of Tirolese cooking to its affluent visitors. Another 8 km (5 miles) ahead on the road from Brunico to Dobbiaco, the **Val di Braies** opens on the right; it is well worth driving the 12 or so km (7 or 8 miles) of this easy road to the famous **Lago di Braies**. Totally enchanting in the middle of thick pinewoods, it mirrors in its limpid water the high mountains that surround it (the lake is three-quarters of a mile by one-quarter, and it is possible to walk around it). Back on the main Val Pusteria road, at Villabassa, a superb Tirolese restaurant awaits visitors: **Friedlerhof**, via Dante 40, where the goulash is the best you will ever have.

Five km (3 miles) east of Dobbiaco is the village of **San Candido**, with the 13th-century La Collegiata, the best-preserved Romanesque church in the Alto Adige. San Candido is a well-developed ski resort. A good and affordable restaurant is the **Vecchia Segheria**, 3 km (2 miles) off San Candido on route 52. From San Candido it easy to reach Lienz in Austria, while from Dobbiaco an easy scenic road leads south for 30 km (20 miles) to **Cortina d'Ampezzo**, the capital of the Cadore (see the Veneto chapter).

Staying in Alto Adige

Two centuries of touristic tradition have endowed the Alto Adige with a number of sumptuous hotels. The remodeling of castles and monasteries has recently added more guest facilities, often striking for their architecture and views (it seems that the ancient monks were very good at siting their retreats). The recent boom of the ski trade has added countless facilities in the middle and low price ranges, all characterized by a love for order and cleanliness that often makes quite a contrast with certain *pensioni* of peninsular Italy.

The Alto Adige Gasthof. In the section on Val Venosta we discussed the farming units called *masi* (*Höfe* in German). Many of them have recently converted part of their space to tourist use, which in some cases has become their main source of income. A publication by the Ufficio Provinciale per il Turismo (piazza Parrocchia 11–12, Bolzano) called "Agriturismo nel Südtirolo" lists more than four hundred of these *masi,* with a photograph of each and detailed information about location and services offered. All of the *masi* listed are very neat and well kept, and the prices for 1988 varied from just 10,000 to 14,000 lire per person per night, breakfast included. For stays of only one to three nights the price is slightly higher. A week or so on a *maso* is a wonderful way to get to know the Alto Adige landscape and its people.

GETTING AROUND

The Trentino–Alto Adige can be entered by train from the north (Austrian border) on the Munich–Innsbruck–Bolzano–Trento line, which continues through Verona to Milan and Venice and is one of the most important international lines in Italy. There are no other railroad lines from the north, and there aren't any from the west. On the east, a railroad connects Lienz in Austria to Bolzano and Trento through Dobbiaco and the Val Pusteria (Brunico, Bressanone).

From the south, in addition to the Verona–Trento–Bolzano line, there is an important train service from Venice to Trento through Bassano del Grappa (in the Veneto) and the Val Sugana (in the Trentino). There are two local railroad lines: from Bolzano northwest through Merano and the Val Venosta, with the line ending at Malles, and from Trento northwest through Mezzolombardo and Lake Santa Giustina to end at Malè (Val di Sole).

The rest of this mountainous region is served by public buses, with the main terminals in Trento and Bolzano. From each of those centers it is possible to reach by bus all the main villages located in the surrounding valleys. Bolzano and Trento are also connected by bus to Milan and Venice. Buses also connect most smaller railway stations to the villages in the area. Many of those local buses, however, run only once a day in each direction.

The best way to enjoy both the landscape and the tourist facilities is definitely by car. The roads are safe, well kept, and as comfortable as the mountainous nature of the region allows; the local drivers are much more disciplined than those in southern Italy. The major car rental firms (Hertz, Avis, and others) have offices only in Bolzano, not in Trento, and offer the usual possibility to drop the car anywhere else in Italy (or elsewhere in Europe, for an extra fee).

ACCOMMODATIONS REFERENCE

Trentino

▶ **Hotel Accademia**. Vicolo Colico 4, 38100 **Trento**. Tel: (0461) 98-10-11.

▶ **Hotel Cristallo**. 38084 **Madonna di Campiglio** (Trento). Tel: (0465) 411-32. This nice hotel's finest feature is the view of the mountains from its rooms; open December through March and July through August.

▶ **Hotel Flora**. 38077 **Terme di Comano-Stenico** (Trento). Tel: (0465) 715-49. Open all year.

▶ **Golf Hotel**. **Campo Carlo Magno** 38084 Madonna di Campiglio (Trento). Tel: (0465) 410-03. A quiet retreat in a pinewood; open December through March and July through August.

▶ **Hotel Henriette**. 38027 **Malè** (Trento). Tel: (0463) 921-10. Reasonably priced, with nice views; open Christmas through March and June through September.

▶ **Hotel Ischia Alle Dolomiti di Brenta**. 38018 **Molveno** (Trento). Tel: (0461) 58-60-57. This hotel has a handsome garden and nice views; open all year.

▶ **Italia Grand Chalet**. **Vetriolo Terme** 38056 Levico Terme. Tel: (0461) 70-64-14. Very quiet and reasonably priced, with good views and excellent service; open Christmas through April and July through September 15.

▶ **Hotel Villa Madruzzo**. 38050 **Cognola di Trento**. Tel: (0461) 98-62-20.

▶ **Grand Hotel Trento**. Via Alfieri 3, 38100 **Trento**. Tel: (0461) 98-10-10; Telex: 401335.

▶ **Hotel Panorama**. 38033 **Cavalese**. Tel: (0462) 316-36. Moderately priced, this beautifully situated hotel is true to its name.

Alto Adige

(When writing to the hotels below, write "Bolzano" after all town names other than Bolzano itself.)

▶ **Hotel Burg Hochnaturns**. Via Castello 30, 39025 **Naturno**. Tel: (0473) 871-38. Located in the old castle of Naturno and surrounded by a garden.

▶ **Hotel Cappella**. **Cappella** 39030 Corvara in Badia. Tel: (0471) 83-61-83; Telex: 400643. Splendid garden, tennis courts, and magnificent views.

▶ **Hotel Elefante**. Via Rio Bianco 4, 39042 **Bressanone**. Tel: (0472) 327-50.

▶ **Hotel Emmy**. 39050 **Fié Allo Sciliar**. Tel: (0471) 720-

06. Reasonably priced, with a splendid view of the Sciliar mountain.

▶ **Hotel Feldhof.** Via Municipo 4, 39025 **Naturno**. Tel: (0473) 872-64. With a swimming pool and garden; open all year.

▶ **Castel Freiberg. Freiberg** 39012 Merano. Tel: (0473) 441-96; Telex: 401081.

▶ **Hotel Garberhof.** Via Nazionale 25, 39024 **Malles Venosta**. Tel: (0473) 813-99. Open all year.

▶ **Sporthotel Gran Baita.** 39048 **Selva di Val Gardena**. Tel: (0471) 752-10; Telex: 401432. This may be the best of the hundred or so hotels and *pensioni* in this very busy summer and winter resort. Covered swimming pool, view of the Dolomites, and a very good restaurant.

▶ **Hotel Grien.** 39046 **Ortisei**. Tel: (0471) 763-40. Perfectly located at the center of the Val Gardena, this hotel has a garden and affords splendid views; open all year.

▶ **Castel Guncina-Reichrieglerhof. Guncina** 39100 Bolzano. Tel: (0471) 463-45.

▶ **Royal Hotel Hinterhuber. Riscone** 39031 Brunico. Tel: (0474) 212-21; Telex: 400650. Unusually quiet, with swimming pool and great mountain views.

▶ **Hotel Irma.** Via Belvedere 17, 39012 **Merano**. Tel: (0473) 301-24. This moderately priced hotel has a beautiful garden and a swimming pool; open from Easter through October.

▶ **Schloss Korb.** Strada Castel d'Appiano 5, **Missiano** 39057 San Paolo Appiano (about 10 km/6 miles west of Bolzano). Tel: (0471) 63-32-33.

▶ **Castel Labers.** Via Labers 25, 39012 **Merano**. Tel: (0473) 344-84.

▶ **Park Hotel Laurino.** Via Laurino 4, 39100 **Bolzano**. Tel: (0471) 98-05-00; Telex: 401088. A luxury-class hotel very close to the city center.

▶ **Villa Mozart.** Via San Marco 26, 39012 **Merano**. Tel: (0473) 306-30.

▶ **Palace Hotel.** Via Cavour 2, 39012 **Merano**. Tel: (0473) 374-34.

▶ **Hotel La Perla.** 39033 **Corvara in Badia**. Tel: (0471) 83-61-32; Telex: 401685. A breathtaking view of the Dolomites and a large heated swimming pool; open June through September and Easter through Christmas.

▶ **Hotel Plavina.** Burgeis 157, **Burgusio** 39024 Malles Venosta. Tel: (0473) 812-23. Open all year.

▶ **Kurhotel Castel Rundegg.** Via Scena 2, 39012 **Merano**. Tel: (0473) 341-00. A bit less expensive than Merano's other luxury hotels; open all year except the last three weeks in January.

▶ **Hotel Scala Stiegl.** Via Brennero 11, 39100 **Bolzano.** Tel: (0471) 97-62-22.

▶ **Hotel Schlossgarten.** Via Pretura 25, 39028 **Silandro.** Tel: (0473) 704-24. Open Easter through October.

▶ **Park Hotel Sole Paradiso-Sonnenparadies.** Via Baranci 8, 39038 **San Candido.** Tel: (0474) 731-20. Affordable, with excellent service and swimming pool and tennis courts; open all year.

▶ **Hotel Sunnweis.** Via August Kleeberg 7, 39025 **Naturno.** Tel: (0473) 871-57. Open Easter through October.

▶ **Sporthotel Teresa.** Pedraces 39036 **Badia.** Tel: (0471) 83-96-23; Telex: 400518. Overlooking the mountains of the Val Badia; open all year.

EMILIA-ROMAGNA

By Peter Todd Mitchell

Emilia-Romagna was created during the unification of Italy in 1860 by the joining of the coastal province of Romagna to the Emilian plain, which skirts the Apennines, the mountain chain that separates the region from Liguria and Tuscany.

For centuries, Romagna was Roman in every possible sense: It was part of Rome when Emilia was still a series of colonies; later, under the Visigoths and then the Byzantines, its leading town of Ravenna served as what was to be the final capital of the Western Empire. Roman again during the Renaissance, along with Ferrara and Bologna, the area ended up as the property of the Papal States.

The historic cities of Emilia—Piacenza, Parma, and Modena—line the ancient Roman road that not only gives the territory its name but also passes through the center of Bologna as well. Founded by Marcus Aemilius Lepidus in 187 B.C., the **Via Emilia** was devised to connect the present Piacenza to Arminium (Rimini) on the Adriatic. The cities of the Via Emilia are not distant from one another, and the road is straight (now paralleled by a modern *autostrada*), so time is no problem until the traveller reaches them and finds that for architecture, for history, and for art they are a miracle to visit.

And for food, too. The wheat fields that extend from the Po to the mountains make the region Italy's pasta basket. The cows grazing in the Enza valley between Parma and Reggio account for Italy's butter and Parmesan cheese. The pigs—who owe their presence to the Ro-

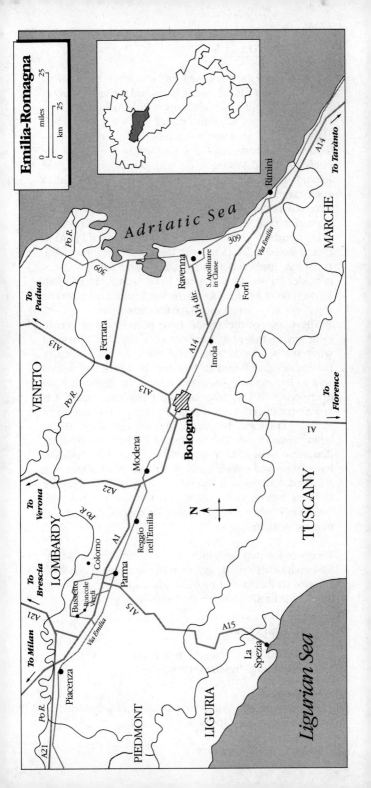

mans, for whom pork was far and away the favorite meat—account for the Parma hams and the vast variety of sausage, some of which ends up as Bologna's mortadella. In warm weather a cornucopia of fruit such as peaches, cherries, and apricots is harvested. The vegetables— asparagus in particular—are the best in Italy. What the chefs of Emilia-Romagna do with all this has become legend, and the legend continues: What Rossini did to celebrate the food of Bologna in the 19th century Luciano Pavarotti has done for Modena's in ours. As it has for centuries, rivalry between the towns continues unabated. Many fastidious palates prefer the lighter fare of Parma to that of Bologna; Modena, with its famous restaurant, Fini, considers itself superior to either. Most foreign critics consider Italy's best restaurant to be Gianni Morini's San Domenico in Imola, also on the Via Emilia. Lucky are the travellers who can go and judge for themselves.

The wines of the region have been open to certain criticism in the past. Lambrusco, a dry, red sparkling wine that is served chilled (and often not cold enough), has for decades found its way into the Christmas parcels sent to Italians living abroad. Here in the region it is on every other table, particularly near Modena, where it is largely produced. Some find it a perfect accompaniment to the local food; for those who do not, there is the hearty Sangiovese. The whites, which hail mostly from Romagna—where they go well with the fish dishes— have improved enormously in recent years. Once the standard local was a sweetish, heavy Albana, but the vintners met modern tastes, and now an icy, pale dry Trebbiano (often a bit *frizzante,* or sparkling) is served in most restaurants.

We cover the two most important cities of Romagna first: Ravenna, on the coast, and then Ferrara, inland. Next we go west to Parma and move southeast from there along the old Via Emilia through Modena to Bologna.

MAJOR INTEREST

Food and restaurants (Emilia)
Mosaics and frescoes (Romagna)

Ravenna
Byzantine and Visigothic mosaics and architecture
Basilica of Sant'Apollinare in Classe

Ferrara
Old palazzi
The castello: Ducal Suite
The cathedral (façade and Cosmè Tura panels)
Palazzo dei Diamanti painting gallery
Palazzo Bevilaqua-Massari museum (Boldoni)

Parma
Galleria Nationale "Pilotta" (Correggio, Leonardo)
Convent of San Paolo (Correggio)
Romanesque cathedral (Correggio, frescoes)
Church of San Giovanni Evangelista (Correggio,
   Parmigianino)
Farnese Palace at Colorno
Verdi birthplace at Roncole
Verdi villa at Busseto

Modena
Galleria Estense (paintings)
Este library
Cathedral
Piazza Grande cafés

Bologna
Pinacoteca Nazionale (Raphael, Giotto, others)
Streets of palaces
Medieval Piazza Maggiore
Byzantine-Romanesque church of Santo Stefano
Basilica of San Petronio (exterior, paintings)
Church of San Giacomo Maggiore (Costa frescoes;
   chapel)

RAVENNA

Of all the towns of Emilia-Romagna, Ravenna remains the
most evocative and the most unusual. Set apart from the
Via Emilia on the Adriatic coast, it retains a distance both in
place and in time. For nowhere else can you find so many
vestiges of Byzantium as in this town of marble, ivory, and
gold that was to be the final bastion of the Western
Empire. Its mosaics and their images outshine anything of
a similar period in Istanbul—where every representation
of the human countenance was destroyed in the Iconoclastic Rebellion—or in Greece, where centuries of earthquakes and Turkish occupation have left little. So you
must come to Ravenna to view a record of these fifth and

sixth centuries that signaled the fall of the Empire in the West. And every stage of that Empire had been witnessed here: from its beginning, when Ravenna was the head-quarters of Caesar in his march on Rome, to its Golden Age, when Augustus created the thriving port of Classe (marked now by the lone basilica of Sant'Apollinare), and then—in a wave of invasions—to the end.

In the fifth century the Visigoths moved their capital from Milan to Ravenna, then a city protected by marshes and lagoons and crisscrossed by canals—an early version of Venice. This was an intelligent move that was to pro-long the life of the Empire by hundreds of years. The monuments of that capital can be seen almost chronologi-cally, one near the other.

Those sights that remain most deeply in the mind are connected with two amazing women. One monument is the **Tomb of Galla Placidia**, off via San Vitale in the northwest corner of the city; the other is next door, the mosaic in San Vitale depicting the Empress Theodora and her court. Galla Placidia's history was far the earlier. Born to a patrician Roman family, she was captured in the sack of Rome by Alaric in 410 and was present at his burial in the river Busento, in Calabria. To the horror of Roman aristocratic society, she married his successor, Ataulf. From then on, she never looked back. The Visigoths by no means considered themselves barbarians; they felt that the mantle of Rome had fallen on their shoulders, and this highly ambitious woman was to take the fullest advantage of that legacy. She ended up as regent to her son, Valentinian III, who became Emperor at the age of six; for 20 years she ran the Western Empire. This in-cluded most of Spain, where her name appears on more streets and squares than in Italy; her palace in Barcelona lies below that of Ferdinand and Isabella. In Ravenna she is buried with her son and her husband (whose reign was brief) in a tomb that glows with blue and gold lapis, with stars on its ceilings and its mosaic panels in the naturalis-tic manner of Rome's early Christian churches. Of Galla Placidia's many palaces and basilicas, this small mauso-leum is all that remains, but its impact goes far beyond its size.

The Visigothic Empire in Spain lasted until the Arab invasion; in Ravenna its life was shortened by a crusade from the East, sparked by the view of the Orthodox Catholic Church of Byzantium (and in particular the Em-peror Justinian) that its Arian form of Christianity was a heresy. Justinian launched a war both with generals and with architects. The generals, of whom Belisarius was the most capable, took Ravenna in 540. The architects, years before, had started pouring money from the imperial treasuries into structures in Ravenna that would illustrate the true faith, and of these the most spectacular remains the **Church of San Vitale**. Distinctly Oriental in design, like the churches of Syria, its interior walls are lined with marble and porphyry; mosaics cover the ceilings and arches, incorporating them with two panels of Imperial portraits that are the finest left to us by Byzantium: On one are Justinian and his court; on the other, his empress, Theodora, with her ladies-in-waiting. San Vitale was finished in the year of the death of this *Basilissa,* who sports a halo hardly earned by her past. By no means of noble birth like Galla Placidia, Theodora was born into the circus—then a sort of burlesque. Even that sounds fine enough compared to Gibbon's immortal description of her in his *Decline and Fall.* She rose to dominate both emperor and empire with just the sort of hard, strong character that is apparent in her image here in San Vitale.

Among the other attractions at the town center is **Sant'Apollinare Nuovo**, built by Theodoric during the sixth century for the Arians and expanded three centuries later with a graceful cylindrical campanile. The mosaics are among Ravenna's most famous—the processions of the virgins, preceded by Magi, toward the Madonna and Angels and the martyrs going from Ravenna toward Christ. The nearby Battistero degli Ariani (Baptistery of the Arians), also sixth century, contains a fine mosaic *Baptism of Christ and Procession of the Apostles.* Behind the Duomo, the **Museo Arcivescovile** boasts the great ivory throne of Maximilian, chef d'oeuvre of sixth-century Alexandrine artists.

San Vitale might be the most unusual of Ravenna's churches, but the **Basilica of Sant'Apollinare in Classe**, near the pine woods that have grown over the silted-up Roman port and reached by frequent bus service from the train station, is in its way the most beautiful. Serene and spacious, built on the plan of an early Christian basilica, its sides are lined with marble columns and sarcophagi leading up to a golden blaze of mosaics dominated by a cross against a sea of stars. The pine forest itself was once a haunt for the horse-riding Byron, when he was living in Ravenna in the palazzo (still there) of his mistress, Teresa Guiccioli, with her, her complacent husband, and his own menagerie of animals. (This affair is lucidly described in Iris Origo's impeccable book *The Last Attachment*.) Ravenna's other guest-poet, Dante, exiled from Florence, died of marsh fever right in town. The citizens of Ravenna used every subterfuge to retain his body, and he still lies here in his domed marble tomb.

With all its museums, baptisteries, and basilicas, Ravenna is difficult to see on a day trip, except perhaps from Ferrara. The churches are best seen in the morning light, so it is a good idea to spend the night. The two most attractive hotels are the **Centrale-Byron** (via 4 Novembre 14) and the **Bisanzio** (via Salara 30), both quiet and central—but small, so reserve. Ravenna itself has had an economic revival, thanks to the discovery of methane gas on its outskirts in what is now an industrial landscape (immortalized by the director Michelangelo Antonioni in *The Red Desert,* one of his many attempts to drive his leading actress, Monica Vitti, mad).

The Old Town itself is intact; it has a delightful miniature piazza from the Middle Ages, the piazza del Popolo, with columns like those near San Marco in Venice, supporting the town's two favorite saints, who look down on the café tables. There are two good restaurants in Ravenna. One, the **Tre Spade**, alongside the cathedral at via Rasponi 37, was started a few years ago by young people who admired Imola's San Domenico. In their neo-Venetian Rococo decor they have done well indeed; carpaccio, tagliolini with smoked salmon, and crepes with artichoke hearts are a few of the specialties. The food of Romagna is akin to that of Venice (the same sea is at hand): *fritto misto* of fish, scampi grilled or boiled, and risotto with *gamberetti.* Some of these last dishes are available at the **Bella Venezia** (via 4 Novembre 16), which is more of a trattoria in style than the Tre Spade. Since the best Trebbiano is produced in the Ravenna area, and since it goes well with all of this food, it is the wine to order.

FERRARA

Ferrara is, like Ravenna, a city of Romagna and set apart from the Via Emilia. Though founded by the inhabitants of the ancient, now ruined, port of Spina in the Po delta, its population became sizable only after the fall of Ravenna to barbarians in the sixth century, when an influx of refugees made its riverfront a working commercial port. By 1208 Ravenna had been taken over by the Este family, and they ran it in a manner that was to make it a center for arts and learning known to all of Europe. Within their castle, which dominates the city center, took place most of their bloody deeds—the most famous being the execution by the Marchese Niccolo III of his young wife, Parisina Malatesta, and his son Ugo, when he caught them in flagrante delicto thanks to a window mirror.

More innovative were the broad, sunny streets of gardens and palaces laid out by Ercole I in the 15th century, making Ferrara one of the first planned cities anywhere. The most advanced contributions to the civilization of the Renaissance came first from the small courts such as those of Ferrara and Mantua, developments that were copied later in Florence and Rome. The Estes had their castle—just as the Bourbons later had the Bastille in Paris—but for pleasure and entertainment they used their outlying palaces, and it was in them that they received the Humanist writers and philosophers, such as Tasso, Ariosto, and Petrarch, who were to make their town into a cultural phenomenon. One of their random inventions was the theater as we know it, with a curtain going up and a play performed in front of an audience.

The Estes were to rule for three and a half centuries, but by the 15th century their way of life had been determined. Even the dread Niccolo was a Greek scholar who invited some of the best minds of Byzantium to found a school here. He also produced a record number of children—at least 30 of them illegitimate—and in the Este tradition raised them together with his legitimate brood, with equal rights to education and succession. One of his offspring was the genial Borso, an able administrator and avid protector of the arts. It is thanks to him that we have the **Palazzo di Schifanoia**, near the town walls on via Scandiana, with frescoes that he commissioned from the three painters who first formed the School of Ferrara: Cosmè Tura, Ercole de' Roberti, and Francesco del Cossa. Cossa's frescoes give us an idea of the pastimes and pleasures of Borso's court, and in them one notes the large part that women played in Este society. Two of the most remarkable were the daughters of Ercole I: Isabella, who was to marry a Gonzaga and become marchioness of Mantua, and Beatrice, who was to marry Ludovico Sforza and became duchess of Milan. They exported their background with them, with results that have filled art galleries and libraries. (In painting alone, Isabella was patron to Andrea Mantegna, and Isabella to Leonardo.)

Apart from the Schifanoia there are three palaces in Ferrara that are not to be missed. (Ferrara's attractions are easy to enjoy, for the flattish city is comfortable to walk and a joy for bicyclists, who count among their numbers many local residents of all ages.) One was built for the retirement of Ludovico il Moro, Beatrice's husband, but fate was to decree an early death for her and prison for him after the French, largely at his instigation, descended into Italy. The **Palazzo di Ludovico il Moro**, with its rose gardens and painted ceilings, now houses the Greco-Etruscan finds from Spina. Not far from it is the **Palazzina di Marfisa d'Este**, decked out with furniture and paintings of its period, and with a garden theater where the plays of Marfisa's friend, Torquato Tasso, were performed. The airiest and most pleasant of the three palaces is the **Casa Romei** (north of the Palazzo di Schifanoia and reached by the borga Vada), built by the merchant husband of Polissena d'Este and later enlarged by the same Cardinal Ippolito who built the Villa d'Este at Tivoli. It is now a museum for the sizable number of frescoes, sculpture, and paintings rescued from convents and churches in Ferrara after the arrival of Napoléon.

Casa Romei also served as a second home to Ferrara's most famous duchess, Lucrezia Borgia, who married Duke Alfonso I. By this alliance the duke appalled the Italian aristocracy, since by his time the Estes had become pillars of genteel society, whereas the Borgias were looked upon as something akin to a Spanish Mafia. As we now know, it was Lucrezia's bloodthirsty brothers who did the poisoning and the killing; but her record—one husband horribly murdered and the other warned in the nick of time to run for his life—was hardly reassuring. It was her stupendous dowry and fear of her loving, dangerous father—Pope Alexander VI—that assured the marriage to Alfonso, and her entrance into Ferrara for her nuptials became one of the most recounted spectacles of Renaissance Italy. The best biography of this fascinating woman is by Maria Bellonci; it reads like a novel of suspense.

Lucrezia was then 20. She was not stupid, and she had a very appealing side to her character. She stayed on in Ferrara, much loved even after her family fell from power, until she died at the age of 39 giving birth to her seventh child. She had renovated part of the **Castello**, the main ducal residence, for her own apartments, and now her *orangerie,* which served as her salon for artists and poets, has been restored, as have the frescoes of its loggia. Gone, though, is her brocaded bathroom; her mania for bathing, most likely an Hispano-Moresque legacy, had scandalized the Italians right from the start, when her mammoth wedding cavalcade stopped for 24 hours on its way from Rome so that she could wash her hair. Her conquests in Ferrara were ardent but most likely platonic, her three suitors having been Pietro Bembo, the dashing poet who was to become a cardinal; Ercole Strozzi, the Florentine who helped her set up the *orangerie;* and finally Alfonso Gonzaga, the husband of her worst enemy, Isabella d'Este. Isabella could never forgive Lucrezia for having so much money; on the other hand, Lucrezia's attempt at a learned court could never rival Isabella's at Mantua because she simply did not have Isabella's education. But she did have a personal warmth perhaps sorely needed by the nonintellectual Gonzaga, who had been treated with nothing but contempt by his bluestocking wife.

Near the Castello is the **Duomo**, with its handsome, pink marble façade—an amalgam of Romanesque and Gothic style—and the **Museo del Duomo**. In this neighborhood of squares and courts are a welter of welcoming cafés and restaurants. The best of the latter are the least pretentious. The **Grotta Azzurra** (piazza Sacrati 43) serves Northern Italian food (risottos and grilled meats); the **Vecchia Chitarra** (via Ravenna 13) has local specialties such as *saluma de suga* with *purea,* a spicy sausage served with mashed potatoes.

North of the center along corso Ercole is one of the most handsome of Ferrara's palaces, that known as **dei Diamanti**, so called for the diamond-shaped marble facets on its façade. It now houses Ferrara's painting museum, or **Pinacoteca**, which contains a creditable collection of the School of Ferrara. Even so, the finest Cosmè Turas are his panels in the Museo del Duomo; the best Cossas are his frescoes in the Schifanoia; and a lot of the best of everything was hauled off to Modena when the Estes had to leave Ferrara at the end of the 16th century thanks to a papal refusal to accept their last possible heir as duke. Many an illegitimate Este had been recognized over the centuries, but Rome had long coveted Ferrara and so in 1598 refused to accept the grandson of Alfonso I as heir. When the family left, they were in quite a bad mood and took just about everything movable with them, including their vast libraries and lots of paintings. Something else that left with them was the luck of Ferrara; ineptly administrated by cardinal legates, it fell victim to flood and plague, then to the depredations of Napoléon's troops—and finally to the bombings of World War II.

Ferrara was one of the worst-bombed cities in Italy, sharing the fate of the other towns of Emilia-Romagna that happened to be incorporated in the German "Gothic Line." The miracles lie in what was saved and in the restoration of the rest.

One local painter was born too late to have his work evacuated by the Estes. The magical virtuosity of Boldini had made him celebrated by 1900, his reputation being largely achieved by his portraits of the rich, the famous, and the fashionable: from *demi-mondaines* such as Cleo de Merode to Italy's titled women of the d'Annunzio period such as the Marchesa Casati. These and others are in the **Museo Boldini e dell'Ottocento Ferrarese**, sumptuously housed in the **Palazzo Bevilacqua-Massari** near the Diamante, off the corso Porta Mare. The best surprise for many will be the views that Boldini painted of Paris and Venice, for they show what a really fine artist he was.

Also off the corso Ercole is the house of the writer Ariosto, who wrote that best-seller of the late Renaissance, *Orlando Furioso,* and spent his last years in Ferrara. By no means humble, his home is worthy of an internationally known writer. His book was translated in England at the forceful request of Queen Elizabeth I, who caught her courtier Sir John Harrington reading its raciest chapter to her ladies-in-waiting and sent him into exile until he could bring back the whole book.

From these sights you can walk to what is certainly Ferrara's best and most attractive restaurant: **La Provvidenza**, at corso Ercole 92. The arched interior is like that of a rustic manor, and in warm weather you can dine in the garden. Before ordering it might be a good idea to survey the tables of antipasti, where you can serve yourself from a mosaic of scampi and other shellfish, tuna with *fagioli,* every sort of salami and mortadella, and a rainbow of cooked vegetables and salads. The crepes *alla parmigiana* are excellent, and so—for the sturdy—are the veal chops and grilled meats. The house wine is good, too.

Ferrara is worth a night's stay, being perfect for evening walks, whether around the animated squares of the

Medieval section or in the nostalgic shadows of the later palaces and the greenery of its more open areas. These nighttime scenes will remind you, in their perspectives, of Giorgio di Chirico—who spent years of his early life here. These pink and ocher palaces have become familiar through his artistic vision. Their gardens turn up in a book and film of our own time—*The Garden of the Finzi-Continis*—which is set in Ferrara.

The most convenient central hotels are the **Ripagrande**, installed in a palace in the Medieval section, and the gracious and quiet **Astra**, near the Castello. Also near the castle—and more modest—is the **Touring**.

THE CITIES OF THE VIA EMILIA

The road built by Marcus Aemilius Lepidus began at the Roman town of Placentia, where it was crossed by the Via Postumia running from the Roman equivalent of Genoa to Concordia in the Veneto. Placentia became a very busy town; **Piacenza**, the city that later replaced it, remains a commercial center, and—with its sturdy Palazzo Communale fronted by two Farnese equestrian statues on their pillars—a monumental one at that. It has one very good restaurant, the **Antica Osteria del Teatro**, and a lively trattoria, **Agnello-da Renato** (via Calzolai 2). Most travellers, however, will probably want to keep moving southeast along the Emilia to its next large city, Parma.

Parma

The city of Parma, laid out with such spacious elegance by the Farnese family, has a history that is not just the usual one of survival: It is a success story. The Farneses, during their centuries of rule, united with a bridge the two towns that now make up Parma, opened up the Medieval sections with avenues and parks, and made their duchy a powerful force in the international politics of Europe. When Isabella Farnese assumed the throne of Spain in the early 18th century, though, the Farneses left—taking even their furniture with them; their town could easily have gone the way of Ferrara, which, with the departure of the Estes, simply fell to pieces like a clock with the center of its mechanism removed.

A flood of lucky events kept Parma on the map. The beginning of the 19th century brought Marie Louise, the

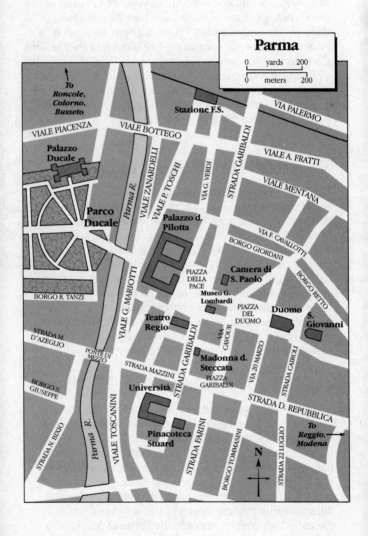

Parma

| 0 | yards | 200 |
| 0 | meters | 200 |

To
Roncole,
Colorno,
Busseto

Stazione F.S.

VIA PALERMO

VIALE PIACENZA

VIALE BOTTEGO

STRADA GARIBALDI

VIA G. VERDI

VIALE P. TOSCHI

VIALE ZANARDELLI

Parma R.

VIALE A. FRATTI

VIALE MENTANA

Palazzo
Ducale

VIA F. CAVALLOTTI

BORGO GIORDANI

BORGO RETTO

Parco
Ducale

Palazzo d.
Pilotta

PIAZZA
DELLA
PACE

Camera di
S. Paolo

VIALE G. MARIOTTI

BORGO R. TANZI

Museo G.
Lombardi

PIAZZA
DEL
DUOMO

Duomo

S.
Giovanni

Teatro
Regio

VIA
CAVOUR

STRADA CAIROLI

STRADA M.
D'AZEGLIO

PONTE DI
MEZZO

STRADA GARIBALDI

Madonna d.
Steccata

VIA 20 MARZO

BORGO S.
GIUSEPPE

STRADA MAZZINI

PIAZZA
GARIBALDI

Università

STRADA D. REPUBBLICA

To
Reggio,
Modena

Parma R.

VIALE TOSCANINI

STRADA FARINI

STRADA N. BIXIO

Pinacoteca
Stuard

BORGO TOMMASINI

STRADA 22 LUGLIO

N

Hapsburg wife of Emperor Napoléon, to rule the duchy when her husband was sent into exile. Both she and her consort, Marshal Neipperg, were efficient administrators. Devoted to music, painting, and books, they soon set their noble city back on its feet—commercially, too, and in the most various ways. Parma's violets had always been celebrated; Marie Louise created a perfume industry around them. Parma's hams had been produced since Roman times; now they became *jambons de Parme* and were exported as the region's main product. The local cheese, Parmigiano, had been made by the Romans, too; now it became a sine qua non for Italian pasta anywhere. (Parma cheeses and other goods, everything from paintings to clothes, are for sale at the **Ghiaia**, an open-air market beneath the bridge at the end of via Mazzini.) Cultural publicity was soon to come as well. A minor French functionary, Marie-Henri Beyle, came to see Parma's paintings; later, as the writer Stendhal, he was to set the action of *La Chartreuse de Parme* here.

Music, a passion with Marie Louise as it had been with her aunt, Marie Antoinette, was housed in a handsome new opera house. Soon, in the hamlet of Roncole just to the north, a composer worthy of filling it was born. Giuseppe Verdi made Parma a place of pilgrimage for opera-lovers even to our day, and his last librettist, the composer Arrigo Boito, was to give his name to the local conservatory of music. Today, in the streets of Parma in the evening, music seems to emerge from every corner: from private homes, from churches, in the piazzas.

The painter whose work Stendhal came to see was Correggio, and his paintings can still be seen in the same places. One is in the **Pinacoteca** of the Farnese Palace, the **Palazzo Pilotta**, on piazzale Marconi, where his paintings are joined by the works of Van Dyck, Leonardo, and many others, including works taken from various convents and villas and brought here for safety by Napoléon. Alongside the galleries is the **Teatro Farnese**—older than Vicenza's Palladian theater but, though damaged in the war, now thoroughly repaired and used for concerts.

The most delightful work of Correggio, however, is found in the **Convent of San Paolo** near the Pilotta: frescoes the abbess commissioned for her dining room. The subjects are mythological, done as trompe l'oeil in colors as fresh as the day they were painted.

Correggio's most ambitious work in Parma remains his frescoed cupola in the **Duomo**, a masterpiece of light and perspective. The Duomo was of course started long before Correggio came along, as its 12th-century façade testifies. It is adorned with some of Italy's most interesting Romanesque sculpture, mostly by one artist, Benedetto Antelami, whose neo-Byzantine reliefs grace the baptistery as well. The latter, octagonal in form and built in pink Veronese marble, is remarkable for its bright 13th-century ceiling murals.

Nearby is the **Church of San Giovanni Evangelista**, which is more Renaissance in style than the Duomo, with frescoes both by Correggio and by Parma's other major painter, Parmigianino, who did much to create the Mannerist style later developed by the school of Fontainebleau. San Giovanni also has a cloister sheltering a 13th-century pharmacy, its shelves laden with faïence medicine jars and mortars.

One of the joys of wandering about Parma is the number of cafés—for a cappuccino or a *frizzante*—set in squares all over the town: smaller ones are near the cathedral or the opera house, with the greatest expanse of tables on the **piazza Garibaldi**, and catering to tastes that range from "family" on the edges to highly sophisticated toward the center.

The best restaurants of Parma are strategically located, too. Near the aperitif center of the Garibaldi is **Parizzi** (strada della Repubblica 71), which is entered by an alleyway; the restaurant itself is in a patio beneath a skylight. In the center of the space is a choice of antipasti: the best ham and charcuterie available—since the owners' family ran a *salumeria*—and a tempting choice of *ripiene*—stuffed zucchini, eggplant, and tomato. In season the local favorite, fresh asparagus *alla parmigiana,* is very much in evidence: with melted butter, grated Parmesan, and here with eggs boiled just to the point at which they can be chopped over the asparagus tips. Crepes *alla parmigiana* are a specialty here, and so are the veal scallopine filled with ham and cheese and sautéed in butter and lemon. Parizzi also serves a zabaglione so heavy with Marsala that you won't need a *digestif*—which would be a shame, since Parma produces some of the best, whether nut-flavored Nocina or the aromatic herb liqueur Erbe Luigia. As for wines, the surest bets remain Sangiovese for red and Trebbiano for white—along with a particularly good Pinot Grigio brought down from the north.

If you leave the galleries of the Pilotta at lunchtime, you

can walk right across the palace square to **La Greppia** (strada Garibaldi 39), a bright, white eatery where a plate-glass window at the end of the room fully reveals the kitchen and gives a concrete idea of the fresh pasta and vegetables at hand. These can be combined, as in a delicious pasticcio of asparagus. You can spend days in Parma without seeing a drop of tomato sauce; instead, the *agnolotti* and *tortelli* are served with *panna* (based on cream), or shaved white truffles, or just butter and freshly grated Parmesan. The main courses at La Greppia range from a smooth *vitello tonnato* to liver sautéed in sage. The desserts can feature the taste of bitter chocolate that the Hapsburgs took with them from Vienna to wherever they ruled.

Near La Greppia and on the same via Garibaldi is the **Museo Civico Glauco Lombardi**, dedicated to Marie Louise and filled with souvenirs, paintings, and furniture rescued from her town palace, which nestled alongside the Pilotta and was bombed off the face of the earth during World War II. As you can see here, she herself was an excellent watercolorist, taught, like her aunt, by Redouté. She and Marie Antoinette shared a problem: they were Austrian, one trapped in France by the Revolution and the other ruling in an Italy where the Risorgimento was beginning to stir. In France Marie Louise had been confronted by the problem of replacing the enormously popular Josephine de Beauharnais as Napoléon's wife, but in Parma her goodwill and good works won over the population. The Neoclassical tomb she built for Neipperg can be seen in the church of La Steccata, across from her opera house, surrounded by more frescoes by Parmigianino. Her second city palace has survived: the Ducale, or *dei Giardini,* with its shaded gardens in the style of Le Nôtre, across the river from the Pilotta.

Parma seems to have congresses for just about everything, and its hotels are often full. The least pretentious of the grander hotels is the **Park Hotel Toscanini** (quiet in back). The Toscanini is convenient to the best trattorias—**Il Tribunale** and **La Campana** are two—and to the spectacular shopping street for food products: the **strada Farina**.

Outside Parma

Excursions from the town can combine lunching with sightseeing. At **Colorno**, about 15 km (9 miles) north of Parma, is the country palace used by Marie Louise. Built as a summer residence by the Farneses, it has been restored to something like its former state thanks to antiques fairs periodically held in it. And this **Palazzo Ducale** is worth preserving; it is a Baroque building set on the foundations of a former castle of the Sanseverinos, surrounded by trees, and reflected in its river—an open invitation to romance.

This is just how it served in the case of Stendhal. Always searching through old papers and documents for ideas, he fell upon a history of the Farnese family from its origins and in it found the story of the seductive Vannozza, sister of Pier Luigi Farnese and a woman of few scruples who was infatuated with her young nephew Alexander. She was mistress to many, including a certain Cardinal Roderigo, who was to become Pope Alexander VI. Once installed in Rome she sent for her nephew, whose interests she energetically advanced, and from a libertine he was transformed into the serious man who was one day to become Pope himself. Stendhal took these figures from history and put them into *La Chartreuse de Parme*. It should be reread by any traveller approaching these lands.

Stendhal-da Bruno, a restaurant on the site of the inn where the author stayed, is a busy series of rooms aromatic with the scent of herbs on roasting lamb and pork. The restaurant moves out of doors in good weather, overlooking the stream below, which is a haven for fishermen. Both salmon and *fritto misto* of freshwater fish remain favorites on the menu.

Fans of Giuseppe Verdi have several choices for lunching in the country near places associated with the life of the composer. Northwest of Colorno is **Roncole Verdi**, his birthplace, where his father's general store and tavern is now a national shrine. Next door to it is very good restaurant called **Guareschi**, named after the author of the Don Camillo books but with musical tribute aplenty to the composer inside. From Roncole the young Verdi moved to the town of **Busseto**, a few miles away. There he worked as organist in the church and was taken under the wing of Antonio Barezzi, a music-loving grocer of means who ran the local orchestra society and was able to help further the career of the already promising composer. Verdi's first wife, Margherita, was Barezzi's daughter; their marriage ended in the tragedy of her death and that of their two children when the couple were desperately trying to make good in Milan. Busseto remains a bustling, prosperous town. The atmospheric restaurant, **I Due Foscari**, is appropriately run by the singer Carlo Bergonzi, but for food, **Ugo**, at via Mozart 3, is the better place to go.

After his first success, with *Nabucco,* Verdi's luck changed, and he returned to the environs of Busseto to build in 1849 the **Villa Verdi di Sant'Agata**, which was largely paid for by *Trovatore* and *Rigoletto.* His companion here was the well-known soprano Giuseppina Strepponi, who had befriended him in his early days and who was later to become his wife. Their marriage, however, only took place in 1859, and Verdi never forgave the people of Busseto for their bad treatment of Giuseppina. Sant'Agata, open to the public, is filled with mementos of Verdi and Giuseppina: her favorite parrot, stuffed; a portrait of his Maltese terrier. It's a rather gloomy house, but comfortable. We even see his death bed, brought from a Milan hotel. His last years at Sant'Agata were sad and lonely; Giuseppina and most of his friends had already died, and he had to count on the visits of his younger collaborators, among them Arrigo Boito and an enthusiastic young conductor from Parma, Arturo Toscanini.

From Parma, the Via Emilia descends southeast, passing through the rich commercial town of Reggio, which shares the honors with Parma in the production of Parmesan cheese. About 20 km (12 miles) farther on from Reggio is the ancient city of Modena.

Modena

The Via Emilia serves as the main street of Modena, which, of all the towns in its path, is perhaps the most exquisite; with a Romanesque cathedral that is a masterpiece; a superb museum of paintings; and streets of palaces, churches, arcades, and squares that have not changed since the days of Stendhal—so that the town itself is a work of art. Modena was scarcely hit in the last war; whatever damage has been done to the Medieval quarter was perpetrated not by bombs but by the Este family when they arrived from Ferrara at the end of the 16th century. Modena was to be their new capital; Baroque was their style; and money was no object. New avenues were cut through the old city, and the Palazzo Ducale, second in size only to that of the Gonzagas in Mantua, was built to dominate the center, which it still does. Later, a small, elegant opera house was built (both Luciano Pavarotti and Mirella Freni are Modenese). When the city walls came down after the unification of Italy they were replaced by tree-lined promenades. Many an avenue was once a canal—as is revealed by the names—and Modena must have had a Venetian air; some of the piazzas near the cathedral do. Like Venice, Modena is a city best appreciated when explored on foot.

The **Galleria Estense** is the painting museum, housed in the Palazzo dei Musei (at the far end of Via Emilia), along with the Este library. It took years to reorganize the picture galleries, but the result has been worth waiting for: one of Italy's best arranged collections. The Estes arrived—as would be expected—with cartloads of works of Cosmè Tura and the school of Ferrara, but they went right on collecting. Duke Francesco I went to Madrid and had his portrait painted by Velázquez (who in turn came to Modena on a buying trip for the king of Spain and was proudly shown it in the palace). He also commissioned a flamboyant bust from Bernini, and that we see, too, along with a selection of Veroneses, Tintorettos, Guardis, and even an El Greco. On the floor below the gallery is the **Biblioteca Estense**, and though all of its 600,000 books and 15,000 manuscripts are hardly on permanent view, one room is open to the public to show the library's prizes. Featured is the Bible of Borso d'Este, with 1,200 pages illuminated by a team of artists including Taddeo Crivelli. It is certainly the most valuable illustrated manuscript we have from the Italian Renaissance. It is in good company, with priceless Byzantine codices, French miniatures, and a fascinating collection of maps. One of the latter represents countries by their fauna; the coast of Brazil is the curved back of a green cockatoo.

Towering over Modena is the cathedral's Romanesque campanile, called the **Ghirlandina** thanks to the bronze garland on its weather vane; it reminded the Spanish Sephardim of their Giralda in Seville. The **Duomo** itself has been returned to its original Romanesque self, yet its interior nonetheless has a Byzantine air, with its painted crucifix glowing over the raised main altar backed by arches and separated from the nave by a magnificent rood screen. The cathedral is closer to San Marco in Venice than to its Norman contemporaries in Apulia. It is a veritable museum of sculpture, with the work of the Lombard Wiligelmo later added to by the Campionese artists who came down from Lugano. There is even more in the cathedral museum, with its remarkable metopes brought down from the buttresses to rooms where they can be properly seen. More treasures surround the tomb of San Geminiano in the crypt; and lovers of wood intarsia shouldn't miss the Coro.

The lateral side of the Duomo facing the **piazza Grande** at the center of Modena is worth contemplation—best done over an aperitif in one of the cafés opposite (providing that it is not a weekend, when a hurly-burly antiques fair descends with its carts and stands).

Modena's main shopping street is the **via Farina**, which leads to the dominating façade of the Palazzo Ducale. Mary of Modena, who was to be queen of England, was born in the palace. Ripped away to become the tearful child-bride of the enormously unattractive James II, she ended up as a devoted wife who lent dignity to his 30 years of exile, and she gave her dark good looks to the Stuart line. The Stuarts were eventually to return to Italy, in the 18th century, but Mary never came back here, and for most visitors, the palace is haunted by the mad duke of *La Chartreuse de Parme*—who was modeled on one of the last of Modena's Este rulers.

The more fanatic gourmets who come to Modena look at nothing at all and head speedily for the famed **Fini** on the largo San Francisco. Practically an institution, Fini was founded in 1912 alongside a *salumeria;* since redecorated, it has nevertheless retained its relaxed atmosphere and superior service. You would hardly suspect that the family has organized its own export service for many of the delicacies that find their way to your table here: their own salamis, hams, and pâtés; their *zampone,* or stuffed pig's foot (which is sliced like a sausage when served); and (certainly the best buy for a traveller) the *aceto balsamico,* a heady vinegar for which the region is famous and which is strong enough so that a little goes a long way. The Finis have their own vineyards, where they produce the best of Lambruscos: the Sorbara. But in case this doesn't appeal to you, the restaurant has a wine list of 150 labels, both Italian and French, noted by province. Their pâté of prosciutto and chicken is an ideal opener; their pastas change with the season. If you are lucky, the menu will have a pasticcio of tortellini, served with a rich béchamel and encased in a crisp pastry shell. The cuisine of Modena—and the town considers it completely apart from that of Bologna and Parma—involves a great deal of labor; the sort of chopping and mincing done in Genoa goes on here, too. So to accompany the boiled meats, *zampone,* and fowl of the *bollito misto* a bevy of sauces are wheeled up, among them *salsa verde,* then a *peperonata* of diced peppers, and the piquant mixture of preserved fruits known as *mostarda de Cremona.* Truffles lace the dishes here as they do all over the north, turning up in risottos, shaved over veal cutlets, or topping chicken already swimming in whiskey and cream. The dishes at Fini need not be heavy, though: witness the lightly fried brains and sweetbreads, the kidneys *trifolati,* and the liver cooked with sage. A chocolate *semi-freddo* is one of the best desserts of the house; of course, all the cakes and tarts are made on the premises. Tel: (059) 22-33-14.

There are many other good restaurants in Modena. On the grand side there is the **Borso d'Este** at piazza Roma 5, facing the palace, and in a more modest bracket, **Oreste** (piazza Roma 31), or **Enzo,** upstairs at via Coltellini 17.

For the pleasure of walking in Modena, the more central your hotel, the better. (It should be noted that the Hotel Fini, on Modena's outskirts, is a completely separate establishment from the restaurant, which is in the middle of town.) A list of Italy's most beautiful hotels would have to include Modena's **Canalgrande**, set as it is in a former bishop's palace, its lobbies hung with Baroque portraits and sparkling with chandeliers, and its rooms overlooking the parterres of a small garden. There is a choice of simpler lodgings, in particular the **Roma**, right on the via Farini, and the **Libertà**. It isn't a bad idea to remember that Modena is the next city northwest of Bologna on the Via Emilia, a scarce 39 km (24 miles) away; that it is a particularly pleasant town to stay in; and that it is far less expensive than Bologna. So, if Bologna is packed because of one of its innumerable trade fairs, it can be visited from Modena quite easily.

Bologna

The capital of Emilia-Romagna, and one of Italy's richest cities, Bologna was already celebrated in the Middle Ages—for its university. That same university still gives it a taste of youth that many a historic Italian town lacks. Its arcaded streets have remained wonderfully intact, all 21 miles of them. For urban conservation, Bologna is thought by many to be second only to Venice.

Luckily for visitors, not all of these leagues of arcaded thoroughfares have to be traversed. Walkers can easily

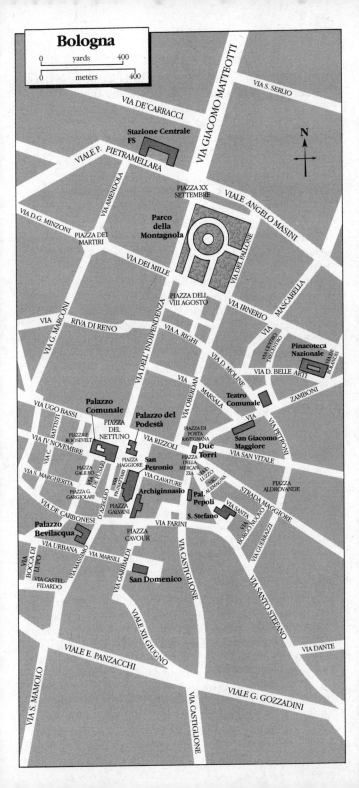

manage the sights at the center of town by starting in the
piazza di Porta Ravegnana, where the tallest landmarks of
Bologna stand: the two Medieval towers, Due Torri. From
there, like rays of a star in an older version of the Parisian
étoile system, issue the streets that harbor most of the
town's treasures: the **via San Vitale**, the **via Zamboni**, and
the **strada Maggiore**.

You can follow the history of Bologna in the churches
and palaces of these streets, beginning with the most
ancient of all: the conglomeration of buildings that form
the **Church of Santo Stefano**. Bologna's San Petronio
constructed this 12th-century church as a replica of the
church of the Holy Sepulcher in Jerusalem; his version
remains much more like the original than does the 19th-
century hodgepodge of the actual sepulcher today.

By the time of Petronio, Bologna's university, the oldest
in Europe, had been founded. It specialized in civil law,
was modern to the point of having women teachers, and
by the 13th century was attracting up to 10,000 students at
a time from all over Europe. For this deluge of outsiders,
lodgings had to be created, food provided, and hostels
opened, so the expansion of Bologna began as pure
necessity. The town's arcaded streets served to leave the
sidewalks open for commerce and discussion in any
weather, while the center remained for traffic. Many of
the students were by no means poor: Thomas à Becket
was one, and later came many an English lord as well as
the sons of Italian aristocrats. One of the latter was Ercole,
the son of Isabella d'Este, who, like many, arrived to fill a
rented house with his own furniture and paintings (with a
mother who was the patron of Andrea Mantegna, one can
imagine). Other students could stay in one of the 14
national "schools" opened for foreigners (the one for the
Spanish is still there), or they could rent rooms.

The 13th century also brought the wars between the
papacy and the German Emperor Frederick II. In Bologna, the papal, or Guelph, side won, and the emperor's
son Enzo, already resident in Bologna, was taken prisoner and lodged—in luxury—in the palace on the **piazza
Maggiore** that still bears his name. Then as now Bologna's
central square, the piazza is the location of the Palazzo
del Podestà, the Palazzo Communale, and the cathedral,
or **Basilica of San Petronio**. The basilica, planned to be
larger than St. Peter's in Rome, was designed by Antonio
di Vicenzo, who also provided the other major buildings
of Gothic Bologna, including the Loggia dei Mercanti.

Much of the piazza Maggiore was his, and there as elsewhere in town a certain Medieval heaviness was lightened by later additions—in the case of the piazza, by the
bronze fountain of Neptune, the work of the Flemish
sculptor Jean Boulogne (Giambologna). It wasn't long
before the Renaissance city began to take shape, with its
colors of ocher, rose, and rust (from the terra-cotta trimmings), the copper domes of the churches lending a glow
of sulphur green.

Bologna never remained for a long period under the
dominion of any one family, unlike the Ferrara of the
Estes or the Mantua of the Gonzagas. Here there were
three important families: the Pepoli, the Visconti, and the
Bentivoglio. These last, who intermarried with the Sforzas and modeled themselves on the de Medici, were the
most influential. Even they were so disliked, however,
that their palace was destroyed by a mob. It was situated
across from their charming chapel in the **Church of San
Giacomo Maggiore** on the via Zamboni, its frescoes by
Lorenzo Costa depicting a day in the life of a Renaissance
court.

During this period Bologna's artists were usually called
in from elsewhere, the painters largely from Ferrara, and
the sculptors (Nicola Pisano, Jacopo della Quercia, and
others) mainly from Tuscany. These artists turned the
churches into veritable museums. Apart from San Giacomo, with its Bentivoglio chapel and oratory, there is
San Domenico for Pisano and **San Petronio** for the sculptures over the doors and the paintings inside. One of the
great pleasures of Bologna is the work of Nicolo dell'
Arca. Inside the church of San Domenico one of his
delicate angels flanks a robust early work of Michelangelo's. His, too, is the bust of San Domenico in the sacristy.
In the Pinacoteca, his Pietà of lifesize figures, raw with
emotion, is on loan from its former home in Santa Maria
della Vita. The finest palace of the Renaissance in Bologna
is the **Palazzo Bevilacqua**, near San Domenico, where the
Bentivoglios moved when their own palace burned down.

The quarrels of these reigning families and the communal government itself were to come to an abrupt end in
1506, when the papacy took over Bologna and ruled the
town until the arrival of Napoléon. Here the reign of
Rome was not to be as negligent as it was in Ferrara; a
large portion of the city was given over to convents and
monasteries. The Popes had decided to make Bologna
the Rome of the north, a decision concurrent with the

beginning of the Counter-Reformation, whose first conference, the Council of Trent, was held here in the Palazzo
Bevilacqua in 1543. Emperor Charles V already had been
crowned here by the Pope in 1530, and soon the Inquisition was to arrive. So did an era of prosperity, due to the
production of silk and hemp in the city. A wave of Baroque architecture engulfed the city in churches and in
palaces—which you must search out, because the arcades
draw our attention instead to their courts, which regale
us with splendor. Most palaces, like the **Hercolani** and the
Pepoli Campogrande, are on these same streets near the
Due Torri; lovers of Baroque should get a list of the many
others at the tourist office. The largest building of all was
the Archiginnasio, built as a center of the **University of
Bologna** behind San Petronio by the papacy. Baroque
theater came later, introduced by Bologna's Bibbiena family, all ten of them, who were to construct theaters and
settings for the courts of Europe, and who left a gem in
Bologna with their **Teatro Communale**, on via Zamboni.

Most important of all here was Baroque painting: the
school of Bologna started by the Carracci brothers and
carried on by Guido Reni, Domenichino, and Il Guercino,
among others. They—along with Correggio—were the
Italian painters whose work the later visitors on the Grand
Tour came to see, visitors such as Liszt, Goethe, Stendhal,
Byron, and the Romantics. After a century of being shelved
thanks to "modern" taste, these works are all now back
being reconsidered, featured in massive shows in London,
New York, and of course in the very large **Pinacoteca** on
Bologna's via Zamboni. This gallery was founded by the
city fathers in 1797 after the arrival of Napoléon. Its contents were largely taken from the church property the
French put up for sale or turned into prisons, barracks,
and hospitals. All this had to be done quickly, before the
occupying forces could indulge in their favorite game of
packing masterpieces and sending them back to the Louvre. The resulting museum gives a complete survey of
Bolognese artists from the Gothic masters to the Baroque, as well as of the schools of Ferrara and of Giotto.
The *Santa Cecilia* of Raphael, which sent many a 19th-
century viewer into a swoon, remains the most famous
picture here.

The French naturally moved the headquarters of the
university from its Catholic cradle in the Archiginnasio
into a building that had been used for physics and science. One of the later Bolognese graduates who studied

there was the inventor Marconi. With the unification of Italy the old city walls came down, Bologna's commerce expanded, and a period of bourgeois prosperity was ushered in. One of the chief things that these newly rich were interested in was food.

For a foretaste of Bologna's table and to whet your appetite, there is nothing better than a stroll from the Due Torri to the streets surrounding the main market, the **Pescherie Vecchie** and its satellites. There you can see *salumerias* without rival, their windows chockablock with the local mortadellas, salamis, and huge wheels of cheese from all over Emilia. The pyramids of wild mushrooms, vegetables, and fresh fruit are worthy of any still life in the Pinacoteca. As for the restaurants, they are of such renown that they produce the same sort of "news" that flashes through Paris: whether it be that Bologna's Ristorante Dante has changed management, or that Morini of Imola has taken a part-interest in the Pappagallo, or that the best of all is the new **Tre Frecce**, installed in Medieval quarters on the via San Vitale.

Michelin, ever stingy with its stars (rosettes) outside of France, lights up Bologna with three. The **Pappagallo** (piazza della Mercanzia) remains the most popular, but in the upper echelons there are many more. The **Notai** (via de' Pignattari 1) sits serenely elegant in its 1900 setting, while **Grassilli** (via del Luzzo 3) offers not only superb food but an additional treat for opera-lovers. Its walls are emblazoned with signed photos of its past clientele— Maria Callas, Tebaldi, Mario del Monaco, the names of some of them etched into brass plaques on the backs of the chairs they used to occupy—and a bust of Verdi presides over the main room. In all of these restaurants the big three of Bolognese pasta are featured: tortellini, tagliatelli, and lasagna. When green (from being mixed with spinach) the last two are unbeatable here. They are treated in myriad ways, so by no means do you have to stick to the local staple *salsa* Bolognese. These pastas can be flavored with *funghi porcini* or topped, in season, with diced vegetables or sauces of green pepper *(pepe-verde)* or cream *(panna)*. Nor are you limited to the big three: gnocchi with a dressing of gorgonzola can be delicious, as are the Pappagallo's crepes stuffed with *mortadella*. Of the main courses, the best known are the turkey breast *(tacchino)* or veal *costollete alla Bolognese,* richly cooked with grated Parmesan, butter, and sliced ham. Veal also turns up in *involtini* (veal birds), with mushrooms (*farcite*), or with truffles, sweetbreads, and chicken giblets (*in cassoto*).

Many chefs, to counter the charge that the food of Bologna is heavy, have come up with new ideas for salads, galantines, and mousses. The client can counter heaviness, too, by intelligent ordering. There is no reason to precede a Rabelaisian meat dish with pasta; with a copious pasta dish you need only salad and dessert. Another escape route can be economic, too: lunch in a starred restaurant, but dine more simply with locals in a reliable trattoria (such as **Leonida**, on the vicolo Alemagna 2). Because of its young population, Bologna is great fun at night and is one of the few Italian provincial towns where a curtain of melancholy doesn't come thundering down at nine o'clock. Not all of the local *jeunesse* can afford the Pappagallo, and the trattorias are where the animation can be found.

Of the hotels in the higher categories, the newly reopened **Baglioni**, a delight of Carracci frescoes, is one of Italy's most exquisite hotels. The next most appealing is the **Internazionale** (via dell'Indipendenza 60): it is old-fashioned in its decor and in its courteous service. On a small scale, but still with four stars, is the **Al Cappello Rosso**, on a pedestrian street (via de' Fusari 9) a stone's throw from the piazza Maggiore, and thus convenient for sightseeing. Of the more modest lodgings, the **Dei Commercianti** (via de' Pignattari 11) and the beautifully renovated **Corona d'Oro** (via Oberdan 12) are good bets, but they both get very full, so reserve ahead.

Bologna is by no means the last city on the Via Emilia. Fans of both the architect Alberti and the painter Piero della Francesca will drive farther southeast down the A 14 to **Rimini** on the Adriatic at its very end to see the **Tempio Malatestiano**, one of the great monuments of the Renaissance, a church glorifying Sigismondo Malatesta, who is buried within; and then perhaps dip down to Umbria. Others will take advantage of Bologna's rapid Autostrada A 1 south over the Apennines to Florence and Tuscany.

GETTING AROUND
This region may be the best connected of all Italian regions. Most of the major cities are on train lines, with frequent service to one another. From Bologna there are many trains a day to Parma, Piacenza, Modena, Ferrara, Ravenna, and Rimini. The railroad is so thorough in its

routing that buses are rarely necessary, except to visit the smallest towns.

Bologna is also well connected to Florence and Venice by train, and by air to all other Italian airports directly or with good continuing flight service. (Several major European cities also include regular service to Bologna on their schedules.)

By highway Emilia-Romagna is on a direct line from Parma to Bologna and Rimini across the old Via Emilia, which is now approximated in part by Route A 1, with clearly marked turnoffs for the western part of Emilia-Romagna. Major arteries connect the other cities and most of the important towns.

ACCOMMODATIONS REFERENCE

▶ **Astra.** Viale Cavour 55, 44100 **Ferrara**. Tel: (0532) 262-34.

▶ **Grand Hotel Baglioni.** Via dell'Indipendenza 8, 40121 **Bologna**. Tel: (051) 22-54-45.

▶ **Bisanzio.** Via Salaria 30, 48100 **Ravenna**. Tel: (0544) 271-11.

▶ **Canalgrande.** Corso Canal Grande 6, 41100 **Modena**. Tel: (059) 21-71-60; Telex: 510480.

▶ **Al Cappello Rosso.** Via de' Fusari 9, 40123 **Bologna**. Tel: (051) 26-18-91.

▶ **Centrale-Byron.** Via 4 Novembre 14, 48100 **Ravenna**. Tel: (0544) 222-25; Telex: 551070.

▶ **Dei Commercianti.** Via de' Pignattari 11, 40124 **Bologna**. Tel: (051) 23-30-52.

▶ **Corona d'Oro 1890.** Via Oberdan 12, 40126 **Bologna**. Tel: (051) 23-64-56.

▶ **Internazionale.** Via dell'Indipendenza 60, 40121 **Bologna**. Tel: (051) 24-55-44; Telex: 511038.

▶ **Libertà.** Via Blasia 10, 41100 **Modena**. Tel: (059) 22-23-65.

▶ **Park Hotel Toscanini.** Viale Toscanini 4, 43100 **Parma**. Tel: (0521) 28-10-32.

▶ **Ripagrande.** Via Ripagrande 21, 44100 **Ferrara**. Tel: (0532) 347-33.

▶ **Roma.** Via Farini 44, 41100 **Modena**. Tel: (059) 22-22-18.

▶ **Touring.** Viale Cavour 11, 44100 **Ferrara**. Tel: (0532) 260-96.

FLORENCE

By Anne Marshall Zwack

Florence does not evoke love at first sight, unlike the instant infatuation one has with Rome or Venice—which has been compared to eating a box of chocolate liqueurs all at once. And yet it is the most Anglo-Saxon of Italian cities, where expatriates from Robert and Elizabeth Barrett Browning onward have felt most at home. It is, as Mary McCarthy writes in *Stones of Florence,* "a manly city, and the cities of art that appeal to the current sensibility are feminine." The three dominant figures of the Renaissance—Donatello, Brunelleschi, and Michelangelo—were, after all, bachelors. There are no sweeping vistas in Florence, with the exception of the Technicolor sunset from the piazzale Michelangelo; the *palazzi* are forbidding. "Magnificently stern and somber" are the narrow streets, according to Charles Dickens, streets crammed today with honking vehicles between token sidewalks and frowning eaves. Ezra Pound claimed that Florence—Firenze—was the most damned of Italian cities, with no place to stand or sit or walk.

Likewise, the Florentines themselves, compared with the extroverted, warm southern Italians, are a dour folk who tolerate tourists as a necessary evil. The Florentine is iconoclastic and frugal, not to say stingy. Dante, himself a Florentine, called them *"Gente avara, invidiosa e superba"* (a stingy, envious, and proud people). They are also well groomed, well educated, and very civilized. Florence is a northern European city where—though since Mussolini the trains may not always run on time—people are punctual, reliable, and hard-working. Indeed, the Florentines' understated lifestyle and undemonstrative, almost puritanical nature is not dissimilar to the so-called WASP ethic.

Florence is not an industrial city—within less than half an hour from the center the Chianti wine-growing country is at hand—and hence there has been no mobile population to melt in the Florentine pot. Not only the aristocracy, known as the *dugento* (meaning, descending from the 1200s), who still live in their patrician palazzi, but the clerks and tradespeople have been Florentines for centuries before the Mayflower landed, and they have the arrogance of people who know that their ancestors invented the modern world. Now as then a Saint Bernardino of Siena could preach from the steps of the church of Santa Croce, "Italy is the most intelligent country in Europe, Tuscany the most intelligent region in Italy, and Florence the most intelligent town in Tuscany."

The Renaissance

Florence, after all, *is* the Renaissance, the first city to be raised like Lazarus from the dead when the rest of us were, if not exactly painted blue, still plunged in the Dark Ages. "It is inside these walls," exclaimed the young Stendhal as he rode over the Apennines into Florence, "that civilization began again." It is interesting to reflect on the fact that Michelangelo, the culminating figure of the Florentine Renaissance, died the year Shakespeare was born. "This century, like a Golden Age, has restored to light the liberal arts, which were almost extinct— grammar, poetry, rhetoric, painting, sculpture, architecture, music, the ancient singing of songs to the Orphic lyre—and all this in Florence," wrote Marsilio Ficino, protégé of the Medicis, in 1492.

For three and a half centuries, Florence and larger-than-life figures like Leonardo da Vinci and Galileo set the world a new standard, not only in the arts, but in medicine, science, engineering, astronomy, physics, political thought, even economics (there were 72 banks in the center of the city alone, and the Florentine florin was the dollar or Deutsche mark of the Middle Ages). Dante and the Florentines invented the Italian language as it is spoken today, while Florence also pioneered mapmaking. By following the Florentine Toscanelli's map, Columbus was able to discover the New World, although both thought it was a new route to Asia. Another Florentine, Amerigo Vespucci, disproved this and gave his name to two continents, while Giovanni da Verrazzano sailed up the North American coast as far as Nova Scotia, calling new landmarks by Tuscan names such as Vallombrosa and San Miniato. It could thus be argued that all of us—Old World or New—have roots in Florence, and that, as the present mayor Massimo Bogianchino said when criticized for not stemming the flood of tourists, "Florence belongs to the world."

"When one great genius is born, it is in the very nature of things that he shall not stand alone." So observed Vasari, Renaissance architect and chronicler, when writing about Masaccio. His theory is that Renaissance men were "impelled by nature and refined to a certain degree by the *air they breathed* to set to work, each according to his own talent." It is nevertheless difficult to explain how so many great talents lived in this "Etrurian Athens," as Byron called it, at the same time. It may simply be that the 15th century was an age of individualists, many of whom happened to be artists. Florence was as modern and as aggressively progressive in the quattrocento as New York is today—one might even say the Medicis were the Rockefellers of the Renaissance.

The River Arno

Florence is divided, like Paris, into a right and left bank, here by the yellow river Arno—and indeed yellow is the dominant color in Florence. "She sits," says Henry James, "in the sunshine beside her yellow river like the little treasure city that she has always seemed"; the "sallow houses" vary in shade from ochre to withered lemon, while the roofs and domes are a rusty orange.

In the 13th and 14th centuries the foundations of Florentine wealth were built on wool, a full quarter of the population being involved in the many facets of the cloth trade. Artisans washed and rinsed their fleeces in what a perennially disgruntled Dante called that "cursed ditch," the river Arno. Even Mark Twain thought it would be "a very plausible river if they could pump some water into it." The Arno sinks so low in summer that the fish die, while in winter it can rise so high that it floods its banks, as in 1966, when much damage was done to the city and its works of art. (You will see plaques all over the city showing the height of the floodwaters.) In the old days carts came rumbling over the Ponte alla Carraia (from *carro,* meaning cart), bringing wool from the English Cotswolds and from France and Flanders to be dyed and spun in Florence; the cloth guilds, the Arte della Lana and the Calimala, were so wealthy they could finance the building of the Duomo, the Baptistery, and the basilica of San Miniato.

The Medici family, who ruled Florence officially and unofficially from 1434 until 1737, with only a few interludes—such as Savanarola's ascendancy and several attempts at a true republic—were merchants, lords of commerce rather than an aristocracy, and it is due to their affluent patronage that so much of the city was built and adorned. Their coat of arms, a varying number of balls, surmounts many a portal and cornice to this day. (It has been suggested that these balls are meant to be pills, a pun on the name Medici, which means doctors.)

The two banks of the Arno are linked by a number of bridges, of which only one, the **Ponte Vecchio**, or Old Bridge, spanning the river at its narrowest point, survived the war. Hitler fell so in love with the kitsch conglomeration of jewelry stores lining its sides that the Luftwaffe was ordered to spare it for posterity. It is called the Old Bridge to distinguish it from the Ponte alla Carraia, which was "new" (in 1220), although the present structure of the Ponte Vecchio dates from 1345. Goldsmiths and jewelers have plied their trades on the bridge since the 16th century, in stores that were once a bazaar for butchers, hosiers, greengrocers, and blacksmiths.

Other, more beautiful bridges, such as the **Ponte Santa Trínita**, whose arches were drawn by Michelangelo, had to be fished piece by piece out of the river after the war and rebuilt with funds raised by the sale of tickets for individual bricks and stones; $160,000 was collected by a committee led by Bernard Berenson.

The right (north) bank of the Arno is the more pompous, monumental side of the river, where you will find all the banks, boutiques, and car-rental and travel agencies, the train station, and most of the museums and churches.

MAJOR INTEREST ON THE RIGHT BANK

Galleria degli Uffizi (comprehensive collection of Renaissance art)

Palazzo Vecchio (Florence's town hall)

Galleria dell'Accademia (Michelangelo's *David*)

Museo Nazionale del Bargello (sculpture by Donatello and others)

Duomo, Baptistery of San Giovanni, and Campanile and the Museo dell'Opera di Santa Maria del Fiore

Church of Santa Croce (Giotto frescoes) with the
Museo dell'Opera di Santa Croce
Church of Santa Maria Novella (Uccello frescoes in
the Green Cloister)
Monastery of San Marco (Fra Angelico frescoes)
Church of San Lorenzo and the Cappelle Medicee
(sculpture by Michelangelo)

SPECIAL INTEREST

Palazzo Davanzati (Medieval nobleman's home)
Museo di Storia della Scienza (Galileo's
telescopes)
Cenacoli (frescoes depicting *The Last Supper*)
Opificio e Museo delle Pietre Dure (Renaissance
stone workmanship)
Palazzo Medici-Riccardi (Gozzoli frescoes)
Museo Archeologico
Biblioteca Medici Laurenziana

The left (south) bank, or *Oltrarno* (literally, "over the
Arno"), is traditionally the poorer side of the river, the
artisan quarter, and the greener side of Florence.

MAJOR INTEREST IN THE OLTRARNO

Palazzo Pitti with the Galleria Palatina, Museo degli
Argenti, and the Giardino di Boboli
Church of Santo Spirito (Filippino Lippi altarpiece)
Church of Santa Maria del Carmine (Masaccio
frescoes)
Piazzale Michelangelo (panoramic view)
Church of San Miniato al Monte (Romanesque
architecture)

Most museums in Florence are open from 9:00 A.M. until
2:00 P.M. except Mondays, unless otherwise noted here;
on Sundays and public holidays, until 1:00 P.M. Churches
are open from 7:00 A.M. until noon and 2:30 or 3:00 P.M. to
6:30 or 7:00.

THE RIGHT BANK

Although central Italy was first civilized by the Etruscans,
and the little hilltop village of Fiesole was an Etruscan
settlement, Florence itself is a Roman town. The main

thoroughfares used to converge on the corner where Upim, the city's main department store, stands today; the piazza della Repubblica is on the site of the Roman Forum; and it was long believed that the Baptistery was originally a temple to Mars, built to celebrate the Roman victory over the Etruscans in Fiesole. No traces of its Roman past remain in contemporary Florence, however, although excavations are being carried out in the piazza della Signoria, and further evidence of the buried Roman city may yet come to light. Florence today is overwhelmingly Renaissance, her treasures still lived in and part of everyday life. "The ancient city of the 15th century still exists and constitutes the body of the city," remarked the 19th-century philosopher Hippolyte Taine, without being "enveloped in medieval cobwebs," while someone else has said that Florence is "like a town that has survived itself."

It is to the architect Arnolfo di Cambio that the Duomo (cathedral), the Palazzo Vecchio (or Town Hall), and the church of Santa Croce have all been attributed. He was the son of a German "Maestro Jacopo" who was invited to Florence after building a Franciscan church in Arezzo and was immediately rechristened "Lapo," a local name still very popular today. In Florence he built the Palazzo del Bargello, which was the law courts (now a museum containing the Medici collections), while his son Arnolfo, born in 1232, was responsible for as much progress in architecture, according to Vasari, as Cimabue was in painting. At the age of 30 Arnolfo was considered the best architect in Tuscany.

Il Duomo

The word "Duomo" comes from the Latin *Domus Dei* (House of God). Even today the cathedral of Santa Maria del Fiore looks inordinately large, but in 1294, when the cornerstone was laid, the project must have seemed as vast and wondrous as the launching of the *Titanic* 500 years later. Even now, no building in Florence can be built higher than the cathedral, which dwarfs the rest of the city, as Mark Twain says, "like a captive balloon." Vasari claimed "The ancients never dared so to compete with the heavens as this building seems to do, for it towers above the hills which are around Florence." The city fathers had decided that their cathedral should be *"più bello che si può"* (as beautiful as can be), a require-

ment stipulated in this and subsequent Florentine building contracts throughout the Renaissance. Italians today
are still city patriots rather than nationalists; in those days
there was a definite one-upmanship among the rival cities
of Tuscany as to which would have the biggest and the
best. When Arnolfo di Cambio died, the Florentine elders
were left with the problem of raising the biggest dome
since the Roman Pantheon above his vast edifice. A competition was held for the design, but before Brunelleschi's project was finally accepted, many decades were
spent in theorizing and arguing. One scheme was to
build a mound of earth full of coins, construct the dome
above it, and then invite the townspeople to scavenge for
the coins. Meanwhile, to finance the building a tax was
levied on anyone caught blaspheming—a bad habit still
notoriously rife among Florentines today.

Genius and Beauty do not always go hand in hand. Both
Brunelleschi and Giotto were ill-favored youths—and apparently even Michelangelo had protruding ears—but Vasari comforts us with the notion that "under the clods of
earth, the veins of gold lie hidden." Filippo Brunelleschi's
father wanted him to become a notary like himself, and
was impatient with the doodlings of someone who was to
give the world "the most noble, vast, and beautiful building of modern times" (Vasari). Like many Renaissance
artists—Ghiberti, Botticelli, Donatello, Uccello, Verrocchio, and Luca della Robbia—he was first apprenticed to a
goldsmith. Donatello was Brunelleschi's best friend, and
together they went to Rome to dig up and measure the art
and architecture of antiquity. Contemporary Romans, who
had not yet awakened to the importance of their Classical
past, thought the two of them eccentric treasure-seekers.
Filippo came back with his project for the biggest dome in
Christendom: to build *two* cupolas, one within the other,
bearing each other's stresses and strains—an idea that
initially made him the laughingstock of Florence. Fourteen years later, when several marble quarries had been
depleted in the process of building it, the laugh was on
the other side. Overcoming all opposition, Brunelleschi
supervised the building, which began in 1420, down to
the minutest details, personally designing the pulleys and
hoists and constructing kitchens and wine shops between
the two walls so that the masons need not descend for
lunch. He illustrated his answers to architectonic queries
submitted by the craftsmen by whittling away at a handy
turnip. Today visitors can walk around the dome between

the double walls, 300 feet above the ground, every day except Sundays.

The maintenance of the Duomo is a full-time job. Around the corner in the via dello Studio, a little band of craftsmen called the *scalpellini* work on damaged buttresses or cornices and on the strips of green and white marble from the cathedral's façade all year round. The dome is currently supported by scaffolding, because some telltale cracks have appeared on the ceiling.

The Renaissance architect Alberti wrote of the dome that, rising above the skies, it was "large enough to shelter all the people of Tuscany in its shadow." As you walk in the echoing interior of the cathedral today this is believable, especially since all the statuary and furniture of the cathedral have been moved to the nearby Museo dell' Opera di Santa Maria del Fiore. As an 18th-century traveller observed, "The architect seems to have turned his building inside out; nothing in art being more ornamented than the exterior, and few churches so simple within." The **Museo dell'Opera di Santa Maria del Fiore** (the cathedral museum) must be the least well signposted in Florence, but in it are the splendid organ lofts, or *cantorie,* by Luca della Robbia and Donatello, whose *putti* are surely the most roguish urchins of the Renaissance. Here too is a Michelangelo *Pietà,* one of his four great sculptures of the mourning Madonna receiving the body of Christ from the Cross (the others are the one in St. Peter's in Rome, the *Pietà da Palestrina* in the Galleria dell'Accademia in Florence, and the *Pietà Rondanini* in the Castello Sforzesco in Milan). The one here was never finished, and Michelangelo actually tried to destroy it, although he had originally intended it as his own funerary monument. The figure of Nicodemus supporting the body of Christ is a self-portrait. The museum is open every day (half-days on Sundays), until 6:00 P.M. in winter and 8:00 P.M. in summer.

The Baptistery of San Giovanni

The Baptistery, opposite the cathedral, was called the "bel San Giovanni" by Dante, who was baptized there—as were all the children born in Florence during the year—in a communal ceremony, a practice still in use today. Every time a boy was born a black bean was dropped into an urn in the Baptistery, while a girl was signified by a white bean, thus establishing the annual birthrate. The

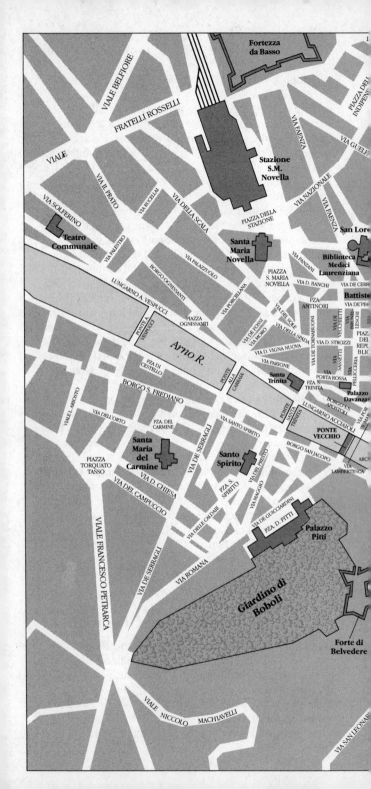

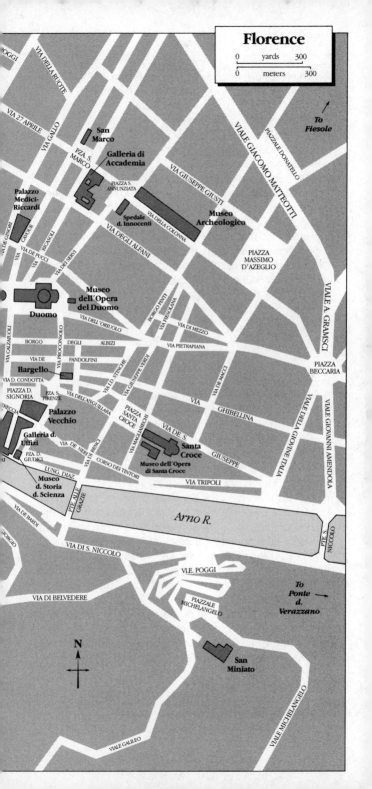

structure, a pure octagon, is above all remarkable for its **Ghiberti bronze doors**, notably the famous "Gates of Paradise," as Michelangelo called them.

Brunelleschi and Ghiberti were rivals. When, in 1400, the Calimala (cloth guild) announced a competition to see who would forge the doors of the Baptistery, Brunelleschi was 23 and Ghiberti 20. Ghiberti won. It took the Ghiberti bronze foundry 24 years to finish the Gates of Paradise, during which time many leading Renaissance artists, such as Donatello, Uccello, Michelozzo, Gozzoli, and Antonio Pollaiuolo, passed through his workshop, the artists of the Renaissance being first and foremost superb craftsmen. Both the casting in bronze of the Ghiberti doors and the raising of Brunelleschi's cupola were unprecedented technical as well as artistic achievements. Today the restored panels of the Gates of Paradise are also to be seen in the Museo dell'Opera di Santa Maria del Fiore.

The Campanile

In 1334 a public decree announced the building of a *campanile* (bell tower) in these terms: "The Florentine republic desires that an edifice shall be constructed so magnificent in its height and quality that it shall surpass anything of its kind produced in the time of their greatest power by the Greeks and Romans." The project was assigned to Giotto, who when asked by Pope Benedict IX to submit samples of his work drew a perfect circle in red pencil. If the seeds of the Renaissance can be said to have been sown somewhere, it is with Giotto, a pupil of the great Cimabue, whom he surpassed and, again according to Vasari, "threw open the gates and showed the path to that perfection which art displays in our age." Although Giotto did not live to finish it (he died in 1336), the Campanile remains, to quote Longfellow, "the lily of Florence blossoming in stone." Visitors can climb to the top of it for a bird's-eye view of the city. Unlike the Duomo and the Baptistery, the bell tower, right next to the cathedral, is open all day every day (not closing for lunch) until 5:00 P.M. in winter and 7:00 P.M. in summer.

The Palazzo Vecchio

Goethe concluded that for Florence to have accumulated such a rich heritage of art and architecture she must have enjoyed "a long succession of wise rulers." And yet throughout the 13th century Florence was split by bitter strife between the two warring factions, the Guelphs and the Ghibellines. Like the Montagues and Capulets of *Romeo and Juliet,* some families belonged to the Guelphs, the merchant party with allegiance to the Pope, others to the Ghibellines, the aristocratic and feudal party whose sympathies were with the Hohenstaufen Holy Roman Emperors. These feuds were carried on between cities as well—Guelph Florence against a Ghibelline Siena, Pisa, and Arezzo. However, even among the Guelphs themselves there were bitterly opposed White Guelphs and Black Guelphs. Depending on which party momentarily held sway, Florentines of the opposite allegiance were forced, as Dante (himself a White Guelph) was, to eat what he called "the bitter bread of exile."

The Palazzo Vecchio, on the piazza della Signoria, was built to celebrate a definitive Guelph victory at Benevento in 1266. The tower, which has variously been compared to a rocket or a hypodermic needle, soars upward from the **piazza della Signoria**, the center of Florentine civic life, the square that was paved over the ruins of Ghibelline property so that they could never set foot in their *palazzi* again. Later the Palazzo Vecchio became the official residence of the Medicis, acquiring the epithet *"Vecchio,"* or old, when Cosimo de' Medici moved into his new apartments in the Palazzo Pitti. Today it is Florence's town hall, where births and deaths are registered and where Florentines are married—the bride always being presented with a bouquet of *gigli,* or irises, the city's emblem. Seemingly endless flights of stairs lead up to the great rooms, seat of the city's administration in the 15th century, and to the Medici apartments, all of which can be visited, except on Saturdays.

Church of Santa Croce

Dante left Florence, never to return, and is buried in Ravenna—a fact to which the Florentines are still not resigned. But there is a commemorative plaque to Italy's greatest poet in the Franciscan church of Santa Croce, together with flamboyant marble tombs of great Italian figures such as Galileo, Rossini, and Michelangelo. Santa Croce, at the eastern edge of the city center near the river, is Florence's Pantheon, a center for the cult of famous men. The most beautiful tombs are of two chancellors of the

Republic and prominent humanists, Leonardo Bruni and Carlo Marsuppini, that face each other on either side of the nave. Humanism in the Renaissance was *humanitas,* a word that Leonardo Bruni, who was chancellor in 1427, borrowed from Cicero, meaning studies that are "humane," worthy of the dignity of mankind. It is therefore appropriate that the portrait of the man himself dominates each tomb, the Bruni monument being the more austere of the two, the solemnity of the Marsuppini tomb relieved by some entrancing little *putti* blithely standing guard.

Giotto

The church of Santa Croce is where Lucy Honeychurch of E. M. Forster's *A Room with a View* finds herself at a loss without a Baedeker while looking for the frescoes of Giotto, "in the presence of whose tactile values she was capable of feeling what was proper." With these frescoes in the **Peruzzi and Bardi chapels**, Giotto, who flourished in the early 14th century, imposed a new and more human vision of the arts of Western Europe. Not since antiquity had the human body been represented in such a realistic way. He also had a genius for selecting the most dramatic psychological moment in a story and making every component of the fresco echo this. His people are experiencing real emotion; the grief-stricken brothers mourning the death of Saint Francis are human in their suffering at a time when faces in other paintings were only conventional masks. The epitaph on a monument to Giotto erected by Lorenzo the Magnificent reads in Latin, "I am he by whom the extinct art of painting was revived."

The flood of 1966 did much damage to the church of Santa Croce, especially to the frescoes and to the giant 13th-century crucifix by Cimabue—widely pictured in the press dragging in the mud when the waters had receded. What is left of it is in the **Museo dell'Opera di Santa Croce** in the old convent refectory next door. The leather school that adjoins the church was founded by the monks and is now, besides a school, a series of little workshops where you can purchase leather goods and have them initialed on the spot.

Other Frescoes in Florence

Although Florence is a treasure trove of painting, Renaissance and otherwise, it is the frescoes that as a group make the most moving statement, with an expressive power never since equaled. The Masaccio frescoes of the **Cappella Brancacci (Brancacci chapel)** in **Santa Maria del Carmine** in the Oltrarno have been under restoration and girded by scaffolding for years, but should be unveiled by 1989. The frescoes of Paolo Uccello are in the so-called Green Cloister, adjacent to the church of Santa Maria Novella across from the train station at the piazza della Stazione.

Masaccio's real name was Tommaso, but they called him Masaccio, which means "Slovenly Tom," because of his disregard for appearances. Masaccio was a people's painter, with the straightforward honesty of a Florentine artisan. About a century after Giotto, Masaccio revived the earlier artist's approach to fresco painting. He painted in a sculptural way, departing from the International Gothic style by emphasizing mass and light over line and color.

Masaccio was the first painter of his time to apply the new principles of perspective worked out by sculptors and architects such as Donatello, Ghiberti, and Brunelleschi. Although he died at the age of 27 (in 1428), in only five or six years he managed to revolutionize Florentine painting. He used the new knowledge of anatomy to paint, as Vasari says, "many attitudes and movements that had never before been painted." The tax collector collecting the tribute money from Saint Peter is appropriately avid; Adam and Eve express their shame with gaping mouths as they are expelled from the Garden of Eden. Since being restored, Adam and Eve are now as Masaccio painted them—without the fig leaves of puritanical afterthought—something that recently caused quite a stir.

No lesser painters than Filippino Lippi, Andrea del Castagno, Verrocchio, Ghirlandaio, Botticelli, Leonardo da Vinci, Perugino, Michelangelo, and Raphael recognized Masaccio as a master and came to study these frescoes in the Brancacci chapel.

Paolo Uccello was obsessed by perspective. His wife said that he would crawl into bed late at night saying, *"O, che dolce cosa è questa prospettiva"* (how fair a thing is this perspective). He was called *Uccello,* or bird, because of the many birds and beasts that appeared in his paintings. Although he relied largely on illustrations of birds and beasts, the animals featured in Renaissance paintings often were drawn from life. Lions were caged behind the Uffizi from the 13th century onward, and a camel, a giraffe, and other exotic animals arrived in the suite of the

Emperor John Palaeologus when the Western and Eastern churches met in Florence. This historic event, sponsored by the Medicis, was as momentous then as a Reagan-Gorbachev summit is today, and was immortalized by Benozzo Gozzoli in his *Procession of the Magi* in the chapel of the Palazzo Medici-Riccardi.

Uccello spent a disproportionate number of hours (scolded for it not just by his wife but by his friend Donatello) studying the perspective of the *mazzocchi,* the intricate straw scaffolding used for the extravagant headgear of the time, as shown in the equestrian portrait of Niccolò da Tolentino by Andrea del Castagno and in Uccello's twin fresco of Giovanni Acuto, the English mercenary whose real name was John Hawkwood. (The two frescoes are side by side in the Duomo.) Typically parsimonious, the Florentines owed this *condottiere* a memorial, but to save money they commissioned Uccello to do a fresco giving the illusion of sculpture.

Paolo Uccello's 15th-century studies of perspective are most evident in his frescoes in the **Green Cloister**, adjacent to Santa Maria Novella, in the piazza Santa Maria Novella. These depict scenes of the Creation and the Universal Deluge; the panic and anarchy in the latter are underlined by a vanishing focal point that seems to act like a magnet, drawing in the entire biblical cast.

The Green Cloister is so called because of the *terra verde,* or greenish grisaille, that was Uccello's favorite medium for frescoes. The cloister follows most Florentine museum opening and closing times but is closed Fridays.

Church of Santa Maria Novella

Leading off the Green Cloister is the **Cappellone degli Spagnoli (Spanish Chapel)**, "Spanish" because the Spanish suite of Eleonora of Toledo, wife of Cosimo de' Medici, used to hear mass there. The murals here, painted by Andrea Bonaiuti and others around 1366–1368, were the most ambitious work of pictorial theology of their time. Salvation, they suggest, is possible if sinners listen to the Dominican monks to whom Santa Maria Novella and the cloister and neighboring pharmacy all belonged. "Dominicans" colloquially was said to mean *"Domini Canes,"* hounds of the Lord; the Dominicans fought heresy mercilessly. No doubt when the Black Death of 1348 struck Florence and more than half the population of the city died, many townsfolk must have felt a cold wind blowing "I told you so" down their necks.

The side chapels in the church of Santa Maria Novella were all financed by leading citizens thankful for survival or in memory of their dear departed: for example, the **Strozzi Chapel** with frescoes by Filippino Lippi or the **Tornabuoni Chapel** with frescoes by Ghirlandaio, who also made the magnificent stained-glass window that dominates the nave.

The church is very badly lit, or as Edward Hutton politely puts it, "full of a sort of twilight," which can be illuminated by inserting some coins into a machine. You must seek out *The Trinity* by Masaccio in the main nave. Here Brunelleschian architectural forms are used—the arch is an exact copy of part of the façade of the Ospedale degli Innocenti—as a setting for figures that are represented for the first time in a human dimension rather than larger than life, as divine figures traditionally were. Above the door in the sacristy, where postcards are on sale, is an ample, very beautiful wooden cross by the school of Giotto (currently under restoration).

Look, too, for Brunelleschi's crucifix, which hangs with an almost chilling solemnity in a chapel all by itself. Hereby hangs the tale of the competition between Donatello and Brunelleschi as to who would carve the most beautiful crucifix. When Brunelleschi pronounced Donatello's Christ "a boor," Donatello is supposed to have answered, "Take wood, then, and make one yourself," a saying that became a byword in Renaissance Florence. Some time later, the two friends came back to Brunelleschi's studio, having shopped for lunch. Donatello was so bowled over by the just-completed ascetic Christ hanging on the wall that he dropped the provisions—eggs, cheese, and all—out of his artisan's apron onto the floor.

The **Pharmacy** of Santa Maria Novella in via della Scala 16, originally run by the Dominican monks, has been functioning since 1612. It still makes and sells herbal remedies 400 years old. In times of plague the pharmacy made a lotion called *Aceto dei Sette Ladri*, or Seven Thieves Vinegar, an unguent that was rubbed on the body to prevent contagion, named after the seven thieves who used to go around the city at night to rob the corpses of unfortunate victims of the plague. The pharmacy still does a surprisingly brisk trade in this lotion, which it sells as smelling salts. It also sells soaps, colognes, and pot-pourris in old-fashioned packaging that make unusual little gifts to take home.

Brunelleschi's Architecture

The exploration of space, be it of a canvas, a continent, the celestial realms, or the concentric circles of the Inferno, was a Florentine fixation from Dante to Galileo. Brunelleschi himself represents a transition from wall decoration, albeit sculptural, to true, three-dimensional architecture. Although his most famous achievement is the *Cupolone,* as the dome is called, Brunelleschi is also responsible for the Ospedale degli Innocenti (foundlings' hospital), the Old Sacristy of San Lorenzo, the church of San Lorenzo, the Pazzi chapel in Santa Croce, and the church of Santo Spirito, west of the Palazzo Pitti in Oltrarno.

The **Ospedale degli Innocenti,** on the piazza Santissima Annunziata northeast of the Duomo along via dei Servi, was the first Renaissance building in Florence. Begun in 1419, the hospital shows Brunelleschi's debt to the Classical and Romanesque past in its colonnaded loggia.

The hospital also has a picture gallery that is worth a visit for an inhabitant's view of a pure Renaissance building, as well as for the *Adoration of the Magi* by Ghirlandaio, who was Michelangelo's mentor. In color and detail it is magnificent, with sheep grazing on the Tuscan hills in the background and the Arno seemingly flowing on forever behind the stable in Bethlehem. The bearded, richly accoutred figures were all members of the Silk Guild, the *Arte della Seta,* who were the orphans' affluent benefactors.

Church of San Lorenzo

In the Old Sacristy in the church of San Lorenzo, between the Duomo and the train station, and in the **Cappella dei Pazzi (Pazzi chapel)** off the cloisters of Santa Croce, Brunelleschi uses a basic design—a circle within a square—that formed the basis of quattrocento architecture. Renaissance people believed strongly in the mysticism of mathematics: The geometrical figures of the circle and square corresponded exactly to the symmetry of a human figure with all four limbs outstretched; the Deity could best be represented by a triangle. Mankind belonged to a lucid, geometrically ordered universe.

Brunelleschi also designed the main body of the church of San Lorenzo, a virtuoso exercise in perspective. The church is a geometrical progression of columns, arcades, cornices, and window frames in *pietra serena* (the local stone that is the hallmark of Florentine Renaissance interiors), each element echoing the central theme and receding into a well-ordered distance, as though rippling toward the same vanishing point.

The Della Robbias

Many Brunelleschian designs are enhanced by roundels in glazed terra-cotta, such as the swaddled infants that line the façade of the Ospedale degli Innocenti, by Andrea della Robbia, who died in 1525. The Della Robbias were the only "dynasty" of the Renaissance—Luca's nephew Andrea had three sons, Luca, Girolamo, and Giovanni, all of whom were sculptors. It was Luca who invented the terra-cotta glaze that gave this fragile medium an almost endless durability. The Della Robbias have works in nearly every museum and church in Florence.

Michelangelo

The **Cappelle Medicee (Medici Chapels)** in the church of San Lorenzo were designed by Michelangelo, who was given what amounted to a state funeral in this church when he died in 1564. Michelangelo believed that architecture was fundamentally based on anatomy, with man as the measure of all things. He himself said, "Those who do not know the human body cannot be good architects." Indeed the architecture of these chapels, built as a Medici final resting place, can be described, like their creator, as superhuman—in concept and design. Until Michelangelo, sculpture was considered an ornament to architecture; in the Medici chapels the roles could be said to be reversed—Michelangelo's architecture *is* sculpture.

On the tombs the figures are not reclining, their feet in floppy chain mail, as on earlier funerary monuments, but are sitting up ready for the Resurrection, with Michelangelo's statues of *Day* and *Night, Dawn* and *Dusk,* signifying the passing of time, at their feet. Much has been written about the statue of *Night,* perhaps most poignantly by Walter Pater, who said, "No one ever expressed more truly than Michelangelo the notion of inspired sleep, of faces charged with dreams."

While you are visiting the church of San Lorenzo and the Medici chapels, it is worth pausing in the **Biblioteca Medici Laurenziana** (Laurentian Library), in the piazza San Lorenzo. Most remarkable for its staircase, also designed by Michelangelo, the library houses priceless manuscripts and codices, including the *Medici Virgil*.

Most of the Renaissance artists came from simple backgrounds, village boys brought up among the stonecutters. Even Michelangelo, the only one from the minor nobility, maintained that he had imbibed his genius with the milk of his wet nurse, a stonecutter's wife from Settignano. His most famous work is the **David**, carved out of an 18-foot block of marble. Contemporary Florentines called it *Il Gigante* (the Giant), so that you wonder how large Goliath would have been. Indeed, Michelangelo believed that the artist should have his measuring tools in the eye rather than in the hand, as it is the eye that judges, and he saw his *David* as a civic symbol. The arrogant youth is Florence, the little city on the Arno, triumphing over a whole cast of Goliaths—the papal court, the Medici power, and the rest of the world put together. *David* remains to this day the most popular Florentine, as D. H. Lawrence said, the "presiding genius of Florence."

The *David* is in the **Galleria dell'Accademia** (the world-famous museum northeast of the Duomo on via Ricasoli, which leads off the Duomo's piazza), along with a large collection of paintings from the 13th to the 18th century. There are also two copies of *David* in Florence, one in the piazza Signoria and one on **piazzale Michelangelo**.

The Monastery of San Marco

An entirely different figure from Michelangelo was **Fra Angelico**, an unworldly and retiring monk—he once refused a bishopric, pleading unworthiness—from the Dominican monastery of San Marco. He was commissioned by Cosimo de' Medici to paint frescoes in the cloisters and chapter house of San Marco, and to him we owe what is perhaps the most reproduced **Annunciation** of all time. However, despite the delicacy and pastel colors of Fra Angelico's paintings, he shares with the architects of his day (the first half of the 15th century) a keen architectonic sense; there is depth and perspective in the colonnades that frame the Angel Gabriel appearing to Mary.

A fellow Dominican, whose cell here can also be visited, was Fra Girolamo Savonarola, whose rabid puritanism, which urged artists to throw their works onto his Bonfire of Vanities, almost nipped the blossoming Renaissance in the bud in the last years of the 15th century. Even great artists like Botticelli fell under the spell of his thundering sermons. It was his spirit that inspired the Florentines to suggest putting a golden fig leaf on Michelangelo's *David,* much to the master's distress. Off the cloisters is another pharmacy that, although functioning as a modern pharmacy today, with a street entrance on the via Cavour, still has antique apothecary jars on the shelves. Hanging from the ceiling in an adjoining room is a crocodile the monks brought back from the Nile in the 17th century.

The Galleria degli Uffizi

The Galleria degli Uffizi, next to the Palazzo Vecchio, was once the offices, or *uffizi,* of the Medici government. The building was designed by Vasari, who also built a corridor to enable the reigning grand duke to leave his apartments in the Palazzo Pitti and cross the Ponte Vecchio without ever having to descend to street level. It was completed in only five months and claimed five lives in the building. Today the gallery houses the most important collection of Renaissance art in the world. The museum is open afternoons as well as mornings, from 9:00 A.M. to 7:00 P.M. daily and a half day on Sundays.

The main gallery, on the top floor, starts with the early Sienese painters (almost Byzantine in style), including Duccio, Lorenzetti, and Simone Martini, and continues through the International Gothic style of Gentile da Fabriano and Lorenzo Monaco to the early Renaissance. Here Masaccio is joined by Masolino, who also collaborated on the frescoes in the Brancacci chapel in Santa Maria del Carmine, and Uccello, with what is often considered his masterpiece, the *Battle of San Romano.* This battle scene, which used to hang in Lorenzo de' Medici's bedroom, is one of three panels—the other two are now in Paris and London.

The two best-known paintings of the Uffizi are surely the **Birth of Venus** and **Primavera** by Sandro Botticelli—

huge canvases, recently restored, that once hung in a Medici villa outside Florence. Botticelli's popularity is a relatively recent phenomenon; he was rediscovered during the Victorian Grand Tour period at the end of the last century. In his own lifetime he would have died a pauper on crutches if Lorenzo de' Medici had not supported him during his last years (he died in 1510).

Both the *Birth of Venus* and the *Primavera* would seem to be pagan subjects, but they are in fact offshoots of the Neoplatonic thought subscribed to almost slavishly at Lorenzo the Magnificent's court—interpretations of the Venus myth in Christian terms. The *Primavera* is an allegory of civilized living, while *Venus* is a pagan Madonna. Marsilio Ficino, tutor to the Medici children, wrote to one of his charges that Venus symbolizes humanity, "herself a nymph of excellent comeliness."

Another recently restored work is the *Tondo Doni,* a round picture of the Holy Family that Michelangelo painted for Agnolo Doni, who, like a good Florentine, haggled over the price (it was a new idea that artists should be paid differently from artisans, who got so much per hour); the patron was shamed into paying double. (During a similar argument, Donatello smashed a statue to pieces, declaring that his patron was obviously more used to purchasing beans than art.) In the *Tondo Doni,* the only canvas he ever completed, Michelangelo shows his mastery of contour, his sculptural style emphasizing movement and expressive line.

The Uffizi also houses an *Annunciation* by **Leonardo da Vinci,** one that, like most Annunciations, seems to have taken place in Tuscany, with cypress trees and umbrella pines punctuating the skyline. Leonardo's treatment of the angel's wings is highly innovative—they have evidently been studied in detail from real birds' wings—while the folds of the Madonna's draperies have been copied from an actual piece of cloth.

Leonardo was the archetypal Renaissance man, who excelled at everything he turned his hand to. The illegitimate son of a village squire, he was the first to apply reason to everything in the universe. He discovered the meaning of fossils, understood the solar system far ahead of his time, realized a hundred years before it was pronounced a certainty that the blood circulated in the body, understood optics and the role of the retina, and nearly invented the airplane. At the Antico Setificio in San Frediano the silk weavers still use a giant bobbin invented by Leonardo to wind the silk—no one has yet thought of a better system.

Leonardo was so busy inventing he had little time for painting, where perhaps his greatest genius lay. He himself wrote, as an afterthought when offering his services as an architect and an engineer, "In painting I can do as much as anyone, whoever he may be." To Leonardo we owe the tender mysterious smiles, not just of the Mona Lisa, but of all his female figures, sacred or otherwise. He conceived objects as bathed in space, inventing *lo sfumato,* in which he defined his forms without abrupt outlines. When just a youth he was apprenticed to Verrocchio, and painted the left-hand angel in a canvas of his master's, *The Baptism* (now in the Uffizi), after which it is said that a chagrined Verrocchio vowed never to paint again, concentrating on sculpture from then on. Also in the Uffizi is Leonardo's *Adoration of the Magi,* which, with its pyramidal composition—a solution to the problem of cramming a picture with spectators around the central group of the Madonna and Child—is considered a watershed in Renaissance art: a break with all that had gone before, and one of the most important works in Florence in the last quarter of the 15th century.

The Uffizi collection includes works by Filippino Lippi, Mantegna, Perugino, Raphael, Bellini, Giorgione, Correggio, Titian, Rubens, Veronese, Caravaggio, Tintoretto, and every other major Renaissance painter in Italy and abroad. When the High Renaissance began to wane, we have the Mannerism of Pontormo and Bronzino, with his portraits of Medici courtiers, in the magnificent circular room with its mother-of-pearl inlaid domed ceiling.

The Bargello

The Bargello, built 50 years before the Duomo and the Palazzo Vecchio (which is just to the southwest of the Bargello) was originally the seat of the *podestà,* or chief city magistrate. Criminal offenders were often hung out of the windows of the tower, and their pictures were painted on the walls of the tower and inner courtyard by well-known artists like Andrea del Castagno, who acquired the nickname Andreuccio degli Impiccati, or "Andy of the Hanged." Medical students and investigators such as Leonardo could claim the bodies of the condemned men for dissection, as long as the condemned had been born more than two miles beyond the city walls and were therefore "foreigners."

The Museo Nazionale del Bargello today is to sculpture what the Uffizi is to painting. Here are Michelangelo's *Drunken Bacchus* and *Brutus;* Cellini's *Perseus* in a number of poses: with his mother, Danae, slaying the Medusa, and rescuing Andromeda; Giambologna's *Mercury;* and two more *David*s: bronze statues by Verrocchio and Donatello, the latter reputedly the first nude statue of the Renaissance.

On the first floor, Donatello's *David* is flanked by his magnificently austere *Saint George* and his irresistible *Amore*—a cupid in wading trousers reaching up to be hugged; his *Marzocco* lion of Florence, a *St. John the Baptist* by Desiderio da Settignano, and some of the better-known Della Robbias.

Donatello was, after the death of Masaccio, the major Florentine artist of the 15th century. Sculpture at that time was a question of either accepting Donatello's ideas or reacting against them; the latter solution usually meant following in the more conventional wake of Ghiberti. Donatello challenged the subordinate role of sculpture as mere decoration of architecture. His work has a dramatic quality and a passionate sense of tragedy, especially in works like his *Mary Magdalen* in the Museo dell'Opera di Santa Maria del Fiore.

Donatello's *David* is very different from Michelangelo's. It is a boyish, almost effeminate statue, with curly locks and a dandyish hat—in many ways a flashback to the Classical past in which Donatello found his inspiration. At the same time, it is not a mere copy of Roman art but the work of an equal who is doing very much "his own thing." Verrocchio's *David,* on the other hand, is typical of the late quattrocento in its elegance and finesse of workmanship, and is said to have been inspired by his pupil, the young Leonardo.

Music and Literature in Florence

Not all of the greatness of Florence lies in its paintings, statues, and buildings. Besides seminal Renaissance thinkers and philosophers such as Leonardo Bruni, Marsilio Ficino, Giovanni Pico della Mirandola (*Oration on the*

Dignity of Man), and Niccolò Machiavelli (definitely not, however, under the patronage of the Medicis), Florence is very important in both music and literature.

The seeds of opera as we know it today were sown in Florence in 1580 at the house of Count Giovanni Bardi—the same family as Dante's Beatrice—when a group of musicians, together with Vincenzo Galilei (father of Galileo and a composer), decided to revive the ancient music dramas of the Greeks. In former times there had been no song catchier than the "Kyrie Eleison" until the troubadours brought love ballads to the courts of Italy and France. Slowly, *musica profana* in the form of madrigals, and choral singing in general, took over from psalms and religious chants; the angels in Renaissance painting are equipped more often than not with lutes and mandolins, while Boccaccio's *Decamerone* resounds with joyous voices singing worldly songs in unison.

La Camerata Fiorentina, as it came to be called, went one step further, and in works like *Dafne* by Jacopo Peri (1594) and *Euridice* (1600) by Peri (with Caccini) the dramatic values of the story were enhanced by the expressive quality of the music, inventing musical speech, or "recitative," gradually to be enriched by arias, duos, and set choral pieces. In this way the groundwork was laid for Claudio Monteverdi at Mantua, who in turn opened the way for the later great operatic composers such as Gluck, Mozart, Rossini, Verdi, and Wagner.

Florence's Teatro Comunale has an opera season in the fall and features ballet and concerts in the spring. The musical director is Zubin Mehta, but other famous conductors as well as singers and performers come to Florence all year round, especially in May and June during the Maggio Musicale (Musical May Festival).

Dante Alighieri, born in 1265, was a Florentine and the first great figure of the Renaissance. He was not only a poet but a philosophical thinker, a politician, and a religious visionary. He gave expression to the mind and spirit of an age in which the conflicting realms of religious thought and an Aristotelian vision of the cosmos formed the basis of contemporary writing but—because it was expressed exclusively in Latin—was available only to a scholarly elite. In *De vulgari eloquentia* Dante advocated the use of Italian, and his *Divina Commedia* was written in the language of his native city's streets.

Exiled from Florence in his early 30s because of his

political activities, Dante was a wanderer until the end of his life in 1321. Don't bother to visit his house in Florence; it is a 19th-century reconstruction, not to say a fake.

Giovanni Boccaccio, one of the world's greatest storytellers, half French, half Tuscan, was born in 1313. He grew up in his family home of Certaldo, between Florence and Siena. He was a great admirer of Dante, and one of his earlier works was a biography of Italy's leading poet. In his last years he received an allowance from the city of Florence as public expositor of the *Divina Commedia*. The Florentine gardens of the Villa Schifanoia were the setting for his famous *Decamerone*.

Florentine Stone Inlay

The art of semiprecious stone inlay flourished under the Medicis and is still very popular in Florence today, although instead of the lapis lazuli, jasper, sardonyx, porphyry, agate, and chalcedony of the Renaissance, the materials used now are more likely to be marble, alabaster, or even stones from the bed of the Arno. Although the workmanship is still excellent, it can't compare with the days when there was a Medici patron to foot the bill. At that time there was an artisan whose sole function was to select the semiprecious stones to fit the designs of wreaths of flowers, baskets of fruit, and miniature Tuscan landscapes. At the **Opificio delle Pietre Dure** (via degli Alfani 78, near piazza della Santissima Annunziata) you can see the workmanship of the Renaissance on tables and panels where the garlands of roses have an almost velvety sheen, with pearly drops of dew nestling among the petals, the pips of the pomegranates juicy and red.

The Palazzo Davanzati

The Palazzo Davanzati, a few streets to the west of the piazza della Signora, is a unique example of a domestic building of the 14th century, when the Medieval tower was evolving into the Renaissance palace, the fortress into the home. Once a nobleman's house, it has been restored as it was in the days when Florentine matrons sat at the loom or the spinning wheel, filling their bedroom chests with handspun linen, their kitchen shelves stacked with the utensils and crockery typical of the time, all of which is still there on view. The Palazzo Davanzati is also remarkable for its *agiamenti,* a genteel Renaissance word for toilet—a rare luxury in those days.

The Palazzo Medici-Riccardi

This was the Medicis' private home, completed in 1460, where Cosimo, Piero, and Lorenzo all lived, although Cosimo complained that it was "too large a house for so small a family." Later they moved into the Palazzo Vecchio and then, as Grand Dukes of Tuscany, to the Palazzo Pitti.

Benozzo Gozzoli was a quattrocento Florentine painter who studied under Fra Angelico, and whose fresco of the *Procession of the Magi* in the tiny chapel of the palazzo is perhaps his best work, among the most unforgettable of the many frescoes in Florence. His approach to his work was lighthearted: When Piero ("the Gouty") de' Medici complained about two little seraphim on the horizon, he was told not to worry, "two little cloudlets will take them away." The *Procession of the Magi* contains more Florentines than Wise Men, with the depiction of the Medicis and their courtiers. There is Piero the Gouty himself, his motto, *Semper,* engraved on the horse's trappings. The three Medici girls are dressed as pages with feathers in their caps, and Gozzoli has painted himself into the procession together with his mentor Fra Angelico. The palace, catercorner from the church of San Lorenzo, is closed Wednesdays.

Museo Archeologico

If you are not planning to include important Etruscan centers like Volterra or Chiusi in your itinerary, you may want to visit the Museo Archeologico in Florence; officially it is in the piazza Santissima Annunziata, although the main entrance is now in a side street, via Colonna. Here are the alabaster ash chests from Volterra and little bronzes of startling artistic merit, as well as the most famous Etruscan bronze in Tuscany, the Chimera. A mythical creature—part lion, part goat, its tail like a snake biting one of its own horns—this statue was found in Arezzo and restored by Cellini. If you are lucky you may catch one of the exhibitions that the museum, a world center for restoration, holds periodically of works restored after being rescued, usually from the bottom of the sea; in recent years these have included the Riace bronzes and the gilded bronzes of Cartoceto.

The Cenacoli

Florence has a number of *cenacoli,* or frescoes of the Last Supper, painted on the walls of monastery refectories. The first Renaissance refectory in Florence belonged to the Benedictine nuns of Santa Appollonia. The *Last Supper* by **Andrea del Castagno** here, in via Aprile 1, near the piazza San Marco and west of the train station, is a tense, dramatic work with a very sinister Judas sitting alone on the other side of the pristine tablecloth. Andrea del Castagno was a glowering peasant painter, what the French call *ténébreux,* and his bloodthirsty reputation may be due in part to his appearance, in part to the harsh realism of his work. He is one of the most important painters to follow in Masaccio's footsteps, although he owes the linear rhythms and dramatic quality of his work to Donatello.

A very different *cenacolo* is the *Last Supper* by **Domenico Ghirlandaio**, in the reflectory at Borgognissanti 42, where Jesus and his apostles are enjoying a peaceful domestic reunion, with pewter flagons on the floor and a beautifully embroidered tablecloth. In the background, songbirds wheel above the lemon trees. (Open till 12:45 but closed Sundays.) Domenico Ghirlandaio was the son of a goldsmith whose craft also gave the family their name: *Ghirlande* means garlands, or wedding crowns. Ghirlandaio was the master of the young Michelangelo, who as a mere boy was drawing at his feet while he was painting the Tornabuoni chapel in Santa Maria Novella, causing the elder painter to exclaim, "but he knows more than I do!"

Andrea del Sarto painted his *Last Supper* at San Salvi much later, in the mid-16th century. The ballooning draperies and flamboyant gestures of the apostles are typical of the High Renaissance. Although he was among the best draftsmen of his time, and Michelangelo is said to have told Raphael, "There is a little fellow in Florence who would make you sweat if he ever got a great commission to do," Andrea del Sarto had a weak character. He married a shrew, but unlike Petruchio he never tamed her, and with Madonna Lucrezia he had, says Vasari, "his work cut out for him for the rest of his days." However, every woman that Andrea painted—"his handsome vague-browed Madonnas," as Henry James called them in his *Florentine Notes*—had something of his wife in her, because not only were she and her numerous and demanding family always before him, but "he carried her image in his heart."

The painter died of the plague at the age of 44, untended by his wife, who was scrambling to leave the city. The church of San Salvi is at via Andrea del Sarto 16, a short taxi or bus ride from the center of Florence (take bus number 6, which can be caught in piazza San Marco).

Galileo

Galileo was the last of the great Florentines at the end of a Golden Age. He originally wanted to be a painter, but his father discouraged this as an unprofitable profession. Instead, Galileo's work on the science of dynamics and statics, and his discovery and formulation of the laws of motion, are the basis of modern engineering, even of spacecraft. Such avant-garde ideas brought him into conflict with the Church, and he spent much of his life trying to justify his theories before the Inquisition. He lived out his last years, blind and embittered, in exile at his villa in Arcetri on a hill above Florence, where the Florentine Observatory stands to this day. The **Museo di Storia della Scienza** (Museum of the History of Science), open until 1:00 P.M. but closed Sundays, contains Galileo's telescopes, compasses, astrolabes, and the lens with which he first identified Jupiter and the "Medici" planets, as he christened them. There is his armchair, telescope stand— and even the pickled third finger of his right hand. The museum is in the piazza de' Giudici, two blocks from the Ponte Vecchio on the river, going east.

THE OLTRARNO
The Palazzo Pitti

The Pitti palace is the largest, most overwhelming palazzo in Florence. It was built by Luca Pitti, who was the equivalent of a modern-day industrialist and self-made man who wanted to have a bigger and better home than any of the noble families of Florence, especially the Medicis. The Pitti was criticized at the time, as there was already a housing shortage in Florence, and never before had a private residence been conceived on such a large scale, with blocks of stone that to Taine seemed more like "sections of mountains." Never before, too, had a palazzo been built, as Machiavelli complained, in such royal isolation, although this became an advantage later on when the Pitti became the palace of the ruling families of Tuscany, first the Medicis. The Medicis were followed by the Hapsburg Lorraine archdukes, in the days when Florence was part of the Austro-Hungarian Empire, and by the House of Savoy when Florence was briefly capital of Italy. Today it houses no fewer than six museums, of which two—the Monumental Apartments, as they are called, and the Carriage Museum—are temporarily closed.

The **Museo della Porcellane** and the **Galleria del Costume** are both well worth a visit, but if you are on a tight schedule you may have time only for the Galleria Palatina and the Museo degli Argenti—the same ticket gives access to both.

The **Galleria Palatina** houses pictures from the High Renaissance by Raphael, Titian, Tintoretto, and Andrea del Sarto, as well as some beautiful landscapes by Rubens. Apart from Andrea del Sarto, none of these masters was born in Florence, even though Vasari describes Raphael as a "Florentine painter born in Urbino," perhaps because his stay in Florence and because his study of the works of Masaccio, Leonardo, and Michelangelo had a lasting effect on his work. "I must not fail to mention that Raphael so much improved his manner after his visit to Florence that he seemed to be an entirely different and much greater artist," says Vasari.

The **Museo degli Argenti** (Silver Museum) is chiefly remarkable for the collection of vases and *orfèvrerie* that belonged to Lorenzo de' Medici. Unlike his father, Cosimo, he was not a patron of large works of art, preferring to collect ornaments and accessories. For him love was the *appetito di bellezza,* the appetite for beauty. Don't miss the jewels of Maria Luisa de' Medici in a little alcove of their own.

Behind the Pitti palace is the **Giardino di Boboli** (Boboli gardens), which is open to the public from 9:00 A.M. until sunset every day. This is a Classical Italian garden with ilex walks, box parterres, and a whole cavalcade of statuary, such as the grotesque pot-bellied figure of a dwarf, Cosimo's court jester Morgante, astride a turtle. The gardens are the favorite venue of children and their nannies in the mornings and are an ideal place to picnic, with an 18th-century coffeehouse halfway up the hill. The Medicis planted a plethora of imported seeds and bulbs in the gardens; even today when a child says,

"*Voglio* . . ." (I want), he will be told, "The grass called 'I want' doesn't even grow in the Boboli gardens."

The Medicis also sponsored every aspect of the arts, and goldsmiths, silversmiths, engravers in crystal and cameos, seamstresses, wood-carvers, leather craftsmen, and artisans working in baser metals like bronze and copper all flocked to the Medici court and competed to produce the jewels, the trinkets, the knickknacks and ornaments that adorned the ruling family's apartments.

Today this thriving artisan life still exists in the streets that fan out at the feet of the Palazzo Pitti. One of the joys of the Oltrarno is to lose yourself on purpose in the narrow little streets and peer into dingy workshops where wood shavings fly and strong smells of glue and varnish assail the nose. As Mary McCarthy says, "The Florentine crafts, out of which the arts had grown, the severe tradition of elegance that goes back to Brunelleschi, Michelozzo, Donatello, Pollaiuolo has been transmitted to the shoemaker and the seamstress."

With the death of Galileo in 1642, the Golden Age of Florentine arts and architecture came to an end, but Florence is still a world center for craftsmen and for art restoration. There are artisans like **Bartolozzi**, in via Vellutini 5R, whose workshop pieced together and recarved the abbey of Monte Cassino after it was bombed by the Americans during the war. Inch by inch it took 30 artisans ten years. Or **Brandimarte**, whose workshop at via Bartolini 18 rings with the sound of chisels like the chorus from *Il Trovatore,* making timeless silverware, goblets, and large silver plates ringed with fruit and flowers that could have graced the tables of Lorenzo the Magnificent himself. Next door, the **Antico Setificio Fiorentino** is still working with looms more than a century old, into which up to 40,000 hairlike strands of silk are threaded by hand one by one, while the patterns are punched on wooden blocks, the quattrocento version of a computer. Emilio Pucci is president of the Setificio; to this day only women, and only women from the Oltrarno San Frediano district of Florence at that, can work here.

The Churches of Santa Maria del Carmine and Santo Spirito

These two churches are west of the Pitti in neighboring squares bearing their names. In the Carmine is the **Cap-**

pella Brancacci, of which much has already been said on the subject of Masaccio's frescoes. The church of Santo Spirito was Brunelleschi's last church, which he did not live to finish. It belonged to an Augustinian order whose members gave up lunch for half a century in order to finance its building. Even though Brunelleschi's designs were not entirely carried out, it is still, according to Vasari, "almost the most perfect church in Christendom." There is a fine altarpiece by Filippino Lippi, as well as a small, eye-catching painting quaintly called *Saint Mary of the Relief,* with a Madonna in a magnificent orange gown brandishing a wooden club at a sour-looking little orange devil, who stamps his foot on an orange-checkered marble floor.

Piazza Santo Spirito is a neighborhood square, with old men dozing on benches while their wives knit and gossip and children, dogs, and pigeons tumble about the fountain. In the mornings there is a market for vegetables and, among other things, shoes and secondhand clothes.

Church of San Miniato al Monte

The church of San Miniato is reached by a steep but very rewarding climb, up steps behind the Porta San Niccolò, less than a mile east of the Pitti. It is the most beautiful Romanesque church in Florence and dominates the city, sharing with the nearby **piazzale Michelangelo** the view to end all views, especially at sunset, "when the sun from the west, beyond Pisa, beyond the mountains of Carrara / Departs, and the world is taken by surprise" (D. H. Lawrence).

San Miniato himself was the first Christian martyr in Florence. After having been decapitated in the arena, he carried his head up the hill and across the river to the present site of the church, which is built on an early Christian cemetery. The mosaic floor with its zodiac symbols dates from 1207. At 4:45 P.M. sharp every day, the monks sing Gregorian chants in the crypt; the doors are shut the moment they begin, so be punctual.

GETTING AROUND
Shod in a pair of comfortable shoes, you can see the whole city on foot. A car is a liability because of a trigger-happy civic system for towing away vehicles that have strayed from the straight and narrow paths and parking lots. Recently, to combat traffic anarchy and pollution,

most of the "historic center" has been closed to all vehicles, and female police, like Scylla and Charybdis, bar your way at every turn. If you do have a car, your only hope is to try to park outside the main train station or on the lungarno in the piazza di Cestello on the Oltrarno side of the river, where there is a parking lot in the Porta Romana; if you can find the devious route into the midst of things, there is also parking outside the church of Santa Maria del Carmine. At all of these lots, payment by the hour escalates in price as every hour goes by.

The only destinations that might call for a bus are the church of San Miniato and piazzale Michelangelo (line number 13) and the *Cenacolo* of San Salvi (line number 6). Tickets can be purchased at tobacconists. The main bus stops are outside the main train station of Santa Maria Novella on arrival, or near the Duomo in the stretch of via Martelli that runs into via Cavour from piazza del Duomo to piazza San Marco, or in the piazza San Marco itself.

Taxis are yellow and fairly ubiquitous; they can also be summoned by telephone from a bar: 4798.

When to Go

Florence lies in a hollow ringed by hills, which makes it one of the hottest cities in Europe in summer. It is to be avoided if possible during July and August—which is also when tourists descend on the city like locusts. Spring and autumn are the best times to come; the winter is relatively mild and short-lived, from December to mid-March, and it rains rather than snows.

Arrival at Major Gateways

For years the only airport near Florence was at Pisa, which has a rail service direct from the airport to Florence, but Florence has just inaugurated its very own airport, called Peretola. Neither of these is an intercontinental airport. Pisa handles flights to Great Britain and Germany, while Peretola is mainly for domestic flights, linking Florence to Milan and Rome for overseas travel. If you are arriving directly from North America, you will have to land in Rome or Milan and take another plane or a fast train to Florence. The slowest train in Italy is called an *accelerato,* followed by a *diretto,* then a *direttissimo,* an *espresso,* a *rapido,* and finally the super-superlative *super-rapido* and *inter-city,* which will get you to Florence in under three hours from Rome or Milan (first class only, but worth the extra money for one of the best trains in Europe).

ACCOMMODATIONS

Finding room at the inn in Florence is never easy; when the tourist season is over, the buyers come pouring in for the various Pitti fashion shows, while the *Maggio Musicale,* the annual music festival in May and June, fills the hotels in spring. (The telephone area code for Florence is 055.)

Florence has a number of large hotels, including two belonging to the CIGA group, the Excelsior and the Grand, both on piazza Ognissanti on the right bank west of the center. After a hibernation of over a decade, the **Grand** has recently reopened, the bedrooms redecorated in pristine pink-and-white Napoleonic stripes. The reception rooms still echo the architectural themes of the end of the 19th century, when the Grand was built, including the magnificent Winter Garden, which is still being restored and should be ready by 1989. Piazza Ognissanti 1. Tel: 27-87-81.

The most exclusive, the most elegant of the five-star luxury hotels is the **Regency**, in the quiet piazza Massimo d'Azeglio at number 3, east of the Duomo near viale Gramsci. More like a stately town house than a hotel, the expensive Regency has an almost sinister chic, with William Morris-style wallpapers and dusky mirrors. A twin hotel to the Byron in Rome, the Regency keeps a very good restaurant. Tel: 24-52-57; Telex: 571-058.

Expense should be no object either at the **Villa San Michele**, a former monastery halfway up the Fiesole hill, northeast of the center, in via di Doccia 4. The villa was designed by Michelangelo, who today has a suite with a marble Jacuzzi tub named after him. Flowers are everywhere, with wisteria tumbling down the walls; there is also a heated pool. Not all the exquisitely furnished rooms share the spectacular view of Florence with the restaurant under the loggia. Via di Doccia 4, Fiesole. Tel: 59-451; Telex: 570-643.

If you like the idea of that setting but can't afford the prices, the **Pensione Bencistà**, a little lower down the hill in via Benedetto da Maiano 4, Fiesole, offers the same view and the same wisteria for less money in a Tuscan country-house atmosphere. However, one meal of home-cooking per day is an obligatory part of the service. Tel: 59-163. The Villa San Michele has a private bus, while the Bencistà has to rely on the services of the municipal number 7. Both hotels are seasonal, open approximately from April to the end of October. (No credit cards accepted at the Bencistà.)

Prices at the four-star hotels are still high, but reasonable for the service and location offered. The **Hotel Berchielli** at lungarno Acciaioli 14, west of the Ponte Vecchio, was an old-fashioned hotel with that brand of well-worn gentility beloved of middle-aged English tourists in flat heels. Recently it has been entirely revamped and modernized and brought almost too forcibly into the 20th century, but it should now appeal to a much wider clientele. Tel: 26-40-61.

Almost facing the Berchielli, on the Oltrarno side of the river, is the **Hotel Lungarno**, with one leg knee-deep in the river and the other in the quaint little street of borgo Sant'Jacopo, at number 14. The Lungarno has become something of a cult hotel with a large international following, many of them buyers, who will stay only there, even if it means a room without a view. The little downstairs sitting room looking onto the river is a cheerful, comfortable place to meet, and there is a garage next door. Tel: 26-42-11; Telex: 570-129.

Another hotel that has been redecorated recently is the very central **Hotel Bernini**, behind the Uffizi gallery in the piazza San Firenze 29. When Florence was the capital of Italy, from 1865 to 1870, members of parliament met in the magnificent room that is now the breakfast room, and portraits of heroes of the Risorgimento stare down from the frescoed and stuccoed ceiling, which has been restored to its former splendor. The rooms are elegantly furnished, and some of them offer a view out over the rooftops at the Palazzo Vecchio or toward San Miniato. There is a small garage. Tel: 27-86-21.

In summer some of the hotels open small rooftop pools; for example, the delightful little terrace restaurant and pool at the **Hotel Kraft**. This is reasonably priced, though still in the four-star category, and stands in a quiet street behind Florence's theater, the Comunale, in via Solferino 2. The hotel is owned and efficiently run by a family of Swiss hoteliers; the clientele has a correspondingly ample and burgherlike appearance. Tel: 28-42-73; Telex: 571-523.

Alternatively, the **Villa Cora** is a five-star hotel in the viale Machiavelli (number 18), one of the sweeping, tree-lined avenues that wind up toward the piazzale Michelangelo in Oltrarno. A grandiose 19th-century edifice, Villa

Cora looks like a Beethoven concerto cast in stone and gilded stucco. The rooms, which have been furnished in fake Victoriana to match, look out on the park and a poolside restaurant. Expensive. Tel: 229-84-51.

Cheaper and less luxurious accommodation is to be had in Florence's various *pensioni,* of which there are many. The **Pensione Beacci Tornabuoni**, one of the better ones, has hotel prices but a pensione atmosphere: cozy little sitting rooms and old-fashioned Tuscan country-house-style furniture right on the via de' Tornabuoni (number 3), Florence's shopping street. The rooms vary greatly in size, but you can pay extra for a large one. There is a passable restaurant, and although the Beacci usually is fully booked months ahead, the management will give preferential treatment to those who want half or full pension terms. Tel: 21-26-45.

A cheaper pensione overlooking the Arno at lungarno Diaz 2 on the right bank is the **Rigatti**, with a definite *Room with a View* flavor, high ceilings, and polished terra-cotta floors. This pensione has been in the same family since 1907. Some of the rooms and a loggia over-look the river as it gurgles under the Ponte alle Grazie. No telephones in the rooms, and no credit cards accepted. Tel: 21-30-22.

DINING

The Florentines, of course, also invented cuisine. When Catherine de' Medici went to France as the bride of King Henri II d'Orléans, she is said to have taken a flagon of olive oil and a bag of beans with her, and reputedly introduced the French court to the use of forks and the subtleties of duck à l'orange and sauce béchamel. When it comes to cooking, the Florentines are reactionary in the extreme. Any variation on the food that *la mamma* or *la nonna* made is viewed with suspicion, and menus in the different restaurants and trattorias in Florence tend to be much the same.

Florentine food is, however, always full of flavor, whether it is the tart taste of new olive oil on toasted bread (*fetta unta*) or on white beans (*fagioli*), the fragrance of fresh basil garnishing *la pappa al pomodoro* (a local soup made with tomatoes), the full-bodied taste of red meat in the *bistecca alla fiorentina* (T-bone steak), or the piquancy of *pecorino,* the local sheep's-milk cheese.

Italy, said D. H. Lawrence "is like cooked macaroni—yards and yards of soft tenderness raveled round everything." Yet although pasta is on every menu the real Tuscan start to a meal is a bowl of soup such as *ribollita*, made out of yesterday's bread and cabbage.

Although only two hours from the sea, Florence is a meat-eating city, and fresh fish is served in very few restaurants. The many varieties of hand-picked salad, of which arugula is only one, are very tasty; vegetables are always ordered separately, under the menu section *Contorni*. Desserts are not Florence's strong point, except in the better restaurants. All the frothy confections of *profiterolles* and meringue in town may be made by the same person, who delivers them to the restaurants every morning.

Florence is surrounded by the Chianti wine-growing area. The best local wine is the Chianti Classico, the bottle with a little black rooster on the neck label. Chianti Putto (with its little *putto,* or cupid, on the neck of the bottle) is grown in a less restricted area and can also be a very palatable table wine. Most restaurants have an unlabeled house wine that you pay for *al consumo*—according to how much you drink.

The only restaurant in Florence with two Michelin stars is the *very* expensive **Enoteca Pinchiorri**, which is rather like experiencing a reception at a society wedding. Waiters, like ushers, whisper in your ear, and there are hothouse blossoms everywhere: in the vaulted dining room and in the palazzo courtyard—five bouquets in the ladies' room alone. Annie Féolde is French and is the power behind the scene in the vast kitchens, which have recently introduced a Tuscan *nouvelle* menu. Her husband, Giorgio Pinchiorri, is in charge of the 70,000 bottles in their cellars, which you can visit upon request. It is best to take the *dégustation* menu, which gives you a little taste of everything. Closed Sundays and lunch Mondays. Via Ghibellina 87; Tel: 24-27-77.

Da Noi literally means *Chez Nous,* and *nous* in this case is Sabine and Bruno, who were part of the Enoteca's staff before branching out on their own in a cozy restaurant, with muted lighting and frugal elegance, in a narrow little street crammed with artisans' workshops and tiny stores, a brisk walk north from Santa Croce. Bruno is in a kitchen the size of most people's refrigerator, while Sabine waits at tables, explaining the constantly varying menu—a creative, very personal rendering of local food—in English if necessary. There are few tables and only one sitting, so that guests are spared any postprandial rush. Reservations should be made as far in advance as possible. No credit cards. Via Fiesolana 46R; Tel: 24-29-17.

Il Cibreo is just around the corner from one of the two main food markets and halls (the Mercato S. Ambrogio, northeast of Santa Croce); it is a small, pleasantly bohemian restaurant like a sophisticated downtown bistro, Fabio and Benedetta being the kind of people who reject plushness on principle rather than out of necessity. Both decor and food bear the stamp of their very individual style. There is no pasta, but instead an array of unusual, mouth-watering antipasti, a choice of delicious soups, and some very good homemade desserts. Like Da Noi, quite expensive, but good value for the money. Reservations are a must. (Both close Sundays and Mondays.) There are a few cheaper tables at the back of the Cibreo for students, locals, and the New Poor. Fabio also has a fascinating gourmet store around the corner from the restaurant. Via dei Macci 118R; Tel: 234-11-00.

Another culinary couple are Giuliano and Sharon, at **Garga,** in a little street between the train station and the river. He is the chef with the basset-hound jowls who peers around the window of the visible kitchen; "I don't like to feel isolated," says Giuliano. Sharon is Canadian and can explain their personal brand of Tuscan cooking in transatlantic terms, dishes such as their *crostini,* a traditional Florentine antipasto, chopped chicken livers on crisply toasted peasant bread; their excellent risottos; and pasta dishes like *Il Magnifico.* They are enlarging their tiny restaurant in 14th-century premises next door, and Garga should be less of a squash, but make reservations anyway. Closed Sundays and lunch Mondays; priced like Cibreo. Via Moro 9; Tel: 29-88-98.

A contradiction in terms—a quiet, restful trattoria—is **Le Quattro Stagioni** (no connection to New York's Four Seasons), where the food is well prepared, the service smooth and polite, the decor blandly unobtrusive. It is the only restaurant in the via Maggio, once the main thoroughfare of Renaissance Florence (Maggio is a shortening of Maggiore) and now the antique-store row, around the corner from the piazza Pitti. Piero, the diminutive chef/owner whose ruddy face beams from under his chef's hat, makes different kinds of *gnocchi* for every season, as well as a Renaissance version of a Caesar salad, called, of course, the Catherine de' Medici salad. Priced like Cibreo; closed Sundays. Via Maggio 61R; Tel: 21-89-06.

Cammillo, on the other hand, is very noisy and bustling, the way Italian trattorias usually are. In the Oltrarno part of town, it has been family-owned for generations. Father sits behind the old-fashioned cash desk while Son weaves in among the crowded tables, and the waiters in long white flapping aprons boom orders into the kitchen with voices like foghorns. *Always* bursting at the seams, not just with Florentines but with an increasing number of Americans and Japanese, for whom Cammillo has become a landmark. They may not yet have managed to turn it into a tourist restaurant, but they have succeeded in inflating the prices, although it is still within the same range as the establishments already mentioned. Just about the only restaurant of note open on a Sunday, Cammillo is closed Wednesdays and Thursdays. Borgo Sant'Jacopo 57R; Tel: 21-24-27.

A light, vinous lunch is to be had at the **Cantinetta Antinori** in the palazzo of the same name, belonging to the Antinori wine-making family, in the piazza Antinori, southeast of the piazza Santa Maria Novella. Although a fancy menu is now available, the Cantinetta is at its best in its original role of patrician snack bar, providing food as accompaniment to the wine. Medium priced, if you stick to the snacks. Closed Saturdays and Sundays. Piazza Antinori 3; Tel: 29-22-34.

Typical of Florence are what could be described as "kitchen" restaurants, with white-tiled walls, communal tables, a quick turnover of patrons, clanging of saucepans, and a noisy, steamy, convivial atmosphere. The most famous of these is **Sostanza**, around the corner from the Excelsior Hotel. This is a Florentine institution where it is important to remember that it is they who are doing you a favor and not vice versa. Closed Saturdays and Sundays. Via Porcellana 25R. A less-known "kitchen" restaurant is **La Vecchia Bettola**, on the other side of the Arno on the piazza Torquato Tasso—closed Sundays and Mondays. Viale Ludovico Ariosto 32R. At "kitchen" restaurants it is impossible to make reservations, and you may end up standing in line. They often don't serve coffee—and can't cope with credit cards. They are cheaper than some of the restaurants given above, but not as cheap as you might think they would be.

A restaurant beloved of professional Florentine businesspeople—always the most discerning and demanding eaters—is the **Taverna del Bronzino**, behind the piazza della Indipendenza. It is difficult to find without a taxi but decidedly worth the detour for excellent food and an impressive wine selection. The decor is sober, solid, and unostentatious—the way Florentines like it—with serious food such as their black tortellini (the pasta dough is tinted black with the lining of walnut shells), and steak baked whole in the oven, sliced, and served with a green pepper sauce. Here is the place to try one of Italy's northern Piedmont wines. Closed Sundays. Via delle Ruote 25–27R; Tel: 49-52-20.

L'Antico Fattore, just around the corner from the Uffizi gallery, features typical Tuscan food and is very good value for the money. Having a bare-bones trattoria atmosphere with well-worn white tablecloths, dark wood furnishings, and bottles standing to attention against whitewashed walls, L'Antico Fattore has a groaning board of antipasti and fresh-tasting, well-cooked food. The three partners, one in the kitchen and two waiting on tables, are very friendly—and speak English. Closed Sundays and Mondays. Via Lambertesca 1R; Tel: 26-12-15.

Very few restaurants in Florence have a garden for outdoor dining in summer; you may want to escape the city heat north toward Fiesole and **Le Cave di Maiano**, although this involves an expensive taxi ride. Here the stone tables are like petrified toadstools, and fireflies wink among the cypresses. Cave di Maiano has been serving the same menu for more than 20 years, but nobody seems to mind. Beware of filling up on the antipasto, which is a meal in itself; you are supposed to follow it with a selection of pastas, grilled meats, and homemade ice cream topped with fresh fruit. Maiano is not expensive for the amount of food you get. Closed Thursdays, and Sunday nights. Via delle Cave 16, Fiesole; Tel: 591-33.

If you must have fish in red-meat country, **La Capannina di Sante**, Sante's little cabin on the banks of the river Arno east of the center at the Ponte da Verrazzano, serves just that—and only that—excellent fresh fish from the Tyrrhenian Sea for every course except dessert. Fresh fish, as opposed to frozen, or *congelato,* is always expensive, but not outrageously so, and Sante also has a very good white wine list. Like Moses' basket of rushes, Sante's little cabin looks as though it might float down the Arno at any moment, although care has been taken with details, such as soft lighting and a red rose on every table. When the restaurant is full the service can be flustered. And, despite

Guernica tactics, the mosquitoes are not always kept at bay.
Ponte da Verrazzano; Tel: 68-83-45.

Giuseppe Alessi used to run one of the Florentine
restaurants most sought after by gourmets from far and
wide. Reservations were made months in advance, and
every one of a wealth of dishes was set before the rever-
ent diners accompanied by a dissertation on its exact
historical and gastronomic context. Today this very talented chef has made a full somersault and now runs an
inexpensive neighborhood eatery where simplicity is the
order of the day, and customers line up outside on the
narrow street, waiting to sit shoulder-to-shoulder at communal tables covered in rough paper tablecloths. Among
the best buys in town, the few dishes are wholesome and
tasty, especially the riotous salads, but this is not the place
to linger over your meal—the next shift is already salivat-
ing at the doorway. No reservations and no credit cards;
closed Sundays. Via di Mezzo 26R; Tel: 24-18-21.

The most scenic pizza place in town is **Le Rampe**, a
restaurant on a bend in the road that winds up from the
river to the piazzale Michelangelo, with terraces overlooking the city's best profile. There is a regular menu as well
as a choice of pizzas (pizza is cheap wherever you go).
Closed Mondays and also at lunchtimes during winter.
Viale Poggi 1; Tel: 681-18-91.

For a sandwich in town off the main shopping street,
the via de' Tornabuoni, go to via del Parione, where three
steps down is a simple little *alimentari* (grocery store)
that makes copious sandwiches to order with crusty
baguette-type bread. Try the prosciutto with *mascarpone*
cream cheese and nuts, downed with a glass of very
ordinary wine. Cheap. Open 8:00 A.M. to 3:00 P.M. and
4:30 P.M. to 7:30 P.M.; closed Wednesday afternoons and
Sundays. Via del Parione 19R.

BARS DURING THE DAY

The three most famous bars in Florence are **Gilli**, in the
only unattractive square in the city, piazza della Repubblica; **Giacosa**, on the main shopping street at number
83R via de' Tornabuoni; and **Rivoire**, in the piazza della
Signoria. All are reasonably priced if you take your refreshment standing up, and all become ruinously expensive the moment you sit down at one of the little tables
with pink tablecloths.

Gilli has Belle Epoque ceilings, a dab hand at cocktails,

very light lunches, and in the evenings music that wafts over the hedge from a little palm-court orchestra at a neighboring bar. Closed Tuesdays. Piazza della Repubblica 39R; Tel: 21-38-96. Giacosa is ideal for shoppers, with dainty little pastries to combat that buying fatigue, as well as expensive light lunches. Closed Sundays. Tel: 29-62-26. Rivoire has the best location in town, being the watering hole nearest to the Uffizi gallery, with sidewalk tables in the square facing the Palazzo Vecchio. Its big specialty is hot chocolate topped with an oversized wedge of double cream. Closed Mondays. Piazza della Signoria 5R; Tel: 21-44-12.

Also in the via de' Tornabuoni, at number 64R, is **Leopoldo Procacci**, a deluxe grocer who sells English marmalades and superior cookies behind glass-fronted cabinets. There is also a small, old-fashioned bar dispensing truffle-paste-filled sandwiches with your aperitif, hence the musty smell of truffles that fills the store. Closed Sundays and Wednesday afternoons, Procacci follows a timetable of its own: 8:30 A.M.–1:00 P.M. and 4:30 P.M.–7:45 P.M. Tel: 21-16-56.

ICE-CREAM BARS

The most famous is **Gelateria Vivoli** in via Isola delle Stinche at number 7R, on the site of an old debtors' prison. The Vivoli family is an institution in Florence, and the bar is a major landmark for visiting Americans, too. The large assortment of ice creams and *semi-freddi*— Piero Vivoli maintains you can make ice cream out of *anything*—is labeled in English as well. Closed Mondays, and on Tuesdays as well during the winter.

Not as well known, but just as good, is the **Gelateria Villani** at the piazza San Domenico number 8, halfway up the Fiesole hill (by the number 7 bus). There are a few tables outside where the ice cream is served, in parfait glasses and smothered in fruit. You can also take it out in little cardboard cups. The specialty is Crema Villani, a creamy caramel flavor. Closed Mondays.

BARS AT NIGHT

There is big action in a small bar, officially called the Antico Caffè del Moro, in the via del Moro 4R, but which everyone calls the **Art Bar**. The best drinks in town, and an international clientele. Closed Sundays. No credit cards accepted.

La Dolce Vita is very much in vogue with the young

crowd, who gather at this simple, streamlined bar in the piazza Santa Maria del Carmine 6R as soon as it is dark, spilling out into the square, glasses propped on the nearest cinquecento car. Closed Sundays.

DISCOS

Rome's *dolce vita* rather passed Florence by. So, compared with other cities, has disco dancing. Your best bet is the **Yab Yum** in the central via Sassetti 5R. Not expensive; the cover charge buys your first drink. Closed Mondays.

SHOPS AND SHOPPING

After Milan, Florence is the number-one shopping city in Italy, more elegant and with more variety and verve than either Venice or Rome. Above all, much of what you see in the stores has been produced in or around Florence itself. It is enough to say that over 90 percent of the "Made in Italy" output exported to North America comes from Tuscany, and the city is full of buying offices for all the major stores.

The Bond Street/Fifth Avenue of Florence is the north-south **via de' Tornabuoni**, which leads down to the S. Trinita bridge, along with such streets as the via della Vigna Nuova branching off to right and left. Here you will find local fashion landmarks like Gucci and Ferragamo, both of whom live and produce in Florence, side by side with big fashion names from all over Italy, and a few French intruders as well: Valentino couture from Rome, Armani and Versace from Milan, Ermenegildo Zegna from the Piedmont, the Neapolitan Mario Valentino for shoes, as well as the Fendi sisters, Yves Saint-Laurent, Vuitton, Cartier—the list goes on. For the very fashion-conscious, two local stores called **Alex** and **Emmanuel Zoo**, both in the via della Vigna Nuova, 5R and 18R, have a very up-to-date collection, while the real style-seekers go to **Luisa** in via Roma at 19–21R. All the avant-garde clothes labels are to be found there, as well as Maud Frizon shoes. Funkier, more accessible fashion is available at **Sandro P.** in the Corso at 38R or at **Mujer**, right next to the bar Rivoire in via Vacchereccia 6R. The ultimate in casual fashion is at **Enrico Coveri**, via della Vigna Nuova 27–29R, or—for designer work shirts—at **Ermanno Daelli**.

The **borgo San Jacopo** is a fascinating shopping street in the Oltrarno for people for whom the designer label is not everything. There is Giachi for bags, La Bottega

Artigiana for shirts, Lo Spillo for Victorian jewelry and knickknacks, the gourmet store Vera, stores selling everything from fun clothes, shoes, and prints to hams, together with a cluster of bars and restaurants. Also here are **Pagliai** for period silver, and **Manetti**, one of the last artisan goldsmiths in Florence.

Florentine stores are open from 9:00 A.M. to 1:00 P.M. and from 3:30 or 4:00 P.M. to 7:30 or 8:00 P.M., and close on Monday mornings throughout the winter, Saturday afternoons in summer. All the larger stores take credit cards. (Some of the smaller boutiques tend to open later in the morning.)

Leather

Florence has always been famous for its leather. To judge from the streets of Florence, it would seem that the only things locals shop for are shoes and pizza by the slice. One of the sad things about Florence today is that whenever an old-fashioned store closes, the space is instantly snapped up by a shoe store or a snack bar. Leather magnates like Beltrami and Raspini have stores all over the city selling not only shoes but bags and leather clothes; you must remember that the prices include their not inconsiderable frontage costs. **Mantellassi** in the piazza della Repubblica 25R still produces handmade shoes—at a price—but you will find cheaper stores, too, around the market in the borgo San Lorenzo, or in the Oltrarno.

The best leather store in Florence is **Cellerini**, in via del Sole 37R. Cellerini is an artisan of a kind that has survived from the days of the Medicis; his upstairs workshop is littered with soft, supple strips of different colored leathers and patterns of bags for the famous people he has been serving for the last 30 years. **Taddei** in the piazza Pitti 6R is a tiny workshop making solid leather objects like boxes, frames, and jewelry cases, a painstaking process involving the pressing of different layers of leather, like the soles of good shoes, over molds and then highly polishing them until they look like wood. **Il Bisonte** is a leather store at via del Parione 11 that now has branches in other cities in Europe and whose goods are also sold in a few select stores in the United States. A Falstaffian figure, the creator of Il Bisonte makes bags, suitcases, and belts out of natural leather, and multicolored canvas bags for summer.

Jewelry

Florence has been a city of goldsmiths since Renaissance times, although nowadays much of the gold and gems sparkling behind the storefronts is factory made. The most famous jeweler in Florence is **Settepassi**, who has recently merged with a Milanese jeweler, Faraone, and moved off the Ponte Vecchio—the goldsmiths' traditional home since the 16th century—to via de' Tornabuoni 25R. The bridge is still the place to go for gold, new and antique jewelry, some silver, and necklaces of coral, ivory, and semiprecious stones. Each tiny store has its own personality, its own history, its own prices. The Ponte Vecchio is like a bazaar, and it continues on into the via Por San Maria on the right bank. **Bijoux Cascio** in via Por San Maria 1R and via de' Tornabuoni 32R makes costume jewelry so perfectly it looks like the real thing, while **Ylang-Ylang**, also in the via de' Tornabuoni, makes the real thing look like modern costume jewelry, and **Angela Caputi** in borgo San Jacopo 78 and 82 makes stunning parures out of plastic.

Linens

In the last century, young girls came from all over Europe, assiduously chaperoned, to buy linens in Florence for their trousseaux. Today few can afford to pay for genuinely hand-embroidered linens trimmed with handmade lace, and much of the merchandise displayed in the windows of Por San Maria is machine made or imported from the Orient. Some is still handmade by the seamstresses of Greve, an hour away from Florence, however; you just have to pick and choose. **Cirri's**, at Por San Maria 38–40R, makes smocked dresses and sailor suits for the kind of children who are seen but not heard, while **Bruna Spadini**, on the lungarno Archibusieri 4–6R, makes very fine linens for the table, boudoir, and bed. The undisputed grande dame of the boudoir, however, is **Loretta Caponi**, in borgo Ognissanti 12R, who makes nightgowns from the stuff that dreams are made of. She has recently opened a store opposite with a second entrance at lungarno Amerigo Vespucci 11, with enchanting outfits for little girls. The most famous linens in Florence came from **Navone**, a second-floor shop on the via de' Tornabuoni, whose name is still sculpted in stone on the corner of the via Spada. Navone made sheets for the Russian grand duchesses and tablecloths embroidered with huntsmen and hounds for the hunting lodges of the aristocracy. Today, Navone's great-grandson, **Giorgio Calligaris**, has a frescoed, stuccoed second-floor showroom on the via delle Caldaie 14, a little side street off the piazza Santo Spirito, where he sells outrageously beautiful and expensive linens using his famous ancestor's designs. Call for an appointment. Tel: 21-09-09.

Antiques and Crafts

Florence is also a center for antiques, old and new, with antique stores on either side of the via Maggio in the Oltrarno as well as in the borgo Ognissanti.

The *settore degli inganni* (trompe l'oeil) has long been one of the minor Florentine arts—a plaster column can be made to look like Carrara marble, a fireplace like chalcedony. At **Ponziani Mario**, via Santo Spirito 27, what at first glance seems an expensive antique store is in fact a rambling workshop where artisans hand-paint in a variety of styles, from chinoiserie to Old Florentine, on furniture that is then treated to look like the most precious of antiques. There are workshops specializing in marbleizing, such as **Cappellini Marino** in via Presto di San Martino 10R, while at stores like **Giannini** in piazza Pitti 37R, or at **Il Papiro** all over the city (via Cavour 55R, piazza Duomo 24R, lungarno Acciaioli 42R), you can buy Florentine paper in an infinity of marble look-alike shades pasted onto frames, boxes, pencils, bookends, diaries, and so on.

Markets

An important part of Florentine shopping is provided by the markets. The main market is in **piazza San Lorenzo**, where stalls are set up every day selling souvenirs, gloves, bags, belts, sweaters, T-shirts, shoes, and jeans, around the corner from the main food hall and fruit-and-vegetable market—which is itself well worth a visit to see the profusion of local produce.

The straw market, **Mercato del Porcellino**, is in the little square at the end of via Por San Maria under covered arches. "Bring me a straw hat from Florence . . ." used to be a popular song, but today the straw goods probably come from the Orient—the market sells cheap linens, bags, umbrellas, small leather goods, and fake Gucci bags instead.

Otherwise, every space in Florence large enough to qualify as a piazza has a morning market for fruit and vegetables and a few other odds and ends thrown in. On Tuesday mornings there is a huge market at the **Cascine**, the big public gardens on the right bank of the Arno west of the center, where you can buy unhemmed Gucci scarves (seconds), antique nightshirts, all manner of clothing, and kitchenware for unbelievably cheap prices. Finally, in **piazza de' Ciompi**, four blocks north of Santa Croce, there is a permanent flea market; bargains are rare but rummaging is fun.

TUSCANY

By Anne Marshall Zwack

There are many things to see in Tuscany outside Florence, and many ways to see them. Our way is to start with the Etruscan sites—after all, everything began with the Etruscans here—and then go south of Florence into the wine-growing areas, the center of which is Siena. Due south of Siena is the most appealing part of the Tuscan seacoast—the Argentario.

Then we follow another route out of Florence to the northwest. There, we'll journey to Prato (practically a suburb of Florence); the hot springs at Montecatini; Medieval Lucca; the marble-quarry areas at Carrara and Pietrasanta; and finally to Pisa.

MAJOR INTEREST

Etruscan sites at Volterra, Cortona, Arezzo, and elsewhere

Wines and country restaurants around Siena in Chianti, Montalcino, and Montepulciano

Trecento art and architecture in Tuscan hill towns

Siena's art and architecture

Monte Argentario and other southwest coastal resorts

The islands: Giglio, Giannutri, Elba

Fra Filippo Lippi's works at Prato

Thermal spas at Montecatini

Walled Medieval city of Lucca

Marble artisans at Carrara and Pietrasanta

Pisa's Campo dei Miracoli (Leaning Tower, cathedral, baptistery, cemetery

Italy is better known for her cities than her countryside, and indeed few Italian landscapes live up to the beauty of the Eternal City—no one ever wanted to "see Latium and die"—while all the Veneto has in common with Venice is the first syllable. The transcendent exception is Tuscany, which some people actually prefer to the Renaissance grandeur of Florence.

Tuscany is a word with a unique resonance that conjures up alluring vistas, so much so that a new perfume has been named after this region of central Italy. Beautiful as they are, no perfume could ever be named after England's Lake District or France's valley of the Loire.

Despite the inroads of the 20th century—concrete posts now support the vines that once clung to the trunks of olive trees or trailed along wooden stakes; tractors replace the white, wide-horned oxen with pendulous chins that used to pull the plows; and the Autostrada has made a gash through the Tuscan hills—Tuscany is substantially still the same as when Lorenzo de'Medici, a fervent Tuscan, wrote: *"Tiene il cipresso qualche uccel segreto . . . l'uliva in qualche dolce piaggia aprica/Secondo il vento par or verde, or bianca"* ("Shelters the cypress a secret bird . . . the olive on its gentle sun-warmed slope blows first green, then white with the wind").

The carefully husbanded hills, combed with vines and crested with cypress trees, still look like the *Allegory of Good and Bad Government,* painted over three walls of the Palazzo Pubblico in Siena by Ambrogio Lorenzetti in the 14th century. Indeed, while painters from other Italian cities are essentially urban, the great Tuscan painters of the Renaissance fill their paintings with the familiar landscapes and rural scenes in which they grew up. Many of those whom we call Florentine painters are in fact Tuscan village boys—Leonardo from Vinci and Masaccio from San Giovanni Valdarno. Madonnas and saints pose before backdrops of vineyards, the banks of the Arno, and umbrella pines. Tuscany has always attracted artists, now as then. "You learn for the first time in this climate what colors are," said Leigh Hunt.

Tuscans are as rooted in their soil as the century-old olive trees that dot the slopes, their philosophy of life based on the country proverbs of their forefathers. Theirs is a crusted charm. They are, as a 17th-century traveller wrote, "ravished with the Beauty of their owne Countrey," and although they may have seen the rest of the world only on television, Tuscans are convinced that the Arno valley is this side of Paradise. Country people forced to leave their land following the decline of agriculture come back a generation later to restore the broken-down farmhouses, called *case coloniche,* as do expatriate English, Germans, Americans, and Milanese.

Tuscan food has an immediacy, a straight-from-the-*orto* (vegetable garden)-to-the-pot flavor about it. Soups like the *pappa al pomodoro* or *ribollita,* both good ways to use up old bread, are topped off with a flourish of olive oil. The herbs are always fragrantly fresh, the salads often hand-picked wild greens. The beef for the famous *bistecca alla fiorentina* comes—when it is not imported—from the Chianine cattle raised in the Maremma region; the homemade pasta is filled with spinach and ricotta cheese, while a typical Tuscan meal is rounded off with *pecorino* (a local sheep's cheese) and fresh fruit. You eat well in any little country trattoria, and so here we will mention chiefly the more elusive and exclusive restaurants, which often are also the most expensive, in a region where eating is generally cheap.

ETRUSCAN PLACES

"Italy today," wrote D. H. Lawrence, "is far more Etruscan in its pulse than Roman and will always be so." The word *Tuscany* comes from *Etruscan,* the ancient civilization that flourished between the river Arno, the river Tiber, the sea, and the Apennines during the eighth to fourth centuries B.C. The Greeks called the Etruscans *Tirreni;* hence, this part of the Mediterranean is known as the Tyrrhenian Sea.

We still do not know where the Etruscans came from. Some say from the lost city of Atlantis, or that they emigrated from the north, or that they originated in Lydia and fled after a great famine struck Asia Minor. Others claim that the Etruscans came from Lemnos, an island in the Aegean, and left when the smiths of Vulcan became short of iron, or that they were Phoenicians who settled in colonies along the coast during their navigation of the Tyrrhenian Sea. The most likely is perhaps the thesis put forward by Dionysius of Halicarnassus in the first century B.C.: "The Etruscans emigrated from nowhere. They have always been there."

Wherever they came from, the Etruscans were as culturally advanced and commercially affluent as the Greeks who were colonizing southern Italy (Magna Graecia) during the same period. Etruria consisted of a league of 12 cities, called the *dodecapolis,* among which were the Tuscan cities of Volterra, Populonia, Chiusi, Arezzo, Vetulonia, and Cortona. Fiesole, the hilltop town above Florence, was Etruscan until subdued by the Romans, as was Saturnia with its hot sulfur springs. Each city was governed by a king, called a *lucumone.* The Etruscans grew grain in abundance on what Livy called the *"opulenta arva Etruria,"* and bequeathed polenta to Italian cuisine. They planted vines; their Trebbiano is still one of the grapes used in Chianti wines and in the Tuscan whites. They were the first to mine iron and copper on the island of Elba and at Populonia, where there are still iron pebbles on the beaches. They were sufficiently advanced architecturally to invent the cupola, and the paintings they have left on vases and amphorae are of astonishing artistic merit.

The Etruscans believed that mankind was governed by an implacable destiny, as was the life of an individual or an entire civilization. They thought Etruria would, like the Third Reich, last a thousand years. They shared with the National Socialists and the ancient Romans the belief that the state and the city were more important than the individual, who could be sacrificed to the general good. The Roman symbol of power, subsequently the symbol of the Italian Fascist party, was the fasces, borrowed from Etruscan lore.

Nonetheless, the Etruscans were a joyous, insouciant folk, with a passion for music and dancing and with what D. H. Lawrence called "an inner carelessness" that, although crushed by the heel of the advancing Roman legions, has survived to the present day. Sumptuous banquets were followed by theatrical performances; *ister,* the Etruscan word for actor, has given us our word *histrionics.*

Most of what we know of the Etruscans comes from objects excavated from their tombs. Although their dead were always cremated, the Etruscans believed in taking everything with them when they went. There are tombs at, for instance, Populonia, Vetulonia, and Chiusi—but when you've seen one Etruscan tomb, you've seen the lot. (Henry James also complained about the "trudging quest for Etruscan tombs in shadeless wastes.") The more fascinating Etruscan heritage is to be found in the contents of these tombs—the painted amphorae and carved funerary

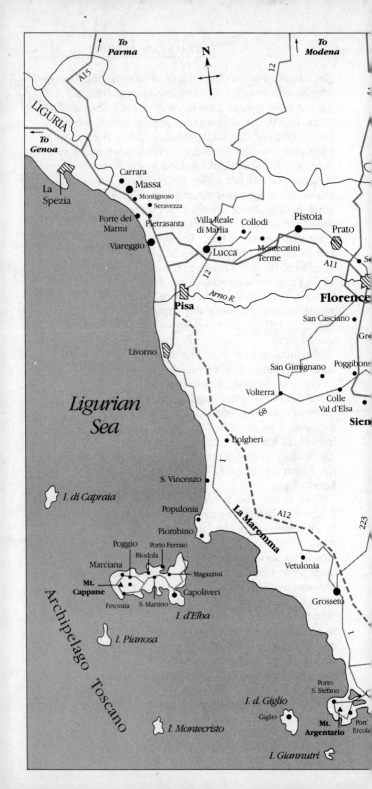

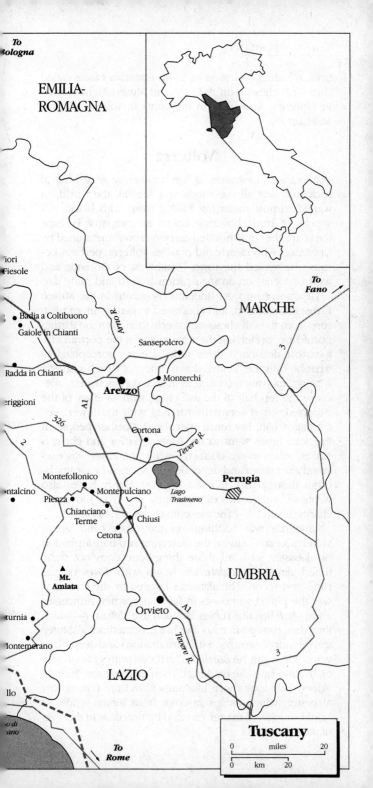

To Bologna

EMILIA-ROMAGNA

To Fano

MARCHE

Fiesole

Badia a Coltibuono
Gaiole in Chianti

Sansepolcro

Arno R.

Radda in Chianti

Monterchi

Arezzo

eriggioni

A1

326

Cortona

2

Tevere R.

Montefollonico

Perugia

Montepulciano

Lago Trasimeno

ntalcino

Pienza

Chianciano
Terme

Chiusi

Cetona

UMBRIA

Mt.
Amiata

Orvieto

A1

turnia

Tevere R.

ontemerano

LAZIO

3

llo

o di
ano

To Rome

Tuscany

| 0 | miles | 20 |
| 0 | km | 20 |

urns, which D. H. Lawrence in his *Etruscan Places* called "little ash chests"—in the splendid Museo Archeologico in Florence, as well as in museums in Volterra, Chiusi, and Cortona.

Volterra

Volterra, said Lawrence, is "on a towering great bluff of rock that gets all the winds and sees all the world," a walled, almost menacing hilltop town with black, still specks of birds hovering above its ramparts. Perhaps these are the "gray-hooded carrion crows" mentioned by Lawrence, who clearly did not like Volterra, perhaps because he visited the town (southwest of Florence and west of Siena) on an inauspiciously cold and rainy day.

He cheered up considerably, however, in the **Museo Etrusco Guarnacci**, and confessed to getting more pleasure from the ash chests of Volterra than from the Parthenon frieze, preferring the immediacy of the portrait effigies that decorated these little alabaster sarcophagi to what he calls the "boiled down" effect of Greek aesthetic quality, "too much cooked in artistic consciousness." Because the top half of the ash chest, with its effigy of the departed, often seems ill-matched with the lower, sarcophagus half, Lawrence speculated whether people in Etruscan times went to the funeral parlor and chose a casket, much as we do today, while the effigy was executed after death and depended on what end your implacable destiny had in mind for you. Henry James also wrote of "reliquaries of an infinite power to move and charm us still. . . ." (The museum closes at 1:45 P.M.)

Lawrence was scathing, on the other hand, about Volterra's main activity, the quarrying and transformation of alabaster into "all those things one does not want: tinted alabaster lampshades, bowls with doves on the rim," and so on. The alabaster favored by the Etruscans was the purest white—as in fairy tales, when princesses always had lips like rubies and skin like alabaster—which they then painted in rusts and black. Sometimes alabaster can be more like onyx, with dark shadows and deep black veins. Or it can be *bardiglio,* grizzled with gray or reddish arabesque-like markings. Then there are the "blonde agates" that look more like amber, and the rare yellow alabaster, which ranges in color from lemon-yellow to bright orange. Alabaster can also be tinted, as in the case of most souvenirs.

Alabaster lends itself to an infinite variety and fluidity of designs, as it is one of the softest stones. Its heyday was in the 18th and 19th centuries, when merchants braved the oceans of the world to bring their wares to marketplaces as far away as Bombay. In Volterra you can walk down the narrow, cobbled streets and peer into workshops where artisans sit at their workbenches, chipping away at a vase or the head of a horse, almost up to their ankles in snow-white shavings that crunch underfoot. Although much of the output answers to Lawrence's description, Volterra has many gifted artisans who can execute orders to your specifications relatively cheaply.

Fun gifts to take home are the alabaster ice creams, coffee cups, fried eggs, etc., which *Vogue* calls "half pop, half metaphysical," made by the young **Marco Ricciardi** in his workshops in via Guarnacci 26 and via Porta Diana 9.

The rather grim aura of Volterra perhaps comes partly from the high-security prison within its ancient walls. In Lawrence's day, two imprisoned artisans managed to escape by carving old bread into realistic effigies of their faces—curls, warts, and all—which fooled the guards while they made their getaway. Today the prison houses some of Italy's most notorious terrorists, including members of the Red Brigade.

Populonia

There is not much left of the grandeur of Etruscan Populonia except its splendid isolation and the view. From the top of a hill covered in Mediterranean scrub, where wild boar snuffle for acorns, Populonia overlooks the coastline and the island of Elba. And yet in Etruscan times it was important enough to be able to send 600 men to the aid of Aeneas, as Virgil tells us in the *Aeneid.*

Populonia was named for the Etruscan god of wine, Fufluns, which became Fofluna and eventually Popluna. Vestiges of the Etruscan walls are still visible in this one-street, one-coffee-shop village, which belongs in its entirety to a doctor living in Rome. The Populonian necropolis is at the foot of the hill, near the Gulf of Baratti, which was the port for Etruscan Volterra and where now in summer flocks of little yachts and fishing craft come to roost. The Gulf of Baratti has a beautiful beach ringed with umbrella pines; it does get very crowded, however, in the summer.

The working of iron ore moved from Elba to Populonia in the fourth century B.C., when wood for fuel became scarce on the island. It is estimated that the area occupied by the furnaces was about 40 acres, while the mountain of *scoriae* (tailings) accumulated to around two million tons. Populonia became famous throughout the Mediterranean, and as Phoenicians and Ionians came with ships full of artworks to exchange for tools and arms, the city grew in stature and prestige. Just how elegant the villas and temples of Populonia became can be seen from the statue of Apollo, now in the Louvre, that was found in the bay, tangled in seaweed, by a group of 19th-century fishermen looking for octopus.

Populonia is in the Maremma region, where cattle are raised and wild boar still hunted. Bristly heads with awe-inspiring tusks adorn many a restaurant wall, and menus here lean heavily to red meats and wild-boar roasts or stews. Surprisingly few restaurants serve fresh fish from the Tyrrhenian Sea, although one exciting exception is the **Gambero Rosso** in San Vincenzo, a ten-minute drive from Populonia. Fulvio Pierangelini has recently emerged as one of Italy's most talented young chefs, and for those who shun the sophistication and expense of Il Gambero Rosso he has opened a more casual beach restaurant just next door, **Il Bucaniere**. Both restaurants serve superlative fish menus. (Only the Gambero Rosso takes credit cards.)

Chiusi

Chiusi was one of the most important Etruscan centers in Italy, and its **Museo Nazionale Etrusco** is well worth a visit. Porsenna, legendary king of Etruscan Chiusi, summoned goldsmiths from all over the known world to make him a golden sarcophagus drawn by 12 golden horses, but although Chiusi has its share of Etruscan tombs, this treasure has never been found. Chiusi, south of Arezzo near the Autostrada, shares a railway station with Chianciano Terme, a busy, modern spa about 120 km (75 miles) from Florence and 65 km (40 miles) from Arezzo. Chianciano has about 200 hotels and one famous restaurant, **La Casanova**, elegant and secluded— and expensive—in a sylvan setting. The chef-owner is German and brings Teutonic precision to Tuscan dishes such as *tortelloni nazionali*. Underneath the restaurant is a fascinating store selling local produce, especially pecorino cheese. Closed from October 31 to March 1, La Casanova is open every day in summer and closes on Wednesdays the rest of the year.

Cetona

Only about 15 km (10 miles) from Chiusi and Chianciano, Cetona has become famous in recent years thanks to Padre Eligio, a Capuchin monk who used to be the chaplain of the Milan soccer team. He has since started a restaurant, **La Frateria di Padre Eligio**, in a restored monastery outside the Etruscan village of Cetona, together with graduates of his Mondo X drug-rehabilitation program, who not only cook and serve in the restaurant but tend the vegetable gardens and orchards as well. What could have been just a laudable exercise in philanthropy has become a very good restaurant for which gourmets make a detour.

Cortona

Cortona, a town near Lake Trasimeno south of Arezzo and east of Siena and the Autostrada, has long been something of a cult corner of Tuscany for expatriate intelligentsia and people like Germaine Greer. Even older than Troy, Cortona was a flourishing little township well before the Etruscans colonized it. During the Renaissance it basked in the reflected glory of its most famous native son, Luca da Cortona, or Luca Signorelli. Fra Angelico also lived here for some ten years and painted an *Annunciation* that makes an interesting comparison with the one in the monastery of San Marco in Florence. This painting and Luca Signorelli's work are in Cortona's **Museo Diocesano** (closed Mondays).

Luca Signorelli was considered one of the most important artists in the mid-15th century—he was commissioned to paint a whole cycle of frescoes for the Sistine Chapel in Rome, as well as for the cathedral at Orvieto. He was much influenced by his time in Florence, and his obsession with the dramatic possibilities of the male nude hark back to Masaccio and forward to Michelangelo. A pupil of Piero della Francesca, he shows a wild imagination and rude vigor in his best work; his later paintings, churned out together with his school during his retirement in Cortona, are somewhat wooden.

Cortona also has its share of Etruscan tombs and an archaeological museum—the **Museo dell'Accademia Etrusca**—whose most important exhibit is a monstrous Etruscan lamp from the fifth century B.C. (currently under restoration). The museum is closed Mondays.

Today Cortona is a magical town, "perched on the very pinnacle of a mountain, and I wound and doubled interminably over the face of the great hill, while the jumbled roofs and towers of the arrogant little city still seemed nearer to the sky than to the railway station," as Henry James put it in his *Italian Hours*. There are at least two pleasant trattorias in the center of Cortona, while the **Hotel Gugliemesca** is 10 km (6 miles) away on a wooded hillside.

Saturnia

Saturnia, between Orvieto and Grosseto about 220 km (135 miles) south of Florence and frequented more by Romans than Tuscans, is the Etruscan equivalent of a Jacuzzi tub. At the **Cascatelle del Mulino** hot sulfurous water cascades down the hillside, while the banks are lined with the kind of mud that would cost $20 a thimbleful in London or New York. Whole families strip off fur coats and down jackets and wallow in natural pools at a temperature of 100 °F, leaving the skin like satin, well-being oozing from every pore. Some 7 km (4 miles) south at Montemerano is **Laudomia**, a rustic, relatively inexpensive trattoria with rooms above, which offers very good food. And although the cascades are public, there is room for everyone and no need to fight over the mud, especially on weekdays.

Arezzo

Although Arezzo was one of the chief cities of the Etruscan league, today we go to this little Tuscan town 80 km (50 miles) southeast of Florence to see the work of Piero della Francesca. Piero, called "della Francesca" because he was the son of a woman who was widowed before he was born, painted a cycle of frescoes in Arezzo's **Church of San Francesco** that are among the most beautiful in Italy. They have a moonlit quality, an unearthly austerity and immense expressive power. Giorgio Vasari, himself a native of Arezzo, says that in this work "Piero shows the importance of copying things as they really are"—a novel concept at the time. The frescoes tell the legend of the "Triumph of the Cross."

Piero was first and foremost a mathematician, "a most zealous student," we are told, "using a knowledge of

Euclid to demonstrate the properties of rectilinear bodies better than any geometrician." He went blind before he died, and his mathematical works were published posthumously by a pupil. His other painting in Arezzo is a *Saint Mary Magdalen* in the cathedral, but it is worth driving the 40 km (25 miles) northeast to his birthplace at Sansepolcro to see his most famous work, *The Resurrection,* which D. H. Lawrence claimed was the most beautiful painting in the world. Some 17 km (10 miles) south of Sansepolcro at Monterchi is another Piero della Francesca masterpiece, the *Madonna del Parto,* or *Madonna of Childbirth.*

Giorgio Vasari, whose house at number 55, via XX Settembre, he himself lovingly furnished and frescoed, is another famous Aretine. Petrarch was born here (his house has now become an academy), as were Maecenas (in 68 B.C.) and the humanist Leonardo Bruni, whose tomb is one of the loveliest in the church of Santa Croce in Florence. Many Renaissance figures were born and grew up in the surrounding countryside, among them Michelangelo, Masaccio, and Paolo Uccello. Said Lady Morgan, travelling in the early 19th century: "It's subtile air has been asserted to be peculiarly favorable to genius."

The best time to come to Arezzo is the first Sunday (and preceding Saturday) of every month, when an antiques fair is held in the town's Medieval center. Stalls are set up in the piazza San Francesco and continue past the church into the piazza Grande or piazza Vasari and around the corner up the street leading to the Duomo, "the stately, dusky cathedral," as Henry James called it.

Another church to be visited is **San Domenico**, for the Cimabue crucifix over the main altar, similar to the much damaged cross of the church of Santa Croce in Florence (now in the adjoining museum), and a beautiful *Annunciation* by another native of Arezzo, Spinello, also known as Aretino.

On the first Sunday of September every year a tournament called the "Saracen Joust" is held, a tradition going back to the 13th century. The breast-plated Saracen is armed with a whip that he uses to lash at charging horsemen wearing the colors of the four Medieval neighborhoods of Arezzo.

There is quite an adequate little restaurant in the main square, while the best place to stay is 28 km (17 miles)

southwest of the city at Gargonza, a tiny 13th-century
village belonging to Count and Countess Roberto Guicciardini, of one of the oldest families in Florence. You can
either rent one of the renovated, doll-like Medieval houses
for the week or stay in the guest house for a night or two.
In summer the Guicciardinis organize music festivals.

THE WINE-GROWING AREAS
OF TUSCANY

The word *Chianti* comes from the Etruscan name *Clante*.
Chianti wines as such have been grown throughout the
heart of Tuscany since the 12th century; Chianti Classico,
most prized of the Chianti wines, grows in a more restricted area between Florence and Siena. Chianti Classico has a black rooster on a gold background as its neck
label, an emblem inspired by a Vasari painting on the
ceiling of the Sala del Cinquecento in the Palazzo Vecchio
in Florence. Only those wines that are grown within strict
geographical confines and that meet the exacting regulations of the Gallo Nero (Black Rooster) Consortium may
call themselves "*classico*." "Riserva" on the bottle means
that the wine has aged for at least three years.

The quickest route from Florence to Siena is the Superstrada. But the via Chiantigiana (route 222) will give
you more of the feel of Tuscany, especially as you near
Radda and Gaiole east of 222, a bit more than halfway to
Siena. Every bend in the road (and these are frequent)
brings more undulating hills combed with vines, and
more rows of cypresses that seem to march up the slopes
and then stop abruptly halfway, as though pausing to get
their bearings. Silver-green olive trees, ravaged by the
brutal winter of 1984–1985, still peep over the old stone
walls that line the route. Alternating with the trees is a
tangle of bushes and stunted oaks that are highlighted in
spring with a blaze of yellow broom, and in winter by red
rose hips and old man's beard.

In Tuscany, as in Italy as a whole, it is almost inconceiv-
able to consume food and wine separately. That may
explain why, despite the large quantities of grapes grown
and consumed each year, public drunkenness is virtually
nonexistent. It also means that where there are vines,
there are restaurants, too many to mention, or, as they say
in France, an *embarras du choix*.

Greve

This town, about a third of the way to Siena on route 222, is considered the capital of Chianti Classico, and every year in the second half of September a wine fair is held here. Individual growers preside over stands where you can sample and compare the different Chianti wines. In the main square, with its sloping arches on three sides, there is an *enoteca* (wine-tasting room) open year round, as well as a butcher, Falorni, where they still make their own sausage and prosciutto the old way, curing the meat on the ashes of a wood fire.

The Chianti region has always been very industrious, as opposed to industrial, although small industries have mushroomed in recent years. The road to Greve takes you through the area where the huge terra-cotta vases for the lemon trees are produced, as well as the bricks and tiles—some still made by hand—that are used for so many Tuscan floors. In Greve itself the women are famous for their needlework. They can spend up to three years on a tablecloth, which they then bring to stores like **Azina Valoriani** on via C. Battisti, just off the main square, to be sold at prices that may sound high but are in fact a fraction of the real worth.

Just above Greve is the tiny village of **Montefioralle**, paved with rugged flagstones and dating from the 11th century. Montefioralle is the birthplace of Amerigo Vespucci. This is such an unusual rock pool of history, left behind by the tides of time, that it is worth stopping here at the otherwise undistinguished little **Trattoria del Guerrino** for a simple Tuscan lunch.

South of Greve

Two delightful hotels are at Castellina on 222 and Radda to its east. The **Tenuta di Ricavo** at Castellina, once a Medieval village, has old stone houses tucked away among gardens, trees, and bushes around a swimming pool—the ultimate in getting away from it all. The Swiss management ensures that everything works and that guests are on time for meals.

The newly opened **Relais Fattoria Vignale** at Radda was once the manor house of a wine-growing estate, now faithfully restored so that a stay in the almost monastic elegance of its rooms and lounges grouped around the pool is like Tuscan country life when people could afford to live it up in style. It was here that the Gallo Nero Consortium was formed in 1924, and the Relais is still the legal headquarters of Chianti Classico. Neither of these hotels is expensive for what it offers, and both are near enough to Florence and Siena to permit easy day trips to both.

From Radda east to Gaiole the road winds past the entrance to vineyard after vineyard, most of which can be visited; these wine makers sell their wine directly from their cellars as well as send it all over the world. The **Castle of Brolio**, since 1141 the seat of the Ricasoli family, who make Brolio Chianti, is open to the public every day and is well worth a visit for a walk along the castle walls. A left turn as you leave the castle will take you to Badia a Coltibuono, a tiny village grouped round the ancient tower of the Benedictine monastery, now privately owned by the Badia a Coltibuono wine-making family (Lorenza de'Medici, the owner's wife, runs a well-known cooking school in spring and fall). The restaurant outside the monastery's thick walls is also called **Badia a Coltibuono**, and although the food is not very imaginative, it is not expensive and is wholesome, with fresh ingredients from the surrounding countryside, including *porcini* mushrooms that grow in the woods behind the restaurant.

A right turn from the castle, on the other hand, will take you to Villa a Sesta, to the **Bottega del Trenta**. This restaurant has a courtyard at the back where you can sit in summer and where the villagers come once a year, on Saint Catherine's Day, to cook a festive dinner in the 150-year-old wood oven. All the ingredients, especially the olive oil on toasted bread, called *fett'unta,* and the tiny homemade sausages, are of the best quality, and the peasant soups and hearty pastas are the kind of fare you would serve at home. You can buy some of the local produce in an old-fashioned store sandwiched between the dining room and the kitchen, where Stefano, Gianni's nephew, who learned to cook on a ship in the Italian navy, cheerfully stirs the bubbling cauldrons of soup. The wine is the excellent Villa a Sesta. No credit cards accepted, but the Bottega is not expensive.

San Casciano

If, instead of route 222, you take the Superstrada south from Florence, your first exit will be at San Casciano, a busy market town. Machiavelli wrote his treatise *The*

Prince only 3 km (2 miles) away at Sant'Andrea in Percussina. He spent the days of his country exile snaring thrushes, selling wood from his estate, and reading Dante and Petrarch while lunching on "such food as this poor farm and my slender patrimony provides." The afternoons were spent with the locals at the inn, where Machiavelli would "act the rustic for the rest of the day," playing cards until the ensuing arguments could be heard as far away as San Casciano. In the evening he would strip off his muddy workaday clothes and change into his court robes to work on his masterpiece, "plumping and grooming" it for four hours every day.

Incongruously located at the corner of a dusty square and a parking lot in San Casciano is one of the best restaurants in Italy, the **Antica Posta.** For those of us who prefer to find rustic charm in rustic places, the almost excessive sophistication of the Antica Posta, with its exquisitely prepared nouvelle cuisine meals and rigorously selected Italian wines, may seem out of place in what was once the *Posta,* or post-house, of San Casciano. Expensive, but a must for those interested in eating as an art.

Colle di Val d'Elsa

Another worthwhile stop close to the Superstrada is Colle di Val d'Elsa (about two-thirds of the way to Siena), a glassmaking town since the Middle Ages. Since the 18th century, when an Alsatian firm chose Colle as its headquarters because of the abundant supply of wood for the furnaces, the town has specialized in crystal. Today there are about a hundred artisans working in glassblowing, engraving, and cutting crystal in and around this walled Medieval town, which was the birthplace of Arnolfo di Cambio, architect of Florence's cathedral.

Every year in September there is a Crystal Fair here. Because this is the countryside, the fair is more like a village festival than a trade fair, but you will get a good idea of the range and artistry of these glass artisans, whose work is as fine as any produced in Europe today (a fact the Tuscans themselves do not even know, Tuscany being a land that rarely honors its own). There is a glass store in the center of town called **Mezzetti,** where you can buy work by all the factories and engravers in Colle di Val d'Elsa.

There are three good restaurants in town, but perhaps the best is **L'Antica Trattoria,** on three floors with an Art

Nouveau decor. Antica serves unusual dishes such as *risotto verde all'ortica* (green risotto with nettles), which, despite its name, is delicious.

San Gimignano

The Poggibonsi exit off the Superstrada leads you west to San Gimignano, home of one of Tuscany's few white wines, the Vernaccia. The wine is golden yellow, dry, fresh, and smooth in taste, with a hint of bitter almond; it should be drunk young and cold.

San Gimignano is one of the few Tuscan towns that still has its towers, which appear on the horizon like a mirage or a fairy castle as you round a bend. Of the legendary 72 towers, only 14 remain; the highest, like the "Rognosa," which was once the courts of justice and prison, are more than 160 feet high. The others belonged to leading San Gimignano families—the higher your tower, the bigger a shot you were—like the rival Ardinghelli and Salvucci families, one Guelph, the other Ghibelline. From the holes in the walls that are still visible, ramps and passageways were constructed so that friendly families could visit one another without venturing out into the streets. San Gimignano was involved in all the important battles between Guelph and Ghibelline cities, such as the Battle of Montaperti, when—according to Dante—the waters of the river Arbia ran red. Dante also mentions the battle of Colle di Val d'Elsa in his *Divine Comedy*.

San Gimignano was an important stopping place for pilgrims on their way to Rome, and was such a bustling trade center that the to-ing and fro-ing of mules bearing merchandise must have looked not unlike the prosperous township in Ambrogio Lorenzetti's *Allegory of Good and Bad Government* in the Palazzo Pubblico in Siena. Besides wine, one of the main products handled here was saffron, used in cooking, dyeing, and medicines. The merchants of San Gimignano traded far and wide; one of the Ardinghelli family is recorded as taking his wares to Egypt, Libya, and Syria.

Where there is prosperity, there is art, and the **Cathedral of San Gimignano** is a treasure trove of artworks. The cathedral contains two wooden statues by Jacopo della Quercia: a very Aryan-looking Angel Gabriel announcing the birth of Jesus to a masterfully self-effacing Madonna. Taddeo di Bartolo's dire vision of Hell here verges on the grotesque, not to say the obscene. Barna di Siena was one of the few artists of the late *Trecento* who can bear comparison with the earlier innovators, like his maestro, Simone Martini. The cycle of frescoes in the cathedral, depicting episodes from the life of Christ, was Barna's last work; he fell off the ladder while stepping back to admire his portrayal of the Crucifixion, with fatal consequences.

Benozzo Gozzoli did some of his best work during his last years in San Gimignano in the **Church of Sant' Agostino**. In this cycle of frescoes it is the *bambini* who charm us most, whether the infant Saint Augustine and his fellow students being handed over to a Nicholas Nickleby–type schoolmaster, or the baby Christ himself, petulantly playing with a wooden spoon while the mature Saint Augustine holds forth on the mysteries of the Trinity.

An important figure in San Gimignano's lore and legend was Santa Fina, a little saint who was as delicate as the violets that bloom on the towers on the anniversary of her death in 1253. There are pictures of this saint in the Museo Comunale and in the cathedral; Ghirlandaio painted the 15-year-old Santa Fina on her deathbed being comforted by a vision of Saint Gregory borne aloft by crimson-winged cupids. To Ghirlandaio we also owe another *Annunciation,* showing a very bookish Madonna surprised at her studies, under the arches of the Piazza Pecori next to the cathedral.

The **Museo Comunale** is the forbidding palazzo to which the Torre Grossa, or Big Tower, belongs. Among the many artworks housed here is a *Maestà* by Lippo Memmi, another pupil of Simone Martini, in what is sometimes called "Dante's Hall" because Dante spoke here in 1300 to drum up support for the Guelph party.

San Gimignano also has a high-security jail girded by the ancient walls (as does Volterra to the west). In Medieval cities like these a jail doesn't seem out of place, and the thousands of tourists who crowd into San Gimignano every year scarcely cast a glance in its direction as they shop in the many little stores selling very tempting and tasteful basketware and ceramics, or eat in the main square overlooking the 13th-century cistern, or *cisterna,* which gives the square its name. This well was still in use until 50 years ago; you can see the marks of seven centuries of ropes chafing against its sides.

The hotel and restaurant **Cisterna** cannot fail to please, located here in one of the most picturesque squares in Italy. The rooms are full of period charm, and the restaurant offers an unambitious but pleasant meal with a view, at affordable prices.

Wine cellars beckon on both sides of the narrow main street, where you can sample the different Vernaccias and buy a bottle or two to take home. One of the best is called Guicciardini Strozzi, from a vineyard belonging to the princely Tuscan family of the same name.

Monteriggioni

The last stop going south on the Superstrada before you reach Siena is tiny Monteriggioni, another miragelike fortress with squat square towers punctuating the 6-foot-thick walls that surround the flagstoned square and the well, or *pozzo,* which gives the one restaurant its name. Built in the early 13th century, Monteriggioni merits a passing mention in Canto 31 of *L'Inferno: "Come su la cerchia tonda/di Monteriggioni di torri si corona"* ("As with the circle of turrets Monteriggioni is crowned").

Il Pozzo is a family-run restaurant with a welcoming atmosphere and good food prepared by the owner's wife. The dishes include *panzerotti,* a bubbling-hot mixture of crêpes and cream, and also meat grilled over an open fire. A meal, accompanied by the house Vernaccia, is not cheap, but it is good value.

Vino Nobile di Montepulciano

The other two wine-making areas of Tuscany—Montepulciano and Montalcino—are within a short drive of each other and make a very rewarding day's outing southeast from Siena.

First mentioned in documents dating from the eighth century, the Vino Nobile di Montepulciano is less well known than Chianti, but experts from the Farnese Pope Paul III onward have been loud in its praise. The pope said, *"Questo vino ha odore, colore, e sapore"* ("This wine has bouquet, color, and taste"). It is a more purplish red than Chianti Classico and has a delicate bouquet of violets. It becomes Riserva after three years' aging.

In the old streets of **Montepulciano**, southeast of Siena and not far from the A 1, are several cellars where you can taste and buy the Vino Nobile. Among the most prestigious are the Avignonesi wines in the cellars of the 16th-century palace of the same name in Montepulciano's main street, the corso. The cellars are opposite a modest and inexpensive family-run hotel, the **Marzocco**, which gets its name from the Marzocco lion atop a column before its windows. (Montepulciano was involved in a tug of war between Florence and Siena for centuries, and the Marzocco lion, a symbol of Florentine dominion, replaced the she-wolf of Siena in 1511.)

Montepulciano is one of the best-preserved historic towns in Italy. The imposing façades of the Bucelli, Gagnoni-Grugni, and Cervini palaces belonging to the once powerful local families seem too large for the narrow little corso, which winds up the hill with Medieval dignity, past the Michelozzo façade of the church of Sant' Agostino to the spacious, grandiose **piazza Grande** that commands a view of the valley.

The **Palazzo Comunale** (town hall), also by Michelozzo, is a squatter version of the Palazzo Vecchio in Florence, a symbol of the town's allegiance to Cosimo de' Medici's Florence. Medici influence can also be seen in the square, where the well by Antonio Sangallo the Elder is surmounted by the famous Medici coat of arms, supported by Florentine lions, while the griffins of Montepulciano stand respectfully to one side.

The dusky interior of the **Montepulciano Cathedral** contains a number of interesting artworks, including a funerary monument to a certain Bartolomeo Aragazzi, bits and pieces of which are distributed all over the church. A frieze of putti and garlands, once the base of the monument, is now in the main altar, which is surmounted by a magnificent triptych of the Assumption, painted in 1401 by one of the most gifted of Sienese painters, Taddeo di Bartolo. In one of the panels Saint Antilia is shown carrying the 14th-century town of Montepulciano on a large tray, as if it were a ceremonial cake.

The piazza Grande, with its splendid square palazzi Nobili-Tarugi and Contucci, is also the location of a **school for mosaics** whose works are on sale to the public.

Montepulciano's most famous son was Angelo Ambrogini, known as Poliziano, one of the leading poets and humanists of his time (1454–1494). When he was 16, his translations of Homer earned him the tribute *juvenis Homerus,* or young Homer. Lorenzo de'Medici became his patron, and he was tutor to the Medici household and taught at the university in Florence. Among other things, he wrote the first play in Italian of any literary merit, *Orfeo,* one of the finer works of the Italian Renaissance.

The **Museo Civico/Pinacoteca Crociani** in the Palazzo

Neri-Orselli is well worth a visit, especially for its earliest paintings, a *Saint Francis* by Margaritone d'Arezzo and the *Crowning of the Virgin* by Jacopo di Mino del Pellicciaio, with its almost Oriental hues.

Halfway down the hillside is the **Abbey of San Biagio**, also built by Antonio da Sangallo the Elder and once a place of pilgrimage for its miraculous frescoed Madonna, whose eyes were said to move. Today the hallowed precincts should still be visited for a 16th-century architectural feast. Meanwhile, Montepulciano remains best known for a bit of Old World kitsch, a life-size figure of the Neapolitan clown Pulcinella, who chimes the hours on top of a 16th-century tower in the main street.

A 15-minute drive northwest from Montepulciano is **Montefollonico**, where Dania Lucherini has made a name for herself as one of the best chefs in Tuscany. Her food owes its flavor and flair to the freshness of the herbs and greens that come from her vegetable garden beneath the **Ristorante La Chiusa**'s walls; cheese and meats are supplied by country people from round about. La Chiusa has a few rooms, country-cottage style except for the bathtubs, which are pure California, large enough for a whole family to congregate in.

Pienza

Enea Silvio Piccolomini, whose life story is told so vividly in the frescoes by Pinturicchio in the Libreria Piccolomini in Siena's cathedral, was born in the town of Cosignano, later renamed Pienza in his honor (west of Montepulciano on route 146). After he became Pope Pius II in 1458, he asked Bernardino Rossellino, architect of the Marsuppini tomb in Santa Croce, to transform his native town. Pienza was to be the first example of Renaissance urban planning, its piazza and adjacent buildings rebuilt according to Renaissance principles of architecture and lifestyle.

And so it remains today, a lived-in museum where you can visit the pope's palace and apartments, with their hanging gardens overlooking the rolling, misty green hills of the Val d'Orcia, with Monte Amiata in the background. No wonder Pope Pius insisted that the windows of the cathedral, which he called *domus vitrea,* look out toward what is perhaps the most uplifting and unspoiled vista in Tuscany. He even threatened to excommunicate anyone who dared to modify the interior's decor; the pictures by Il Vecchietta, Sano di Pietro, and Giovanni di Paolo—which he commissioned—are still in their original places. These are the last works of the glorious Sienese era, which by the 15th century had faded into insignificance beside the bright star of Florence.

Pius himself was so pleased with Pienza that he forgave Il Rossellino for exceeding his budget, praising him thus: "You did well, Bernardo, in lying to us about the expense involved in the work. If you had told the truth, you could never have induced us to spend so much money, and neither this splendid palace nor this church, the finest in all Italy, would now be standing." He then gave the architect an additional 100 ducats and a scarlet robe, an honor awarded to few.

The **Club delle Fattorie**, or Farmsteads' Club, is a very successful concern specializing in all-natural products from all over Tuscany. Recently it has opened a store just inside the main gateway to Pienza, where you can buy the honeys, jams, olive oils, pickled preserves, and other produce of the region. Pienza is famous for its cheese, perhaps because the sheep have rich pastureland in the Val d'Orcia, and feast on herbs like absinthe, mint, and leopard's bane; the cheese is wrapped in walnut leaves while it seasons. Every year on the first Sunday of September there is a *cacio* fair, when local producers bring their cheese to town to be sold.

Monticchiello

Another little hilltop village, between Pienza and Montepulciano, is Monticchiello, famous for its *Teatro Povero* (Poor People's Theater), which puts on a play in the main square in the second half of July, entirely written, acted, and directed by the villagers. Although Monticchiello is the essence of "off the beaten track," its theatrical background has brought the villagers total literacy since the 1700s, unusual in a country community in the days when distances seemed greater and communication was slow. The 13th-century church houses a very lovely *Madonna and Child* by Pietro Lorenzetti that—despite the severity of the *Trecento* style—shows great tenderness and bonding between mother and child. If you prefer to stay for lunch in this hilltop hamlet, try the **Taverna di Moranda**, a rather dark but comfortable little restaurant that will serve you an honest Tuscan meal.

Brunello di Montalcino

This wine, considered Tuscany's most "serious," grows around the town of **Montalcino**, 46 km (28 miles) south of Siena. Again a very old wine, Brunello is mentioned continually in documents narrating the vicissitudes of Tuscan history, such as the time the Maresciallo di Monluc rubbed it on his cheeks to give them color during the siege of Montalcino in 1553, so that the populace would not realize how serious the food shortage had become. It was the wine, we are told, that the Medicis preferred to send their popes, although Cosimo de' Medici complained more than once about the highly intoxicated state in which his guests left his dinner table after the Brunello had been flowing too freely.

Brunello is aged in casks for four years before bottling and continues to age in the bottle, becoming more full-bodied and velvety as time goes by. It can be called Riserva only after five years; it's one of those wines that really needs to breathe and should be uncorked up to a day before consumption. The most famous—and expensive—Brunello is Biondi Santi, but other, less-renowned Brunellos can be equally good. The **Fattoria dei Barbi Colombini** has opened a rustic restaurant a few minutes' drive from Montalcino. You can drink your fill of Brunello here during an inexpensive meal outside on benches in summer or around a log fire in winter. Alternatively, at the **Caffè Fiaschetteria Italiana**, a wine bar and coffeehouse left over from the Belle Epoque in the center of Montalcino, you can taste and compare different Brunellos by the glass.

Legend has it that Charlemagne laid the foundations of the **Abbey of Sant'Antimo**, 9 km (5 miles) from Montalcino, one of the most beautiful Romanesque buildings in Italy. With its pale yellow stone and bucolic silence, Sant'Antimo is unforgettable, whatever your credo.

SIENA

Siena, south of Florence in the heart of the wine country of Tuscany, is a distillation of all things Tuscan, like a Cognac or, more to the point, a grappa. The Sienese speak the purest Italian; their city has been a highly civilized place since the Middle Ages. The Madonnas in their 14th-century paintings are draped in ornate robes

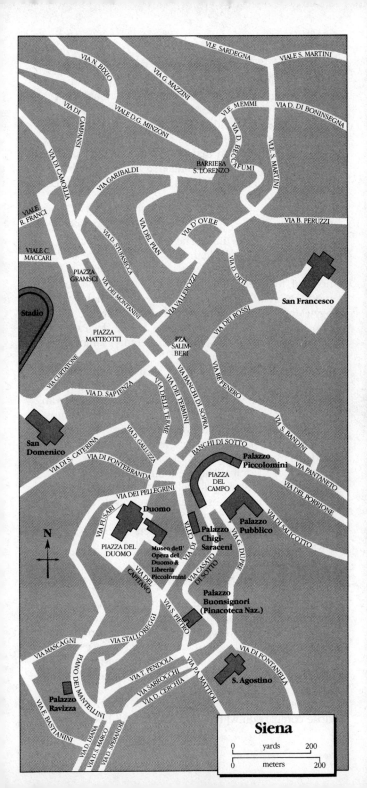

made of mouth-watering silks and damasks, and even today the velvets and brocades for the costumes used in the *Palio,* the historic horse race run twice a year in the main square, are handwoven and cost hundreds of dollars a yard. Unpolluted by industry and unspoiled by the locust sort of tourism that afflicts some of Italy's larger cities, affluent Siena has maintained the same high standards of excellence and elegance for centuries and needs no tourism to boost the city's economy.

For four centuries the city's archives were kept in wooden bindings called *Biccherna,* each painted by a leading artist of the time. (These are well worth a visit, in the State Archives of Palazzo Piccolomini). Dante studied at the university in Siena, one of the oldest in Italy. The hospital, founded in the ninth century, is still one of the most important in the country, especially for ophthalmology (Mrs. Sakharov came from Russia for an eye operation here). Siena's own bank, the Monte dei Paschi di Siena, was founded in the 17th century, although its origins go back even further.

"The Siena of today is a mere shrunken semblance of the rabid little republic which in the 13th century waged triumphant war with Florence, cultivated the arts with splendor, planned a cathedral ... of proportions almost unequaled and contained a population of 200,000 souls." So said Henry James, but the Sienese have none of the Madame Bovary complexes of provincial towns. In the 18th century Horace Walpole found Siena "very smug," and Ghibelline Siena still feels superior in every way to the rest of Tuscany—especially Florence, its traditional Guelph enemy. After all, was Siena not founded by Senus, son of Remus, one of the twin founders of Rome who was suckled by the she-wolf, Siena's symbol to this day?

The Sienese Trecento

In the 1300s it was Siena that led the way in painting and determined the course of Florentine art at the dawn of the *Quattrocento.* "Like a leaven working through the whole lump, so the outstanding quality of Tuscan art during the fourteenth century slowly permeated the whole of Western European painting," wrote Peter and Linda Murray in *The Art of the Renaissance.*

However, the only Sienese artist who can withstand close comparison with Giotto is Duccio di Buoninsegna.

He was an unruly genius; there are records of at least nine fines levied against this great painter, for a number of offenses. All the other leading figures in Italian art were pupils of someone or another, but Duccio seems to have blazed a trail out of nowhere, although he was certainly affected by the work of Nicola and Giovanni Pisano from Pisa, who at that time were working on the pulpit in Siena.

His most famous work in Siena is the *Maestà,* or *Majestic Madonna,* a supremely important figure for the Sienese, who revered her not just as the Mother of God but, more intimately, as patron saint of the Sienese Republic. When this painting was completed in 1311, the people of Siena bore it in triumph to the cathedral, accompanied by the music of trumpets and bagpipes.

Originally the *Maestà*—now in the **Museo dell'Opera del Duomo**—was painted on both sides. The central scene of the Madonna on her throne was surrounded by 60 panels, two of which are now in the United States, in the National Gallery in Washington and the Frick Collection in New York.

Another transcendent figure of the Sienese *Trecento* is Simone Martini, a pupil of Duccio. He, too, painted a *Maestà,* for a 40-foot wall of the Palazzo Pubblico, where she could observe the judicial procedure of the councillors of the Sienese Republic. Even more famous is his painting, on the opposite wall, of Guidoriccio da Fogliano, a knight and charger caparisoned in a rather loud black-and-yellow checked cloak (checks and plaids are very popular in Sienese painting), all the more remarkable because the horse is standing on two left feet. In recent years a shudder has gone through the international art world at the suggestion that this masterpiece of Simone's might be a fake.

Perhaps Simone's most brilliant work is his *Annunciation,* which, although painted for the cathedral in Siena, is now in the Uffizi in Florence. Also in Florence is his *Madonna* in the Guilds' church of Orsanmichele, while in Pisa his polyptych—six panels surrounding a Madonna and Child—is in the Museo Nazionale.

After Simone Martini's departure to Avignon (then seat of the papacy), where he spent his last years, the brothers Ambrogio and Pietro Lorenzetti stepped into his shoes. Pietro's earliest work is a haunting polyptych to be found in Arezzo (east of Siena across the A 1) in the church of

Pieve di Santa Maria. The sloe-eyed Madonna, in an ermine-lined mantle, looks at her guileless *Bambino* with a passionate intensity, almost with foreboding.

In 1340 Pietro was summoned by the Florentines to paint another Madonna for a church in Pistoia (that painting is now in the Uffizi). This would seem to confirm that in the century following Giotto's death and before the emergence of Masaccio—a period marked by a devastating plague—there were no Florentine artists to match the painters of Siena. Pietro's work is best represented in Siena by his *Birth of the Virgin,* now in the Museo dell'Opera del Duomo.

Pietro's brother, the gentler, more introspective Ambrogio, has left Siena an incomparable masterpiece, the *Allegory of Good and Bad Government,* which covers three sides of the **Sala della Pace**, also known as the Sala del Nove (Room of the Nine) in the **Palazzo Pubblico**. Never before in the whole history of art had anyone attempted such an ambitious project, a detailed panorama of daily life in both city and countryside, and it is one of the most exciting things to see in Siena. (Another key painting by Ambrogio, also in the Uffizi, is the *Presentation in the Temple,* showing a depth and sense of architectural perspective that was revolutionary in those two-dimensional days, as was the expressive quality of the main characters.)

The gradual evolution in Sienese painting from the *Trecento* onward can be seen in the **Pinacoteca Nazionale**, where Byzantine Madonnas slowly give way to rosier cheeked, ampler forms in the new perspective of the Renaissance, painted by artists like Giovanni di Paolo, Matteo di Giovanni, and Il Vecchietta. There are also the first pure landscapes, executed on wooden panels, to be painted in Europe: *City by the Sea* and *Castle on the Shore of a Lake* by Ambrogio Lorenzetti.

Frequently represented in Sienese painting—see the last saint in the front row on the left-hand side of Duccio's *Maestà*—is Saint Catherine of Siena (1347–1380), usually depicted with a lily, a flower generally absent from Sienese painting, as it was the symbol of hated Florence. Although she never learned to read and write and had no formal education, Saint Catherine dictated learned treatises and missives to leading ecclesiastical figures (not least Pope Gregory XI, whom she persuaded to transfer the papal seat from Avignon back to Rome), and became a Doctor of the Church and later patron saint of Italy. Her house can be visited, although not much is left of the original decor except her cell, which contains a few personal belongings, including the walking stick that was necessary because of the arthritis she willed on herself in atonement for her father's sins. In the **Church of San Domenico** are further relics of this saint, frescoes by Sodoma of her swooning in ecstasy, and her only recognized likeness, in a chapel at the end of the nave.

The Piazza del Campo

The square in front of San Domenico is the best place to leave your car, as no motorized vehicles are allowed in the old flagstoned streets of Siena. The urban layout is like a Gothic game of Snakes and Ladders, with a magnificent finishing post, the piazza del Campo, acclaimed by Montaigne as the most beautiful square in the world. Don't attempt to visit Siena in high-heeled shoes; you'll either be slithering down the narrow streets that trickle toward the piazza (fanning out like a peacock's tail at the foot of the Torre del Mangia) or resolutely climbing up again.

Henry James, who regretted how few of the world's wonders can "startle and waylay," was quite bowled over by the piazza del Campo: "The vast pavement converges downward in slanting radiations of stone, the spokes of a great wheel." These spokes divide the piazza into nine segments in honor of the government of the Nine, leading merchants and bankers who ruled Siena from 1283 to 1353. The Nine was the only really stable government Siena ever enjoyed in that era; the city's history is otherwise punctuated by the internecine fighting between Guelphs and Ghibellines and its century-long feud with Florence. The Nine built the cathedral and the Palazzo Pubblico, from which the Torre del Mangia, as Henry James saw it, "rises slender and straight as a pennoned lance planted on the steel shod toe of a mounted knight, and keeps all to itself in the blue air." Few things inspired James as much as the Torre del Mangia, "the finest thing in Siena," whose 332 steps you can climb today.

In the center of the square, where people sit and watch the pigeons scatter in clouds every time children or dogs gambol past, is a copy of a fountain surmounted by she-wolves, by Jacopo della Quercia. This great Sienese sculptor (without whose heritage, the Sienese claim, Michelangelo could never have reached the exalted peaks of Mount Olympus) was one of the first, according to Vasari, "who showed that sculpture might make a near approach to nature." His *Fonte Gaia* (Gay Fountain), which took years to complete, earned him the nickname of "Jacopo della Fonte," although his best-known work is the tomb of Ilaria del Carretto in the cathedral in Lucca.

Siena Cathedral

Ruskin wrote that he found the cathedral "in every way absurd—over-cut, over-striped, over-crocketed, over-gabled, a piece of costly confectionery." For the non-purist, Siena Cathedral is an architectural *Maestà,* an overwhelming edifice that inspired Wagner, during his Sienese sojourn, to write *Parsifal.* One of the most remarkable facets of this profusion of decorative arts is the cathedral floor, covered in elaborate graffito technique, while the **Libreria Piccolomini**, off the left nave, was a favorite haunt of Henry James, with its illuminated manuscripts, "almost each of whose successive leaves gives the impression of rubies, sapphires and emeralds set in gold and practically embedded in the page."

The Libreria Piccolomini is frescoed by the Perugian Pinturicchio, whose paintings narrate the life of that "most profanely literary of Pontiffs and last of would-be crusaders," Enea Silvio Piccolomini, who became Pius II. Much of the revenues of his papacy went into this library, and at times, judging from the fresco of his caravels lashed by a violent storm in the port of Genoa, the future pope lived dangerously. Later he was to rebuild the center of his native town, Pienza, one of the loveliest in Tuscany (discussed above). In this cycle of frescoes, reputedly Pinturicchio's best work, some of the rather stereotyped faces are of unusual quality and may have been painted by the young Raphael.

The Palio

Siena's famous horse race, an event that is in no way intended as a mere tourist attraction, is a dusty, noisy, tense, and sometimes frightening occasion that the townspeople relive every year with passionate fervor. Neighborhood feeling here is intense: Every child in Siena is baptized draped in the flag of its *contrada* (a little group of streets), which bears the name and colors of the local insignia—the Dragon, the Porcupine, the She-Wolf, the Noble Goose, and so forth. The first Palio was run in

1656; since then it takes place twice a year, on July 2 and August 16—with full Renaissance panoply—and sometimes three times if there is a special event to commemorate, as when the first man walked on the moon. Every year, voices of protest condemn the riotous, unruly race around the main square on a thin layer of sawdust. A riderless horse can win the race, no matter how or by whom the rider was unseated, and casualties, both human and animal, are not uncommon. The winning horse is adequately rewarded, however, at the victory banquet of his *contrada,* when tables are set out in the narrow streets and he stands at the head of the table, his hooves painted gold, with an overstuffed nosebag of fodder and sugar. Every *contrada* has a museum that can be visited on application to the Azienda Autonoma di Turismo on via di Città 43.

In July the **Accademia Musicale Chigiana**, the music festival held in the Palazzo Chigi-Saraceni, draws music lovers and well-known musicians from all over the world.

Staying in Siena

A large hotel in a magical position on a hill 3 km (2 miles) north of Siena is the CIGA-run **Park Hotel**—strictly for people who feel comfortably cocooned by the amenities and ambience of a major hotel. The rampant William Morris–style wallpaper in the not over-large rooms may intrude on your dreams, while the service is not always what it should be at the price. The hotel has a minibus that takes guests into the center of Siena at infrequent intervals.

Another choice, the beautiful **Certosa di Maggiano**, is a Relais et Châteaux hotel 3 km (2 miles) south of the city, in a converted monastery with the quiet elegance of a Tuscan country house—peach trees surround the pool, and old, leather-bound books line the library walls.

If your budget doesn't rise to Certosa prices, try the **Pensione Palazzo Ravizza** in a charmingly old-fashioned 17th-century palazzo five minutes from the Duomo. Long *the* place to stay for the discerning tourist, the Ravizza offers quite acceptable accommodation—although it's not what it once was.

Food in Siena

Siena is better known for its culture than its cuisine, which, although palatable enough, has settled into a com-

fortable gastronomic rut—thanks no doubt to the unde-
manding tourists who hardly notice what they are eating
as they sit out at tables in the piazza del Campo, one of
the most splendid open-air dining rooms in the world.

A restaurant a little out of the ordinary—and certainly
trying harder—is the **Osteria Le Logge**, just around the
corner from the Palazzo Pubblico. A bohemian place, the
venue for Siena's university fauna and what could be described as swinging Sienese, it looks less like a restaurant
than an Old Curiosity Shop, with old-fashioned glass-
fronted cabinets around the walls; prewar radios and similar props punctuate the decor. Le Logge's food is imaginative, like the *Terra di Siena,* veal baked with peperoncino
and tomato, and a risotto with bacon and sweet corn. A
good selection of *pecorino,* the local sheep's cheese,
rounds off the meal, a perfect partner for the house wine, a
Brunello del Paradiso. The owners of Le Logge have recently restored a 14th-century cellar beneath the restaurant, and it will be visible from above through glass. No
credit cards accepted.

A more comfortable, if staider and more expensive,
restaurant is **Al Marsili**, near the Duomo at via del Castoro
3, with a very comprehensive collection of Chianti Clas-
sicos stacked around the walls, giving a wine-cellar look
to the place. The food is good, wholesome Tuscan, which
is the same as Florentine in most respects. The Sienese
are famous, however, for their salami and their sheep's
cheese, and they make much use of *dragoncello,* or
tarragon, which was first planted in Siena by Charlemagne's troops. A local pasta is *pici,* hand-rolled spaghetti, which Al Marsili serves with a mushroom and meat
sauce.

The real eager-beaver gourmet drives a little way out of
Siena (a taxi will also oblige not too ruinously) to the
Antica Trattoria Botteganova. Here great care goes into
the choice of dishes resuscitated from the menus of
Siena's past, into decanting the impressive choice of
wines, and into procuring the freshest ingredients, such
as the *erbette* (herbs) that are an integral part of many
dishes here. Allow the helpful staff to advise you on the
constantly varying menus, and try one of the soups made
of potatoes, mushrooms, or onions, or *acqua cotta* (literally, cooked water), a Sienese specialty of vegetables left
to cook for a long time and served with bread and grated
pecorino cheese. Botteganova is not as expensive as it
could be.

Siena has Tuscany's sweet tooth. It's famous not only for its *panforte,* which tastes like a very solid mince pie, but also for cookies called *ricciarelli.* At **Nannini** in via Banchi di Sopra you can sample all these local delicacies and also buy boxes in varying sizes to take home.

Siena is not a fashionable shopping town, but the little boutiques on via Banchi di Sotto and via di Città, the streets encircling the Piazza del Campo, are well worth a browse. You can pick up local pottery there, with designs inspired by the colorful flags of the *Palio,* at stores like **Zina Provvedi.**

THE TYRRHENIAN COAST

There are 203 miles of coastline in Tuscany, not counting the islands—not quite enough to accommodate comfortably the many thousands of Italian holiday-makers and sun-worshippers from northern climes who descend on its beaches and coastal resorts, especially in July and August. The Versilia district, to the north, was once the haunt of artists and poets as well as the local aristocracy, who still have summer homes there. But a broad band of concrete has wedged itself between the mountains and the sea, leaving windswept pines to tower forlornly over the countless *villette* (bungalows) and hotel billboards.

A busy four-lane road roars past the beach, which is divided into different *bagni* where you have to pay, sometimes through the nose, for your corner of a foreign land complete with deck chair and umbrella. At best, like the Bagno Piero at Forte dei Marmi, these *bagni* look a little like Deauville in Impressionist paintings; at worst, like Viareggio, which has become more famous for its spectacular carnival than for its seashore, they can verge on Coney Island.

Farther south is the **Maremma,** Tuscany's Camargue (see also the section on Etruscan Places, above), where people raise white oxen and hunt wild boar and where you can still find local cowboys, called *butteri,* riding on old American-style saddles. However, the area's wild beaches, lined with dunes and dense Mediterranean *maquis,* are often part of wildlife protection areas, such as the Lago di Burano and the oasis of Bolgheri. Those beaches readily accessible to visitors are always crowded in summer; few have the kind of hotels and facilities the discerning traveller is accustomed to.

L'Argentario

Readers should therefore concentrate on the southernmost tip of the Tuscan coast, the Costa d'Argento (Silver Coast), more often called simply **L'Argentario** after the rocky promontory that dominates the coastline and the islands of Giglio and Giannutri. Sixteen miles of panoramic coast road on L'Argentario dip and swerve around dazzling corners, linking Porto Santo Stefano and Port' Ercole, the two fashionable resorts on what is virtually an island joined to the mainland by narrow causeways. Argentario is about the same distance south of Siena as it is northwest of Rome: 120 km (75 miles).

There are two sandy beaches here, the **Giannella** and, better still, the **Feniglia** (where Caravaggio is said to have died), but the real joy of the Argentario is to rent a boat and bathe in the blue depths of the rocky inlets or among the grottoes that corrugate the islands' coastline—a paradise for deep-sea diving. The **Hotel Pellicano**, with a beach and swimming pool of its own, sits in a dreamlike setting on a hillside; you can watch the yachts billowing by on their way to Cala Galera, a marina where up to 700 boats can moor in summer. You pay for this vista by the inch.

Porto Santo Stefano and **Port'Ercole** are for people who love the sea and who like to be seen. The boutiques lining the port at Ercole sell designer seamen's sweaters or shell-like jewelry at **I Gioielli del Mare**, while the seafaring jet set step into their rope-soled shoes and off their yachts to go eat at one of the restaurants on the port, like **Il Gambero Rosso**, which, despite ups and downs over the years, is still the place to people-watch in Port'Ercole. Or "Let's go to the Monastery," they say, and pile into cars to drive up to the Convento dei Frati Passionisti, where the food at **Il Sorgente** may be cheap and undistinguished, but the view of the lagoon of Orbetello glittering at your feet is priceless. After dinner there is dancing in the open air on top of a hill at **Le Streghe**, a small and intimate night club that has been the venue of chic young Romans for the past 20 years.

Another favorite haunt in Port'Ercole is **Il Bacco in Toscana**, an *enoteca*. It also serves very good food while you sip the wines of, among others, Prince Agostino Chigi, of one of the noble families who have made Italy's history. His estate, the **Cantina dell'Aquilino** near Port'Ercole, has a few rustic rooms grouped around an open-air trattoria that serves good home cooking in the middle of the family

vineyard. Open from June until harvest time in the beginning of September; its prices are more than reasonable—
and credit cards are a thing of the future here.

THE ISLANDS

The archipelago of the Argentario was a strategic stretch
of coastline, a prey to Saracens and marauding pirates,
including Barbarossa, who carried off 700 inhabitants of
the island of Giglio in 1544 to sell as slaves at the market
in Constantinople. The last time raiders came, so the story
goes, they got drunk on Ansonaco, the famous wine of the
island—Stendhal talks of it—and were ignominiously captured by the islanders.

Giglio

Giglio, 14 km (9 miles) from Porto Santo Stefano, is
famous not only for its wine but for its granite, out of
which many Italian churches have been built, as has the
Medieval fortress of Giglio Castello that dominates the
island. Here, at **Le Tamerigi**, you can enjoy a delicious
meal of fish and the local wild rabbit and game. The most
magical hotel on the island, if not the most luxurious, is
the **Hermitage**, which can be reached only by sea. (If you
have no boat of your own, the hotel will pick you up at
Giglio Porto.) Allowing for the inevitable drawbacks of its
secluded position, Hotel Pardini's Hermitage, as it is
called in full, is the perfect retreat, and a base from which
to sally out and discover the grottoes and hidden bays,
where shoals of Mediterranean fish bask on the sandy
seabed.

Giannutri

The Greeks called this island Artemis because it is shaped
like a quarter moon. Fourteen miles from Port'Ercole by
private boat, it has no hotels or restaurants, but it does
have fascinating sea depths where sunken Roman galleons, half submerged by sand, can be explored.

Elba

"Lucky Napoléon!" wrote Dylan Thomas to friends in
1947. Whether the Little Emperor shared his opinion is

unclear; the most lyrical passage he writes about Elba in his *Memoirs* concerns his departure: "I left the island of Elba on the 26th February, 1815, at 9 o'clock in the evening. I boarded the brig *Inconstant,* which flew the white flag studded with bees throughout the journey."

Unfortunately a great many people seem to share the Welsh poet's enthusiasm. This largest island in Tuscany, reached by boat from the mainland town of Piombino (about 75 km/50 miles south along the coast from Pisa), is overrun by tourists—especially Germans—in the summer months. But it *is* possible to get far from the madding crowd by renting rowboats at the beautiful beaches of Cavoli or Fetovaia on the southwest coast and rowing around the headland to bathe in deserted coves.

There are two Napoleonic landmarks on Elba: his villa in San Martino, 5 km (3 miles) from Portoferraio, and the **Palazzina dei Mulini** in the historic center of Portoferraio. The villa has a pleasant setting and a good view, but there is little of Napoléon except for his bed, which probably looks the same as Napoléon's beds everywhere else, while at the Palazzina there are manuscripts, his library, the flag with three bees that he had made especially for his Elban interlude, and a picture of his dog.

Some of the most fascinating parts of the island, where the Etruscans mined iron ore—the Greeks called it Aethalia (Soot Island)—and where the Romans built their summer villas, are off the tourist track. At **Magazzini**, a small port on the north coast near Bagnaia, there are gardens like the Villa alle Palme, where almost every kind of palm tree grows, as well as exotic plants brought over the centuries from all around the world. At her estate in Magazzini, **La Chiusa**, Giuliana Foresi, one of the leading citizens of Elba, sells her wines from a centuries-old manor house, including the velvety dessert wine for which Elba is famous, Aleatico. In the hills above Marina di Campo is **Sant'Ilario**, a little village most tourists haven't even heard of, which has one of the most stable populations in Italy; for centuries no one has left his or her native village, nor have there been infiltrations from elsewhere. Here a man known as Pietro delle Pietre (Peter of the Stones; ask at Sant'Ilario's only bar) has accumulated one of the most interesting collections of semiprecious stones in the world.

Marciana, on the slopes of Monte Capanne, Elba's highest mountain (the 3,340-foot peak can be reached by funicular railway), boasts an interesting archaeological museum, the Antiquarium Comunale. In the neighboring Medieval hamlet of Poggio Alto you can eat a hearty meal of wild boar and game at **Publius**. The best restaurant on the island, however, is **Il Chiasso** at Capoliveri, which serves exquisitely prepared fish from the surrounding seas. The hotel with the most charm is the not overpriced **Hermitage** in the gulf of La Biodola.

From the Elba (Piombino) and Argentario areas, route 1 leads southeast to the A 12 into Rome.

From Florence again, another route through Tuscany is through Prato and Montecatini to Lucca, Pisa, and up toward the Ligurian coast.

PRATO

Prato, 19 km (12 miles) from Florence to the northwest, is its industrial alter ego. It is the ladies of Prato whose sleek cars are parked outside the boutiques and jewelers of Florence's via Tornabuoni, something the Florentines with their old money and ancient heritage find—not without a tinge of envy—rather vulgar.

The Pratesi owe their wealth to wool, as Prato is the largest wool-producing city in the world. Known as *cenciaioli* (ragmen), the Pratesi invented the recycling of wool on an industrial scale. Huge trucks trundle through the center of the city carrying bales of rags destined for recycling into short-fibered wool, the kind most overcoats are made of.

Less well known are the ancient origins of Prato and the considerable artworks within its 14th-century walls. "Prato," says Edward Hutton, "is like a flower that has fallen by the wayside, that has faded in the dust of the way." Squares like the piazza del Comune and the surrounding streets have the same Medieval charm as Lucca or Arezzo, and the cathedral is a cornucopia of artworks. The statue in the middle of the piazza is of Francesco di Marco Datini, the first great merchant of Prato, who has gone down in the annals of commerce as the 14th-century inventor of the letter of credit.

Filippo and Filippino Lippi

Filippo Lippi was a Carmelite monk who spent his boyhood, brush in hand, studying the Masaccio frescoes in the Brancacci chapel. Despite his vocation, Fra Filippo was a hot-blooded youth, "so great a sensualist," we are told by Vasari, "that he would stop at nothing to gratify his immediate longings." His lusty nature no doubt interfered with his work, because his patron Cosimo de' Medici once locked him in his room until he had finished a painting. After two days, the frustrated artist tucked up his robes and shinned down a rope made of bed sheets. "And here you catch me at an alley's end," wrote Robert Browning in his poem "Fra Lippo Lippi," "Where sportive ladies leave their doors ajar."

While in Prato, Fra Filippo became enamored of a novice, Lucrezia, and (incredibly) persuaded her Mother Superior to let the young girl sit as a model for the Virgin in a painting on which he was engaged. One thing led to another—Shaw's life force—and Lucrezia bore him a son, Filippino, the next year; brought to Florence by his father when he was ten years old and placed under Sandro Botticelli's wing, Filippino was destined to become one of the great masters of the Renaissance.

Meanwhile, his father the monk was being paid 2,000 florins, the highest fee ever earned by a Renaissance artist, to paint the main chapel of the cathedral at Prato with scenes from the lives of Saint Stephen and Saint John the Baptist, with an enchanting Salome dancing the dance of the seven veils. One of the stricken observers staring at Saint John's severed head is none other than Fra Filippo himself.

St. Stephen's Cathedral

The cathedral in Prato, dedicated to Saint Stephen, is guardian of a precious relic, the *Cintola,* or girdle of the Virgin Mary. Legend has it that the Mother of Christ gave her girdle to Thomas, the doubting apostle, when she was assumed into heaven. Saint Thomas entrusted the girdle to a priest, whose daughter Maria fell in love with a boy from Prato who had come to the Holy Land as a crusader. The two eloped to Prato, with the girdle hidden in a basket of rushes. Today the girdle is shown to the populace five times a year from the circular pulpit on the right side of the cathedral's façade, which is decorated with a frieze of putti by Donatello, not unlike his frieze of gamboling urchins in the Museo dell'Opera del Duomo in Florence. The rest of the year the girdle is kept in the chapel of the Cintola, the altar surmounted by a small but very expressive statue of the *Madonna della Cintola* by Giovanni Pisano—the mother looks in mock severity at the Christ Child, who evidently is intent on pulling off her crown. An altogether better behaved *Bambino* sits on the lap of the *Madonna dell'Ulivo* (*Olive-tree Madonna*), by Benedetto da Maiano, also in the cathedral.

Other churches well worth a visit are **Santa Maria delle Carceri**, by Giuliano da Sangallo, built according to the classical *Quattrocento* plan (devised by Brunelleschi) of the circle within a square, and the **Convent of Sant' Niccolò**, with its Della Robbia–style lavabo in the sacristy and its nuns' private chapel. Knock on the door to the left of the main altar and the nuns will show you around; they appreciate a little offering in exchange.

If you have time, visit the **Galleria Comunale**, open from 9:00 A.M. to 1:00 P.M. and from 3:00 to 5:00 P.M. except Sundays. It contains, along with some beautiful works from the *Trecento,* paintings by Prato's most famous son, Filippino Lippi, including his *Madonna del Ceppo* and the *Tabernacolo di Santa Margherita,* which the artist originally painted on the corner of the house he bought for his mother. When the house was bombed in 1944, the tabernacle was also smashed and has been entirely reconstructed in the Galleria Comunale.

For a change from art of the past there is the new **Prato Museum of Contemporary Art**, an immense exhibition space that resembles a saw-tooth-roofed factory—and which has indeed been endowed by a textile industrialist.

The Metastasio Theater draws avant-garde and exotic theater groups from all over the world; whether it is New York's Living Theatre, Chinese acrobats, or Russian puppets, it is very popular among Florentines and Pratesi alike. It's around the corner from the church of Santa Maria delle Carceri.

There is a delightful hotel, the **Villa Santa Cristina**, on a hill above Prato in a vine-covered villa. Both the hotel and its excellent restaurant are expensive.

People come especially to Prato to eat at **Il Pirana**, a fish restaurant with an unfortunate "executive suite" decor but with very good seafood dishes, such as spaghetti with lobster, a meal in itself. (Fresh fish is expensive everywhere in Tuscany.) Pirana is in a rather unattractive part of Prato, the via Valentini 110; Tel: (0574) 257-46. Il Pirana is closed on Saturdays and Sundays and all of August.

MONTECATINI TERME

People have been "taking the waters" at the spa of Monte-catini Terme since Roman times. One of the springs, the **Tettuccio**, has just celebrated its sixth centenary. The unforgettable scenes of turn-of-the-century spa life in the award-winning film *Oci Ciornie* (*Dark Eyes*) were shot here: Marcello Mastroianni in impeccable white trousers and spats walking with enviable sangfroid into the mud bath to retrieve his lady love's hat from among the water lilies.

Montecatini, off the A 11 west of Prato, is an unexpect-edly lush and languorous corner of Tuscany, with a balmy atmosphere conducive to the healing of psyche and phy-sique for which this spa is famous throughout Italy. Many Italian families take their holidays in Montecatini to un-wind after the stresses and strains of the working year and to cure their gallstones and gastric ulcers in the most natural and congenial way.

It is difficult to talk about the beneficial effects of the waters of Montecatini without descending into the nether regions of the human anatomy. However, "the purgative effect only represents a part, and not the most important, of the activity of the Montecatini waters," the learned little booklet issued by the spa assures us. Basically, Monte-catini's springs are recommended for the treatment of diseases of the liver, digestive tract, and metabolism, including the extensive pathology of arthrosis. The wa-ters can be classified into two groups: the salt-sulfate-bicarbonate-sodium for drinking purposes and the salt-iodine-sulfate-alkaline for thermal baths, irrigations, and showers. The beverage waters are mainly found in the Tettuccio, Regina, Excelsior, Torretta, and La Salute estab-lishments, while mud cures, baths, inhalations, and so on are to be found in the Leopoldina, Excelsior, and Redi establishments. High season is from August 1 to October 15. The Excelsior establishment is the only one open all year round.

After a bracing shot of salt-sulfate water before break-fast, visitors to Montecatini evidently spend the rest of their time pampering themselves. For a small provincial town, it has an impressive array of boutiques lining the corso Roma and its continuation, the corso Matteotti, and there are also extensive facilities for sports, including golf.

A light but highly sophisticated lunch at the **Enoteca da Giovanni**, accompanied by a crescendo of local vintages, is hardly a dietician's dream; neither is the more substantial fare at **Lido's** in Montecatini Alto, where, although the menu is based on fish, the lobster and oysters feature more prominently than steamed cod. A funicular railway leaves Montecatini every half-hour for **Montecatini Alto**, an ancient hilltop hamlet 1,000 feet from the spa; Lido's is worth a visit for the view alone.

Cakes and coffee are an important part of the afternoon ritual here, and Montecatini's main specialty is *cialde*, plate-sized wafers filled with a nutty-tasting cream, to be sampled at, among others, the **Nuovo Caffè Biondi** on the corner of the main shopping street. The most famous *pasticceria* in Montecatini is **Giovannini** at corso Matteoti 4. In the evenings, visitors to Montecatini take a constitutional walk along spacious, tree-lined avenues like the viale Verdi, where at the large outdoor **Caffè Gambrinus** a palm-court orchestra plays.

Montecatini has 500 hotels and pensioni, of which the most famous is the **Grand Hotel e la Pace** with its adjoining "natural health center" in five acres of luxuriant park. Built in 1870, this Belle Epoque palace was once the most exclusive "fat farm" in Italy, where the likes of King Farouk recovered from their excesses; it is correspondingly expensive, although special terms can be worked out at all times. (Open April to October.)

About 25 km (15 miles) west from Montecatini is the walled Medieval city of Lucca.

LUCCA

From the air Lucca looks like a pinball game about the size of New York's Central Park, the tourist like the little lead ball dribbling along the tortuous jumble of streets and bouncing off churches at every corner. Lucca seems less a town than a film set for a Medieval epic, the kind where halberds clash beneath mullioned windows. You will find yourself wondering why the men are not in doublet and hose, the ladies in high-necked ruffs—in every other way the city seems to be caught in a Gothic time warp. The corners of the narrow streets are so eroded by centuries of elbows brushing past that the walls are noticeably indented about three feet above the ground.

The Lucchesi have a reputation for being even stingier than the Florentines, but perhaps they are just careful of their wealth, as for centuries Lucca has been a prosperous town.

Lucca was to silk what Florence was to wool in the Middle Ages, and under Paolo Guinigi (about whom more later) the silk industry reached its apogee. Silk is still woven in Lucca and sold at the **Tessiture Artistiche Lucchesi** at via Anfiteatro 15 and at via del Duomo 12. Luccan mastery of the art of wrought iron can still be seen in the 16th-century lanterns, doorknobs, and knockers that stud the façades of the city's palazzi.

The old center of Lucca is surrounded by two and a half miles of massive 17th-century ramparts and walls, so wide that the top has been turned into a tree-lined avenue. One of the most rewarding things to do in Lucca is to rent a bicycle and peddle along the top of this "circular lounging place of a splendid dignity," as Henry James called it, looking down at the city below. There is a certain snobbism among the Lucchesi as to who lives within and who without the city walls, the two "classes" being *Lucca fuori* and *Lucca dentro* (literally, Lucca out and Lucca in). As a visitor you will definitely be Lucca in, as everything you want to see is *dentro*.

Lucca used to be a very important city, despite its diminutive size, bristling with over 200 towers, each belonging to one of the leading families, with trees sprouting on top of them. Over the centuries these towers have either been demolished, the bricks recycled into other buildings, or have collapsed of their own accord. The only tower left standing, as opposed to a house-plus-tower like the Palazzo and Torre Guinigi, is the **Torre delle Ore** (Tower of the Hours), saved for posterity because it sported one of the two public clocks in Lucca.

Castruccio Castracani, whom Machiavelli is said to have taken as his model for *The Prince,* was literally found in a cabbage patch here at the end of the 13th century by a widow who raised him as her son. He led Lucca into feats of valor that this placid little Tuscan city had never dreamed of, and became a local Napoléon, master of all of western Tuscany, from Pistoia to Volterra.

Another important Lucchese is the 15th-century artist Matteo Civitali, whose work is almost ignored by encyclopedias and art historians. His works adorn many of Lucca's churches, together with works by other members of his family: Vincenzo, Masseo, and Nicolao.

The Churches of Lucca

Lucca was apparently the first city in Italy to receive the light of the Gospel, and has 99 churches to its name, "ecclesiastical architecture being indeed the only one of the arts to which it seems to have given attention," said Henry James. But in this art they excelled. Even Ruskin wrote of one of the smaller churches, the Santa Maria Forisportam, better known today as Santa Maria Bianca: "Absolutely for the first time I now saw what Medieval builders were and what they meant. I took the simplest of façades for analysis, that of Santa Maria Foris-Portam, and thereon literally began the study of architecture."

You cannot visit all 99, but three churches are of prime importance: San Martino, San Michele in Foro, and San Frediano.

"All that is best in Lucca, all that is sweetest and most naive may be found in the beautiful Duomo," says Edward Hutton about **San Martino**. However, the cathedral's interior is so dark that it almost seems foggy, as though centuries of incense had stopped trying to filter out of the windows high up under the vaults. Take a handful of 100-lire coins to put into a machine that will illumine for an if-you-blink-you-miss-it moment the beautiful tomb of Ilaria del Carretto, the wife of Paolo Guinigi, who died in 1405. The figure of this child-wife, by the Sienese sculptor Jacopo della Quercia, looks as though she were asleep, with a little dog at her feet waiting expectantly for his mistress to wake up, "neither alive with the life of the body, nor dead with the death of the body." This truly moving funereal statue is not just a work of art but conveys—as it did to Charles Morgan's Sparkenbroke—a feeling of "private communication," as though "her silence had whispered in his ear." The *Last Supper* by Tintoretto, on the other hand, seems to shine with a light of its own, the table where the apostles are dining depicted vertically for once, instead of the usual transversal scene.

Among other things, Matteo Civitali worked on the octagonal chapel in the middle of the church that houses the wooden crucifix, or *Volto Santo,* which has been venerated in Lucca since 782. Legend has it that the crucifix with Christ's face was carved by Nicodemus (who helped to bury Christ) out of a cedar of Lebanon, the angels guiding his hand. To save the holy work from religious persecution, Nicodemus put it out to sea in a rudderless boat, which eventually beached on the coast near Lucca. The relic was brought to Lucca in a cart drawn by untamed oxen. Every year on September 13 and 14 the people of Lucca relive this tradition with the *Luminara,* a candlelit procession through the streets. The *Volto Santo* became famous throughout Europe in the Middle Ages, and even King William II of England used to swear, *"Per Sanctum vultum de Luca."*

The façade of the **Church of San Michele**, typical of the Pisan style, is like a crescendo of notepad doodles, layer upon layer of blind arcades. It is crowned by one of the city's landmarks, a 10-foot-high statue of the Archangel Michael in bronze and stone, with a magnificent pair of wings, and with the defeated dragon at his feet.

Matteo Civitali's contribution to this church, the *Madonna Salutis Portus,* erected to mark the end of the plague of 1476–1480, is presently undergoing restoration.

Santa Zita is buried in the **Church of San Frediano**, one of the best examples of Lucca's Romanesque style. Saint Zita, who died in 1278, is the patron saint of housemaids, mentioned by Dante in Canto 21 of *L'Inferno.* She was a maid in the household of the noble Fatinelli family, and her master discovered her distributing bread from his larder to the poor. When challenged, Zita held open her apron to find that, by divine intervention, the bread had been turned into flowers. On her feast day in April there is a ceremonial blessing of the newly blossomed daffodils, and the streets of Lucca turn into a flower market. In death, this homely saint joined the Irish Saint Richard, who died in Lucca on a pilgrimage in 722 and also is buried in this church. (These churches are open from 9:00 A.M. to noon and 3:30 to 5:00 P.M.)

Paolo Guinigi

Like the Medicis in Florence, Paolo Guinigi was a merchant and patron of the arts. He was only 24 when he became "Captain and Defender of the People," and he was Lord of Lucca for 30 years, from 1400 onward. It was he who brought Jacopo della Quercia from Siena to make a sarcophagus for his young wife, Ilaria. Commerce flourished during his rule. He had a monopoly of the local marble quarries, and his ox carts brought marble to Florence and Venice to build the cathedrals of Santa Maria del Fiore and San Marco. He brought a foretaste of Renaissance grandeur and an unfamiliar joie de vivre into the sober lives of the Lucchesi, traditionally an austere and parsimonious folk. His library could boast works by Dante, Boccaccio, and Petrarch, and he had a passion for precious stones, sending scouts to Paris and Venice to bring back gems for his collection.

The Guinigi Tower, with its seven ilex trees growing on top, is a worthwhile climb to enjoy a view of what Hilaire Belloc called "the most fly-in-amber little town in the world," with its rust-colored roofs like crumbling gingerbread and the Apuan Alps in the background.

Paolo Guinigi also built the Villa Guinigi, today the **Museo Nazionale**. Again Matteo Civitali is represented, with a *Madonna and Child,* but the most interesting exhibits are the carved wood and intarsia, some of which come from Paolo Guinigi's library and some from the cathedral of San Martino, especially the work by Cristoforo Canozzi de Lendinara (a friend of Paolo della Francesca), with his views of Lucca in different shades and grains of wood.

Lucca was originally a Ligurian settlement, which became Roman around 180 B.C. The city still retains its Roman layout, its *cardo* and *decumanus* (intersecting major streets) and, above all, the oval **Amphitheater** tucked away right in the center of the city, where you come upon it completely by surprise. The arches from which hungry lions and gladiators once issued into the arena are now little boutiques.

Lucca may not have given the world as much art as some other Tuscan towns, but it gave us more than its share of musicians. From the 16th century onward musicians such as Guami, Malvezzi, Gregori, Gasperini, Geminiani, and Boccherini left Lucca for the courts of Europe, while Giacomo Puccini's family had been Lucchesi for generations. You can visit the house on the via di Poggio where he was born and where, among other things, his *Turandot* piano and his greatcoat are preserved. (Open from 10:00 A.M. to noon and 4:00 to 6:00 P.M. in summer and from 10:00 A.M. to 4:00 P.M. in winter. Closed Mondays.)

Outside Lucca

During Napoléon's occupation of Italy, he gave the city of Lucca to his sister Elisa, who was married to Felice Baciocchi. In 1811 she took over the **Villa Reale in Marlia**, about 15 km (9 miles) northeast of Lucca, redecorating all the rooms in Neoclassical style. Here she listened to concerts conducted by Niccolò Paganini, her private conductor, and supervised the embellishment of the villa's beautiful gardens, which can be visited all year. (Hourly tours of gardens on Tuesdays, Thursdays, and Sundays, July to October, from 9:00 A.M. to noon and 4:00 to 6:00 P.M.; daily except Mondays the rest of the year.)

A bit farther out to the northeast of Lucca are some of the most famous gardens in Italy, at the **Villa Garzoni** at Collodi, birthplace of the author of *Pinocchio*. (From April 1 to November 6, the gardens are open from 8:00 A.M. to 1:00 P.M. and from 2:30 P.M. to sunset, and from November 7 to March 30, from 9:00 A.M. to noon and from 2:30 P.M. to sunset.)

When choosing a hotel in Lucca, it is best to fall between the two extremes. The **Villa la Principessa**, 3 km (2 miles) from the center of the city, is indeed princely, having been the private home of the Bourbon Parma family, with a park to match, but one could argue that it is more expensive than it is worth. The **Hotel Universo** in the center of Lucca, on the other hand, despite some splendid stucco in the lobby, has definitely seen better days. The middle of the road, the three-star **Hotel Hambros**, is in a large garden five minutes from Lucca.

Food in Lucca does not differ substantially from the rest of Tuscany, but the Lucchesi do have their own wines—the Montecarlo whites—and their own olive oil, which many prefer to the classical Tuscan olive oil produced around Florence and Siena. Little trattorias abound in the center of Lucca, all similar, so choose one that doesn't look too touristy and that has good smells wafting from the kitchen—such as **Da Giulio in Pelleria** (piazza San Tommaso 29; closed Sundays and Mondays). However, some of the best food in Tuscany is to be had 10 km (6 miles) due north of Lucca at Ponte a Moriano, a hamlet on the banks of the river Serchio.

A predecessor of the **Ristorante la Mora** in Ponte a Moriano was probably offering refreshment to travellers on their way to Florence in Roman times, as the word *mora* is Latin for a stopping place. What is sure is that the great-great-uncle and -aunt of today's owners, Sauro and Angela Brunicardi, were already cooking for their guests in 1867. The restaurant serves traditional dishes from the Lucca region, including a thick soup called *gran farro* made from spelt, a type of wheat that grows on the local hills and was used in cooking by the Roman legionnaires as they tramped up the peninsula. Other dishes include chicken breasts in balsamic vinegar, beef with fresh *porcini* mushrooms (which are also good with *straccetti,* a local pasta), and what can only be described as a Tuscan cheesecake. Closed on Wednesday evenings and Thursdays; expensive but worth every penny for a fine culinary experience.

In Lucca the streets around the via Fillungo are the main shopping venue. The largest stores must be all of three yards across, and their names are still in traditional black and gold. There are jewelry stores in particular, like **Carli** at via Fillungo 95, that look as though they haven't changed since they were founded—in Carli's case, in 1655. The coffeehouse **DiSimo** at via Fillungo 58 has been a haunt of litterateurs and artists since the days when Giovanni Pascoli, one of Italy's most famous poets, took his morning coffee there; the atmosphere is such that he could still be propping up the bar. In keeping with the pervading sense of antiquity in Lucca, the most sensible thing to buy is old prints at **Silvano Spinelli** at via Sant'Andrea 10. Another art connection in Lucca: Every other year, in November, a festival of cartoons brings cartoonists from all over the world.

Night life in Lucca is the streets, thronged with people as if they were in an outdoor salon until the early hours.

CARRARA AND PIETRASANTA

A side trip from Lucca (or from Pisa) would be a visit to the Tuscan marble-quarrying areas northwest up the coast toward La Spezia in Liguria. The marble quarries of the Apuan mountains above Carrara and Pietrasanta have been providing giant blocks of marble for the façades of temples and churches, equestrian statues, and monumental flights of stairs from Roman times to the present day. In the old days the huge slabs were sent sliding down the mountainsides, hoisted onto carts, and dragged by the traditional Tuscan white oxen to the big cities or to the nearby seashore, where they were loaded onto ships and sent all over the world.

Today the quarrying still goes on day and night, and the mountains yield 700,000 tons of marble a year, much of which you can see stacked like packs of cards in the yards of the innumerable workshops huddled around the little towns of Carrara and Pietrasanta in northwest Tuscany. It is worth driving up to the quarries of Monte Altissimo, 5,200 feet high, between the two towns. From the top of the sheer white marble face—said to be the source of the marble for many of Michelangelo's famous sculptures—you can see as far as the Côte d'Azur on a good day. (Take the Seravezza exit from the Aurelian Way.)

If you like marble in the kitchen—cutting slabs, rolling pins, pestles and mortars, and so on—there is a store in Carrara on via Piave called **Nuova Marmotecnica**, run by Giordano W. Baudoni, that is well worth a visit.

On the other hand, if you have your heart set on a marble statue like the ones in the windows of Romanelli, the famous marble store on the lungarno Acciaioli in Florence, the artisans of Carrara or Pietrasanta will carry out orders to your specifications, however outrageous these may be. It is interesting to know that these marble artisans actually execute the giant masterpieces that adorn the main squares of cities all over the world and find their way into famous collections and art galleries. The sculptor submits a model in plaster or marble and the artisan here then reproduces it to scale in the outsize dimensions required, chiseling and honing the work to its finished perfection.

In the workshop of **Carlo Nicoli** at piazza XXVII April 9, the oldest and best-known workshop in Carrara, are artisans who are responsible for some of the most famous works of art today. If your requirements are more modest, CAMP (the syndicate for artistic marble products and typical handcrafts from the town of Pietrasanta, at viale Marconi 5) will send you to whichever artisan is most qualified to carry out the type of work you have in mind.

About ten minutes southeast of Carrara in Montignoso, in an unlikely setting tucked away among small industrial centers, is **Il Bottaccio**, which would be impossible to find if the signs along the road were not so good. At this supremely elegant Relais et Châteaux hotel, white Persian cats prowl around the indoor fish pond in the dining room in an atmosphere redolent of the early James Bond (perhaps the vaguely ghoulish waiters who hover at your elbow, assiduously pouring vintage wines, feed recalcitrant diners to the exotic fish lurking beneath the water lilies). The five suites also have a Hollywood setting: The rooms are on several levels, and high-tech four-poster beds share the space with an antique stone oil press (where Dr. No gets ground up in the final scene?) and a mosaic-lined, sunken Jacuzzi tub. Very expensive—for an unforgettable, unique experience.

PISA

The people of Pisa believe in keeping their jewels in the bank and use their front parlor only on Sundays. Pisa's "jewels," or main sights, lie not on a velvet cushion but on the lushest of green lawns within the campo dei Miracoli (Square of Miracles), while the rest of the city leads a humdrum life outside its limits. Two-thirds of your time in Pisa will be spent at the campo, visiting the Leaning Tower, the Duomo, the Baptistery, and the cemetery.

It should not be forgotten that Pisa—due west of Florence near the coast, and now its poor relation visited chiefly for the Leaning Tower—is one of the oldest cities in Europe and was a great maritime republic long before the Florentine Renaissance. Florentine sculpture and architecture owe much to architects like Buscheto, who started work on the cathedral here in 1063, 200 years before the Duomo in Florence, while sculptors like Nicola Pisano and his son Giovanni gave Tuscany its most beautiful pulpits—not overshadowed even by those of Donatello—in the 13th century.

Despite a succession of overlords, Pisans have always remained Pisans rather than Etruscans, Romans, or even Tuscans. From earliest times they have turned their backs on the rest of Italy and looked toward the sea that gave them the Medieval equivalent of an empire. Their supremacy on the sea and their victories over the Saracens provided Pisa with the funds to build the campo dei Miracoli and influenced the so-called Pisan style that was imitated by so many later Tuscan architects: the black-and-white striped marble and the lacy tiers of blind arcades that are Gothic and Romanesque with a strain of Muslim.

All the great Pisan sculptors are called quite simply Pisano, although they are not all related—Bonanno, who was the original architect of the Leaning Tower; Nicola and his son Giovanni; Andrea da Pontedera and his sons Nino and Tommaso. Nicola, helped by the young Giovanni and his pupil Arnolfo di Cambio (later the architect of Florence's Duomo), was responsible for the pulpit in the baptistery, while Giovanni executed the breathtaking pulpit, or *pergamo,* in the cathedral itself. Later they were

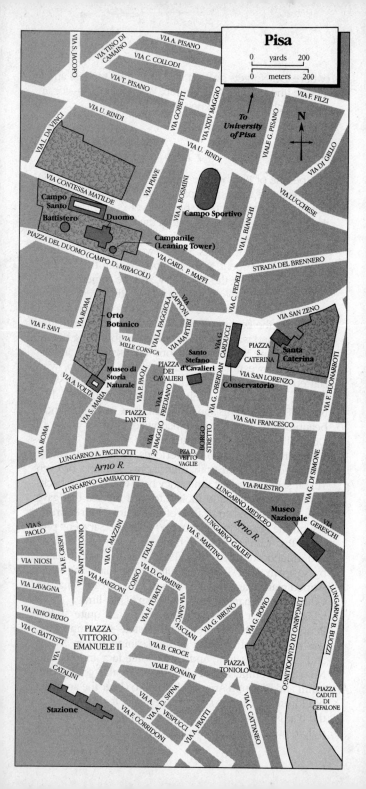

all called to Siena to work on the pulpit for the cathedral there.

Pisano works adorn nearly all the churches in Pisa, such as the lovely **Church of Santa Maria della Spina** (Saint Mary of the Thorn; so called because it once housed a thorn from Christ's crown) on the banks of the river Arno. Together with other treasures of Pisan sculpture and painting, the works of the Pisano sculptors—including the nursing *Madonna of the Milk* by Nino Pisano—are to be found in the impressive **Museo Nazionale di San Matteo**, on the lungarno Mediceo.

Pisa, said Shakespeare, is "renowned for grave citizens." The University of Pisa on via XXIX Maggio, still one of the most important parts of city life, is among the oldest in Italy—founded in the 12th century—and was frequented by, among others, Galileo Galilei. He carried out experiments from the top of the Leaning Tower, demonstrating that a 10-pound weight and a 1-pound weight dropped from the maximum height of the tower (186 feet) would hit the lawn at the same time. Hanging from the magnificent ceiling of the Duomo is the "Lamp of Galileo," which, according to popular legend (as in Newton and the apple), inspired the great astronomer's theory of the movement of the pendulum.

Campo dei Miracoli

"Pisa and its monuments," according to Henry James, "have been industriously vulgarized, but it is astonishing how well they have survived the process." Despite the fact that the tower has become one of the seven wonders of the world and an outsized cliché, you will not be disappointed by a visit to the campo dei Miracoli. After the hollow emptiness of Florence's Duomo, the Pisan **cathedral**'s rich and busy interior will come as an uplifting experience, not just for the pulpit, but, among other things, for the Byzantine-style mosaic in the apse, the last work of Cimabue, who died in Pisa in 1302; for the oval dome; and for the bronze doors by Bonanno Pisano.

Another jewel, more like a giant marble tiara, is the **baptistery**, with its beautiful octagonal font for baptism by total immersion and its ascetic statue of John the Baptist. The baptistery has remarkable acoustics: If you bribe a choirboy to sing for you, suggests Edward Hutton, you will hear "a thousand angels singing round the feet of San

Raniero." (San Raniero, or more correctly, San Ranieri, is the patron saint of Pisa, and on the eve of his feast day—June 16—the entire city, including the tower, is lit up with flaming torches. The next day the whole town takes part in the Medieval *Gioco del Ponte,* a mock battle held on the ponte di Mezzo, Pisa's main bridge over the Arno.)

The enclosed **Camposanto** (cemetery), built on earth brought back from Mount Golgotha by the crusaders, was enriched by the seafaring Pisans with souvenirs of their travels to foreign lands, making the cemetery's cloister the oldest museum in the world. During World War II it was badly bombed, and the splendid frescoes by Benozzo Gozzoli and the unknown Maestro del Trionfo della Morte were severely damaged. Restored, they now hang in a special room here.

The most remarkable thing about the **Leaning Tower** is, of course, that it leans. As Herman Melville said, we wait for it to crash, like a pine cone poised to hit the ground. It continues to tilt, a millimeter more every year. Although it is not expected ever to fall, international contests are periodically launched to find a remedy for the tower's increasing slant. Should it topple, 14,500 tons of marble will come crashing down onto the green lawns of the campo dei Miracoli. In the meantime, it is almost *de rigueur* to climb to the top for a view of the coastal plain with the Apuan mountains in the background.

Piazza dei Cavalieri

The campo dei Miracoli continues into the piazza dei Cavalieri, site of the **Church of San Stefano dei Cavalieri,** with its spectacular wooden ceiling by Vasari. The Knights of St. Stephen were a military order founded by Cosimo I de' Medici, whose statue stands in the square. Opposite is the **Palazzo dell'Orologio** (Clock Palace), once two towers with sinister associations for the Pisans. Pisa, like many Tuscan cities, once bristled with towers—10,000, according to the chief European rabbi at that time, Beniamino da Tudela, although surely this was an exaggeration. In one of these towers, the Pisan Ugolino della Gherardesca, considered responsible for one of the city's resounding naval defeats, was starved to death along with his sons and grandsons, while the *Pasquareccia*—one of seven bells atop the Leaning Tower—rang to announce his end, an episode that inspired both Dante and Shelley.

Shelley was also inspired by the river Arno, one of the few jewels that the Pisans do wear every day. The river winds its way in an elegant curve through the center of the city, and nearly everything you will want to see here (besides the campo dei Miracoli) is on the river. One place not to miss is **Sergio**, the best restaurant in Pisa, a welcoming, unpretentious trattoria famous all over Tuscany. Sergio offers menus at varying prices—none of which you could actually call cheap—based on fish from the nearby shore, seasoned with local herbs like wild fennel and *santoreggia,* a kind of thyme. The **Caffè dell'Ussero** in the Agostini Palace is also a landmark where patriots and poets forgathered in the last century.

Although the leading hotel in Pisa is **Dei Cavalieri**, opposite the train station, it is worth sacrificing its undoubted comfort for the turn-of-the-century charm of the somewhat dilapidated second-category **Hotel Victoria**, also overlooking the river. This hotel has been in the same family since 1839 and was, in its heyday, the best hotel in Pisa; members of the English royal family, the Iron Duke of Wellington, and Shelley all stayed here. Rooms like 211 and 212 still have the original frescoes and old tiled bathrooms.

The port of Pisa has long been silted up, but the city today still has a melting-pot, casbah atmosphere. There is none of Florence's understated chic in the **corso Italia**, Pisa's main street. Behind the Hotel Victoria is the market square, the **piazza delle Vettovaglie**, more North African than Italian, where the fishmongers sell *cee,* Pisa's main specialty in winter—baby eels. You can eat here with the vendors themselves in the cheap and unceremonious little **Trattoria della Mescita**, tucked between two market stalls.

GETTING AROUND

The Etruscan sites and the winegrowing areas around Siena are best seen by car, rented in Florence or Siena.

Volterra is difficult to get to without a car. From Florence, take the Superstrada down to Colle di Val d'Elsa, where you can have lunch, and then drive half an hour west on route 68 through an unspoiled Tuscan landscape up the hill to Volterra. Colle di Val d'Elsa is also a good place to shop for glassware, at **Giovanni Mezzetti** on via Oberdan.

Cortona, also an Etruscan town, is two hours by train from Rome (Terontola station) and about one-and-a-half hours from Florence (Camucia station). It is roughly the same distance by car; there's an Autostrada exit at Arezzo, which is only 30 km (18 miles) from Cortona.

Siena is an hour's drive from Florence south along the Superstrada, and buses leave regularly from the Florence bus station, opposite the main train station. The bus usually makes a stopover at San Gimignano on the way.

L'Argentario on the coast is about two hours by car from Rome and three-and-a-half hours from Florence. The train stop for l'Argentario is at Orbetello.

Ferries to the Giglio and Giannutri islands leave from Porto Santo Stefano. For Giglio the ferry company is Società Toremar; Tel: (0564) 81-46-15. For Giannutri it is Mare Giglio; Tel: (0564) 819-20.

Elba is an hour by car ferry (Toremar and Navarma lines) from Piombino, and 30 minutes by Hovercraft. In summer there are flights to Elba from Pisa.

Montecatini Terme is about 40 km (25 miles) from both the Pisa airport and Florence. It is an easy, short drive or bus or train trip from Lucca as well as Pisa and Florence.

Lucca is about 70 km (45 miles) west of Florence and less than 25 km (15 miles) east of Pisa; it's easily accessible by train or by car on the Autostrada. The city is so small that the only way to visit it is on foot. (The author of this chapter literally got stuck in a Mercedes between the narrow sides of a street in Lucca, like Winnie-the-Pooh in the rabbit hole.)

Pisa has its own airport, with flights to all major European cities, and is an important railway junction. It is an hour's drive from Florence, but parking is a problem in Pisa—which anyway is small enough to be seen on foot.

ACCOMMODATIONS REFERENCE

▶ **Il Bottaccio**. 54038 **Montignoso**. Tel: (0535) 34-00-31.

▶ **La Cantina dell'Aquilino**. 58018 **Port'Ercole**. Tel: (0564) 80-90-34.

▶ **Dei Cavalieri**. Piazza Stazione, 56100 **Pisa**. Tel: (050) 432-90.

▶ **Certosa di Maggiano**. Strada di Certosa 72, 53100 **Siena**. Tel: (0964) 28-81-80; Telex: 574221.

▶ **Ristorante La Chiusa**. Via della Madonnina 88, 53040 **Montefollonico**. Tel: (0577) 66-96-68.

▶ **Hotel Cisterna**. Piazza Cisterna 23, 53100 **San Gimignano**. Tel: (0577) 94-03-28.

▶ **Relais Fattoria Vignale.** Via Pianigiani 15, 53017 **Radda in Chianti.** Tel: (0577) 73-83-00.

▶ **Grand Hotel e la Pace.** Via della Torretta 1, 51016 **Montecatini Terme.** Tel: (0572) 758-01; Telex: 570004 GRANDHOTEL.

▶ **Hotel Hambros.** Via Vecchia Pesciatina 197, 55010 **Lunata.** Tel: (0583) 93-53-55.

▶ **Hotel Hermitage.** La Biodola, 57037 **Portoferraio** (Elba). Tel: (0565) 96-99-32.

▶ **Il Marzocco.** Piazza Savonarola, 53045 **Montepulciano.** Tel: (0578) 772-62.

▶ **Hotel Pardini's Hermitage.** 58013 **Isola di Giglio.** Tel: (0564) 80-90-34.

▶ **Park Hotel.** Via di Marciano 16, 53100 **Siena.** Tel: (0577) 448-03; Telex: 571005 PARKSI.

▶ **Il Pellicano.** Località Sbarcatello, via Panoramica, 58018 **Port'Ercole.** Tel: (0564) 83-38-01; Telex: 500131.

▶ **Villa la Principessa.** 55050 **Massa Pisana.** Tel: (0583) 37-91-12; Telex: 590068.

▶ **Palazzo Ravizza.** Piano dei Mantellini 34, 53100 **Siena.** Tel: (0577) 28-04-62.

▶ **Hotel Villa Santa Christina.** Via Poggio Secco 58, 50047 **Prato.** Tel: (0574) 59-59-51.

▶ **Tenuta di Ricavo.** 53011 **Castellina in Chianti.** Tel: (0577) 74-02-21.

▶ **Tuscan Rentals.** Box 2125, Jenkintown, PA 19046. Tel: (215) 887-6948. This firm rents some 400 villas and apartments in all price ranges throughout Tuscany.

▶ **Hotel Universo.** Piazza Puccini 1, 55100 **Lucca.** Tel: (0583) 436-78; Telex: 621840.

▶ **Hotel Victoria.** Lungarno Pacinotti 12, 58100 **Pisa.** Tel: (050) 233-81.

UMBRIA AND THE MARCHES

By Joanne Hahn

Joanne Hahn has lived and studied in Italy, and travels there frequently. Formerly on the staff of Travel & Leisure *magazine, she writes for several consumer magazines.*

Umbria is a landlocked fortress of Medieval treasures, built on the remains of an Italic, Etruscan, and Roman past. Somewhat overshadowed by Tuscany, its celebrated neighbor to the north and west, this land of saints and sinners, with its serene hills, tranquil lakes, silent valleys, and steep mountains, is more quietly seductive. Stepping into these Medieval hilltop villages, you can experience life much as it existed hundreds of years ago, when the rising communes began cutting their feudal ties and experimenting with self-rule.

Perhaps the most striking feature of the area is its peacefulness. The landscape seems transcendent and perpetually shrouded in a blue-green haze, which may account for the impressive number of saints born here—said to number over 20,000—whose names read like a *Who's Who* of holiness: They include Saint Francis of Assisi, founder of the Franciscans, and his friend Saint Clare, who created a sister order, the Poor Clares; Saint Valentine, third bishop of Terni; and Saint Benedict of Norcia, whose monastic Rule helped spread Christianity and kept Western civilization from totally succumbing to the barbarians.

Noble cathedrals, graceful monasteries, and resilient manors dot hills and cluster around tiny villages. Tradition is kept alive not only through crafts and festivals but in the converted monasteries offering comfortable lodgings and retreats from the congested cities—accommodations that range from a few rooms in a convent to a sprawling Benedictine monastery like Bevagna's.

Distances between towns are short, making it possible to visit major sights and surroundings on day trips from such nearby major cities as Rome and Florence, though Umbria is quite appealing as a destination in itself. The more popular towns of Assisi, Perugia, and Spoleto can become crowded, especially during the summer, but most of the other towns are off the beaten track—though easily accessible by car and bus—and therefore rarely thronged.

The Marches (pronounced MAR-kay in Italian) lie between Umbria to the west and the Adriatic coast on the east. The best-known city is Urbino, one of the great centers of the birth of Renaissance humanism. Except for the Byzantine influence (from Ravenna to the north)—and some Venetian influence, too—the Marches underwent much the same historical movement as Umbria.

With Perugia as a starting point, we follow a clockwise elliptical track through the center of Umbria—Assisi, Spoleto, Todi, Orvieto—and then take another track north from Perugia to Gubbio and on to the Marches, Urbino, and the Adriatic.

MAJOR INTEREST IN UMBRIA

Perugia
Piazza IV Novembre and its Fontana Maggiore
Palazzo dei Priori (Galleria Nazionale dell'Umbria)
Collegio del Cambio (frescoes of Perugino)
Duomo
Corso Vannucci (shops, cafés, people)
Musical events

Deruta (pottery)

Assisi
Basilica of San Francesco (frescoes of Giotto)
Church of Santa Chiara
Tempio di Minerva
Eremo delle Carceri
Religious festivals

Spello (Pinturicchio frescoes)
Fonti del Clitunno, Tempietto del Clitunno

Spoleto
Festival of Two Worlds
Ponte delle Torre (Bridge of Towers)
Duomo

Todi

Lago Trasimeno (boating and fishing facilities)

Orvieto
Duomo (frescoes of Fra Angelico and Signorelli)

Gubbio
Palazzo dei Consoli (Eugubine Tablets)
Roman theater
Basilica and monastery of San Ubaldo
The race of the Ceri, May 15
Palio della Balestra (crossbow contest)

MAJOR INTEREST IN THE MARCHES

Urbino
Palazzo Ducale (Galleria Nazionale delle Marche)

Fano and Pesaro, on the coast

UMBRIA

The "green heart of Italy," as Umbria is known, lies in the center and is bordered on the west and north by Tuscany and on the east by the Apennines, that sweep of wooded mountains and limestone hills that runs from the Alps to the tip of Calabria. (On the other side of the Apennines are the Marches.)

Over three million years ago the sea covered most of western Umbria. The largest lake left when the waters receded is **Lago Trasimeno**, a popular resort area west of Perugia. This is where Hannibal outmaneuvered the consul Flaminius and slaughtered more than 16,000 Roman soldiers in 217 B.C. Trasimeno is rich in trout, pike, eels, perch, and the delectable *lasca,* a favorite fish of the popes since the Middle Ages.

Now you too can eat those same fish—and very well prepared—at the rustic **Ristorante da Luciano,** on the north shore at Passignano sul Trasimeno (the main restaurant, overlooking the lake, is expensive *prix fixe,* but the meals are huge; right next door is an adjunct where you can get dishes à la carte, and spend less). At Passignano you can also hire boats to go out on the lake, maybe for a visit to Isola Maggiore, a beautiful moody island with the church of San Michele Arcangelo, which has 14th- to 16th-century frescoes. You'll also find lovely examples of Irish lace-making, which the Irish servants of the Marchioness Guglielmi passed on centuries earlier.

The Tiber (*Tevere*), which transported Cleopatra on her visit to Julius Caesar in 46 B.C., meanders south through Umbria on its way to Rome and is joined by the Nera, which runs the width of Umbria. Critical to agricultural development during early settlement days, the Tiber was replaced as the main thoroughfare by the Flaminian Way, which the Romans built as they were consolidating their power throughout the region. They sited many of their military colonies throughout the Tiber valley and along this road, which runs north from Rome through Umbria before terminating at the Adriatic city of Fano. Since that time, popes, emperors, dukes, and armies have travelled it on their way to Rome. Today, route 3 (and 3 *bis*) more or less traces this ancient road and connects many of the region's cities and towns.

The Etruscans

The region is named for the Umbri, a rather peaceful tribe dispersed around 500 B.C. by the Etruscans, who travelled from the western coast to Tuscany, Latium, and Umbria, where they formed a religious and cultural federation. According to Herodotus, the Etruscans came from Lydia in Asia Minor, although some scholars believe them to be indigenous. The Tiber was the ancient frontier; the Etruscans occupied the lands on the western side, while the Umbrians set up on the eastern side. To this day, natives claim they can detect differences in dialect from one town to the next, even though the distances between them may be a mere ten miles. Towns were built on hills, the so-called Etruscan position, to avoid the malarial lowlands and provide defense against invaders; Perugia and Orvieto are among the best examples.

Wars and truces with the Romans, who arrived in the fourth century B.C., greatly diminished Etruscan power, and many cities became Roman. Tombs record the losses of this period and are markedly more sober than the richly ornamented ones of earlier, prosperous times. The Etruscans' language, with Greek elements, continues to captivate scholars, and their sculpture, elaborate funerary objects, rich metalwork, and intriguing tombs reveal their vivid religious beliefs and preoccupation with the after-life. To prevent the spirits from intruding into the world of the living, their burial cities (*necropoli*) usually were built some distance from the towns—which accounts for their discovery in isolated locations.

Skilled engineers, the Etruscans cleared thickly wooded areas and used the timber to build ships and homes. Their advanced agricultural and engineering techniques proved invaluable to the Romans, who by 396 B.C. had captured the Etruscan city of Veii in the south. Orvieto and Perugia resisted the Romans for a while, but fell toward the end of the century. The glorious days of Augustus (40 B.C.–A.D. 14) brought great peace and prosperity to Umbria, the results of which can be seen in the numerous Roman bridges, amphitheaters, and temples that are incorporated com-fortably into the Medieval fabric of the Umbrian cities.

The Middle Ages

Umbria's arts and customs reflect its strong religious and papal ties. With the arrival of the barbarians and the fall of Rome in the fifth century, Umbria sank to a low point and turned in on itself. During this time, bishops exercised both ecclesiastical and civic responsibilities and fought against many of the barbarian kings, who later came to rely on their literate skills. The numerous wars decimated the countryside and made it easy prey for the Lombards, who conquered the area, eventually became Christian, and established roughly a dozen duchies. Spoleto was one of the most important, and it ruled most of Umbria from the sixth to the ninth centuries. From the fourth century, with the Empire ruled from Constantinople, the popes began accruing power, as they marched in the imperial footsteps of the Romans.

While the Lombards fought the Byzantines, the papacy rose through the skillful rule of Pope Gregory the Great

(A.D. 590–604); his pontificate established a high mark in the development of the papal states, which came to rule much of Umbria centuries later. Another ally of the papacy during this time was monasticism, which had arisen in the East during the early Christian era and had greatly diversified by the time it reached the West. Just a few years after the last Roman emperor was deposed, the tiny town of Norcia in southeastern Umbria gave birth to Saint Benedict, who in 529 founded the great monastery in Monte Cassino (between Rome and Naples) according to a strict Rule he had devised, which combined work with prayer, regulating almost every detail of a monk's life. This Rule of Saint Benedict became a model for other monasteries, and Benedictine monasticism spread throughout Western Europe. Cultural and civil lifeboats during those dark years, the Benedictine monasteries flourished, banishing the great Medieval sin of *accidia* (sloth) and providing safe havens and centers for the preservation of ancient and early Church thought.

Charlemagne's creation of the Holy Roman Empire set the stage for the papal and imperial rivalry that shaped the political arena for the next few hundred years. A reading of the battlements that mark the skyline of the Umbrian cities reveals initial loyalties: square crenellations for Guelph (pope); swallowtail for Ghibelline (emperor). In Perugia, the papacy prevailed from 1540 to 1860.

In the 12th century, after the growth of commerce fostered ecclesiastical abuses, the Church took stock of itself morally, and there followed a great tidal wave of reform that had been gathering force since the tenth century. Saint Francis of Assisi took the emotional lead, and his mendicant friars reached out directly to the confused masses. His spirit covered Umbria like a blanket of peace, turning ferocious Medieval demons into sweet birds and bees, taming wolves, softening the stoic Madonnas into tender ladies of love, and bringing the heavens down to earth, narrowing the gap between rich and poor.

The collapse of the Carolingian dynasty ultimately left a power vacuum that was quickly filled by the merchants and landowners, and free communes arose. From the 11th through the 13th centuries, trade with the East (which the crusades helped unleash) and trade with Flanders and France stimulated the growth of towns in Umbria. With this came a measure of freedom and local self-

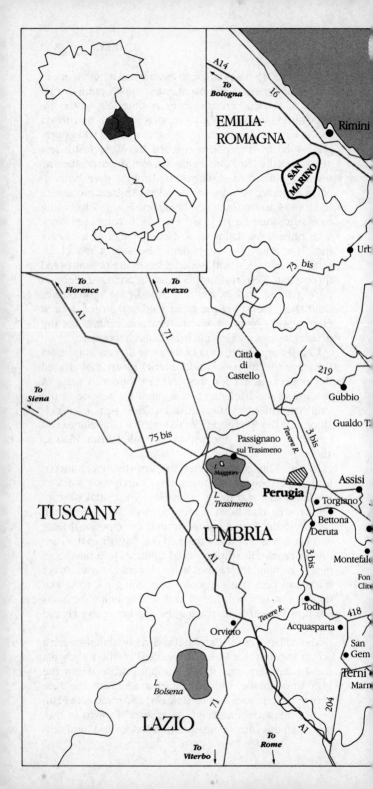

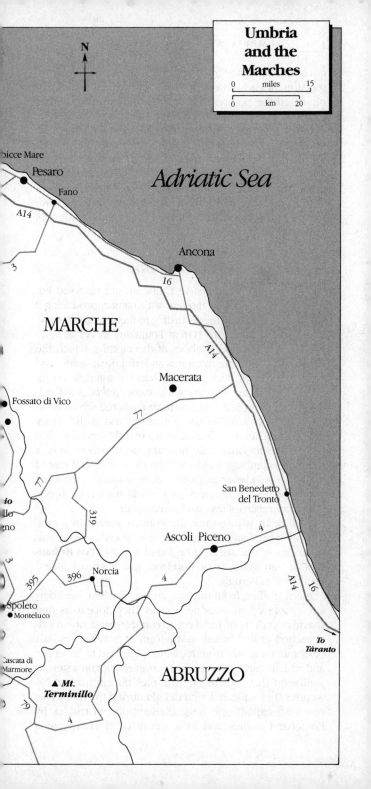

0   miles   15

0   km   20

N

bicce Mare

Pesaro

Fano

A14

3

Adriatic Sea

Ancona

16

MARCHE

A14

Fossato di Vico

Macerata

77

io
llo
gno

77

319

San Benedetto
del Tronto

Ascoli Piceno

3

395   *396*   Norcia

4

A14

16

Spoleto

Monteluco

To
Táranto

Cascata di
Marmore

ABRUZZO

79

▲ *Mt.*
Terminillo

4

government. Heady from their newfound independence, they fought each other with appalling regularity and manipulated the powers that be, which then meant either the pope or emperor.

Cities trafficked not only in goods but in ideas. The introduction of Aristotle's works via Arab and Greek scholars—in direct contrast to the prevailing Christian Neoplatonism—and the revival of Roman law created great intellectual excitement and yielded new modes of abstract thinking, which were expressed in business, commerce, and religion. This ferment led to the founding of universities.

Umbrian Food

Like their quiet countryside, Umbrians are reserved but friendly. They work in tandem with nature, producing a simple but royal cuisine according to the season's bounty. The Fontana Maggiore (Great Fountain) in Perugia impressively records the labors of the months, which the restaurants celebrate in their wonderful meat, game, and vegetable dishes, such as *palombacci,* roasted wood pigeon often in an intricate wine sauce; *gobbi,* fried cardoons; and *porchetta alla perugina,* roasted whole suckling pig with wild fennel, rosemary, and garlic. Spicy sausages are another treat and are usually served grilled or in a cream sauce, *alla norcina,* over pasta. Norcia, a mountain-climbing region and butchering capital east of Spoleto, provides a sumptuous array of salamis, the most exotic being the *mazzafegato,* made with pork livers, pine nuts, raisins, sugar, and orange peel.

Wild boar, whose meat the Romans stewed in a mixture of honey and vinegar, remains popular here, and variations of the dish can be found at the **Ottavi Restaurant** at San Mariano di Corciano, just 6 km (4 miles) southwest of Perugia.

Black truffles, from the area around Spoleto, are liberally employed in cooking; usually they appear as fine shavings on top of hand-cut *strengozzi* pasta or on oil-drenched grilled bread, in the form of *crostini.* Festivals celebrate these musty gems, which pigs used to ferret out and which scientists recently discovered contain a steroid similar to that secreted by the pigs during mating. No wonder they squealed with delight during the hunt. This may also explain the huge consumption of truffles by Emperor Claudius and King Henry IV of France, who believed their sexual prowess would thereby be enhanced. Today, dogs hunt them, though in a much less frenzied fashion.

The gnarled olive trees that hug the slopes yield the pale gold oil that culinary cognoscenti consider the finest in Italy. It is best sampled on *bruschette,* oil-slathered grilled slabs of bread.

The abundant walnuts here find their way into the Indian-type cornmeal pudding called *brustengolo* and the typical Christmas dish of *maccheroni con noci e cacao,* pasta with a walnut and cocoa sauce. The most fertile Umbrian land, in the Tiber valley and lowlands between Perugia and Spoleto, is lined with olive trees and grapevines that look out over plains sprinkled with corn, wheat, tobacco, and alfalfa.

The rich vineyards produce a wide variety of wines, from the prized Orvieto—which the popes loved in its *abboccato* (sweet) form but which today is mostly dry— to the superb DOCs of the Colli Altotiberini and Montefalco and grand crus and rich Rubescos of Torgiano.

PERUGIA

Perugia, the capital of Umbria, is a logical place from which to explore the region. Easily reached from Rome, Siena, or Florence, it has excellent transportation to neighboring cities such as Todi, Gubbio, Assisi, Spoleto, and Orvieto.

An important agricultural and commercial center, it takes the lead now much as it did during its Etruscan period in the sixth century B.C., when it was one of the most important strongholds of the 12 confederated cities. Fragments of these early times pervade the city, especially around the Old Town. The **Museo Archeologico Nazionale dell'Umbria**, in the monastery of the church of San Domenico at piazza Giordano Bruno in the southeast part of the city, has fine examples of Etruscan and Roman antiquities—especially the Cippus slab, inscribed with 150 Etruscan words.

Angered by Perugia's support of Antony following the death of Caesar, in 40 B.C. Octavian (later called Augustus) ravaged the city, which he "starved into surrender," according to Suetonius. After he became emperor, Augustus rebuilt the city and inscribed his signature, "Augusta Perusia," on the Etruscan arch at the end of via Ulisse

Rocchi. During the barbarian invasions, Perugia resisted the advances of Totila for seven years, ultimately—in 546—succumbing.

The Old Town

The Medieval and Renaissance area of Perugia—site of its principal attractions—sits atop an uneven cluster of hills that rise high above the central Tiber valley. From the **Giardini Carducci**, graced by dark fir and ilex trees and located just off the corso Vannucci (the main street), you can take in the surrounding countryside, confirming Henry James's description of Perugia as the "little city of infinite view."

Scarce parking for cars at the top is relieved by several lots below, the most convenient one being near the entrance to the **Rocca Paolina**, the famous fort erected by Pope Paul III in 1540 to help control the city's despotic family, the Baglioni, whose scandalous behavior he couldn't tolerate. All but destroyed in 1860 when the Perugians shed the last reins of papal rule, the fort (incorporated into the city's administrative building at piazza Italia) now contains a series of escalators and walkways that connect the lower and upper parts of the city. A ride through this Perugian Pompeii, incorporating the remains of the rebel family's holdings, reveals traces of ancient roads, piazzas, and buildings. It stood as a symbol of papal authority over the Perugians, papal partisans who nevertheless rebelled against the Pope's salt tax. (To this day, Perugia's bread remains saltless, as does most of the region's).

During the papal exile in Avignon and the Great Schism that followed (which divided the Church and created rival factions, each claiming its own pope), princely despots arose and began menacing the Umbrian cities. Perugia, never quite comfortable under papal rule, produced two of the most vicious families, the Oddi and the aforementioned Baglioni, whose shameless behavior sent tremors of fear throughout the region. The Baglioni, who eventually drove out the Oddi, wore their cruelty like a badge of honor. Even their names—Astorre, Grifone, Atalanta, Zenobia—have a mythic ring to them, suggestive of warriors of some dark saga; their actions did at times seem superhuman. The historian Jacob Burkhardt describes the climate of fear they created, when the city was turned "into a camp and the houses of the leading citizens swarmed with bravos; scenes of violence were of daily occurrence . . . and the city became a belea-guered fortress under the absolute despotism of the Baglioni, who even used the cathedral as barracks." The young artist Raphael, who was studying with Perugino at the time, witnessed these horrors and painted his world-famous and moving *Deposition* (now in the Galleria Bor-ghese in Rome) for the mother of one of the men killed in battle.

Both Perugia's play and piety were tinctured by vio-lence, as its rather unpleasant game called *la battaglia dei sassi* (the battle of the stones) shows. Revived by the condottiere Braccio Fortebraccio, who controlled the city from 1416 to 1424 after he'd defeated the papal forces, it resembled a dress rehearsal for war—one lightly pro-tected team, the *lanciatori,* would pelt the more heavily padded *armati* in a fight for control of the piazza, leaving the wounded groaning among silent corpses. The *battuti* (flagellants), popular during the reform movement in the Church, originated here, and in acts of great public pen-ance they would whip themselves into a frenzy. Unlike the gentle followers of Saint Francis, they spread a tortured fervor throughout a good part of Europe before the pope halted them.

In the 15th century the Franciscan preacher Saint Ber-nardino of Siena travelled here, attempting to reform the city, delivering his impassioned pleas from the golden balcony that juts out from the cathedral. The **Oratorio di San Bernardino** at piazza San Francesco, with wonderful bas-reliefs by Agostino di Duccio marking the façade, is dedicated to this outraged Franciscan.

The City Center

Today the city's aggressions are sublimated in the produc-tion of the exquisite Perugina chocolates (available practi-cally everywhere in Perugia), Buitoni Pasta, and the activi-ties of the sizable university, whose students flood the city.

The hub of activity is the **corso Vannucci,** named after the city's master painter, known as Perugino (Pietro Van-nucci), a wide majestic street with buildings scarred by time and human struggle that is used as an open-air sa-lon—people shop, students congregate, men and women debate the latest political intrigues, children play, and dogs scramble for handouts. The corso runs from the

VIA R. D'ANDREOTTO

VIA S. SIEPI

VIALE ORAZIO ANTINORI

Ber

PIAZZA S. FRANCESCO

PIAGGIA COLOMBATA

VIA D. SPOSA

VIA D. S. PAO

VIA S. PROSPERO

GALLERIA

VIA D. PRIORI

V

VIALE POMPEO PELLINI

VIA DELLA CUPA

VIALE F. DI LORENZO

VIA D. FORZE

PIAZZA MARIOTTI

VIA CAPORALI

VIA D. LUNA

VIA D. PRIORI

VIA BONAZZI

San Costanzo

Collegio d. Cambio

PIAZZA D. PARTIGIANI

VIA DEL PARIONE

VIALE INDIPENDENZA

PIAZZA ITALIA

CORSO VANU

VIA MASI

Giardini Carducci

VIA BAGLIONI

VIA DANZ

VIA MAZ. ZINI

Rocca Paolina

VIA MARZIA

PIAZZA N

LARGO CACCIATORI D. ALPI

VIALE INDIPENDENZA

VIA OBERDAN

VIA G. MARCONI

CORSO CAVOUR

VIA XX SETTEMBRE

VIA

VIALE ROMA

Museo Archeologico Nazionale

BORGO XX GIUGNO

San Pietro

Basilica d. S. Domenico

VIA BONFIGLI

VIA RIPA DI MEANA

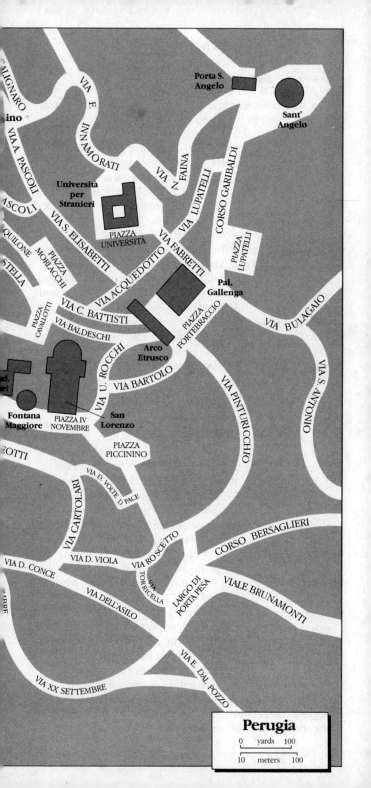

Porta S.
Angelo

Sant'
Angelo

VIA F. INNAMORATI

VIA Z. FAINA

VIA LUPATELLI

CORSO GARIBALDI

ALIGNARO

ino

VIA A. PASCOLI

Università
per
Stranieri

PIAZZA
UNIVERSITÀ

VIA FABRETTI

PIAZZA
LUPATELLI

ASCOLI

VIA S. ELISABETTI

VIA ACQUEDOTTO

QUILONE

PIAZZA
MORLACCHI

Pal.
Gallenga

VIA BULAGAIO

STELLA

VIA C. BATTISTI

PIAZZA
CAVALLOTTI

VIA BALDESCHI

PIAZZA
FORTEBRACCIO

VIA S. ANTONIO

Arco
Etrusco

VIA U. ROCCHI

VIA PINTURICCHIO

VIA BARTOLO

Fontana
Maggiore

PIAZZA IV
NOVEMBRE

San
Lorenzo

PIAZZA
PICCININO

EOTTI

VIA CARTOLARI

VIA D. VOLTE D. PACE

CORSO BERSAGLIERI

VIA D. VIOLA

VIA ROSCETTO

VIA D. CONCE

VIA TORRICELLA

LARGO DI
PORTA PESA

VIALE BRUNAMONTI

VIA DELL'ASILO

BRE

VIA E. DAL POZZO

VIA XX SETTEMBRE

Perugia

0   yards   100

10   meters   100

Giardini Carducci at the piazza Italia to the piazza IV Novembre and is totally closed to automobile traffic. The best hotel in town, the stately **Brufani** in the piazza Italia, combines luxury rooms with practical business facilities and has marvelous views from every room. Next door is the somewhat less expensive but comfortable **Palace Hotel Bellavista**. A more moderately priced hotel, **La Rosetta**, also nearby, has a highly regarded restaurant (the ravioli with walnut sauce is sublime) as well as a pleasant, sheltered patio with a partial view of the avenue's goings on.

Dominating the corso Vannucci is the Gothic **Palazzo dei Priori** (Priors' Palace). This former home of the ruling magistrates is a somber, arrogant building that houses the **Galleria Nazionale dell'Umbria**. Notable within are the large painted crucifix by Maestro di San Francesco and the Bonfigli works: the lovely *Adoration of the Magi,* the *Annunciation with Saint Luke* and the animated fresco, *The Siege of Totila,* recalling the city's barbarian phase.

Other impressive works are Piero della Francesca's polyptychs and his *Annunciation.* In the two rooms devoted to paintings of Perugino and Pinturicchio, the mystical Umbrian countryside and rich religious piety—hallmarks of Umbrian art—are distilled. Also worth noting are a collaborative work of Pinturicchio and Perugino, the *Miracle of the Saints,* which is rich in architectural detail, and the luminous *Madonna and Child* by Gentile da Fabriano.

On the ground floor of the Palazzo dei Priori is the hall of the **Merchants Guild**, and next door is the **Collegio del Cambio**. Two of the most powerful guilds in the city were the merchants and the money changers, whose members (two from the merchants and one from the exchange) could be elected as priors. The richly carved audience room of the exchange houses the real gem here—the masterful frescoes of Perugino and his students, who included Raphael. Classical and Christian worlds unite, presided over by the pudgy-faced painter Perugino, whose self-portrait sits on the dividing pilaster. Vasari describes Perugino as a man "of little or no religion, who could never bring himself to believe in the immortality of the soul." Nevertheless his deft treatment of space opened up the compositional plane for the Renaissance masters.

North on the corso Vannucci is the piazza IV Novembre, and the 13th-century **Fontana Maggiore**, built to celebrate the completion of an aqueduct that brought water to

Perugia from Montepulciano in Tuscany. Its striking bas-reliefs by the sculptors Nicola and Giovanni Pisano, whose works are amply represented in Pisa and Siena, carve out rich symbols of civic and religious pride on the upper basin and the rhythms of nature on the lower. Culinary pride is in evidence nearby as well, at the simple vaulted restaurant **Il Falchetto**, on via Bartolo 20, right behind the Duomo. They make a fine *pappardelle alla lepre* (pasta in a rabbit sauce), hearty *palombaccia al rubesco* (wood pigeon in a wine sauce), and tasty *falchetti* (spinach dumplings). The Gothic **Cathedral of San Lorenzo**, whose unfinished façade gives it an equivocal presence, is undistinguished except for the inlaid wooden choir, a particularly lovely *Deposition* painted by Barocci, and the beautiful altarpiece of Luca Signorelli (in the cathedral museum).

Around the other side of the cathedral on piazzi Danti you find the via Ulisse Rocchi; at number 16 is the **Enoteca Provinciale**, where you can sample over 150 local wines. At the end of the street is the **Arco Etrusco**, where the Etruscans' engineering skill is immediately apparent. The massive stone blocks, blackened by the Octavian fire and surmounted by a 16th-century loggia, were one of the seven gateways to the old city. Just beyond, at piazza le Fortebraccio, is the renowned **Università Italiana per Stranieri** (Italian University for Foreigners), opened in 1926 and responsible for the international flavor of the city. It has a superlative library of Italian, English, French, and German books. From here the via Fabretti leads northwest to Perugia's 14th-century university, housed in an old Olivetan monastery on sprawling grounds.

The quintessential Medieval streets in this area are evocative, brimming with secrets. Among the best of them are the via delle Volte della Pace, a dark and mysterious covered walk, and the via della Gabbia, where criminals once dangled in cages from the Palazzo dei Priori. Close by is piazza Morlacchi, where the eponymous 18th-century Rococo theater hosts many of the city's musical events. Indeed, the jazz festival in July electrifies the city—which is then soothed during a festival of sacred music in September. Check for listings with your hotel concierge or at the tourist office on the corso Vannucci. Two other Perugian churches worth seeing, if time permits, are the early-fifth-century **Church of Sant'Angelo**, at the northern edge of town, and the **Church and Abbey of**

San Pietro on via Borgo XX Giugno to the south, where hangs the solemn *Pietà* of Perugino.

Outside Perugia

The Etruscan necropolis **Hypogeum Volumni**, about 6 km (4 miles) to the southeast on route 75 *bis,* evokes the mysterious charms of the Volumni, an important Etruscan family of the second century B.C. A small green door marks the entrance to these chambers, dug directly into the volcanic rock, which contain Greek stylized cinerary urns and fascinating funerary pieces, many of which display the intensely emotional Etruscan personality. Note the interesting urn of Arunte Volumni, who reclines on the top in the manner of a bored Caesar.

Wine enthusiasts will find the **Wine Museum** at Torgiano appealing. It's roughly 16 km (10 miles) south of Perugia, off route 3 *bis,* and is also the site of the superb Relais et Châteaux hotel **Le Tre Vaselle**. Many travellers prefer to make this their base for exploring the area. Gracious gardens enhance the dignified old palazzo, which was restored by the vintner Giorgio Lungarotti; its restaurant serves Umbrian dishes (many of which appear in the restaurant's cookbook) plus—as you'd expect—fabulous wines. Try the *cinghiale sulla griglia con rosmarino* (boar steak grilled with fresh rosemary). The hotel will make arrangements to pick up guests at the Ponte San Giovanni train station in Perugia, or you can take a taxi.

Those interested in pottery will find **Deruta**—roughly 16 km (10 miles) south of Torgiano on 3 *bis*—a good place for the traditional blue, orange, and green majolica ware, along with other designs, all of which are sold in the many outlet stores on the via Tiberina, the main street of the lower town. You should visit the town's Ceramic Museum, which is lavishly stocked with examples of majolica and pottery.

ASSISI

Only 25 km (15 miles) east of Perugia is Assisi, indelibly connected with Saint Francis, whose life is the greatest riches-to-rags story ever told. The grand, two-tiered basilica with the adjoining sacred convent of San Francesco announces its identity right up front and dominates the plains below. The **Sacred Convent**, the sprawling building attached to the basilica, was built at the same time and enlarged and modified several times over the next few centuries. Pilgrims once slept beneath the portico that lines the courtyard. The large cloister was commissioned by Sixtus IV in 1470 and contains lovely frescoes of scenes of the life of Saint Francis by the artist Dono Doni.

The valley below Assisi cradles the domed basilica of Santa Maria degli Angeli, about 5 km (3 miles) away in the town of the same name. Francis began his pastoral mission in the small chapel, known as the **Porziuncola**, beneath the grand cupola, and returned there to die years later. It was here also that Saint Clare was received in the Franciscan order after she had fled her rich father; her hair shorn, her garb gray, her life now sacrifice and poverty.

The rosy hue of Assisi is nature's doing—part sun, part pink limestone quarried from Mount Subasio, from which the entire city gets its unified character. Flowers and rosemary spill over ancient walls, providing extra color and fragrance.

The storm preceded the calm here; from the fall of the Roman Empire to the end of the 15th century, Assisi was the scene of occupation and warfare: Totila, Lombards, Perugian menace, the plague. During Saint Francis's time the hilltop contained the castle of the feudal baron, Conrad of Lutzen, duke of Spoleto, ever ready to receive the Holy Roman Emperor, who might stop on his way to Rome. The town was divided politically into the nobles, who idled away at their estates; the merchants selling their wares; the artisans grouped in guilds; and the serfs, who labored in the fields. When the duke was finally driven out (4-year-old Frederick II, Barbarossa's grandson, was visiting at the time and barely escaped), the merchants attempted to overthrow the nobility, who quickly fled to Perugia for help—and Perugia was only too happy to feed its aggressive instincts. Fields were devastated and the peasants, being the low men on the totem pole, were terrorized.

The merchant class, to which Francis was born in 1182, was perhaps the best off. Son of the wealthy textile merchant Pietro de Bernardone, he lived well, helped his father in the shop, and probably accompanied him on the customary expeditions to the south of France, where they would buy sumptuous fabrics to bring back to the city. Passionate in play and love, he fought against Perugia and was captured and held prisoner for a year—during which he experienced his conversion to Christ. Knights, courtly love, and the crusades shaped these times, and Francis was very much a man of his time, who referred to himself as the *jongleur de Dieu*.

Exchanging a cloak of silk for one of poverty did not exactly endear Francis to his merchant father, a consummate businessman who gave credit to his customers and calculated the collateral of land he would have should they default. Besides, who would carry on the business? Nevertheless, the burgher's son was transformed into the *poverello* (poor one), and he courted poverty much the way Dante wooed Beatrice.

Some thought Francis mad, but he attracted many, including some prominent noblemen who willingly renounced their wealth to follow him. In 1209 he petitioned Pope Innocent III for approval to establish an order of preaching friars. The pope hesitated initially, partly because he understood the threat Francis's radical poverty would pose to the wealthy prelates. But he also realized its salutary effects. A dream in which Innocent saw the church of St. John Lateran falling and the barefoot Francis supporting it (chronicled in one of the Giotto frescoes in the basilica) coincided with Francis's desire, and the pope granted him oral approval, which later was formalized into the Franciscan Rule by Honorius III in 1221. (Fifty years later, when the order had become institutionalized, the Friars began segregating themselves into the strict Spirituals and reformed Conventuals.)

Francis preached throughout the country and beyond. In 1219 he accompanied the Fifth Crusade to Egypt, where he unsuccessfully sought to convert the sultan. His life offered great aesthetic possibilities to artists who for centuries chronicled the saint's love of nature and mankind in ever-widening fashion.

Two years after Francis's death Pope Gregory IX began building the great **Basilica**, and it is one of life's ironies that a saint dedicated to simplicity and poverty should have such an imposing church erected in his name. Or, as Henry James comments in his *Italian Hours,* "the Saint whose only tenement in life was the ragged robe which barely covered him, is the hero of this massive structure. Church upon church, nothing less will adequately shroud his consecrated clay."

This basilica, constructed over a period of 25 years, reflects the twists and turns of an increasingly humanized religion. The Romanesque lower church has short squat

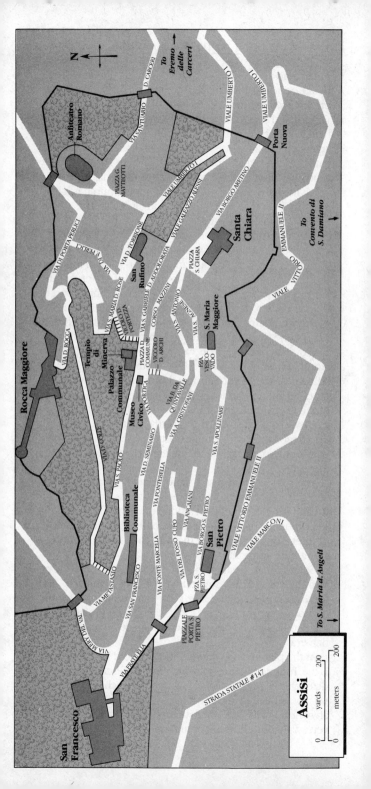

pillars and an ornamented vaulted ceiling, lightened only by an occasional streaming sunbeam. The walls are covered with moving frescoes by Cimabue, Simone Martini, Giotto, and Pietro Lorenzetti. Henry James found it particularly holy, claiming "it would be hard to breathe anywhere an air more heavy with holiness." The body of Saint Francis, which the Assisans hid from Perugian body snatchers, lies in the crypt; it was only rediscovered in 1818. In sharp contrast, the Gothic upper church is a leap into light, both architecturally and literally. The unforgettable Cimabue frescoes, particularly the *Crucifixion,* point the historical way to the wonderful Giotto fresco cycles here, painted between 1296 and 1304, that depict the life of the saint. What Dante did for literature, Giotto did for painting—two great journalists of character and nature, respectively. The 32 frescoes on the upper part of the nave walls, with scenes from the Old and New Testament, were attributed by Vasari to Cimabue, though they may be the work of Cavallini and his pupils.

From the basilica, you can almost touch the gracious **Hotel Subasio** on via Frate Elia. From one of this hotel's balconies, the poet Gabriele D'Annunzio delivered his mock sermon to his lover, Eleanora Duse, to the applause of the forgiving Franciscans. Although the hotel fronts on a noisy, crowded street, the attractive restaurant and magical terrace offer a marvelous setting in which to enjoy a view of the countryside; the quietest rooms look out over the valley.

The via San Francesco, unfortunately festooned with tawdry memorabilia of St. Francis, extends from the basilica and traverses the town's slope on its way to the piazza del Comune. There are Medieval buildings and a number of interesting sights along the way, such as the **Biblioteca Comunale** at number 12, which contains the oldest copy of Saint Francis's nature poem, *Canticle of the Creatures.* Midway, where the street becomes via Seminario and then via Portica, delectable pastry shops appear (try the *panforte assisano*). Here, too, is the **Museo Civico**, housing replicas and lapidary inscriptions of the early Christian era.

At the piazza del Comune, site of the old Roman forum, is the **Tempio di Minerva**, which caused Goethe to rhapsodize over its proportions, "just right for such a small town yet so perfect in design that it would be an ornament anywhere." He preferred this temple, which was converted to the church of Santa Maria in 1529, over the "monstrous basilica," as he described it. The piazza, where troubadours sang of idealized love and today grandmothers trudge across on their daily marketing rounds, is within a stone's throw of many hotels and restaurants. Just beyond the temple, a steep flight of stairs leads to the family-run and moderately priced restaurant **La Fortezza**, a cozy refuge for simple but delicious fare. Try their mixed salamis, grilled pork, and *maccheroni alla Fortezza,* pasta in a rich green vegetable sauce.

The quiet **Hotel Umbra**, situated at the end of a cul-de-sac on vicolo degli Archi, right off the piazza, has a good restaurant with lovely terrace dining, and its pleasant rooms are reasonably priced. And not too far is another hotel/restaurant combination, the small, genteel **Hotel Fontebella**, on via Fontebella, where more refined Umbrian fare is served at its **Il Frantoio Restaurant**, which occupies a 17th-century olive-oil pressing room. The garden terrace with its thatched roof is delightful, and the tortelloni with sage butter is especially good.

From the piazza runs the corso Mazzini, a shop-lined street and site of the moderately priced **Hotel dei Priori**, with some 19th-century furnishings and 20th-century conveniences. The street leads to the **Basilica of Santa Chiara**, where the body of the saint lies in a subterranean tomb. Impressive for its massive pink buttresses, it also contains a 12th-century crucifix said to have spoken to Saint Francis, telling him to rebuild "His" church.

The immense basilica of San Francesco may reflect the sweeping influence of Francis, but the **Convent of San Damiano**, south of Porta Nuova about 2 km (1.5 miles), best expresses his simple, eloquent love of God through humanity. A lonely and silent place amid gnarled olive trees and soaring cypresses, it was here that Francis composed his *Canticle of the Creatures,* and where St. Clare and her order lived.

Assisi is a pilgrimage town and teems with visitors who come for the many festivals and religious ceremonies, but it manages the crowds well. During Holy Week the Deposition is reenacted with a torch-lit procession through the streets. Calendimaggio, held on April 30 and May 1, sees a flourishing of Medieval pageantry. The Festa del Voto, celebrating the miracle when Saint Clare repelled the Saracens from the city, is on June 21. On October 3 and 4, the Transito di San Francesco commemorates the death of the saint with a simple service at sunset; the light from hundreds of candles gives the city a surrealistic glow.

In addition to religious sights, there are several interesting artisan workshops along via Fontebella.

Also worth a visit is the **Eremo delle Carceri** (Hermitage of the Prisons), just a ten-minute drive up forested hills, or a one-hour hike (recommended only if you are a decathalon champion). Saint Francis and his companions frequently sought solace at this monastery, which was nothing more than a few caves until Saint Bernard built it up. The interior resembles an errant Henry Moore sculpture and there are compelling views from its grounds. Descending a steep flight of steps, you arrive at Saint Francis's stone grotto, the original core of the monastery, where you can see the saint's stone bed and oratory.

SPELLO AND MONTEFALCO

About 33 km (20 miles) from Assisi, southeast on Route 75, is the charming town of Spello, a rosy oasis of pristine narrow streets nestled on a foothill of Monte Subasio. The main gateway at the bottom of the hill, the Roman Porta Consolare, introduces the town's history. During the Augustan reign the city enjoyed wide territorial power (the poet Propertius lost much of his land during this time and was quite bitter over it). The 12th-century **Church of Santa Maria Maggiore** on via Cavour contains wonderful Pinturicchio frescoes, painted for the Baglioni family, a favorite of Pope Martin V who gave Spello to them; the frescoes are set off by brilliant Deruta majolica floors. Many visitors to Assisi spend the night in Spello and find the comfortable lodgings and restaurants a good value. On via Salnitraria, at the highest point in the city, is the **Hotel Bastiglia**, "rustic modern" with some hillside rooms and a fine restaurant in a lovely space with giant wooden beams and fireplace. This small city boasts two other good restaurants: **Il Molino**, in a converted 18th-century mill at the bottom of town at piazza Matteotti 6, and **Il Cacciatore**, via Giulia 42, with terrace dining available offering sweeping views.

There are many diminutive towns in the hills close by: the Etruscan **Bettona**, girded by Etruscan walls, west of Spello, and the Umbrian Montefalco. **Montefalco** sits like a Medieval aerie on what seems the highest point in the region just south of Spello, earning it the title "balcony of Umbria." This old Roman colony, sacked by Frederick II and later taken by the papacy, is surrounded by inviting hills that are great places to picnic; take along a bottle of the local wine, Sagrantino, a hearty wine made from twice-pressed grapes.

Montefalco is a sunny town where old men with sun-baked faces sit around playing the popular Italian card game *scopa,* while their apron-clad wives stand vigil in doorways, oblivious to the treasures of their art museum, the former **Church of San Francesco**—the superlative fresco cycle of Saint Francis's life by Benozzo Gozzoli. A popular trend of the 14th century was to depict Francis's life as paralleling Christ's; the cycle begins with Francis's birth in a stable and ends with the appearance of the stigmata—corresponding to the crucifixion. In the piazza del Comune, knock at the door of number 10 and ask the attendant to take you to the bell tower in the **Palazzo Comunale**, from which you can get a superb view of the majestic Umbrian landscape.

Fonti del Clitunno

South of Spello on route 3 (the Flaminia Way), near the village of Pissignano, are the Fonti del Clitunno, the ancient pure springs that were a Roman religious outpost and the source of the river Clitumnus. The notorious emperor Caligula prayed here at his villa, which stood on the banks of this limpid pool rimmed by weeping willows and poplars. Its powerful effects have charmed many writers throughout time—Virgil exclaimed about its beauty, Byron included it in his *Childe Harold,* and Corot painted its sublime poetry. Nearby is the miniature **Tempietto del Clitunno**, built in the fifth century over a pagan oratory and containing the oldest frescoes in Umbria (seventh century). Its delicate proportions inspired Palladio. The rambling **Mulino Inn**, adjacent to the temple, is a good bed-and-breakfast spot, open from late spring to the end of summer.

SPOLETO

South of Assisi on route 3, east of Orvieto and Todi and north of Rome via Terni, is Spoleto. The densely wooded forests of Monteluco, which rise over 2,000 feet, shelter this tiny gray town, so full of charm and cultural excitement each summer during the famous **Festival of Two**

Worlds that was launched by Gian-Carlo Menotti 30 years ago.

The city's history is contained within the compact format of its shadowy corridors and twisting narrow Medieval streets that barely accommodate the tiny Fiats that somehow tear through. Already an episcopal see in the fourth century, Spoleto suffered under the barbarian Totila and subsequently became the headquarters of the Lombard duchy that ruled over most of Umbria for three hundred years. After the Guelph versus Ghibelline battles in the 14th century, Spoleto became part of the Papal States.

Each summer, the festival turns this sleepy town into a Mediterranean Chautauqua, with world-famous artists in attendance. The giant Calder sculpture in the faceless modern part of town, where the train arrives, is the first clue to Spoleto's other nature. If you expect to attend the festival, plan well in advance; tickets are snatched up early and hotels fill fast. (The festival runs from mid-June to mid-July; for information, write: Festival dei Due Mondi, via Margutta 17, Roma; Tel: 06-678-3262.)

As for ancient times, Roman ruins predominate here, but the giant stones that form part of the wall surrounding the Rocca (see below) recall the Umbrians who lived here in the seventh and sixth centuries B.C. Fiercely loyal to the Romans, who had colonized the city in 241 B.C., Spoleto repulsed an attack by Hannibal. The **Porta Fuga**, near the Palazzo Pompili, commemorates this impressive victory, and the splendid theaters, basilicas, Roman baths, houses, and arches throughout Spoleto act as palpable guides to this rich Roman period.

The area from the Roman arch, Porta Monterone, around to the Duomo (cathedral) and sweeping up to the Rocca includes the most interesting sights. Viale Matteotti, the main road, skirts the public gardens and passes the **Hotel Dei Duchi**, an agreeably modern place with an adequate restaurant and pleasant terrace. (It is a ten-minute walk from the center of town.) The street leads to the piazza della Libertà, once the private courtyard of a 17th-century palazzo and now where the tourist office is located. The office has designed some good walking tours of the city, which include nature walks with altitudes indicated. Off the piazza stands the remains of a Roman theater that has been beautifully restored and that you can visit. From here the corso Mazzini, the main artery sprinkled with attractive shops, slices through the heart of town, passing the delightfully lively **Sabatini**, where you can dine on sumptuous *stringozzi* pasta with truffle sauce in either of two lovely garden terraces. Another fine restaurant, in a more secluded spot, is the formal **Taverna il Tartufo**, located at the foot of corso Garibaldi at the city's exit point (Tartufo is a healthy walk from Sabatini). Specialties to try here are the game and truffle dishes.

A short drive from the piazza Garibaldi is the **Basilica of San Salvatore**, a remarkable fourth-century church built by Oriental monks out of a Roman temple and modified in the ninth century. Its naked quality reflects the simple character of early Christian devotion.

Back at the center of town, and off the via Brignone, is the petite 12th-century **Church of Sant'Ansano**, decorated with Romanesque frescoes. Alongside is the **Arco di Druso**, built in A.D. 23 by the Roman Senate in honor of Tiberius' son Drusus, who had repelled the Germans. Below the arch are the remains of a Roman temple, part of which has been incorporated into the crypt of the church. Entry is through a flight of stairs in the church.

Nearby is the lively piazza del Mercato, once a Roman forum and now the town's bustling marketplace. From the piazza a series of galloping steps, the via del Mercato, runs down to the piazza Collicola, where there is parking and a few modest hotels.

At the end of piazza del Mercato, the via del Municipio leads to the piazza Comunale, beneath which lie the remains of the home of Vespasian's mother. (You can visit there and other Roman ruins; ask the caretaker at the entrance on via di Visiale for keys.) A short stroll from here is the brooding **Rocca**, a six-towered fort constructed in the 14th century by Gattapone on orders from the papal legate. The Rocca served as residence to papal governors and even to Lucrezia Borgia, whose father, Pope Alexander VI, appointed her governor of Spoleto in 1498.

To the south of the Rocca is the overwhelming **Ponte della Torri** (Bridge of the Towers), spanning the ravine through which flows the river Tessino. The dramatic 14th-century bridge, built on the foundation of a Roman aqueduct that still carries water from the hills of Monteluco, has ten soaring arches. The bridge dwarfs the tiny **Hotel Gattapone** (13 rooms); this multilevel gem has gleaming wood-paneled walls and a shiplike feeling; it looks out over rich green mountains studded with evergreens, oaks, and ilex, and dappled by wild sweetpeas.

Long held in reverence by the Umbrians, who worshiped here, and then the Romans, whose laws protected them, the hills of Monteluco were also home to Saint Francis, who carved out a little sanctuary that was enlarged a few hundred years later by Saint Bernard of Siena and today is used by the Capuchin brothers. It is 8 km (5 miles) from Spoleto; follow the via di Visiale.

From piazza Campello (at the foot of the Rocca; there is long-term parking here) head toward via Saffi and then turn right on via dell'Arringo, a lyric flow of steps named after the *Arringo,* the general assembly of men who decided the politics of the day. One of the prettiest walks in town, it brims with orchestras and chamber groups during festival time. At the end of via dell'Arringo is the piazza del Duomo. The walk passes the little 11th-century **Church of Sant'Eufemia**, a fine example of Lombard architecture, which contains an interesting seating gallery for women (*matronei*) and the lovely Cosmatesque sculpture decorations.

The wide fan of steps, the via dell'Arringo, opens onto the piazza del Duomo, where the **Cathedral** stands, plain and proud and adorned only by its great rose windows that twirl around the lovely fresco on the tympanum and the intricate carvings surrounding the main door. The Duomo was sacked by Frederick Barbarossa in 1155. Rebuilt and consecrated by Pope Innocent III some 40 years later, the church contains splendid frescoes of Pinturicchio and Annibale Carracci. In the apse are the peerless frescoes of Fra Filippo Lippi, the monk who wore his habit rather loosely and whose sweet Madonnas were inspired by his lover, a nun with whom he had two children. His son, Filippino Lippi, designed his tomb, which you see here, and the Medici family paid for it. Actually, it was Lorenzo de' Medici who helped the monk out of some hot water during one of his amorous escapades and who landed him the commission to paint the frescoes.

Also in the square, next to the baptistery, is the 17th-century **Teatro Caio**, where the major performances of the festival take place.

Monteluco

An excursion to Monteluco, a mountain just 8 km (5 miles) southeast of Spoleto on route 2, is a beautiful drive deep into the densely wooded Monteluco hills and takes you to the ancient **Church of San Pietro**, built on the site of an old necropolis encircled by cypress trees. The Romanesque façade is a profusion of carvings of animals and religious themes, a stony guidebook to the Medieval mind of faith and superstitions. Farther up is the **Convent of San Francesco**, an intriguing stony honeycomb of cells nestled into the sanctuary that Saint Benedict built over it. Today, Capuchin brothers use the hermitage, just as Saint Anthony of Padua, Saint Benedict, Saint Francis, and generations of other brothers have before them.

South of Spoleto and Monteluco, off route 3, and a little to the southeast of Terni, is the **Cascata delle Marmore** (Marble Cascade). Built by the Romans, who diverted the waters of the Velino river to drain the Rieti marshes, the cascade drops about 500 feet, in three successive waves, over marble-lined clefts. A breathtaking view can be had of them, but only on weekends. A short run from Terni, northwest on Route 3 bis, you'll come to the fascinating **Carsulae**, the pure Roman town where you can walk unimpeded by any Medieval structure among ruins of temples, baths, theaters, and arches.

TODI

On route 79 *bis,* west of Spoleto and about 25 minutes east of Orvieto, is the picturesque town of Todi, whose history is revealed in its three sets of walls: Etruscan, Roman, and Medieval. The gods had a hand in creating Todi: According to legend, an eagle swept over the plains and snatched the Umbrians' building blueprints and delivered them to the top of the hill. The superstitious Umbrians read this as an omen and re-sited their city at the summit, unwittingly making it an attraction for the Etruscans (400 B.C.)—who never could resist a hilltop village. When the Romans conquered Tutere (the Etruscan name), they changed its name to Tuder and shaped it into a ferocious military power, also endowing it with amphitheaters, forums, and many temples, some of whose fragments survive to this day. Sprawling down very steep slopes of over 1,300 feet against the backdrop of the Apennines, Todi contains one of the loveliest squares in Italy, the **piazza del Popolo**, once a Roman forum, which is surrounded by buildings whose stern walls summon up the vigorous civic and commercial life of the city: the

Palazzo del Capitano, linked with the 13th-century Lombard Palazzo del Popolo, one of the oldest public buildings in Italy, and the Palazzo dei Priori, former seat of the *podestà* (mayor), and marked by a sprawling bronze eagle (a symbol that recurs on many buildings) on its façade.

The 12th-century **Cathedral**, standing at the end of the square where the temple to Apollo once stood, almost in defiance of the civic buildings, contains some fine Renaissance art and 16th-century inlaid stalls. Because of its strategically superior site and the clever ministrations of its bishop, Todi eluded the barbarian Totila—as it would Frederick II years later. The **Church of San Fortunato**, at piazza della Repubblica, commemorates this period. Within is a crypt containing the tomb of Jacopone da Todi; a lawyer with a taste for luxury and excess, he became a Franciscan monk after the death of his wife—whom he discovered had been wearing a hair shirt for years. He was a staunch critic of Pope Boniface VIII (his Frati Minori were instrumental in the final persecution of the pope) and an accomplished poet, composing biting *laude* (prayer ballads, and Italy's first protest songs) that exposed papal corruption. His devotional lauds, especially the Stabat Mater (which the Church added to its liturgy and had set to music in the 18th century) are particularly beautiful. Some of his lauds are performed here during Holy Week.

As a center of woodworking and antiques, Todi is host to the national antiques fair each spring. There are two good restaurants in town—the **Jacopone-da Peppino** and **Umbria** (try their special *spaghetti alla boscaiola,* with wild asparagus, and the local wine, Grechetto; in good weather, you must eat outdoors on the Umbria's terrace, which overlooks miles of spectacular Umbrian landscape)—and a few modest hotels. The more luxurious hotels lie a few miles outside of town. A rocky road reaches the **San Valentino**, south of town. Much money went into restoring this 13th-century monastery, nestled on a wooded hillside in the town of Fiore (and open year-round). Nearby, in Terminillo, there are some respectable ski slopes. Another good choice is the converted convent **Hotel Bramante**, about a km (less than a mile) west of town on the road to Orvieto. It sits opposite the lovely Renaissance church of the Consolation, has some rooms overlooking the valley, and is reasonably priced.

There are several good restaurants just outside of Todi. The simple **Cibocchi**, a few miles outside the town on the road to Fiore, is an especially pleasant choice. Home-made tagliatelli, simple grilled food, and the traditional flat bread of Umbria known as *torta al testo,* with pros-ciutto, are served in a warm setting.

ORVIETO

Talk about being placed on a pedestal: No defensive walls were needed at Orvieto. The giant upthrust of reddish tufa rock, a jagged remnant of volcanic days, lifts Orvieto some 900 feet above the wide valley of the river Paglia. Approached by route 71 from Lago Bolsena in the south-west, the city appears a mirage, especially during the sizzling Umbrian summer when the air is wavy like a moiré fabric. (Orvieto, about 20 km (12 miles) west of Todi, is also easily reached by the A 1 from Rome to the south.)

Although its cathedral and its wine have taken top billing, Orvieto's history stretches back to the Etruscans, whose sharp eye for defensive positions made this an important stronghold of their confederation in the sixth century B.C. Then known as Volsinii, this thriving pottery town developed a prosperous economy, trading widely with Greece, and established a powerful agricultural mo-nopoly in the area. The Romans sacked it in the third century B.C. and forced the inhabitants to build a new city, Volsinii Novi (modern Bolsena). Later the *urbs vetus,* or old city—from which Orvieto's name derives—was re-built. Numerous artifacts taken from Etruscan tombs are on view at the **Museo Archeologico Faina** in the Palazzo Faina across from the cathedral.

The Roman period was followed by the familiar bands of Medieval marauders—Goths, Byzantines, and Lom-bards—the last of whom set up a duchy here in the sixth century A.D. During the Guelph-Ghibelline battles, the Monaldeschi and Fillipeschi families, whom Dante com-pared to the Montagues and Capulets, scandalized the city and their neighbors. The plague and their quarrel-ing frayed the fabric of the city and made it easy prey for the takeover in 1354, when the papal legate, Cardinal Albornoz, annexed it to the Papal States.

Orvieto is quite flat up top, where it is laced with narrow streets sporting stately 13th-century palaces and shops that sell traditional majolica ware. Overwhelming the piazzale Cahen at the eastern edge of the city is the

Rocca Fortress, built in 1364 by Cardinal Albornoz as a way of keeping the papal embers burning while the pope lived in Avignon, similar to the fortresses in Spoleto, Assisi, and Urbino. Nearby is the **Well of San Patrizio**, commissioned by Pope Clement VII who, having recently fled Rome after Charles V sacked the city, wished to prepare the town should it be placed under siege. Two spiral staircases, which never intersect, descend into the well.

The focal point of the city is the **Cathedral**, which stands in the spacious piazza Duomo directly across from the tourist office. The zebra-like Duomo, with its striped sides and bejeweled façade, is a masterpiece of exuberant details and dominates the spacious square, if not the entire city. Gothic architecture, introduced into Italy by the Cistercians, never really captivated the Italians (their version is always with a small "g"). Uncomfortable with the standard Gothic proportions, which they considered inimical to the widely spaced Roman plan they loved, the Italians did what they were best at: They *decorated* the cathedral in Gothic style but never wholly embraced the Gothic form.

The Miracle of Bolsena gave birth to Orvieto's cathedral. A skeptical priest, Peter of Prague, doubted the theory of transubstantiation (a hotly debated issue in the Church at the time, when heresies were cropping up regularly), which holds that at the time of consecration of the host, the wafer is transformed into the body and blood of Christ. While he was once celebrating mass, his misgivings were relieved when the host spouted droplets of blood on the altar cloth. The miraculous news spread fast, and when Pope Urban IV heard it (he was in residence at the time, to escape the heat of Rome—and its political factions), he declared an official feast day, Corpus Christi, and enlisted the brilliant Thomas Aquinas—who was lecturing in theology at the convent of San Domenico—to write the sacred Office of the day. The plan for the cathedral took some 30 years to flesh out; in 1290 Pope Nicholas IV laid the cornerstone. Since 1264 the feast has been celebrated here every summer (on the ninth Sunday after Easter) with a lavish festival, during which buildings are draped, citizens don Medieval costumes, and the sacred altar cloth, housed in an elaborate reliquary shaped like a little Duomo, is paraded through the streets.

The cathedral's construction, spanning three centuries,

was begun in the Romanesque style by Arnolfo di Cambio; it took on a Gothic appearance when the Sienese architect Lorenzo Maitani began work in 1309. The façade is a symphony of color, harmony, and grace, lifted to the heavens by soaring pinnacles that divide the surface into a three-part scheme. The mosaics, restored over time, are especially spectacular at sunset. The modern hand of the Sicilian sculptor Emilio Greco (1964) created the richly ornamented bronze doors, whose themes of charity and mercy blend harmoniously into the overall scheme of the façade. The austere, striped interior contains outstanding works, including the marble *Pietà* of Ippolito Scalza; a monumental organ with 5,585 pipes; and the gilt-and-enamel reliquary, by Vieri, where the linen cloth is kept.

A major attraction over the years has been the incomparable frescoes of Fra Angelico, Benozzo Gozzoli, and Luca Signorelli in the cathedral's **Chapel of the Madonna di San Brizio**. Begun by Fra Angelico and Gozzoli around 1447, they were completed some 40 years later by Signorelli. In the fresco *The Damned in Hell,* Signorelli modeled the woman being carted off by the devil after a lover who had spurned him. The human modeling is so superlative that Michelangelo came here to study the frescoes, as did Augustus John several hundred years later. If you want to get a glimpse of the artists, take a look at the Antichrist fresco and note the two black-robed gentlemen in the corner—Luca Signorelli and Fra Angelico. The iconography of the frescoes is enriched by the figures of Dante, Homer, and Ovid, to name a few.

South of the cathedral is the severe-looking Palazzo Soliano dei Papi, which sheltered 32 popes in its time. Today it houses the **Museo dell'Opera del Duomo** and contains a fine collection of regional art (look for the Signorelli and Martini works) as well as exceptional Medieval gilt work.

Near the cathedral, off the Palazzo Faina on via Maitani, is the small first-class **Hotel Maitani**. Graciously appointed and skillfully managed, it offers a good view of the cathedral and the rooftops of Orvieto from its terrace. The same management runs the dignified **Ristorante Morino** on via Garibaldi, serving rich Umbrian meals, such as pasta with fondue and truffle sauce, and tasty spit-roasted goat. A few doors down from the Maitani, a simple but reliably good meal can be had at **Trattoria Rocchio**, a favorite of the locals. And at number 1, the **Cantina Barberani** wine bar is a good place to sample the local wines. To the north of the cathedral, in the piazza, is the modern but tiny **Hotel Virgilio**, set in an ancient building. On via Duomo there are many fine pottery shops and, at number 41, a good jewelry store, **Adami**. At number 78, **Ristorante Maurizio** serves a delicious agnolotti (pasta dumpling) stuffed with mushrooms. Follow the via Duomo to the corso Cavour. Take a leisurely stroll down Cavour, a street of attractive shops and Medieval homes. The **Montanucci Bar** at number 21 serves a delicious *frullata,* a concoction of mixed fresh fruits blended to a creamy froth—and sometimes spiked with vodka.

One of the charms of Umbria is its thriving artisan workshops. Perpendicular to the corso Cavour is the quaint artisan street of Bottega Michelangeli, named after the local wood sculptor whose works are abundantly featured in the shops. Number 3 has a whimsical collection of handmade wooden puppets and dolls.

At the western end of corso Cavour is piazza della Repubblica, where the Roman forum once stood, and still the city's nerve center. On one side of the square is the 13th-century Palazzo Comunale, built over the remains of the previous town hall. To the east is the lovely 11th-century **Church of Sant'Andrea**, built over the remains of a Roman temple. The church has a vibrant historical past; it was here that Innocent III announced the Fourth Crusade and that Pope Martin IV was crowned in 1281 in the presence of Charles of Anjou. The sacristan will admit you to the Etruscan and Roman remains below.

Radiating from the piazza is via Garibaldi, where the **Hotel Aquila Bianca** is located. This restored Renaissance palazzo, with coffered and painted ceilings, has an understated beauty. It is first class but reasonably priced and well located. It can be a bit noisy, so request a room facing the courtyard.

The Medieval quarter stands at the western edge of the piazza della Repubblica, dotted with old ocher churches and tiny homes clinging tenaciously to the hills. Bright geraniums and lilting sounds of families gathered for lunch add a gentle touch to a stroll. Via Ripa Serancia snakes through here and ends at the **Grotte del Funaro** restaurant, a cavernous but cozy restaurant located in a restored grotto, popular for its spicy sausage and rich antipasti. The piano bar (it opens at 10:00 P.M.) nicely prolongs an evening and offers an alternative to the only other form of nightlife, the *passeggiata* (promenade), which takes place in front of the cathedral. At the end of via Malabranca is the **Church of San Giovenale**, dedicated to Saints Giovenale and Savino, who first brought Christianity to Orvieto, and worth seeing for its 12th-century altar.

The piazza del Popolo is wonderfully alive, especially awash with activity on Thursdays and Saturdays, when the open-air markets are in operation. On the piazza, the Palazzo del Popolo, an ecclesiastical palace dating from Hadrian IV's pontificate (1157), faces the palazzo of the Bracci family, which today is the **Grand Hotel Italia**. The hotel *is* grand, and romantic, and a little worn—though there's ongoing renovation. For those who are willing to sacrifice a little convenience for the sake of charm and history, this moderately priced hotel offers good value.

Orvieto was a holy place for the Etruscans, and the **Croce del Tufo necropolis** (dating from the eighth to the third centuries B.C.), located at the foot of the city, offers a fascinating excursion into the elaborate world of the dead. There is a convenient parking lot near the entrance to the walkway, which is lined with chambers. The tombs, built right into the tufa rock, bear the names of the deceased over the archways.

Just 5 km (3 miles) south of Orvieto is a former Christian abbey, today the incomparable **Hotel La Badia**. The eighth-century Benedictine abbey of Saints Severo and Martirio was for centuries a sanctuary for popes, cardinals, and nobles, and has now been transformed for the comfort of travellers. Everything here, from the graceful courtyards and fountains to the splendid Romanesque architecture and elegant rooms, is designed to induce peace and comfort. The hotel's restaurant is also superb, and for the more active there are a small pool and tennis courts.

GUBBIO

About 40 km (25 miles) northeast of Perugia, just over a stretch of the Apennines and on the way up to the Marches and Urbino, is Gubbio, standing hard and gray. Of all the Medieval towns it is perhaps the best preserved, probably because it's a bit remote and can be reached only by car or bus (the nearest train station is at Fossato di Vico, 16 km/10 miles away—there is bus service from Fossato to Gubbio). The city began at the foot of the hill as an Umbrian town during the sixth and fifth centuries

B.C., then became an ally of Rome. In the early years of the Roman Empire its position made it an important communications point between Rome and Ravenna, and it prospered greatly during those times. The sprawling, well-preserved 2,000-year-old **Teatro Romano** lies just outside the town walls, about a five-minute walk from the piazza Quaranta Martiri, entry point for cars and buses, and a good place to park. The theater, with solitary arches and columns, set apart from the city like an exiled king, makes a comeback each year from mid-July to August, when classical plays are performed here (mostly in Italian). The frescoes of the city's celebrated painter, Ottaviano Nelli, can be seen in the **Church of San Francesco** in the piazza.

Gothic invasions pushed the city up the treeless slopes of Monte Ingino. In 413 Gubbio was the seat of a bishopric, and in the 10th and 11th centuries it developed into a powerful free commune before being drawn into the Montefeltro Duchy of Urbino in 1384. The patron saint, Ubaldo, who lived at a time of civic and religious alliance, is credited with saving the city by convincing Frederick Barbarossa to release it from allegiance to the Holy Roman Empire. His withered remains can be seen in a glass coffin in the **Basilica** at the top of the hill.

The **Palazzo dei Consoli**, grand dame of civic pride, dominates the city from its lofty position on the piazza della Signoria, strewn with stark modern sculptures that seem the only tie to the modern world.

Built by Gattapone between 1332 and 1346, the palazzo contains the grand Salone dell'Arenga (top floor, and also site of the Communal Art Gallery), where the town's consuls met to plan the city's affairs. Inside are the fascinating two-thousand-year-old Eugubine bronze tablets, the Rosetta Stones for Umbrian culture. Written in Etruscan and Latin characters, they are sketchy clues to the language and sacred rites of this holy city that was once governed by a council of priests. Also worth inspecting here are the collection of Roman coins and sarcophagi; the sweet, faded frescoes of Nelli and Palmerucci; and the beautiful *Madonna of the Pomegranate*.

Several of the best restaurants in Gubbio are grouped near the Palazzo: the homey, ribbed-vaulted **Taverna del Lupo**, via B. Ansidei, which serves a great lasagne, and the gracious **Fornace di Mastro Giorgio** restaurant, on via Mastro Giorgio, noted for its exceptional truffle-laced dishes and soothing Baroque music. Close by, near the upper part of the town, is the old Palazzo Raffaelli, now a hotel, the **Bosone**. Dante was a frequent visitor of the Raffaelli family here, and its halls still seem to echo with the sounds of his voice.

With May come the spirited festivals of the **Palio della Balestra** (Crossbow Competition), on the last Sunday in May, and the **Race of the Ceri**, May 15, when the city of silence erupts into a riotous Medieval pageant and recalls the city's victory over a league of cities, headed by Perugia, which attempted to subdue the city. You can just picture the time when the Gubbian knights and their men-at-arms marched off to join the First Crusade. Neighborhood teams march up the steep hill to the basilica of San Ubaldo, hauling their *ceri* (candles)—actually 16-foot, half-ton wooden poles each topped by a representative saint. As you'd expect, Saint Ubaldo's team always finishes first.

Medieval buffs hankering for a crossbow or some other Medieval weapon should go to the **Bottega del Artigiano di Antonio Bei** at via Borghetto Nuovo, number 9. (Crossbows were so deadly and penetrated with such force that in 1139 the Lateran Council voted to prohibit their use; the attempt was unsuccessful.) Bibliophiles will find the wide selection of books and old maps at **Gabriel**, a book and print shop at via dei Consoli 24, worth a look.

At the top of town the Palazzo Ducale and the Duomo face each other. The **Palazzo Ducale** is built on the remains of an older building, where Charlemagne and Frederick II had stayed, and was redone for Federico da Montefeltro, Duke of Urbino, who seized Gubbio during its waning days of independence. The palazzo is notable for its lovely Renaissance courtyard, a subtle blend of flowing arches and Corinthian columns rising from a herringbone brick pavement. Across the small piazza is the **Duomo**, a 13th-century church with a graceful façade constructed of lavender-gray brick. The interior is quite magnificent, with an elegant geometry created by rows of Gothic arches and some lovely frescoes of Nucci, Doni, Gherardi, and Viti.

The snug alleys and streets around here feature stark homes with everyday doors as well as *porte dei morti* (death doors). Coffins are said to have passed through these portals, which have long since been bricked up. A more convincing explanation, though less colorful, establishes them as openings through which ladders passed to upper living quarters, thus protecting the family from intruders.

The most picturesque streets within the Medieval center are the via dei Galeotti, via Piccardi, and via Baldassini, where, at number 28, the **Ceramiche Casagrande Giorgio** features the impressive ceramics for which the city is famous—particularly the black *bucchero* and lusterware.

Umbria is a beehive of artisans who furnish everything from hand-loomed tablecloths to gaily colored pottery and fine lace. **Gualdo Tadino**, southeast of Gubbio on route 3, is known for its rich polychrome and metallic pottery. The International Pottery Exhibition and Competition is held there every July and August.

THE MARCHES

Near Gubbio, route 3 heads north toward Urbino, lying on the eastern edge of the Apennines in the area known as the Marches. The region, which abuts Umbria on the west, extends along the Adriatic side of the Apennines from Pesaro down to San Benedetto del Tronto; it is marked by a series of very high slopes, paralleling the coast, that gradually soften as they approach the sea. The coast is strewn with overcrowded, undistinguished seaside resorts, although there are some lovely hillside towns above that are worth exploring. The Gauls and Piceni, who had settled here, were early incorporated into the Roman hegemony, around the third century B.C. Some impressive Roman works remain, like the **Arco d'Augusto** in Fano and the **Arco di Traiano** in Ancona, capital of the region. During the Middle Ages the Lombards ruled the southern part; the northern area fell under the Byzantine exarchate of Ravenna. Later the entire region was handed to the pope as a gift from the Franks. The 12th and 13th centuries were followed by activities of the powerful signorial families, including the Malatestas of Rimini and the Montefeltros of Urbino. The area's economy is largely agricultural. Ancona, the principal port, is a jumping-off point to Greece and Yugoslavia and shows Venetian influence.

URBINO

The star of the region is Urbino, where, nestled between two hills, a court of humanistic splendor took shape toward the latter half of the 15th century —a singular occurrence whose effects would resonate throughout history.

The honey-colored city traces its origins to the Umbrians, centuries before Christ, and it became a Roman municipality in the third century B.C., but its zenith came during the 15th century under the great condottiere Federico da Montrefeltro, whom Castiglione describes as the "light of Italy."

The Montefeltros were placed here as overlords by the Holy Roman Empire after the Byzantine and Lombard invasions. During the growth of the free communes, Urbino became caught up in the strife between the pope and emperor. The full flowering of the city came in 1444 when Federico, the philosopher-warrior, assumed control after the citizens murdered his tyrannical half-brother, Oddantonio. Federico's court exemplified the best in Renaissance style and tradition, and in the words of Castiglione, his palace "seemed more like a city than a mere place."

Federico was a remarkable man by any standards, dividing his time between soldiering and scholarship. Along with his wife, Battista Sforza, he created one of the most illustrious cultural centers of his time. As a mercenary he was in great demand, serving both kings and popes, and earning a reputation for loyalty in a line of work synonymous with treachery. At one point Venice, which was at war with Ferrara (under whom Federico was engaged), offered him money to withdraw from fighting. He refused. Milan and Florence as well as the papacy were among his employers; Edward IV of England awarded him the Order of the Garter.

In addition to the great warrior-humanist, two other luminaries are associated with the city: the architect Bramante, who expressed his love of antiquity in many a palace and church in Italy, and the painter Raphael.

Urbino is small and compact and is still girded by its great Roman walls. The scenic path of the **via delle Mura**, which traces these walls, offers splendid views of sloping manicured fields set off by rows of cypress. Because the city is a bit off the main travel routes, there are no grand hotels or restaurants. One of the city's best hotels is the

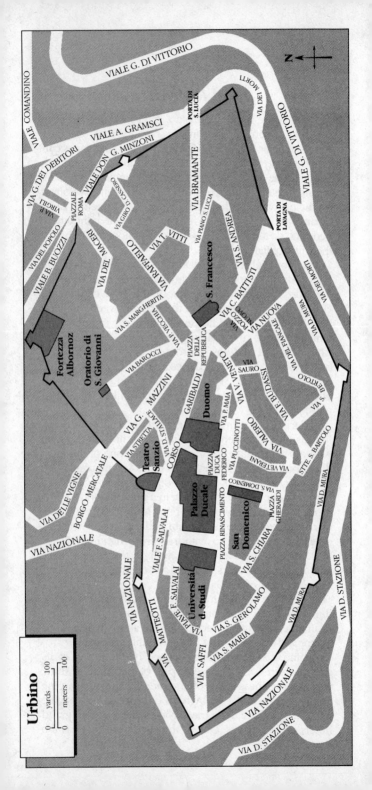

Bonconte, which sits like a small jewel box on the via delle Mura and offers comfortable (though smallish) accommodations at reasonable prices. The front rooms afford a magnificent view of the undulating fields. The Bonconte is within walking distance of the town's center and a stone's throw from Gabriele Monti's endearing restaurant, **Vecchia Urbino**, on via dei Vasari. Strictly a family affair, it serves some of the region's best dishes— try the *olivette alla pesarese,* a thin rolled veal cutlet with a paste of capers, or the *spaghetti alla chitarra "Vecchia Urbino,"* made with bacon, red pepper, and cheese—all prepared by the loving hands of Signor Monti's mother. Verdicchio, the leading wine of the Marches, goes well with these dishes. The dessert wine, Moscato, is superb.

The train station for Urbino is just over a mile south of the Old Town; there are buses to the piazza della Repubblica in the heart of town. Clearly the Ducal Palace of Federico is the city's main attraction; it is only a five-minute walk from the piazza della Repubblica. As the corso Garibaldi snakes up from the piazza, you immediately become aware of the 16th-century university, which has a surprisingly complete bookshop where you can obtain translations of many of the classics.

The Ducal Palace

The Renaissance Palazzo Ducale is located at piazza Duca Federico. Commissioned in 1444 by the duke, who called in the Dalmatian architect Laurana to incorporate the two existing and dismal Gothic palaces, it was completed by the Sienese Francesco di Giorgio Martini in 1482. The top floor now houses the **Galleria Nazionale delle Marche**; the graceful courtyard, *Il Cortile d'Onore,* is one of the world's most ennobled spaces, rimmed by a lovely colonnade. The grand staircase leads to the private apartments of the duke. In the gallery, Pedro Berruguete's portrait of the duke sums up his character: bedecked in shimmering armor and silk robes, the duke sits serenely reading, with his small son, Guidobaldo, at his knee. But the most riveting portrait remains that of Piero della Francesca's (in the Uffizi), the unmistakable hawk-nose of Federico etching a fierce and noble pose against a golden sky.

Everything here reflects Federico's passion for antiquity. During his time the place brimmed with the best art and furnishings, and scholars, poets, and artists flocked to his halls. Today imagination is needed to recall these lively times, since most of the furnishings were carted off when the popes took control and are now on view in the Vatican Museum. However, the space itself is masterful; it captivated the likes of Lorenzo de Medici and Montaigne (and is well known to viewers of Sir Kenneth Clark's television series *Civilisation*).

Although the throne room contains magnificent 17th-century Gobelin tapestries, the duke's study is one of the most riveting rooms in the palace. Lustrous wood inlay work designed by Botticelli and Pontelli manifests the ideals of the Renaissance. The room is a triumph of *trompe l'oeil* with books and armor that seem to magically spill out of closets. Beyond the optical effects, the room is a key to the Renaissance preoccupation with mathematics, science, and the classical world.

There are a few masterpieces in the palace. Raphael's silent portrait of a lady, called *La Muta,* is strong and tender, with a Leonardesque mystery. Piero della Francesca's compelling *Flagellation* is a triumph of perspective, with which the artist was obsessed. His other work here, the *Madonna of Senigalia,* is ferociously silent, with a deep emotional gravity.

Another artist tied to perspective, though less successful at it, is Paolo Uccello. His *Profanation of the Host* here, done in six panels, is especially vibrant. The *Ideal Town,* an architectural rendering, is also of interest.

Federico received classical training at the Gonzaga court in Mantua, where he studied with the great tutor Vittoriano da Feltre. The school, open to rich and poor, girls and boys, had merit as its only qualification for entrance. Distinguishing himself in the classics, including Latin and Greek, and in mathematics and athletics, Federico carried on the tradition at his own court. One of his passions was book collecting, and he established a comprehensive library—though he was suspicious of the newly invented art of printing, and insisted that all his books be hand lettered.

Records reveal some 500 people in attendance at his court, from knights, soldiers, servants, and teachers to readers, astrologers, transcribers, and musicians. His son, Guidobaldo, and daughter-in-law, Elisabetta Gonzaga, further expanded the tradition of learning. During Guidobaldo's reign, the poet and diplomat Baldassare Castiglione was in service at Urbino, and conceived his famous book, *The Courtier,* here. Written in the form of conversations and consciously modeled after Plato's *Republic,* it examines the ideal of the perfect courtier, as the *Republic* explored the subject of the philosopher-king and the ideal state.

The **Duomo**, near the palace, is a Neoclassical reworking of an older church and contains some interesting works of Barocci. The diocesan museum, the Albani, has a good collection of ceramics, vestments, and chalices.

Off the piazza della Repubblica, the via Raffaello snakes up a steep hill, passing the house, at number 57, where Raphael spent his youth. It is an interesting period piece and provides a good feel for the economic level of his father, Giovanni Sanzio, a mediocre court painter in Federico's court.

The street crests at piazza le Roma; just to the west, the public gardens and the great fortress of Cardinal Albornoz offer a superb view of the city.

Also from the piazza della Repubblica, the via Barocci leads to the **Oratorio di San Giovanni Battista**, where the colorful frescoes of the Salimbeni brothers can be seen.

THE COAST

From Urbino, route 3 continues to the seaside town of **Fano**, home to the Malatestas for more than two hundred years, which has some interesting Roman features, such as the **Arco d'Augusto**. The Renaissance period is handsomely represented here by the imposing Palazzo della Ragione, which has the Teatro della Fortuna. Plays and many musical events take place at the lovely Open Theater of the Malatesta Court. In summer, the Fano Festival of Festivals includes many cultural and sporting events, and there are also lively folkloric festivities. **Ristorante Da Pep**, at via Garibaldi 21, serves very good seafood in comfortable surroundings.

A half-hour north along the coastal highway is the charming resort town of **Pesaro**, birthplace of Rossini. The city is handsome; its main artery, corso Rossini, is lined with attractive shops and runs past the composer's home (to which a small museum is attached). The great **Palazzo Ducale**, remnant from the signorial days, is particularly noteworthy, and there are numerous good hotels and pleasant bathing facilities (many are closed in the off season). The Rossini Opera Festival takes place here in August and September.

One of the most spectacular drives, though, is north

from Pesaro in the direction of Gabicce Monte. The majestic hills here, crowned with wild flowers and pines, offer an oasis of silence and beauty. Random exploration of the hills and valleys will reveal many wonderfully preserved Medieval towns and graceful monasteries.

GETTING AROUND

There is no airport in the region, the nearest one being Rome's. There are several ways to explore this region. Most of the interesting sights and cities can be visited following a circular route. For instance, as we've laid out our narrative, a tour by car might begin at Perugia, continue to Assisi, down to Spoleto, across to Todi and Orvieto, back up to Perugia, and on to Gubbio before heading to Urbino.

Or you can start at Orvieto and proceed to Todi and Spoleto, then up to Assisi and Perugia before continuing on to Gubbio and Urbino.

If you are travelling by rail, there are two daily trains making the three-hour trip from Rome to Perugia on the Rome-Ancona line. Change at Foligno for the train to Perugia and Assisi. There are frequent trains directly from Rome to Orvieto on the Rome-Florence line; the train arrives beneath Orvieto's Old Town; buses and taxis take you up to the piazzale Cahen or piazza Duomo. There are also trains from Florence to Perugia.

The F.C.U. (Ferrovia-Centrale Umbra), one of Italy's few remaining privately operated railroads, has a route beginning in Terni (an uninteresting industrial town) in southern Umbria and following the valley of the upper Tiber through the heart of Umbria. Terni is about an hour and a half from Rome by train. It is fun—if not always entirely comfortable—to travel on these trains, packed as they are with housewives and students on their way to Perugia. Schedules tend to be "flexible," so allow plenty of time. The train passes through some ancient towns, like the spa towns of San Gemini and Acquasparta, and proceeds to Todi, Deruta, and Perugia. F.C.U. schedules are available in the Italian Railways' Orario Generale. Local bus service between towns is good, with stations in all the major centers.

ACCOMMODATIONS REFERENCE

▶ **Aquila Bianca**. Via Garibaldi 13, 05018 **Orvieto**. Tel: (0763) 412-46.

► **La Badia**. 05019 **Orvieto** (5 km/3 miles south). Tel: (0763) 903-59.

► **La Bastiglia**. Via Salnitraria 21, 06038 **Spello**. Tel: (0742) 65-12-77.

► **Bonconte**. Via Delle Mura 28, 61029 **Urbino**. Tel: (0722) 24-63.

► **Bosone Hotel**. Via XX Settembre 22, 06024 **Gubbio**. Tel: (075) 927-20-08.

► **Hotel Bramante**. Via Orvietana, 06059 **Todi**. Tel: (075) 884-83-82; Telex: 661043.

► **Brufani**. Piazza Italia, 06100 **Perugia**. Tel: (075) 625-41; Telex: 662104.

► **Dei Duchi**. Viale Matteotti 4, 06049 **Spoleto**. Tel: (0743) 445-41.

► **Fontebella**. Via Fontebella 25, 06082 **Assisi**. Tel: (075) 81-28-83.

► **Gattapone**. Via del Ponte 6, 06049 **Spoleto**. Tel: (0743) 231-25.

► **Grand Hotel Italia**. Piazza del Popolo, 05018 **Orvieto**. Tel: (0763) 412-47.

► **Maitani**. Via Maitani 5, 05018 **Orvieto**. Tel: (0763) 420-11; Telex: 564021.

► **Palace Hotel Bellavista**. Piazza Italia, 06100 **Perugia**. Tel: (075) 207-41.

► **Hotel Dei Priori**. Corso Mazzini 15, 06081 **Assisi**. Tel: (075) 81-22-37.

► **La Rosetta**. Piazza Italia 19, 06100 **Perugia**. Tel: (075) 208-41.

► **San Valentino Hotel & Sporting Club**. 06059 **Fiore**. Tel: (075) 88-41-03.

► **Subasio**. Via Frate Elia 2, 06081 **Assisi**. Tel: (075) 81-22-06; Telex: 662029.

► **Le Tre Vaselle**. 06089 **Torgiano**. Tel: (075) 98-24-47; Telex: 564028.

► **Umbra**. Vicolo degli Archi 6, 06081 **Assisi**. Tel: (075) 81-22-40.

► **Virgilio Hotel**. Piazza del Duomo 5/6, 05018 **Orvieto**. Tel: (0763) 418-82.

ROME

By Dwight V. Gast and Barbara Hults

Dwight V. Gast is the author of our chapters on Apulia and Calàbria. Barbara Hults is the author of our chapters on Sicily and Campania as well as the Overview. They have both lived and worked in Rome, and return frequently.

Ever whirling in water arcs of fountains, citizens chattering and gesturing wildly, traffic like metallic legions going into combat—Rome rushes at you. It can be overwhelming, overblown, exaggerated. The city is as colossal as the Colosseum, as pompous as the Baroque popes, as melodramatic as a street vendor. But just when you've had enough and given up on it, suddenly something unexpected happens. You see the Tiber sparkling sapphire in the night light, a waiter brings you a fresh taste from the oven as a gift, you're charmed by a cat admiring a column once reserved for the Caesars, and you decide to reconcile.

Federico Fellini once praised the city's expansive aspect: "Rome allows you all sorts of speculation, vertically. Rome is [also] a horizontal city, made of water and earth, spread out, and is therefore the ideal platform for flights of fancy. Intellectuals, artists, who always live in a state of friction between two different dimensions—reality and fantasy—here find an appropriate and liberating stimulus for their mental activity, with the comfort of an umbilical cord that keeps them solidly attached to the concrete. Because Rome is a mother—the ideal mother because she's indifferent. She's a mother who has too many children and who, not being able to take care of any one of them, doesn't ask anything of you, doesn't expect anything of you. She welcomes you when you come, lets you go when you leave."

Though quoted when he made his film *Roma* in the early 1970s, Fellini's words have an ageless quality about them—as befits the Eternal City. They recall the flights of fancy that created the legend about the foundation of Rome by Romulus and Remus, nursed by the she-wolf, the original mother of Rome.

That the contemporary reflects the ancient is the glory of Rome, a relationship immediately apparent on arrival. If your point of entry is the airport at Fiumicino, on your way to the city you'll pass the expanse of the E.U.R. suburb, begun under Mussolini for the Esposizione Universale di Roma, a world's fair that never took place. The use of Classical elements in its buildings portends the post-modern movement in contemporary architecture, and Classical Rome itself is the reason most people visit E.U.R.—its Museo della Civiltà Romana houses a famous model of ancient Rome (currently closed). If instead you arrive at the train station, Stazione di Termini, you'll also be confronted by a piece of modern architecture—the station itself. Immediately outside, however, are the remains of an ancient wall, and across the piazza stand the ruins of the Terme di Diocleziano (the Baths of Diocletian).

Between the deep red of the ancient brick and the stark white of modern marble and concrete are the mellower tones, now fixed by law, that dominate Rome, which might have come out of a fruit basket in a Caravaggio painting. Peach, apricot, pomegranate, and honeydew hues decorate its palazzos and villas, the colors made even more striking in combination with the stately Renaissance style imported from Florence, or the exuberant Baroque born in Rome and favored by the popes. Rome's present look is a blend of all such styles, with a touch (but just a touch) of order added when the government of a newly united Italy lined the Tiber with travertine embankments when the city became its capital.

Rome's principal attractions are covered in the narrative below, but don't anticipate—or even attempt—seeing everything the first time around. The jumble of the centuries is simply too confusing, even to longtime residents, who expect the distractions of the unexpected church closures, the signs announcing *chiuso per restauro* (closed for restoration) and *chiuso per mancanza di personale* (closed for lack of personnel), the delightful tangent of discovering a hidden courtyard, witnessing a dramatic bit of street theater (though it's just the Romans going about their daily business), or lingering a little at table over a meal enlivened with good wine and better conversation.

Begin your visit on a leisurely note and let Rome's charms wash over you slowly. One way is by taking the free English-language tours given regularly by Foyer Unitas (Tel: 654-16-18). Include a Sunday or public holiday in your plans in order to see the city free of the traffic that normally engulfs its streets and monuments. If it's a nice day (and it usually is, for the south begins in Rome, as evidenced by the palm trees and the slower pace), rent a bicycle or sit in one of the cafés or restaurants in piazza Navona and watch the drama unfold in front of you against the piazza's Baroque backdrop. As a visitor, you'll be as much a part of the street scene as the "real" Romans, whose heroine Anna Magnani personified their fierce vitality. For despite nostalgic laments among many residents that the real Romans have been overrun by other Italians drawn to the capital to take patronage jobs, they are still here in force. A visit to campo dei Fiori or Trastevere will verify that.

And the city, which together with the Vatican is capital of church and state, is just as intensely bureaucratic and chaotic as any Fellini fantasy. But don't let it overwhelm you. Above all, take your time. Toss a coin into the Trevi Fountain to ensure you'll be back, for that oft-quoted expression about Rome, *non basta una vita* (one life is not enough), is true.

MAJOR INTEREST

The Roman Forum
The Palatine hill
The Colosseum
The Pantheon
Piazza Navona's Baroque splendor
Walking through the Centro Storico (Old Rome, the historic center) for its large and small architectural pleasures
Piazza del Popolo's churches and cafés
The Spanish Steps
Shopping in the via Condotti area
The especially Roman areas of campo dei Fiori and Trastevere
Rome's restaurants, cafés, and bars

The museums at Villa Borghese, Palazzo Barberini,
the Capitoline Hill, the ancient Roman Terme di
Diocleziano, the Vatican (including the Sistine
Chapel), and elsewhere
St. Peter's basilica and piazza

The visitor is constantly confronted with visual reminders
of more than two thousand years of history: From the
evidence newly excavated in the Forum supporting
Rome's traditional founding date of 753 B.C. (to this day
the city celebrates its birthday on April 21 by illuminating
the Capitoline Hill with candles), to such modern architecture as Pier Luigi Nervi's 1971 New Audience Hall at
the Vatican. The Sabine and Etruscan kings ruled for
more than two centuries (traces of the fortifications
known as the Mura Serviane—traditionally attributed to
the Etruscan king Servius Tullius, who ruled from 578 to
534 B.C.—may still be seen near Mercato di Traiano
[Trajan's Market]) until the Republic was founded around
500 B.C. The defeat of Carthage in 146 B.C. coincided with
the conquest of Greek colonies in southern Italy, thus
beginning the Greek influence on monumental Roman
architecture, which expanded greatly during the Empire
(27 B.C.–A.D. 395). It was during this era that most of what
we see of ancient Rome was built, as well as when the
engineering feats of the Aurelian Wall in the city (270–
282) and the roads and aqueducts throughout the Empire
were constructed.

Despite a series of sacks of Rome (by the Goths in 410,
the Vandals in 455, the Saracens in 845, the Normans in
1084, and the German troops of Charles V in 1527) the
papacy steadily established itself in the city, raising religious monuments and palazzi. The popes' effective political power began under Gregory I (590–604), but the
development of the Holy Roman Empire—established
when Leo III, in Rome, crowned Charlemagne emperor
in 800—led to a series of conflicts between popes and
emperors and eventually to the transfer of the papacy to
Avignon (1309–1378). Rome's political and cultural importance was greatly diminished during this period.

With the end of the pope-antipope schism, and beginning with Martin V in 1417, Rome entered the Renaissance, and the popes began to commission great works
from such artists as Michelangelo and Raphael. Sixtus V
(1585–1590) began the first serious planning and development in the city in centuries, with straight roads, and

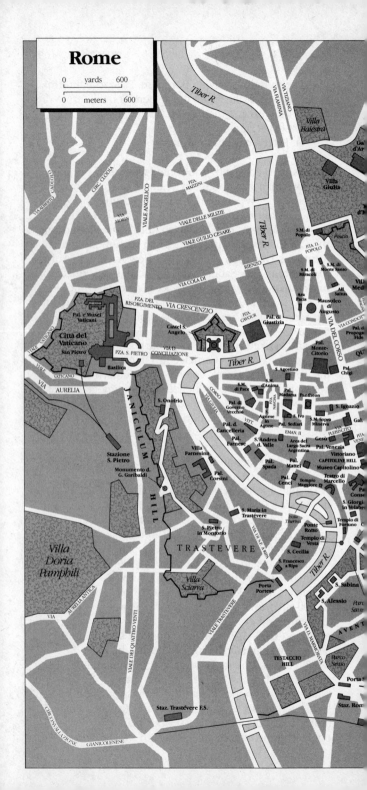

under Urban VIII (1623–1644) and Innocent X (1644–1655) the Baroque we so associate with Rome today reached its peak. During the relatively quiet political period that followed, such 18th-century works as the Spanish Steps and the Fontana di Trevi were built. Napoléon's troops occupied the city in 1798, and the French taste for Neoclassicism, typified by the works of Antonio Canova, Napoléon's favorite sculptor, also invaded the city's arts.

Following the defeat of Napoléon in 1814, the Italian revolution (Risorgimento) began, and Rome became the capital of the united Kingdom of Italy in 1870. The overblown monument to King Vittorio Emanuele, completed in 1911, set the stage for Mussolini's march on Rome in 1922, and the Fascist government he established imposed its order on the city by cutting such broad avenues as via dei Fori Imperiali and via della Conciliazione.

The liberation of Rome by the Allies in 1943–1944 brought about the Italian Republic we know today, and except for such scattered modern buildings as the New Audience Hall and a few hotels, the most important contribution to postwar building in Rome seems to be the Grande Raccordo Anulare (the 44-mile-long highway that rings the city)—an impressive feat of engineering, given Roman bureaucracy, almost in the tradition of the ancient Romans.

The discussion of the city that follows begins at the beginning, with *ancient Rome*. It continues chronologically with the monuments of the Pantheon and piazza Navona (formerly Diocletian's stadium), in the area where the mixture of ancient, Baroque, and Renaissance is most apparent: the *Centro Storico*. You'll then go south of the Centro Storico and see how the real Romans of today live, in the lively neighborhoods of *campo dei Fiori* and—across the Tiber—*Trastevere*. Then we return to ancient history in the *Capitoline* and *Aventine* hills back across the river west of the Roman Forum.

After a breather in Rome's largest park, *Villa Borghese,* you can trace the presence of foreigners in Rome (among them Napoléon's sister Pauline, who lived in the Villa Borghese), then, from the *piazza del Popolo,* take in that high point of the Grand Tour, the *Spanish Steps,* and from there go on to the haunt of the Hollywood stars, the *via Veneto*. That area becomes a springboard to the city's Christian past, in the general neighborhood of the *Quiri-*

nal and *Esquiline hills,* beginning with Palazzo Barberini, built for Pope Urban VIII, and then going generally south (into the area east of the Roman Forum) and back in time to Michelangelo's conversion of a portion of the Terme di Diocleziano into a church, to early Christian churches, and to two of Rome's major basilicas, Santa Maria Maggiore and San Giovanni in Laterano. Finally, you'll traverse the Tiber once again to the separate state surrounded by the city of Rome—*the Vatican.*

ANCIENT ROME

Traces of old Rome—an arch, a column, a fragment of sculpture, or even the colossal marble foot that gave via di Piè di Marmo its name—are strewn around the modern city. The ancient city itself, however, inhabits its very own zone. Behind the Vittorio Emanuele monument radiate the forums and the Palatine Hill, the Colosseum, the Circus Maximus, and the Terme di Caracalla. It is a world of venerable ruins intersected by avenues of rushing Roman traffic.

Before entering, pick up a copy of the red loose-leaf book *Rome: Past and Present,* with plastic overleafs that show the Forum now and then; it is essential in re-creating the whole from the assembly of stray columns and fragments you'll see before you. (Buy the book in a store as opposed to a stand near the monuments. It should cost about 12,000 lire, but will be double that or more on the grounds—unless you want to bargain.)

The Palatine Hill evokes the Rome of Classical fantasy, umbrella pines shading fragments of ancient palaces. It's reached from the Forum Romanum, whose main entrance is around to the left of the Vittoriano, as Romans call the modern-day monument, and is the best place to get an overview of the otherwise complicated Forum. When you reach the Forum grounds from the main entrance on via dei Fori Imperiali, you will see the Palatine ahead of you, rising above the ruins, an irregular mass of pine, oleander, and cypress interspersed with yawning arches. These arches are the ruins of the grand palaces that lined the hill (which gave us the very word "palace"): residences of Augustus, Nero, Caracalla, Tiberius, and Domitian. To reach the belvedere of the Palatine, from which you'll have a grand overview of the Forum, walk left through the Forum to its far side and then follow the path up the hill. Turn right and take the steps up to the terrace.

The Roman Forum

Few monuments so clearly represent the history and life of an entire civilization as does the great complex usually called the Roman Forum (Foro Romano). There are many forums, and the Roman is only a small part of the entire archaeological site, but for clarity the Roman Forum is considered to be that section entered from via dei Fori Imperiali through the admission gate.

Built in the valley between the Capitoline and Palatine hills, the Roman Forum reached the peak of its importance under Julius and Augustus Caesar. Both these emperors—and later ones—enlarged the area with their own forums, but it was here at the original Roman Forum that the structure of Western civilization was forged. Much of our government system derives from this forum. Even the names here are standard in Western thought: "capitol" from the Capitoline Hill next to the Forum; the word "forum" itself; "rostrum" from the Rostra, where Mark Antony gave Caesar's obituary; "money" from the mint at the Tempio di Giunone Moneta on the Capitoline; these are only a few examples.

Early spring is the time to come here, if you can, when flowers blanket walls with pastel colors and delicate fragrances; on the Palatine the air is especially sweet under the umbrella pines, where the birds sing. But even in summer the Palatine is a joy; the air here is cooler than in the rest of the city, and the rose gardens are in bloom; tiny lizards dart around the ruins under acanthus leaves. In fall and winter the ruins are moodier, and the Palatine seems full of wandering ghosts, although not all of the hill's past inhabitants are people we would want to conjure up—Tiberius, Caracalla, and Nero can rest in peace.

The original Forum predates most of the buildings you'll see, which were built during the time of Augustus, the beginning of the Roman Empire. At the right, just past the entry ramp, stands the ruins of the **Basilica Emilia**. It was built in 179 B.C. and was later nearly destroyed by fire and the Vandals. The original basilicas had no religious purpose but were commercial buildings with halls for conducting business. The building style was primarily functional, allowing light and air to circulate inside. The shape was rectangular and monumental, with two aisles

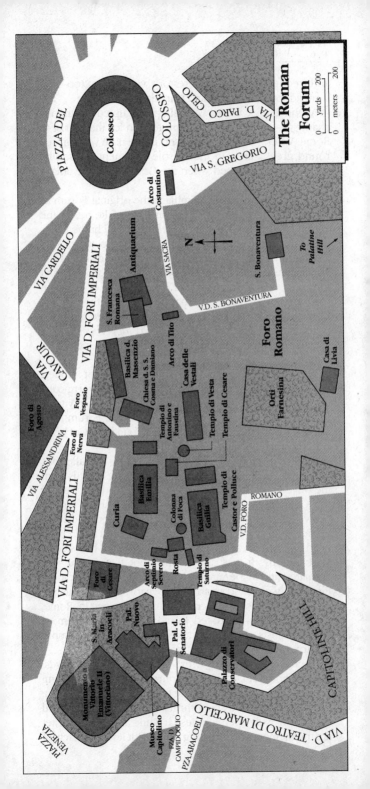

The Roman Forum

0 yards 200
0 meters 200

PIAZZA DEL COLOSSEO

Colosseo

COLOSSEO

VIA D. PARCO CELIO

VIA S. GREGORIO

Arco di Costantino

Antiquarium

VIA SACRA

N

S. Bonaventura

To Palatine Hill

V.D. S. BONAVENTURA

S. Francesca Romana

Arco di Tito

FORO ROMANO

Casa di Livia

VIA CARDELLO

VIA D. FORI IMPERIALI

Basilica d. Massenzio

Chiesa d. SS. Cosma e Damiano

Casa delle Vestali

Templo di Vesta

Templo di Cesare

Orti Farnesina

VIA CAVOUR

Foro di Agosto

Foro Vespasio

Foro di Nerva

Tempio di Antonino e Faustina

VIA ALESANDRINA

Curia

Basilica Emilia

Colonna di Foca

Basilica Giulia

Tempio di Castore e Polluce

ROMANO

V.D. FORO

VIA D. FORI IMPERIALI

Foro di Cesare

Arco di Septimio Severo

Rostra

Tempio di Saturno

S. Maria in Aracoeli

Pal. Nuovo

Pal. d. Senatorio

Palazzo di Conservatori

CAPITOLINE HILL

Monumento a Vittorio Emanuele II (Vittoriano)

Museo Capitolino

PIA. D. CAMPIDOGLIO

PZA ARACOELI

PIAZZA VENEZIA

VIA D. TEATRO DI MARCELLO

and frequently a row of clerestory windows on top—the form adopted by many early Christian churches.

At the Emilia there were shops occupied by money changers—still an important profession for the tourist in Rome. When you walk up closer, in the nave you can see round green stains in the marble pavement, caused by copper coins dropped when the Goths set Rome ablaze in 410.

In front of the Basilica Emilia is the original Forum as devised by Tarquin, the Etruscan king of Rome, in the eighth century B.C. He and other kings brought the tribes who inhabited these marshy hills together to accomplish a communal project—draining the malarial marsh of the Forum area. This done, the stage was set for the first forum—really an early piazza. The **Tempio di Vesta** on the east side was there at that time, as was the original Curia—next to the Basilica—that was the meeting place of the senate. The black stone called *lapis niger* is in a sacred enclosure dedicated to Romulus, as legend would have it.

The look of the place at that time was of modest buildings made of tufa with a stucco coat and terra-cotta decorations. Since wars absorbed much of Roman vitality for centuries, little was done to beautify the Forum until Augustus, who then boasted that he'd found a city of brick and transformed it into a city of marble.

City life was concentrated in the Forum, and all roads led there. Political candidates addressed the crowds from the once grand **Rostra**, now just a stone platform behind the Column of Phocas. The Rostra was named for the prows (*rostra*) of ships captured as war booty and lined up here as war trophies. A later trophy would be Cicero's head and hands (43 B.C.), when he got on the bad side of Mark Antony. It was also at this spot that Caesar was cremated and Mark Antony delivered the funeral oration. Elections were held nearby, and victorious generals paraded along the **Via Sacra** (the oldest street in Rome, currently being excavated by an international team of archaeologists), to the Capitoline Hill, where the **Tempio di Giove** (Temple of Jupiter) stood.

Plautus, in his comedy *Curculio,* described the crowds: "In case you want to meet a perjurer, go to the Comitium; for a liar and a braggart, try the temple of Venus Cloacina; for wealthy married spendthrifts, the Basilica. There will be harlots, well-ripened ones . . . while at the fish market are the members of the eating clubs." But Roman society of that time—well before the wild days of Tiberius—was relatively reserved in dress and manners. Women were forbidden to wear jewelry or expensive clothes, partly because of the war efforts. Later, when Carthage was subdued in the Punic wars and Gaul was pacified—both events that filled the treasury—Rome changed, and its first capitalist class was born, for whom wealth was not in land but in money. After that, temples and basilicas sprang up in all the forums, including the adjacent Foro di Cesari, and the Foro Traiano—Trajan's Forum—across the present-day via dei Fori Imperiali (built by Mussolini and covering further riches known at this moment only to the gods).

At that time, in the middle of the second century B.C., cast concrete was invented—and the Romans took to it with characteristic gusto. Arches and vaults, Rome's quintessential architectural forms, could leap wide spaces, giving the city what it wanted: majestic, impressive space. With a base of pebbles, stone, and rock chips, plus whatever other matter was at hand, concrete vaulting could spread throughout the Empire. The far-flung provinces were no longer dependent on their local resources and could produce similar effects. Soon the look of Rome filled all Roman conquests. Gaul had its aqueducts, and the North African desert had a coliseum, and citizens everywhere felt part of a whole, for better or worse. Roman buildings, in their imposing vastness and colossal statuary, were political statements in an era that had no other media to promote the concept of the Empire. Political and military themes were thus conveyed to the world far beyond the Forum.

Beyond the basilica stands the **Curia**, a brick building begun by Sulla in 80 B.C. that replaced the original Curia that is thought to have been built by King Tullius. Before the days of the Empire senators had considerable power. Judgments were sometimes helped along by augurs, who revealed the workings of fate by reading patterns in flights of birds or in the feeding movements of chickens. The Curia was a consecrated building, with an altar and statue to a pagan god of victory. Christians hundreds of years later objected to the statue, and Saint Ambrose, archbishop of Milan, finally had it removed by appealing to reason: "Where was Jupiter [when the Gauls attacked]?" he asked. "Was he speaking to the goose?"

In A.D. 203 the **Arco di Settimio Severo** (he was in charge of Britannia) was erected to him and his two sons, and on top of the arch was a sculpture of all three in a chariot. One of his sons, however, was Caracalla, who murdered his brother, Geta, to ensure that he himself would become emperor—and erased Geta's name from this and other monuments throughout Rome, though the original inscription can still be made out under the obliterated fourth line across the top of the arch. Romans often used columns decoratively rather than structurally, which can be seen in the freestanding examples of the arch's portico.

To the side and slightly behind the Arch of Septimius Severus is the **Tempio di Saturno**, whose eight columns can still be seen. Dedicated to the god Saturn, it was the site of the Saturnalia, celebrated in December of each year. It was a time of wild public festivities and gift giving, and the quality and amount of the gifts were no less carefully observed than they are today.

In front of the Rostra is the **Colonna di Foca**, dedicated to the tyrannical Eastern emperor who gave the Pantheon to Pope Boniface IV in 608. Next to the Temple of Saturn is the **Basilica Giulia**, named for Julius Caesar, who was murdered (not in the Forum but in Pompey's Theater near campo dei Fiori) before its completion. Some stones in the pavement were used as ancient gaming boards, traces of which can still be seen.

The most beautiful fragment in the Forum is from the **Tempio di Castore Polluce**: the three elegant columns east of the basilica, often photographed as a symbol of Classical grace. The temple was created during the fifth century B.C. because Roman troops saw the divine twins Castor and Pollux (the Dioscuri) fighting at their side in battle far from Rome. Then the heavenly twins appeared at this site, proclaiming the Roman victory.

The round **Tempio di Vesta** nearby is a favorite site, where the goddess's flame was kept burning by the Vestal virgins. It was modeled on the circular hut used by the area's earliest known inhabitants. The Vestal virgins, women of noble birth pledged for 30 years to this cult, were charged with never letting the flame die. If it went out, they were severely thrashed; if they lost their virginity, they were buried alive after being driven in a covered hearse through the streets and forced to descend to their own tomb on a ladder. Because they enjoyed great privileges in Rome, it is sometimes assumed that Vestal virginity was a sought-after honor, but Suetonius tells of noble families doing everything to keep their daughters' names from getting on the list when a virgin died.

The house of the Vestal virgins was like a luxurious convent, a self-contained unit surrounding a central garden court with pools and statues of the virgins. The name Claudia has been erased below the figure of one who converted to Christianity, as a reminder of her ignominy.

The **Tempio di Antonino e Faustina** (at the right of the entrance to the Forum area) is named for the emperor and his wife who adopted Marcus Aurelius and ruled after Hadrian in A.D. 138. Impressively set atop a long staircase, Etruscan style, it has nicely carved columns and a fragment of a statue on the porch. Alongside it is the **Church of Santi Cosma e Damiano**, once part of the Vespasian Forum. If the Forum-side entrance is open, you can see a delightful Neapolitan *presepio* (an exuberant, expansive Nativity scene). The church also merits a visit to see its sixth-century mosaics, among the earliest in Rome. Christ as the Lamb Enthroned is on the triumphal arch.

The name of the large **Basilica di Massenzio e Costantino** sounds as if the building was a collaborative effort, but wasn't: It was begun under Maxentius, but after Constantine beat him at the battle of the Milvian bridge in 312 it assumed his name as well. Its original form is easy to imagine, and part of the coffered ceiling can still be seen. In the Museo Capitolino are some disembodied fragments of the 40-foot statue of the emperor Constantine that stood inside the basilica. Encountering the enormous head and hand is an unforgettable Roman experience.

Three massive cross vaults of the nave rose to 114 feet above the floor, their lateral thrust strengthened by concrete piers 14 feet in diameter. A Barberini pope appropriated the bronze tiles for St. Peter's, giving rise to the saying, "What the barbarians didn't take, the Barberini did." One of its gigantic marble columns ended up in front of Santa Maria Maggiore on via Cavour. This sort of papal modularism makes it seem probable that everything is really still here in Rome; if only massive rearranging could be done. But, of course, the jumble of the centuries is part of Rome's charm.

The **Arco di Tito** at the end of the expanse of the Forum was built in A.D. 81 to celebrate the sack of Jerusalem by the emperor; the friezes show the spoils being transported back to Rome in A.D. 70.

Next to the church (Santa Francesca Romana) between the basilica of Maxentius and Constantine and the Arch of Titus is the **Antiquarium**, a museum that has some interesting objects excavated from the Palatine and models of the huts in sarcophagus form. (A complete model of ancient Rome is on display at the Museo della Civiltà Romana in the suburban district of E.U.R.—currently closed. E.U.R. is accessible by Metro.)

The Palatine Hill

But now look at the Palatine Hill behind you.

> Come and see
> The cypress, hear the owl, and plod your way
> O'er the steps of broken thrones and temples.
> Ye whose agonies are evils of a day
> A world is at our feet as fragile as our clay.

This atmosphere of antiquity enchanted Byron when he wrote *Childe Harold* and is readily evoked on the Palatine. Here you can wander amid the umbrella pines of Rome that must have inspired Respighi, and for the moment the world is perfect in classical beauty. The Farnese spread gardens along the hill, fragrant with roses and orange blossoms in the spring. Down the steps are the excavations of Livia's house, with its delicately painted walls, and beyond that the unearthed huts of Romulus and Remus's time. To the southeast are remains of emperors' villas, including that of Augustus, which looks out over the Circus Maximus, on the other side of the hill from the Forum.

The Circus Maximus

Although an oblong field, with wild flowers here and there, is all that's left of the circus's great chariot track, it is enjoyable to walk where four chariots raced together for seven laps around the 2½ miles. Originally, as many as 385,000 spectators sat there amid marble columns—nothing Rome did was less than colossal. Caligula loved the chariots, and during his reign the number of races doubled to 24 per day. In the stands, touts and wine-sellers worked the crowds. The last race was held in A.D. 549.

The Arco di Costantino

On a nice day you'll notice lots of people on the Palatine reading (or amorously occupied) under the trees, and you may want to follow suit. Otherwise walk back down the hill and past the Arch of Titus and out on the via Sacra to via San Gregorio and the Arch of Constantine, the largest and best preserved of the ancient arches. It was erected to the emperor after his successful encounter with Maxentius. That battle is famous partly because of the vision that Constantine had before it began: He saw a flaming cross formed in the sky and heard the words, *"In hoc signo vinces"* ("In this sign thou shalt conquer").

The arch's unusual collection·of reliefs was partly assembled from various other Roman monuments. On the inside of the central archway are reliefs from the frieze of a monument that commemorated Trajan's Dacian victories, but Constantine's head has been substituted for Trajan's. The frontality of the figures, a Byzantine convention, here foreshadows Constantine's transfer of the imperial capital from Rome to Byzantium (rebuilt as Constantinople) in 330, and the end of the glory days.

Beyond the arch looms the great oval mass that is the Colosseum, which may be contemplated alfresco with lunch at the **Hostaria Il Gladiatore** on the piazza in front of the Colosseum entrance.

The Colosseum

It was its colossal size that gave the Colosseum its name, but it was its games of bizarre cruelty that made this the most famous building in Rome. The Empire had many coliseums, and some exist today in better condition than Rome's, but this will always be *the* Colosseum. During the years when Christians were literally thrown to the lions, along with other "criminals," Claudius used to arrive at dawn to see the spectacle.

The building was begun in A.D. 72, during the reign of the emperor Vespasian, on the site where Nero had excavated a lake for the gardens of his Golden House (now in ruins across the street and rarely open). Outside stood a 96-foot colossal statue of Nero. Vespasian's spectacles of persecution were so sadistic that even Romans turned from them in disgust.

The niches that now seem open arches on the sides of the Colosseum were actually created to house Greek sculpture—including athletic motifs from Greece's unbloody games. The Greek athletic contests were introduced to the Romans but were apparently too tame for a time when combat to the death was the daily diet. Roman architects used niches not only for statuary but to glorify

the massiveness of the walls by emphasizing their depth—
something Greek architects with their airy colonnades
would never have dreamt of.

The Colosseum was built of blocks of travertine excavated from quarries near Tivoli and brought to Rome
along a road created just for that purpose. It was apparently modeled after the Teatro di Marcello (see below),
built during Julius Caesar's time. It rises in three levels,
each decorated with columns, from the plain Doric at the
bottom to Ionic and Corinthian; the fourth level held the
cables that supported the huge awnings that could be
billowed out across the spectators to protect them from
rain or excessive sun. Scents were also sprayed on the
crowd to keep the smell of blood away from their delicate nostrils.

At the first row of seats we can still see the names of
important boxholders. In the second circle sat the ple-
bians, with women and then slaves at the back. Galleries
constructed between the seats and the outer walls provided a place to mill during intermissions. The Roman
use of the crossed vault made such galleries possible.

Almost 50,000 could be seated with enviable efficiency.
There were 80 entrances (four for the select boxholders),
and each had a number that corresponded with the
game-goer's ticket. Leaving was also facilitated by the
vomitoria that "disgorged" the crowds down numerous
ramps. Every detail was ingeniously worked out by the
architects, sensitive to public comfort while they watched
gladiators and animals die agonizing deaths.

The games, too, were organized carefully. Gladiators
were recruited from the ranks of those condemned to
death or of war prisoners—both groups with little to lose
and the possibility of a dazzling future. They were housed
nearby in the recently excavated *ludus magnus*. The floor
could be flooded to create *naumachiae* (sea battles), and
sometimes the gladiators fought in the water.

Not every program was just gladiatorial strife, of
course. There were circus acts with panthers pulling
chariots and elephants that wrote Latin inscriptions with
their trunks.

Gladiators did not fight beasts. That was the work of the
bestiarii. During the inauguration of the Colosseum more
than 5,000 beasts were killed in one day. The actual
gladiatorial combat was called the *mumus,* and it usually
was preceded by days of mock combat called the *lu-
siones,* a warm-up period for the fighters and the crowds.

One major event lasted 117 days, during which 4,941 gladiators fought. Even if not every defeated gladiator was killed, the loss must have been more than a thousand men. But it began in glory. They sauntered around the arena, nonchalant, with their valets bearing their arms. They wore purple embroidered with gold, and when they came to the emperor's box they saluted by raising their right arm, and saying, *"Ave Imperator, morituri te salutant"* ("Hail, Emperor. We who are about to die salute you"). The crowd screamed and cheered at each blow: *Verbera!* (Strike!) and *Ingula!* (Kill!). To ensure that a fallen warrior was dead, he was struck on the head with a mallet. A gladiator unable to continue could lie on his back and raise his left arm in appeal. Then the crowd could wave their handkerchiefs and show their raised thumbs to the emperor, who might take their advice and raise his, granting life. Or they might consider him cowardly and turn thumbs down. The emperor's downturned thumb could not be contested.

Winners were given gold and the adoration of young girls. Cicero thought it a good way to learn contempt for pain and death, and Pliny the Younger thought the trials fostered courage. (Cicero and Pliny, however, did not have to fight.) What was fostered among the spectators was something basic to the Empire: Rome was about conquering.

Of the forms used by Roman architects, the amphitheater, a huge bowl structure such as the Colosseum, survives well today in the sports stadium. It is the nearest to modern taste of all historical styles—in its utilitarianism and in its striving for grandiose and overwhelming effects.

The Baths of Caracalla

For more of ancient Rome, take a bus or taxi to the Terme di Caracalla south of the Colosseum. They were luxurious even for imperial Rome, their massive space shining with multicolored marble, the pools filled by jets of water spouting from marble lions' mouths, the nymphaeum of gardens and pools and statues, gyms, theaters, and libraries. Everyone—rich and poor—went to the baths to socialize and gossip. Caracalla began this project in 212, and his successors added to the glamorous surroundings. The ruins today, the evocative site of Rome's summer opera season, provide important insights into the social organization of ancient Rome.

Trajan's Column and Other Forums

Successive emperors laid out their own forums, and most are found across the via dei Fori Imperiali, Mussolini's idea of a triumphal highway, which split the forums in two parts. (Plans are underway to dig up the street and return the area to its historical state, but motorists are protesting the plan vigorously—and Rome is a city where motorist rights are often given precedence over pedestrians.)

Foro di Cesare (Caesar's Forum) is mostly on the Foro Romano side of the avenue. On the far side, close to the Vittoriano, the **Colonna Traiana** (Trajan's Column) has just been undraped after years of painstaking restoration, and so you will now be able to see this brilliant work, a depiction of the emperor's battle (triumphant, of course) long classified as one of the wonders of the world. Its spiral frieze rises 100 feet. It would, if marble could be unrolled, extend 215 yards. This masterpiece of intricate composition contains 2,500 figures, and was once more easily seen by a spiral staircase. Now binoculars would be handy.

Although you can see the column and much of the several forums by walking along the sidewalk, go inside the **Foro Traiano** (Trajan's Forum; entrance at via Quattro Novembre 94), because then you can see **Mercato Traiano** as well; besides, there may be an exhibition going on, as there often is. Trajan's Market has the intimate fascination of ordinary places. It was a mall of 250 small shops on three levels where oil and wines, perfumes and shoes could be bought, and much of the original structure is well preserved. Beyond the Foro Traiano is the **Foro di Augusto** and then the **Foro di Nerva**—where two fine Corinthian capitals have been restored, above a relief of Minerva; the friezes tell the story of Minerva's jealousy of Arachne, when she heard the peasant girl could spin more beautiful garments. She slit the web Arachne had created, and Arachne hanged herself in shame. Repentant Minerva changed her into a spider, restoring her skill in spinning.

Returning to Mercato Traiano to leave, you'll see the Torre delle Milizie rising above it, part of what was the fortress of Gregory IX (pope 1227–1241). The dramatic, hilly streets that radiate from here, and around nearby piazza del Grillo (off via di Sant'Eufemia), are so Medieval in aspect they could be part of an Umbrian town, especially on Sunday when traffic is slow. The glimpses they afford of the forums through windows and arches and from parapets dramatize the ancient by contrasting the eras. From piazza del Grillo you can enter the Casa dei Cavalieri di Rodi, ancient seat of the crusading Order of St. John of Jerusalem. Go inside if it is open for the excellent view of ancient Rome from the loggia.

THE CENTRO STORICO

The Centro Storico, Rome's historic center, sometimes also called Old Rome, is the name traditionally given to the part of the city that occupies the bend of the Tiber across from the Vatican, where the Pantheon, piazza Navona, and a world of Renaissance palaces and piazzas, Baroque drama, and spacious courtyards unfold—sometimes gradually but often abruptly, seducing the senses.

Begin at the Palazzo Venezia, on the right corner of the via del Corso facing the Vittoriano, where the traffic is so frenetic that only nuns and mothers with small children (the only pedestrians for whom Roman drivers apply the brakes) dare cross. A traffic light eases some of the trauma, and once across you can weave a splendid path for yourself through streets that hold surprises even for those who tread their cobblestones daily. Most palaces along the way were created for noble families that numbered cardinals and one or even more popes among their members. The area was called the Campus Martius (Plain of Mars), taking its name from an altar to Mars that was once located here. After the second century B.C. it was the scene of athletic contests and military drills. The piazza Campo di Marzio is nearby.

Peek into courtyards and look up at building decorations and tiny shrines. The traffic in this area is dreadful, and you might consider walking through it on a Sunday. Shops will be closed then, but almost everything else on this walk will be open, including the churches, though you will have to stop just before or just after mass to find them open to nonworshipers. If you can hire a bicycle to sail the virtually car-free streets, so much the better.

Palazzo Venezia's crenellated, fortresslike mass was once the home of the Venetian Pope Paul II, but now it's better known for its balcony, at the center of the façade, from which Il Duce told Rome the Empire would rise again. Inside you sometimes can see his war room (Mappamondo). The museum in the palazzo has a good

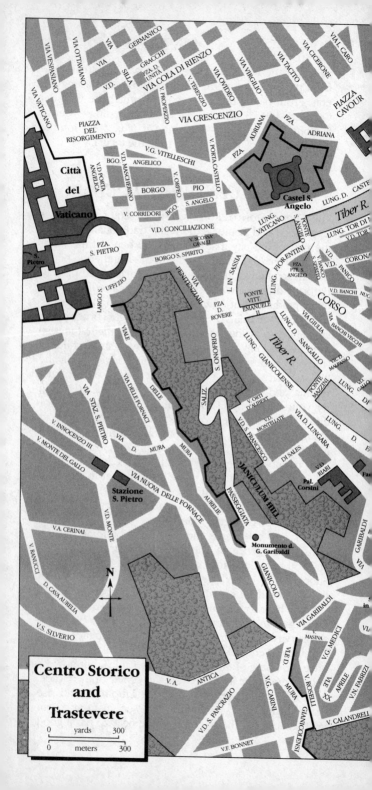

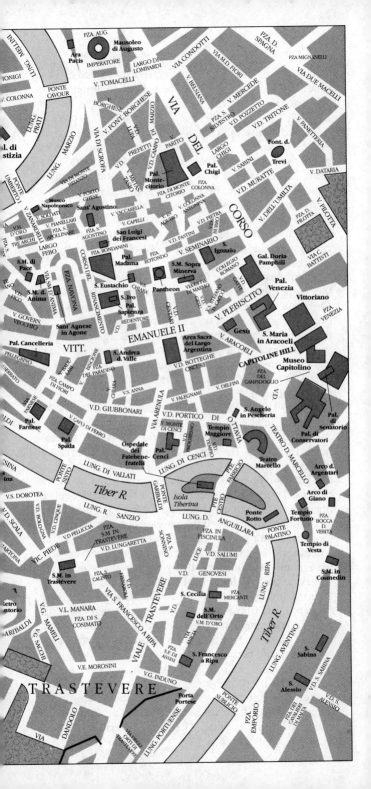

Medieval collection and hosts frequent shows and exhibitions. In 1564 the pope gave the palazzo to Rome as the Venetian Embassy, but now it belongs to the Italian Republic.

Tucked almost out of sight behind the palace is one of Rome's Byzantine jewels, the **Basilica of San Marco**. On its porch the popes once blessed the crowds as they do now from St. Peter's, but this small church usually escapes notice in a city where everything is grandiose.

The interior glows with mosaics and a coffered ceiling of blue and gold, with the heraldic crest and the crossed keys that always signify a pope. In the apse is a ninth-century mosaic of Pope Gregory IV offering Christ this church.

As you leave, notice the left side of the porch, where the large plaque at the bottom is the gravestone of Giovanna Catanei, called La Vannozza, mistress of Rodrigo Borgia when he was a cardinal and after he became Pope Alexander VI. Cesare and Lucrezia Borgia came into the world as a result of their union. The mystery is: How did the stone get here, since she actually was buried at the church of Santa Maria del Popolo, where she paid for the chapel herself?

Across via del Plebiscito is the **Palazzo Doria Pamphili**, still partly inhabited by the noble Doria family, whose anti-Fascist resistance during World War II is remembered by Italians. The Genoese admiral Andrea Doria is a prominent ancestor. Cross via del Plebiscito and follow the little street behind the palace around to its inner courtyard and the museum, which is well worth seeing not only for the paintings but also for the apartment tour, a rare opportunity to see the interior of a Roman palace. (You must wait for a small group to be assembled, but you can see the paintings in the meantime.) The paintings have numbers only, so you may want to buy a catalog.

Among the highlights of the collection are *Salome* by Titian, Caravaggio's *Penitent Magdalen* and *Rest on the Flight to Egypt* (the angel is superb but the gallery lighting isn't—it takes angling to see the painting without glare). Farther along is Parmigianino's *Adoration of the Shepherds;* then the bizarre *Olimpia Maidalchini,* whose less-than-sweet face, in a bust by Algardi, is found at the corner. The brother-in-law she bedeviled is around the corner: Innocent X, as seen in one of the greatest portraits in the world, by Velásquez, and also in a portrait by one who knew him better, Gianlorenzo Bernini. We owe much of the neighborhood to Innocent's forcefulness, until Olimpia cheated him out of all worldly goods, taking his last coin when he was on his deathbed, according to some reports. Notice also, in Room IV, the lunettes by the Carracci family and the *Flight into Egypt* by Annibale Carracci.

When you leave, follow the street in front, via di Piè di Marmo, past the large marble foot lying nonchalantly at the side of the street. If fabric shopping is on your itinerary turn left at via del Gesù to **Bises** at number 93, the 17th-century palace that has sold fine yard goods to Roman matrons for many years. The frescoed ceilings help maintain a remembrance of times past.

At the Gesù intersection, you see **piazza della Minerva** rearing its lovely obelisk, placed atop Bernini's small elephant. The elephant seems quite undisturbed by the size of the obelisk on his back; his trunk curls out cheerfully, like a horizontal bazaar snake. The obelisk was found near here and presumably came from the Temple of Isis that stood close by this spot. In fact, the marble foot may be the only remaining part of the figure of Isis. A nearby street called via Santo Stefano del Cacco was named for the god Anubis, who was mistaken for a type of monkey called *macacco,* which was shortened to *cacco.*

The **Church of Santa Maria sopra Minerva** has a plain façade that hides its considerable riches. It's one of the only ancient Gothic churches in Rome, and it stands on the site of a temple to Minerva, as the name says, to Isis, and Serapis—Egyptian religions having been brought to Rome when the Empire spread to Egypt. The first Christian church on the site was built during the eighth century, and much of the existing one dates from the 13th century—the work of Dominican brothers Fra Sisto and Fra Ristoro. As you advance along the impressive, dark right aisle, the first large chapel is the Aldobrandini crypt, where the parents of Clement VIII were laid to rest with a memorial by Giacomo Della Porta and Girolamo Rainaldi. At the transept is the delightful Carafa chapel, merrily frescoed with the life of Saint Thomas Aquinas painted by Filippino Lippi between 1488 and 1492.

To the right of the high altar is the Capranica chapel, with a *Virgin and Child* attributed to Fra Angelico. Beneath the altar is the crypt of Saint Catherine of Siena, the main patron saint of Italy and a Doctor of the Church. She lived near here and was instrumental in persuading the popes to return from their "Babylonian captivity" in Avignon. At the left is the tomb of the mystical Fra Angelico. Beyond is *Christ with the Cross* (1514–1521) by Michelangelo, apparently finished by another when the master found a flaw in the marble. Cardinal Bembo is buried at the altar (plaque in floor), as are Popes Leo X and Clement VII, in tombs sculpted by Sangallo the Younger. Works of art are clearly not lacking in this church; an inexpensive booklet is for sale here, detailing each of them, or take a look at the diagram near the entrance. Behind the altar you can see a small museum and rooms Saint Catherine occupied.

As you leave, notice the restaurant across the piazza—the Santa Chiara: **Archimede**, where you might return for *fiori di zucchini fritti* (fried zucchini flowers) and wonderful artichokes if in season. Their *tiramisù* is nicely frothy.

If shrimp and lobster sound good, go to nearby **Angoletto**, a relatively inexpensive trattoria with wonderful seafood and pasta. Their terrace is a pleasant retreat, even though the piazza Rondanini in front has become a car park for government officials and their friends from the nearby ministries. (A special permit is needed to park in the Centro Storico.) By night bureaucracy lifts and youth emerges, to linger, stylishly dressed, in the piazza sipping a drink that **Le Cornacchie** provided, or to wander down, drink in hand, to **Hemingway**, in piazza delle Coppelle.

The Pantheon

As you walk toward the right, the mass of the Pantheon seems to sit in wait for you, as it has for millions of admirers for centuries. Its massiveness is what seizes you first, then the grace of its columns and the piazza (piazza della Rotonda) that opens in front. The obelisk-topped fountain of wonderfully absurd faces spraying water, the students sitting at the base, the open windows—always someone leaning out—make this one of the loveliest piazzas in Rome for people watching while paying respects to the Pantheon, the best preserved of all Rome's ancient buildings. Have a drink or coffee at one of the cafés and savor the day.

Across the top of the Pantheon's façade you'll see the name Agrippa in the inscription, signifying the son-in-law of Augustus who built the original Pantheon (27 B.C.), which later burned down. The existing structure is the work of the ever-building Hadrian, and was begun in 118.

In 609 it was consecrated as a Christian church, having originally been a temple to all the gods.

You won't be prepared for the interior, because the outside gives little hint—and there is nothing like it in the world. The circular opening, way on top—with clouds passing some days, or even raindrops or an occasional snowflake—comes as a shock. The immensity of the round space so high above and the coffered ceiling around it are awe-inspiring. The tomb of Raphael, especially, and of the Italian kings Vittorio Emanuele II and Umberto I, are impressive, of course, but it is the space that hushes chattering visitors when they come through the door. In fact, it was the first building ever conceived as an interior space, aided by the use of concrete and cross vaults that allowed Roman architecture to soar.

Walk around the Pantheon to the left as you leave, until you see the stag's head and antlers of the church of Sant'Eustachio, the saint being the nobleman who converted to Christianity when hunting. His bow and arrow were aimed at the stag when suddenly Christ's face appeared in the antlers, according to the legend. Have coffee or cappuccino at the **Caffè Sant'Eustachio**, long considered by many the best in Rome, although the other coffee bar on the piazza allows you to move your table in sight of the swirling tower of Sant'Ivo, Borromini's masterpiece (see below). Coffee and deer heads are now so intimately mingled in the Roman psyche that one recalls the other, Pavlov fashion.

Continue to the right into via della Scrofa for two streets, to the **Church of San Luigi dei Francesi** (Saint Louis). You'll want to run inside to see the Caravaggios, but stop outside for a moment to see a bit of drollery. At the bottom right of the façade is a salamander that bears the head of François I of France. The salamander was his insignia, but in his version did not wear his face.

Inside, the Caravaggios are in the last chapel on the left. *The Vocation of Saint Matthew* glows with unreal light that hits each person in a different way, some to follow Christ, some to remain in shadow. *Saint Matthew's Martyrdom* is one of the most dramatic of his works in lighting effects. The plumed figure at the top left is thought to be the artist himself. *Saint Matthew and the Angel* was painted in 1602 and shows Matthew writing what the angel dictated.

Turn left from the church of San Luigi for two blocks, then left again to the **Church of Sant'Agostino** for Caravag-

gio's *Madonna di Loreto*. This painting was not at all what
was expected, because he used the poor and humble as
her supplicants instead of the usual rich patrons. The
model for the Madonna was a local woman who had
rejected a lawyer who sought her hand. The lawyer called
Caravaggio a "cursed ex-communicant" for painting her;
the artist wounded him with a sword and had to escape to
Genoa until things cooled down. Raphael painted the
Prophet Isaiah in fresco here after he had seen the Sistine
ceiling; the high altar is the work of Bernini.

From back at San Luigi it's a short walk south on via
della Scrofa to Sant'Ivo. Turn right into corso del Rinascimento, past the well-guarded Palazzo Madama, named for
Madama Margaret of Austria, illegitimate daughter of
Charles V, who married a Medici and then a Farnese. The
palace is now the Palazzo del Senato, named for the
government body whose traditions go back to the Curia
of the Forum.

While on the corso del Rinascimento stop at number 72,
Ai Monasteri, where honey from sweet-pea-frequenting
bees and anchorite elixirs for curing colds made by Car-
melites, Benedictines, and Trappists throughout Italy are
sold.

Just beyond, at number 101, is the Palazzo della Sapienza, whose Renaissance façade is the work of Della
Porta. Inside now are the state archives, but the reason to
enter is to see Borromini's tower and **Church of Sant'Ivo**
and the courtyard there that Borromini also designed. The
Barberini bees that have been worked into the design
indicate that a Barberini pope, Urban VIII, was the instiga-
tor. The courtyard is elegantly planned to lead the viewer
to the campanile's upward movement. The church, constructed from 1642 to 1660, is an intricate play of convex
and concave shapes inside, with a hint of the Rococo.
Borromini's search for geometric perfection as a spiritual
state comes close to fulfillment here.

Piazza Navona

Just across the street, behind a row of palaces, is piazza
Navona. The façades that grace the piazza make the owners of these buildings among Rome's most envied people.
The piazza is beautiful in all lights and moods: in early
morning when the street-sweepers swoosh through, and
by the golden light of sunset when shadows make casual
encounters seem dramatic. On Sunday it is still the village

piazza, with the entire family here to watch the youngest balance his first two-wheeler while papa hovers above him. Artists set out their paintings, Africans sell belts, pigeons swoop, and rendezvous are agreed on with the eyes.

Festivity has always characterized piazza Navona. In ancient Rome it often took the form of *naumachiae,* when the piazza was flooded to create a sea for real ships to play war in—but it was not play, and deaths were part of the "excitement." During this time the piazza was the stadium of Domitian, which accounts for its elongated shape. Athletic contests (*agone*) were frequent, and gave the name to the church facing the center, Sant'Agnese in Agone.

During the Renaissance the Pamphili family built a large palace (closed to the public) on the piazza, begun by Rainaldi and completed by Borromini, who also designed part of the adjoining Sant'Agnese church. Innocent X's sister-in-law Olimpia, who lived here, was called La Pimpaccia by local residents, a name to which many meanings have been ascribed, none of them favorable.

The Pope, wanting a symbol of his family to be indelibly imprinted on Rome, as well as to beautify the city, called in Bernini to create a monument, stipulating that an obelisk be fetched from the Circus Maximus to be part of the design. Bernini's fountain shows four rivers and their continents, each represented by a person. The head of the figure representing the Nile was covered to indicate that the source was then unknown, but Romans said it was because Bernini's statue couldn't bear to look at his rival Borromini's dreadful façade (on the church of Sant'Agnese). The Danube's outstretched arm, meant to connect the fountain visually with the façade, was said to be raised to ward off the church's imminent collapse. The Plate and the Ganges make up the rest of the four. Bernini himself, it's thought, finished the horse, rock, lion, and palm while working here in situ. His poetic use of realistic objects in an exuberant style has made the Fontana dei Fiumi (Fountain of the Rivers) symbolic of Rome itself.

The other two fountains in the piazza were finished by Bernini and his studio: Fontana del Moro con Tritone (the Moor) and Fontana del Nettuno (Neptune); the latter was largely rebuilt during the 19th century.

Inside the **Church of Sant'Agnese** is a bas-relief of Saint Agnes by Algardi, showing the miracle in which she was stripped naked in preparation for martyrdom, only to be covered immediately by her long, luxuriant hair, which suddenly grew to conceal her body from her persecutors.

Piazza Navona is the place to eat a creamy *tartufo* at **Tre Scalini**—so what if it's crowded with tourists; the tartufo and Bernini together are not to be scorned. **Mastrostefano**, the terrace restaurant on the piazza, is another good place to sit to observe the piazza life, and the food can be surprisingly good for such a major attraction location. Prints are found at **Nardecchia**, a 30-year-old institution at number 25. The finest of cameos and corals are to be found past Tre Scalini at **Giovanni Api**.

The streets off the western side of the piazza are fashionable with the young and trend-conscious. Wine bars and shops have sprung up, enlivening the area at night. Walk down to the north end of piazza Navona (on your right when facing Sant'Agnese), turn left to the church of Santa Maria dell'Anima, designed by Giuliano da Sangallo, past the charming, vine-covered Hotel Rafael—protected by *carabinieri* because of its government guests—to the lovely **Church of Santa Maria della Pace**. Be there just after 10:30 mass on Sunday to see the Raphael frescoes of the sibyls. If it's closed, the façade and the polygonal piazza are delightful anyway. But if the church is open, you also can see its cloisters, Bramante's earliest Roman creation.

So popular it's often overflowing, the **Pace Bar** on via dell'Anima is an old-fashioned, pleasant place to have an expensive drink. **Blue Lab Music** on nearby vicolo del Fico and **Music Inn** on largo dei Fiorentini (also nearby) are popular jazz spots.

One block north of Santa Maria della Pace is the merry **via dei Coronari**, which holds regular antiques fairs and is the antiques-sellers' street, often carpeted as if for royalty, festooned with flowers and banners. Paralleling the street to the north is the Medieval via dei Tre Archi, and all around for strolling are delightful streets near the bank of the Tiber.

Along the river at piazza di Ponte Umberto I is the **Museo Napoleonico**, with family portraits, the chaise on which Pauline reclined for her famous statue, now in the Museo Borghese (see below), and a Rome devoted to the time Napoléon "detained the popes" in France.

From here you can follow the via dell'Orso, the street of the bear, through its romantic meanderings. The **Hostaria dell'Orso** is as atmospheric a place as Rome offers—a Medieval hostelry where you can stop for a drink at the beautiful bar on the ground floor or for dinner upstairs (though the food does not match the decor in quality). At night the lights from the river make the window views softly romantic.

For lunch stop at **L'Orso '80**, at number 333, where freshly baked bread, an exceptional antipasto table, and grilled meats attract a stylish clientele. If unusual theater and movie posters and books for the devotee of these performing arts interest you, go to **Il Leuto** at via Monte Brianzo 86; they have a foreign mail-order business as well.

Continuing back to the *corso* you may want an ice cream at Rome's venerable *gelato* institution, **Giolitti**. If so, make a detour when you reach via degli Uffici del Vicario. The *semi-freddo* (partly frozen) varieties and fresh fruit flavors are sought after; in pastry the *bigne a zabaglione* (a cream puff bursting with Marsala-laced cream) is one of their rich favorites. Farther along the same street, the **Gelateria delle Palme** is a relative upstart favored by younger *gelato* addicts.

Via degli Uffici del Vicario leads to piazza di Montecitorio, where, in **Palazzo Montecitorio**, the lower house of parliament meets—thus the heavy security and milling journalists when congress is in session. The palace itself was completed by Fontana in 1634, as requested by the ubiquitous Pope Innocent X Pamphili. The back of the palace has one of the few Art Nouveau touches in Rome—the stairway and portal designed by Basile, the Sicilian master of Liberty style, as Art Nouveau is called in Italy.

The obelisk at the center of the piazza was brought to Rome by Augustus, according to Pliny in his *Natural History;* it is one of the 13 that remain out of the nearly 50 that once enhanced the cityscape.

At the far end of the piazza a short street leads to **piazza Colonna**, dominated by the **Palazzo Chigi**, where the cabinet offices of the government are located. The Chigi Palace was designed by Giacomo Della Porta in 1562 for the Aldobrandini family, but the famous Chigi family of banking interests bought it. During the 18th and 19th centuries this piazza was sufficiently off the beaten track for coffee to be roasted here in the open air; the scent was then considered disagreeable. The column for which the piazza is named will show you (if the scaffolding and tarpaulins are ever removed) the commemoration of the campaigns of Marcus Aurelius and his victory over the Germanic tribes. The emperor's statue at the top was replaced by one of Saint Paul in 1588.

For a grand finale to your walk, cross the via del Corso to the right of the arcaded Galleria and continue straight ahead until the rush of water tumbling over boulders tells you that the **Fontana di Trevi** is near. This Baroque version of a nymphaeum, bursting with gods and steeds, was just another fountain until Hollywood, with *Three Coins in the Fountain,* and Fellini, who splashed Anita Ekberg in it in *La Dolce Vita,* made it part of the standard itinerary. It's most magical at night when fewer tourist cameras are clicking. (Restoration is being carried on at present, and so you may find a dry fountain to toss your coins in.)

THE REAL ROMANS: CAMPO DEI FIORI TO TRASTEVERE

Baroque style was not appreciated until recently by North Americans, whose aesthetic schooling in Gothic and Renaissance styles caused them to be put off by the expansive emotionality that many Baroque artists used to convey their message. The essential quality of the Baroque, the drama that forces the spectator to become a participant, was gladly received by more expressive Latin cultures.

The Counter-Reformation, when the Roman Catholic church was attempting to draw back the parishioners who had strayed northward, was a time when popes commissioned artists, notably Bernini and Borromini, to seduce the viewer into the church's mysterious excitement. Façades waved convex and concave, statues gestured, putti cavorted over ceilings and dangled chubby legs from balustrade perches. What realism didn't accomplish, trompe l'oeil did. For a scholarly account of this relationship between religion and Baroque art, read Rudolf Wittkower's *Art and Architecture of the Baroque.*

No art form better expressed Italy's own vitality, and especially the exuberance of the land from Rome southward. To see Baroque at its most opulent, start at the church of Sant'Ignazio (Saint Ignatius, founder of the Jesuit movement) and continue to the Gesù, where he is buried. The contrast between today's Jesuits—sometimes condemned by the Vatican for leftist policies—and the priests who accumulated the Gesù's gold and precious stones is as dramatic as the art itself.

The **Church of Sant'Ignazio** is near the Palazzo Doria, on a piazza best appreciated on a car-free Sunday. Sit on the church steps and you will discover yourself on a stage, the center of attention of the palaces that curve around the piazza, whose waving convex and concave lines caused critics to call them "the bureaux"; the name spilled over into the tiny adjoining street, via del Burrò.

The church's visual impact starts with the façade, designed by the Jesuit Father Orazio Grassi, Algardi, and others, and financed by Cardinal Ludovisi, whose collection of antiquities is exhibited at the Museo Nazionale. Inside, a blaze of marble, stucco, and rich altar decorations set the tone. Algardi created several large statues for this church, but the pièce de résistance is the nave's vault, entirely frescoed by the Jesuit Andrea Pozzo, which shows Saint Ignatius's ascent into Paradise. Stand at the marble disc on the floor for the trompe l'oeil effect. (Baroque churches relied on viewer participation.)

The simple trattoria **Cave di Sant'Ignazio**, with an outdoor terrace on the piazza, is still a favorite with Romans at night, when the setting is even more scenic.

Several blocks south of the church is the via Plebiscito. Turn right into it and soon you will see the **Church of the Gesù**, whose opulence makes Sant'Ignazio seem stark. The façade was designed by Della Porta with Jesuit Father Valeriani. The church is the prototype for Counter-Reformation churches, with room for the congregation to hear the priest's address comfortably, and wide aisles for seating. The church design was by Vignola, for Cardinal Alessandro Farnese, and the idea was to lead the spectator into contact with the mystical by artistic means. According to Wittkower, "Confidence in the victory of Catholicism had never been expressed so vigorously in sculptural terms and with so much reliance on overpowering sensual effects."

At the chapel where Saint Ignatius is buried, Wittkower continues, "Unrivaled is the colorful opulence of the altar, its wealth of reliefs and statues; but a typically Late Baroque, diffuse, picturesque pattern replaces the dynamic unity of the High Baroque. In this setting one is apt to overlook the mediocre quality of the over-lifesize marble groups."

Father Pozzo again created a great ceiling in the chapel. The master of the quadrature painters, who treated entire ceilings as canvases, he organized the groups of heavenly participants by dark and light areas. Bernini's influence is seen here in the rays of light at the center, to which your eyes gravitate. There appears the monogram IHS, signifying the Name of Jesus, a subject for contemplation in Ignatian meditation. But not everyone saw it as mystical: The grand duke of Tuscany said it meant "*Iesuiti Habent Satis*"—"the Jesuits have enough."

Another story attached to the church is that of the devil and the wind. The two were out walking in Rome when they came upon this church. "Wait for me," said the devil, entering the Gesù. Since he never came out, the wind is still waiting, which explains why that corner is one of the windiest in Rome, and reveals one view of the Jesuits.

Continue along corso Vittorio Emanuele II to the **Area Sacra del Largo Argentina**, where some of Rome's oldest buildings, temples from the period of the Republic (fourth century B.C.), can be seen—in the traditional home of Rome's largest stray cat colony, whose benefactors are numerous. Continuing on the same street, on the left is where *Tosca* begins: the **Church of Sant'Andrea della Valle**, designed by Maderno but publicized by Puccini and Zeffirelli. Domenichino's contribution has been considerable: the frescoes of the *Life of Saint Andrew*. The dome is the next highest and largest to St. Peter's in the city. A recently canonized saint of the family of Tomasi di Lampedusa (the Leopard) is buried here to the right of the high altar. Along corso Vittorio Emanuele II, and off to the left on via Baullari (the trunkmakers' street), are the busy streets that surround piazza Campo dei Fiori.

The Campo dei Fiori Area

On sunny mornings there is no merrier market scene—a Medieval Covent Garden of cheeses and meats, fruits and flowers, greens and vegetables like none you've ever seen before, and all fresh from the fields, with the bakery **Il Forno** to provide fragrant bread and the **Enoteca Campo dei Fiori** for wine. A fixture is the knife sharpener who sharpens as he pedals a stationary unicycle, flicking the knife or scissors with calm assurance. On gray or stormy days the Campo is more fascinating and moody. Then the Middle Ages at their most intense permeate the atmosphere around the statue of Giordano Bruno, who was burned as a heretic in 1600. **Da Francesco** on the piazza is a good trattoria for lunch; the crowded Carbonara rests on its shaky old laurels. The **Grotte del Teatro di Pompeo** on via Biscione is a favorite in the evening for the stylishly light dishes and the pizza from their wood-fired oven.

To the north of the campo is the lovely Palazzo della Cancelleria, whose court with a double loggia is a Renaissance masterpiece that is thought to be partly the work of Bramante. (A glimpse through the gate may be all you'll get, though its hallowed halls ring with chamber music during the Christmas season.) To the southwest of the Campo, the next square is the **piazza Farnese**, reached from the via del Gallo. There stands one of the most influential of Renaissance palaces—it was reproduced all over Europe. The **Palazzo Farnese** was begun by Sangallo the Younger for Cardinal Alessandro Farnese, who would be Pope Paul III. Exactly what part Michelangelo played is disputed, but it appears that the central balcony, the cornice, and the third floor were his contribution. The palace is today the French Embassy; for admission, which may or may not be granted, apply to the French Cultural Attaché. The courtyard is sometimes open on Sunday mornings. While on the piazza, have a look at the tiles in the **Galleria Farnese** boutique. If you are antique hunting, stroll along the via Giulia, which runs parallel to the Tiber.

Continue along via di Monserrato southeast to the **Palazzo Spada**, in piazza Capo di Ferro. The piazza was designed by Francesco Borromini, who built a wall to screen the palace's resident, Cardinal Spada, from encircling eyes. Windows later broke the wall, however, and the fountain was replaced by a more modest one.

The palazzo's busy façade blends whimsy and artistry, depicting heroes of ancient Rome fêted with garlands of stucco. The palace was built about 1550, but Borromini wasn't called in until 1632. Because the Italian Council of State is the present occupant, access is not easily obtained, but the gallery and the garden are open. When you enter the courtyard—a fantasy of tritons, centaurs, and delicate garlands—stop at the custodian's corner office and ask him to show you the gardens (*giardini*) and the palace (*palazzo*). He often waits to assemble a small group—so you will know whether to stay there or to go into the gallery, which has regular hours.

The garden has a charming secret—a colonnade that leads to a life-size figure . . . but no, it's an illusion created by diminishing columns; the figure is only about a foot tall in reality. We owe this fancy to the Augustinian priest Giovanni Maria da Bitonto (1653), not, as was thought until recently, to Borromini.

If you can enter the palace, you'll see the statue of Pompey under which Caesar was murdered (or a reasonable facsimile thereof). It's the "dread statue" to which Byron addressed this question: "Have ye been victors of countless kings, or puppets of a scene?" Borromini's stairway, the Corridor of Bas-Reliefs, and the state rooms are appropriately impressive.

The gallery is interesting partly because it is housed in its original setting, four rooms of the cardinal's palace. Of the artworks note especially Titian's *Musician,* the *Visitation* by Andrea del Sarto, and a portrait of Cardinal Spada by Guido Reni.

The Ghetto and Isola Tiberina

From piazza Mattei, south of the largo Argentina, via Sant'Ambrogio leads south to **via del Portico d'Ottavia,** named after the monument at the end of the block to the left. Augustus rebuilt the second-century B.C. portico of Cecilius Metellus, which surrounded the temples to Jupiter and Juno, and created two libraries—one Greek and one Latin—dedicating the portico to his sister, Octavia. It became a fish market (*pescheria*) during the Middle Ages and houses the fishmongers' church, Sant'Angelo in Pescheria, named in the fishmongers' honor.

Today, via del Portico d'Ottavia is the main street of what was Rome's Jewish **Ghetto.** Formerly residents of Trastevere, the Jews of Rome moved to the Isola Tiberina following the pillage of Rome in 1084. Then, crossing over the ponte Fabricio (which was once known as the pons Iudeorum, or the Bridge of the Jews), they moved to the area next to the Portico d'Ottavia, ironically the very site where Vespasian and Titus had convened the senate the day Rome conquered Jerusalem. Paul IV officially confined the Jews to the Ghetto in 1555, and although much of it was razed in 1885 to destroy what had become a crowded and insalubrious district over the centuries, many of Rome's Jews chose to remain here. People still come to the area for its characteristic cuisine, which may be sampled at **Da Luciano** on the via del Portico d'Ottavia, or more expensively at **Piperno** on via del Monte dei Cenci. There is also an excellent pastry shop, Il Forno del Ghetto, at number 119 (try the cheesecake).

Another unfortunate site nearby is **Palazzo Cenci**, in piazza Cenci. Never a part of the Ghetto, the palazzo was the home of the bloody Cenci family. In a 16th-century scandal, the brutal and perverted Francesco Cenci was murdered by a killer hired by his wife and three of his 12 children. Although public opinion held that this was legitimate self-defense, his wife and daughter Beatrice were beheaded near the ponte Sant'Angelo, his son Giacomo was drawn and quartered, the other son was sentenced to life imprisonment, and the pope confiscated all the family property. The Cenci exploits inspired many literati, including Shelley and Antonin Artaud, and every year on the anniversary of their deaths a mass is celebrated for the repose of Beatrice's soul in the church of San Tommaso next to the palazzo.

One block away is lungotevere dei Cenci, where, to your left, is the Tempio Maggiore, Rome's synagogue. Built in 1904, it also houses a museum of Roman Jewish memorabilia. Across from it is the boat-shaped island called the **Isola Tiberina**, reached by ponte Fabricio, Rome's oldest bridge, which dates from 62 B.C. (Farther downstream may be seen the remains of the older ponte Rotto, or Broken Bridge, which collapsed in 1598, the year Francesco Cenci was murdered.) The Isola Tiberina was sacred to Aesculapius, the god of medicine, and had hospitals on it long before the present-day Ospedale dei Fatebenefratelli (literally, the do-good brothers). The island's history will soon be commemorated in a museum to be opened by the American journalist Milton Gendel, a longtime resident. Until then it is pleasant enough to stroll along its embankment, where many before you have continued the longstanding Roman tradition of graffiti with declarations of love. From Isola Tiberina the ponte Cestio leads south into Trastevere.

Trastevere

After walking through the ever-rushing center of the city, crossing the Tiber to Trastevere (tras TAY-var-ay) can be like entering a country town (after the speedway along the Tiber is bested; push buttons for lights are found about every 50 feet). Go to Trastevere late in the afternoon, when the light on the buildings glows rose and gold, and at night (money-belt-only zone). You can stroll through lanes where green tufts of grass from little cracks in thick-walled buildings sprout; tiny shrines are lit to the Madonna; the smell of fresh bread entices; artisans repair statues, sand tables, solder tin pots; children play in long smocks and dark stockings; fountain steps harbor meetings; and on enviable roof gardens the long arm of gentrification is seen. The people of Trastevere consider themselves the true Romans and have made little accommodation to the "foreigners" who have adopted their quarter, although they are warm and friendly by nature.

Start in the southern part of Trastevere at the **Church of Santa Cecilia in Trastevere**, whose large, tranquil courtyard is sought by local mothers watching their *bambini* taking first steps. Life was far from tranquil for Santa Cecilia, however, who lived in a patrician villa on the site (excavations have been made of her rooms below ground; entrance from inside the church). Her husband, Saint Valerian, was beheaded because, as a Christian, he refused to worship the Roman gods. Cecilia was locked in the steam room of her house, heated by a roaring fire; instead of dying, she was found singing in a heaven-sent shower. Three days of heat did not kill her, and even blows of an ax failed. By the time she died, hundreds had converted, inspired by her courage. Thus armed with the legends, enter the church to see her statue by Stefano Maderno at the high altar, a figure lying down with her head turned away, as she was when her sarcophagus in the catacombs was opened. On November 22 concerts honor her; and the Academy of Santa Cecilia in Rome, among the most prestigious of music academies, was named for her. During the late afternoon, you may hear the nuns sing mass from behind the grate.

In the nearby **piazza in Piscinula** (named for an ancient Roman bath) stands the 12th-century Palazzo Mattei (now private), once home of the family that reigned over this neighborhood in Medieval days with intrigue and murder. Though both acts were common in the Middle Ages, apparently the Mattei went too far and were thrown out of Trastevere. They landed on their feet, amassing a great fortune and a cluster of palazzi at piazza Mattei across the river, by the Fontana delle Tartarughe.

The spiritual side of the Middle Ages is also well represented at the piazza, with the church at the opposite side built above the house where Saint Benedict spent his childhood, and which he left to create one of the most widespread monastic organizations in the world. The tiny campanile (the smallest in Rome, with the oldest bell) can be seen to best advantage along via in Piscinula. Ceramics from all over Italy are beautifully displayed at the Centre d'Arte on via della Pelliccia, a good place for gift buying.

Stop at nearby via dei Genovesi 12 and ring for the *guardiano* to see the *chiostro,* one of the loveliest small cloisters in the city. Follow via Anicia south from via dei Genovesi, past the church of Santa Maria dell'Orto, with the odd little obelisks on its façade, to piazza San Francesco d'Assisi. Here the **Church of San Francesco a Ripa** shelters Bernini's statue of *Blessed Ludovica Albertoni,* strikingly similar to his more famous Saint Teresa. Bernini was in his seventies when he made this statue but was still in command of his formidable powers. The chapel is a domed space, strangely illuminated over the body of the saint lying in her final agony. Howard Hibbard, in his book *Bernini,* describes it in terms that recall a host of Baroque scenes in Rome: "The waves of draperies in front echo her position, their heaving billows reflect her agony, their colors accentuate her pallor... the chiaroscuro of this drapery and the diagonal of Ludovica's arms, broken by [the position of] her hands, create an almost symphonic treatment of physical suffering and death... the frieze of bursting pomegranates below the painting signifies the immortality to which her soul is passing."

A living Baroque scene takes place daily (except Sundays) at the produce market in **piazza San Cosimato**, across the viale di Trastevere (a major bus artery) from the church of San Francesco. If the market doesn't have something to entice you, the streets that surround it are likely to. On **via di San Francesco a Ripa**, which runs from piazza Santa Maria to San Francesco, you'll find freshly made mozzarella and ricotta, and banks of new cheeses to try, plus fresh bread, pizza squares, and pastries—the *bignè* (cream puffs) *con zabaglione* are rich with Marsala. On Sunday mornings the bakeries are open and filled with people seeking *sfogliatelle* (a Neapolitan transplant), the traditional *cornetti,* and their more sugary associates.

Come early (8:00 or 9:00 A.M.) on Sunday morning for the Porta Portese flea market, which extends for blocks and is filled with banks of sometimes interesting antiques, old books and prints, stacks of jeans and shoes, fresh coconut and raw fava beans (*fagioli*) to munch on, and a liberal assortment of pickpockets. Roman authorities would close the market, but the *populus Romanus* yells a resounding No. Stop first at the bakeries on via di Francesco a Ripa (above) for fresh *cornetti* and coffee to fortify you. After 11:00 A.M. only the crowd-loving need apply—it's the thing to do on Sundays for many Romans. The entrance where the "antique" dealers ply their trade, off via degli Orti di Trastevere, is the easiest. The section around Porta Portese, on the Tiber, is often mobbed by 11:00. (Remember that state museums are open Sunday mornings, however.)

From here to the famous **piazza Santa Maria in Trastevere** is only a short walk. The church of Santa Maria is enchanting, especially by night light, when the façade mosaics glisten. By day it's a mini–piazza Navona, with crowds of local residents and visitors, soccer games, and entangled lovers on the fountain steps.

The church's portico, embedded with ancient relics, was built by Carlo Fontana in 1702. Its campanile (restored) has surveyed the piazza since the 12th century. Although the church we see dates from then, it was erected over what is traditionally thought to be the oldest church (first century) in Rome dedicated to the Virgin Mary. Inside is a gilded ceiling designed by Domenichino; the wonderful polychrome marbles and mosaics sparkle above the Cosmatesque pavement. In the mosaic of the *Madonna with Christ,* a very real woman sits with her son's arm about her in touching tenderness.

Sabatini's on the piazza is a popular place to dine, especially for the view, or stop at **Noiantri**, another landmark nearby. The English-speaking (or -learning) crowd in Rome turns out in force at the Pasquino, a second-run movie house on vicolo del Piede. **Vicolo delle Cinque** to the north is an attractive old street of stylish boutiques and trattorias; **Mal di Mare** is currently popular. On via della Scala the **Pub della Scala** is the spot for jazz and drinks. Trastevere has several jazz clubs (Billie Holiday, Folkstudio, Big Mama) with American musicians in regular attendance. For a more elegant note, sit in the garden at the **Selarium** (just off via dei Fienaroli) and listen to live music. When it's late, the **Manuia** will follow up with Brazilian music and food, for a variation on Roman *cucina.*

Janiculum Hill

High above Trastevere to the northwest, and overlooking the Centro Storico on the other side of the river, the Gianicolo (Janiculum Hill) is frequently climbed (or driven) not only for the superb views of Rome it affords but also for the **Church of San Pietro in Montorio**, built over the spot west of Santa Maria in Trastevere where Saint Peter was once believed to have been crucified. In the courtyard is Bramante's lovely Tempietto, smug with Renaissance harmony. Beatrice Cenci is buried in the church, within sight of her place of execution.

If you walk farther west up via Garibaldi and then to the passeggiata del Gianicolo, you'll see the monument to Garibaldi, hero of a united Italy. The passeggiata continues past the statue of his wife, Anita, who fought and died at his side.

If you descend via Garibaldi almost to the river and turn left on via della Lungara Settimiana, you'll arrive at the **Palazzo Corsini**, which houses an impressive collection of masterworks of the Renaissance and beyond—Fra Angelico to Poussin. Across the street, the **Villa Farnesina** contains several rooms frescoed by Raphael with voluptuous and dramatic tales of the gods. (The two museums are open mornings only, so may be left to another day.)

CAPITOLINE HILL TO AVENTINE HILL

An exhilarating walk (mostly downhill) leads with very few street crossings from the piazza Venezia to the Tiber (stopping off at the Capitoline museums, Santa Maria d'Aracoeli, and piazza Bocca della Verità) and turns up the Aventine Hill, where the simple charms of early Christian basilicas are entwined with the scent of rose gardens and the orangery, exquisite in spring.

The monument to Vittorio Emanuele II, or the **Vittoriano**, as it is frequently called, has few redeeming features as architecture, and its never-darkening white marble in a city of apricot and honey tones is a shock. But to the Italian tourists who come to Rome to see their capital of only a little more than a century, it is a powerful image of unity and durability. The Tomba del Milite

Ignoto (Tomb of the Unknown Soldier) midway up the steps, guarded 24 hours a day by the military, adds to its nationalistic appeal. An oddity just in front on the left is a fragment of ancient wall—left there because, when the area was being razed for the monument, it proved to be the tomb of one Caius Publicius Bubulus, who died about 2,000 years ago. Since graves had to be outside the city limits, this provided a historical marker of the first century B.C. city walls.

Around to the right as you face the monument are the steep steps that lead to the Aracoeli church. These are suitable for penitents, but if you feel guilt-free you might opt for Michelangelo's Cordonata, the sloped staircase on the right that leads to the Capitoline Hill's summit and piazza del Campidoglio.

The **Church of Santa Maria d'Aracoeli** (pronounced *ara-chéli,* or *-shéli* in Roman dialect) was built on the site of an ancient temple to Juno Moneta (source of the word "money") and to Jupiter—a holy place above the Forum where every Roman offered sacrifices. The earliest church on the site dates from the sixth century. In the ninth century a Byzantine monastery occupied the hill, and the present basilica was built around that time. Saint Bernard of Siena lived here, and his life is celebrated inside in a series of frescoes by Pinturicchio. The flight of 124 steps was built by the architect Simone Andreozzi, in gratitude for being spared from the plague in 1348; the parishioners contributed the funds. The church's name, which translates as Saint Mary of Heaven's Altar, is derived from the 12th-century *Mirabilia,* which tells of the time when the emperor Augustus consulted the sibyl about a problem: The senate wanted to deify him, but that idea didn't appeal to Augustus as it had to his predecessor Julius Caesar. The sibyl prophesied that "from the sun will descend the king of future centuries." At that moment the Virgin Mary with the Christ Child in her arms descended from heaven and voices said to him: "This is the Virgin who will receive in her womb the Savior of the World—this is the altar of the Son of God." On that spot Augustus created the altar that was called the Ara Coeli. Later chroniclers mention the altar, which is now lost. A column in the church came from Augustus's bedroom in his palace on the Palatine hill. It's marked *a cubiculo Augustoranum* and stands third on the left in the nave.

The sumptuous ceiling of gilt-coffered panels was built to honor the victory at Lepanto, which ended the Turkish fleet's rule of the Mediterranean—the papal fleet had taken part in the rout.

Pinturicchio's frescoes of Saint Bernard, painted in 1486, are among the best examples of the artist's work. In the right transept is a Roman sarcophagus festooned with fruit and flowers. Across from it at left is the octagonal tomb of Saint Helen, mother of Constantine. The altar beneath her burial urn is what was thought to be the Ara Coeli but is instead a fine 13th-century work that depicts the miracle. Also in this transept is the tomb of the 13th-century Cardinal Matteo d'Acquasparta, an exceptional work by Arnolfo di Cambio.

In the sacristy, or in the left aisle, at Christmas, is the little gold- and gem-encrusted figure of the *Santissimo Bambino,* the Most Holy Child, whose intercession is still sought. Among the many legends of the Bambino is one of a very wealthy woman who was so ill she wanted desperately to keep the Bambino with her through the night. In the morning she felt better but decided she couldn't part with him and had a replica made to return to the church. One Medieval night, stormy to be sure, the monks at the church were aroused by a loud knocking at the outer door. It was the Bambino come to his rightful home. At Christmas every year, children come to the church and recite poetry to him; and Christmas Eve mass here is among the most festive celebrations in Rome.

Piazza del Campidoglio

The adjoining piazza del Campidoglio is one of the most pleasant places in Rome to sit, and especially so in the evening. The museums here are open certain weeknights and Saturday evenings. Though you may have to make do with a bit of curbing to sit on, the beauty of the piazza and the lack of cars make it exceptionally conducive to a respite. Since Michelangelo was the planner, this is not entirely surprising. Even the approach along the Cordonata alerts the senses to something out of the ordinary at the top.

The Campidoglio (Capitoline Hill) is the smallest of Rome's famous seven hills, but it is the most imposing because it was the spiritual and political center of the Roman world, since the Forum was built on its slope, and remains today the seat of the city government.

Although the equestrian statue of Marcus Aurelius has been removed for restoration, the dramatic if less bril-

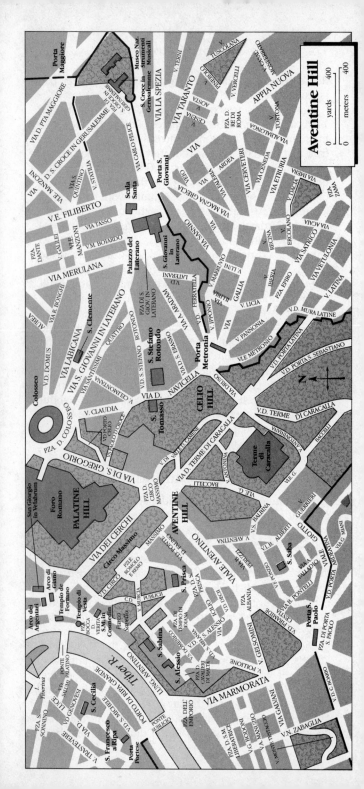

Aventine Hill

0   yards   400
0   meters   400

Porta Maggiore
Museo Naz. Strumenti Musicali
S. Croce in Gerusalemme
VIA LA SPEZIA
VIA TARANTO
APPIA NUOVA
VIA D. PTA MAGGIORE
D. S. CROCE IN GERUSALEMME
VIA CARLO FELICE
V. TUSCOLANA
V. TERNI
V. OTTOMENIA
V. VERCELLI
GRABERIMINOV
TESSOA
V. AOSTA
V. CESENA
PZA. D. RE DI ROMA
VIA ALBALONGA
VIA TORTONA
VIA MANZONI
V. S. QUINTINO
V. STATILIA
VLE. QUINTINO
V.E. FILIBERTO
VIA TASSO
V.M. BOIARDO
Scala Santa
Porta S. Giovanni
VIA
V. ARDEA
VIA CERVETERI
VIA MACENEDA
VIA ETRURIA
VIA DUCIA
VIA IMERA
PZA. ZAMA
VIA ACAIA
PZA. DANTE
V. GALLEI
VLE. MANZONI
Palazzo del Laterano
S. Giovanni in Laterano
VIA SANNIO
V. FALERIA
VERO
V. REGINA
VIA ERCOLANO
VIA SATRICO
VIA VETULONIA
VIA MERULANA
V. BONGHI
V. STEFANO ROTONDO
QUATTRO
VIA DI S. GIOVANNI IN LATERANO
V.D. LATERANI
V. FERRATELLA
V. TIPONIO
V. MARONNITO
V. LIJINI
V. BRITTI
V. GALLIA
V. LICIA
PZA. EPIRO
V. IBERIA
V. LATINA
ALTIERA
VIA LABICANA
S. Clemente
V.D. DOMUS
VIA SANTISSIMI
V.D.S. STEFANO
S. Stefano Rotondo
Porta Metronia
V. IPPONIO
V. PANNONIA
V.D. MURA LATINE
Colosseo
V. CELIMONTANA
V.D.
NAVICELLA
VIA D.
CELIO HILL
VLE METRONIO
V.D. PORTA LATINA
V. CLAUDIA
V.D. PORTO CELIO
S. Tommaso
V.D. VILLE CAMENE
VIA DRUSO
V.D. TERME DI CARACALLA
V.D. PORTA S. SEBASTIANO
PZA. D. COLOSSEO
V.D. PAOLO D'ERCE
Forto Romano
San Giorgio in Velabrum
PALATINE HILL
VIA DI S. GREGORIO
PZA. D. CIRCO MASSIMO
V.D. VILLE CAMENE
V.D. TERME DI CARACALLA
Terme di Caracalla
V. ANTONINIANA
VIA ANTONINA
V.D. TERME DI CARACALLA
VLE. G.
BACCELLI
V. GUERRIERI
Arco di Giano
Tempio di Fortuno
Tempio di Vesta
Arco dei Argentari
S.M. in Cosmedin
VERITA
BOCCA
Parco Savello
VIA DEI CERCHI
Circo Massimo
V.D. CIRCO
C.D.
V. MURCIA
PUBLICII
VIA AVENTINO
AVENTINE HILL
VIALE AVENTINO
V. AVENTINA
V.S. BALBINA
V.T.B. ALBERTI
GIOTTO
V.S. BALBINA
BACCELLI
VLE. G.
S. Saba
V. GUERRIERI
Fiberina
S. Cecilia
S. Michele
PORTO DI RIPA GRANDE
Tiber R.
S. Sabina
S. Alessio
V.D. CAVALIERI DI MALTA
PZA. DI TEMPIO DI DIANA
V.S. PRISCA
S. Prisca
PZA. D. S. PRISCA
VIA S. ALESSIO
V.D. DECII
VIA DI S. SABA
V. GALVANI
VIA MARMORATA
VIALE AVENTINO
V. MAZZINI
PZA. ALBANIA
V. POLLIONE
V. GELSOMINO
V. PALLADIO
VIA A. FONTELLI
V.D. PORTA ARDEATINA
S. Sabina
PONTE SUBLICIO
PZA. DELL' EMPORIO
V.G. BODONI
V.G. MANUTIO
PZA. S.M. LIBERATRICE
VIA GALVANI
PZA. DI PORTA S. PAOLO
Porta S. Paolo
V.D. PIRAMIDE
CESTIA
V.D. PORTA S. PAOLO
V.N. ZABAGLIA
V.D. C. CIAGOMO
MONTE TESTACCIO
PZA. S. SONNINO
S. Francesco a Ripa
Porta Portese
VIA DI RIPA GRANDE
VIA D. GENOVESI
VIA S. MICHELE
LUCE
VIA D. TRASTEVERE
PONTE PALATINO
PZA. DELLA BOCCA DELLA VERITA

liant statues of Castor and Pollux stand at the top of the steps. At the right is the **Palazzo dei Conservatori**, in which the Conservators' Palace Museum is found. Its courtyard is unmistakably Roman; the enormous head and hand of Constantine, and odds and ends of muscles from the statue that was in his basilica in the Forum, line the warm apricot walls of the court.

On the stairs is the figure of Charles of Anjou, whose ambitions were ended by the Sicilian Vespers revolt; it is the only Medieval portrait statue in Rome. In this extensive classical collection—the statues are mainly copies of Greek originals—the *Thorn Extractor* is notable, but the portrait busts from Augustus to Nero and Tiberius are the prizes. Here Roman art did not follow the Greek patterns but showed the rulers in unidealized portraits. The Etruscan bronze statue of the she-wolf, with the nursing twins, Remus and Romulus, that Pollaiuolo added, is here; its imprint is on everything in Rome, from state seals to sewer covers. The Museo Nuovo wing is devoted to the Renaissance: paintings by Bellini, the Carracci, Caravaggio, Lotto, Reni.

Directly across the piazza, in the Palazzo Nuovo, is the **Museo Capitolino**, where the ancient god Marforio lies in seductive indolence in the courtyard. His name is assumed—he's one of the "talking statues" to which verses were attached, usually satiric poems directed at the celebrities of the time.

Hadrian's villa at Tivoli was awash with splendid mosaics, and some of them are now here, in the Room of the Dove. The theme is Love: Eros and his Roman counterpart, Cupid, with Psyche and the Capitoline Venus. Among the fine statuary are the poignant *Dying Gaul;* the *Marble Faun* (a satyr figure attributed to Praxiteles, and the faun of Hawthorne's last novel); and the *Wounded Amazon* (copy), which was sculpted for a competition at Ephesus, where the cult of Diana thrived.

The remaining building on the piazza is the Palazzo del Senatorio, where the local government meets. In back of it splendid views of the Forum unfold (by night as well).

Toward the Aventine Hill

To the left a couple of blocks on the via del Teatro di Marcello, in front of piazza del Campidoglio, is the **Teatro di Marcello**, Julius Caesar's first contribution to the dramatic world (his second was made by Shakespeare). Its impressive if fragmentary current state is enhanced by the oddity of having apartments above. Known as the Palazzo Orsini, it is still inhabited by the Orsini family, who have the best view in Rome. (The stylish **Vecchia Roma** restaurant is close by, for lunch.)

Down via del Teatro di Marcello toward the Tiber, before piazza Bocca della Verità, stands the sturdy **Arco di Giano** (Arch of Janus), newly restored, in a valley (now behind a parking lot) where cattle dealers gathered in the days of the Empire, sheltering themselves inside the arch. On the far side of the arch is the delightful **Church of San Giorgio in Velabrum**, named for the marsh in which Romulus and Remus were found. (The Palatine Hill is just beyond.) The church often bears the red carpet that awaits a wedding party, presided over by 13th-century frescoes.

The beautifully sculpted arch adjoining the church has recently been restored, like many monuments in Rome. Called the **Arco degli Argentari** (Arch of the Money Lenders), it was erected in 204 in honor of Septimius Severus and his sons. And again, after Caracalla murdered his brother, Geta, he removed Geta's name from the arch, as on the Arch of Septimius Severus in the Forum. On the pilasters contemporary views of the Forum provide the background.

As you turn back toward the Tiber, across the broad boulevard is the exquisite, round marble **Tempio di Vesta**, (second century B.C.), really a temple to Hercules, some think, and the so-called **Tempio della Fortuna Virilis**.

At the end of the street is the Medieval **Church of Santa Maria in Cosmedin**, famous for the open mouth of truth, the *Bocca della Verità,* on the porch. Hordes of tourists wait in line to see if it will snap off their hand if they tell a lie. The face was a Medieval drain cover, but its appeal is not diminished by that knowledge. The sixth-century church was later enlarged and given to the colony of Greek refugees. The floor is a rare example of mosaics produced by the Cosmati themselves, most floors being only Cosmatesque; geometrical designs signal their work.

The Aventine Hill

Turn left at the corner by Santa Maria and walk to the next wide street, via del Circo Massimo. Across it, a winding road from the piazzale Romolo e Remo ascends the

Aventine Hill; by following it you'll see the loveliest rose gardens in Rome (in season) and the orange trees of the **Church of Santa Sabina**—and the view of Rome from the balustrade in the little Savello park by the church. The church is an elegant example of a fifth-century basilica, wonderfully lit by clerestory windows and impressive with Corinthian columns, but the drama is in its simplicity. In 1222 it was given to Saint Dominic, who was founding a new religious order, and the Dominicans still preside at the church. On the porch is a carved cypress door (under glass); the crucifix at the left top is apparently the oldest known representation of Christ on the Cross.

Continue southwest after Santa Sabina to **piazza dei Cavalieri di Malta**, a Piranesi-designed space most famous for the keyhole at number 3 that frames St. Peter's dome so beautifully. The Aventine is an obviously wealthy residential neighborhood (money belts, please), and it is a joy to stroll up and down its slopes, away from the hubbub of the city. If you have time, stop also at the ancient churches of Santa Prisca, built over a Mithraic temple (being excavated), and San' Saba, on the other side of piazza Albania to the southeast of the hill.

For lunch, go across via della Marmorata from the Aventine to the outskirts of **Testaccio**, an old neighborhood where the slaughterhouse once stood, and that is still famous for cooking innards. Wonderful vegetables are also a specialty of the inexpensive trattorias that dot the area. **Perilli** is a favorite on via della Marmorata, which leads from the ponte Sublicio to the Porta San Paolo, but stop first up the street at **Volpetti** (number 47) to see one of the most marvelous shops for cheese and other delicacies including a mortadella like no other. Try the very strong Pugliese *ricotta forte* and varieties of fresh mozzarella; tasting is encouraged.

ROME'S LEGACY OF FOREIGNERS

Begin one of your days in Rome early, at the **Museo Borghese** in the small palace of the **Villa Borghese** (not a villa but a large park built for Cardinal Scipione Borghese, the pleasure-loving nephew of Pope Paul V, on the Pincio Hill). Today the Villa Borghese, just north of the Spanish Steps/via Veneto area, is one of the greenest and most relaxing public places in Rome, a favorite spot for a picnic, a trip with the children to its modern zoo, or a promenade to its piazzale Napoleone I on the west side of the **Pincio** for a traditional view of Rome over piazza del Popolo.

For the purpose of this one early-morning visit, however, go primarily for the museum, where the cardinal amassed, by patronage and plunder, an extensive collection of paintings and sculpture. The display begins dramatically, if not scandalously, with the statue of Napoléon's sister Pauline, who, when she married Prince Camillo Borghese, commissioned it as a wedding present for him from Antonio Canova and insisted on posing as Venus, almost entirely in the nude. (When asked how she could have done so, she replied, "Oh, there was a stove in the studio," anticipating Marilyn Monroe's remark about having a radio on in similar circumstances.) Scipione Borghese was an early patron of Bernini, a number of whose most outstanding sculptures are on display here, including *David, Apollo and Daphne,* and *Pluto and Persephone.* Upstairs are such paintings as Raphael's *Deposition* (stolen from a church in Perugia by the cardinal), Caravaggio's *Sick Bacchus* and *Boy with a Basket of Fruit,* and a roomful of Venetian paintings, including Titian's Neoplatonic allegory *Sacred and Profane Love.*

From the museum it is a pleasant walk (or, perhaps better for scheduling your time, taxi ride) to Villa Giulia at the northwest corner of the park, which actually *is* a villa, housing the **Museo Nazionale di Villa Giulia**—a vast collection of the art of the mysterious Etruscans who once inhabited central Italy. Highlights include the *Apollo of Veii,* found in the excavations there, and the *Bride and Groom,* a sarcophagus depicting a dreamy-eyed, smiling couple reclining as if at a banquet, with an equality that shocked other ancient societies. Upstairs are attenuated bronze statues and other objects covered with drawings that, to our eyes, look strikingly modern.

If modern art is what interests you, go then to the **Galleria Nazionale d'Arte Moderna**, which you passed on your way from the Museo Borghese. It contains works of modern painters such as De Chirico, Boccioni, and Pistoletto, as well as some foreign works.

Piazza del Popolo Area

From Villa Giulia, ride or walk west to the ancient via Flaminia; turn south on it and you'll be entering Rome as travellers have traditionally done for centuries, through the grand gate called **Porta del Popolo** at piazza del Popolo. One such arrival was Queen Christina of Sweden, who converted to Catholicism and came to Rome in 1655, on the occasion of which Bernini decorated the inside of the great arch and Pope Alexander VII composed the arch's inscription: *Felici faustoque ingressui MDCLV.* Across the piazza are the twin churches of Santa Maria di Montesanto (on the left) and Santa Maria dei Miracoli (on the right), playful exercises in the art of illusionary design begun by Carlo Rainaldi. The church on the left is narrower than that on the right, so Rainaldi topped the left church with an oval dome and the right with a round one in order to make them look symmetrical, and they do.

Immediately to the left of the gate is the **Church of Santa Maria del Popolo**, which was constructed with funds from the *popolo* (people) and gives the piazza its name. It was built originally in the Middle Ages over what was thought to be Nero's grave, in order to exorcise his malign spirit. Best known for its two paintings by Caravaggio, *The Conversion of Saint Paul* and *The Martyrdom of Saint Peter,* it also contains the Cappella Chigi by Raphael and works by Pinturicchio, Annibale Carracci, Sebastiano del Piombo, and Bernini (who also was responsible for the restoration of the church). In the farthest chapel on the right is buried Giovanni, duke of Candia, the son of Pope Alexander VI, who probably was murdered by his brother, Cesare Borgia, in 1497; the gravestone of their infamous mother, La Vannozza, seems to have been moved to the portico of the Basilica di San Marco. At Christmastime, the adjacent former convent has an exhibition of *presepi,* or Nativity scenes, from throughout Italy.

Between the twin churches runs the renowned **via del Corso**, named after the horse races that were run during Carnival along its entire length between piazza del Popolo at the north and piazza Venezia and the Vittoriano at the south. To the left (looking south) is via del Babuino, (which leads to piazza di Spagna), and to the right is via di Ripetta. Either of the cafés at the beginning of these streets is a nice place to pause for some morning refreshment. Most evocative of the dolce vita era is **Canova**, on the left, since it is modern in style and popular with employees of the nearby Italian television office (RAI). **Rosati**, on the right, with its original Art Nouveau decor, comes alive at night, when it is frequented by slick young lotharios on the prowl in noisy sports cars and motorcycles.

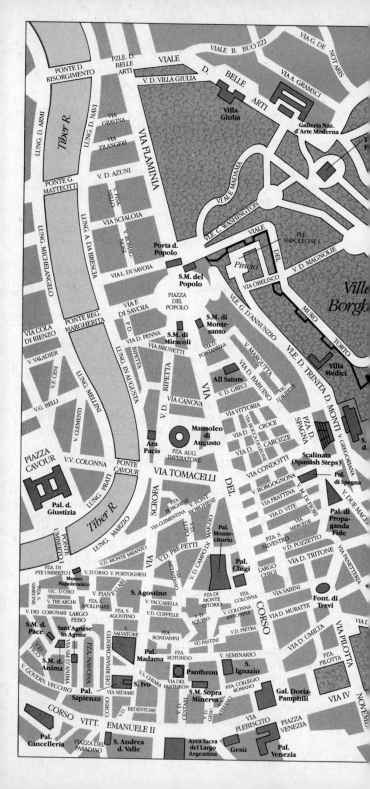

Piazza
del Popolo —
Via Veneto

0 yards 300

0 meters 300

N

ALDROVANDE
ULISSE

VIA P. RAIMONDI

VIA GIOVANNI PAISIELLO

OTHELLO

VIA PO

V. RASINTO

ADDA

VIA

V.D. UCCELLIERA

Museo
Borghese

VIA ALLEGRI

VIA SALARIA

D. V. ALBANI

VIA

d
di
io

V.D. CAV. MARINI

VONICA

V.D. MUSEO BORGHESE

PORTA PINCIANA

VIA PO

VIA ISONZO

VIA

SAVOIA

NIZZA

V. BRESCIA

VIA

D. P. PINCIANA

2

V.D.

TEVERE

VIA PIAVE

V. BERGAMO

PORTA PINCIANA

CORSO D'ITALIA

CORSO

D'ITALIA

VIA CAMPANIA

VIA LUCANA

Porta
Pia

VIA AURORA

VIA LUDOVISI

VIA SARDEGNA

V. MARCHE

VIA ROMAGNA

VIA

VIA CALABRIA

PZA.
SALLUSTIO

V. PALESTRO

PORTA PINCIANA

VIA BONCOMPAGNI

PIEMONTE

VIA GOITO

VIA VITTORIO VENETO

VIA XX SETTEMBRE

ita
nti

QUIRINALE
HILL

V. PURIFICAZIONE

V. SISTINA

S. Maria di
Concezione

VIA SALLUSTIANA

DA TOLENTINO

V.L. BISSOLATI

S.M. di
Vittoria

VIA FLAVIA

VIA CERNAIA

Museo
Nazionale
Romano

V.S. NICOLO

VIA BARBERINI

S.
Susanna

VIA VITT.
EMAN. ORLANDO

S.M.
Angeli

Terme di
Diocleziano

PZA.
BARBERINI

VIA AVIGNONESI

VIA RASELLA

Pal.
Barberini

VIA TORINO

PZA. D.
REPUBBLICA

VIA EINAUDI

Stazione di
Termini F.S.

VIA SCUDERIE

Pal. del
Quirinale

VIA DEL QUIRINALE

S. Carlino

S. Andrea al
Quirinale

VIA NAPOLI

VIA D. QUATTRO FONTANE

Teatro
d'Opera

VIA VIMINALE

PIAZZA DEI
CINQUECENTO

VIA G. GIOLITTI

ARIA

PZA. D.
QUIRINALE

VIA NAZIONALE

VIA
PALERMO

BALBO

CAVOUR

VIA F.

VIA GIOBERTI

TURATI

VIA XXIV MAGGIO

MILANO

V.D. BOSCHETTO

S. Pudenziana

VIA C.
VIA URBANA

PZA.
ESQUILINO

S. Maria
Maggiore

VIA C.
ALBERTO

VIA SERPENTI

VIA PANISPERNA

VIA

V.Q. CANTONI

V.D.
OLMATA

PZA. S.M.
MAGGIORE

S. Prassede

First follow the narrow **via di Ripetta**. For a look at the building where Antonio Canova's studio once was located, turn onto via Antonio Canova, the third street on the left. You'll find the studio on the right, a low building with bits of classical sculpture set into the apricot-colored façade, which also displays a bronze copy of a self-portrait bust of the artist.

Two streets ahead on via di Ripetta is the **Ara Pacis Augustae**, an altar finished in 9 B.C. to celebrate the Augustan peace, which not only brought peace to the Empire but ushered in the Augustan Age lauded by Vergil in the *Aeneid* and by other writers such as Livy, Ovid, and Horace. Much of the altar was rediscovered in Rome in the 1930s and transported to its present site, now covered with a protective piece of Fascist-era architecture. Missing segments were reclaimed from museums throughout the world or replicated.

On one side of the altar, Augustus walks first but remains, modestly, almost unseen in the procession. Sir Mortimer Wheeler wrote of the marble, "If we would understand the Augustan period—its quiet good manners and its undemonstrable confidence—in a single document, that document is the Ara Pacis Augustae." As a work of art it is brilliant, and as a portrait gallery it gives us an image of the Augustan *dramatis personae.* His daughter Julia (banished to the Tremiti Islands for her sexual exploits), and her husband, Agrippa, who built the Pantheon, are at the center. The scenes of everyday life here are superb: A child pulls at his mother's robe, and a woman silences a chattering couple with a finger to her lips. The child who wears the laurel crown would be grandfather to Nero. The floral motifs on the far side are some of the finest examples of decorative art in Roman times.

Across the street is the odd mound that is the **Mausoleum of Augustus**. Now stripped of its original travertine covering and obelisks, it was once counted among the most sacred places in Rome. Like Hadrian's tomb (Castel Sant'Angelo), it took the cylindrical Etruscan form, and Augustus's ashes and those of his family were buried within. At his funeral pyre, which was nearby, an eagle was released when the emperor's body was committed to the fire, symbolizing his immortal soul soaring to divine heights.

Continuing along via di Ripetta, the first piazza you will encounter is **piazza Borghese**. Here, in the morning, stalls

are filled with antique books and prints, often of high
quality and reasonably priced. From the piazza, via Clem-
entina and via Fontanella Borghese lead to the Corso,
across which begins via Condotti. Lined with designer
shops, **via Condotti** is Rome's most famous shopping
street, though the two streets parallel to it on the south—
via Borgognona and via Frattina—are lined with equally
luxurious shops. If you're interested in serious shopping
(see Shopping), avoid the area on a Saturday, when the
nearby Metro stop of piazza di Spagna disgorges hordes
of young people from the suburbs who look but don't
buy, much to the consternation of the owners of Gucci,
Ferragamo, Fendi, and other shops in the area. Via
Condotti goes straight to the Spanish Steps. Along the
way, peek into number 68, the palazzo where the Sovereign Military Order of the Knights of Malta has its headquarters. Granted extraterritorial rights by the Italian
state, it issues a limited number of passports and license
plates with its S.M.O.M. insignia. If the Vatican is the
world's smallest inhabited state, this is the only one entirely enclosed in a palazzo.

The Spanish Steps

Piazza di Spagna is in the shape of a butterfly, and without
doubt it is a steamy subtropical species. The tall palms
that greet you immediately and the languid crowds on the
steps are beautiful reminders of how balmy Rome really
can be. The piazza takes its name from the Palazzo di
Spagna at number 57, the Spanish Embassy to the Holy
See. Many other foreigners, however, have been active in
the area. The Spanish Steps (Scalinata della Trinità dei
Monti, in Italian), which rise in the middle of the piazza,
actually were paid for by the French to create an easier
access to the church of Trinità dei Monti, built by their
kings at the top of hill, and the piazza once was known
locally as piazza di Francia. The whole area, in fact, was
called *er ghetto del'Inglesi* by the Romans, assuming that
all foreigners were English, just as the Greeks before
them had referred to all outsiders as barbarians. Keats
lived and died in the house at number 26 piazza di
Spagna, and is commemorated with a death mask and
cases full of memorabilia (as are Shelley and Byron) in
the Keats-Shelley Memorial there, where you can purchase tiny volumes of the poets' works.

Goethe and Dickens also knew the Spanish Steps. In

his *Pictures from Italy,* Dickens described the characters of the day who went to the steps to hire themselves out as artists' models. "There is one old gentleman, with long hair and an immense beard," he writes, "who, to my knowledge, has gone through half the catalogue of the Royal Academy. This is the venerable, or patriarchical model." He then goes on to describe other colorful types who posed as "the *dolce far niente* model," "the assassin model," "the haughty or scornful model," and writes that "as to Domestic Happiness, and Holy Families, they should come very cheap, for there are lumps of them, all up the steps; and the cream of the thing, is, that they are all the falsest vagabonds in the world, especially made up for the purpose, and having no other counterparts in Rome or in any other part of the habitable globe." The theatricality of the Italian street scene is nothing new. These days, though, you're likely to encounter all sorts of vendors as you climb the steps, for amid the pots of azaleas in the spring and throughout the steps are the people selling crafts and offering modern-day Daisy Millers a coffee that turns out to be drugged, as the tale of her robbery will reveal in the next day's *Il Messaggero.*

You'll need some sustenance to scale the 137 steps, however. Fortunately, the historical presence of travellers and the piazza's contemporary guise as a center for luxury shops (increasingly affordable, it seems, only to Italians) have ensured a number of cafés and restaurants in the area. If you're feeling fancy, try **Ranieri's** on via Mario dei Fiori, a remnant from the Grand Tour days. Otherwise, **La Campana,** on vicolo della Campana, is a long-lived, typically Roman trattoria; on a nice day the pleasant outdoor courtyard of **Otello alla Concordia** on via della Croce is a fine spot for lunch. For a postprandial pickup, the old **Caffè Greco** on via Condotti has been offering coffee and other refreshment since the early 18th century. **Babington's,** to the left of the steps in the piazza, serves high-priced tea, and the bar at the Hotel D'Inghilterra serves as a watering hole for the elegant locals.

Or you may simply want a sip of water from the fountain called the Fontana della Barcaccia, at the base of the steps. Designed by Pietro Bernini, or possibly his son Gianlorenzo, it takes its shape from the boats that once came to the papal port of Ripetta, formerly nearby on the Tiber.

Before making your ascent up the steps, follow via del

Babuino off the piazza to the left. Turn right on vicolo d'Alibert to the charming **via Margutta**, lined with an open-air art show every spring and fall (and art galleries year-round), and double back at via della Fontanella to via del Babuino, where amid the elegant antiques shops you'll notice the statue of Silenus, dubbed by residents "the baboon" and giving the street its name. The Anglican church of All Saints is at number 153, and the English-language **Lion Bookshop** is at number 181. Cross piazza di Spagna to its southern triangle, where you'll see the column dedicated to the Immaculate Conception. Here each December 8 the pope crowns the statue of the Virgin with a garland of flowers; its height requires that the deed be performed by a member of Rome's trusty brigade from the ladder of a fire truck. The building behind the column is Palazzo di Propaganda Fide (Palace of the Propagation of the Faith), the missionary center of the Catholic world. Bernini and Borromini both worked on its façades, but not at the same time. The side facing the piazza is the work of Bernini, and his rival's concave façade is to the right.

Perhaps braced with another sip of water from the Fontana della Barcaccia, you're now ready to climb the delightfully curving travertine steps to Trinità dei Monti and views of the shoppers below. In honor of the Trinity, the staircase is divided into three landings; each in turn is divided into three. The French occupy not only the church but the adjacent **Villa Medici**, just to the left as you face the church, on viale della Trinità dei Monti. It was here that Louis XIV established the Académie de France and the Prix de Rome in 1666. French artists still come to study at the academy within, which also hosts important art exhibitions. The street eventually leads to the view from the Pincio, but come back at sunset to enjoy that at its best, preferably from the **Casina Valadier** café-restaurant. Now is the time to turn around and head down via Sistina to piazza Barberini and the beginning of via Veneto. The piazza's centerpiece, the Fontana del Tritone by Bernini, will be under restorers' wraps for a while, but at the corner of via Veneto is the (badly) restored Fontana delle Api (Fountain of the Bees), named after its numerous symbols of the Barberini family, who commissioned the work from Bernini. (The Palazzo Barberini here is the starting point of our Centuries of Christianity section below.)

Via Vittorio Veneto

The shady curves of via Vittorio Veneto recall the days when it was a cow path only a century ago but mask the more frenetic activity that has taken place there in recent years, most famously in the 1960s, when it was the center-piece for the extravagances of international film stars working at Rome's film studio, Cinecittà. The way of life was dubbed la dolce vita (the sweet life) and fictionalized by Fellini in a movie of the same name. Before musing on that time, however, stop into the **Church of Santa Maria della Concezione** for a memento mori about where the sweet life eventually leads. Its five chapels were deco-rated in bizarre Rococo patterns formed by the bones of some 4,000 Capuchin monks.

The heady climate of la dolce vita was described by Italian journalist Lieta Tornabuoni. "Rome fills up with American divas," she writes, "the most mythical and the most restless.

"They live in the grand hotels of the Via Veneto.... Their wealth, flamboyance, temperament, hard drinking habits, and professional courtesy amaze Italian film peo-ple and journalists but don't shock them.

"They require spoken English. They animate the nights with amorous or alcoholic squabbles and fake suicides; they nourish journalism and photojournalism.... In Rome, Audrey Hepburn will find a husband and Anita Ekberg will find success with Fellini. Liz Taylor falls in love with Burton and poisons herself. Ava Gardner and Anthony Franciosa fight to the death over Walter Chiari, Anthony Quinn changes wives, Sinatra comes to blows over a perfor-mance. Everybody buys everything, everyone drinks."

These days the climate is quieter, interrupted occasion-ally by the tension of terrorist incidents at the American Embassy or the nearby British Airways office, or the click-ing heels of the prostitutes who walk the street at night and the cars that screech to a halt to meet them. But the overall atmosphere is peaceful, and the street activity can be taken in slowly over refreshment at **Café de la Paix**, the best-known café from the days of the sweet life.

CENTURIES OF CHRISTIANITY

Ever mindful of museum hours, begin one day's tour on via delle Quattro Fontane at the entrance to **Palazzo**

Barberini. Begun in 1625 for Pope Urban VIII (Maffeo Barberini) by Carlo Maderno, construction of the palazzo was taken over by Borromini, who was responsible for the oval stairs on the right, and then by Bernini, who designed the central façade and the rectangular staircase on the left. The palazzo remained in the hands of the Barberini family for years. Among its tenants was the American sculptor William Story, who entertained the Brownings, Henry James, and Hans Christian Andersen in his apartments there. In 1949 it was sold to the Italian government and now houses the **Galleria Nazionale d'Arte Antica**, which is not a gallery of antique art at all. The gallery contains paintings by such artists as Fra Angelico, Filippo Lippi, Bronzino, Caravaggio, Tintoretto, and El Greco, as well as Raphael's recently restored portrait of *La Fornarina,* the baker's daughter who was his mistress. The sumptuous Baroque and Rococo decoration of the rooms, especially Pietro da Cortona's ceiling fresco *Allegory of Divine Providence* (note the ever-buzzing Barberini bees in the center) in the salon gives some idea of the splendor in which the popes lived.

Southeast up via delle Quattro Fontane, where it intersects via del Quirinale, are the four facing Baroque fountains for which the street is named. This is also the crossroads of the wide streets laid out under Sixtus V (1585–1590), with sweeping views leading to Porta Pia to the northeast, and to the obelisks of the Quirinal Hill to the southwest, the Esquiline Hill to the southeast, and Trinità dei Monti to the northwest.

On the far corner of via del Quirinale is Borromini's **Church of San Carlo alle Quattro Fontane**, known affectionately as San Carlino, with a lovely adjacent cloister. The geometric complexity of the church's interior provides an obvious contrast (and convenient comparison) to the interior of Bernini's **Church of Sant'Andrea al Quirinale** just down the street, which is relatively simple in spite of its rich marble and gilt decor.

Farther down the street is the **Palazzo del Quirinale**. Designed by Maderno, Bernini, and many others, it was formerly a summer residence of the popes, and later used by the kings of Italy. It is now occupied by the president of the republic. Its rich decoration by such artists as Melozzo da Forlì and Pietro da Cortona can be seen only by permission (write the Ufficio Intendenza della Presidenza della Repubblica, via della Dataria 96, 00187 Rome). No appointment is necessary, however, to

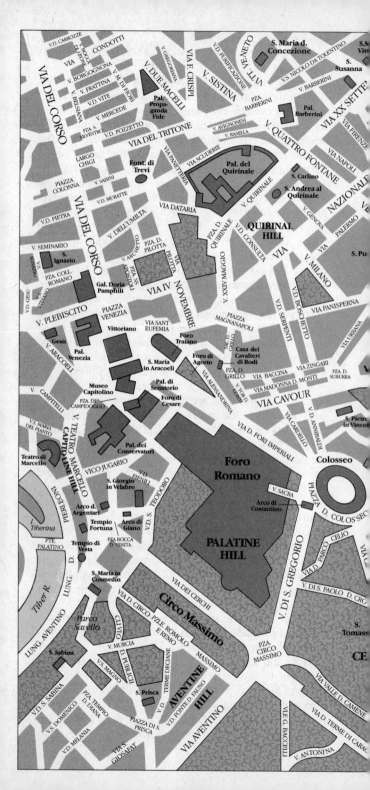

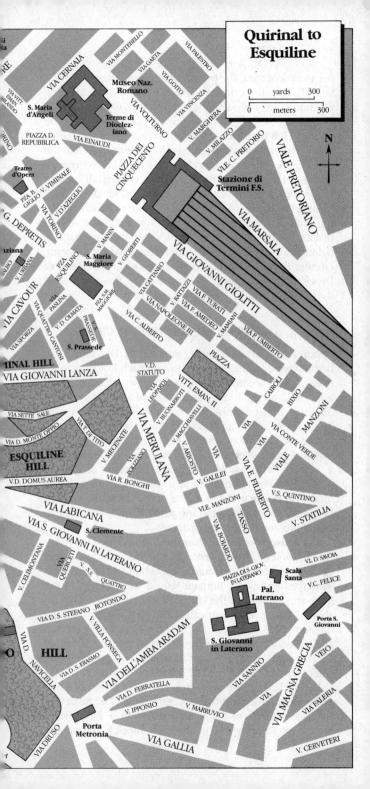

see the *corazzieri,* the presidential guard, all over six feet tall, dashing in crimson and blue uniforms, wearing gleaming boots and shining helmets with tossing plumes.

Take via della Consulta south off piazza del Quirinale and turn left on bustling via Nazionale (where you'll pass many places for a midmorning refreshment, as well as the neo-Gothic American church of St. Paul on the corner of via Napoli) to piazza della Repubblica, with its tall spray of water shooting out of the Fontana delle Naiadi, an 1885 bronze fountain by Alessandro Guerrieri of naiads cavorting with sea monsters. The piazza is commonly called piazza Esedra because the arcades of the two curving palaces around it are built where the *exedrae,* or semicircular benches, of the Terme di Diocleziano (Baths of Diocletian) once existed. (Coincidentally, the ring around the fountain is still a popular trysting place.)

Baths of Diocletian Area

Begun by Maximilian and completed by Diocletian, the baths (*terme*) were the largest of all such Roman institutions, able to accommodate 3,000 people and covering an area of 32 acres. Today, the church of Santa Maria degli Angeli is housed within the original Tepidarium. It was begun as a Carthusian church by Michelangelo, who converted the baths' vast central hall into the nave, but when Vanvitelli took over the design, he changed the nave into a transept. What has not changed is the sense of space, a uniquely Roman contribution to the course of architectural history. Near the entrance of the church is a statue by Jean-Antoine Houdon of Saint Bruno, the French founder of the Carthusian order.

The **Museo Nazionale Romano** (often closed for restoration), entered from piazza dei Cinquecento, forms part of this complex. Its extensive collection of antique art is displayed just as the Romans would have seen it, in the halls and gardens of the baths. Best known for the chair-shaped Greek sculpture called the *Ludovisi Throne,* the museum also contains a copy of the Greek sculptor Myron's *Discobolus,* the *Daughter of Niobe,* the *Venus of Cyrene,* and a bronze *Boxer,* as well as mosaics, frescoes, stuccos, and portrait busts of Roman patricians.

Before leaving the area, stop into the **Church of Santa Maria della Vittoria** on via XX Settembre. (The American Catholic church of Santa Susanna, with a magnificent façade by Maderno; is in the next block.) The simple interior of Santa Maria della Vittoria also was designed by Maderno in the Counter-Reformation style of the Gesù, and Bernini's theatrical Cappella Cornaro is Baroque at its most flamboyant. There, members of the Cornaro family are portrayed in marble as spectators in theater boxes to the statue of Saint Teresa of Avila, whose ecstasy seems decidedly secular. If her sensuality gets the best of you, cool off in front of the horned statue of Moses in the Fontana del Mose around the corner. The fountain was designed by Domenico Fontana, who allegedly died after seeing how badly his work compared to Michelangelo's statue of Moses in the church of San Pietro in Vincoli (see below), though the story is held to be apocryphal.

Better to sublimate your desires into lunch and take the five-minute taxi ride from piazza della Repubblica in front of the Terme di Diocleziano a few long blocks south to the simple setting of the restaurant **Cicilardone** at via Merulana 77. There you'll be able to sample the endless varieties of homemade pasta by ordering *assaggini,* or little tastes, and they go a long way. (A less expensive alternative would be to buy provisions at the boisterous food market in nearby piazza Vittorio.)

If you haven't already done so on your travels, give a passing glance to **Stazione di Termini**, the railroad station often overlooked in the context of the city's more venerable architecture. Begun under the Fascists, as the neo-Roman side sections show, the construction of the station unearthed part of a wall built after the invasion of the Gauls in 390, the ruins of which in front of the station provide a stark contrast to the sweeping travertine curve of the entrance.

Santa Maria Maggiore

From Cicilardone take via Merulana to the double-domed **Basilica of Santa Maria Maggiore**, one of the four so-called major basilicas of Rome, built on the Esquiline Hill. Many myths and legends surround the basilica, dedicated to the Virgin Mary after the Council of Ephesus in 431 affirmed that she was the mother of Christ. One of the most charming is that the Virgin appeared on this site on the night of August 4, 352, saying that her church should be built on an area she would cover—and did—with a snowfall the following morning. The event is commemorated each August 5 with a pontifical mass in the Cappella Borghese, accompanied by white flower-petal flurries from the dome of the chapel as well as much celebration in the piazza outdoors. (The chapel is also where the tiny coffin of Pauline Borghese lies.) The basilica preserves the relic (displayed each Christmas) of the Holy Crib in which the infant Jesus was laid, mentioned by Petrarch in a letter to Pope Clement VI in Avignon as one of Rome's sacred treasures, to lure the papacy back.

The basilica has a magnificent vaulted ceiling covered with what is supposedly the first gold to have arrived in Europe from the New World, but even more precious are its mosaics, best seen with binoculars. The nave mosaics contain scenes from the Old Testament; the triumphal-arch mosaics depict the infancy of Christ; and the apse mosaics illustrate the Coronation of the Virgin. In the afternoon it is also likely you'll find a sacristan to admit you to the oratory of the manger beneath the Cappella Sistina, which houses the remains of Arnolfo di Cambio's original 13th-century decoration.

Outside, notice the campanile, which is the tallest in Rome. Its bells are said to speak in Roman dialect. When they ring, try to make out the words *Avemo fatto li facioli, avemo fatto li facioli* (We made the beans). The bells of San Giovanni in Laterano then ask, *Con che? Con che?* (With what?), and Santa Croce in Geru-salemme responds, *Co' le codichelle, co' le codichelle* (With *cotechino* sausage).

Nearby are Santa Prassede and Santa Pudenziana, two early Christian churches dedicated to sister saints, the daughters of a Roman senator named Pudens, who was a Christian and a friend of Saint Peter. Off the piazza di Santa Maria Maggiore is the side entrance to the brick **Church of Santa Prassede**, on via Santa Prassede. The church was a *titulus,* a private residence where Christians were sheltered and rituals took place during the time of persecution. In the apse mosaics the sisters are being presented by Saints Peter and Paul to the Re-deemer, but the most spectacular Byzantine mosaics entirely cover the Cappella di San Zenone, which contains a column, brought from Jerusalem, on which the flagellation of Christ is believed to have taken place. Many relics are found in the church, among them a circular porphyry stone under which Santa Prassede is said to have placed the blood and bones of thousands of Christian martyrs.

On the other side of Santa Maria Maggiore, off piazza del Esquilino (with its obelisk that originally stood in front of the Mausoleo di Augusto), you'll find via Urbana, where the **Church of Santa Pudenziana** stands. Its apse contains one of the oldest mosaics in Rome, dating from the fourth century.

San Pietro in Vincoli Area

Follow via Urbana down the hill to piazza degli Zingari, then to piazza della Suburra, named after the most notorious district of ancient Rome—which today seems quite peaceful, even trendy, with restaurants and rents both rapidly on the rise. Taking the steps up to via Cavour (where you could slip into the **Enoteca** at number 313 for an afternoon refresher), cross the busy street and, on your right, locate the steep staircase to the church of San Pietro in Vincoli. The church preserves a relic said to be the chains (*vincoli*) that shackled Saint Peter during his imprisonment in Jerusalem as well as in Rome, but most people come here to see Michelangelo's statue of Moses. (The horns are an artistic convention meant to indicate the subject's status as a prophet.) The figure is part of Julius II's ill-fated tomb, originally intended for St. Peter's and supposed to contain some 40 statues but never finished; some of its statuary was dispersed to the Louvre and to Florence's Galleria dell'Accademia. The *Moses* was completed, however, and Vasari writes about how the Jews of Rome went there "like flocks of starlings, to visit and adore the statue." Many legends surround the statue: The mark on the knee supposedly comes from Michelangelo throwing his hammer at it, commanding it to speak.

Descend the Esquiline Hill on via degli Annibaldi and take the stairway that leads to piazza del Colosseo; around to your left, via San Giovanni in Laterano will bring you east to piazza di San Clemente. On the left is the fascinating **Basilica di San Clemente**, a three-level house of worship run by Irish Dominican brothers since the 17th century. Its upper level has a lovely 12th-century marble pavement by the Cosmati family, 12th-century mosaics, and 15th-century frescoes by Masolino da Panicale. Underneath, reached by the right aisle, is the lower church, which has frescoes dating from the ninth century. Beneath it, accessible at the end of the left aisle, are the remains of a first-century *domus* and third-century Mithraic temple, which has a bas-relief representing the sun god Mithras slaying a bull. And even farther below is another evocative phenomenon: If you listen carefully, you'll hear the Charonic sounds of an underground river, which leads to Rome's ancient Cloaca Maxima sewer.

San Giovanni in Laterano

Continuing along via San Giovanni in Laterano, lined with nondescript residential apartment buildings, you will soon come across another of the major basilicas of Rome, San Giovanni in Laterano. It is the cathedral church of Rome and the titular see of the pope as bishop of Rome; he usually celebrates Maundy Thursday services there. The basilica takes its name from the patrician family of Plautius Lateranus, whose huge estate on the site was confiscated by Nero but later was returned to the family and became the dowry of Fausta, wife of Constantine, who built the original basilica on the site. It subsequently underwent a series of disasters: a fifth-century sacking, a ninth-century earthquake, and a 14th-century fire; and the present church has more historical than aesthetic appeal. The original Palazzo del Laterano next to the church was the residence of the popes until they moved to Avignon, and many important events in the history of the church took place there, including the 1123 Diet of Worms. (The current palazzo dates from the 16th century and is the seat of the Rome vicariate.)

Today, you see an 18th-century façade on the church, crowned with gigantic statues of the saints surrounding Christ. Borromini designed the nave and aisles of the interior, which has a magnificent ceiling and statues of the apostles by followers of Bernini. Among the other sights of the church are a heavily restored fresco by Giotto in the Cappella Corsini; reliquaries containing the heads of Saints Peter and Paul and a piece of the table on which the Last Supper took place; and cloisters dating from the 13th century. The baptistery next door was built in the fifth century and is the only part of the complex remaining from its original incarnation.

The Scala Sancta, on the opposite side of the Palazzo del Laterano from the baptistery, contains the **Sancta Sanctorum**, the old private chapel of the popes, and, leading up to it, what are believed to be the steps Christ climbed in Pilate's house; today, the faithful still climb them on their knees.

Farther ahead, at the other end of via Carlo Felice, is the **Church of Santa Croce in Gerusalemme**, one of Rome's seven pilgrimage churches. It contains two 15th-century works of art worth stopping for—an apse fresco, *The Invention of the True Cross* (the church was built to house the relics of the True Cross brought back from Jerusalem: three pieces of wood, a nail, and two thorns from Christ's crown), and a mosaic in the Cappella di Santa Elena—as well as another lovely marble floor by the Cosmati. The **Museo Nazionale degli Strumenti Musicali** next to the church, at piazza di Santa Croce in Gerusalemme 9A, houses an impressive collection of musical instruments from ancient times to the 19th century.

It is unlikely that the Diet of Worms attracted one of Rome's best fish restaurants, **Cannavota**, to the area, but nevertheless you can find it back in piazza San Giovanni in Laterano near the obelisk—Rome's oldest, dating from the 15th century B.C.—and the restaurant is worth a dinner reservation. If you need to cast about beforehand, have a look at the colorful street market outside Porta San Giovanni in via Sannio, or check out the local branch of Italy's Coin department-store chain.

THE VATICAN

If all roads lead to Rome, they soon after lead across the Tiber to the Vatican. Since 1929, when Benito Mussolini and Cardinal Pietro Gasparri signed the Lateran Treaty between Italy and the Holy See, Vatican City—the seat of the Roman Catholic church and the cradle of all Christendom—has been an independent state ruled by the pope, the only absolute sovereign in Europe. The Vatican, as it is most commonly known, has its own flag and national anthem, mints its own coinage, prints its own postage stamps (many Romans even have more faith in its postal system than in Italy's, and go to the Vatican just to mail their letters), has its own polyglot daily newspaper (*L'Osservatore Romano*), Latin-language quarterly (*Acta Apostolicae Sedis*), and multilingual radio station. All these activities take place in an area just over 100 acres, a considerable part of which is taken up by St. Peter's, the world's greatest basilica in the world's smallest state. In addition to establishing the sovereign territory contained within the high walls of the Vatican, the Lateran Treaty granted special extraterritorial privileges to the churches of San Giovanni in Laterano, Santa Maria Maggiore, and San Paolo Fuori le Mura: Together with St. Peter's they constitute the four major basilicas of Rome.

Because of the limited opening times of many of the Vatican's attractions, you'll need careful planning to see the sights in the span of a day. *Begin early,* on Italian territory in piazza ponte Sant'Angelo across the Tiber from the Castello Sant'Angelo. You will be facing Rome's most beautiful bridge, the glorious ponte Sant'Angelo, which Bernini intended as the initial part of the approach he designed to St. Peter's. Statues of Saints Peter and Paul greet you as you walk over the Tiber, virtually escorted by the ten angel statues Bernini created to herald your visit.

Looming like a Medieval flying saucer over the other side of the Tiber is **Castello Sant'Angelo**. The ancient mausoleum of Hadrian, it was once landscaped, clad in travertine, covered with sculpture, and topped by a bronze statue of the emperor himself. In the Middle Ages it became part of the Aurelian Wall and, through a gate on the castle grounds called Porta San Pietro, became the main point of entry to the Vatican for religious pilgrims. It also has served as a refuge for the popes, who entered it through a private passageway from the Vatican, and as a prison. One of its illustrious captives was the Renaissance goldsmith Benvenuto Cellini, whose escape is one of the most gripping moments of the dashing life he recounted with bravura, if not braggadocio, in his *Autobiography.* Bypass the castle's grim displays of weapons and prisons and opt for the sumptuous papal apartments on the top floor. From there take the staircase that, after a display of military paraphernalia, leads to the terrace familiar from the last act of *Tosca,* from which the heroine jumped to her death in the Tiber. (The river is actually too far away from the castle for her to have done this, and it would be physically impossible even for the sinewy-legged boys who play soccer on the landscaped moat below, where she most likely would have landed.) The terrace has one of the best views of Rome and offers a close-up of Peter Anton Verschaffelt's recently restored 18th-century bronze statue of the Archangel Saint Michael, commemorating Pope Gregory the Great's vision during the plague year of 590, when Saint Michael appeared over Hadrian's tomb, sheathing his sword, an act that signified the end of the plague and gave the castle its name.

In Bernini's day, a walk down the narrow Medieval streets from Castello Sant'Angelo directly west through the area known as the Borgo led to the delightful surprise of his expansive piazza at St. Peter's. Now, however, the grandiose **via della Conciliazione**, named after the Lat-

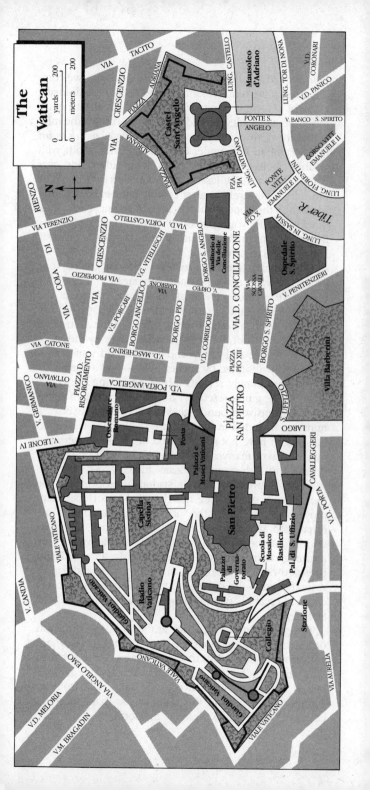

The Vatican

yards 200
meters 200

N

VIA TACITO
VIA CRESCENZIO
VIA ADRIANA
PIAZZA ADRIANA
VIA RIENZO
VIA TERENZIO
VIA COLA DI RIENZO
VIA CRESCENZIO
VIA PROPERZIO
VIA CATONE
VIA OTTAVIANO
PIAZZA D. OTTAVIANO
VIA GERMANICO
V. LEONE IV
V. CANDIA
V.D. MELORIA
V.D. ANGELO EMO
V.M. BRAGADIN

Castel Sant'Angelo

Mausoleo d'Adriano
LUNG. CASTELLO
LUNG. TOR DI NONA
V.D. PANICO
V.D. CORONARI
PONTE S. ANGELO
V. BANCO S. SPIRITO
CORSO VITT. EMANUELE II
LUNG. FIORENTINI
PONTE VITT. EMANUELE II
LUNG. VATICANO
Tiber R.
LUNG. IN SASSIA
VIA PIO X
PZA PIA

VIA D. PORTA CASTELLO
VIA G. VITELLESCHI
BORGO S. ANGELO
V. ORFEO
V. OMBRONE
BORGO PIO
BORGO ANGELICO
V.S. PORCARI
V.D. MASCHERINO
BORGO PIO
V.D. CORRIDORI
V.D. PORTA ANGELICA
BORGO S. SPIRITO
V. PENITENZIERI
V. SCOSSA CAVALLI

Auditorio di Via della Conciliazione
VIA D. CONCILIAZIONE
PIAZZA PIO XII
Ospedale S. Spirito
Villa Barberini

PIAZZA SAN PIETRO
Osservatore Romano
Posta
Palazzi e Musei Vaticani
Capella Sistina
Radio Vaticano
Giardini Vaticano
Palazzo di Governatorato
San Pietro
Scuola di Massaico Basilica
Pal. di S. Uffizio
V.D. PORTA CAVALLEGGERI
LARGO S. UFFIZIO
Collegio
Stazione
Giardini Vaticano
VIALE VATICANO
VIA AURELIA
VIALE VATICANO

eran accord, has ludicrously overextended the welcoming arms of Bernini's colonnade and ruined the dramatic element of turning into piazza San Pietro. In all fairness, a monumental boulevard had been planned since the middle of the 15th century; it was unfortunate that *domani* finally came in 1936 under Fascism. The wide swath, with double obelisks goose-stepping along either side, was completed in 1950, just in time for a Holy Year (they officially occur every quarter century but can be declared as often as the pope wishes, as seen in recent years). Walk quickly, and fix your gaze on St. Peter's. Head straight for the tourist information office in the colonnade on your left as you face St. Peter's.

The **Vatican Gardens** are now open to guided tour groups only, so make the most of your time if not your money (the price of admission to most things at the Vatican is lofty) and get to the office by at least 10:00 A.M. to sign up for the daily tour. It begins at the Arco delle Campane (Arch of the Bells), watched over by the Swiss Guards, whose red-yellow-and-blue striped uniforms—supposedly designed by Michelangelo—add a playful air to the increasingly serious job of protecting the pope. From there, guides escort visitors to a number of sights on the extensive grounds, given an occasional assist by a minibus. Included in the tour are sights most visitors to the Vatican have not seen—**Circo di Nerone**, where the first Christian martyrs (including Saint Peter) met their deaths; the 18th-century mosaic studio, which still sells stones as souvenirs; the train station (used primarily for the delivery of duty-free merchandise to fortunate employees and friends of the Vatican); the Palazzo del Governatorato, where the governor has his office; the radio station; and the prison. The most pleasant part of the tour is the gardens themselves, meticulously groomed and presided over by cypresses, umbrella pines, and—most magnificently—the only good views of the largest brick dome in creation, part of Michelangelo's original plan for St. Peter's.

The garden tour ends back at the tourist information office, and whether or not you've gone on it, this is where you should take the bus to a side entrance of the Vatican Museums. The bus also goes back through the gardens and is a pleasant alternative to the long walk from St. Peter's Square around the walls to the main museum entrance on the viale Vaticano to the north.

The Vatican Museums

The Vatican Museums have become so crowded that the authorities have come up with four color-coded tours to impose order. The only one that covers all the important sights is the yellow tour, which supposedly lasts five hours, but by following the yellow route and stopping only at the highlights listed below you can cut that time in half. (In general—check the exceptions—the museums close at 2:00 P.M. and on Sundays.)

The Egyptian Museum. Head straight for Room V, where the most impressive relics are the colossal granite statue of Queen Tuia, mother of Ramses II, and the sandstone head of Pharaoh Menuhotep across from it. Before leaving the room, peek through the door into the outdoor niche, which contains the giant bronze fir cone found near the Thermae of Agrippa, to which Dante compared the giant's face ("just as wide as St. Peter's cone in Rome") in the *Inferno* (XXXI, 58).

Chiaramonti Museum. Rather than dwelling on any single works of art here, take a look at the display, which was laid out in the early 19th century by Neoclassical sculptor Antonio Canova. If you can't resist lingering just a little, concentrate on the realistically human portrait busts of ancient Romans.

Pio-Clementine Museum. Two of the most celebrated antique sculptures in the world are exhibited in Room VIII. The undisputed star is the *Laocoön,* described by Pliny the Elder as "a work to be preferred to all that the arts of painting and sculpture have produced." The first original Greek work of art to be discovered in Rome (it was unearthed in 1506 on the Esquiline Hill), it depicts a passage from the *Aeneid* in which Vergil describes the wrath the gods released on the priest Laocoön for warning the Trojans about the horse, by sending two serpents to destroy him and his two sons. In the same room is another famous work, the *Apollo Belvedere* (a Roman copy of a fourth-century B.C. Greek statue once displayed in the Agora in Athens), which influenced Canova's nearby Perseus. Other highlights of this museum are the *Apollo Sauroktonos* (Room V), the *Cnidian Venus* (Room VII), the *Belvedere Torso,* so much preferred by the Romantics and Pre-Raphaelites to the Apollo Belvedere (Room III), the *Jupiter of Otricoli* (Room II), and the sarcophagi of Helen and Constantia (Room I).

Gregorian-Etruscan Museum. Highlights here are the Etruscan Regolini-Galassi Tomb (Room II) and *Mars of Todi* (Room III), the Greek *Head of Athena* and funerary stele (Room of Greek Originals), and the Greek amphora of *Achilles and Ajax Playing Morra* (Room XII).

Raphael Stanze. These four rooms were the official apartments of Julius II, who commissioned frescoes from Raphael, the masterpiece of which is *The School of Athens.* According to tradition it contains portraits of Leonardo as Plato, Michelangelo as Heraclitus, and Raphael himself as the figure in the dark cap second from the extreme right.

The Borgia Apartments. Here, Alexander VI had Pinturicchio paint frescoes, of which the richly decorated Room of the Saints is considered the major work.

Sistine Chapel. The Japanese have financed the restoration of the ceiling of the most famous single section of the Vatican Museums, work that will continue through 1992. Much of Michelangelo's ecstasy is covered by scaffolding, and the Vatican management has seen to it that an agonizing alarm goes off when the noise reaches a level they deem inappropriate to the sanctum built under Sixtus V—and still the scene of the conclaves held to elect the pope. One happy result of the painstaking approach, however, is that placards have been set up throughout the chapel, explaining the complex arrangement of the biblical scenes depicted by Michelangelo and the many other artists who were active here.

The Vatican Library. Two paintings predominate here, the Greek Odyssey landscape series and the Roman *Aldobrandini Wedding,* and temporary exhibits display the wonders of the library's rare book and manuscript collection.

Pinacoteca. Paintings by Giotto, Melozzo da Forlì, Raphael, Bellini, Reni, Domenichino, and Poussin here will delight the retina still capable of retaining anything after having taken in the rest of the museums.

Before leaving, have a look at the museum gift shop, which, among its many reproductions and religious articles, sells men's ties patterned with papal coats of arms.

The sin of gluttony is not exactly catered to around the Vatican. However, take via del Pellegrino from the museum exit to **Borgo Pio,** the east-west street parallel to via Corridori/via Borgo to the north, where you'll find a number of prim little restaurants, the nicest of which is probably **Marcello.** It has tables in a vine-covered courtyard during the warmer months, and, like its neighbors, it serves a standard Italian menu.

St. Peter's Square

After lunch, return to the immense oval of St. Peter's Square, which can now be enjoyed at a leisurely pace without having to worry about the pearly gates of the morning's attractions slamming shut. At noon on Sundays Pope John Paul II gives a blessing from his window in the Apostolic Palace, the second from the right on the top floor. At variable times on Wednesday mornings he holds an audience. In the summer it takes place in the piazza until the pope moves to his summer residence at Castel Gandolfo (see the Rome Day Trips chapter). In the winter the audience is held in the new audience hall designed by Pier Luigi Nervi in 1971, for which permission must be received by writing to the Prefect of the Pontifical Household, Città del Vaticano, 00120 Rome, or applied for in advance in person at the bronze door to the right of the piazza.

On audience days the square is filled with religious pilgrims, often grouped together and carrying banners announcing their places of origin. Even at other times the square is bustling with large-scale activity, as befits a monumental space. Tight phalanxes of black-clad nuns and priests scuttle back and forth on official Vatican business. Schoolteachers lead groups of their uniformed charges and try to distract them from the grandeur with lectures. Fatigued tourists squint at the immensity of the piazza and the façade of St. Peter's. And the occasional self-contained honeymoon couple from the provinces wanders dazed toward the basilica. Keeping watch upon it all are the 140 stone saints above Bernini's colonnade and the 13 giant statues over the façade of St. Peter's. For aerial variation, flocks of pigeons swoop freely to and fro, and if you're especially fortunate, it's all topped off by the colossal clusters of cumulus clouds that God seems to have designed especially for Baroque Rome.

The focal point of Bernini's oval piazza is the obelisk at the center, originally from Alexandria, where it had been erected by Augustus, and brought to Rome by Caligula. Not until much later was it erected on its present site; in 1586, chroniclers tell us, 900 men, 140 horses, and 44 winches accomplished the feat. Another account tells of a Ligurian sailor who, defying the papal order to remain silent during the dangerous enterprise, saw that the ropes were about to give out and cried, *"Aigua ae corde!"* an admonition to wet the ropes. He thus saved the day and Pope Sixtus V not only spared his life but rewarded him by starting the tradition of supplying the palms for Palm Sunday from his native port of Bordighera. Apocryphal as the tale may be, it is a charming example of the innumerable legends that surround the Vatican.

On either side of the obelisk shoot the jets of two Baroque fountains, and between the two fountains and the colonnades is a circle of black marble in the pavement. If the squealing schoolchildren will allow you to stand on it, look toward the colonnade and you'll see the four rows of columns blend magically into one.

St. Peter's Basilica

Built under Constantine on the site of the tomb of Saint Peter, the original St. Peter's basilica, constructed in 326, was a sumptuous early Christian edifice almost as large as the present one. When the basilica began showing signs of age, the popes decided to build a new one and appointed a succession of architects to supervise the project. Bramante, Raphael, Sangallo, Michelangelo, and others were involved at one point or another, and their designs alternately called for Greek- and Latin-cross plans. Michelangelo's design for a Greek cross and dome was being carried out at the time of his death in 1564, but under Paul V it was decided to extend the front portion to conform to the outlines of Constantine's original basilica. This unfortunately makes Michelangelo's dome appear to sink as you approach the entrance, although it is the glory of the Roman skyline from elsewhere in the city. Carlo Maderno designed the façade and portico (where Giotto's *Navicella* ceiling mosaic from the old basilica was installed) in an early Baroque style.

As you step inside (you will not be admitted wearing shorts, skirts above the knees, or sleeveless dresses—St. Peter's dress code is stricter than Lutèce's or Claridge's, but the ambiance is worth it), the effect is as dazzling as was intended. Perfect proportions mask the vastness of St. Peter's, but spotting the minuscule forms of other visitors beneath the gigantic statues, or a look at the comparative lengths of other European churches—traced in metal on the floor of the nave—confirm its enormous size. The immensity of history is also immediately present at the round porphyry slab set into the pavement in front of the central door: On this stone, on Christmas in the year 800, Leo III crowned the kneeling Charlemagne the first emperor of the Holy Roman Empire.

In the first chapel on the right, Michelangelo's *Pietà* stands behind the glass erected after the sculpture was assaulted in 1972. At the right end of the nave is Arnolfo di Cambio's bronze statue of *St. Peter Enthroned,* its foot worn by the touches and kisses of the faithful over the centuries. Over the high altar soars Bernini's gilded bronze *baldacchino,* its four fluted columns spiraling up to support a canopy crowned by an orb and cross a hundred feet from the floor. Be sure to note the more down-to-earth, human dimension of the carvings of a woman's features in the marble pedestals that support the columns; the facial expressions become progressively more contorted, culminating in the smiling visage of a newborn infant. Legend has it that Pope Urban VII asked Bernini to add the sequence in gratitude for his favorite niece's surviving a difficult childbirth.

Bernini was entrusted with the decoration of the interior of St. Peter's, and his works abound throughout. In the apse behind the *baldacchino* is his reliquary of the throne of Saint Peter, topped by a stained-glass representation of the Holy Spirit. His tomb of Alexander VII in the passage leading to the left transept is but one highlight among many magnificent monuments in the church by other artists. The Treasury, reached from the left aisle near the transept, houses a valuable collection of sacred relics. Room III contains Pollaiuolo's tomb of Sixtus IV.

Back near Arnolfo's statue of Saint Peter is the entrance to the Vatican Grottoes, a dimly lit church containing a number of chapels and tombs. Beneath them (visitable, again, by written permission from the Prefect of the Pontifical Household) are the famous excavations of what is held to be the original tomb of Saint Peter, where in the 1940s an ancient crypt containing bones and the remains of a garment fitting the description of Saint Peter's were discovered by archaeologists.

For a final survey of your visit to the Vatican, take the elevator at the front of the left aisle for a walk on the roof. Inspired souls may then continue up the 537 steps to the lantern for a last inspirational view of the Vatican, Rome, the Alban Hills, and the surrounding blessed countryside.

GETTING AROUND

International flights generally land at Leonardo da Vinci airport in Fiumicino, about 30 km (20 miles) southwest of Rome. Taxis are available at the airport, as are regularly scheduled buses that take you to the Stazione di Termini railroad station in Rome, from which you can get a taxi to your hotel. Bus tickets can be purchased inside the airport terminal.

Ciampino airport, about 16 km (10 miles) southeast of the city, is used mainly by charter flights. ACOTRAL buses provide service to the Cinecittà metro stop, from which you can take the subway to Rome, but unless you know the system, taxis are your best bet.

Be forewarned that you will be charged about double what the meter reads when coming in from the airport, a total of about 50,000 lire from Fiumicino.

International (and most national) trains arrive at Rome's central station, Stazione di Termini, from which you can take taxis, buses, or the subway (*Metropolitana*).

Though construction of Rome's subway line often screeches to a halt when digging unearths some ancient relic, the *Metropolitana* (marked by a large M at the entrances) connects many of Rome's main tourist sights. Tickets may be purchased with exact change, in coins only, in the subway stations. Some tobacconists, newsstands, and bars also sell subway and bus tickets.

Rome's bus system is extensive, and various types of tickets—and a valuable map—are available at the ATAC booth in piazza dei Cinquecento across from Stazione di Termini. (Telephone information is available by dialing 4695.) If you buy the week-long tourist pass, you have the advantage of entering the bus from the front during crowded rush hours; watch your belongings. Tickets for single rides are also available at most tobacconists, newsstands, and bars. With these tickets you must enter from the back of the bus and put the ticket into a machine that stamps it. The same applies to the city's more limited tram service. The main office of ACOTRAL, which serves the surrounding area, is at via del Telegrafisti 44; Tel: 575-31. Surburban cities also are serviced by trains from Stazione di Termini.

Taxis are found at numerous stands throughout the city, or may be called by dialing 3570, 3875, 4994, or 8433. There are numerous extra charges, such as for baggage, night service, and holidays, but the additional fee should never be more than a few thousand lire.

ACCOMMODATIONS

"We were well accommodated with three handsome bedrooms, dining room, larder, stable, and kitchen, at twenty crowns a month," wrote Montaigne's secretary of their lodgings in Rome in 1580. "The inns are generally furnished a little better than in Paris, since they have a great deal of gilt leather, with which the lodgings of a certain class are upholstered. We could have had lodging at the same price upholstered with cloth of gold and silk, like that of kings. But Monsieur de Montaigne thought that this magnificence was not only useless but also troublesome on account of the care required by this furniture, for each bed was worth four or five hundred crowns."

Then as now, lodgings in Rome range from the simple and efficient to the unabashedly luxurious, for the city has a tradition of taking care of strangers that goes back to the days when Greeks and Romans first exchanged visits, giving rise to the word *ospite,* which means both guest and host, and is the root of our word hospitality.

Most Roman hotels are conveniently clustered into neighborhoods, so you can choose accordingly. The Centro Storico (Old Rome) area offers proximity to major monuments; Villa Borghese affords welcome glimpses of green park; piazza di Spagna is close to Rome's most elegant shops; via Vittorio Veneto has the city's highest concentration of luxury hotels and an active nightlife; and the area near Termini (the train station) is convenient for those travelling with lots of luggage or who need to come and go in a hurry. Hotels in other areas also have advantages described below.

(The telephone area code for Rome is 06; omit the 0 when dialing from outside the country.)

Centro Storico

The service is as plain and efficient as the decor at the **Bologna**, but the moderate price and large number of single rooms near the center of town, convenient to both piazza Navona and the Pantheon, make it a popular choice for lone travellers.

Via di Santa Chiara 4/a, 00186; Tel: 656-89-51; Telex: 621124.

Montaigne would have felt right at home at the expensive **Cardinal**, appropriately decorated in red fabrics with a heavy touch of leather. Housed in a palazzo attributed to Bramante on Rome's most famous Renaissance street (the rooms on the upper floors have great views of the whole Renaissance quarter), the hotel possesses antiques that include cardinals' chairs donated by the Vatican and huge stones from the Forum, taken in the days when the site was considered a quarry and now displayed behind the bar.

Via Giulia 62, 00186; Tel: 654-27-19; Telex: 612373.

Stendhal, Mazzini, and Garibaldi were all once guests at the **Cesari**, and although it hasn't changed on the outside, the inside of this moderately priced hotel has been modernized and provides a quiet respite from the bustle of the nearby via del Corso or the lively activity at the hotel's bar.

Via di Pietra 89/a, 00186; Tel: 679-23-86.

The 150-year-old **Portoghesi**, located in one of Rome's priciest neighborhoods for hotels, is small and inexpensive, and recent efforts to update it have hardly touched the slightly bohemian atmosphere. Depending on your point of view, the service is laissez-faire or lackadaisical.

Via dei Portoghesi 1, 00186; Tel: 656-42-31.

Discretion is the rule at the vine-covered **Raphael**, a favorite of Italian politicians long before Prime Minister Bettino Craxi made his home here because of its proximity to the Italian parliament. The lobby, an interior decorator's dream, blends antiques with modern marble, and though the rooms are small, the views from the upper floors are quite expansive—and expensive.

Largo Febo 2, 00180; Tel: 65-08-81; Telex: 622396.

Dating from 1493, **Sole al Pantheon** is considered the oldest hotel in Rome; its façade displays plaques attesting to the stays here of Ariosto (author of *Orlando Furioso*) in 1513 and Pietro Mascagni (composer of *Cavalleria Rusticana*) in 1890. Opening the shutters on to Western architecture's most venerated monument—the Pantheon— would be worth any price to many, but the fact that the rooms are moderately priced, and were recently renovated, makes it all the more appealing.

Via del Pantheon 63, 00186; Tel: 678-04-41; Telex: 622649.

Conveniently located near piazza Navona and on the busy main route to the Vatican, the moderately priced **Tiziano**, housed in a Renaissance palazzo, has just been refurbished to include phones and the like. Avoid the traffic noise by requesting a room in the back.

Corso Vittorio Emanuele 110, 00186; Tel: 687-50-87.

Villa Borghese

The **Eden** is located in the chic Ludovisi area off via Veneto, and is one of the best values in the luxury price range, with views of more green per lira than any hotel in Rome. Built at the turn of the century, the hotel has been given a facelift that leaves guests with a choice of antique or modern accommodations, and its roof-garden bar and restaurant is a favorite Roman rendezvous spot (see the Dining and Nightlife sections).

Via Ludovisi 49, 00187; Tel: 474-35-51; Telex: 610567; in U.S., (212) 838-3110 or (800) 223-6800; in U.K., (800) 181-123.

For a view of the green expanses of the Villa Borghese (albeit jaundiced by the gold-tinted windows), try the **Jolly**, a somewhat expensive modern hotel convenient to both the park and via Veneto.

Corso d'Italia 1, 00198; Tel: 8495; Telex: 612293.

Also near both the Villa Borghese and via Veneto is the **Golden Residence**, which offers modern accommodations at a more modest price, and each room comes equipped with heating, air conditioning, mini-bar, telephone, and radio.

Via Marche 84, 00187; Tel: 49-37-46.

Perhaps because of its past as a house of ill repute, the luxury-class **Valadier** has some of the largest bathrooms in Rome. Located just below Pincio Hill, the Art Nouveau villa also has spacious rooms and lounges.

Via della Fontanella 15, 00187; Tel: 361-05-92; Telex: 610506.

Marvelous views of the park may be had from the upper floors and roof garden of the **Victoria**, on the via Veneto side of the Villa Borghese. Its facilities are chic and modern, and are among the few in Rome with good services for the handicapped.

Via Campania 41, 00187; Tel: 47-39-31; Telex: 610212.

Piazza di Spagna

The moderately priced **Carriage** is named after the street where the touring carriages of yesteryear used to stop for repairs. That atmosphere is preserved in this small, moderately priced hotel furnished in antique style with modern bathrooms. The nicest rooms are clustered around a terrace on the top floor.

Via delle Carrozze 36, 00187; Tel: 679-51-66; Telex: 625487.

Rooms with views of the surrounding area may also be had at **Condotti**, located just off Rome's chic-est shopping street. Accommodations are rather mannered, but what you spend on leather goods you'll save on shoe leather and on the bill in this establishment.

Via Mario dei Fiori 37, 00187; Tel: 679-46-61; Telex: 611217.

With its Oriental rugs, crystal chandeliers, and marble tables, the **Hotel De La Ville** is for many the quintessence of Old World charm, and you pay for it. Located at the top of the Spanish Steps close to the Hassler, its upper floors and roof garden (which recently began serving Sunday brunch) share the same views as its even more expensive counterpart, while lower rooms overlook a central courtyard.

Via Sistina 69, 00187; Tel: 6733; Telex: 620836.

The now pricey **D'Inghilterra** was a refuge for writers (Henry James, Mark Twain, Anatole France, Ernest Hemingway), musicians (Franz Liszt, Felix Mendelssohn), and royalty (the king of Portugal) in Rome for over a century. Its recent renovation placed it beyond most writers' means. Whether or not you're a guest (and if you are, request an upper room with a terrace and a view), its bar makes a refreshing stopover while shopping the streets in the nearby via Condotti area.

Via Bocca di Leone 14, 00187; Tel: 67-21-61; Telex: 614552.

The small and stylish **Gregoriana** was decorated by Erté, and the rooms bear his anthropomorphic letters rather than numbers. Located in the area at the top of the Spanish Steps in a former convent on the architecturally appealing street of Rome's *haute couture* houses (and take a look at the amusingly grotesque palazzo façade at number 30), the 19-room hotel does not take credit cards.

Via Gregoriana 18, 00187; Tel: 679-42-69.

The sumptuous **Hassler–Villa Medici** is the preferred hotel of many of Rome's most distinguished visitors, from American presidents to movie stars, whose presence seems to have given it an air of prewar luxury travel reminiscent of an ocean liner. Firmly moored at the top of the Spanish Steps, it is crowned with one of the city's most elegant restaurants, which recently began serving Sunday brunch. At these prices, ask for a room with a view of the city or the gardens behind the hotel. No credit cards accepted.

Piazza Trinità dei Monti 6, 00187; Tel: 678-26-51; Telex: 610208; in U.S., (212) 838-3110 or (800) 223-6800; in U.K., (800) 181-123.

A reasonably priced alternative for those who want to stay in the neighborhood is **King**, just down the street from the Hassler. Its sparsely decorated rooms are comfortable, and the rooftop terrace has more of those wonderful views.

Via Sistina 131, 00187; Tel: 474-15-15; Telex: 626246.

Another reasonably priced hotel in the area (nearer piazza del Popolo) is **Margutta**, decorated in bold colors that reflect the artistic spirit of the nearby street from which it takes its name. Two of its 21 rooms are on the roof, and come with fireplaces and terrace.

Via Laurina 34, 00187; Tel: 679-84-40.

Reflecting its name, the **Suisse** is efficiently run with a charming roof terrace characteristic of the area and a clientele loyal enough (and rates low enough) to require reservations well in advance.

Via Gregoriana 56, 00187; Tel: 678-36-49.

Reservations are also required for the moderately priced **Scalanita di Spagna**, opposite the Hassler at the top of the Spanish Steps, and sharing those gorgeous views. It too has a roof terrace for even better views to go with your breakfast.

Piazza Trinità dei Monti 17, 00187; Tel: 679-30-06.

Via Vittorio Veneto

At the low end of Rome's smartest street for a hotel address, the **Alexandra** is at the high end of the moderate price range. Like the street, its lobby and rooms are large and have seen better days, but its location makes it convenient both to the dolce vita and the Spanish Steps.

Via Vittorio Veneto 18, 00187; Tel: 46-19-43; Telex: 622655.

Opposite the American Embassy, the **Ambasciatori Palace** offers large and luxurious accommodations in a modern setting, and has a lively bar popular with embassy types and their guests, as well as one of the better restaurants if you happen to be in the vicinity, the **ABC Grill Bar**.

Via Vittorio Veneto 70, 00187; Tel: 474-93; Telex: 610241.

Despite its monotonous modern marble façade, the **Bernini Bristol**, at the foot of via Veneto, has luxurious rooms furnished in a modern style reminiscent of the dolce vita days. All rooms are soundproofed to keep out the constant traffic noise, and the ones on the upper floors, like the roof terrace, have pleasant views of the surrounding area.

Piazza Barberini 23, 00187; Tel: 46-30-51; Telex: 610554; in U.S., (212) 838-3110 or (800) 223-6800; in U.K., (800) 181-123.

The **Excelsior** excelled as the residence of Liz Taylor and Hollywood stars during the dolce vita era, and its roomy, luxurious suites and well-appointed rooms, recently redecorated in the French Empire style characteristic of the CIGA hotel chain, once again live up to the hotel's glorious past.

Via Vittorio Veneto 125, 00187; Tel: 4708; Telex: 610232; in U.S., (212) 935-9540 or (800) 221-2340; in U.K., (01) 930-4147.

Offering the most conservative service of the via Veneto hotels, **Flora** has Old World decor to match. Its location just inside the Aurelian Wall on the other side of Villa Borghese gives the upper floors great views of the park.

Via Vittoria Veneto 191, 00187; Tel: 49-78-21; Telex: 622256.

One of the few moderately priced hotels in the area, the **Oxford** has functional and modern decor, a bar, and a reasonably priced restaurant—all of which make it popular with North Americans.

Via Boncompagni 89, 00187; Tel: 475-68-52; Telex: 614387.

Another favorite spot for North American visitors, but slightly more expensive, the **Savoia** is a modern hotel equipped with large rooms, bar, and restaurant.

Via Ludovisi 15, 00187; Tel: 474-41-41; Telex: 611339.

Quirinal

The name of the **Anglo-Americano** has served to draw a proper Anglophone clientele to its modern facilities, an upholsterer's apotheosis. Set next to Palazzo Barberini, its rear rooms face the palazzo's gardens.

Via delle Quattro Fontane 12, 00184; Tel: 47-29-41; Telex: 626147.

Originally built during the Renaissance with material taken from the nearby Imperial and Roman forums, the luxurious **Forum** overlooks both sites in a setting that transcends time, and a meal in its roof restaurant is one of the most relaxing ways of appreciating ancient and contemporary Rome with an enchanting view of its namesake.

Via Tor de' Conti 25, 00184; Tel: 679-24-46; Telex: 622549.

The smallish **Quattro Fontane** is a favorite with Italian businessmen, who appreciate its central location, modern facilities (not all the rooms have baths, but those that do would meet the most demanding Milanese design standards), and moderate price.

Via delle Quattro Fontane 149/a, 00184; Tel: 475-49-36.

The expensive **Quirinale** was designed by Achille Sfondrini, the architect of the adjacent Teatro dell'Opera and the passageway that leads to it from the hotel lobby. Its rooms are modern, and the ones that face the garden are the preference of its substantially North American clientele. Verdi's sojourn here in 1893 for the premiere of *Falstaff* set the stage for the hotel's bar as a popular place for a drink before a night at the opera.

Via Nazionale 7, 00184; Tel: 4707; Telex: 610336.

Also near the opera is the **Viminale**, a small, moderately priced hotel offering modern accommodations and a rooftop terrace with a view of the twin domes of the basilica of Santa Maria Maggiore.

Via Cesare Balbo 31, 00184; Tel: 474-47-28.

Near the Station

The grandness of the **Le Grand Hotel** is not diminished by its location near piazza Esedra, officially called the piazza della Repubblica, the latter having fallen from the glory it once enjoyed at the turn of the century. The standard in Rome for luxury and service, the hotel boasts rooms and suites whose elegance is matched by the appointments of the expansive public areas, where an elaborate tea is served in the afternoon accompanied by lobby music (in the old sense of the term). Its romantic, apricot-colored **Le Grand Bar** is still the place for a business or romantic rendezvous, and just this year its **Le Restaurant** opened (see the Dining section).

Via Vittorio Emanuele Orlando 3, 00185; Tel: 4709; Telex: 610210; in U.S., (212) 935-9540 or (800) 221-2340; in U.K., (01) 930-4147.

The modern facilities of the moderately priced **Londra e Cargill** are masked behind an unassuming turn-of-the-century palazzo, but its simplicity, efficiency, and convenient location between the station and via Veneto make it a favorite for businessmen.

Piazza Sallustio 18, 00187; Tel: 47-38-71; Telex: 622227.

Also moderately priced, the tastefully modern **Marcella** is another option in the area between the train station and via Veneto, and has a roof garden with a panorama stretching from St. Peter's to the Alban Hills.

Via Flavia 104, 00187; Tel: 474-64-51; Telex: 621351.

Large rooms and a location convenient to the train station and public transportation make the **Massimo d'Azeglio** popular and the service manages to remain courteous. Begun as a restaurant over a century ago, the hotel maintains its reputation for Old World courtesy, and its restaurant (see the Dining section) is still among the best in Rome.

Via Cavour 18, 00184; Tel: 46-06-46; Telex: 610556; in U.S., (212) 599-8280 or (800) 223-9832.

Like its sister hotel the Massimo d'Azeglio, the recently renovated **Mediterraneo** does a brisk business in tour groups, and also has in common with its counterpart an efficiency and courtesy that make it an elegant oasis in a nondescript area.

Via Cavour 15, 00184; Tel: 46-40-51; Telex: 610556; in U.S., (212) 599-8280 or (800) 223-9832.

Both the friendly and helpful English-speaking management of the **Morgana** and its rates set it apart from the other options on this otherwise undistinguished street a block from the train station and therefore also convenient to the Fiumicino (Leonardo da Vinci) airport bus. Ask for one of the recently renovated rooms on the first floor.

Via Filippo Turati 37, 00185; Tel: 73-48-74.

Located opposite Le Grand is the **Sitea**, whose eclectic decor and sprawling layout reflect the character of its Italian owner and his Scottish wife. The reception desk is made from an antique altar, and other period pieces are displayed in showcases scattered about its five rambling floors. Topping it all off is a display of 18th-century Neapolitan Nativity scenes on the roof terrace and bar.

Via Vittorio Emanuele Orlando 90, 00185; Tel: 475-15-60; Telex: 614163.

The Vatican

Housed in a Renaissance palazzo with appropriately splendorous lobby decor, the **Alicorni** is inexpensive if inconsistent in the size and services of its rooms. Ask to see one first.

Via Scossacavalli 11, 00193; Tel: 687-52-35.

The modern, expensive **Atlante Star** has a roof garden with unusually close views of St. Peter's, and the (in Rome) unique policy (along with its sister hotel, the

Atlante Garden) of picking up its guests at the airport free of charge.

Via Giovanni Vitelleschi 34, 00193; Tel: 656-41-96; Telex: 622355.

The **Atlante Garden** is the proper older sister of the Atlante Star, offering efficient Old World–style accommodations at the same rates along with free airport service.

Via Crescenzio 78/a, 00193; Tel: 653-04-90; Telex: 622355.

Formerly the Renaissance palazzo of Pope Julius II, the moderately priced **Columbus** maintains some of its sumptuous trappings in the lobby and public rooms, though management has opted for simplicity in the private rooms. The combination, and the fact that the hotel is a block from St. Peter's, might account for the large numbers of clergy among the clients.

Via della Conciliazione 33, 00193; Tel: 65-65-435; Telex: 620096.

Other Places in Rome

With pool, tennis courts, bars, and restaurants (see the Dining and Nightlife sections), the luxurious **Cavalieri Hilton** is such a self-contained unit that many of its guests never get into the city. Nevertheless, its privileged position high atop Monte Mario (north of the Vatican) gives it some of the best views of Rome, and a bus shuttles guests to the Spanish Steps and returns them—usually laden with luxury goods—to the hotel.

Via Alberto Cadlolo 101, 00136; Tel: 3151; Telex: 610296.

Located in the quiet Prati quarter just north of the Vatican, the inexpensive **Forti's Guest House** is a block from the Tiber and convenient to all forms of public transportation, and the Italian-American management is friendly and helpful.

Via Cosseria 2, 00192; Tel: 679-93-90.

Located in a residential area between piazza del Popolo and the Tiber, the **Locarno** offers small, comfortable rooms and an attractive bar and roof terrace in a relatively untrafficked spot ideal for romantic walks along the river and café-sitting in piazza del Popolo; it's not too far from the Borghese Gardens or the shopping district near the Spanish Steps.

Via della Penna 22, 00186; Tel: 361-08-41.

In the exclusive residential neighborhood of Parioli

behind the Villa Borghese, the luxurious **Lord Byron** is one of the quietest hotels in town, and its restaurant (see the Dining section) is one of the city's best.

Via Giuseppe de Notaris 5, 00197; Tel: 360-95-41; Telex: 611217.

—Dwight V. Gast

DINING

Rome's penchant for the table is legendary. Its roots go back to the Lucullus-style banquets satirized by Petronius in his *Satyricon* and re-created by Fellini for the cinema in our time. Even today, nothing gives a Roman more pleasure than an outing at the local *osteria*—the simple neighborhood eatery more abundant in Rome than anywhere else in Italy—for a loud and lengthy meal accompanied by many a *fujetta* (the glass carafe introduced by the ever-efficient Pope Sixtus V) of Colli Albani wine.

The *osteria* is the essence of Roman dining, for the best restaurants in town are neither trendy nor fussy. The *osteria* traditionally serves such regional Roman dishes as *coda alla vaccinara* (oxtail stew), *rigatoni e pajata* (tubular pasta prepared with veal intestines), tripe, and sweetbreads, but if you have a weak stomach (or are not particularly fond of eating one), there are a number of other Roman specialties found in *osterias* and the more formal Roman restaurants.

A complete Roman meal begins with *antipasti* of everything from vegetables to salami and shellfish, often selected from a large table set up as a lure near the entrance of the restaurant, or *bruschetta*, a garlic bread topped with tomato sauce. The most popular pasta dish is spaghetti, served *alla carbonara* (with bacon, egg, cheese, and pepper), *all'amatriciana* (in a tomato sauce with onions, bacon, and cheese), *all'arrabbiata* (with a peppery tomato and garlic sauce), and *alla puttanesca* (with a sauce made from tomatoes, capers, and black olives). The hollow spaghetti called *bucatini*, the quill-shaped pasta called *penne*, and *fettuccine* are also popular forms of pasta, and on Thursdays restaurants in Rome offer *gnocchi* (potato dumplings) as a first course.

An increasingly popular choice for a light main course is grilled *scamorza* cheese (due to inevitable changes in eating habits, and the profusion of cooks from Abruzzi, where the cheese originates), but meat dishes are as abundant as ever. The best-known is *saltimbocca alla romana* (sliced veal prepared with prosciutto, cheese, and sage); other typical entrées are *abbacchio* (baby lamb), *capretto* (kid), and *porchetta* (suckling pig roasted with herbs), which are often eaten with a salad of one of the local greens unknown outside the Rome area, such as the crunchy *puntarelle,* served with a dressing made with anchovies and garlic, or the more traditional arugula or roast peppers.

Accompany your meal with the local Colli Albani, Frascati, or Marino wines, or try the Latium Est! Est!! Est!!!, the wine that was considered so good by the servant and wine scout of a certain 12th-century Bishop Fugger that an establishment selling it was enthusiastically marked with these words (they mean "it is" in Latin) for the good bishop. Traditional Roman digestives are sambuca (an elder-flavored liqueur—reminiscent of anise—in which you are supposed to place three coffee beans, referred to as *mosche,* or flies), the sweet, saffrony Strega, or the ever-popular grappa.

Rome's role as the country's seat of government brought one good side effect along with the nightmarish bureaucracy. There is a profusion of regional restaurants in the city, perhaps a better argument for making Rome the nation's capital than Garibaldi could ever have made. You can become acquainted with some of the best aspects of the entire Italian peninsula in a taxi ride just a few minutes long.

Though *cucina nuova,* the Italian counterpart of nouvelle cuisine, has proved to be antithetical to the nation's way of eating, it did serve to foster experimentation among restaurateurs, and *cucina creativa* (creative cuisine) is the current term for their efforts, which may best be sampled at some of the restaurants listed below.

Romans eat late (lunch is usually served between 1:00 and 3:00 P.M.; dinner begins at 8:00 P.M. at the earliest), a practice often attributed to their need to discuss restaurant candidates for the meal ad infinitum before deciding where to settle in. This habit may leave some visitors hungry early; however, there are a number of snacks that are often available in neighborhood coffee bars between restaurant hours. *Tramezzini* are the finger sandwiches found throughout Italy, but peculiar to Rome are *supplì,* rice croquettes stuffed with a dollop of mozzarella cheese, then breaded and fried; *filetti di baccalà,* strips of dried cod batter-dipped and fried; and sandwiches made of *porchetta.*

The following restaurants, organized in the same neighborhood order as our narrative, should guide but not limit your dining choices. Don't forget to note the weekly closing days and the summer and Christmastime holiday schedules, and remember that the loyalty of the regular clientele usually makes reservations necessary.

If you find it difficult to get a reservation, remember that Rome has some five thousand such establishments, and the joy of discovery that characterizes the city also applies to its eateries. As a rule of thumb, to ensure quality when choosing an unfamiliar restaurant, look for a handwritten daily menu, a fresh display of antipasto, and an appreciative local crowd. Once you've sat down, don't expect to get up for some time, for you'll have become part of Rome's time-honored ritual of *sapersi contentare*—that distinctively Roman knack for knowing how to enjoy oneself.

Ancient Rome

The owner of **Alvaro al Circo Massimo** on via dei Cerchi 53 is shaped like the Circus Maximus, from which his place takes its name. The fish dishes are generally the better choice here during the summer, when there are a few outdoor tables for alfresco dining, and game is appropriate during the winter, but let Alvaro order for you if money is no object. Closed Mondays and August. Tel: 678-61-12.

Located at piazzale del Colosseo 15, **Hostaria Il Gladiatore** is best appreciated during the warm weather, when outdoor tables spill out onto the street. Abundant portions of Roman food are served here. Closed Wednesdays and national holidays. Tel: 73-62-76.

Located in the former stable of a Medieval palazzo near the Foro Traiano on the salita del Grillo 6, **La Tana del Grillo** is the only restaurant in Rome to feature the cuisine of Romagna. Spicy sausage antipasti, pasta with meaty ragù sauce, and rich desserts are the order of the day here, to be downed with sparkling red Lambrusco wine and finished with *nocino,* a digestive liqueur made from walnuts. Closed Sundays and August. Tel: 679-87-05.

A unique marriage of a Sicilian and an Emilian makes the cuisine of the tiny and quiet **Ai Tre Scalini Rossana e Matteo** at via Santissimi Quattro 30, a side street near the Colosseum, one of the most unusual dining experiences in Rome. This, as they say in Italian, is a *ristorante serio,* a serious restaurant, and the devotion both owners have to creating original and refined dishes based on simple

Italian ingredients is apparent to the eye, palate, and pocketbook. Closed lunch Saturdays, dinner Sundays, Mondays, and July and August. Tel: 73-26-95.

Ulpia overlooks the basilica of the same name in the Foro Traiano. Its menu is standard Italian, but if it's food with a view you want (with a decided emphasis on the latter), this is the place. You'll be sharing both with the legions of cats that inhabit the grounds of the forum below, waiting for scraps; the foreboding statue of the goddess Ulpia indoors might force you to make just such a sacrifice. Closed Sundays. Tel: 679-62-71.

Pantheon

Seafood reigns supreme at **Hostaria Angoletto**, in the corner (*angoletto*) of piazza Rondanini 51, just off piazza della Rotonda. New management has transformed the simple cooking, and the outdoor tables sit on one of the only wooden decks in Rome, surrounded by flowers. Closed Mondays. Tel: 656-80-19.

A block off the via del Corso at piazza Sant'Ignazio 169, **Cave di Sant'Ignazio** is a great place to try simple Roman specialties (the waiters ask you immediately if you want *bianco o rosso*—red or white wine), preferably from the outdoor tables overlooking the piazza in the summer. Closed Sundays. Tel: 679-78-21.

On the street of the same name, **La Rosetta** ranks high among Rome's fish restaurants, with the catch from Sicily arriving fresh daily. Everything is prepared simply, out of respect for the taste of the fish, but the Sicilian influence becomes evident in pasta dishes accompanied by sardines, grapes, or fennel, and in the deeply chilled Corvo wine. Closed Sundays, lunch Mondays, August. Tel: 656-10-02.

On the other street leading to the Pantheon is **Da Fortunato**, which serves classic Roman cuisine popular with politicians and North Americans who can afford it. The Saturday-night special is *trippa alla romana,* tripe served in a tomato sauce with ham, garlic, parsley, and mint. Closed Sundays and national holidays. No credit cards. Tel: 679-27-88.

Piazza Navona

The Venetian-inspired menu and glamorous, discreet surroundings make the **El Toulà** at via della Lupa one of the best of this Italian chain—for those who can afford it. Stick with the simpler items on the menu if you're here for the food. Most people aren't: Italian politicians and movie stars like to be seen dining here, sometimes together. Closed Sundays and August. Tel: 678-11-96.

If you eat in one non-Italian restaurant in Rome, make it **Chez Albert**, at vicolo della Vaccarella 11. The French owner-chef of this small establishment serves the Gallic standards (nothing *nouvelle* about this cuisine) in such classic fashion that local French clubs make field trips here. At Christmastime, if you absolutely have to have stuffed turkey, *voilà*. Closed Sundays, lunch Mondays, Tuesdays, Wednesdays. Tel: 656-55-49.

L'Orso Ottanta, at via dell'Orso 33, passes the antipasto test with flying colors. There's a generous table of it at the entrance, and the husband-and-wife team from the Abruzzi sees to it you eat your fill. The pasta dishes and main courses are equally abundant, but after all that antipasto, you'll probably just want a pizza. Closed Mondays. Tel: 656-49-04.

More Abruzzese specialties are to be had at **La Majella**, piazza Sant'Apollinare 45, a favorite with the Roman rich and famous. *Maccheroni alla chitarra* (pasta sliced thin on a guitarlike instrument), various types of risotto (with everything from zucchini flowers to Champagne), *abbacchio* (baby lamb), *porchetta* (roast pig), and game dishes are all highly recommended here. Closed Sundays, one week in August. Tel: 656-41-74.

The view of piazza Navona is the drawing card of **Mastrostefano**, where you'll eat practically in the mist of Gian Lorenzo Bernini's *Fontana dei Quattro Fiumi* (*Fountain of the Four Rivers*), overlooking the considerable activities of the piazza. As if that weren't enough in itself, some of the food—especially the Roman dishes such as *porchetta* and *abbacchio* (lamb)—isn't bad either. Closed Mondays and last two weeks in August. Tel: 654-16-69.

Osteria dell'Antiquaro serves highly refined Italian cuisine such as *lasagne con melanzane al sugo di anatra* (lasagna with eggplant in duck sauce) and *coscio di anatra alle erbe in casseruola* (herbed thigh of duck in casserole) in the tiny piazza San Simeone, which makes it one of the most intimate summer dining experiences in Rome. Dinner only. Closed Sundays, and one week in August. Tel: 65-96-94.

For those to whom dining must be an educational experience, **Papà Giovanni**, at via dei Sediari 4, is a tasteful classroom. Basing the menu on the freshest ingredients of the season from Campo dei Fiori and his own undisclosed sources, the owner-chef takes great pains to create highly personal gastronomic statements that vary with the vagaries of the market and the chef, but *vermicello cacio e pepe* (thin spaghetti with cheese and pepper) is available year-round. Though some French wines are on the list, pay attention (and pay you will, for everything) to the ones from Latium. Reservations are a must at this Roman temple of gastronomy. Closed Sundays and August. Tel: 656-53-08.

With a recent change of management, **Pino e Dino** is now run by Peppino and Tonino, but has retained its name and maintained its fame. The two new young chefs' inventive dishes include *risotto al castagno con tartufo d'Alba* (chestnut risotto with Alban truffles) and *funghi porcini e salsa di tartufo nero in crosta* (porcini mushrooms and black truffle sauce in a crust), and the hand of their Calabrian chef is also felt in the spicier dishes. Food here is reasonably priced. Closed Mondays, one week in August, three weeks in January. Tel: 656-13-19.

Pizzeria Baffetto, at via del Governo Vecchio 114, is an active and inexpensive location filled with young Romans. Outdoor tables right on the busy street enliven the festivities. Closed Sundays and August. Tel: 656-16-17.

Once a not-so-simple inn that hosted Dante and Rabelais, **Hostaria dell'Orso**, at via dei Soldati 25, has retained its palatial look, with cuisine and prices to match. Many diners go from table to the **Cabala Discotheque** upstairs. Dinner only. Closed Sundays. No credit cards. Tel: 656-42-50.

On via de Baullari, near campo dei Fiori, **Filetti di Baccalà** is always filled with young people, especially on Friday evenings when they come from all over Rome to taste the specialty for which the restaurant is named—fried cod, served at paper-covered communal tables and accompanied by the strong house white. Closed Sundays.

Campo dei Fiori
As if it wasn't enough to dine in the entrance of the Theater of Pompey, where Julius Caesar was assassinated, how nice to be able to sample some classic local cuisine. **Costanza**, at piazza del Paradiso 65, offers some of the best Roman cuisine in town. All the grilled meats and fish are highly recommended, and the influence of the nearby Jewish ghetto may be tasted in the *carciofi alla giudia,* artichokes fried Jewish-style. Closed Sundays. Tel: 656-17-17.

Patrizia e Roberto del Pianeta Terra is another rarity in Rome, run by a Tuscan rugby player and his Sicilian lawyer wife. Its inventive menu includes such dishes as *ravioli d'oca al Barolo* (ravioli stuffed with goose prepared with Barolo wine) and *petto d'oca in salsa di prugne* (breast of goose in plum sauce). French wines have made inroads here, too, as have prices that would hold their own on the international market. Dinner only. Closed Mondays and August. Tel: 686-98-93.

The dowager of campo dei Fiori, **La Carbonara** is still going strong since it was founded by the daughter of a coal merchant in the early 1960s as a place for local food sellers to have their early morning meal. Though now few workers can afford it, those who can are particularly fond of its specialty, *penne alla carbonara.* Closed Tuesdays and three weeks in August. Tel: 656-47-83.

To call **Il Drappo** (at vicolo del Malpasso) "Sardinian-inspired" is missing the mark. The cuisine here is inspired, period. Sister Angela recently joined the original brother-and-sister team of Paolo and Valentina, and together they produce loving variations on the hearty cuisine of their native island. The menu is seasonal, but try any one of their risottos or *maialino arrosto* (roast pig), accompanied by *carta di musica* (sheet music) bread, and a strong Sardinian wine such as Malvasia. Closed Sundays and two weeks in August. Tel: 687-73-65.

The numerous small dining rooms of **Vecchia Roma**, at piazza Campitelli 18, are an intimate setting for classic Roman cuisine or the restaurant's specialties of *gnocchi Vecchia Roma,* served with cheese sauce, or the *fantasie di polenta* menu, on which all listings are made with the cornmeal mush called *polenta.* Closed Wednesdays and two weeks in August. Tel: 656-46-04.

Ghetto

Da Giggetto, at via del Portico d'Ottavia 22, is the least fancy of the ghetto restaurants, and the most reasonably priced. It serves all the specialties in the Roman Jewish *cucina povera* (poor man's cuisine) tradition, such as *carciofi alla giudia* (fried artichokes) and *filetti di baccalà* (fried batter-dipped dried cod), along with basic Roman fare. Closed Mondays. Tel: 656-11-05.

The liveliest of the ghetto restaurants, at via del Portico d'Ottavia, is **Da Luciano**, another reasonably priced choice in the area. Closed Tuesday lunch. Tel: 687-47-22.

The most established of the ghetto restaurants, **Piperno** is also the most pricey, but if you want exemplary (though nonkosher) versions of the Jewish classics in a setting slightly removed from the hustle and bustle of the ghetto's main street, this is the place (at Monte de' Cenci 9). Closed Sunday dinner, Mondays, Christmas, Easter, and August. Tel: 654-06-29.

Trastevere

If you prefer your fish on the refined side, try **Alberto Ciarlà** (piazza San Cosimato 40), which has an international menu of everything from Maine lobster to Scottish salmon, and a wine list to match. The freshest catch is usually local, however, and the same goes for the olive oil and the Bianco di Velletri Vigna Ciarla white wine, both produced by the owners. Dinner only. Closed Sundays. Tel: 581-86-68.

The ultimate tourist experience, **Da Meo Patacca**, piazza dei Mercanti 30, advertised up and down the streets of Rome, puts on a kitsch dinner show of singing minstrels who encourage the tables full of North Americans and Germans to sing along. Though its authenticity is reflected in its name (*patacca* is Roman dialect for fake), the experience can be good fun if you're in the right mood. Dinner only. No credit cards. Tel: 581-61-98.

To many, dining in Trastevere still means **Sabatini I**, in the piazza facing Santa Maria in Trastevere. The main dining room reeks of atmosphere, with beamed ceilings and frescoed walls, but even better are the crowded and noisy outdoor tables overlooking the church (and watched over by the local pickpockets). Closed Wednesdays and two weeks in August. Tel: 58-20-26.

Sabatini II absorbs the spillage from its namesake listed above, and for those who prefer less boisterous surroundings, this is the place. It has the same menu and prices as Sabatini I. Closed Tuesdays, and for two weeks in August when the other is open. Tel: 581-83-07.

The full name of **Tentativo** (via della Luce 5) reads like the title of a Lina Wertmuller film: Tentativo di Descrizione di un Banchetto a Roma (Attempt at a Description of a Banquet in Rome). The creative and pricey attempts, such as *ravioli d'anatra* (duck ravioli) and *filetto di manzo affumicato con funghi porcini* (fillet of smoked beef with porcini mushrooms) are usually quite successful. Closed Sundays and last two weeks in August. Tel: 589-52-34.

Piazza del Popolo

The late Roman restaurateur Alfredo, self-proclaimed King of Fettuccine and creator of *fettuccine all'Alfredo*, has been popular with Americans ever since he served fettuccine to Douglas Fairbanks and Mary Pickford with a golden spoon and fork. **Alfredo all'Augusteo l'Originale** continues his tradition at piazza Augusto Imperatore with what they say are the original utensils, and the drama is enhanced by live music, which makes this place an enduring character in the cast of Roman street theater. Closed Tuesdays. Tel: 678-10-72.

Dal Bolognese in the piazza del Popolo specializes in the cuisine of Bologna, considered the gastronomical capital of Italy. The pasta is all homemade, and any such dish should properly be ordered *al ragù,* with the meat sauce typical of Bologna. Though *cotolette alla bolognese* (breaded veal cutlet with ham) is the most characteristic dish, the *bollito misto* (boiled meats accompanied by a green sauce of parsley, capers, and onions) is an equally good choice. Closed dinner Sundays, Mondays. Tel: 361-14-26.

The setting on Pincio Hill in Villa Borghese is what sells **Casina Valadier,** best for a light alfresco lunch, with plenty of room to let the kids loose while you engage in pleasant people-watching. Closed Mondays. Tel: 679-20-83.

One of Rome's most creative fish restaurants, **Porto di Ripetta** is run by the daughter of a fisherman, Maria Romani. Impulsively, imaginatively, and impeccably, she works her magic on the catch of the day in this quiet and chic restaurant a few steps from piazza del Popolo, at via di Ripetta 250. Closed Sundays, three weeks in August. Tel: 361-23-76.

Piazza di Spagna

A Roman institution, **La Campana** (located on the street of the same name) traces its origins to an *osteria* sited here more than five hundred years ago that later became a front for a house of ill repute on the other side of the courtyard. It now serves, impeccably, a classic Roman menu to a lively and sophisticated crowd largely composed of journalists and Italian television personalities, and at a moderate price. Closed Mondays and August. Tel: 656-78-20.

Pizzeria La Capricciosa (largo dei Lombardi 8) credits itself with the invention of pizza *alla capricciosa,* a capricious blend of just about everything, and the version in this lively, reasonably priced place is as good as any. Closed Tuesdays. Tel: 679-40-27.

Nino (via Borgognona 11) is one of the nicest Tuscan restaurants in town, serving *pappardelle al sugo di lepre* (wide pasta noodles in a hare sauce), *bistecca alla fiorentina* (thick Florentine steak), and *cannellini* beans, to be eaten with Chianti *a consumo,* meaning you pay only for what you drink from the flask on the table. Closed Sundays and August. Tel: 679-56-76.

Otello alla Concordia (via della Croce 81) provides simple meals in a trattoria-type indoor setting covered with paintings, or beneath a vine-covered pergola during the warmer months. Closed Sundays, two weeks at Christmas. No credit cards. Tel: 679-11-78.

Ranieri 1843, at via Mario de' Fiori 26, has been around at least as long as the date in its name. Giuseppe Ranieri was the restaurant's original owner, and chef to Queen Victoria. A classic stop on the Grand Tour itinerary, some find its Old World ambience a bit stuffy, but the ingredients that go into its venerable fish and meat dishes are as fresh as any in town. Closed Sundays. Tel: 679-15-92.

Via Veneto

Andrea is considered one of the best restaurants in Rome, and such dishes as *gamberetti con rughetta* (shrimp with rughetta greens), *stracetti di manzo con porcini e tartufi* (strips of beef with porcini mushrooms and truffles) certainly uphold any such claims. Flawless service and an intelligent list of Italian wines enhance the pleasures of Andrea's pricey tables, at via Sardegna 26. Closed Sundays, three weeks in August. Tel: 49-37-07.

Chef to the stars during the dolce vita days, Mario Zorzetto is now the owner of **Elefante Bianco** (via Aurora 19), one of the most elegantly appointed restaurants in town. Wood paneling, piano music, silver, and crystal are the backdrop to the Venetian-inspired menu, abundant with succulent risottos and fresh fish. His selection of wines from the Veneto is also excellent, as is the grappa, but expect to pay dearly. Closed Sundays, national holidays. Tel: 48-37-18.

Giancarlo Castrucci, formerly the "Charles" of the Eden Hotel's famous rooftop restaurant, recently retired to open his own place, **Charles Rasella 52**, at the street address of the new restaurant's name. Fish reigns supreme here, as does Charles, who pampers the loyal clientele who followed him over from the Eden. Try whatever the catch of the day may be, along with the fashionable Locorotondo white wine. Closed Sundays, two weeks in August. Tel: 46-04-57.

The hearty specialties of Emilia are served in a trattoria-type setting at **Colline Emiliane** at via degli Avignonesi 22, near piazza Barberini. Homemade pasta (made in front of your eyes), *culatello* (a mouth-watering type of prosciutto from Parma), and *l'anitra all'arancia* (duck with orange sauce) are the dishes to order here. There is an excellent selection of Lambrusco and other Emilia Romagna wines. Closed Fridays. Tel: 475-75-38.

Near the Station

At via Merulana 77, **Cicilardone** is inexpensive and extensive in its selection of pasta, various types of which can be sampled at once if you ask for *assaggini,* or little tastes, but the other light selections on the menu make it perfect for lunch if you're in the Santa Maria Maggiore area. Closed dinner Sundays, Mondays, late July to early August. No credit cards. Tel: 73-38-06.

One of Rome's least expensive fish restaurants, **Cannavota** (piazza di San Giovanni in Laterano) is of the old school in that, despite his appearance, its reedy owner (his nickname means "empty cane") believes in copious portions and generous amounts of house wine served in hand-painted Faenza pitchers. Large dining rooms and a quick turnover keep things hopping, but the atmosphere is festive, never pressured. Closed Wednesdays, first three weeks in August. Tel: 77-50-07.

The pizzeria **Est Est Est** claims to be the oldest in Rome. Its copious pies are quite inexpensive and good, served in a boisterous setting on via Genova 29 that encourages sampling the ancient wine for which this place is named. Closed Mondays, August. Tel: 46-11-07.

Don't be fooled by the stage-set Neapolitan trappings of **Scoglio di Frisio**, at via Merulana 256, decorated with fishnets and murals of Vesuvius. The food is genuine, largely made up of fish but including such meat dishes as *bistecca alla pizzaiola,* beef stewed in a spicy tomato sauce. Musicians lead diners in rousing choruses of "O Sole Mio" and other Neapolitan standards, adding to the theatrical atmosphere. Closed Sundays in spring and summer, Mondays in fall and winter. Tel: 73-46-19.

The Vatican

Taverna Giulia specializes in Ligurian cuisine such as pasta *al pesto* (a sauce made from basil) and serves a large number of fish dishes and wines from the same area, in the sumptuous setting of a Renaissance palace (vicolo dell'Oro). Closed Sundays, August. No credit cards. Tel: 656-97-68.

At borgo Pio, **Marcello** is one of the most pleasant of the rather standard restaurant offerings near the Vatican, but its courtyard, open during the warmer weather, sets it apart from its otherwise indistinguishable neighbors. Closed Fridays, August. Tel: 656-44-62.

Other Places in Rome

Located at via Ancona 14, just outside Porta Pia (north of Termini where the corso d'Italia and via Nomentana meet), **Coriolano** offers outstanding versions of Italian classics, including *ravioli di ricotta e spinaci* (ravioli pasta stuffed with ricotta cheese and spinach), and such Roman dishes as *abbacchio* (lamb) and *capretta* (kid). Closed Sundays, Saturdays in July, and August. Tel: 844-95-01.

The chic place to eat the Roman specialties of various animal innards is **Checchino dal 1887**, at via di Monte Testaccio 30, across from an old slaughterhouse in the trendy neighborhood of Testaccio. The restaurant recently celebrated its centennial, but in fact goes back even before 1887, when it was called Osteria dell'Olmo, after the elm tree (*olmo*) that shaded it. The original Checchino invented *coda alla vaccinara* (oxtail stew), which is the most palatable item on the menu for the squeamish. The house Frascati is quite good, and is kept cool in wine cellars carved out of the mountain of broken pottery that makes up Monte Testaccio. Closed Sundays, Mondays, August, one week at Christmas. Tel: 574-63-18.

More conventional Roman specialties may be sampled at **Da Severino**, at piazza Zama 5 beyond the Terme di Caracalla, which serves excellent *bucatini* and *tagliatelle* pasta, as well as *saltimbocca* and *abbacchio alla romana* (baby lamb). Closed dinner Sundays, Mondays, August. Tel: 755-08-72.

Hotel Restaurants

Charles Roof Garden at the Eden Hotel (via Ludovisi 49) has the greenest views in Rome, made all the more enjoyable by the simple, fundamentally Roman cuisine of this exclusive restaurant, which offers seasonal specialties in an incomparable setting. Lunch is lovely, overlooking the city skyline, while in the evening the night light of the city is further softened at the bar. Closed Sundays, August. No credit cards. Tel: 474-35-51.

A rapidly disappearing Old World elegance is still in evidence at the **Massimo d'Azeglio**, via Cavour 14, which dates from the days when Rome became capital of a newly united Italy. Its copious antipasto wagon rivals anything from the most lavish neighborhood trattoria, and the pasta and main courses are equally generous. Closed Sundays. Tel: 475-41-01.

La Pergola, in the Cavalieri Hilton (via Cadlolo 101), is another restaurant for which Romans go out of their way. Besides the magnificent view of Rome from its setting high above the city on the Vatican side, its menu has a heavy international Italian accent, with dishes such as *carpaccio* (thinly sliced, uncooked beef) and seafood with balsamic vinegar. Try the *degustazione* menu, a sampling of house specialties. Dinner only. Closed Sundays, first three weeks in January. Tel: 3151.

Considered by many locals to be Rome's best restaurant, **Relais Le Jardin** in the Lord Byron Hotel (via Giuseppe de Notaris 5) has a menu that leans heavily toward the nouvelle cuisine implied by its name, though the inventive dishes are all inspired by authentic Italian ingredients. The quiet indoor setting, decorated in cool pastels, attracts upscale neighborhood types from nearby Parioli as well as a crowd of wealthy Romans and foreigners. Closed Sundays. Tel: 360-94-51.

Le Restaurant del Grand Hotel (via Vittorio Emanuele Orlando 3) just opened in an opulent setting straight out of Scarpia's apartment in *Tosca*, with gilded furnishings and private banquettes. The menu is international Italian, with some elegant touches such as the truffle-oil marinade on its *carpaccio*. Closed August. Tel: 4709.

—Dwight V. Gast

NIGHTLIFE

Nightlife is the most fleeting aspect of life anywhere, though it's not nearly as trendy in the Eternal City as in many other capitals. Rather than looking at the after hours as a time for boisterous partying, the Romans take the opportunity to put on their most civilized airs—dressing to the nines, posing, posturing, speaking in hushed tones with knowing expressions—in short, pursuing the night in a characteristically classical way. This practice has given

rise to a larger proportion of reliable and regular estab-
lishments than elsewhere. When the sun goes down, the
Roman expression "One life is not enough" becomes
"One nightlife is not enough."

Not that Rome is devoid of cultural activities to be
taken in during the evening. Its opera (box office, via
Nazionale 64; Tel: 46-17-55) mounts productions outdoors in the summer at the Terme di Caracalla; the season at the Teatro dell'Opera (piazza Beniamino Gigli 1;
Tel: 46-17-55), while not on a par with that of Milan,
Naples, or Bari, runs from November through January.
Concerts are given from October through June by the
Accademia di Santa Cecilia Orchestra (Tel: 654-10-44) in
piazza Campidoglio in July and August, and in the Auditorio di Via delle Conciliazione, near the Vatican.

Film and performing arts events take place all over
town during the summer festival called L'Estate Romana,
widely publicized in such local papers as *Il Messaggero*
and *La Repubblica*.

Since most foreign films in Italy are dubbed, English
speakers in Rome like to congregate at the English-
language Pasquino Cinema in Trastevere (vicolo del
Piede; Tel: 580-36-22), and follow the movies with an ice
cream at one of the many *gelaterie* in the neighborhood.

But there are many other possibilities for an evening's
entertainment. From an after-dinner *espresso* coffee or
prosecco wine in a café or bar, on to live music in a
piano bar or club, and through to dancing and perhaps a
late-night supper in one of many specialized nightclubs
around town, the Roman night can easily extend to the
wee hours. Each step of the way there are ample
chances to observe—and perhaps participate in—the
mating game *alla romana*. Also, Anglophones have an
automatic advantage in the stakes, since speaking English is considered as sophisticated as taking part in the
nocturnal circuit. But communication is hardly a problem under the circumstances.

Activity in cafés and bars starts picking up after dinner,
at around 9:00 P.M. Piano bars and live-music clubs begin
to get lively a couple of hours later, and nightclubs don't
get into full swing until after midnight, though all open
sooner. Most of the clubs charge a cover to get in, and
some may even require a membership fee. In true international style, the more exclusive ones may make you
wait at the door and even then may not let you in.

Cafés and Bars

Many Romans follow their meals with a coffee or ice cream at one of the places in Centro Storico. **Sant'Eustachio** (piazza Sant'Eustachio 82) and **Tazza d'Oro** (via degli Orfani 84) are both equally famed for their coffee as they are for their *granita al caffè,* or coffee ice. **Giolitti** (via degli Uffici del Vicario 40) and **Tre Scalini** (piazza Navona 30) are the best known among the many *gelaterie* in the area. In Trastevere, **Caffé-Bar di Marzio** (piazza di Santa Maria in Trastevere 14/b) serves coffee at the bustling center of the action in the area's main piazza.

Those looking for action still go to **Rosati** and **Canova**, facing cafés in piazza del Popolo. Rosati is currently the more chic of the two, its motorcycles and sports cars winning hands down in the mating display department, often even over their owners. The men here tend to be Roman, the women foreign. The reverse is true of the cafés of via Veneto. **Café de Paris** (no. 90), **Gran Caffè Doney** (no. 145), and **Harry's Bar** (no. 150) have faded from their heyday during the dolce vita era, and tend to fill up with foreign men and domestic ladies looking to keep them company—usually for a price. Nearby is **George's**, one of the most comfortable of the stylish bars for North Americans, where a Negroni is the cocktail of choice.

Piano Bars and Live-Music Clubs

Via Veneto also has some of Rome's nicest piano bars. Practically every hotel in the area has its own, but the **Roof Garden Bar** of the Eden Hotel (via Ludovisi 49) has the most romantic view of all.

For live music the choices are even wider, and are scattered throughout the city. **Big Mama** (vicolo San Francesco a Ripa 18), true to its name, is the leading jazz club in Rome, but there are many others. **Mississippi Jazz Club** (borgo Angelico 16), **Music Inn** (largo dei Fiorentini 3), and **Billie Holiday Jazz Club** (via degli Orti di Trastevere 43) are all just as well established. **Saint Louis** (via del Cardello 13/a) is still enormously popular, but lately has been displaced by **Caffè Latino** (via di Monte Testaccio 96), in the trendy Testaccio neighborhood, as the current favorite.

For other kinds of music, there's **Four Green Fields** (via Morin 40) for Irish music; **Yes Brazil** (via San Francesco a Ripa) for Brazilian; **Makumba** (via degli Olimpionici 19) for African reggae and salsa (weekends only);

Folkstudio (via Sacchi 3) for folk; and **Alexanderplatz** (via Ostia 9), a Roman gathering place for Italian singers from Milan.

Nightclubs

In the Eternal City of night, **Jackie O'** (via Boncompagni 11), in the via Veneto area, is as exclusive as ever. The poor rich kids of the Parioli residential district north of Villa Borghese, so much a cultural phenomenon the name *pariolini* is used in Rome to mean gilded youth, drag themselves to **Bella Blu** (via Luigi Luciani 21) with the same lack of enthusiasm as ever. Jaded jet-set types still frequent **La Cabala** and the **Blue Bar** (via dei Soldati 25), both upstairs from the Hostaria dell'Orso restaurant. Gays continue to put on jacket and tie for **Easy Going** (via della Purificazione 9). **Open Gate** (via San Nicola da Tolentino 4) draws its age-old crowd of rich industrialists, and chic crowds still cram around the piano at **Tartarughino** (via della Scrofa 2).

But most Romans are now talking about other places. The *pariolini* are now going to **Hemingway** (piazza delle Coppelle 10), billed as "Rome's first singles bar," and to **Olimpo** (piazza Rondanini 36). Testaccio has its new gay club, **L'Alibi** (via di Monte Testaccio 44). Jet-setters have started flying to **Atmosphere** (via Romagnosi 11/a) and **Le Cornacchie** (piazza Rondanini 53). **Notorius** (via San Nicola da Tolentino 22) has absorbed some of the moneyed spillage from the nearby Open Gate. And the latest place for the chic crowds, opened by the owner of Hemingway, is **Gilda** (via Mario de' Fiori 97), a "revival" house of Italian pop music from the 1960s and 1970s, which attracts former singers and their fans from that era of protest, many of whom are now Italian politicians. But who knows when the new emperors of entertainment will turn their thumbs down on what Cicero called the *aura popularis,* or popular breeze, of these "in" establishments? Before you go, you'd better have your hotel check to make sure they're still in business.

—*Dwight V. Gast*

SHOPS AND SHOPPING

Though T. S. Eliot's women may "come and go, talking of Michelangelo," when women come and go in Rome today the talk is more likely to be of Valentino, Fendi, and other designers who keep their ateliers here. For despite Milan's prominence in the ready-to-wear fashion world,

Rome still reigns supreme for *alta moda,* the Italian term for haute couture.

Rome's sartorial splendor extends to men as well. The fabrics of made-to-measure shirts rival anything you'll see on Savile Row, and the tailoring is often superior. Quality, and the traditions of pomp and circumstance running from the ancients through the popes and now to the headquarters of Italy's major television networks and film industry, are what distinguish shopping in the capital. Thus clothing, antiques, engravings, jewelry, fabrics, and crafts remain the best buys in Rome, fluctuating exchange rates notwithstanding.

Shops in Rome are generally open from 9:00 or 10:00 A.M. to 1:00 or 1:30 P.M., and unless they're on *orario no-stop* (chic Italian for nonstop schedule), they reopen between 4:00 and 5:00 P.M. until between 7:00 and 8:30 P.M. All shops are closed Sundays and Monday mornings, except around Christmas, and food shops close Thursday afternoons. In addition to national holidays, many shops close on Rome's birthday, April 21.

Most of the shops listed accept credit cards, but if you find that you need cash outside of normal banking hours, try the American Service Bank (piazza Mignanelli 15; Tel: 544-21) or the Banca Nazionale del Lavoro (via Veneto 11; Tel: 475-04-21), both of which stay open *no-stop* until 6:00 P.M.

Spanish Steps

The most elegant shopping in Rome can be had in the area around the Spanish Steps. Off the top of the steps themselves runs via Gregoriana, where top designers such as Valentino have their studios. (It was he, in fact, who was outraged over the opening of Rome's first Mc-Donald's a couple of years back on the grounds that the hamburger fumes would taint his couture, but he has since buttoned his lip.) At the bottom of the steps, directly in front of Bernini's *Fontana della Barcaccia,* is **via Condotti,** where the traffic has been closed off to make way for some of Italy's biggest names in clothing and jewelry. Before you make a beeline for it, have a look around piazza di Spagna, where you'll find the American Express office handy for a quick fix of cash at number 38.

Italy's leading linens may be purchased at **Pratesi,** at No. 10, while Rome's most exclusive jeweler, **Petochi,** is at No. 23. The Missoni men's shop, **Missoni Uomo,** is at No. 78, and next to it is the natty women's clothier **Krizia,** at No.

77. Artsy types might then want to wander up **via Babuino** to the north off the piazza, where besides Armani's (No. 102) and the inexpensive boutique Emporio Armani (No. 140), some of the city's leading antiques dealers are located. **Antonacci** (No. 146) and **W. Apolloni** (No. 133–34) are the most famous, and expensive, but you can still pick up the inexpensive gift item at **Il Granmercato Antiquario Babuino** (No. 150). If trattoria-type painting appeals, double back down **via Margutta** and have a look at Rome's highest concentration of commercial art galleries. A recent addition is the more contemporary **Galleria Apollodoro** at piazza Mignanelli 25, within piazza di Spagna.

Return to piazza di Spagna and head down via Condotti, where you'll immediately recognize Richard Ginori, Gucci, Cartier, Bulgari, Beltrami, Buccellati, and Hermès, and may want to stop to see how their Rome inventories vary from those of the other cities where they ply their pricey wares. There are certain stores, however, to which you should pay particular attention, since they do not exist outside Rome. **Barilla** (No. 29) makes classic hand-sewn shoes for men and women, while **Capuano** (No. 61) sells custom-made jewelry to the stars, and **Battistoni** (No. 61/a) made-to-measure menswear. Before heading south to the parallel luxury streets, aficionados of elegantly designed office supplies might want to venture two blocks north to the two **Vertecchi** stores at the via della Croce (Nos. 38 and 70).

Via Borgognona and via Frattina are filled with more famous-name designers. **Fendi** virtually owns the former venue, its women's shop at No. 36 dominating the street (though **Gianni Versace** has his men's shop at No. 29, and **Gianfranco Ferre** has his men's shop at No. 6 and women's at No. 42/b, and the ever-effete **Franco Maria Ricci** sells the most esoteric cards and books on the face of the earth at No. 4/d).

Via Frattina is home to **Mario Valentino** (No. 84), who also has a women's store on via Bocca di Leone 15 and via Mario dei Fiori 22. More designers line the cross streets: **Basile** has a store for both men and women on via Mario dei Fiori 29, and **Gianni Versace** has a women's store at via Bocca di Leone 26. If it's cheap Italian woolens you want, go to **Anticoli** at via della Vite 28 before leaving the area. You can mail them, or any other purchases weighing less than two kilograms, from the post office in nearby piazza San Silvestro, open *no-stop* from 8:00 A.M. to 8:00 P.M. weekdays, 8:00 A.M. to noon on Saturdays.

Specialty Shops in Centro Storico

The area just to the west across the Corso from the via Condotti area is filled with specialty shops. Since it encompasses the Pantheon, piazza Navona, and campo dei Fiori, it's a wide area to wander aimlessly. Therefore, the following shops are listed by the type of merchandise they sell.

Antiques and engravings. The auction house **Christie's** has its Italian headquarters in Palazzo Lancellotti (piazza Navona 14; Tel: 656-40-32). Besides the open-air print market in piazza Fontanella di Borghese, which sells original antique prints, there are a number of dealers who keep shops in this part of town. **Via dei Coronari** is almost completely lined with antiques dealers, and if you're there in May or October you'll see the street decked out for the antiques fair called the Mostra Mercato di Antiquariato. Some exceptions to the rule of 19th-century English furniture sold in the streets' shops are **Metastasio** (at No. 33–34), which has the unusual specialty of nautical paintings; **Mario Morisco** (No. 136–121), which sells French Empire furniture; and **La Mansarde** (No. 202–203), which deals in Piemontese furniture. Dealers along **via Giulia**, considered the heart of Renaissance Rome, naturally specialize in older antiques. Among the nicer ones are **La Chimera** (at No. 122), which deals in 19th-century Italian furniture, and **La Pinacoteca di Via Giulia** (at No. 188), which handles Italian painting from the same period. Scattered around the area are **Roberto Boccalini** (via del Banco di Santo Spirito), who deals in old prints, books, and engravings, as do **Casali** (piazza del Pantheon 81/a), **Cascianelli** (largo Febo 14), **Nardecchia** (piazza Navona 25), and **Galleria Carlo Virgilio** (via della Lupa 9).

Contemporary art galleries. Rome is currently undergoing a renewed importance as a center for contemporary art, and although there's no one distinct area for them as in other cities, many of the galleries are in Centro Storico. Among the ones to watch out for here are **Galleria Giulia** (via Giulia 148), **Galleria Mara Coccia** (via del Corso 530), **L'Attico** (via del Paradiso 41), **Planita** (via di Ripetta 22), and **Monti** (via di Ripetta 41).

Crafts. **Via dell'Orso** holds a crafts fair every October; there are quite a few artisans working along it and its side streets. For do-it-yourselfers, **Canguro** (via di Campo Marzio 45) sells some of the best yarns in town, as does **Le Vie Delle Lane** (via dei Banchi Vecchi 116). The antique craft of tile making is still practiced at **Galleria**

Farnese (piazza Farnese 50), which makes reproduction and original designs. If you thought candle making was a lost art, step into **Cereria Pisoni** (corso Vittorio Emanuele 127–29), which has kept the popes enlightened since 1803 and will make any size, color, and quantity of candle to order. They are the exclusive manufacturers of the saucer-shaped candles called *torcie a vento,* typically Roman street illuminations found along the city's streets on festive occasions.

Housewares. **Croff Centro Casa** has two stores of their well-designed housewares in the area, at via Tomacelli 137 and via del Corso 316.

Men's made-to-order. **Caleffi** (via Colonna Antonina 53) has been making men's shirts for three generations, as well as their own pajamas and dressing gowns; **Camiceria Piero Albertelli** (via dei Prefetti 11) specializes in men's nightwear.

Unusual shops. The entire street of **via dei Cestari** specializes in sacred vestments and accoutrements, from the chasubles at Luciano Ghezzi (No. 32–33) to the ornamental reliquaries and monstrances at Statuaria Arte Sacra (No. 2). For something more *urbis* than *orbis,* **Art'è** (piazza Rondanini 32) sells witty replicas of urban architecture. Rome's only magic shop is **Curiosità e Magia** (via Aquiro 70). **La Gazza Ladra** (via dei Banchi Vecchi 29) has an extensive stock of 19th-century walking sticks. **Ai Monasteri** (corso del Rinascimento 72) sells liqueurs, perfumes, honeys, and other products made by monks and nuns throughout Italy's monasteries and abbeys. For the young and young at heart, try **Mondo Antico** (via dei Pianellari 17), where miniature stage settings and puppets are the stars. **Zanon** (via Santa Maria dell'Anima 18) continues the venerable Roman art of *tarsia,* or marble inlay, with a vast array of objects such as lamps and tabletops.

More stores in the area. Rome's most central bookstore is **Rizzoli** (largo Chigi 15), which sells the city's largest selection of art and travel books, many of which are in English. Finally, cross back over the Corso to stop for a snack at Rome's oldest chocolate store, **Moriondo & Gariglio** (via della Pilotta 2).

Other Shopping Streets

Via del Tritone offers inexpensive clothing and expensive fabrics; Galtrucco at No. 18–23 has the most luxurious of the latter. While in the area, stop by **Pineider**, the elegant

Florentine stationers, at the via Due Macelli 68–69. More inexpensive clothing and shoes are sold along the entire length of **via Nazionale**, from which runs a designer-seconds outlet called **Discount System** on via Napoli. While in the neighborhood, check out the newly expanded **Economy Book & Video Center** at via Torino 136, which now rents English-language videos (they're on a different system, but may make a nice gift for a Roman friend) in addition to its vast selection of English-language books on every subject. Also nearby is Rome's leading wine and olive oil shop, **Trimani** (via Goito 20), behind the Terme di Diocleziano.

If you're feeling adventurous, at the opposite extremes of the middlebrow via Nazionale (and at opposite ends of town) are **via Sonnio** (near San Giovanni in Laterano), an open-air street market specializing in used clothing, and **via Cola di Rienzo** (near the Vatican), a tree- and boutique-lined modern street that is Rome's closest thing to a suburban shopping mall. All the respectable names are here, but for a touch of the unusual, go to **F.A.M.A.R.** (piazza dell'Unità 51–52), at the end of the street, where you'll be able to buy such unusual items as blazer buttons with designer logos on them.

Finally, don't leave Rome without spending a Sunday morning at **Porta Portese**, the open-air flea market in Trastevere. Everything from *porchetta* sandwiches to vintage postcards to stolen car parts and fake antiques is on sale here. The place is also rife with pickpockets—the common dictum is that if your wallet is stolen on the way in, you'll find it for sale on the way out—but if you take precautions accordingly you should have a great time.

—*Dwight V. Gast*

DAY TRIPS FROM ROME

By Dwight V. Gast

In addition to Orvieto in neighboring Umbria, there are a number of places in Lazio (the region around Rome) that make interesting day trips for lovers of ancient Roman ruins, Renaissance and Medieval architecture, fine rustic dining, remnants of the evocative Etruscan civilization, and war memorials. Most of the sites can be reached by train or ACOTRAL (an acronym for Lazio's bus service).

MAJOR INTEREST

The Catacombs
Ostia Antica, ancient Roman town excavations
Tivoli for Villa d'Este and Villa Adriano: frescoes, gardens, fountains
The Castelli Romani, castles and villas in the Alban Hills: Frascati, Castel Gondolfo, others
Etruscan sites
The ancient Benedictine Abbey of Monte Cassino

THE CATACOMBS

Of the dozens of Early Christian burial chambers around Rome known as catacombs, the three most easily accessible lie one after another southeast of the city along the via Appia Antica, or Appian Way, the ancient road opened in 312 B.C. to connect Rome with the Empire to the south, ending at Brindisi. The catacombs may be visited in half a

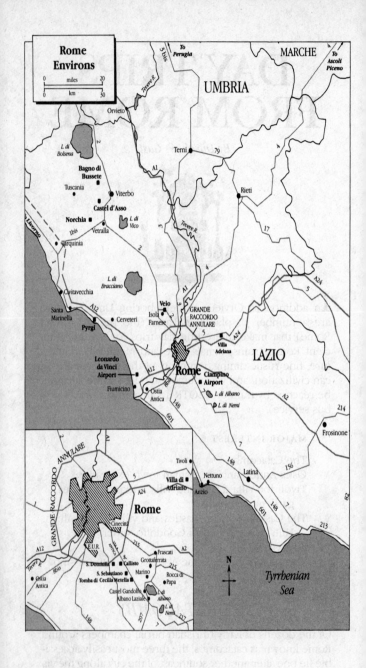

day. The ones mentioned below are staffed with multilingual tour guides.

The **Catacomb of San Callisto** is the most important of all. It constituted the first specifically designated cemetery of the early Christians; named after Saint Calixtus, who was appointed guardian of the site by Pope Zephyrinus (199–217), it was the burial place of the early popes as well as Saint Cecilia, who is commemorated by a copy of the Carlo Madreno statue in the crypt. It is also the most extensive of the catacombs, stretching some 15 miles underground, and has not yet been fully explored. Just behind the catacomb of San Callisto is the **Catacomb of Santa Domitilla**, which contains the fourth-century basilica of San Nereus and San Achilleus, as well as some beautiful paintings, including the first known representation of Christ as the Good Shepherd, painted in the second century.

The **Catacomb of San Sebastiano**, a few minutes away, grew around the spot of the martyrdom of Saint Stephen, and is where the bodies of Saint Peter and Saint Paul were once buried. It is the oldest known catacomb, and consequently has been visited heavily over the centuries and has been damaged by pilgrims. Nevertheless, the tunnels, covered with ancient graffiti, and the nearby **basilica of Santo Stefano** (one of Rome's seven pilgrimage churches) are the most impressive examples of catacombs in Rome.

A Roman monument in the area is the **Tomb of Caecilia Metella**, a huge circular tower built under the Emperor Augustus. Unlike most monuments of the period, it has been preserved with much of its marble facing intact, and is decorated with charming relief scenes. Nearby is the restaurant **Cecilia Metella** (via Appia Antica 125; Tel: 511-02-13), which makes for a pleasant outdoor lunch or dinner during the warm weather.

The number 118 bus from the Colosseum stops at the catacomb of San Callisto; the other sites are all within walking distance from San Callisto.

OSTIA ANTICA

The extensive excavations of the ancient seaport of Ostia are most important to archaeologists for their examples of Roman residential architecture, ranging from the patrician villa, called the *domus* (much more common at the wealthy resort town of Pompeii), to the apartment block called the *insula*. Set in a park unbothered by the intrusions of the centuries and pleasantly planted with cypresses and umbrella pines, the site gives a more vividly focused picture of everyday life in the Empire than anything in Rome does. From the entrance at Porta Romana, follow the Decumanus Maximus, the town's main street, to the Terme di Nettuno (Baths of Neptune), which contain some interesting marine mosaics. Continue on to the theater and the tree-shaded piazzale delle Corporazioni, the former business district, where the mosaic pavement in front of the offices depicts the nature of the various businesses. Several blocks later you'll reach the Capitolium, behind which is the **Museo Archeologico Ostiense**, housing well-displayed sculptures from the excavations, noteworthy among them *Cupid and Psyche, Family of Marcus Aurelius,* and *Lion Attacking a Bull.* Farther on are some remarkable mosaics in the Casa delle Muse (House of the Muses) and the Domus dei Dioscuri (House of the Dioscuri). At the extreme end of the excavations are the remains of one of the oldest synagogues yet discovered, dating from the first century.

The most picturesque way of getting to Ostia is on the boat sponsored by the Amici del Tevere, which leaves from the Ponte Marconi in Rome. Otherwise, the trains that leave from Stazione di Termini for Lido di Ostia stop at Ostia Antica; there is also a subway line from Rome to Lido di Ostia, a short walk from Ostia Antica.

TIVOLI AND VILLA ADRIANA

Medieval in appearance, the town of Tivoli is the bastion of the Renaissance **Villa d'Este**, built for Cardinal Ippolito II d'Este by Pirro Ligorio. The villa itself contains frescoes by 16th-century artists, but more noteworthy are its gardens, awash with hundreds of fountains, some of which once played music or bird songs. Though the *giochi d'acqua,* the sprays of water that surprised unsuspecting visitors, are no longer in use either, the fountains themselves are just as wondrous. The Organ Fountain, Terrace of the Hundred Fountains, Ovato Fountain, Rometta Fountain, and Dragon Fountain are but a few. Dry for centuries, the fountains were restored by the Italian government, which also illuminates them at night during the summer.

Seeing the fountains at Villa d'Este is perhaps best combined with a surreptitious picnic dinner at **Villa Adriana** (Hadrian's Villa), a few km (couple of miles) west of Tivoli. Now in ruins, it was once the largest villa in ancient Rome. The Emperor Hadrian built it for his retirement, reconstructing some of his favorite sights from around the world to keep him company. Among them were the entrance colonnade, called the Poikile, from Athens, and the Canal of Canopus from Egypt. Other monuments include the Lyceum, the Maritime Theater, and the Academy. The extensive grounds serve as an ideal backdrop to a discreet meal, which might be taken as lunch after a visit to the Villa d'Este if you are unable to see its fountains at night.

ACOTRAL provides regular bus service from Rome to Tivoli, depositing passengers near the entrance to Villa d'Este; buses stop at the entrance of Villa Adriana on the way.

CASTELLI ROMANI

The Castelli Romani (Roman castles) are, collectively, the 13 towns where wealthy Romans built castles and villas in the Colli Albani, or Alban Hills, best known for their crisp white wine. **Frascati** is the most popular of the Castelli Romani, and though its lovely 16th-century Villa Aldobrandini has spectacular views of Rome, it is best known as a gathering place for *fagottari,* people who buy or bring bundles of *porchetta* (pork roasted with herbs) and other delicacies to enjoy on open-air terraces next to the wine shops while drinking healthy amounts of the Frascati wine. **Cacciani** (via Armando Diaz 13; Tel: 942-04-40) is an excellent restaurant here, with an expansive outdoor terrace to enjoy in the summer.

Grottaferrata is worth a visit for those interested in its Abbazia, a Basilian abbey where the Greek Orthodox rite was reinstituted with the pope's permission during the last century. The monks will show you around the grounds and the museum of religious artifacts, and also sell olive oil and a good local wine. The wine of **Marino** is considered the best of all the Colli Albani whites, and is especially celebrated during the Sagra dell'Uva (Festival of the Grape) on the first Sunday in October, when, after a procession and an offering to the Madonna, the town's fountain (Fontana dei Mori) flows with wine.

Castel Gandolfo is believed to be the location of Alba Longa, the most powerful city in ancient Latium, founded by the son of Aeneas and destroyed by the Romans. The current town contains the church of San Tommaso da Villanova and a fountain, both by Bernini, in its main square. Its **Palazzo Pontificio** is part of the Vatican State and serves as the the summer residence of the pope, who then gives addresses here on Sundays and holds audiences on Wednesday mornings (apply for admission at the Vatican). **Albano Laziale** is on a lake on the site of the Castra Albana built by Septimius Severus for a Roman legion in the second century. Ruins of the ancient town and subsequent Medieval additions may be seen.

The Nemus Dianae, or Grove of Diana, sacred to a primitive cult with which Frazer opens *The Golden Bough,* gave its name to the town and lake of **Nemi**, today famous for its strawberries. Though very few of them are wild, they are all celebrated in the Sagra delle Fragole, or strawberry festival, in June. **Rocca di Papa**, named after the castle, or *rocca,* built by the popes, is the highest of all the Castelli Romani. The upper portion of the town is Medieval, and if you ascend Monte Cavo above that (as did the Roman legions when the Temple of Jupiter Latialis was located here) you'll have magnificent views of the Castelli, the lakes of Albano and Nemi, and the surrounding countryside as far as the coast.

The most convenient way to see the Castelli Romani in a day is undoubtedly by car, beginning on the Roman via Tuscolana (route S 215) and following signs for the individual towns; otherwise, select the one or two towns that appeal most to you and check train and bus schedules. Trains from Stazione di Termini serve Albano, Marino, and Frascati. ACOTRAL buses from Cinecittà go to all the towns mentioned.

ETRUSCAN SITES

Most of the beautiful objects—sculpture, vases, and gold artifacts—unearthed from Etruscan necropolises over the last century are on display at museums such as the Museo Nazionale di Villa Giulia and the Musei Vaticani in Rome. The tombs themselves, however, which so fascinated D. H. Lawrence (he wrote about them in *Etruscan Places*) and others, are easy to visit from Rome, and a look at their faded frescoes and homelike arrangement makes the ancient civilization seem both closer and more distant.

Begin at the Medieval-looking town of **Tarquinia**, where the **Museo Nazionale Tarquiniese** has an extensive collection of Etruscan art from the nearby necropolises (about 3 km/2 miles west of town)—only a few of which are also open to the public (apply at museum) on any given day, because of their delicate condition and to protect them from grave robbers (*tombaroli*). Toward Medieval **Viterbo**, more necropolises are to be seen surrounding the hill town of Tuscania and farther along the road at Bagno delle Bussete. Castel d'Asso, on a small road southwest of Viterbo, has a large cliffside necropolis, as does Norchia, to the west of Vetralla. From there, after returning to Tarquinia, the coastal road is dotted with both Etruscan and Roman sites at Civitavecchia, Santa Marinella, and Pyrgi. **Cerveteri** was once the most flourishing of the Etruscan cities, and its Banditaccia necropolis about a mile outside of the town gives the best idea of the extent and luxurious furnishings of the civilization's cities of the dead. Closest to Rome, off route S 2, is the necropolis at **Veio**, near the hill town of Isola Farnese.

Since many of the Etruscan sights are tombs in the open countryside, the best way to visit them is by car. Depending on how long you want to stay at the individual sites, this can take one lengthy day or two leisurely days, with the best accommodations for a stopover at Tarquinia's **Tarconte e Ristorante Solengo** at via Tuscia 19; Tel: (0766) 85-61-41. Otherwise, buses leave from via Lepanto in Rome for Tarquinia and Cerveteri, and Veio is on Rome's number 201 bus route from Ponte Milvio.

ANZIO AND NETTUNO

Anzio was the birthplace of both Caligula and Nero, a bloody legacy continued more recently by the landing in World War II of American and British troops. Today it and Nettuno are modern seaside resort towns, Anzio boasting excavations of the **Villa di Nerone** (Nero's Villa). Both are of special interest for their cemeteries: The British Military Cemetery is located at Anzio, the American at Nettuno.

ACOTRAL buses leave for Anzio from Rome at Cinecittà; trains from Stazione di Termini.

ABBAZIA DI MONTECASSINO

The site of a lengthy World War II battle that completely destroyed it, the Abbazia di Montecassino (Abbey of Montecassino), near the town of Cassino, was an important center of learning during the Middle Ages and has been reconstructed in Medieval style. Now as then it is the headquarters of the Benedictine order founded there by Saint Benedict in 529. Its history, breathtaking views, and a collection of Medieval manuscripts make it a worthwhile stop when driving between Rome and Naples.

THE ABRUZZI

By Peter Todd Mitchell

There are few world capitals you can leave and, within a couple of hours, find yourself in a region as high, as wild, and as spectacular as the Abruzzi (actually the regions of Abruzzo and Molise joined). Rome is such a capital, and the province to its east that until recent times was known for being both primitive and remote has suddenly been brought into the orbit of every traveller, thanks to the miracle of Italy's roads. The same Autostrada, A 24, that skirts Hadrian's Villa soon enough delivers you into the center of a mountain world once known for its witches, its superstitions, its wolves, and, just to help things along, its werewolves: *lupi mannari*. The breathtaking mountains themselves—the highest of the Apennines—were largely responsible for cutting the Abruzzi off from the north and directing its traffic of herds and its commercial dealings toward Apulia and the south, or to the port of Pescara on the Adriatic. These peaks are high enough to be snow covered all year round, and can be seen from every side: from the seacoast, where they form a silhouette the natives call "The Sleeping Beauty," and from Abruzzo's capital, L'Aquila, where the white crests of the Gran Sasso tower over the town to the north, forming a barrier 9,000 feet high.

The well-constructed roads to L'Aquila from every other direction glide through a landscape that never fails to delight: lush valleys, rushing streams, and Medieval towns perched on terraced hills. Voyagers who arrived at these villages were once in for a rough night in whatever passed for lodgings; inedible food and beds crawling with "little strangers" were commonplace. Now there are modern hotels not only in the larger towns but in the mountains as well—the latter opened up as ski resorts in the winter and as havens for nature and wildlife lovers in the summer. For those who ski there are outposts in every direction—Campo Imperatore, Campo Felice, Campo di Giove.

If you're searching for interesting flora and fauna, head in particular toward the south, where the hills below Sulmona and Scanno lead to the Parco Nazionale dell'Abruzzo.

MAJOR INTEREST

Wild, mountainous landscape
Medieval villages
Food

L'Aquila
Churches of Santa Maria di Collemaggio and San
    Bernardino
Castello and its Museo Nazionale d'Abruzzo
Fontana delle 99 Cannelle
Tre Marie restaurant

Teramo mountain town
Gran Sasso d'Italia and its ski resorts
Scanno jewelry in Roman style
Sulmona Medieval hill town
Parco Nazionale d'Abruzzo
Chieti (Roman ruins)
Campbasso (ruins of Greek Saepinum)

L'Aquila

L'Aquila is a town of architectural treasures ranging from its Romanesque and Renaissance churches to its perfect Spanish **Castello**, built by Don Pedro of Toledo during the reign of Charles V. The Spanish were here for some time, and they must have felt at home. The spectacle of L'Aquila's buildings, often subtle yet colorful, in contrast with the ever-present drama of their background, is reminiscent of Granada, another favored town of Emperor Charles, even though here the streets are set in a more rectilinear manner. The Castello has been turned into a very well-designed museum, the **Museo Nazionale d'Abruzzo**, with collections of Medieval art and Renaissance sculpture. The natural daughter of Charles V, Margaret of Austria, retired to L'Aquila after two not very happy marriages: one to a Medici (murdered), the other to a Farnese. She was an *amazone,* and sounds like a kindred spirit to Cristina of Sweden. She would ride forth from her palace (now the Palazzo di Giustizia) dressed as a man. The streets of L'Aquila have hardly changed since then, and it is thanks to them, and the inviting promenades they offer, that the town can be best enjoyed if you stay over—to see the *passeggiata* down the corso Federico II at sunset; its small piazzas with their fountains in the evening under the stars; and then the hubbub of the market in front of the Duomo the next morning.

This cathedral, due to the earthquakes that plague the Abruzzi, has survived badly; but it never did compare with the two outstanding churches of L'Aquila. One of them, **Santa Maria di Collemaggio**, is on the edge of town, reached by way of a tree-lined avenue. It has a boldly designed façade of red-and-white marble, its patterned polychrome interrupted by three Romanesque portals and three rose windows. Santa Maria was founded to honor a miraculous image of the Virgin seen by Saint Celestine, an aged hermit who was almost forcibly dragged from his mountain retreat near Sulmona to become pope at the end of the 13th century, at a point when the College of Cardinals had reached a total impasse. Pope was the last thing that the naïve Celestine wanted to be, and once his incapacity was recognized he abdicated, only to be imprisoned by the succeeding pontiff, a former Cardinal Gaetani, who wasn't naïve at all. Celestine was kept in a castle at Fumone until he died at 81, and only then was it considered safe to bring him back here to his own church, to canonize him, and later to build him the fine Renaissance tomb that we see at this church.

The other saint who ended up in L'Aquila was Saint Bernard of Siena, who arrived here just in time to die, to the everlasting fury of the Sienese, who never got his body back. The people of L'Aquila gave him a superb Renaissance church, however: the **Church of San Bernardino**, with an imposing mausoleum sculpted by Silvestro dell'Aquila, who did one almost equally fine for Maria Pereira in the north chancel.

Very much the point of visiting L'Aquila are the smaller churches and their respective piazzas, dotted all over town: San Giusta and San Flaviano (Romanesque); Santa

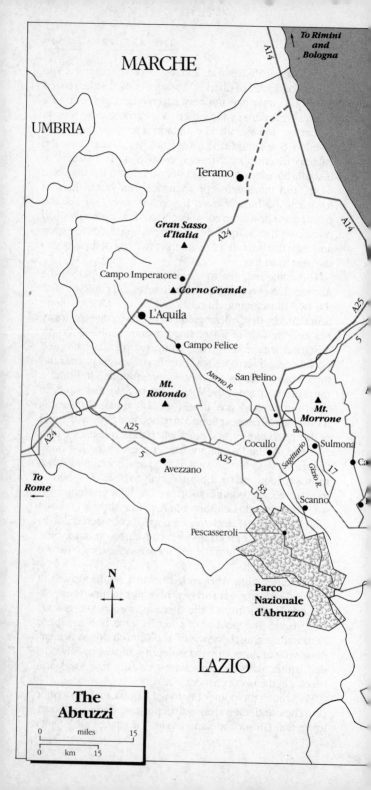

Maria di Paganica, surrounded by Gothic palaces; San Silvestro, with its frescoes; and San Giuseppe, with its Gothic tombs. Near the Porta Rivera is San Vito, and below it is the **Fontana delle 99 Cannelle**, where 99 sculpted masks spout water. According to legend, L'Aquila rose from the earth with 99 of everything: quarters, fountains, churches, and 99 villages around it to come to its rescue in time of need. The truth is that the city was founded in 1240 by Emperor Frederick II, as yet another bastion against Rome.

The Food of L'Aquila and the Abruzzi

Frederick did a great deal for the cuisine of Apulia and his other domains to the south, and it is possible that a whiff of the East inherited from his childhood in semi-Saracen Palermo affected the food of the Abruzzi, too. And varied that food is, coming from the five provinces that make up this region of the Abruzzi, in the plural. The region's red-hot pepper, *diavoletto,* is thrown around with an almost-Moroccan abandon. Every aromatic herb at hand is used as well, including tarragon (supposedly introduced to the French by the Abruzzese chef of Catherine de Medici). Meats are almost always treated with rosemary, white wine, and olive oil, while later additions to flavoring—saffron and capers—also turn up in many dishes. The various cuisines of the province—mountain, hill, and sea—were once more separate than they are now, and the renowned cheeses turn up in every area: *Pecorino* is often used in cooking, and the pear-shaped *scamorza,* made from the milk of cows that graze very high, is exported on a large scale. Vegetables are prepared with great care, and those of the spring, such as peas and fava beans, are thrown—along with lentils—into a *minestra* known as *le virtu.*

The good fish restaurants are naturally confined to the coast, but luckily for newcomers to the Abruzzi, the best of local dishes can be sampled right in the center of L'Aquila, at the venerable **Tre Marie**, tucked away on a side street of the same name right off the piazza del Duomo. Even in the story of its inception, the Tre Marie is typical of L'Aquila's past. In the 19th century the great-grandfather of the present owner went off to the hills to buy cheese and lamb for his inn. He was killed by bandits, and his widow was left with three daughters to raise. The tradition of teaching cooking was by no means new here;

the school known as the Villa Santa Maria had been founded as long ago as the 14th century to teach the *lazaroni* a trade and inundate Europe with Abruzzese chefs. In that tradition, the widow Candelora taught her daughters to cook, and a restaurant was started where they passed on her recipes, in turn, to their children. The present menu changes with the season, of course, but quite conveniently always includes the basic local dishes. For soups there is a minestra of vegetables, or a chicken broth served with light crepes—*scrippelle M'Busse*—and sprinkled with Parmesan. Most will opt for the Abruzzi's favorite pasta: *maccheroni alla chitarra,* cut into very thin strips with the wooden-and-steel harp once found in every household here, the pasta then served with either a sauce of tomato or one of diced meat and pecorino. Polenta with chopped sausage is an alternative, and so are the short, flat *fusilli* served with a game sauce.

The ham of L'Aquila was certainly a Spanish innovation—cured here but resembling that of Serrano. Fresh mountain river trout are served at the Tre Marie on a bed of potatoes and black olives; also from the mountains come the truffles, here sliced and served with breast of chicken. The two favorite local meats are roast lamb and pork, both cooked with herbs. For the spring festivals, pork comes out onto the piazzas, and roast suckling pig is sold at stands with accompanying slabs of bread.

All the local cheeses are on the menu of the Tre Marie, with the *scamorza* served *allo spiedo* (on a skewer). The best of the desserts are the *dolcetti paesani di mandorle,* a selection of every sort of almond sweet, from the rich, soft marzipan made in the southern hills of Maiella to a crisp variation of Spanish *turron.* The wines of the Abruzzi have recently improved: the rosé (Rosatello) has always been worthy of export, but it has now been joined by a red Montepulciano d'Abruzzo and a white Trebbiano.

The cuisine of the Abruzzi has come very much into its own in the past decade, just like that of Apulia. Apart from L'Aquila there are two other centers for sampling it. One, the mountain town of **Teramo**, 75 km (45 miles) to the northeast by beautiful roads, is a capital of its own province within a province, a picturesque place, a Roman town in origin, though much of the city is Medieval and Renaissance in appearance. In the old part of town, visit the 12th-century red-brick Duomo, with a silver altar made of 34 panels. Roman ruins have been excavated near the center of town. At the **Church of Madonna della**

Grazie, in the east end of town, there is a good 15th-century Virgin made of wood, the work of Silvestro dell'Aquila. The Villa Comunale houses a museum with art works by local and Neapolitan artists. In Teramo, the restaurant **Duomo** has been turned by its proprietor, Elio Pompa, into a station both for traditional dishes and some of his own creations, such as rigatoni *alla Candida,* aromatic with olives, herbs, and prosciutto. Lamb or roast kid can follow, and the wines here are particularly good. Another starred shrine is at **Lanciano**, near the coast and just south of another capital, Chieti (south of Pescara). There, in his **Taverna Ranieri**, Nicola Ranieri creates local dishes with his own flair: crepes filled with seafood; *agnolotti* made with eggplant; and (the sea being near) lobster, sea bass, and crayfish, all *alla Ranieri.*

Hotels in L'Aquila include the **Castello**, conveniently located opposite the Spanish fortress, worth booking in advance because it can be quite full (ask for a room in back, away from the traffic). On a grander scale there is the **Duca degli Abruzzi**, also central enough, and with a roof garden boasting a view of Il Gran Sasso d'Italia.

The Gran Sasso

Some might even want to make a day excursion to this snow-capped ridge of limestone, 22 miles long and bare but for the snow. The highest peak, the Corno Grande (9,554 feet), is higher than any peak in southern Italy except Sicily's Etna. Consisting of two chains, almost parallel and separated by a depression, the Gran Sasso divides the Abruzzi from the Marches to the north. Hikers, equipped with good maps that are available at newsstands, can walk to *rifugi* (inexpensive inns). The Club Alpino Italiano, Via XX Settembre 8, L'Aquila, is the best source of information, but a knowledge of Italian is essential. To make the trek to the top of the massif from L'Aquila, take a city bus to Fonte Cerreto and from there the cable car to Campo Imperatore, at the foot of the Corno Grande; the hike to the top will take you about seven hours. **Campo Imperatore**, at 7,029 feet, is also connected by bus with L'Aquila (about 25 km/15 miles away) and is a complete resort. The **Albergo di Campo Imperatore** is at the top of a ski lift.

The Gran Sasso is certainly more accessible to present-day travellers than it was to Otto Skorzeny, who was sent to these mountains by Hitler in 1943 to rescue Mussolini. After his arrest, Il Duce had been shifted from one isolated prison to another, and it took two months for the Germans to discover where he was. Once found, the hideaway—a hotel on the Gran Sasso—was surrounded by German commmandos landing by glider. The Italian guards put up no resistance, and Skorzeny rushed to the room where Mussolini was lodged, explained what was happening, and with the help of a crack aviator named Gerlach managed, in a damaged plane, to get the dictator to Vienna that very evening.

The Southern Ranges

Many travellers will want to head southeast to the range of La Maiella and Monte Morrone above Sulmona, or the Colle Rotondo above Scanno, because this southern region culminates in the **Parco Nazionale d'Abruzzo**: 150 square miles of scenic splendor inhabited by chamois, bears, and golden eagles, and crisscrossed by excellent roads.

The roads south to the Parco Nazionale, however, also pass through or near places of interest: **San Pelino**, with its Romanesque church, and **Pescocostanzo**, off route 84 near route 17, a gabled Medieval town of artisans. In **Scanno**, between routes 83 and 17, the women no longer wear the black Middle Eastern dresses that were once taken for granted (fewer and fewer native costumes are to be seen), but the town is still a center for jewelers whose designs have not changed much since Roman times. There are hotels aplenty, thanks to winter sports, both in town and on the lake, where a rain-bringing Virgin has her shrine. The best hotel is the inexpensive **Mille Pini**, simple, neat, Alpine in style, and, as the name suggests, surrounded by pines. It is situated at the foot of the chair-lift to Monte Rotondo and has a small garden. A nice place to eat is the **Archetti**, an old-fashioned tavern in a 16th-century cellar.

The best known of these hill towns remains **Sulmona**, right off route 17, just south of A 25. Its Medieval monuments, such as the Palazzo dell'Annunziata, line the main street, which leads from the market to the Duomo. It doesn't take long to find out who the favorite native son of Sulmona is. "Sulmo Mihi Patria Est," declared the Roman poet Ovid, and the Sulmonese have taken his word for it. The principal thoroughfare is the corso Ovidio, there is a statue of him in the largest piazza, and there are plenty of indications as to where "Ovid's Villa" can be found. Whether or not it even belonged to his distant kin, its size reminds us, as Ovid himself was wont to do, that he was a knight and born into a wealthy family, in a land "cool and rich in water." (The mountains around Sulmona frame a valley running with streams.) The poet himself, hardly elegiac, was by no means addicted to country life; highly urbane, he preferred metropolitan Rome. His elegant, completely amoral verses described nature of another sort—without, miraculously, ever using an obscene word. Later, the natives of Sulmona became confused about his powers; it was said that Ovid was more literate than even Cicero because he could read with his feet (and his statue in Sulmona has him standing on a book).

As for ski resorts in this region, the town of **Campo di Giove**, 85 km (53 miles) southeast of L'Aquila and just 18 km (11 miles) east of Sulmona, stands at the foot of Tavola Rotonda (6,703 feet), which is one of the peaks of the Maiella mountains. In the old village there are still some houses dating from the 15th century. The **Fonte Romana** is one of the best hotels, near ski lifts and the cable car.

A mountain retreat on a grand scale at a very reasonable price is the **Castello di Balsorano**, a fine outpost on the western side of the national park from which to make forays into the park or into nearby Latium. This 13th-century fortress is one of the few to survive the barbarians and the earthquakes. Inside, the fortress is still Medieval—coats of armor, shields, and daggers abound. Some bedrooms are done up in baronial style with silk wall hangings and ornately carved beds. Proprietor Mary Ricci is English, a help in this land where little *inglese* is spoken. The hotel is very small, so reserve well in advance. Dining room meals are good and moderately priced; even so, you will pay more for them than for the room.

Elsewhere in the Abruzzi

The Abruzzi produced another poet, one of our century, and his birthplace is one of the few sights that the Adriatic port of **Pescara** offers. Gabriele D'Annunzio was to be as famous in his time as Ovid was in imperial Rome—and with some similarities: Both, in their youth, shocked the world with poems of unbridled sensuality; both became the darlings of the aristocracy; and both treated their subject matter as masters of style. But there the resemblance ends. D'Annunzio was born into a humble family, and he was finally a very serious man who loved his country (he lost an eye for it in World War I, and soon after secured Fiume for Italy with his own army of companions). Ovid showed nothing but scorn for the rustic Abruzzese, while D'Annunzio, though born on the coast, was fascinated by the people of the mountainous interior, and in particular by their ventures into sorcery and witchcraft.

The invasion of witches and snake charmers came to the Abruzzi from the west in ancient times, when a people called the Marsi streamed over the mountains to settle around what is now Avezzano, leaving their name on many a village still there: *nei Marsi.* They brought their spells with them, and their ability with snakes, too. Every year at his festival at Cocullo, near Scanno, the image of San Domenico is carried forth covered with a writhing, hissing brood. Children here are taught to handle snakes without fear, and these reptiles even turn up on the coat of arms of the monastic order of San Celestino.

It was in the Abruzzi that the word *Italia* was born; and, whether Greek, Roman, or Italic, remains of classical cultures litter the gentle slopes of Chieti and Molise as they descend toward the sea or toward Apulia to the south. In the town of **Chieti** itself, south of Pescara off A 25, the ruins are Roman, and some of the fine statues found there are displayed in the Museo Archeologico Nazionale in Naples.

Molise

It is in the province of Molise, at the Abruzzi's south, however, that you will come upon the more ancient towns, often Samnite in origin, with some ruins contemporary with the Golden Age of Greece. In the north of the province are the excavations at **Pietrabbondante**: a theater and scattered temples completely in the countryside, raised on a green tableland with views in every direction.

Larger in scale, and not far south of Molise's capital, Campobasso (off route 87), is the city of **Saepinum**. Its forums, temples, and monuments are in a miraculous state of preservation, and still in bucolic surroundings that recall that it was the stopover for the massive movement of herds twice a year between the heights of the Abruzzi and the Apulian plain. The outer wall of the theater has been converted into peasant homes; otherwise, you can wander through a stone Pompeii reminiscent of those untouched towns we see in paintings of the 17th century. For the many travellers who will pass through here on their way south to the wonders of Magna Graecia, the museums of Bari and Taranto, and the temples of Calabria and Basilicata, they are a perfect preparation for things to come.

GETTING AROUND

Service between Rome and Pescara and L'Aquila is at present better by bus (ARPA line) than by train, which is direct but a longer ride by more than an hour. L'Aquila and Pescara are linked by rail and bus to Sulmona. The Parco Nazionale can be visited by taking the bus (ARPA) from Sulmona to Pescasseroli, the park's administrative center; or the train to Avezzano, on the Rome–Pescara line. Other connections can be made by bus within the region.

ACCOMMODATIONS REFERENCE

▶ **Le Cannelle.** Via Tancredi da Pentina 2, 67100 L'Aquila. Tel: (0862) 6981; Telex: 600120. Swimming pool, tennis, and other amenities at this large, 160-room hotel across from L'Aquila's famous fountain.

▶ **Albergo di Campo Imperatore.** 67010 **Campo Imperatore.** Tel: (0862) 66-132.

▶ **Castello.** Piazza Battaglione Alpini, 67100 **L'Aquila.** Tel: (0862) 29-147.

▶ **Castello di Balsorano.** 67025 **Balsorano.** Tel: (0823) 95-236.

▶ **Duca degli Abruzzi.** Viale Giovanni XXIII, 10, 67100 L'Aquila. Tel: (0862) 28-341.

▶ **Fonte Romana.** 67030 **Campo di Giove.** Tel: (0864) 40-111.

▶ **Grand Hotel del Parco.** Via Santa Lucia 3, 67032 **Pescasseroli.** Tel: (0863) 91-356. A luxurious and expensive (especially for this region) hotel near Parco Nazionale d'Abruzzo.

▶ **Mille Pini.** 67038 **Scanno.** Tel: (0864) 74-387.

NAPLES, CAMPANIA, AND THE AMALFI DRIVE

By Barbara Hults

Campania, nature decreed, would be a balm to body and soul, a luxurious coastline of sheltered bays curving past Naples, down to the ancient Roman cities of Pompeii and Herculaneum, and beyond to the beautiful Amalfi coast and the ancient Greek city of Paestum. Running in back of the coastline are the Apennine mountains, and offshore lie Capri and the volcanic mysteries of Ischia. Even Vesuvius, the volcano that once covered Pompeii with ash, is beautiful, its famous double curve completing the symmetry of the Bay of Naples.

While the past is creatively preserved here, the present is also celebrated, at resorts as chic as the San Pietro in Positano or as happily untouristed as Palinuro farther south. Pompeii and Herculaneum are frozen moments, their life stopped suddenly at A.D. 89, when Vesuvius erupted. Paestum's Doric temples have kept their youth because the site was abandoned when malaria swept the south; Tiberius's beautiful villa on Capri fared less well, but the site is so magnificent that ruins are secondary when visiting Capri. At Amalfi the cathedral recalls the

Arab-Norman past, and the churches and palaces of Naples are getting a long-overdue face-lift.

Naples and Campania combine the influences of, in succession, ancient Greeks, Romans, Byzantines, Normans, Hohenstaufens, French Angevins, Spanish Bourbons, the Bonapartes, and Garibaldi's movement toward the *Risorgimento*.

As a place to relax in the shadow of antiquity, Campania still draws dreamers from throughout the world, rewarding them with days of endless beauty, relaxation, and good food—seafood, macaroni (in a thousand shapes, it seems), pizza, fine wines, and fruits and vegetables from the rich volcanic soil.

MAJOR INTEREST

Natural beauty along the coast
Unique mix of cultural influences

Naples
The Old City of Spaccanapoli (Gothic and Baroque churches)
Castel Nuovo
Teatro San Carlo
Castel dell'Ovo
The museums (Archeologico, Capodimonte, San Martino)
The Bay, from Naples to Capo Posillipo

Antro della Sibilla (Cave of the Sibyl) at Cuma
Pompeii, Herculaneum, and Paestum
Capri
Ischia
The Amalfi coast

Campania is one of the easiest regions of Italy to visit because the most sought-after destinations lie along the coast when you travel from north to south. The mountainous interior is rich with towns and valleys that recall the past, but even these are overshadowed by the formidable line of attractions along the seacoast extending from Naples. Despite its drawbacks, Naples remains a fascinating city and a good base for exploring other parts of Campania.

NAPLES

Naples is not kind to the day visitor, who must combat traffic and noise in a city that offers no gracious piazzas in which to relax. The city bestows its favors only on those who take the time to know it and who then often remain loyal friends for life.

Watching a street scene in Naples is like watching a hundred television sets at once, each tuned to a different channel. The variety of expressions one eyebrow can engineer is amazing, not to mention the full repertoire of mime both more subtle and more obvious than most actors use in a lifetime.

Naples is known for having given Italy—and the world—some of its greatest thinkers: Benedetto Croce, for example, and Giovanni Vico, the first modern historian.

To enjoy the best of Naples and avoid the worst confusion, choose a hotel along the harbor at Santa Lucia. The elegant old **Excelsior** looks out to Vesuvius with the perfect view of the Bay of Naples, and the modern **Royal** faces the dramatic Castel dell'Ovo, which is floodlit at night and bordered by crashing waves (hope for a storm). Ask for front rooms at both. Another advantage is that nearby buses will take you anywhere in the city, although from Santa Lucia you can simply walk to the Teatro San Carlo and the Palazzo Reale. (The **Paradiso** at Capo Posillipo is another hotel with a view.)

Take the number 140 bus—never at rush hour—to its last stop, piazza Gesù, the heart of old Naples. (The bus starts at Capo Posillipo, the pretty residential cape beyond the city's western boundary.) At piazza Gesù a tourist office offers color-coded maps of the Old City, called Spaccanapoli, where the Greco-Roman grid pattern of streets marks out one of the most colorful parts of town. The main tourist office in the Palazzo Reale can also provide these maps, which are worth looking for: Ask for *The Old City: A Stratified Multiple Itinerary Map.*

In the piazza del Gesù Nuovo stands the **Church of the Gesù**, and in front of it a *guglia*—curious, dethroned steeplelike monument that seems to be waiting to be lifted back on top of the church. This one is especially Baroque in feeling—festooned with flowers, saints, and

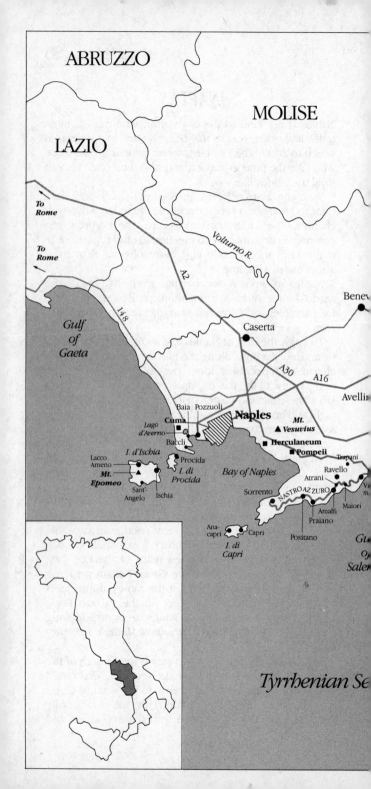

angels, with the Madonna on top, like a country processional object captured in stone.

The rusticated façade of the Gesù itself is created of diamond-pointed *piperno,* a lava stone obviously easy to come by here in the shadow of the volcano. Inside is one of the typical surprises Naples has to offer: a joyous profusion of colored marble and frescoes. Neapolitans love to marry here in May (the month of the Madonna), with pomp and enthusiasm worthy of the setting. Despite earthquakes and bombs, the church has endured and kept its charm through restoration. The Jesuit architect Valeriani built this structure over an older palace between 1584 and 1601, when the Spanish viceroys ruled Naples. Above the door is *Heliodorus Driven from the Temple* by Solimena, which shows why he was unequalled as a fresco painter until Tiepolo appeared in the north. Cosimo Fanzago, a genius with multicolored marble, contributed the Saint Ignatius altar in the left transept.

Spaccanapoli District

After seeing the Gesù, enter the **Spaccanapoli District**, a sort of Baroque souk of flower markets, street-corner transistor hawkers, dark cathedrals of mysterious saints, and grand palace courtyards hung with flapping sheets and towels that signal the owners' presence.

Just left of the Gesù is via Benedetto Croce, named for the Neapolitan philosopher who lived in the 14th-century palace at number 12, where he founded the Istituto Italiano per gli Studi Storici in 1947.

But first there is the lovely **Church of Santa Chiara**, now restored to its Gothic-Provençal charm, where Robert the Wise (who died in the 14th century) is buried. King Robert's court was as close as Naples ever came to Camelot—a time that Boccaccio described in the *Decameron,* though he changed the setting to Florence. Robert's wife, Sancia de Mallorca, had wanted to enter a convent, often a favored alternative to an arranged marriage, but fate or her father decided on Robert. As an act of secular devotion she had Santa Chiara and the cloisters built, giving Naples one of its most loved churches.

Robert's regal tomb at the altar shows the king lying in the Franciscan robes he wore when he entered that order late in life. To Petrarch, of whom Robert was a patron, he was the "consummate king and philosopher, equally illustrious in letters and in dominion." He was also unusual for an Angevin; most were detested for their cruelty.

The adjoining **Cloisters** are a peaceable kingdom hidden from the noisy streets. The columns and garden walls, brightly decorated with majolica scenes of life beyond the convent walls, kept the nuns from being homesick. Italian convents often attracted the aristocracy, who added the good life to good works by enjoying the world's beauty and developing a high level of cuisine, still found in convent bakeries on occasion, when they sell to the public. (Not here, unfortunately, though there is a wonderful baker up the street at piazza San Domenico.)

Past Croce's palazzo is another *guglia*—this one a votive offering against the plague. It marks the **Church of San Domenico Maggiore** (1308), the church of the Aragonese nobility. During the late 1500s, when Naples was ruled by a Spanish viceroy, powerful religious landowners built hundreds of convents, monasteries, and churches here, creating a small ecclesiastical city for themselves, which is why churches pop up on every block, though many are closed or abandoned.

San Domenico is very much alive inside, with its elaborate Renaissance altars. In the candle-lit Cappellone del Crocifisso, the painting of a crucifix is regarded as sacred because it spoke to Thomas Aquinas, one of the most prominent Neapolitan saints, who lived and taught here in the adjoining monastery. Christ asked the faithful Thomas what he could give him for his efforts. "Only thee, Lord, only thee," was Thomas's reply. Although Aquinas's rooms were destroyed by an earthquake and World War II bombs, a few relics are left: the bell he used, a portrait bust, the papal bull that proclaimed him Doctor of the Church. Stop in the sacristy to see the wonderful frescoes by Solimena and the unusual Aragonese tombs set into the walls.

Stop also at **Scaturchio** across from the church for coffee and a *sfogliatelle*, light, triangle-shaped layers of pastry with a soft ricotta center sweetened with lemon or candied fruit bits.

Off the right side of San Domenico is via De Sanctis, where the **Cappella San Severo** serves as crypt/museum for the family of the alchemist Prince Raimondo di Sangro (1711–71). The bizarre statues *Modesty* (veiled) and *Disillusion* (netted) stand at the altar, flanking Sammartino's extraordinary *Veiled Christ*, a virtuoso work in marble that

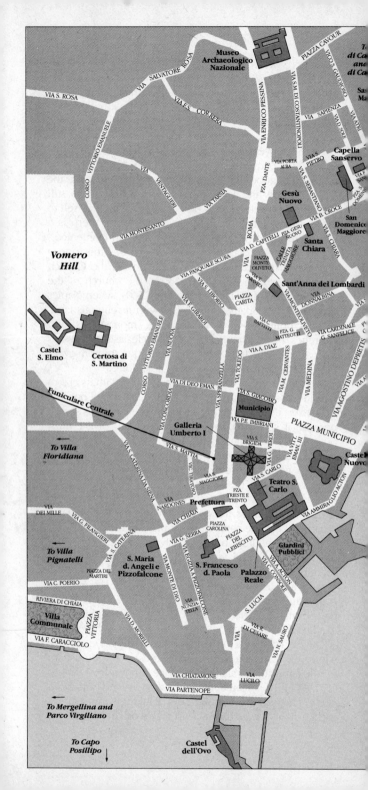

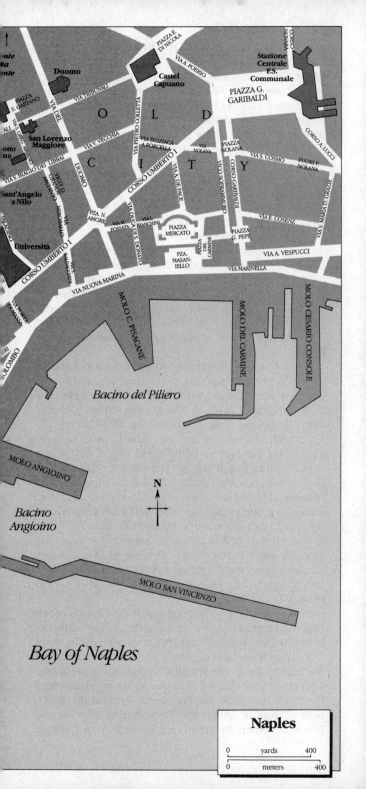

shows even Christ's wounds under a marble veil. Down-stairs is something else again: two mummies, apparently made up of masses of veins and arteries, preserved by an ancient Egyptian formula. Gossip says that the woman, obviously pregnant, was Sangro's mistress, caught with her lover. The likeness of the prince appears on the medallion on his tomb upstairs.

On via Nilo the forever-closed **Church of Sant'Angelo a Nilo** encloses a fine work of Donatello, but how to see it? Ask the portiere at the back of the Palazzo Brancaccio, vico di Donnaromita 15, to see the "*sepolcro del Cardinal Brancaccio*"; the fates may favor you.

The word *Nilo* here comes from the reclining figure lolling in the largo Corpo di Nilo, supposedly the river Nile, sculpted in Nero's time. For some reason the statue was beheaded, buried, and then resurrected. Perhaps it was his mischievous ways—he whispers to women who pass at night, say local residents. An espresso break at the **Bar Nilo** will let you observe wily Nilo and the passing throng.

A few blocks to the east is **via San Gregorio Armeno**, the street of Christmas past and present, where the mak-ers of *presepi* fill their workshops with every object for their miniature Christmas villages. The village is Bethle-hem, Neapolitan style of course: The tiny kitchens are filled with wee pizzas and the utensils used to make them, plus all manner of fruit and vegetables (young family members roll out the pea-size tomatoes and ap-ples); cows and camels; wise men and townspeople; and, of course, the Nativity scene and walls of angels, who also swing from the ceiling on wires. Although Christmas is the time to visit, a few shops stay open all year.

The **Church of San Gregorio Armeno** has charming cloisters and Luca Giordano's frescoes of Saint Gregory the Armenian's life. Giordano painted so many murals in Italy and at the European courts that he was called Luca *fa presto* ("Luca works fast").

At the top of the hilly street stands the **Church of San Lorenzo Maggiore**, built over the ancient pagan basilica of Neapolis (which is currently being excavated). In about 555 a church was built here to honor Saint Lawrence but it was replaced with this grander, Gothic church during the 13th century by Charles of Anjou. In this mystical setting Boccaccio first saw his Fiammetta—supposedly Maria, natural child of Robert the Wise—during Mass on one Easter Eve when the Pascal candle was lit from a brazier and incense permeated the very French setting of pointed arches and parapets. "As San Lorenzo was favored by the Angevin kings and therefore fashionable, there were present besides the devout folk many young men with curled and frizzed hair and many young women more luring than lenten in their dark dresses, who loitered beneath the Gothic arches and perhaps lipped a prayer or two between glances and signals and ogles; for even sinners do sometimes pray. . . . Among them was young Messer Giovanni Boccaccio," writes biographer Francis McManus. Boccaccio, enthralled with the poetic flourishes Provençal troubadours had absorbed from the Arabs at Cordoba, writes: "The shining eyes of the lovely lady looked sparkling into mine with piercing light along which, it seemed to me, I saw coming a fiery arrow of gold."

Petrarch, too, came to mass at San Lorenzo, and in 1345 prayed with the monks throughout the night during an earthquake and tidal wave. Another drama is remembered in the left transept, where Joanna I, Queen of Naples and granddaughter of Robert the Wise, is buried. Her adopted son Charles poisoned her when she supported Louis of Anjou against him. Her body was first displayed in the cloisters of Santa Chiara, though she was not yet dead, according to some observers. Flanking the church is a museum related to its history. The enormous refectory, which can be visited, was once used for the parliament of the Kingdom of Naples.

Across the street, the figure of San Gaetano gestures to the sky, in front of the **Church of San Paolo Maggiore**, built on the site of the pagan temple of the Dioscuri. The columns on the façade come from the early temple, as does the torso under the statues of Saints Peter and Paul. Nero held his singing debut in this temple, despite an earthquake that shook the building.

Since body and soul are intimately related in Spaccanapoli, the *pizzaiolo,* the pizza maker, is also venerated. At the **Trattoria Lombardi**, via Croce 59, *pizzaiolo* Mazza produces the adored Margherita pizza—made with fresh mozzarella, tomatoes, and fresh basil—kept simple so that the delicious crust can be fully appreciated. Drowning pizza or pasta with sauce is not a native tradition; Italians like the taste of the crust and the pasta as much as the topping. The best pizza makers use a brick oven, sometimes throwing a sprinkle of wood chips in at the last minute to singe the cheese and crust perfectly. The simple Margherita was named for Queen Margherita of Savoy, who in 1889 first tasted this version as prepared by *pizzaiolo* Raffaele Esposito. Another pizzeria, the **Bellini**, also in Spaccanopoli (via Santa Maria di Constantinopoli 80), wins approval from Neapolitans with high standards. Hearty, even rough wines accompany pizza; more subtle tastes would be lost.

From San Lorenzo it's easy to find the **Duomo**, off via Tribunali, on via del Duomo. There the patron saint of Naples, San Gennaro, performs a miracle twice yearly by liquefying his congealed blood kept in vials in a dazzling chapel here that has paintings by Domenichino. Multitudes gather for the occasion, waiting to judge the rapidity of the transformation, because the quicker the blood liquefies, the better the outlook for the city. Gennaro, called Januarius by the Romans, was beheaded in nearby Pozzuoli in 305, after which he walked to Naples carrying his head (the story goes). September 19 and December 16 are the days of the miracle. (In the crypt, or Cappella Carafa, a brilliant altar in Renaissance style contains San Gennaro's tomb.)

Among other occupants of the Duomo are Charles Martel and Charles I of Anjou, entombed at the entrance door and surrounded by an elaborate Luca Giordano fresco. Opposite San Gennaro's chapel is the much-restored Basilica of Santa Restituta, the oldest part of the Duomo, founded during the fourth century on the site of a temple to Apollo, with 27 columns that are probably relics of that early temple.

If you retrace your steps to piazza Gesù, detour briefly from the piazza down the Calle Trinità Maggiore to piazza Monteoliveto, where the **Church of Sant'Anna dei Lombardi** is full of wonders, such as a life-size pietà of eight figures by Guido Mazzoni (1492). The chapel at the right of the entrance contains an *Annunciation* by Benedetto da Maiano (1498), who also finished the tomb of Mary of Aragon in the opposite chapel, where there is a fine *presepio* by Antonio Rosellino.

The Museums of Naples

Antiquity was once considered the province of the king, but Garibaldi relieved the royals of that responsibility in 1860, and now museums are open to all. At the **Museo Archeologico Nazionale**, north of piazza Gesù at the far end of via Santa Maria di Constantinopoli, the collection is one of the best in the world, especially the paintings from Pompeii and the small bronzes. Visit this museum before traveling to Pompeii and Herculaneum to get a clearer idea of those cities' original grandeur.

North of the archaeological museum is the **Palazzo e Galleria Nazionale di Capodimonte** (bus number 324 from piazza Vittoria), which occupies a hillside palace that enjoys a panoramic view of the bay. Charles III used the palace as a hunting lodge instead of a castle because it had no water. The art gallery has an important collection of works by Caravaggio, Rubens, Bellini, Titian, and Filippo Lippi. Also represented here is the lesser-known Artemisia Gentileschi. Influenced by Caravaggio, she favored gruesome scenes painted in bright, translucent tones with a strict attention to detail. Her paintings of Judith here and in the Uffizi are especially dramatic. Stop at the Royal Apartments to see the Salottino di Porcellano, an all-porcelain room delicate in chinoiserie motifs—peacocks and flowers and Chinese objects. (A museum devoted to porcelain is located in the **Villa Floridiana** on Vomero hill; see below for Vomero.)

The De Ciccio collection in Capodimonte includes porcelain, tapestry, and small bronzes. Charles was entranced by the *presepio* tradition and started making his own figures from clay while the queen and princesses sewed and embroidered the costumes. As the king did, so did society, and this once-simple tradition of keeping Christmas all year became a new way for the nobles to outdo one another in grandiosity.

On top of Vomero hill, to the north of the Santa Lucia area, is the **Certosa di San Martino**, a 14th-century monastery that is now home to examples of Naples' *presepio* art, with entire *presepi* as well as individual figures—not well presented but interesting nonetheless. Topographical maps, ship models, and the like elicit the city's cultural past, from the Bourbons to Garibaldi. The panorama of the bay and Vesuvius from the belvedere is one of the city's most dramatic.

Fanzago's white cloisters here contrast with the elaborately beautiful marble intarsia of the church, also his creation. The monks' chancel is the most remarkable section, with a superb marble communion table, a *Nativity* by Reni, and *Christ Washing the Disciples' Feet* by Caracciolo, founder of the Neapolitan school that opposed Mannerism in favor of Caravaggio's emotional path. His young rival, the Spaniard Giuseppe Ribera (1591–1652), known in Italy as Spagnoletto, became the court painter because of his sensuous approach. In the treasury is his *Deposition* and Giordano's last work, *The Triumph of Judith.* Caracciolo's frescoes of *The Life of Mary* (1631) decorate the third chapel at the left. On the entryway arches are Ribera's *Twelve Prophets;* the *Deposition* (1638) at the door is the work of Massimo Stanzioni, the leader of the Neapolitan school at mid-century, known for his subtle chromatic values, melodious lines, and lyrical expressions.

From Castel Nuovo to the
Villa Communale

The enormous **Castel Nuovo**, a brick castle at the harbor north of Santa Lucia built (1279–82), by Charles of Anjou presents such a tough-looking, macho aura that it's called the *Maschio Angioino.* Naples, however, is ever the great deceiver: The castle housed more than artillery. The court of Robert the Wise enjoyed a style of life behind its walls that inspired much of the *Decameron.* Boccaccio and Petrarch were there, and Giotto painted frescoes at the castle, though they were subsequently destroyed when the Aragonese redecorated and did away with the Angevin decor. Two magnificent features remain: the Renaissance arch and the Cappella Palatina. The Arco di Trionfo that welcomed Alphonse of Aragon to Naples has recently been restored, thanks to one of the region's greatest assets, the Napoli 99 committee, whose determination not to allow the city's treasures to molder away has led to the restoration of many aspects of Naples' past. In the Cappella Palatina (also known as the church of Santa Barbara) is a Madonna by Laurana— one of the most sensitive sculptors of Madonna and Child themes—and a fine rose window. The Sala dei Baroni, though damaged by fire, gives an idea of the castle's finest hours.

Beyond the castle to the west, at the piazza del Plebiscito, stands the **Teatro San Carlo**, where a 250-year anniversary gala in 1987 brought music celebrities from throughout the world. (Not the first time good musicians were welcomed in Naples; Handel was lionized here in 1708, for example.) The frayed red velvet and gilt interior has seen many of opera's most tearful moments. Although the season begins in December, musical productions are staged through much of the year. Take the tour if you can't see a performance.

Across the street is the Galleria Umberto I, usually less than sparkling clean and too drab to evoke its glamorous sister in Milan, but more interesting for its basic glass-and-steel form than the shops inside. Although few stores here are interesting, finding a table for a coffee in one of the local cafés allows you the pleasure of watching Neapolitans discuss politics. Next to San Carlo is the enormous **Palazzo Reale**, facing a piazza that is probably beautiful at dawn but for the rest of the day is a traffic cop's nightmare. The only effective preparation for crossing the street would be running with the bulls at Pamplona. Inside the 17th-century palace are a museum of paintings and the Bourbons' court theater, both at the top of a wonderfully dramatic staircase.

The piazza to the northwest of the palace, piazza Trieste e Trentino, leads to via Toledo/via Roma, the main shopping street and the boundary imposed by the Spanish Viceroy Don Pedro of Toledo in 1537 to separate royal Naples from the overpopulated streets beyond. The **Caffè Gambrinus** on the piazza still gives a hint of the Belle Epoque. The via Chiaia also starts at the piazza and leads to the most fashionable shopping area at Santa Lucia and Mergellina.

For an interesting stroll through a relatively peaceful quarter back to Santa Lucia, where most of the hotels are located, walk left from the beginning of via Chiaia to piazza Carolina and along via Gennaro Serra to the Pizzofalcone hill, identified by the church of Santa Maria degli Angeli e Pizzofalcone at the end of via Serra. From there walk seaward and to the left at via Nunziatella for a wonderful view of the Bay of Naples.

One of Lucullus' villas stood on this hill, surrounded by gardens of rare plants. None of this ancient luxury is in evidence today, but the harbor views are still exciting. The slope is part of a crater that ends below at the Castel dell'Ovo. Colonizers from Rhodes settled this part of Naples during the eighth century B.C. and founded Partenope on this shore, the settlement named for the nymph washed ashore at Santa Lucia, dead of weeping for Ulysses' unrequited love. Later, Greeks conquered this city, then called Palaepolis (the old city), and named their own area Neapolis (the new city), which of course was later shortened to Naples.

Continue down to the **Castel dell'Ovo** and the harbor, where you can have dinner at one of the seafood restaurants, none particularly good but all entertaining for the view of fishermen and contraband runners plying their courses.

The wonderful Castel dell'Ovo was built over an egg that the Roman poet-magician Vergil placed inside a glass container and secured in the foundation. If the egg breaks, the castle will fall and take all of Naples with it. A castle of Lucullus stood here, too, and then the castle-building Normans erected a structure. It was enlarged by the Hohenstaufen monarch Frederick II, who kept his treasury and held parliament here before embarking on his crusade. Thirty years later his grandchildren, the sons of Manfred, died in prison at the castle. In 1379 Joanna I received the antipope Clement VII here, and later she was imprisoned in the castle until being poisoned (as discussed above). The situation now is happier: The castle has been restored, and you can wander through dungeons and parapets. At night it's brilliantly floodlit, and the tourist office sponsors folk dance performances here.

Turning away from the city along the harbor to the west, you'll soon reach the **Villa Communale**, an attractive area refreshed by a park full of tropical trees and plants. A flea market operates here the third week of each month.

The **Museo Pignatelli**, opposite the middle of the park, is lodged in a splendid 19th-century Neoclassical villa. The carriage museum in the garden is charming; inside the villa there is a major collection of European porcelain. Evening chamber music concerts are frequently scheduled at the museum, and good trattorias are plentiful in the adjoining Mergellina district. A favorite with Neapolitans is **Palummella**, where the antipasto table is worth the trip and the amusing owner adds to the fun. Another small and charming place, **Al Poeta**, on piazza Salvatore di Giacomo, serves a wonderful *rigatoni alla montanara* made with artichokes, chopped meat, prosciutto, and mozzarella. At **Lo Scoglio di Frisio**, a bit fancier, a variety of sea creatures passes through the kitchen to be transformed into imaginative mixes—squid and artichokes, for instance—and even the fritters have a taste of algae.

One of Naples' most fashionable restaurants, on a hill in the Mergellina area, is **La Sacrestia**, set in a charming villa at via Orazio 16, with a grand view. Sacrestia features traditional Neapolitan recipes and interesting experiments in a sophisticated atmosphere. Windows open onto the bay. Reservations suggested. Tel: 66-41-86.

Neapolitan cuisine has touches of the Greek, Arab, French, and Spanish, yet the result is pure Parthenopean. Along the bay, *maccheroni* (macaroni) is prepared in as many ways as fish, meat, vegetables, and cheese require. A classic Neapolitan dish is *spaghetti alle vongole veraci,* made with tiny clams from the Naples area, the tastiest in existence. The sauce is white with garlic and parsley or red with small tomatoes. Vermicelli is sometimes served with a sauce of *polpetielli affogati* (tiny octopus in tomato sauce). *Lasagna alla napoletana, penne all' arrabbiata* (with hot peppers), *linguine alla puttanesca* ("whore's style"—spicy with black olives and capers), and the hearty *pasta e fagioli* all make eating here a joy. Vegetables, too, are given special attention. Eggplant is always a star, especially in *parmigiana di melanzane,* baked with cheese, tomato, and basil. *Peperoni* (large peppers) with cheese and *friarielli* (a kind of broccoli) cooked with a sauce of sausage meat can be eaten alone or in a pasta sauce. Meals often begin with *caprese*—fresh buffalo mozzarella from nearby Caserta's buffalo farms—and tomatoes with fresh basil.

Campania's volcanic soil is kind to grapes. Good whites include Fiano di Avellino, Vesuvio, Ischia, Falerno (of which Pliny spoke), Ravello, and Greco di Tufo. Lacryma Christi, best known because of its name (Christ's tear), can be quite good. Taurasi is a great red for hearty meals. Falerno's red is excellent, as is Gragnano, which can be *frizzante* (sparkling). Ravello also produces a very good red and a rosato (rosé) to finish the meal.

In Mergellina, near the church of Santa Maria di Piedigrotta and near the Galleria Quattro Gironate, steps lead to the Parco Virgiliano and the so-called tomb of Virgil—which it probably is not but was so recorded by Seneca and Petronius.

If you continue out to the limit of the curve of the Bay of Naples you'll reach **Posillipo**, a fashionable residential area that extends out along a cape. From the park a belvedere looks toward Naples and Vesuvius and out to Capri. At the busy fishing harbor at Capo Posillipo **Giuseppone a Mare** (Tel: 76-96-002) has long served fine seafood to Neapolitans. Though lately it hasn't lived up to its old standards, it's still amusing, informal, and a good place to enjoy the harbor sights. You may want to take a taxi out to Cape Posillipo because the number 140 bus stops inland of the cape itself. The trip from Naples is expensive, however.

WEST AND NORTH OF NAPLES

Campania's northern region still steams with volcanic activity; here and there fumaroles (jets of steam and mud) escape the earth. The steamy land seemed magical to the ancients, who were both repelled and fascinated by the dance of gases over the earth, which they called the Campi Flegrei, or "burning fields."

At **Lago d'Averno**, past present-day Posillipo at Baia, between Pozzuoli and Bacoli, Vergil located the mouth of the Underworld, the gate of Hell: "And here the unnavigable lake extends, o'er whose unhappy waters, void of light, no bird presumes to steer his airy flight. Such deadly stenches from the depth arise, and steaming sulfur that infects the skies. From hence the Grecian bards their legends make, and give the name Avernus to the lake."

Lago d'Averno (Lake Avernus) today is not exactly paradise, but the infernal fumes, actually sulfurous vapors, are gone, and the birds have returned. The Greeks created myths around the fumaroles, but the Romans created spas and used the volcanic activity to heat their villas. All the accoutrements of the good life grew quickly, especially around Baia, which became famous for the glamorous and wild lifestyles of Romans by the sea. Though little is left to recall those days, the baths at Baia have been newly excavated.

The **Antro della Sibilla** (Cave of the Sibyl) at **Cuma**, on the coast due west of Naples near Lago d'Averno, is the most intriguing stop. Virgil speaks of the "frenzied prophetess, deep in the cave of rock she charts the fates, consigning to the leaves her words and symbols.... She will unfold for you who are the peoples of Italy, the wars that are to come, and in what way you are free to flee or face each crisis. Worshipped properly, she grants prosperous voyages." The long caverns where the hopeful awaited the prophecy the Sibyl would read in the leaves still resonate with her aura—if you see the cave when the groups are absent. If time is short, however, take a group tour from Naples to Cuma and the craters of **Sulfatara**, where the fumaroles can be seen; alternatively, you can commute about the sites by bus. At the Bocca Grande (Great Hole) at Sulfatara, the vapors shoot up violently, reaching a temperature of 320 degrees F. Cuma itself, founded by Greeks as Cumae around the middle of the eighth century B.C., was the farthest Greek outpost in Magna Graecia; the Etruscans held sway farther north.

Though Sibyls can't be found, a local *mago* often has fliers distributed there, listing the hours he'll be available to tell your fortune, sometimes with a drop of oil in water. Near the entrance to the site, the **Taverna Giulia** conjures up exquisite dishes.

At low tide **Pozzuoli**, the principal town of the region, seems to be sinking into an ancient Roman underworld. The bizarre outcropping of columns is the result of bradyseism, a phenomenon in which the earth shakes and rises. Thus Pozzuoli has become multileveled. A promenade along the harbor leads to several trattorias clustered near the seawall; all serve exceptionally good *frutta di mare* (seafood) in very informal settings.

From Pozzuoli (or Naples) a boat leaves for Procida, to the southwest. Picturesque **Procida**—a green island with clean beaches—is still refreshingly true to its fishing-village past. Since there are boats from Procida to Ischia and Capri as well as to Naples, you could make this a quiet place for island-hopping if tranquillity is your dream. The hotels **L'Oasi** and **Arcate** on Procida provide comfortable places in the sun.

Caserta

Inland from Naples to the north, the **Palazzo Reale** at Caserta is not maintained royally but is still worth seeing for its evocation of the regal splendor of Versailles. Charles III had the palace built in 1752 from the plans of Vanvitelli. Inside, the grand staircase and apartments, the chapel and theater are lavish in their use of marble; and the gardens are stunning—vast fountains, groves, statues, and cascades.

The English gardens are the most beautiful aspect. Lord Hamilton had persuaded the queen to finance a garden with the "natural" look popular in England, and it was in this setting of bucolic bliss that he proposed to Emma—who was soon to meet the young and attractive Admiral Nelson. The lawns, bordered by eucalyptus, palms, yuccas, cedars, and Classical reproductions (Greek temples and Pompeiian nymphaeums), create a world apart—magical and wild, yet gentle and serene. All of this leads inexorably to a desire for wild boar, which you can enjoy in an amazing number of ways—from filet to sausage—at the

Ritrovo dei Patriarchi, where venison and rabbit also star on the menu. It's in Caserta Vecchia, reached by a short bus ride, where you will also see in the cathedral examples of Romanesque style with a dash of 12th-century Arab style, as in many cathedrals in the south.

Caserta is about 45 minutes from Naples by train.

SOUTH OF NAPLES

Ideally, you should allow three days to see Pompeii, Herculaneum, Vesuvius, and Paestum—after spending some time at the Museo Archeologico in Naples to see the collections from the Roman sites. Paestum has a fine museum of its own. Since Pompeii's site is extensive, it requires the better part of a day. You can easily see Herculaneum and Mount Vesuvius in a day, since a bus for Vesuvius leaves from the town of Herculaneum, which is only about 6 km (4 miles) from Naples (closer than Pompeii). Paestum, farther south, can be reached by train from Naples or Salerno. We discuss Pompeii first because, although Herculaneum is closer to Naples, Pompeii is the premier site in this area.

Pompeii

Pliny the Younger tells us what happened on August 24, A.D. 79, from notes his uncle (the Elder) took while watching Vesuvius's eruption from the sea before the fumes killed him. Ashes were falling, hotter and thicker, as his ship drew nearer, followed by bits of pumice and blackened stone. It all seemed a great adventure to him at first. He went home and took a nap and awoke to find his house filling with pumice stone and ash. "Elsewhere there was daylight by this time, but they were still in darkness, blacker, and denser than any ordinary night, which they relieved by lighting torches and various kinds of lamp."

The city of Pompeii itself tells the story clearly after that, especially in the tragic casts of figures caught under the ash, crouching under tables, struggling up stairs, a mother holding up her baby, a horribly contorted dog on a leash. The molten ash made sculptor's molds of them, which have been used to re-create the bodies, displayed in the museum (Antiquarium) at the entrance to the excavations or returned to their original positions.

At both Pompeii and Herculaneum the fascination lies

in the glimpse of everyday life frozen in time. Although Pompeii has a forum, major theaters, and all the trappings of a large Roman city, the private homes and small businesses are the aspects that intrigue archaeologists and social historians. The houses were often in the classic Samnite style (the Samnites were settlers before the Romans arrived), with an atrium at the entrance; then a peristyle, or colonnaded courtyard surrounded by the family bedrooms, then a dining area, or triclinium, where chaise longues were used for family and guests. The Samnites were the most influential in creating the look we see today, although the Romans, who had rebuilt after an earthquake in A.D. 62, added grandiose touches and created a more luxurious lifestyle. The famous Pompeiian red cinnabar dates from this period.

Before starting the tour, which will take a few hours at least, buy the book (sold here) that has transparent sheets re-creating the look of the original buildings, aiding the imagination. Guides and guards are useful because they have the keys to everything, and much of interest is locked for security. It's worth the tips.

A great deal of the artwork from Pompeii is in the archaeological museum in Naples, but the **Casa dei Vettii** has been allowed to keep its treasures and has been partly restored. Researchers have studied friezes and dead roots to re-create the garden's original look. The brothers Vettii, Aulus and Restituti, bought this gracious villa during the first century A.D. Thanks to the beams and roofs that covered it when it fell, it was kept in good condition through the centuries. The house, also Samnite style, faces inward, enclosing both atrium and impluvium (rain-water opening) leading to the colonnaded garden. In the vestibule a phallic symbol—a familiar charm that, along with coiled snakes, was thought to bring good luck—wards off the evil eye. The sight and sound of water was used to refresh the garden, as in the Arab houses Rome saw in Egypt and the East. The dining room is exquisite because of its black borders—bright with *putti* going about their daily chores—and the frescoes of gods and goddesses in the last style of Pompeiian art, which are almost Baroque in feeling.

A few other villas to visit are the Casa del Menandro, the Casa di Loreius Tiburtinus, the Casa del Fauno, and the Villa di Diomede. The Villa dei Misteri was the scene of Dionysian cult rituals, some of which are dramatically portrayed on the walls.

There are four identifiable periods in Pompeii's painting: the first, Samnite, used stucco to imitate marble, as in the **Casa del Fauno**; the second introduced architecture with a skewed perspective, as in the **Casa di Sallústio**; in the third, imaginative architectural scenes abound—whole cities and harbors—as in the **Casa di Frontone**; and the last, as in the Casa dei Vettii, featured fuller perspective and dramatic scenes.

Excavation began on Pompeii during the mid-18th century, after a farmer discovered an enormous stone phallus while he was cultivating the soil of his garden. (At least that's the story told.) In any case, digging began and still continues. Charles III of Bourbon, who had already inaugurated the Accademia Ercolanese in 1755, began the new resurrection. As Goethe summed it up, "Many disasters have happened in the world, but few have brought such joy to prosperity."

Pompeii is about 40 minutes from Naples on the Circumvesuviana railroad, a pleasant ride that begins in the Naples Stazione Centrale, which is less pleasant. A new major music festival, the Panatenee Pompeiane, will present concerts each August at Pompeii's theaters.

Herculaneum

Herculaneum (Ercolano), named for its legendary founder, Hercules (Ercule), is much smaller and more intimate than Pompeii. Because the inhabited section of town above the site looks very similar to Pompeii, if you have seen Pompeii first, it may seem as if Herculaneum is Pompeii come to life. When Pompeii, inland, was drowned in ashes, Herculaneum, at the coast, was flooded with mud churned up by the roiling sea. Consequently even the wood survived in its mud and lava casing. Furnishings and foodstuffs, statues and mosaics still decorate the houses and villas.

Although Herculaneum's past is detailed in this manner, its full history—whether the lovely villas belonged to Pompeii's merchants or to the Romans as another holiday resort—is not known. According to Seneca, Caligula was among the social set in Herculaneum.

The early history of eighth-century B.C. Oscan and later Samnite civilization is similar to Pompeii's; in fact, graffiti in Oscan can be seen on Herculaneum walls. Herculaneum remained packed in mud until 1709, when an Austrian prince who was having a well dug found a theater where the water table should have been. The Bourbon King Charles III got into the picture in 1738, and in 1755 he established the Royal Herculaneum Academy. The *Antiquities of Herculaneum,* a book of engravings published by the academy, influenced European taste for the next half century, from jewelry and clothes to interior design and painting.

As at Pompeii, guides or guards have keys, making them indispensable, and some of them are quite knowledgeable as well. Be sure to see the Casa del Tramezzo di Legno (House of the Wooden Screen), a patrician residence with a garden.

The **Terme**, male and female, are also fascinating, with mosaics of Neptune and dolphins, seats, and ledges for clothing. In the **Casa del Mobilio Carbonizzato** (House of the Carbonized Furniture), the bedroom, painted in the warm red associated with Pompeii, has a bed and table from the original house. The **Casa di Nettuno** has a lovely nymphaeum in mosaic, and adjoining it is a shop with food staples still packed in storage jars. Be sure to visit the Palaestra and serpent fountain, the Casa dei Cervi (House of the Stags) and its fine sculpture, and the Terme Suburbane (Suburban Baths), with marble rooms and windows opening to the sea.

The Circumvesuviana train goes to Herculaneum, as does a trolley (*filovia*) from the piazza del Municipio (but never take the trolley on Sunday or during rush hour; otherwise, it provides a nice way to see the neighborhoods around Naples). From Herculaneum buses go to Mount Vesuvius.

If you have extra time, visit the **Villa di Oplontis** at Torre Annunciata, also on the Circumvesuviana route, between Herculaneum and Pompeii, where brilliant murals have been uncovered in a splendid villa currently being excavated.

Mount Vesuvius

Vesuvius has come through history with a very good press, given the horror it inflicted at Pompeii. Nowadays Neapolitans look fondly at Il Cratere, as they call it, a dear sight on the horizon that means home, not to mention good wines like Lacryma Christi from its slopes and succulent fruits and vegetables. The plume of smoke is no more; only an occasional fumarole escapes to let us know it's down but not out. The famous truncated cone, Mount

Somma, stands 3,714 feet above sea level; and the smaller cone, Mount Vesuvius, rises to 4,190 feet. Probably the best way to see it is to take the bus from Herculaneum. From the bus stop it's about an hour's climb to the top, and you'll need a guide. The views from the summit are spectacular.

PAESTUM

At the ancient Greek city of Paestum, south of the Amalfi coast and Salerno, wonderfully preserved Doric temples are set in a grassy field surrounded by gardens and hills. Although the site is small, it's so charming that you may want to spend time just relaxing here. The museum is also exceptional, especially since the Tomb of the Diver was discovered.

Greek Poseidonia (called Paestum by the Romans) was founded around 600 B.C. and dedicated to Poseidon, or Neptune, in 400. The founding Greeks came from Sybaris (itself an Achaean colony in Magna Graecia near the modern city of Táranto), whose lifestyle made the word *sybarite* synonymous with luxurious comfort. Their influence on the region was considerable, and the city they built impressive. The magnificent **Tempio di Nettuno** (actually dedicated to Hera and misnamed), set in a lovely countryside, re-creates the Hellenic spirit in southern Italy with symmetry, serenity, and grandeur. The interior sacred area, the *cella,* altered by Rome into two, was originally covered with white stucco. The **Basilica** is the oldest structure here (mid-sixth century B.C.). Its columns are curved (entasis), an unusual feature, but Greek Italy was more cavalier in its approach to temple art than was Athens, where the rules of symmetry, variety, number of columns, and such were adhered to strictly.

Paestum is rich in detail. Exceptionally graceful figures, carved on the metopes that stretched across the top of the columns of the **Tempio Italico**, are still on the site and can be admired at close range. In the museum, metopes from the Sanctuary of Hera, 13 km (8 miles) north of Paestum, are exhibited on an impressive model. Hercules' feats, centaur fights, and the *Oresteia* are the themes. The museum's star is the **Tomb of the Diver**, called the find of the century. Outwardly the tomb resembles the others of this vicinity, but when opened in 1968 it was found to be covered with intriguing frescoes, some subtly erotic. The diver is delightful, diving through space into eternity.

For lunch at Paestum go to **Nettuno**, near the site. Paestum can be reached by train from Naples or Salerno; the excursion can also include a relaxing stop at a beach about a mile from the temples or at the little cove resort of **Palinuro** farther south along the coast, where simple accommodations are inexpensive and the coast is beautifully unspoiled. Driving in this area is not the problem it is in Naples.

Palinuro was named for Ulysses' helmsman Palinurus, inspiration for Cyril Connelly's *The Unquiet Grave*. Condemned "to lie naked on an unknown shore," he was finally buried at a place that "will always be called Palinurus," as Virgil tells the story in the *Aeneid*. **Battipaglia**, to the north, is a center of rich buffalo mozzarella.

Just below Palinuro on the coast is the resort of Práia a Mare, where Calàbria begins (see the chapter on it below).

Velia, near Paestum, has a similar history, much that we know having been provided by Strabo. Founded by Greeks fleeing the Persians in Asia Minor, the town (whose ruins are not preserved as well as Paestum's, which were in the middle of a malarial swamp) is of great interest to archaeologists. Elea, which later became Velia, was the center of the Eleatic school of philosophy, and numbered Parmenides and Zeno among its native sons. Parmenides, most significant of the pre-Socratics, represents the appearance of metaphysics in philosophical thought, and with him philosophy became a strict discipline. Parmenides applied his talents to daily life as well and drew up Elea's constitution.

The Phoenician Zeno, Parmenides' most important pupil and his successor in the Eleatic school, is considered the founder of stoic philosophy. Zeno developed the dialectic method of argument, in which the adversary's thesis is examined and the consequences of the thesis are shown to contradict each other or the thesis itself. Zeno and Empedocles in Sicily developed systems that led to the art of rhetoric. Traditional customs and ethical principles were subjected to rational examination, raising the question—which would later cause the Cartesians sleepless nights—of how we know anything at all. (Zeno is well-known even today for his various paradoxes.)

On a more worldly level, under later Roman domination Velia served as a base for Brutus when he was fighting Octavian. When Rome declined, trade routes moved to the Adriatic, depriving Velia of its prominent position and prosperity.

CAPRI

When you look seaward from Naples, two islands in the sun beckon: Ischia to the west and Capri to the south.

"Lucky the mortal who arrives on the summit of San Costanzo during one of those bewitching moments when the atmosphere is permeated with a glittering haze of floating particles, like powdered gold-dust. The view over the Gulf of Naples, at such a time, with its contours framed in a luminous aureole rather than lined, is not easily forgotten." So Norman Douglas saw Capri, one of the world's most famous islands. And so it remains today—at least out of season, not when August's crowds invade the tiny piazzas and narrow, winding streets. Even winter days are beautiful here, when scowling winds stir up the whitecaps so that the *aliscafo* (hydrofoil) has to wait out the weather.

From Marina Piccola, the boat landing, the funicular slides up the hill to the town of Capri, but you can detour from the port to walk up to Tiberius' villa, about an hour's climb, each footstep of which seems to reveal a whole new aspect of Capri as it expands below. It was Augustus who first put Capri's name on the list of chic ports of call. Then his stepson Tiberius, if you believe Suetonius, led a life here that shocked even Rome's X-rated morals, with "little nooks of lechery" where Tiberius had boys and girls dressed up as Pans and nymphs. This aerie of incomparable beauty somehow stirred the old emperor to debauchery and torture. He supposedly tossed the bodies of his victims from the cliff called the Salto di Tiberio.

His **Villa Jovis** has been restored systematically, the structure lines along the coast easily discerned. On the peak facing the mainland, the villa's graduated levels down the hill can be accessed by ramps. From the lighthouse near it a system of semaphores transmitted messages off toward Rome, enabling Tiberius to run his empire from the tiny isle.

The **Giardini di Augusto** are designed to provide a lifetime of panoramas of cerulean sky and sea, bright flowers (Capri blooms with 850 species), and dark trees. A seeming anachronism in the garden is the statue of

Lenin, who enjoyed Capri's charms after the 1905 uprising. From here the Faraglioni, the two famous vertical offshore rocks, are splendidly framed below. When Ulysses sailed up the Strait of Messina to Sorrento, he looked toward Capri: "And lo, the Siren shores like mists arise. Sunk were at once the winds.... Some daemon calmed the air, and smoothed the deep. Hushed the loud winds, and charmed the waves to sleep."

The town of Capri, with pretty boutiques and smart restaurants, does not further Homer's image, so take the bus to Anacapri and from there the chair lift to **Monte Solaro**, the top of the world, or so it seems. The heady feeling of this peak was shared with Capri's prehistoric residents, whose traces have been found in the mountain's grottoes.

At Anacapri the **Villa San Michele** exhibits classical sculpture, the collection of the Swedish writer/doctor Axel Munthe; free concerts are frequently performed in the chapel. From Anacapri the via Tragara leads down toward the Faraglioni for a swim, where you might catch sight of the rare blue lizard reputed to dart about the far rock. Nearby are the vineyards of the **Grotta di Matromania**, where Romans worshipped the goddess Cybele. **La Capannina** in Capri, on via le Botteghe, is the place to try the wines and to have lunch as well; or try **Luigi's**, near the Faraglioni on Strada dei Faraglioni if you're planning a swim.

Capri has a good bus system that connects the remotest parts of the island with each other. The best hotels are away from the tourist throngs, which can be annoying even in spring. Here are some hotels that enjoy superb views and are easily accessible to shops and transportation. To live in luxury even ancient Greek Sybarites would envy, stay at the **Punta Tragara**, where the view, the gardens, the isolation, and the Corbusier-designed villa itself are perfect, and the expensive privacy is honored with a terrace for each room. **La Scalinatella** has similar attributes, and both hotels have private pools.

Just a ten-minute walk from the town of Capri is the less expensive but intimate and luxurious **Villa Brunella**, where 11 rooms share a pool and a flower-bedecked terrace with a grand view. The **Villa Sarah** is another charming place, small and as well appointed, with a solarium. In Anacapri the family-run **Villa Patrizia** is simple and quiet, with the lovely terraces and gardens that flourish on the island.

An appropriately lazy way to enjoy Capri's colors and sweet fragrances is to hire a big taxi, all the better if it's a convertible, to explore the roads lined with movie-star villas and new panoramas, each one more spectacular than the last.

Before the water level rose, the **Grotta Azzurra** was a nymphaeum for Tiberius from which several large statues have been excavated. If you take the boat to the grotto, you'll change to a small rowboat to enter, and in high season the little boats must line up. The three-hour boat ride around the island is a good way to absorb Capri's charm and see some of the 65 other grottoes formed from the soft volcanic stone. You'll probably land at Marina Piccola, near the perennial sun-and-seafood spot **La Canzone del Mare**, where good food competes for attention with year-round tans and minute appraisals of face-lifts and liposuction surgery.

Capri gave its name to those sleek, tapered pants reclaimed from fashion limbo recently and to the very bare thong sandals. Slacks are tailor-made at **Gigino's** on via Ignazio Cerio or **Consentino's** on via Camerelle; sandals are custom-formed at **Faiella's** on via Vittorio Emanuele.

Sightseeing from Capri to Naples, the Amalfi Coast, or Ischia is easily arranged, but you're likely to want to join the terrace lounge lizards and let the world go by.

ISCHIA

Ischia is the quiet sister of chic Capri, beautifully green, with comfortable beaches, friendly people, and bizarre troglodytic dwellings high in the volcanic mountains. Lacco Ameno is the smart resort, where the sister hotels **Regina Isabella e Royal Sporting** sheltered Liz and Richard from the paparazzi when love was new and *Cleopatra* was a wrap. Their spa is one of the best for mud (*fango*) baths; those of the **Jolly** at Porto d'Ischia are also excellent, and one-day treatments are available there. Whatever the volcanic mud from Monte Epomeo does for the body, it introduces an entirely new world of relaxation. The process begins in a darkened room, when a bell signals the approach of a scuttle of hot mud from somewhere below the floor, presumably Vulcan's forge. Then someone appears to spread *fango* over a plastic-covered bed; you sink in and are covered with the rest. Primeval ecstasy ensues, followed by a fire-hoselike shower, herbal wraps, almond rubs—whatever the new creature wishes. All cares are gone.

Little towns like picturesque Sant'Angelo are interspersed with white beaches and gentle seascapes; less gentle but mystical are the mountain roads that seem to go back in time as you climb. At Sant'Angelo have dinner at **Del Pescatore**. Near Lacco Ameno the **Negombo** has a great view of the bay. The **Regina Isabella** has an excellent dining room and a barman who remembers Liz's favorite drinks from those wild days.

THE AMALFI COAST

Beyond Pompeii, where the Salentine peninsula curves seaward, the Amalfi coast begins. The town of Amalfi is farther down the long coastline. From the coast's northernmost town, Sorrento, to Positano, the road called the Nastro Azzuro (Blue Ribbon) rises over the magnificent crest of land at the top of the peninsula, looking north toward Naples and south toward Positano.

One of the most beautiful roads in the world, the Amalfi Drive curves along majestic cliffs terraced with vineyards and lemon groves, bordered by a rocky shore far below dotted with fortress towers that once defended the towns from sea raiders. The sea views are as fresh as watercolors, bordered with pine and cactus, brightened with wild roses and bougainvillea.

Since relaxing is the point of being there, a few days' stay is in order; don't try racing along the hairpin turns—a diversion best left to the locals. Though August is impossibly crowded, July is often surprisingly less so and very pleasant. Weekends bring bumper-to-bumper traffic to the narrow coast road.

Sorrento

Sorrento, hugging the top of cliffs that reach 150 feet in height, is a big city when compared with Positano and Amalfi. Its grand hotels in Belle Epoque style, luxuriant gardens, and splendid views recall Sorrento's former glorious days as a regal summer spot. The rocky shore has bathing pavilions built out like cruise-ship decks. Torquato Tasso, the 16th-century author of *Jerusalem Delivered,* was born in Sorrento, and is feted with a statue and a piazza named for him. The hotels **Excelsior Vittoria** and **Parco** dei Principi, although near the town center, are surrounded by dazzling gardens and panoramic views and look as if guests in white suits or starched dresses play croquet on the lawn all summer. Among the best restaurants in town are **La Favorita** and **La Pentolaccia**, both in the heart of the city. Furniture is now a main industry here, particularly intarsia work, in which paper-thin wood strips of varying patterns are laid one on the other and lacquered. Sorrento is a terminal for trains and buses and has frequent boat service to the islands of Capri and Ischia and to the other towns of the Amalfi coast.

Positano

Pastel sweet by day and as magic as a Christmas village by night, Positano is set into the cliffs. The streets are steep or stepped, so espadrilles or rubber soles are necessary, especially after a rain. Some of Italy's most choice hotels are here, including the splendidly hidden **San Pietro**, dazzling with azaleas and hand-painted tiles, thanks to the inventive whimsy of the late Carlo Cinque, who created this delightful place. Just beyond the town, the hotel has a private bus to provide transport. In the town proper, the **Sirenuse** is a posh hotel sparkling with antiques, huge terraces, and a pretty pool. High above the town sits the **Poseidon**, a fine villa with a wide view of the coast as well as a pool and restaurant. Less pricey is the charming **Palazzo Murat**, in an 18th-century palazzo where Murat, once king of Naples, spent some time. Both the **Casa Albertina** and the **Casa Maresca** are family run and provide perfect views, and both are less expensive than most other hotels in Positano.

Besides hotels and villas, Positano has a tiny harbor, a cathedral, and lots of boutiques—and not much more (aside, of course, from the marvelous scenery). The **Cambusa Buco di Bacco** and the **Covo dei Saraceni** are good places to eat fish while looking at harbor sights. The **San Pietro** has a very festive restaurant; reserve. Tel: (0187) 87-54-55.

Pretty **Priano**, the next town along the coast, is quieter than Positano, with a lovely harbor and beach. The **Grand Hotel Tritone** sits high on the cliffs and looks out at a dazzling panorama; each room has a terrace, and the swimming pool and restaurant are each nestled on their own terrace levels. A late-night disco down at sea level welcomes guests coming by boat or down the cliff steps.

Amalfi

The town of Amalfi, across the Furore Fjord bridge, has an imposing history for a little place nestled beneath ponderous cliffs and wandering up a central street into the mountains. During Amalfi's days in the sun, the city was an important maritime republic, like Pisa and Venice, with trade routes extending as far as Constantinople, where the cathedral's bronze doors were forged in 1066. The **Cathedral** is among the most beautiful in southern Italy, intricate in Arab-Norman design and detail, with a cloisters even more Eastern in its intertwining arches and palm trees. Dedicated to Saint Andrew, patron saint of sailors, it was begun during the ninth century and remodeled three centuries later.

The interior, jubilant even on the darkest day, has been restored in Baroque style, with a ceiling of intaglia woodwork. Even the crypt is radiant, and the altar, the work of Fontana, as well as the statues of Saints Peter and Paul by Pietro Bernini, are magnificent. Under the altar lie Saint Andrew's bones, but not quietly. The bones exude a fragrant oil called the manna of Saint Andrew, and when it miraculously appears, it must flow quickly to portend well, like San Gennaro's blood. Slow manna is less auspicious.

Papermaking is an 11th-century art still practiced here. At the top of the central street (number 92) is a mill where fine paper with Amalfi watermarks is made. If you ring and the time is right, you may see the production process, from pulp to sheets. Watercolor paper sold here is excellent, as is the stationery.

In the piazza near the harbor stands a statue of Flavio Gioia, inventor, they say, of the compass he is consulting. In back of him the Municipio, or Town Hall, houses the Tabula Amalfitana—long accepted as the law of the sea—and the costumes for the Regatta of the Four Maritime Republics (Venice, Pisa, Genoa, and Amalfi), celebrated each year at alternating cities.

Christmas and New Year's bring feasting and fireworks over the sea, making that season a nice time to be here, and there is just a little rain now and then. The **Santa Caterina**, Amalfi's deluxe hotel, serves wild boar along with turkey, *baccalà,* and Champagne; at midnight the coast lights up with pyrotechnics from Positano to Amalfi and Atrani. The hotel curves along the coast, many of its rooms opening onto terraces with only the sea beyond, above lush gardens and lemon groves. These lemons are used by the chef in a sauce for pasta that can be made successfully only with Amalfi's lemons.

High above Amalfi, the hotel **Cappuccini Convento**, reached by cliff elevator, evokes the Medieval monastery it once was, set on a terraced garden with a grape arbor. Nearer to sea level, the **Luna Hotel** recalls its cloistered past, with vaulted rooms and antiques, and, of course, cloisters. Near the harbor the **Hotel Residence** is inexpensively atmospheric. The **Caravella** and **Marinella** are good seafood restaurants.

The white town of **Atrani** is easily missed because the highway covers part of it with an overpass. Walk down into the piazza, from which you will see a maze of houses rising up the hill. These can be reached only by staircases, private and elusive as a North African village. A few al fresco restaurants on high reward the climb; the cathedral bears a bronze door like Amalfi's, made in Constantinople during the 11th century.

Ravello

Above Amalfi, Ravello rises serene and aloof high on the cliffs, embodying a rare elegance of spaciousness, grace, and mood. Even the light at Ravello is rarefied, most beautiful during the afternoon when the air is clear. Have lunch near the Duomo at the **Palumbo Hotel**, still owned by the distinguished Pasquale Vuillemier, who is often in attendance. The Palumbo and the **Caruso** are Ravello's most charming hotels, each furnished with antiques and graced with superb views near the coast; the Caruso also counts spacious grounds among its attractions.

Just a few minutes' walk from the central piazza, the **Villa Rufolo** is so romantic and atmospheric that Wagner, on seeing it, exclaimed, "The magic garden of Klingsor has been found." He was then (1880) living in southern Italy, orchestrating *Parsifal*. Each July a Wagner festival is held on the grounds. During the 12th century the noble Rufolo family had Villa Rufolo built in front of the boundless sea; Boccaccio was one of their guests, and he mentioned it in *The Decameron*. No ruins are more evocative of the period, and the effect is heightened by the gardens, with their palms, Judas trees, papyrus, and flowers—all counterpoint to the arabesques of the arches and the rugged old tower, now tastefully crumbling.

The **Villa Cimbrone**, a short walk away, is in another mood entirely, without this romanticism but with its own humor and panoramas to jolt even the wide-angle weary. Over the central arch at the entry are two boars' heads representing the coat of arms of Lord Grimthorpe, the eccentric gentleman who was behind the villa's creation.

The first unusual sight is in the cloisters: the seven deadly sins, represented by seven little unrepentant heads. Then, across lawns, through rose gardens, past Greek statues, and into a nymph's grotto, a belvedere unfolds that seems to be a terrace above the whole Mediterranean. Grimthorpe is buried nearby. His epitaph (1917) is as bizarre as his villa: "Glad I came, not sorry to depart."

Before leaving Ravello, stop at the cathedral, named for the doctor/saint Pantaleone. The cathedral façade is obviously restored, but the great door, made by Barisano of Trani, is divided into 54 panels containing beautifully executed lives of Christ and the saints. Inside, the pulpit is superb, the work of Niccolo di Foggia, commissioned by the Rufolo family. Topped with a majestic eagle, it glitters with mosaics; its columns rest on lions. In front of it the small pulpit, a rare piece built in 1130, shows Jonah and the whale, a metaphor of Christ's resurrection, delightfully documented in mosaics.

The museum downstairs is singular. The bust of the Signora da Ravello is thought to be of a Rufolo family member, and the elegant silver head is that of Saint Barbara, perhaps with her real skull inside. (During the Middle Ages trade in saints' relics was frantic. For all of these to have had authentic, saints would have had myriad necks and thighbones and hundreds of extra fingers.)

Ravello's wines are quite good and even better on the Palumbo dining terrace, with the coast spread out beyond. Staying in Ravello can be enchanting if getting away from it all is your idea. During the summer months a bus makes frequent connections between the piazza del Duomo and Amalfi's central piazza.

Vietri sul Mare

On a very different kind of day, when you are in the mood to shop for ceramics, head east along the coast from Ravello to Vietri, a town completely devoted, it seems, to ceramics. Vietri shows its colorful wares on every street. The **Solimena factory** is the one to see first; it's in an imaginative building designed by Solari on via Madonna degli Angeli. The little tourist office on the central piazza will guide you to the latest exhibits and other ceramicists.

For a good alternate route when traffic is heavy, follow the coast east to Maiori, and then turn onto the road north toward Tramonti, with fine scenery until you reach the main road, east toward Salerno. A bus from Amalfi's central piazza climbs the high, winding road to Ravello at frequent intervals.

GETTING AROUND

Campania is so well interconnected by boat, train, and bus that it is possible to stay almost anywhere and travel to the main attractions. Staying in Naples is perhaps most convenient; despite the city's reputation, it can be very comfortable. From Naples there are good train connections to western and northern Campania and to Pompeii, Herculaneum, and Paestum. Ferries and hydrofoils (*aliscafi*) leave Naples frequently for Capri and Ischia. In summer the Amalfi Drive can be reached from Naples by hydrofoil to Amalfi or Positano.

In Naples a car is a hindrance; traffic and parking problems make walking or travelling by bus or taxi a much more practical means of transit. The Amalfi Drive should be approached with caution, because it is extremely tortuous, with narrow, cliff-hugging roads. If you want to drive, rent a car as you leave Naples and take an inland route to Vietri, near Salerno; then double back up the drive to Amalfi and Positano, a much easier approach until you know the territory.

Many hotels in Positano and in Amalfi will send a car to Rome or Naples airport for clients if requested—for a healthy fee, of course. A taxi from Naples to Positano costs about $60. To reach Amalfi or Positano from Rome, take the train to Salerno, and a taxi or local bus to your destination. The train from Naples to Sorrento connects with taxis and buses as well. Local buses do not regularly transport luggage, however, so a taxi makes better sense.

If you stay in Positano, Pompeii is convenient to reach by car; there are also regular bus excursions. Bus and train connections are less convenient but possible.

The Naples daily paper, *Il Mattino,* lists train and boat departures. Salerno adjoins Vietri, and from there the train leaves for Naples or Rome—a last-minute swim or a plate of *spaghetti con vongole veraci,* and you're on your way.

ACCOMMODATIONS REFERENCE

▶ **Casa Albertina.** 84017 **Positano.** Tel: (089) 87-51-43.

▶ **Arcate.** 80079 **Procida.** Tel: (081) 896-71-20.

▶ **Villa Brunella.** Via Tragara 24, 80073 **Capri.** Tel: (081) 837-02-79.

▶ **Cappuccini Convento.** Via Annunziatella 25, 84011 **Amalfi.** Tel: (089) 87-26-01.

▶ **Caruso Belvedere.** Via San Giovanni del Toro 52, 84010 **Ravello.** Tel: (089) 85-71-11; in U.S., (212) 599-8290 or (800) 223-9832.

▶ **Excelsior.** Via Partenope 48, 80121 **Naples.** Tel: (081) 41-71-11; Telex: 710043, in U.S., (212) 935-9540 or (800) 221-2340.

▶ **Grand Hotel Excelsior Vittoria.** Piazza Tasso 34, 80067 **Sorrento.** Tel: (081) 878-19-00; Telex: 720368.

▶ **Jolly Grande Albergo delle Terme.** Via de Luca 42, 80077 **Porto d'Ischia.** Tel: (081) 99-17-44. Telex: 710267.

▶ **Luna.** On main road, 84011 **Amalfi.** Tel: (089) 87-10-02.

▶ **Casa Maresca.** Viale Pasitea, 84017 **Positano.** Tel: (089) 87-51-40.

▶ **L'Oasi.** 80079, **Procida.** Tel: (081) 896-74-99.

▶ **Palazzo Murat.** Via dei Mulini, 84017 **Positano.** Tel: (089) 87-51-77.

▶ **Hotel Palumbo.** Via Toro 28, 84010 **Ravello.** Tel: (089) 85-72-44; Telex: 770101, in U.S., (212) 599-8280 or (800) 223-9832.

▶ **Paradiso.** Via Catullo 11, 80100 **Naples.** Tel: (081) 66-02-33.

▶ **Parco dei Principi.** Via Rota 1, 80067 **Sorrento.** Tel: (081) 878-46-44; Telex: 721090.

▶ **Villa Patrizia.** Via Pagliaro 17, 80071 **Anacapri.** Tel: (081) 837-10-14.

▶ **Poseidon.** Viale Pasitea, 84017 **Positano.** Tel: (089) 87-50-14.

▶ **Punta Tragara.** Via Tragara 57, 80073 **Capri.** Tel: (081) 837-08-44; in U.S., (800) 223-6800.

▶ **Regina Isabella e Royal Sporting.** Piazza Santa Restituta, 80076 **Lacco Ameno.** Tel: (081) 99-43-22; in U.S., (212) 599-8280 or (800) 223-9832.

▶ **Residence.** Via Repubbliche Marinare 9, 84011 **Amalfi.** Tel: (089) 87-11-83.

▶ **Royal.** Via Partenope 38, 80121 **Naples.** Tel: (081) 40-02-44; Telex: 710167.

▶ **San Pietro.** Località San Pietro, 84017 **Positano.** Tel:

(089) 87-54-55; Telex: 770072; in U.S., (212) 599-8280 or (800) 223-9832.

▶ **Santa Caterina.** 84011 **Amalfi.** Tel: (089) 87-10-12; Telex: 770093; in U.S., (212) 719-4898 or (800) 223-9832.

▶ **Villa Sarah.** Via Tiberio 3/a, 80073 **Capri.** Tel: (081) 837-78-17.

▶ **Scalinatella.** Via Tragara 8, 80073 **Capri.** Tel: (081) 837-06-33; Telex: 721204.

▶ **Le Sirenuse.** Via Colombo 30, 84017 **Positano.** Tel: (089) 87-50-66.

▶ **Grand Hotel Tritone.** 84017 **Priano.** Tel: (089) 87-43-33; in U.S., (212) 599-8280 or (800) 223-9832.

APULIA

By Dwight V. Gast

Often described as "the heel of the Italian boot," Apulia (Puglia—pronounced POOL-ya—in Italian) has from prehistoric times had the heels of various peoples planted onto its flat and vulnerable topography. It has been occupied to a greater or lesser extent by the ancient Apuli tribes (from which it takes its name), Greeks, and Romans; it was at various times subjugated by Byzantines, Lombards, Franks, and Saracens; heavily built up by Normans and Hohenstaufens; and was then ruled at a distance by Angevins, Aragonese, and Bourbons. Every town seems to have its ruined castle or musty museum to attest to some aspect of that past.

In short, Apulia has a history that would drive the brightest schoolboy mad. The region's most distinctive architectural style, for example, is a complex blend of French and northern Italian architectural forms with Byzantine ornament of Saracen inspiration, brought together under the Normans. Whatever its confusing origins, the Apulian Romanesque resulted in some of Italy's most significant cathedrals, stretching heavenward above the coastal plain. Yet the region draws visitors not just because of its peculiar artistic heritage but also for the natural wonders of its spectacular coastline, caves, and forests; for its own distinct cuisine; and for the chance to venture off the well-beaten tracks in Italy.

MAJOR INTEREST

Multicultural artistic heritage
Less visited and more intact
Coastal drive of the Gargano massif
Romanesque cathedrals in and near Bari

565

Most of Apulia's overlords were either passing through on their way to more strategically protected destinations or occupying territory that formed part of a greater empire. The overwhelming exception—and the dominant figure of Apulia to this day—was Frederick II of Hohenstaufen, *stupor mundi et immutator mirabilis,* a progressive 13th-century leader and man of letters whom Dante called "the father of Italian poetry." With his son Manfred, Frederick was responsible for much of what Apulia still looks like. He not only filled it with castles but stayed on to make use of them. Later the demise of the Hohenstaufen family dragged Apulia's prosperity down with it.

Most modern invaders were as negligent toward Apulia as the rulers who preceded and succeeded Frederick. Apulia was seen as a place to pass through on the way to and from the port cities of the Adriatic. The region's prosperity, however, is on the rebound. Witness Bari's thriving Fiera del Levante, a trade fair, or the bounty of the region's extensive fields, vineyards, and olive groves. The tourist trade has also begun to flourish, and those who go find more and more hospitable hotels and, especially, restaurants.

Luckily, none of Apulia's magic has been sacrificed so far. During the region's scorching summers, Italy's longest coastline is still visited primarily by Italians, and an almost fairy-tale atmosphere persists throughout. The shadowy Foresta Umbra on the Gargano massif is the closest thing Italy has to an enchanted forest; and the burial markers of the Daunian people, who inhabited northern Apulia in ancient times—thin, flat stones with helmet-headed tops—are reminiscent of Alice's pack of cards. The Rubian drinking vessels shaped like animal heads in the Museo Jatta in Ruvo would put Walt Disney to shame, as would the beast motifs on Apulian Romanesque cathedrals. Animals figure prominently in folklore to this day in rural Apulia, where farmers won't slice milk-soaked bread for fear their cows will go dry, and horses wear beads to ward off the evil eye. In the caves of Castellana Grotte, unusual rock formations have prompted imaginative names. And the already exuberant Baroque found especially fertile ground in Lecce, far down the heel of Italy's boot, where the soft tufa stone, as Osbert Sitwell wrote, "allows the rich imagination of the south an unparalleled outlet."

All this provides a fitting backdrop to the traditional spirituality of many of the region's people, some of whom lived and worshipped until recently in the caves of Matera in the neighboring region of Basilicata. (Other unusual dwellings are the beehive-shaped *trulli* in the Murgia of the Trulli, including practically the entire town of Alberobello, where ruminations within the trulli restaurants and souvenir stands seem to be about how to attract tourists.)

When, according to legend, the Archangel Michael appeared in a grotto on the Gargano in the fifth century and left behind his great red cloak (part of which is now at Mont-St-Michel in France), the cult that arose around him merely replaced that of a local oracle on the same sacred spot, mentioned by Strabo in antiquity. And so it goes down the long coast: Saint Nicholas is celebrated in Bari, and an important Holy Week procession takes place in Táranto. Apulia's latest religious cult figure is Padre Pio, a Capuchin monk who died in 1968 and is buried at San Giovanni Rotondo, just a few miles from where Saint Michael made his original appearance. Born in Benevento, Pio, too, was an outsider, but his remains seem right at home in this magic and mystical land.

CAPITANATA

The northernmost section of Apulia (and therefore its most frequent point of entry from the rest of Italy), Capitanata is a union of topographical opposites. Jutting out into the Adriatic to form the spur of the Italian boot is the mountainous and forested Gargano massif, lapped by the waves of the Adriatic; below it is the flat and treeless Tavoliere (Italian for chessboard, from the grid pattern of roads traced there by the ancient Romans), the largest plain on the peninsula, undulating with waves of wheat and barley. Nature lovers might want to stay (with large numbers of northern Europeans) on the Gargano at the quiet **Hotel del Faro**, on its own promontory on the rocky shore near Faro di Pugnochiuso to the east, or the more

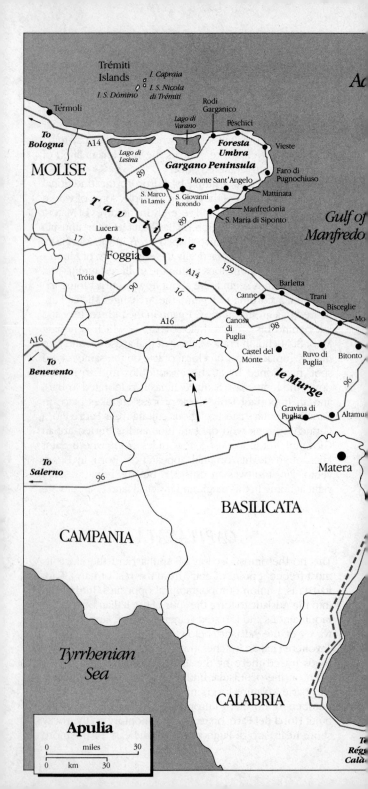

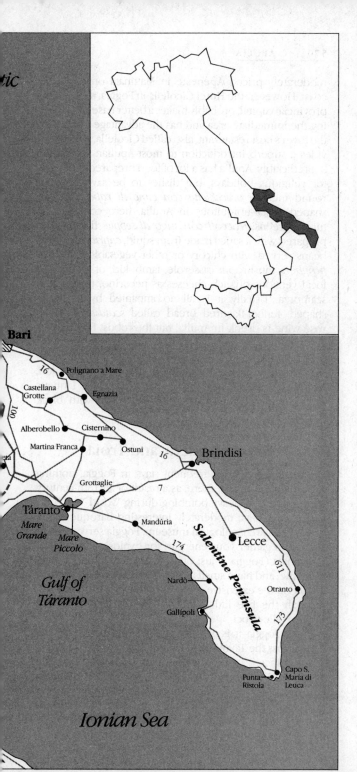

moderately priced **Apeneste** in Mattinata on the south coast. However, the **Hotel Cicolella** in Foggia, the bustling provincial capital, probably makes a better base for exploring the immediate area and has the advantage of housing the town's best restaurant, also called Cicolella, which provides a superb introduction to most Apulian specialties.

Predictably, Apulia has a lot of food prepared especially for religious holidays, but dishes to be savored year-round include *orecchiette con cime di rapa,* the ear-shaped pasta ubiquitous in Apulia, here cooked with turnip greens; *troccoli con sugo di seppie,* flat noodles prepared with a sauce made from squid; *capriata,* pureed beans served with chicory or other vegetables; *tiella di funghi,* a mushroom casserole; lamb, kid, or game; and local versions of such cheeses as pecorino, ricotta, and scamorza. Usually it is all accompanied by the ring-shaped, fennel-flavored bread called *scaldatelli.* Much rosé wine is drunk in Apulia, but the robust food is best accompanied by the mellow reds Cacc' e Mitte or Rosso di Cerignola; lighter foods go well with a refreshing San Severo white. There are plenty of grapes in the region, including some of Italy's best table varieties. Liqueur lovers might try the local Amarella, made with black cherry leaves.

Foggia, Lucera, and Tróia

Despite Frederick II's frequent stays in Foggia, nothing remains of his palace there, as a result of an 18th-century earthquake and heavy bombing during World War II. In fact, except for a moderately interesting Baroque cathedral and an archaeological museum, Foggia serves best as a place to gather your energies for exploring the rest of Capitanata (Foggia is just off Autostrada A 14 and a main train line, and has a small airport), perhaps invigorated by a walk on the extensive grounds of the Villa Comunale or through the five little outdoor chapels leading to the Chiesa delle Croci.

From Foggia it is a short, straight hop by car or bus west across the Tavoliere to **Lucera.** Just outside the city is its magnificent castle, the **Fortezza Angioina,** begun by Frederick II. Norman Douglas begins his *Old Calabria* ("Calàbria" once referred to more of southern Italy than it does at present) with a description of the castle's position, looking toward the Apennines and the Gargano, as the "key of Apulia." The castle itself is equally impressive, with dozens of towers and almost half a mile of encircling walls. Also on the outskirts of town is a Roman amphitheater, currently being restored and used for performances during the summer. In the Arab-looking town proper (Frederick II stocked it with Saracens from Sicily) we get our first glimpse of Saint Michael on the **cathedral**, one of the few intact examples of Angevin architecture in Italy: The archangel is in the center portal, flanked by two lesser angels.

Tróia, directly south of Lucera by car or bus, has another fine view of the surrounding countryside. Though Frederick II destroyed much of the evidence of its noble past, Tróia's **cathedral** remains the happiest marriage of Romanesque architectural forms with Eastern sculptural ornament in Apulia. The intricate latticework of its huge rose window shows Saracen sources, while beneath it the bronze doors burst with Byzantine dragons, animals, saints, and a portrait of the sculptor of the doors, Oderisio da Benevento, less than humbly placed next to Christ.

The Gargano Massif

The Gargano, served by trains and buses from Foggia, gets two types of tourists: nature lovers from Italy and northern Europe during the summer and tour buses full of religious pilgrims from all over the world year-round. From Foggia, pilgrims generally head north across the Tavoliere to the town of San Marco in Lamis to see the convent of San Matteo; then east to San Giovanni Rotondo to pay homage to a statue of the Madonna in the 16th-century convent of Santa Maria delle Grazie, to Padre Pio's tomb in the modern church of the same name, and to see the American-funded Fiorello La Guardia Hospital. The final stop on the route is **Monte Sant'Angelo**, the windswept and rather desolate town perched on a rock, still farther east near the Gulf of Manfredonia, where the Archangel Michael made his appearance to San Lorenzo, Bishop of Siponto, on May 8, 490. Subsequently, the **Santuario di San Michele** became one of the most important religious sanctuaries in the Christian world. Its miraculous grotto was consecrated in the fifth century, and works of art followed over the years. The bronze door at the entrance to the inner vestibule comes from Constantinople and is the oldest in Apulia; also significant is the stone bishop's throne in the grotto, where a marble statue of the saint, attributed to Andrea Sansovino, presides. Devotees often make the steep descent to the inner sanctum in their bare feet, and some continue their penance by licking the floor of the grotto.

The **Gargano coast route** from Foggia begins with a stop at **Santa Maria di Siponto**, a recently restored 12th-century cathedral; it is a survivor of the earthquake that leveled the important port town of Siponto, east of Foggia, in the 13th century. From there, it is a short distance to industrial Manfredonia, founded by Frederick II's bastard son Manfred. Its massive castle houses the **Museo Nazionale Archeologico del Gargano**, which contains the enchanting Daunian stelae, or grave slabs, covered with cartoonlike respresentations of nature. For those interested in art but not in making the entire religious pilgrimage route, it is a short distance from Manfredonia to Monte Sant'Angelo, where in addition to the sanctuary there is an interesting 12th-century structure called the Tomba di Rotari, which originally may have been a baptistery or a mausoleum, and the **Museo delle Arte e Tradizioni Popolari del Gargano**, a museum about daily life in former times. (The folk tradition is still evident in the town's production of wood carving.) Driving back down to the coast you pass through Mattinata, where a curious private collection of local art from Daunian stelae to alabaster statues of Saint Michael is on display in the **Farmacia Sansone**.

The coast road around the promontory is spectacular. Odd rock formations and intriguing grottoes rise above beautiful beaches. Medieval Vieste, whitewashed Péschici (where **Solemar**, a peaceful, modern hotel with beach and private pool, is located), and hillside **Rodi Gargánico** are pleasant towns, if not of overwhelming historical significance. Equally pleasant is the **Foresta Umbra**, an extensive forest of old beech, oak, pine, and chestnut trees. It is surprisingly clean and peaceful—almost spookily so, but companionship may be found at the Centro Visitatori, a visitors' center with exhibits about the human and natural history of the forest.

The Isole Trémiti

The Isole Trémiti take a full day's trip from the mainland no matter how you go to them—by ferry during the summer from Térmoli, Manfredonia, Vieste, Péschici, Rodi Gargánico, or Vasto; by hydrofoil from Péschici, Rodi Gargánico, or Térmoli; or even by helicopter from

Foggia. The large number of hotels on **San Dómino**, the largest of the islands, allows visitors to stay overnight as well, provided they have reservations. The *Insulae Diomediae* of Greek mythology, these were the isles inhabited by Diomedes' Illyrian companions, who were transformed by a vengeful Aphrodite into herons and are still said to be heard crying for their hero at night. The islands have been a place of exile, self-imposed or otherwise, from the era when Augustus's granddaughter Julia was banished to them for adultery through to the Fascist years, when they held political prisoners. These days, the preference is to escape *to* them, and pine-covered San Dómino becomes especially overrun each summer. Its **Kyrie** hotel, with beach, pool, tennis court, and private garden, gets the cream of the local agriculture-magnate crop; the less expensive **Gabbiano** gets a more mixed crowd. Of the other two main islands, **Capraia** (rarely visitable) is known for its rock formations, while **San Nicola** has the most cultural pursuits, with a Medieval fortress offering lovely views of the archipelago, and the abbey church of Santa Maria a Mare, which contains a well-preserved mosaic pavement, a Byzantine crucifix, and a Venetian polyptych.

THE ROAD TO BARI

Apulia's most famous Romanesque cathedrals and more may be taken in during a day's drive from Foggia southeast to Bari, weaving in and out to towns and other places along the Adriatic coast. Most of the towns also are served by trains and buses, but allow ample time to make connections. The first stop is **Canosa di Puglia**, legendarily founded by Diomedes. Its cathedral contains the oldest bishop's throne in Apulia and the tomb of Bohemond, son of the crusader Robert Guiscard. Continuing toward the coast, you pass the site where Hannibal won the battle of Cannae (Canne in Italian) in 216 B.C., only to lose the war later. It takes a lot of imagination to make this archaeological site come alive; it's best not to linger but to move on to **Barletta** on the coast. Its Romanesque cathedral, now in rather sad repair, houses a sensuous Madonna commemorating the "Disfida di Barletta," a 16th-century battle reenacted with much pageantry each July. Outside the basilica of San Sepolcro stands Barletta's major monument, a 16½-foot-high **Colossus**. An ancient

Roman bronze washed ashore in the 14th century, it was almost immediately dismembered by Dominican monks, and the arms and legs melted down to make bells for their church in Manfredonia; new limbs were later added to the original head and torso.

Heading inland again, drive due south to Apulia's most famous single piece of architecture, **Castel del Monte**. Built by Frederick II, it was his favorite hunting lodge and retreat, and it was here that he composed *De arte venendi cum avibus,* still the standard text on falconry. The golden octagonal stone castle, sitting like a crown on an isolated hill, still conveys a sense of majesty and peace. The nearby restaurant **Ostello di Federico** offers a relaxing spot for lunch and an excellent opportunity to sample Castel del Monte wines, which come in red, white, and the ever-popular rosé. Back on the coast southeast of Barletta in the white town of **Trani** is one of Apulia's most impressive Romanesque cathedrals, standing dramatically at the edge of the Adriatic. Farther along the coast, past Bisceglie (its Romanesque cathedral was much altered during the Baroque period and can be skipped in good conscience), is **Molfetta**, a commercial town whose old cathedral (ask directions to the Duomo Vecchio, since there is also a less interesting Baroque Duomo Nuovo) is also on the sea. Back inland, **Ruvo di Puglia** has another lovely Romanesque cathedral as well as the **Museo Jatta**, an extensive private collection of terra-cotta vases, especially noted for its rhytons (drinking vessels in the shapes of animal heads) from the city's ancient incarnation as Rubi. From there it is a short drive to see the cathedral at **Bitonto**, considered the culmination of the Apulian Romanesque, and on to Bari.

BARI AND ENVIRONS

La gente di Bari o vende o muore (the people of Bari sell or die) is a saying that aptly describes the city, whose September Fiera del Levante is the most important trade fair in Italy after Milan's. Apulia's largest and busiest city, Bari is primarily a port and a commercial and administrative center (it is the regional capital of Apulia), but it does have some sights worth seeing. These are found mainly in the **Città Vecchia** (Old City), which contains the prototypical Apulian Romanesque church **San Nicola di Bari**, housing an important bishop's throne as well as Saint Nicholas's tomb in the crypt below. (He *is* the same as Santa Claus. Saint Nick is also the patron saint of sailors, and the anniversary of the arrival of his remains in Bari, brought by local sailors from Asia Minor, is elaborately celebrated each May.)

Another Frederick II castle stands in the Città Vecchia, and is most comfortably explored if you leave your valuables elsewhere. Points of interest outside the Old City are the **Museo Archeologico**, an important archaeological museum; an art gallery (Pinacoteca Provinciale); and Italy's third-ranking opera house (Teatro Petruzzelli). Apulia's most prestigious publisher, Laterza, operates an excellent Italian-language bookstore in Bari, and at the other end of the spectrum, a lively flea market takes place Monday mornings on via Calfati.

Though modern Bari's efficient-looking grid plan belies a horrendous traffic problem, the city is nonetheless a relatively reliable base for trips throughout central Apulia. Virtually all the city's accommodations are geared to businessmen and thus are of the practical and pricey persuasion. You should expect efficiency to overrule charm in such places as the relatively expensive **Palace Hotel** near the castle or the moderately priced 7 **Mari**, also centrally located, which has some views of the Adriatic. Expect crowds during the September Fiera del Levante, when reservations are a must. A luxurious alternative to the Bari hotels is **Il Melograno** in nearby Monópoli. The hotel is in the peaceful setting of a converted *masseria,* or farmhouse, and boasts one of the area's best regional restaurants.

Bari also has excellent restaurants. **Ai 2 Ghiottoni** (via Putignani 11), **La Pignata** (via Melo 9), and **Vecchia Bari** (via Dante Alighieri 47) are all places to try Apulian classics along with such local specialties as seafood and lamb dishes (make sure the latter is local—a lot of lamb from New Zealand and Australia passes through that busy port). Recommended regional wines are Rosso di Barletta, a tart red, and dry whites from Castel del Monte and Locorotondo. The local liqueur, flavored with walnuts, is the potent Padre Peppe.

Inland from Bari

Some odd spots in the rocky, rolling inland plateaus known as the **Murge** make a pleasant day trip from Bari by car; again, trains and buses service the area, but such a trip requires precise schedule-juggling. You begin innocently enough in the hilltop town of **Altamura**, southwest of Bari, admiring the delicate rose window and richly carved door of its cathedral, begun by Frederick II when he re-established the Saracen-sacked city on its ancient, privileged site, stocking it with neighboring Latins, Greeks, and Jews, who were given further privileges. In **Gravina di Puglia**, to the west of Altamura, built into the side of a ravine, you will notice strange stone skeletons reclining above the door of the Purgatorio church. On a narrow street farther down the ravine is the church of San Michele dei Grotti, completely carved out of the rock, where more bones—this time real—are on display, left over from the Saracen attack.

The neighboring province of Matera (once part of Apulia but since redesignated to the otherwise largely undistinguished region of Basilicata) is the site of another ravine city, **Matera**. Inhabited since Paleolithic times, it is famous for its *sassi*, the extensive area of dwellings carved into the side of the ravine, whose inhabitants' poverty was so poignantly described by Carlo Levi in *Christ Stopped at Eboli*. By now most of the residents have been relocated to proper housing projects in the modern upper town, but urchins still prowl the rocks and will divulge the secrets of the caves' chapels and cubbyholes for a fee, though they're not needed to explore the town's Apulian Romanesque cathedral and the macabre façade of its Purgatorio church. For those who want to try Basilicata's cuisine, there is the restaurant **Il Terrazzino** on vico San Giuseppe 7. It serves pasta, lamb, and kid dishes adorned with the region's spicy sausages, all to be respectfully downed with an appreciative toast to Horace (he was born in the Basilicatan city of Venosa) with the extremely robust red wine Aglianico del Vulture. (*Aglianico* means Hellenic, another example of the mix of history here.) On the way back to Bari, movie buffs may want to loop over to **Castellaneta**, perilously perched over yet another ravine. This town was the birthplace of Rudolph Valentino, and the ceramic monument erected there in his honor stands as silent as the screen star, as odd and devout as any piece of Apulian religious sculpture.

Southeast of Bari

Some of Apulia's most primitive and most sophisticated sights can be seen as a day trip by car in the area southeast of Bari; more time is necessary to see it using public transportation. This area makes one of the region's most pleasant drives, filled as it is with gnarled gray-green olive trees often planted side by side with almond trees on red earth sectioned off with dry-laid walls made of weathered gray stone. This same stone is used for the area's most singular architectural feature, the conical dwellings known as *trulli*, most of which are less than 300 years old (although the construction method is prehistoric). In this part of Apulia you also begin to notice a large number of old *masserie*, fortified farmhouses, some of which date from Roman times.

Castellana Grotte, southeast of Bari, is the site of the largest and most spectacular caverns in Italy. Though people have left their imprint on nature through litter and the inevitable coins tossed in any body of water that can be loosely construed as a fountain, the names of beautiful colored alabaster rock formations—such as the Madonna, the altar, and the Leaning Tower of Pisa—attest to the Italians' devotion to the caverns; the in-depth two-hour tour is recommended over the hour-long one.

Alberobello, southeast of Castellana, is a town with a central area of more than 1,000 *trulli* that, despite concerted panderings to the tourist trade such as the omnipresent billboards advertising a liqueur called Amaro dei Trulli, is still something out of a fairly tale. Lunch may be taken in one of the *trulli*, at the **Trullo d'Oro** on via Cavallotti 29, which offers a number of lamb specialties along with local wines.

An alternative for lunch is farther southeast, in the elegant town of **Martina Franca**, famous for its sausages, spit-roasted meats, and strong white wine, some of which is sent north to make vermouth and spumanti. Just out of town is *its* restaurant in a *trullo*, **Trattoria delle Ruote**, on via Ceglie E. Closer to the Baroque churches and palazzi (the town hall is attributed to Gianlorenzo Bernini) is an excellent inexpensive restaurant: **La Rotonda**, at the Villa Comunale.

On the way to Ostuni near the coast you may pass through **Cisternino**, a whitewashed hill town that gives a tiny taste of the splendor to come in Ostuni. Built on three hills, with a Gothic cathedral and some Renaissance and Baroque buildings, **Ostuni** itself is most remarkable for the immaculate appearance of its slopes of whitewashed houses, giving the city the nickname *la città bianca* (the white city). Ostuni offers two relaxing accommodations (also white): the modest and modern **Incanto** in town (with views of the city, plains, and the Adriatic), and the huge **Rosamarina** resort on the coast, with private beach, tennis facilities, and restaurants much frequented by the more prosperous local gentry.

Alternatively, the coastal road back to Bari makes a lovely drive. Along the way is **Egnatia** (Egnazia, in Italian, from the Greek Gnathia), a town written about by Horace and inhabited until early Christian times. Today it is a vast, flat archaeological site with a recently opened museum housing examples of Gnathian ware, the delicate black pottery that takes its name from the town. Closer to Bari, at Polignano a Mare, is the hotel/restaurant **Grotta Palazzese**, on via Narciso 59. Its seafood, regional cheeses, desserts, and wines are all quite good, but the location of the place—in a cave overlooking the Adriatic—is what makes it so spectacular.

THE SALENTINE PENINSULA

The southernmost part of Apulia is the true "heel" of Italy's boot. Called the Salentine peninsula (Salento, in Italian), it is easily explored from Lecce, which has two comfortable hotels, the modern **President** and the more charming and centrally located **Risorgimento**. Both have good regional restaurants.

Brindisi

From Bari southeast to Lecce by car or train, the routes hug the coast to Brindisi, a city worth a short visit even if you are not passing through its port to Greece, the city's raison d'être since ancient times. Strabo praised its wines (*fare un brindisi* means to make a toast, in Italian), Horace mentions it in his first *Satire,* Virgil died here, and many other ancients saw Brindisi because it was the end of the Appian Way. One of the two columns that marked this terminus may been seen near the harbor (Lecce took the other one). The Museo Archeologico, the cathedral of San Benedetto (where Frederick II married his second wife), and the churches of San Giovanni al Sepolcro and Santa Maria del Casale (just north of town) are also worth seeing, but expect tumultuous traffic during the summer.

Lecce

Lecce's 16th- and 17th-century literary academies gave it the nickname "The Athens of Apulia," and its architecture from the same period earned it the epithet "The Florence of the Baroque." The soft and golden local tufa sandstone is easily carved and was handled with such vigor that it gave rise to an indigenous style called *Barocco Leccese,* a religious and secular architecture known more for its lavish decorative elements than formal innovation. (The decorative tradition continues with a flourishing production of papier-mâché and terra-cotta figurines available in many shops.) You can easily spend a day in Lecce, a bustling provincial capital. In addition to seeing the cathedral, the churches of Santa Croce, Rosario, and Santi Nicola e Cataldo, and the Palazzo Vescovile and Palazzo del Governo, you must also wander the streets and look for the rich Baroque decorative details on the humblest of buildings. The town's long history is further evidenced by a half-excavated Roman amphitheater and the **Museo Provinciale**, which is noted for its collection of Italian archaeological artifacts dating from Paleolithic times.

Some of the Salento's regional food specialties include *ciceri e tria,* tagliatelle pasta cooked in chick-pea broth; *cappello da gendarme,* a pastry shell stuffed with veal, eggplant, and zucchini; and *mercia,* a hard-to-find sheep's-milk mozzarella cheese. The robust Salice Salentino is the area's best-known red wine; the mellow Malvasia is the popular choice for white. Gran Liquore San Domenico, made in Lecce's convent of San Domenico, is the local liqueur. These specialties can all be well sampled at the **Risorgimento** restaurant on via Imperatore Augusto 19.

The Salentine Coast

The Greek influence in Apulia becomes most apparent toward the end of the peninsula, where cultural ties with Greece are still evident in the local dialects. The coastal drive is the most pleasant way to see it, since train and bus routes are generally inland.

Otranto, the easternmost city in Italy, was founded by the Greeks and became an important center of the Byzantine Empire. Until recently, residents practiced the Greek Orthodox religious rite, and they still call themselves

Idruntini, a reference to the town's ancient name of Hydruntum. In 1480 Otranto was the site of a vicious Turkish attack, and its castle, made famous by Horace Walpole's Gothic novel *The Castle of Otranto,* was built soon afterward for defensive purposes; these days it is more likely to serve as a backdrop to a lazy game of bocce played by the elderly men of the town. ("I did not even know there was a castle of Otranto," Walpole later wrote. "When the story was finished, I looked to the map of the kingdom of Naples for a well-sounding name, and that of Otranto was very sonorous.") The extensive mosaic floor of Otranto's cathedral is currently being restored, but still visible are its rose window and the chapel containing the bones of the martyrs slain by the Turks—a gruesome sight explaining why the townspeople continue to speak of the tragic event.

Apulia's natural drama has its denouement at **Capo Santa Maria di Leuca,** a lonely white limestone cliff at the very tip of the peninsula. On this site is the church of Santa Maria Finibus Terrae, usually visited by romantic types who thrill at the idea of being at the ends of the earth. (The southernmost end of Apulia, however, is actually at Punta Ristola, a nondescript beach a short distance ahead.)

Up the western coast of the Salento is **Gallípoli,** a fishing town and agricultural center founded by the Greeks, who gave it the name Kallipolis (beautiful city). The name is still a true description of the town, as evidenced by the lavish, almost Spanish Baroque interiors of its cathedral and the church of San Francesco, which contrast with the simple whitewashed façades of the Old City. There is also the inevitable imposing castle and museum, but Gallípoli's setting will put you in the mood instead for lunch at its fine seafood restaurant **Marechiaro,** overlooking the Ionian Sea on lungomare Marconi. An excellent, if expensive, place to linger in the area is the modern resort **Costa Brada,** on its own private beach just out of town. Inland to the north, the city of **Nardò**'s noble Baroque churches and palaces, reminiscent of Lecce, are worth inspecting, as is the town's oddly Oriental-looking pavilion, the Osanna.

From Lecce to Táranto

The highway and railroad from Lecce west to Táranto pass through **Mandúria,** another dignified-looking town with interesting Renaissance and Baroque buildings but known mostly for the nearby ruins of the Messapian civilization that ruled the Salentine peninsula before the Greeks arrived. The archaeological site contains ancient walls (where the Messapians battled the Tarantines), numerous tombs, and the Well of Pliny, so called because the phenomenon of its constant level is thought to be the one mentioned in Pliny's *Natural History*.

Most of the colonies of Magna Graecia were in what is now Calàbria. But the port of **Táranto** (the ancient Spartan colony of Taras, or Tarentum), situated between two bays called Mar Piccolo and Mar Grande, was its greatest city, with a population exceeding the present one. Then, as now, it was famous for the oysters plumped in the Mar Piccolo, but the city's current aspect as Italy's second largest naval dockyard and headquarters of the country's largest steel corporation, Italsider, should make you wary of finding more than pearls when biting into them. Táranto's seafood is safely sampled at its best restaurant, **Al Gambero**, which overlooks the harbor at vico del Ponte 4. Whatever is fresh goes well with Verdea Bianca, a local white wine; the local vanilla-and-chocolate–flavored liqueur is called Amaro San Marzano.

Under the Spartans, Táranto became a center of Pythagorean philosophy, though Pythagoras himself lived in Croton, in what is now Calàbria. Táranto was the birthplace of the mathematician Archytas, whom Plato visited, and Aristoxenes, who wrote the first known treatise on music. Crafts flourished in the ancient colony: The city produced its own pottery and was famous for a purple dye extracted from the murex, a type of shellfish. (The nearby town of Grottaglie has become noted for its ceramics in more recent times, and the colorful wares produced there in blue floral patterns on beige backgrounds may also be found in many shops in Táranto.)

Táranto's *Città Vecchia* (Old City) occupies an island. Like Bari's Old City, it has a magnificent if somewhat rundown castle and cathedral and is the scene of important religious processions during Holy Week. Also like Bari's Città Vecchia, it is poverty-stricken and reputedly dangerous. The remains of a Doric temple dedicated to Neptune, which is the only outdoors remnant of Táranto's Greek past, is also located there. The city's real Greek treasures lie in the **Museo Nazionale**, just over the Ponte Girevole, a swinging bridge connecting the old city with the newer part of town. The collections of sculpture, jewelry, and pottery make this the world's most important museum regarding Magna Graecia; at least half a day should be spent seeing it. (Hotels, again as in Bari, are generally pleasant but impersonal in appearance; try the expensive waterfront **Grand Hotel Delfino** or the more moderate **Plaza**. Both are modern and centrally located.)

To further the study of Magna Graecia, each year in October Táranto hosts the Convegno di Studi sulla Magna Grecia, an important meeting on various aspects of the ancient civilization.

GETTING AROUND

Foggia, Bari, and Brindisi all have airports served by Aliblu Airways or Aerea Trasporti Italiani from Rome and Milan. Trains connect the major cities from Rome, Naples, and Milan; the smaller towns can be reached by local train and bus services. Since connections can require some time, a car (hired at the airports or in the larger cities) offers the most freedom, although it should be closely watched when parked, especially in Bari and Táranto.

Monte Sant'Angelo celebrates Saint Michael on May 8 and September 29. Barletta's Disfida (a reenactment of the battle of 1503) takes place on the third Sunday in July. In Bari Saint Nicholas's feast takes place from May 7 through May 10, and the opera season at Teatro Petruzzelli runs from January to March. In Táranto the processions of Our Lady of the Sorrows (L'Addolorata) and the Mysteries (Misteri) take place on Maundy Thursday and Good Friday, respectively.

ACCOMMODATIONS REFERENCE

▶ **Apeneste**. Piazza Turati 3, 71030 **Mattinata**. Tel: (0884) 47-43.

▶ **Hotel Cicolella**. Viale 24 Maggio 60, 71100 **Foggia**. Tel: (0881) 38-90; Telex: 810273.

▶ **Costa Brada**. Lungomare Costa Brada, 73014 **Gallípoli**. Tel: (0833) 225-51.

▶ **Grand Hotel Delfino**. Viale Virgilio 66, 74100 **Táranto**. Tel: (099) 32-05; Telex 860113.

▶ **Hotel del Faro**. 71019 **Faro di Pugnochiuso**. Tel: (0884) 790-11; Telex: 810122.

▶ **Gabbiano**. San Domino, 71040 **San Nicola di Trémiti**. Tel: (0882) 66-30-44.

▶ **Incanto**. Via dei Colli, 72017 **Ostuni**. Tel: (0831) 97-17-81; Telex: 813284.

▶ **Kyrie**. San Domino, 71040 **San Nicola di Trémiti**. Tel: (0882) 66-30-55.

▶ **Il Melograno**. Contrada Torricella 345, 70043 **Mónopoli**. Tel: (080) 80-86-56.

▶ **Palace Hotel**. Via Lombardi 13, 70122 **Bari**. Tel: (080) 21-65-51; Telex: 810111.

▶ **Plaza**. Via d'Aquino 46, 74100 **Táranto**. Tel: (099) 919-25.

▶ **President**. Via Salandra 6, 73100 **Lecce**. Tel: (0832) 518-81; Telex: 860076.

▶ **Risorgimento**. Via Imperatore Augusto 19, 73100 **Lecce**. Tel: (0832) 421-25; Telex: 860144.

▶ **Rosamarina**. 72017 **Ostuni**. Tel: (0831) 97-00-61.

▶ **7 Mari**. Via Verdi 60, 70123 **Bari**. Tel: (080) 44-15-00.

▶ **Solemar**. Località San Nicola E, 71010 **Péschici**. Tel: (0884) 941-86.

CALABRIA

By Dwight V. Gast

Having been extensively colonized by the Greeks from the eighth century B.C. as part of Magna Graecia, subsequently inhabited by Byzantines, and finally overrun in turn by the Saracens, Normans, Hohenstaufens, Angevins, Aragons, and Bourbons, Calàbria should be used to outsiders. But as recently as 1911, when Norman Douglas, the author of *Old Calabria,* visited San Demétrio Corone, he discovered that "within the memory of living man no Englishman has ever entered the town. This is quite possible; I have not yet encountered a single English traveller during my frequent wanderings over South Italy."

Douglas travelled on foot throughout the "toe" of Italy, but even with the improved highways built during recent years Calàbria attracts fewer visitors than practically any other region in Italy. Most of those who do go are drawn not by its rich history or ethnic diversity but by invitations from distant relatives or the beauties of some of Italy's most unspoiled beaches and panoramic mountain country. A half-century ago Walter Starkey wrote that "one of the charms of a journey through Calàbria is that it sets in continual antithesis the coast and the mountain," a phenomenon that is still true; Calabrians trying to impress their American friends have characterized the region as "Calabrifornia."

Calàbria is slow to reveal its historical and cultural secrets. Many artistic treasures still remain buried beneath the earth. The exact location of the ancient colony of Sybaris, for example, has never been determined, let alone excavated. Furthermore, much of what is above ground lies hidden in small seaside and mountain towns that retain the attitudes, customs, and occasionally even the dress of centuries past. Such places are more common in Calàbria than in any other region in Italy, and, for the imaginative visitor, happening upon them presents a picture of what life must have been like in much of preindustrialized Italy, when cows grazed in the Forum, women turned themselves out in full skirts and peasant blouses, and mustachioed men dashed about in capes and hats.

MAJOR INTEREST

Italy as it used to be
Ethnic diversity
Medieval charms of the old city of Cosenza
Natural Alpine beauty of the Sila massif
Picturesque fishing villages and fabulous views
    along the southern Tyrrhenian coast
Art of Magna Graecia at the Museo Nazionale in
    Réggio di Calàbria, especially the Riace Bronzes
Windswept Medieval town of Gerace
Byzantine monuments of Rossano
Extensive archaeological ruins of the ancient
    Greek colony of Metapontum in neighboring Basilicata

Calàbria's scenic terrain is the most seismic in Italy, a fact that, coupled with centuries of feudal and baronial rule, accounts for the region's alienation, isolation, and poverty. These aspects of modern Calàbria are especially ironic considering the same area's magnificence as Magna Graecia as late as the fifth century B.C.: Rhegion (modern-day Réggio di Calàbria) was a prosperous trading center; Locri Epizephyrii (Locri), lauded by Pindar for its good government, was the first Greek city to write a code of laws; Croton (Crotone) was where Pythagoras developed the ideas of freedom and self-reliance that eventually became permanent themes in Hellenic thought; and the very name of Sybaris (Síbari) was a synonym for luxury. Spiritually and physically, however, there is little present-day evidence of the Greeks in Calàbria outside of the museums.

The centuries of alienation eventually gave rise to romantic brigands, male and female, who roamed the mountains of the Sila and Aspromonte (still favorite hiding places for fugitives from the law) until the last century. Now the local version of organized crime, the

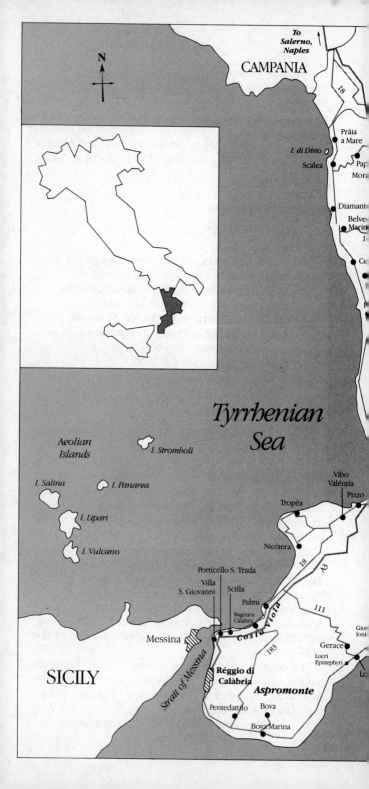

'ndrangheta, has dispelled, with its sporadic bloody out-
bursts, most of the romance of the outlaw.

Isolation brought about a spiritual side to the superstitious nature of the Calabrians, however. Gazing at the
stars in the deep night skies of the mountains, it is easy
to imagine how the Pythagoreans conceived the notion
of celestial music. That same mystical terrain has attracted monks—from Byzantines to Carthusians—the
last of whom even now are busy praying for the sins of
the world at their far-removed monastery in Serra San
Bruno, in the mountains of south-central Calàbria.

Though the government's special fund for the south,
Cassa per il Mezzogiorno, is gradually improving economic conditions, much of Calàbria's historical poverty
remains, though the traveller need no longer be wary of
brigands, or expect to have to share a hotel bed with a
stranger, as Douglas did. A number of comfortable and
efficient, if not altogether luxurious, hotels have been
built in recent years in the larger cities and resort towns.
Even in remote rural areas the grimness and suspicion
that has traditionally greeted strangers is giving way to
increasing invitations to share homemade *paisanella*
brandy or *vino greco* in a toast to the memory of some
relative who long ago left Calàbria for the outside world.

THE NORTHERN
TYRRHENIAN COAST

The entry point to Calàbria by car or train from the north
is the Tyrrhenian coast below Naples and Salerno. The
short stretch of beaches here is so spectacular that this is
the final destination of many travellers attracted to the
civilized amenities as offered by the lavish **Grand Hotel
San Michele** at Cetraro (with its gorgeous views of the
sea, private beach, garden, and pool) or the less expensive beachfront **Mondial** at Práia a Mare, to the north. The
area is an appropriate beginning for an exploration of
Calàbria, since it was one of the first parts of the region to
be inhabited. **Isola di Dino**, reached by boat from Práia a
Mare, is a tiny island where prehistoric relics have been
unearthed in its grottoes, and where Ulysses allegedly
landed on his journeys. (One of its grottoes is also the
home of the statue of the ancient Madonna della Grotta,

celebrated in an annual religious procession.) More prehistoric relics may be seen down the coast, at Scalea, and
at the inland town of Papasidero.

The resort town of Diamante, between Práia a Mare
and Cetraro, is a good place to stop for a meal. Its
moderately priced **La Pagoda** restaurant in the beachfront
Ferretti hotel gently eases the palate from the cuisine of
Campania, just to the north, to the cuisine of Calàbria,
serving equally excellent seafood and eggplant dishes.
Farther down the coast, past the citron groves of Belvedere and Cetraro, and up a winding mountain, is one of
southern Italy's most ethnically important communities,
Guardia Piemontese. Founded by Waldensian refugees,
the town has retained its Provençal dialect and distinctive
folk costumes to this day, and a walk among its stone
houses and along the promenade overlooking the Mediterranean gives a preview of the ethnic diversity and
visual splendor of Calàbria to come. The final stop in this
stretch of Calàbria is **Páola**, birthplace of Saint Francis of
Páola, where an important monastic complex attracts religious pilgrims, especially during this saint's feast on May
5, when his miraculous passage to Sicily—he was blown
over in his own robes—is celebrated by rowing his statue
out into the sea.

COSENZA AND ENVIRONS

Cosenza, reached by train or car from Naples, and just
inland from Páola, is a busy, modern city with an extensive Medieval quarter. Located in a mountain valley near
some of the region's most interesting sights, it also makes
a good base for side trips to the northern Tyrrhenian
coast just described, to the unusual Medieval and Albanian towns in the highlands to the north, or to the Sila
massif, each of which can be seen in a day's drive from
here. The contemporary **Hotel Centrale**, true to its name,
is central, and convenient to both the modern and Medieval city on foot, which accounts for its popularity with
everyone from businessmen to the occasional visiting
artists in town for theatrical and musical activities. The
Centrale also has a good, reasonably priced regional
restaurant and a garage, but travellers with cars might
prefer the even more up-to-date conveniences and swimming pools of the **Europa** and **San Francesco** hotels in

suburban Rende. **La Calabrisella** restaurant at via Gerolamo De Rada 11/a in Cosenza provides the best local introduction to Calabrian cuisine. The region is known for antipasti such as *rosa marina* or *mustica*—a spicy spread made with fish fry, referred to as "the caviar of the south"—or the pungent *soppressata* and *capocollo* sausages; pasta dishes served with eggplant or artichokes, or *con lumache,* with a snail sauce, as well as *schiaffettoni* stuffed with meat and cheese; spicy main courses of roast lamb, kid, or eggplant; and buttery *caciocavallo* cheese or luscious prickly pears for dessert. La Calabrisella also has ample stocks of Calabrian wine. Cirò, which comes in red, rosé, and white varieties, is the best-known wine of the region: Its supporters say its origins in Magna Graecia make it the oldest wine in the world. Other robust reds— Donnici Savuto and Pollino—produced even closer to Cosenza, are descendants of the wines praised by Pliny. Desserts such as *mostaccioli* (animal-shaped cookies made with honey and white wine), *chinulille* (dough fried with ricotta cheese), and *crucette* (figs stuffed with nuts and citron) are typical of the region. The local liqueur is called Amaro Silano.

Cosenza

Cosenza is Calàbria's most culturally lively city, home to the Teatro Rendano, where operas, concerts, and classic and contemporary theater are performed; the Accademia Cosentina, a literary academy that has been active for centuries; and Italy's newest university. Of its Medieval quarter, which comprised the entire city until World War II, George Gissing wrote in his *By the Ionian Sea* at the turn of the century, "Cosenza has wonders and delights which tempt to day-long rambling." In fact, the area, relatively untouched by the disasters that have ravaged much of Calàbria, is still lined with narrow streets that wind up the side of a hill. It makes, if not a day-long rambling, a pleasant half-day's stroll. Of particular interest are the **church of San Domenico**, which has a beautiful rose window, and the **Cathedral**, allegedly consecrated in the presence of Frederick II (its Byzantine reliquary cross, donated by the emperor, is usually kept in the adjacent Palazzo Vescovile but is currently in Florence for restoration). The **Museo Civico** houses a collection of prehistoric bronzes, and at the church of San Francesco di Assisi, exhibitions are often held in the former monastery next door. Dominating the city is a **Norman castle** housing a restored baronial hall. Though the castle is often closed, it affords great views of the old city, and the adjacent olive grove is an ideal spot for a picnic. Provisions can be picked up in the modern part of town before starting out: The Ente Sviluppo Agricolo Calàbria (viale degli Alimena 72–74), selling Calabrian wines, olive oil, dried mushrooms, stuffed figs, cheeses, and other regional produce, is the local branch of a chain of stores throughout the region.

North of Cosenza

The inland towns north of Cosenza are difficult to see conveniently without a car, but for those not dependent on public transportation or with more than a day at their disposal they provide a glimpse of unexpected artistic riches and an ethnic diversity unlike anywhere else in Italy. Farthest north, almost on the border of Basilicata (and east of Práia a Mare), is **Morano Càlabro**, a lovely hill town descending a slope beneath its Norman castle. Its church of San Pietro contains statuary by Pietro Bernini, and two other churches, the Maddalena and San Bernardino, are also worth your attention. Back in the direction of Cosenza is Castrovillari, a bustling regional seat where the local women occasionally still wear red, white, and blue folk costumes. The Old Town has a castle, an abandoned synagogue, and the church of Santa Maria del Castello, with Byzantine beginnings oddly elaborated by Baroque additions. Just outside the town is the **Alìa Restaurant** on via Jetticelle, considered by many to be the best in Calàbria. In an incongruously upscale setting, two brothers have set out to initiate the locals to the ways of the contemporary table, but as didactic as the means may be, the moderately priced results are delicious renditions of regional dishes.

The next town worth visiting is **Lungro** (southwest of Castrovillari), location of the oldest salt mine in Italy, where the ancient Romans extracted the *salarium* they paid their soldiers. Today, Lungro's cathedral of San Nicola di Mira is the seat of the bishop of the largest expatriate Albanian community in Italy, descendants of refugees who settled throughout southern Italy hundreds of years ago to escape the Ottoman Turks. Called *Arbereshi* in local dialect, they continue to practice Greek Orthodox rites and maintain Albanian dialect, dress, and customs. Except for its TV antennas, beat-up Alfa Sud cars, and other modern infringements, this caped and costumed citizenry, which puts on its finery to celebrate many Albanian festivals throughout the year, could have stepped out of the 15th century.

Up a narrow mountain road from Lungro is **Altomonte**, a peaceful, well-kept hamlet seemingly constructed by artists and craftsmen who got lost on their way to Siena. Its church of Santa Maria della Consolazione, recently restored, is a gem of Gothic architecture, and the adjacent museum houses a number of minor masterpieces, including a tiny painting of Saint Ladislas attributed to Simone Martini. A stroll through the town leads to the Municipio (municipal building), housed in a lovingly restored former convent of the Minim order. If you find yourself caught by Altomonte's bucolic charms you can ask at the Municipio's Agroturismo office about taking one of the comfortable, rustic rooms offered in the nearby countryside. Almost as tranquil, on a hill opposite the town, is the modern **Hotel Barbieri**, which houses an unassuming, moderately priced regional restaurant—an excellent spot for a meal overlooking Altomonte—as well as a shop selling tempting local produce.

On the way back to Cosenza are two other Albanian communities, less important politically if more attractive visually than Lungro. **San Demétrio Corone** (east of E 1/ A 3), Douglas's discovery, was originally settled by emigrants from Corone, Albania, and is the site of an Albanian festival each spring. Its church of Sant'Adriano, with its Roman, Byzantine, Basilian, and Norman elements, even predates this 15th-century Albanian settlement. The other worthwhile detour is to the little town of **Luzzi** farther south to see its Medieval churches and the nearby Cistercian abbey of La Sambucina.

The Sila

Rising in the middle of Calàbria is the Sila, a massif known to Strabo. Considered "the great woods of Italy," its name derives from the Latin word for woods, *silva;* its pinewood, *pino larico calabro,* was used by the ancients to build ships, and by early Christians for churches in Rome. Its northern third is called the Sila Greca (Greek Sila) and is home to most of Calàbria's Albanian communities; the central part, Sila Grande (Great Sila), has other ancient settlements and modern facilities for skiing; Sila Piccola

(Little Sila), as its name implies, is the small, southern section. Panoramic views and pine-scented air make a drive in the Sila refreshing, especially during weekdays, when it is completely free of crowds. Its forests are home to wolves and all types of game, its streams and lakes filled with trout (freshwater fishing licenses can be obtained at the Ufficio Caccia e Pesca in any town hall for a small fee), and wild strawberries and *rosito* mushrooms ripen for gathering during the summer and fall, respectively.

A large part of the Sila's villages, lakes, forests, and meadows may be seen in a day trip from Cosenza, to which the massif is connected by train and bus service, but those who want a maximum dose of mountain air can stay at one of the Sila's modest hotels: The rustic, lakeside **Grand Hotel Lorica** in the town of the same name is perhaps the most pleasant, for its views of Lago Arvo. Closest to Cosenza to the east is the town of Camigliatello Silano, of little interest except for its modest ski facilities, and even those are frequented mostly by locals during the long winter season. (One such lodge is the plain but efficient hotel **Aquila-Edelweiss**.) Farther on to the northeast, past the placid shores of Lago Cecita, is Longobucco, a town of Medieval origin known for its weavers, who display their wares (carpets and bed covers with Oriental motifs) each August in a crafts fair.

To the south is San Giovanni in Fiore (east of Cosenza on 107), another town of Medieval roots, where the women wear black-and-white costumes said to have been designed by the town's founder, Gioacchino Da Fiore, a 12th-century abbott. The town is the Sila's largest, and is also home to a thriving community of weavers (this time Armenian inspired), whose work is on sale year-round at the Santa Lucia hotel. An inexpensive restaurant in San Giovanni is **Florence**, which serves such specialties of the Sila as trout and wild boar, as well as *butirro,* a dollop of creamery butter encased in *caciocavallo* cheese. A few hours at one of its simple tables, enjoying the local delicacies—perhaps over a bottle of Savuto or Pollino—is one way of paying homage to Pliny or any one of the ancients who praised the bounty of the Sila. The lazy drive west back to Cosenza may be interrupted with a stop for a digestive stroll in the quiet town of Lorica (perhaps taken literally with a glass of Amaro Silano) on the slopes of Monte Botte Donato, the latter easily scaled in the comfort of an automobile for a last look at the great woods of Italy as they spread out beyond the shores of Lago Arvo.

THE SOUTHERN
TYRRHENIAN COAST

Most people explore the southern Tyrrhenian coast as a
day trip by car from their hotel in Cosenza, or one of the
nearby coastal towns, south to Réggio di Calàbria. Seen
from train or car, the coast offers spectacular views of
the Tyrrhenian Sea and, at its southern end, the Aeolian
Islands and Sicily. Some 59 km (35 miles) south of
Cosenza on the Autostrada is **Pizzo Calàbro**, known for
its castle and its small church, Piedigrotta, carved out of
the stone cliffs. Just ahead is **Vibo Valéntia**, admired by
Cicero for its good government when it was the ancient
colony of Hipponium, and today an active little town
whose modern and moderately priced **Hotel 501** makes
an appealing place from which to base excursions along
the coast. The hotel also houses two fine restaurants,
both of which serve superb meat and seafood dishes
along with the local specialty of *pecorino* cheese. The
city has a surprising range of monuments, including a
recently restored Norman castle, the Renaissance church
of San Michele, and the Baroque cathedral of Leoluca
and church of the Rosario. Artifacts from the excavations
at Hipponium may be seen at the Museo Civico in
Palazzo Cordopardi, and in the private collection housed
in Palazzo Capialbi.

Travelling down the coastal route, what you see next
are the tile roofs of the town of **Tropéa**, almost as red as
the onions for which the town is famous. An earlier
visitor, Hercules (Pliny called the town Portus Herculis),
supposedly first glimpsed its cliffs from the sea. The
cliffs have since been graced with a lovely castle and
cathedral, the latter containing a painting of the Madonna allegedly by Saint Luke. Visitors should also stroll
through the Old Town and out to the abandoned Benedictine sanctuary of Santa Maria dell'Isola. Farther down
the coast, around Capo Vaticano, is **Nicótera**, another
picturesque town with a minor castle and a Museo
Archeologico. It is best appreciated, however, for its
tonnetto all'aceto, a tuna dish garnished with mint
leaves, and the dry Limbadi wine produced nearby.
Palmi, a short distance onward, is where the so-called
Costa Viola (Violet Coast) begins. Outwardly modern (its

huge palms are very old, though), the town has an important ethnographic museum, **Museo Calabrese di Etnografia e Folklore**, which has an extensive collection of antique crafts, useful for honing your eye before you consider purchasing any of their contemporary counterparts, readily available in local pottery shops. The town was also the birthplace of one of Calàbria's most famous personages, Francesco Cilea, composer of *Adriana Lecouvreur,* and though Palmi has no official memorial to him, the mere mention of his name inspires snippets of his operas from the locals.

Down the coast is **Bagnara Càlabra**, a hardworking community with a long-standing tradition of division of labor. Its men, using age-old methods, catch swordfish in late spring and summer, and spend much of the rest of the year working on their wooden boats, while the women of the town prepare the catch *alla bagnarese* (with oil, lemon, capers, garlic, parsley, and oregano) and make a hard-nougat candy called *torrone,* which is prized throughout Italy. People from all over Italy come to take part in the town's swordfish festival as soon as the season has ended, in July. A good place to sample swordfish year-round is the restaurant **Kerkira**.

Just ahead along the coast to the west is **Scilla**. The fishing village and castle are Medieval in appearance, but the rock crowned by the castle is none other than the one mentioned in the *Odyssey* as the dwelling place of the six-headed monster Scylla. (The whirlpool of the monster Charybdis is across the Strait of Messina.) The treacherous seas that gave rise to the myth have calmed through the centuries, but the action continues in a youth hostel and discotheque in the castle. The Costa Viola ends with a bang at **Porticello Santa Trada**, a tourist center full of even more discotheques, and temptingly close to Sicily. This is the point at which the mainland and the island come closest—2 km (just over a mile)—and will be the site of a bridge if the government ever decides to go through with its long-discussed plans for one. (The next town, **Villa San Giovanni**, however, is where the car and train traffic is acually ferried across to the island.) Just ahead is Réggio di Calàbria, where the elegant **Grand Hotel Excelsior**, located just behind the town's most important tourist attraction—the Museo Nazionale—or the less expensive but also comfortable **Palace Hotel Masoanri's** provide convenient local accommodations.

REGGIO DI CALABRIA
AND VICINITY

The ancient Greek colony of Rhegion has had quite an extraordinary series of misfortunes since its founding: It has been sacked by invaders, racked by earthquakes, and was heavily bombed during World War II. Virtually nothing remains of its glorious past. Its current incarnation has a pleasant but uninspiring appearance, yet offers some otherworldly elements. Looking into the Strait of Messina under the right conditions, for example, you may see what appears to be a sunken city, a phenomenon named after a sprite called the Fata Morgana and described in meteorological detail by Swinburne in his *Travels in the Two Sicilies*. (It is actually an optical illusion, a reflection of Réggio di Calàbria and the city of Messina on the other side.)

Most visitors come to Réggio, as it is commonly called, for the **Museo Nazionale della Magna Grecia**, but the indoor treasures of the museum can be complemented by the outdoor pleasures of a stroll in the nearby Lido Comunale, a panoramic promenade designed by Pier Luigi Nervi. The museum is the most important such institution in Calàbria, and the single most significant in the world for its rich archaeological remnants of Calabrian Magna Graecia. A half day is recommended to take in the entire collection, which extends from prehistoric artifacts through two Renaissance paintings by Antonello da Messina. The museum's main attraction, however, is its classical section. As the numerous replicas on sale near the museum entrance and throughout the city attest, the undisputed stars of the Museo Nazionale are two fifth-century B.C. statues of warriors, dubbed the **Riace Bronzes** after the Calabrian town near which they were discovered underwater in 1972. In the same downstairs room is another rare Greek bronze dating from the same period, a bust called the *Head of a Philosopher*.

One of Réggio's best regional restaurants, the moderately priced **Conti** at via Giulia 2, is located near the museum and is as good a place as any to sample Calabrian cuisine and the spicy local seafood influenced by nearby Sicily, perhaps finishing off with sweeter Sicilian specialties that have made their way across the strait—marzipan or *granita,* an ice usually flavored with almond, coffee, or lemon.

Around the Toe
of Italy

There is much to be seen in a half-day's drive from Réggio rounding the toe of the Italian boot along the coast of the Aspromonte, the usually dry massif, which, like much of mountainous Calàbria, becomes riddled with violent torrents called *fiumare* during the spring thaw. The land is planted with almonds, citrus, jasmine, and other fragrant trees, and is the only place in the world where the bergamot orange, used in eau de cologne, is cultivated. Driving along the Costa dei Gelsomini (Jasmine Coast), you pass **Pentedattilo**, a tiny village set beneath the breathtaking hand-shaped rock formation that gives the town its name. Farther along the coast is **Bova Marina**, site of Italy's oldest synagogue (it dates from the fourth century B.C.), uncovered during the construction of the highway. Inland is the town of **Bova**, the center of Calàbria's Greek community, where the inhabitants speak a dialect of Greek and hold an annual summer festival for the region's Greek communities. The somewhat severe-looking Renaissance architecture of the town frames beautiful views of the Ionian Sea. Up the coast, just before the modern town of Locri (where the seaside **Demaco Hotel**, with its sweeping views of the Ionian, is a convenient place to spend the night), are the excavations of the ancient Greek colony **Locri Epizephyrii**. The extensive site also houses a modern museum of the finds, though most of the major works are in Réggio. From Locri, a scenic road leads inland to **Gerace**, dramatically perched on a small mountain plateau overlooking the surrounding plain. Calàbria's largest cathedral (with interior columns possibly taken from the temples of Locri) is here in Gerace, as are other Byzantine and Medieval churches. The town also has a thriving crafts industry, notable for its weavers as well as its potters, who reproduce the ancient vases and tablets of Locri Epizephyrii. A sampling (in one of the many cantinas) of Gerace's strong, sweet, amber-colored *vino greco* is also recommended.

THE SOUTHERN
IONIAN COAST

Continuing north along the Ionian, the peaceful coastal route alternates with awe-inspiring excursions to the *serre,* inland villages set dramatically overlooking gorges. From Locri, modern resort towns (Siderno and Roccella Ionica are among many such crowded, family-oriented places along the Calabrian coast) are interwoven with ghosts of ancient ones like Giososa Ionica. Past Riace Marina, where the famous bronzes were discovered, is **Caulónia**, the site of another excavation of artifacts on display in the museum in Réggio, though some impressive foundations of a Doric temple may be seen in situ.

Stilo and Serra San Bruno

The road inland from Monasterace up the coast from Roccella leads to Stilo, birthplace of the philosopher Tommaso Campanella, where tiny **La Cattolica**, a restored and highly important Byzantine church, leads a list of monuments that includes a Gothic cathedral and a Norman castle. A series of sharp, spectacular curves then leads to **Serra San Bruno**, a town developed in the 11th century as an adjunct to the **monastery of Santo Stefano del Bosco**, begun by Bruno of Cologne, founder of the Carthusian order. The monastery, on the outside of town, offers tours twice daily, at 11:00 A.M. and 4:00 P.M. However, only men are permitted to visit, accompanied by one of the monks (who make a refreshingly delicious cheese for sale at the entrance). Yet both sexes may glimpse the monks on Mondays, when they take their weekly walk in the woods of the abbey. Near the abbey is the church of Santa Maria del Bosco, where Bruno of Cologne resided and died, as well as a pool of clear, pure water that Bruno allegedly made miraculous. In the town proper are the Baroque churches of San Biago and L'Addolorata, and shops selling wood, stone, and wrought-iron crafts, as well as the local sweet, *inzudda,* made with almonds and honey. The invigorating drive on 182 down to Soverato back on the coast will put you in the mood for lunch in the restaurant of the seaside **San Domenico Hotel**.

Catanzaro and Taverna

Pass the resort town of Copanello and make a quick detour inland to **Squillace**, birthplace of Cassiodorus (the great minister of the Ostrogoth Theodoric, conqueror of Italy, who is also remembered for having executed the Roman philosopher Boethius). This ancient town is also noted for its early Christian cathedral and its Norman castle, as well as its own sweet white wine and the production of pottery. Return to the coast, then head inland again at Catanzaro Marina. Drive through the plains that were once considered the Garden of the Hesperides, past (for now) golden Catanzaro, and up the mountain road to **Taverna**, in the foothills of the Sila Piccola. This town should be on the itinerary of every art lover, for it is famous as the birthplace of Calàbria's most famous painter, Mattia Preti, known in the art world as Il Cavaliere Calabrese. Though he painted extensively throughout Italy and in Malta during the 17th century, the churches of San Domenico, Santa Barbara, and San Martino in Taverna contain several of his early works.

From Taverna return to **Catanzaro**, famous in Medieval times as *la città dei tre V: venti, velluti, e San Vitaliano.* Of the three Vs referred to—wind, velvets, and the protector San Vitaliano—little remains except the first, but Catanzaro's role as the regional capital of Calàbria has endowed it with agreeable accommodations and restaurants. The few sights to be seen include the Baroque church and oratory of the Rosario, the Museo Provinciale (a museum with a *Madonna and Child* signed by Antonello da Messina), and a promenade in the adjoining Villa Margherita, which offers a lovely view of the sea across a plain held to be the Garden of the Hesperides of ancient mythology. Modern Catanzaro offers such amenities as the basic comforts of the **Hotel Guglielmo** and **Uno più Uno**, a moderately priced restaurant in galleria Mancuso, good for sampling *rosito* mushrooms from the Sila, the local dish *murseddu,* veal and pork innards seasoned with a peppery tomato sauce, and the local *pecorino* cheese. The dry Lamezia red wine makes a good accompaniment to the hearty fare. If the view of the sea is too tempting, try staying at **Stillhotel e Ristorante La Brace** at Catanzaro Lido, a modern hotel situated right on the water. Its restaurant also serves many regional specialties.

THE NORTHERN IONIAN COAST

The main points of interest on Italy's instep spark the imagination; most of the glories here are ghosts of their former greatness. Rounding Capo Rizzuto from the south, you reach the ruined castle **Le Castella**; it's worth wading through the water to inspect the ancient stone structure supposedly built by Hannibal but actually erected by the

Aragons. (Le Castella is also the site of a contemporary, family-style resort hotel, **Da Annibale**, with a top-notch regional restaurant.) You can bypass Isola di Capo Rizzuto (actually a tiny Medieval town, not an island) farther on and head directly to **Capo Colonne** to see the single column left (there were once 48) from a Doric temple dedicated to Hera and erected earlier than the Parthenon. Isolated on a rocky shore above the crashing surf, the spot is one of the most conducive in all of Italy to Byronic fantasies, and still the location, each spring, of an important religious procession of a Byzantine Madonna from Crotone to the tiny church next to the temple site.

Just ahead is **Crotone**, the ancient Greek colony of Croton, home to Pythagoras and his school. Unfortunately, little geometry or any other trace of the pre-Socratic Greeks is left in this modern commercial city. Its cathedral houses the Byzantine Madonna of Capo Colonne, and there is also an Aragonese castle and an archaeological museum nearby, but as is the case throughout the region the most significant finds from local excavations have been sent to Réggio. **Pino**, on via San Leonardo, is a good restaurant in which to sample an updated version of the local specialty, *zuppa di pesce* (a spicy fish stew), taste Crotone's version of *pecorino,* and drink the wines from Cirò and Melissa, which lie just to the north.

Pass through both these wine-producing areas on the long coastal route from Crotone to Rossano Stazione, from which you take a steep road—with wonderful views of the Gulf of Táranto—to **Rossano**, another of Calàbria's inexplicably untouristed (except perhaps because of its lack of good hotels and restaurants) hill towns. Rossano's church of San Marco ranks with La Cattolica as the most important example of Byzantine architecture in Calàbria, as the town was one of the most monumental cities in the Byzantine Empire; the churches of Panaghia, Santa Maria del Pilere, Santa Anna, and Ospedale are also Byzantine constructions. The town's **Museo Diocesano** houses another Byzantine masterpiece, the Codex Purpureus, an extremely rare illuminated manuscript of the Gospels, on purple vellum. Outside Rossano the Byzantine Santa Maria del Patire, a former monastery, is important for its mosaic pavement but equally rewarding simply as a restful spot in the woods for a picnic on provisions picked up in town. Back at Rossano Stazione the modern, modest

Europa Lido Palace provides the best accommodations for the night.

Beyond Rossano

Archaeology afficionados will find the trip to neighboring Basilicata worth the distance involved, continuing north along the lovely Gulf of Táranto. The town of **Policoro**, halfway from Rossano to Táranto, houses the **Museo Nazionale della Siritide**, a contemporary museum displaying artifacts from excavations at the nearby colony of Heracleia. Farther north is the vast and important archaeological site of the former Greek colony of **Metapontum** (modern-day Metaponto), founded by the Sybarites, where Pythagoras transferred his school after being exiled from Crotone. Its modern **Antiquarium** provides elaborate documentation of the excavations, and an impressive collection of coins, vases, and statuary unearthed at the site. The grounds are extensive enough for an hour or two of pleasant ruminating in the ruins, which contain the remains of a Greek theater and the Doric temple of Apollo Lycius.

(Beyond Metaponto on the coast road to the northeast is the city of Táranto, the end point of the chapter on Apulia, above.)

Otherwise, you can settle for **Síbari**, a small site just a short distance northeast up the coast from Rossano, named after ancient Sybaris. The exact location of the corrupt and luxurious Greek colony (according to legend, destroyed in 510 B.C. by the men of Croton, who flooded it with the waters of the river Crati) still has not been determined, but it probably lies somewhere on the vast floodplain surrounding the train station of Síbari. Near the station is a small museum, the Museo della Sibartide, which displays objects unearthed during local attempts to uncover Sybaris. The most comfortable accommodations for the Rossano–Síbari area are to be had in nearby Cosenza, on the western side of the Sila.

GETTING AROUND

Calàbria has airports in both Réggio di Calàbria and Lamezia Terme; the latter is midway down the region's Tyrrhenian coast and about an hour to both Catanzaro and Cosenza. Each airport is served by Aerea Trasporti Italia from Rome and Milan. Trains run frequently along the coast, visitable all times of year with its mild climate, and they also go inland. Be forewarned, however, that some of the train routes are operated by the small-gauge Ferrovia Calàbro-Lucane, for which separate tickets must be purchased, and that many stations in Calàbria are named after communities miles away from where the trains actually stop. Bus service also connects many coastal points with the inland cities. The Sila, still snowbound at times during the winter but usually kept passable for the ski resorts, is reached by regular train and bus service from Cosenza.

However, because public transportation in Calàbria is not geared to the tourist, a car (rented at either airport or in the larger cities) is more highly recommended here than in practically any other Italian region. Over the past few years roads have been improved, government intervention (some say guilt) has kept the Autostrada in Calàbria free of tolls, and driving—whether along the coast or in the mountains—is almost always scenic.

In Práia, the feast of the Madonna della Grotta al Santuario takes place August 15; in Páola, the feast of Saint Francis of Páola is held May 5; in Cosenza, opera season at the Teatro Rendano runs from December through February; in Lungro, the largest Albanian festival takes place December 6; in San Demétrio Corone, the week-long Albanian festival, Primavera Albanese, takes place each spring; in Bova, the Graecanic Festival is held in either June or July; and at Capo Colonne the procession of the Madonna di Capo Colonne takes place the second Sunday in May.

ACCOMMODATIONS REFERENCE

▶ **Da Annibale.** 88076 **Isola di Capo Rizzuto.** Tel: (0962) 79-50-04.

▶ **Aquila-Edelweiss.** 87052 **Camigliatello Silano.** Tel: (0984) 57-80-44.

▶ **Hotel Barbieri.** Altomonte, province of Cosenza. Tel: (0981) 94-80-72.

▶ **Hotel Centrale.** Via del Tigrai 3, 87100 **Cosenza.** Tel: (0984) 736-81.

▶ **Demaco.** 89044 **Locri.** Tel: (0964) 202-47.

▶ **Europa.** Contrada Roges, 87036 **Rende.** Tel: (0984) 46-50-64.

▶ **Europa Lido Palace.** Strada Statale 106, 87068 **Rossano Stazione.** Tel: (0983) 220-95.

► **Grand Hotel Excelsior**. Via Vittorio Veneto 66, 89121 **Réggio di Calàbria**. Tel: (0965) 258-01.

► **Hotel 501**. Via Madonnella, 88018 **Vibo Valéntia**. Tel: (0963) 439-51.

► **Hotel Guglielmo**. Via Tedeschi 1, 88100 **Catanzaro**. Tel: (0961) 265-32.

► **Grand Hotel Lorica**. 87050 **Lorica**. Tel: (0984) 99-70-39.

► **Mondial**. Via Roma 54, 87028 **Práia a Mare**. Tel: (0985) 722-14.

► **Palace Hotel Masoanri's**. Via Vittorio Veneto 95, 89121 **Réggio di Calàbria**. Tel: (0965) 264-33.

► **San Francesco**. Contrada Commenda, 87036 **Rende**. Tel: (0984) 86-17-21.

► **Grand Hotel San Michele**. Strada Statale 16, 87022 **Cetraro**. Tel: (0982) 910-12.

► **Stillhotel e Ristorante La Brace**. Via Melito Porto Salvo, 88063 **Catanzaro Lido**. Tel: (0961) 328-51.

SICILY

By Barbara Hults

Sicily is mysterious. Even though the island lies in full view of mainland Italy, across the Strait of Messina from Calàbria, Italians from other regions still regard Sicily as a region apart, a seductive puzzle. Sicilians, for their part, still talk of "going to Italy" when they travel 20 minutes across the Strait by hydrofoil.

In many ways Sicily *is* a world apart. Life is lived more intensely there, even today, when the highway system has interconnected the island's cities and television has entered almost every home, for better, for worse. Colors, too, are more intense: The sea is bluer on the southern coast, the contrasts of light and dark greater in the almost tropical sun; the pottery has taken on the hues of its natural backdrop and exploded in reds, yellows, and greens. Jasmine and orange blossoms, mint and wild fennel here produce strong scents, and the perfumed air of a cloister garden or private patio recalls *The Arabian Nights*. Food is tinged with sweet and sour blends from the East and from North Africa, and desserts—sweet mulberry ices or super rich cassata—could be served by Sheherazade. The architecture, too, recalls other times and places—especially Agrigento's Vallata dei Templi, a line of Greek temples above the sea, softened by pink and white almond blossoms each spring; and the massive Norman walls lightened with interlacing arches, opened with cloisters of lemon and orange trees, bamboo and papyrus. Sicilians themselves are intense: glances become penetrating stares—not hostile, just fascinated; each moment seems savored, as emotions run their course.

The Sicilian writer Tomasi di Lampedusa and director Luchino Visconti captured some of this spirit in *The*

Leopard—the colors of the plains, the love of show inherited from the Spanish Bourbons, the feasts, feuds, passions. Francis Coppola and Mario Puzo unveiled a less savory aspect in *The Godfather,* which is still true to some extent, although at least today the Mafia is less secret— almost 300 were jailed recently for Mafia-related crimes, some for life. This could not have happened even the year before.

Although it takes time to see beneath surface impressions in Sicily, spending a week or two there will open some doors to this fascinating conundrum that remains a mystery even to Sicilians.

Sicily has been inhabited for more than 20,000 years. Cave drawings dating back to the Ice Age have been found on Mount Pellegrino near Palermo and on the island of Levanzo. In fact, the early tribes, Sicani and Siculi, along with the Elymi, were already established residents when globe-sailing Phoenicians dropped anchor here during the eighth century B.C.

Greek settlement began along the east and north coasts and soon spread throughout most of the island. By the fifth century B.C. Sicily as a group of Greek colonies was more powerful than Greece itself. Its sophisticated cities, although ruled by tyrants, attracted Plato and Pindar; Empedocles and Archimedes were native sons. Legend-loving Greeks found a natural home on an island that worshiped the Mediterranean fertility goddess Astarte in a mystical temple high on Erice's peak and where Sicilian myth had Persephone kidnapped near Lago Pergusa. Carthage had a foothold here, too, contesting control of the island first with the Greeks and then with the Romans. Not until Garibaldi and the Thousand landed at Marsala about 2,500 years later would Sicily be rid of foreign domination.

The intricate web of historical roots has created an emotional tug-of-war in the Sicilian of today. Contemporary novelist Leonardo Sciascia writes, "They love their island, but they constantly escape or dream of escaping from it. And when they are away from it, they love it even more and dream of returning." Young Sicilians, surrounded by TV, rock music, and video tapes, often think of themselves as Italians or even Europeans, rather than just Sicilians as their grandparents did. The modern world here, as everywhere, is a mixed blessing; greater conveniences but conflicting values and less direction.

To see Sicily in all its aspects, start at Palermo and

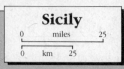

Sicily

0	miles	25	
0	km	25	

Tyrrhenian Sea

Mondello

▲ *Mt. Pellegrino*

Gulf of Castellam- mare

S. Vito lo Capo

Soluto

Egadi Islands

Erice

Monreale

Palermo

I. di Lévanzo

Bagheria

I. Maréttimo

Trápani

I. Favignana

Segesta

Calatafimi

I. Mozia

Marsala

Sambuela di Sicilia

Selinunte

Menfi

Caltabellotta

San Calogero

Sciacca

Agrigento

Mediterranean Sea

Porto Empédocle

I. di Pantelleria

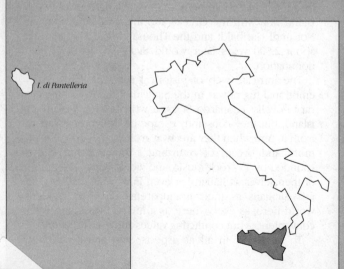

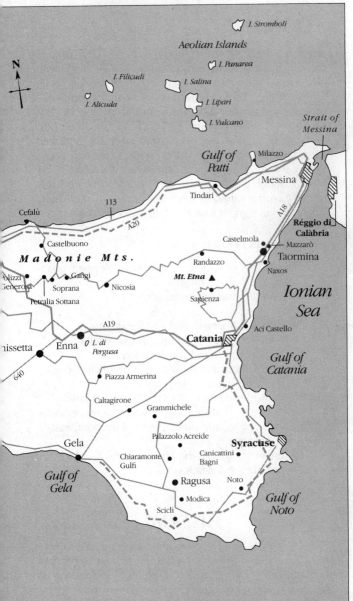

travel counterclockwise around the coast (from Palermo, though, make a short detour east to Cefalù first), with occasional forays into the interior. Before Messina and a return to the mainland make your last stop Taormina— so extravagantly beautiful that it's difficult to leave. But avoid the summer months, especially August, when heat everywhere in Sicily is extreme and Taormina is packed with vacationing Europeans and movie-festival goers. Spring is best: April through June, when the wild flowers bloom. March can be lovely, too, but showers are likely in early spring (almond trees flower in early February, celebrated in Agrigento with a folk-dance festival).

MAJOR INTEREST

Unique mix of Greek, Roman, Arab, Norman, Spanish, and Italian cultures

Lush Mediterranean vegetation

Food

Palermo for Norman sites and for dining

Segesta, Agrigento, Syracuse, and Taormina for Greek temples and amphitheaters

Erice and Taormina for Medieval mountaintop villages with unparalleled views

Piazza Armerina for a Roman villa and mosaics

Caltagirone for ancient and contemporary ceramics

Syracuse, Noto, and other towns of the southeast for Baroque splendor

Mountain villages of the Madonie near Cefalù

The Aeolian and Egadi islands

PALERMO

This chaotic capital of Norman kings and Spanish viceroys has panache and poverty. An interesting and sometimes beautiful city, it's intriguing to explore on foot for its street sounds, its wonderful street snacks (many found only in Sicily), and for conversations with Palermitani, who often speak some English and, like most Sicilians, usually have a relative in America, England, or Australia. When walking about take big-city precautions (a money-belt and an eye on the camera). Passersby will give a tug on the arm and point a finger toward the bag or wallet in jeopardy, and caution "*Attenzione!*"

The Arab-Norman buildings are incomparable. Next in

interest come the Baroque oratories, the museums, and the Vucceria—an outdoor market stretching through a raucous, riveting old neighborhood and lined with carts of olives of every tint, pyramids of blood oranges, mounds of purple cauliflower, and burgeoning banks of sea creatures that would astonish even Jacques Cousteau.

Palermo's grand days, when the Arabs made it their capital, rivaled the splendor depicted in *The Arabian Nights*—a world of jasmine and roses, mosques and fountains, harems and the good life as only Oriental potentates lived it. The Normans and then the great Hohenstaufen Frederick II continued this tradition, even after control of Sicily had been wrested from the Arabs. While their brother Crusaders were attacking Islam in the east, the Normans found coexistence a rewarding system in Sicily.

This exuberant mix is best and most beautifully seen in the **Cappella Palatina** (Palatine Chapel) part of the **Palazzo dei Normanni** that is today the seat of the Sicilian Parliament. King Roger's chapel (constructed between 1132 and 1140) is a rhythmic fusion of the best of Latin, Byzantine, and Islamic traditions. Guy de Maupassant found it the "most amazing jewel ever imagined by human thought." Not only the fine mosaics but even the wooden stalactite-style ceiling is extraordinary, and the Persian-influenced Arab paintings rival anything in Cairo. These paintings are the earliest known of their kind: a magic world of camels and lions, dragons and monsters, scenes of hunting and picnicking with the harem, and Kufic inscriptions praising the Norman King Roger.

Upstairs in the **royal apartments** (which, for security reasons, are not always open, especially when Parliament is in session) court life was as exotic as any ever lived. Frederick II's court rivaled the Normans' as one of the most sophisticated in Europe, a center of arts and sciences where Arab mathematicians and astronomers had their theories translated and propagated to Europe, Greek philosophy and poetry entered European literature, and Italian poetry and music flourished. The extravagance of these days—and his childhood in Palermo—remained with Frederick, the future head of the Holy Roman Empire, who travelled about Europe with entourage—his harem and his elephants—in tow.

Not far from the palace is the **Church of San Giovanni degli Eremiti**, bursting with photogenic vermilion domes, striking from the outside, charming from within

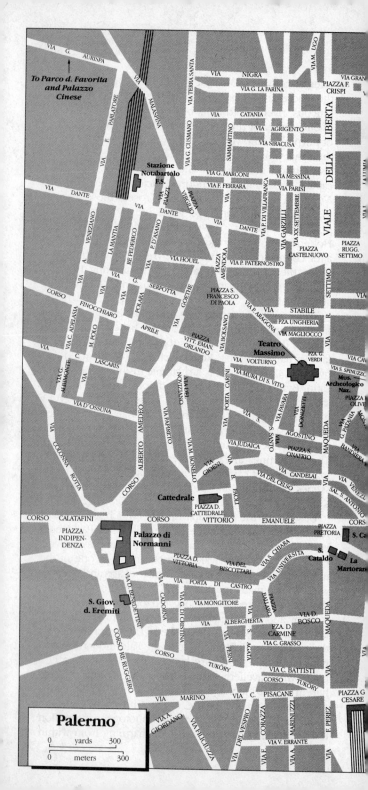

Palermo

0 yards 300

0 meters 300

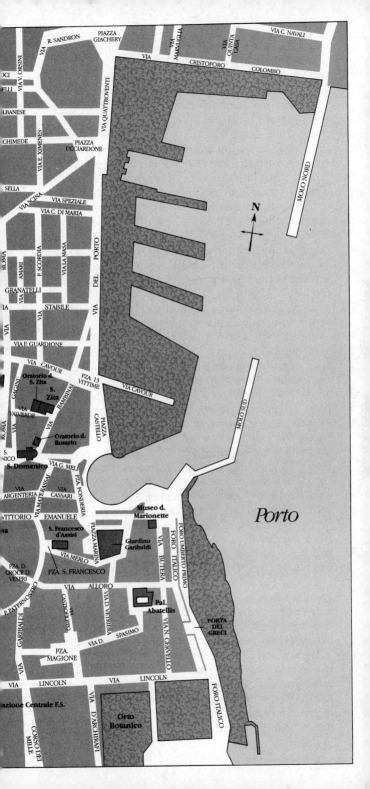

with its courtyard and cloisters of lush palm trees and papyrus.

The **Duomo**, Palermo's cathedral, is a short walk down corso Vittorio Emanuele. Though it suffers from too much redoing, the façade is a record of the city's history, as each new ruler had his era included. The best part is the back, still Norman with some embellishment. Roger II is buried inside, next to his daughter Constance in a simple tomb near the entrance, in back of Frederick II's. (Roger wanted to be interred in the cathedral of Cefalù, east of Palermo, but city politics kept the king here.) The Cappella Novella features the *Madonna della Scala* (1503) by Antonello Gagini, a fine sculptor who, with his family, is responsible for hundreds of little-heralded works throughout Sicily. Francesco Laurana, the great master who was Gagini's teacher, is known for his exquisite Madonna and Child statuary. The *Madonna* in the chapel before the left transept is his work, with student participation.

Ahead on the corso is a famous corner, **Quattro Canti**, at the intersection of via Maqueda. Four palaces face one another at their concave corners, a circular effect recalling Quattro Fontane in Rome. On each façade, figures and symbols represent a season, a king, and a saint who protects that region of Palermo lying behind her.

At the next major street, via Roma, a left turn leads to piazza San Domenico, where **the Vucceria** begins. The Vucceria is not just a market; it's an introduction to the basics of Sicilian cooking. Traditional Mediterranean blends of eggplant, tomato, olives, onions, and garlic are combined with capers, wild fennel, and other bitters— with cheese and pine nuts added to soften the edge—to produce hundreds of sophisticated sweet-and-sour tastes. *Pasta con sarde,* a tradition in Palermo, is the perfect paradigm: a blend of sea and forest derived from fresh (no kin to canned) sardines, fresh wild fennel, sultanas, pine nuts, tomato paste, and saffron. The taste is exotic, and the following devoted. Like many such dishes, a bit more of this or that or a change in flavor because of regional soil differences will create a wholly new taste, so that each dish is orchestrated differently in each kitchen.

The seafood in the Vucceria—sea urchins and lamprey, oysters and swordfish, crabs, and even that blob of gray called *neonata,* the newborn fish that are a delicacy in Palermo—raw or frittered, is difficult to resist, though the cacophony of the hawkers is rarely directed to nonbuying tourists, except to amuse. Two restaurants, the **Shangai**—

which you'll see just above the piazza on a first-floor terrace—and tiny **Da Toto's**, a very simple spot on the side street to the left, will sometimes even cook what you buy or what you point to—if the restaurant isn't crowded and if you can explain to the owner that you want to choose a fish yourself. Fish is often stuffed (*a beccafico*) with bread crumbs, sultanas, pine nuts, and lemon juice and rolled. Swordfish and tuna are staples: broiled, stuffed, *alla marinara,* with lemon and olives, or some home-devised variant. (Fish couscous, another touch of North Africa, is found mainly near Trápani on the western shore of Sicily.)

Try the local wines. Sicily is now a major exporter of very good wine; among the most frequently encountered products are Corvo and Regaleali. The **Enoteca Miceli**, at via Streva, 18, is a good place to sample the island's production, as is **Robinson's** at via Ariosto, 11, a newer *enoteca* (wine-tasting bar).

Since Sicilian lunches are never rushed (the owners at Shangai and Toto sing to the guests when the mood hits), and nothing is open until 4:00 P.M. anyway, retrace your steps to the **Oratorio del Rosario** in back of San Domenico on via Bambinai (if it is closed, ask at the church sacristy). Palermo's oratories are amazing fantasies of Baroque cum Rococo. At the Rosario, in 1720, Giacomo Serpotta created a world of stucco that climbs the walls like ivy and is dotted with tiny figures. Serpotta was not only a master of the *putti,* those cherubs that signal the Baroque, but also a fine sculptor of refined, almost Neoclassical figures such as *Courage,* on view here in the form of a woman with a plumed hat. At the altar is Van Dyck's *Virgin of the Rosary with St. Dominic and the Four Saints of Quattro Canti,* created by the artist after a visit to Palermo. If this oratory interests you, visit **Santa Zita** (next to the church of that name), where extraordinary reliefs of the New Testament and the naval battle of Lepanto reveal more of the Serpotta genius.

Piazza Pretoria, just off Quattro Canti on via Roma, looks awkward by day but intriguing by night. The vast **Fontana Pretoria** (intended for a Tuscan villa) is called the "Fountain of Shame," either because of the nudity or because "Venus is in love with a horse." When fighting was at a brutal pitch in adjoining streets during the 1870 Garibaldi campaign, the Great One showed his powers of leadership by calmly sitting on the fountain steps day after day while local residents brought him flowers and fruit. Though much of the square was destroyed, he was not touched, and his heroism gave the citizens fresh courage.

On the same piazza, the **Church of Saint Catherine** is amazing inside, every inch busily Baroque. Yet even here Sicilian restraint in linear boundaries can be seen. At the right transept is a statue of Saint Catherine (1534) by Antonello Gagini.

In the adjoining piazza Bellini, the red domes bulging beneath a graceful campanile announce the **Churches of the Martorana and San Cataldo**, which together make up a charming Arab-Norman complex, complete with palm trees and cloister. George of Antioch, Roger's admiral, founded the Martorana in 1142; its lovely campanile has survived the church's Baroque rebuilding. Inside, historian John Julius Norwich says you must run the gauntlet "of simpering cupids and marzipan Madonnas" to get to the Norman original. But it's worth the run. The interior, created with marbles and mosaics, has the intimacy of the Cappella Palatina. Services in the Greek rite are still conducted here—most dramatically at Easter. At the west end are original mosaics of Christ crowning Roger (thought to be a true likeness of the Norman king) and of George of Antioch at the Madonna's feet. Across from the Martorana is the **Church of San Cataldo**, restored to its strong Norman simplicity of form (1161).

A morning's walk might begin at the Kalsa, an old section of Palermo where the buildings destroyed in World War II have never been restored. Enter from the harbor side through the Porta dei Greci and turn into the via Alloro where the **Galleria Regionale Nazionale della Sicilia**, housed in the Catalan-Gothic Palazzo Abatellis, exhibits such masterpieces as Antonello da Messina's *Annunciata*. Portraying a transcendent moment, the artist catches the Virgin between two worlds, physically resisting with her hand while spiritually accepting what she is being told. The bust of Eleanora of Aragon by Laurana and the *Triumph of Death* by an unknown painter are among the great works of the gallery, beautifully presented in a newly restored palace setting.

At piazza San Francesco stop for a Palermo favorite, *guasteddu*, a sesame roll with slices of tasty spleen and cacciacavallo cheese. Even if the notion of innards makes you recoil, stop at the **Foccacceria San Francesco** anyway, a wood-and-mirrors place where Garibaldi probably enjoyed his *meusa* (Sicilian for *spleen*). Delicious *arancini*—

rice balls with a bit of prosciutto and cheese inside—and *panelle*—light chick-pea fritters found everywhere in Palermo—are best here or from street vendors. *Sfincioni,* high, light pizzas with tomato and onion, are another street specialty.

Across the piazza, the Gothic doors of the **Church of San Francesco** date from 1302, a period when devotion to the saint was most fervent. Serpotta's statues and Laurana's Mastrantonio chapel (1468) are distinguished.

Just left of the church a gate leads to another of Serpotta's joyful marvels, the **Oratorio di San Lorenzo,** diminished by the loss of a large Caravaggio painting, stolen from the altar some years ago. Ring the bell for entry.

Several other museums merit attention; certainly the **Museo Archeologico Nazionale** in piazza dell'Olivella, where a fine collection of antiquities includes some lovely metopes from temple friezes at Selinunte, a Greek city on Sicily's south coast, and a model of the cave drawings at Addaura on nearby Monte Pellegrino. (To visit the actual cave site, apply at the museum. If you go, stop there also at the shrine to Saint Rosalia, a chaste noblewoman whose bones, an angel revealed, would stop the plague in Palermo. The patron saint of Palermo, she is celebrated with processions and feasting on July 12 to 15 and September 3 and 4.)

Puppet shows based on the Carolingian cycle of Roland (Orlando) battling the Saracens (instead of the Basques, in this version) are a charming form of entertainment in Palermo. You can probably see one at the **Museo delle Marionette** (Marionette Museum) on via Butera or at the **Pitrè,** an ethnographic museum in the outlying Parco della Favorita; check the schedules at the tourist office. These puppets, even originals, are sold in all tourist areas of Sicily, competing with that other superstar, Pinocchio. Originals are sometimes sold at Palermo's flea market and in antique shops (see the section on shopping).

The Pitrè also exhibits carts, ceramics, ex-votos, and other aspects of 19th-century Sicilian life. Not far from it in the park is the curious **Palazzo Cinese,** built in 1799 for Ferdinand III, Bourbon king of the Two Sicilies—as the realm whose capital was Naples was called. This bit of chinoiserie entranced his queen, Maria Carolina, and their guests Lord Nelson and Lady (and Lord) Hamilton at a time when Nelson and Lady Hamilton were the talk of the royals. Harold Acton describes a nocturnal *fête champêtre* thrown by Ferdinand at the Palazzo Cinese to thank his English guests for saving his life: life-size wax figures of the three "were enshrined in a classical Temple of Fame, topped by a goddess blowing a trumpet. Fireworks represented the explosion of *L'Orient* at the Battle of the Nile. Paeans of praise were sung to the deliverer, and the nine-year-old Prince Leonard, his mother's darling, dressed as a midshipman, raised the laurel wreath from the waxen admiral's brow and planted it on that of the living one."

The church that was the setting for the "Sicilian Vespers," the 1282 uprising that began here against the detested Angevin French occupiers, almost all of whom were massacred, stands in the cemetery of Santa Orsola, south of the city, near the railroad station. It was built in 1173 by Palermo bishop Walter of the Mill, an Englishman known in Italian as Gualtiero Offamiglio, who also had the Duomo erected in Palermo.

La Ziza, also near the station, was King William I's earthly paradise, once surrounded by luxuriant greenery. The palace's interior has now been restored to its original grandeur. In Norwich's words, "Nowhere else on the island is that specifically Islamic talent for creating quiet havens of shade and coolness in the summer heat so dazzlingly displayed." At the **Catacombe dei Cappuccini,** near La Ziza, about 8,000 corpses, sitting on the floor or hanging fully clothed from the walls in oddly vivacious poses, provide memento mori for all viewers. Males and females have separate rooms of course; Sicilians are very proper about death.

ACCOMMODATIONS

The important decision is whether to stay in the city or at a nearby resort—Mondello or Cefalù (see the Cefalù and Mondello sections)—and take the train or bus back into Palermo to sightsee. (Don't drive in; chaos and auto theft make that prospect unattractive in the city.) If you choose not to stay in Palermo, you'll have to rise early: Cefalù is almost an hour away by train, though Mondello is closer, by bus.

The **Villa Igiea** is the grande dame, with its own tropical garden, swimming pool, and outdoor dining terrace and bar. The Art Nouveau (Liberty-style, in Italian) rooms are stunningly decorated by Basile. The best rooms face the pool (and the sea beyond); the other part—the main building which includes the late bar and disco—is often noisy, being favored by affluent young Palermo. The management has changed frequently, and staff enthusiasm is not always high. A taxi is required to central Palermo.

Salita Belmonte 43, 90142; Tel: (091) 54-37-44; in U.S., (212) 599-8280 or (800) 223-9832.

The **Grand Hotel et des Palmes**, the stately palace where Wagner wrote parts of *Parsifal,* is now renovated and attractive. Service, however, is less than cordial, apparently because of changing management, who do plan to improve their concept of service. Suites are particularly lovely, but back rooms are dark and crowded. The hotel cannot be beaten for convenience to Palermo's sights. The restaurant, under separate management, is delightful (see below).

Via Roma 396, 90139; Tel: (091) 58-39-33; in U.S., (212) 599-8280 or (800) 223-9832.

The **Jolly Hotel** is not grand but is well equipped to satisfy clients with good service and simple, comfortable rooms. Garden dining is romantic, thanks to a vine-covered crumbling palazzo adjoining the hotel. The quietest rooms face the swimming pool. In front of the hotel lies a stretch of beach that Fellini fans will love—a tired Ferris wheel and other dubious amusements line an enervated, unswimmable sea. Foro Italico 22, 90133; Tel: (091) 616-50-90.

DINING

At **Renato**'s, a little outside of the center of town to the east—and well worth the 15-minute taxi ride—Gian Rodolfo and Francesca Botto have created one of Palermo's best restaurants, where *zuppa di pesce,* crepes stuffed with *frutta di mare,* wonderful raw fish marinated in oil and herbs, and swordfish in almond sauce are happily devoured before the cannoli, especially made at Piana degli Albanesi (a town to the south that has an Albanian population). The attractive seaside setting is enhanced by antique furnishings and the relaxing though fashionable atmosphere. Let the owner choose the wine. Sicily takes olive oil seriously; an olive-oil list is often available. Reserve. Via Messina Marina 28/b. Tel: (09) 47-10-30.

The **Charleston** is still very good and fashionable, despite its ups and downs. It's decorated with gaslight Art Nouveau charm, and the chef has made eggplant a vegetable of Dionysian aspects. *Caponata* here is about the best in Sicily, and pasta with tomato and eggplant (slightly charred for extra flavor) is superb. Angelo Ingrao, the proprietor, and Carlo Hassan, one of Italy's best maitre d's, are known for their ability to make a restaurant work. Piazzale Ungheria 30; Tel: (091) 32-13-66.

A charming outdoor court where a grill braises veal and lamb on cool summer nights is the **Hotel Patria**—not a hotel but a restaurant that has caught on with Sicilians.

La Scuderia, near the Parco della Favorita, is a favorite with well-to-do Palermo—a sizable population. Stuffed perch served with charcoal-grilled vegetables and *caccia-cavallo* cheese is pointless to resist, as is roast lamb with fresh mint. Their super rich dessert *sole* (sun) *di Sicilia* is a *semifreddo* (half-frozen) luxury spiked with Moscato wine from Pantelleria (Sicily's island down near Africa; see Trápani, below). The outdoor terrace in summer is a joy. Via del Fante 9; Tel: (091) 52-03-23.

Another favorite in the center of town is the informal **Bellini's** on piazza Bellini, where a full Sicilian menu has innovations such as the red-leaf lettuce *radicchio* stuffed with meats, cheeses, onions, and eggs. Wonderful pizza can also be enjoyed here at the outdoor tables most of the year.

Al Buco is a cheerful trattoria near the Grand Hotel et des Palmes, with such light, sophisticated specialties as fettucine Angela, a heavenly creation of pasta with smoked swordfish, fresh tomato, vodka, parsley, and olive oil— and hot pepper for those who like it. A good selection of delicate seafood and pasta, as well as more robust classics, is always on the menu. Via Granatelli 33; Tel: (091) 32-36-61.

La Palmetta, whether at the tables inside the Grand Hotel et des Palmes or on its airy roof terrace with mountain views, is one of Palermo's finest restaurants, with a menu of Sicilian and Continental dishes and an attentive staff. Grande Hotel et des Palmes, via Roma 393; Tel: (091) 58-39-33.

CABARET

Nightlife in Palermo might take you to the **Villa Igiea** terrace, to Mondello for a gelato or drink (see the Mondello section below), or to one of the discos in vogue. The **Speak Easy** has lasted a while on viale Strasburgo 34, and even admits those past the usual *jeunesse-dorée* criterion. To dance where the Leopard danced, go to the **Villa Boscogrande**, on the via Natale, where Visconti filmed some of the interiors for his film *Il Gattopardo* (*The Leopard*), but go late (after midnight for dancing). The bar is open earlier. (The place bills itself as a "Whiskey/disco.")

PASTRY SHOPS AND ICE-CREAM PARLORS

Palermo's pastry shops are not hard to come by, and the general quality is high, given the collective Sicilian sweet tooth. An unusual spot is the **Convent of St. Benedict** at piazza Venezia 38A, famous for *minne di Vergini* (virgin's breasts), cannoli, and *trionfo della golla* (the triumph of greed)—the last word on the deadly sin: layers of sponge cake, marzipan, and pistachio with cream fillings. Their *grappola d'uva* is a bunch of grapes made with almond and pistachio paste. Orders are placed and received through a convent wheel by a lay worker or novitiate with the silent order. The more elaborate pastries can be bought only in about four-pound quantities.

For secular sweets, try the **Mazzara**, in via Magliocco 15/17; or **La Martorana**, corso V. Emanuele 196; or **La Rosa Nero**, via Lincoln at via Cervello. Sicilian ice cream is an art form in which all sorts of fruits, nuts, and creams participate. Even *tiramisù* and *zabaglione* are *semifreddo,* and the jasmine-petal ice is a delicate treat. The **Gelateria Ilardo** at Foro Umberto Primo 6 is a popular summer place. (Also see the Mondello section.)

SHOPPING

Antiques, elegant boutiques, and jumbled flea markets have some interesting items, but bargains are rare. Go to the **Mercato di Pulci** (flea market) behind the duomo on corso Alberto Amedeo, where a variety of stores present their wares—often interesting antiques.

Art Nouveau (Liberty) collectibles can be found at **Cravosio** on via Ventidue Gennaio 1 and at **Il Mercato**, via Garzilli 73.

Sicilian ceramics vary with the region: strong patterns of vivid color in Palermo; blue and white in the south and Caltagirone, the ceramics center; and intricate earth-tone patterns at Erice. Contemporary artisans are naturally more experimental. **De Simone** has stores throughout Sicily, with bright, bold patterns and interesting shapes, some for dinnerware, some for decoration. In Palermo, De Simone shops are located at piazza Leone 2 and via Stabile 133. The **Artigianato Siciliano**, via Amari 13, is the largest center, with ceramics from regions throughout Sicily.

Name clothes designers are well represented on via Libertà, piazza Ungheria, piazza Francesco Crispi, and via Ruggero Settimo. Used clothing can be amusing, too: **Baratta**, via Trapani 14, and **Friperie**, at via Nigra 32, are two possibilities. For antique laces and such, stop at **Moda della Nonna**, via Ariosto 17/a, and **Nostalgia**, via delle Croci 33. Traditional Sicilian country hats (*coppola*) can be found along via Garibaldi, at numbers 6 and 39. Spanish-style shawls are sold at **Torregrossa**, via Roma 144.

Mondello

A popular getaway on a summer's night for ice cream is Mondello, up the coast northwest of Palermo, where the **Antico Chiosco** will give you fresh flavors from fruit ice to *tartufo* cream. During the day the beaches here are noisy and crowded, but the town is pretty and certainly animated. At night its streets are lined with fish vendors, and you can eat oysters as you stroll. More likely you'll go to the trattoria **Sympathy**—the origin of its name is a mystery—or to the **Gambero Rosso** for a sit-down meal of one of the sea fantasies you saw at the Vucceria. *Ricci,* or sea urchins, are a great delicacy here. You can reach Mondello easily by bus from Palermo.

Staying in Mondello is a pleasant alternative to a hotel in Palermo if you don't need to be in the city's center. The **Mondello Palace** and the **Hotel Splendid la Torre** both have private beaches, swimming pools, and sea views.

EXCURSIONS FROM PALERMO

A morning bus trip to Monreale and an afternoon train excursion to Cefalù are easily arranged. Each town has a majestic Norman cathedral, and Cefalù adds the pleasures of a beach resort.

Monreale

William II (a.k.a. the Good), Roger II's grandson, was the guiding light behind the Monreale cathedral, which he founded in 1174. According to legend, William was resting in his deer park and the Madonna appeared to him, promising to show him where his grandfather had hidden treasure if he would use it for a holy purpose, and so we have Monreale.

Though William was a man of spiritual depth, his detractors claimed the story was a ruse to excuse the vast sums he spent on construction of the cathedral. As heir to the creator of the Cappella Palatina and the cathedral at Cefalù, he could hardly build a simple shrine. However, politics entered in as well. Walter of the Mill, the bishop of Palermo, was busy creating a political constituency for himself, attracting barons and prelates. By building a new bishopric near and equal to Palermo, William would have a direct link with the Pope, a pipeline the Pontiff supported. When Walter heard this he decided to build a new cathedral in Palermo (the present structure), whose grandeur, it turned out, would never threaten Monreale's.

Monreale is awe inspiring. On gray days, when the mosaics are just decoration and don't create a special light, as they do when the sun is out, it is also cold. "If the Palatine chapel is a Medieval carol, then Monreale is the *Canterbury Tales*," wrote Vincent Cronin in *The Golden Honeycomb*. Against a gold background, cycles of the Old and New Testament unfold, played out in 130 large panels inscribed in Greek and Latin. A curious presence is Thomas à Becket (middle lower right at altar), since William the Good, the cathedral's creator, had Henry II of England for a father-in-law, and Becket had been martyred only a few years earlier by Henry. It's the earliest portrait of Becket yet identified.

The dominating mosaic is of the Pantocrator, brilliantly executed for so vast a work (his hand alone is six feet long). The mosaics represent the beginning of a change from the formal style of Byzantium: draperies swirl, gestures relax, and rhythms are smoother.

Above the royal throne, at left, William receives the crown from Christ, and above the bishop's altar he offers the crown to the Madonna. In a chapel south of the choir the two Williams, the Bad and the Good, are buried, and an inscription marks the place where the body of St. Louis, brother of the later Sicilian king Charles of Anjou, lay on its way back to France from the fateful Tunisian crusade. Some say his heart is buried there, for the Sicilians couldn't bear to part with him entirely. Charles himself was parted with easily, however, during the Vespers revolt, when he and those Angevins who weren't slaughtered were thrown out.

The treasury and the view of Palermo from the roof are

good diversions. So, too, are the cloisters, which are extraordinarily impressive and peaceful, a joy for those who want to read a book in a sunny corner. Intricacy is everywhere, in the patterns of the 104 arches suspended by slender columns, enhanced with mosaic and carved inlays. Taken together, the capitals are a tour de force of Romanesque stone carving, with themes varying from daily life to the Bible to pagan Mithraic sacrifice. A belvedere, reached from outside the cloisters, opens on a panorama of the Conca d'Oro valley—now a victim of urban sprawl.

The Vespers not only ended the Angevin era in Sicily, it brought the house of Aragon into the European spotlight, ending the papal authority's hold on international politics. Sponsoring the Anjou regime had been a disastrous idea for the papacy. According to Steven Runciman, author of *The Sicilian Vespers,* "Their choice of Charles of Anjou is easy to understand; but it was fatal. When Charles's power was broken by the Vespers at Palermo they were too inextricably involved. The story led on to the . . . Babylonian captivity of Avignon, and through schism and disillusion to the troubles of the Reformation."

Cefalù

Cefalù, seen gradually as the train approaches from Palermo, is unforgettable. An enormous cliff rises like a tidal wave; the town huddles below, dominated by the twin campaniles of the **Cathedral of Cefalù**.

Now a lively summer resort, Cefalù (on the coast, some 50 km/30 miles east of Palermo) has been inhabited probably as long as Sicily has, as witnessed by prehistoric relics in surrounding grottoes. Carthage established a colony here, and Greeks, Byzantines, and Arabs followed. In 1063 Count Roger relieved the Arabs of command. It is to his son, King Roger, that we owe the extraordinary honey-colored cathedral. One night when he was caught in a storm at sea, he vowed to build a cathedral—a regal ex-voto—at whatever safe harbor he found. The harmonious Romanesque façade that unfolds as you approach from below is lovely, the church even more so, as you see it in the round. But it is the interior, newly restored to its original simplicity after Baroque errors, that draws the greatest admiration. The Christ who follows you with his mosaic eyes is unlike any other Pantocrator. Many observers consider this an unsurpassed representation, where mercy is mingled with justice. The wisp of hair that has escaped to his forehead, the softened eyes, and the casual robes combine with power and majesty. The Bible he holds is open to "I am the light of the world," in Latin and Greek. The Madonna, too, is a rare creation and would be admired more if the Christ were not of such beauty. The strong-winged angels are transitional in Christian iconography, between the winged bull of Jewish art and the delicate winged messengers who would come later.

In the left transept stands a *Madonna and Child* by Antonello Gagini, and in the narthex is a curious cat on a coat of arms that belonged to Monsignor Chat, who consecrated the cathedral. Via Mandralisca, in front of the cathedral, leads to the **Museum** of that name that contains one of the world's greatest portraits, that of the *Unknown Man* (1465–1470) by Antonello da Messina. His smile, sensuous and sly, has been called quintessentially Sicilian, as mysterious as that of the *Mona Lisa*. Among the archaeological relics here is a rare krater (Greek vase) from the Aeolian island of Lipari, showing a tuna merchant arguing with a customer (fourth century B.C.). The numismatic collection has coins from the principal city-states of Sicily, and Baron Mandralisca's passion for shells provided the 20,000 in the museum's possession.

On the corso Ruggero is a fragment of the **Osterio Magno**, Roger II's palace, with its graceful Norman touches still visible despite the weeds. In front is the **Osterio Piccolo**, residence of the powerful Ventimiglia counts, who dominated the Madonie Mountains to the south.

If you decide to stay here, the best hotels are about a mile from Cefalù. The **Kalura** and **La Calette** are pretty little harbor-side resort hotels with swimming pools. Driving is easier, although you can go by bus or taxi.

From Cefalù, trips to Solunto, Bagheria, and some of the small towns in the Madonie Mountains are convenient by car (and possibly by bus). **Solunto**, a seaside town (about 40 km/25 miles back toward Palermo) dating from the fourth century B.C.—with Phoenician, Greek, and Roman relics on a site above the sea and mountains—is one of the most evocative of the ancient settings.

Bagheria

Bagheria, near Solunto, is something else entirely, a bizarre blend of 18th-century Baroque villas, the most famous of which is the **Villa Palagonia**, creation of a deformed prince who decorated his garden wall with 62 grotesques. Goethe catalogs the eccentricities carefully in his *Italian Journey*. The interior, though in sad ruins, can be appreciated still; it is easy to imagine what the room of cracked mirrors (to make everyone deformed?) looked like in its original state. In the prince's day, entire rooms were decorated with fragments of picture frames and broken glass, pyramids of porcelain teacups, and marble reptiles, and in the chapel there was a huge crucifix from which Saint Francis hung by his neck.

Enjoyable—and less bizarre—is the **Villa Cattolica**, a contemporary-art museum where the works of the late Sicilian painter Renato Guttuso are exhibited. An entirely delightful setting in Bagheria is the little town house restaurant **I Vespri**, especially pleasant when the roof terrace is open. The cooking is exceptional: Sicilian and French, like the owners, with seafood crepes and linguine Wellington—and now discovered by chic Palermo. Reservations are necessary. (Corso Butera 423; Tel: (091) 93-40-40.)

The Madonie Towns

It takes a bit of driving along very tortuous but scenic roads to reach the Madonie towns south of Cefalù. Castles and churches here are preserved from Norman and feudal times, but the charm is the atmosphere, the people, the way of life, the manners, the foods—these things that are the heart of Sicily. From **Castelbuono**, continue to **Petralia Sottano** and **Petralia Soprana**, then west to **Polizzi Generosa**, or east to **Gangi** and **Nicosia**. Stop and enjoy what you see at will.

SEGESTA

Southwest of Palermo, more than halfway to Trápani, Segesta's lonely ruins evoke the romantic spirit: a **Doric temple** on a flower-dotted hillside, the classical ideal of order amid wild nature. Along with nearby Erice, Segesta was settled by Elymi about the 12th century B.C. Although little is known of them, it seems they were of Greek and Trojan ancestry and certainly got along better with the new Greek colonizers than the native Sicani and Siculi did, sharing many aspects of religious and cultural life. The temple's singular charm lies partly in its roughness.

Never finished, the columns were left smooth and pre-pared for fluting; bosses that held the columns' hoist ropes can be seen along the steps. The foundation for the *cella,* the shrine at the interior, was laid but never built. Why it was never completed is the subject of speculation; some think the temple itself was begun only to attract Greek backing for their interminable struggles with Seli-nunte to the south.

Down the hill toward the amphitheater, the two de-fense towers and a fortified gate were used in frequent battles with Selinunte and Syracuse. The **Amphitheater**, still used for performances, is well preserved. Situated with the Greek genius for capturing the best possible view from the *cavea,* or seating area, it looks out on sea and mountains.

Segesta can be reached by train from Palermo; day trips organized by CIT tour operators in Palermo visit Segesta and Erice.

An important detour southward for "Garibaldini" is **Calatafimi**, scene of a famous 1870 battle; red shirts and scarves are sold as souvenirs. The **Mille Pini Restaurant**, at piazza Francesco Vivona 2, is a good road stop.

ERICE

Northwest of Segesta, along the coast above Trápani, Erice (pronounced AY-ree-chay) rises abruptly from the plains of salt fields and windmills. From its peak the coast of Africa can be seen to the southwest, beyond puffs of clouds that drift past the nearly 2,300-foot summit. Once a beacon for Phoenician sailors, Erice has enchanted myth-makers and travellers throughout recorded history.

On Monte Eryx, the town's summit, a temple paid tribute to Astarte, a Mediterranean fertility goddess. "A different goddess, this Eryx Astarte," wrote D. H. Law-rence, "in her prehistoric dark smiling, watching the fearful sunsets beyond the Egades. . . ." The temple stood on the rim of land where Roman, Greek, and Norman ruins now lie. The Pozzo di Venere ("Venus' Well") was the fate of maidens cast down as a sacrifice to the goddess after a ritual orgy. (That version is from guides who tell stories with drama; its real use is unknown.) The histo-rian Jacob Burckhardt describes the festivities as prac-ticed in the eastern Mediterranean to honor this goddess-mother of all living things: "Joyous shouts and mourning

wails, orgiastic dances and lugubrious flute music, prosti-
tution of women and self-castration of men had always
accompanied this cult of the sensual life of nature."

When spring came, a flock of doves would be released
from Erice to fly to Africa. In nine days they would return,
preceded by a red dove, who was Astarte, ensuring a
bountiful harvest after the summer to come.

The Medieval maze of streets and alleys that run steeply
(rubber soles are needed) up and down the town is lined
with gateways that look in on courtyards flowering with
tubs of plants, giving the town a domestic, contented air.
Pottery of dark earth tones and almond pastries are Erice's
specialties. Lots of pretty cafés here serve madeleine-light
sweets to enjoy with coffee. Before leaving stop at the main
piazza to see the *Annunciation* by Gagini in the museum.

The hotels **Ermione** and **Moderno** are attractive places
to stay, the latter consisting of an antique-filled old building and a modern annex nearby. Couscous, the North
African grain, is the thing to eat now that you're in the
west; also sample some new wines, Feudo di Fiori, Donnafugata, Steri, and Etna. Honey-sweet desserts as well as
almond concoctions are found widely in this part of
Sicily, where ties with North Africa are strongest. For
dining in Erice, go to the **Ciclope**, with an outdoor garden, or the **Taverna di Re Alceste**.

You may want to go down to nearby Trápani for dinner
along the harbor (see below). In fact, you might want to
stay there at the beachfront **Astoria Park**, which is simple
and friendly.

If you are driving, which will be easier now that you're
away from Palermo, another possible resort to use as a
base is **San Vito lo Capo**, north of Erice, where the pretty
cape's white beaches are relatively unspoiled by tourism.
The **Hotel Cala'Mpiso** is a comfortable retreat.

TRAPANI

Trápani, which stretches along the west coast below
Erice, is a port city that looks so North African it seems
like a set for Claude Raines as a Foreign Legion officer.
Dockside trattorias make good fish couscous. Go also
to **P & G**, an excellent and popular restaurant, more
in the elegant mode than the dockside places. There
you'll feast on shrimp in Cognac, grilled meats, and fish

such as *palombo* ("dogfish") *alla marinara,* and a nice *cassata.*

A wonderful fish trattoria is **Peppe's**; like P & G it is near the railroad station. The catch of the day is the specialty.

Coral was a local art form during the 17th century, and some notable examples, even a *presepio* ("Christmas village") are found in the **Museo Pepoli**, which also has a good painting collection. The church of **Santa Maria del Gesù** contains a Della Robbia *Madonna* under a marble *baldacchino* by Antonello Gagini.

The Egadi Islands

From Trápani ferries leave for the **Egadi Islands** of Favignana, Lévanzo, and Maréttimo. On **Lévanzo**, which is sparsely populated, the Grotto dei Genovese contains Paleolithic drawings of great beauty and a Neolithic group of paintings, both sets discovered only in 1949. **Maréttimo**, the most distant of the islands, is dramatically beautiful but requires some fancy footwork to explore. Small seafood restaurants are open on the islands during the summer months; rooms are available in private homes, and Lévanzo does have a small hotel, the **Paradiso**. If seclusion is your goal, this would be the place. **Favignana**, the large island, is better equipped for tourism, though its undeveloped western side is the more attractive.

Isola di Pantelleria

From Trápani you can also take a ferry to the island of Pantelleria, which can be reached from Trápani and Palermo by air as well.

Pantelleria, way off by itself, is so close to the African continent it could easily belong to Tunisia. Stark and fascinating, it is famous for raisin wine, Tanit. Made from the *zibibbo* grape, this sweet and sometimes sparkling wine is usually called Moscato di Pantelleria. The dark earth is dotted with vines of capers, too, which make up a sizable part of the economy.

Dammuso houses are tomblike cells used by early inhabitants, somewhat similar to the *nuraghe* of Sardinia. Tourist villages are built in this style to try to keep the island from becoming just another hotel-strewn resort.

The **Cossyra** and the **Mursia** hotels have excellent restaurants; the Cossyra conjures up delightful island combinations such as salads of capers, meat, and potato, or sea bass seasoned with parsley, oil, and capers. For dessert ask for sweet ravioli or *budino de zibibbo*—a pudding made from grape sugar. The **Zzú Natale** is a fine seafood spot. Stay at the pretty **Del Porto** if you're an underwater fisherman.

Mozia

The island of Mozia was an eighth-century B.C. Phoenician base; there you can visit the Whitaker villa museum of ceramics and other objects from that period and a house decorated with fourth-century B.C. mosaics. At Tophet, on the opposite side of the island, is a Punic (Phoenician) sacrificial burial ground dedicated to their goddess Tanit, to whom children were sacrificed, a practice discontinued during the fifth century B.C.

To go to Mozia turn off the highway south of the Trápani airport. Signs say Mozia, Stagnone, or Ragattis. The custodian will row you across the narrow waterway.

MARSALA

Marsala was founded at the westernmost tip of Sicily by Phoenicians during the eighth century B.C. as a trading port and resettled 400 years later by those latter-day Phoenicians, the Carthaginians. Then called Lilibeum, Marsala continued to have strategic importance under the Arabs, who gave it its present name from *Marsa Allah,* the harbor of Allah. In 1773 the Englishman John Woodhouse began a profitable business by shipping the local wine—with alcohol added as a preservative—to England. Marsala, so-called, became a popular drink, rivaling sherry. In 1806 Benjamin Ingham and his nephew Whitaker founded another prosperous Marsala-exporting company, which was taken over by the Sicilian entrepreneur Vincenzo Florio. The house of Florio, with new owners, still flourishes, and the premises on via Florio 1 can be visited. The Rallo family produces Donnafugata as well, a good wine now exported.

Marsala's cathedral contains some fine work by Gagini. A Punic ship, temporarily stored at the former distillery of Baglio Anselmi on the town's western promontory, was found offshore in 1971. Now restored, it's the only warship we have of the period. Marsala's big day in modern times was May 11, 1860, when Garibaldi and the Thousand landed, the first footfall of the revolution.

A harbor-side dinner at **Zio Ciccio** may be in order before heading south.

SELINUNTE

Southeast along the coast about 40 km (25 miles), you'll see the extensive remains of the seventh-century B.C. Greek city of Selinunte spread over three hills. Much of the marble (travertine) would still be there if the Spanish hadn't carted it off to build their palaces and churches. Segesta and Selinunte were always at odds over territory, but Segesta had the edge because Carthage was an ally; Hannibal destroyed much of Selinunte in 409 B.C. An earthquake during the seventh century A.D. delivered the coup de grace.

At the center of the area is the **Acropolis**, and to the west is the sanctuary of Demeter, where more than 12,000 votive objects have been found around the graves, which stretch for miles along the coast. The three temples to the east are in the process of being restored; the one called Temple E is now recognizable, with its righted columns. It is missing the lovely metopes from the frieze across the top of the columns, however, because they are in the archaeological museum in Palermo. Temple G was one of the largest in Greek Sicily, left unfinished when the slaves saw Hannibal's ships heading toward them in 409. Some of the huge unworked column blocks lie on the ground nearby; other half-cut ones can be seen at the nearby Cusa quarries, with the chisel marks of the laborers still visible. On the Acropolis the familiar grid plan is evident; there are remains of the residential section to the north.

SCIACCA AND AREA

This part of Sicily is a little out of the way. If time is no problem for you it's a pleasant place to explore for a few days. Especially tempting are the spa town of Sciacca, the white village of Caltabellota, and the Baroque town of Sambuca in the interior. Stay at the **Torre Macauda** at Sciacca, which, though large and modern—and apt to have tour groups—has little apartments in villas down by the shore cliffs, where it's more comfortable, with swimming pool and tennis courts. Sea-view rooms in the main building are very pleasant as well.

One advantage of this corner of Sicily is **Il Vigneto**, the hacienda-style restaurant run with confident passion by Marco Bursi, who adds imagination to traditional dishes. It's located at the crossroads (*bivio*) of Menfi and Portopalo. In winter the meat couscous is wonderful; in summer, the fish. Call ahead (Tel: 0925-717-32) and ask for *tre assagi* (three samples) of pasta, and you will be treated to some combination of pasta with eggplant, peppery tomatoes, squid ink (a specialty), shrimp, or whatever's available in the market. Grilled meats and fish, even pizza, are regularly on the menu. *Involtini alla siciliana* may be, too; they are thin slices of rolled meat with cheese, bread crumbs, and onions inside. If you let restaurateur Bursi know what you like ahead of time or you let him choose, you'll dine royally—on an open porch looking out on fields of grain and vineyards and fruit trees.

Sciacca, on two levels above the sea, is a pleasant surprise: quaint enough to draw some tourists but not enough to be overrun. It's a thermal spa, as a stop at the **Grande Albergo delle Terme**, overlooking the sea at the east end of town, will show. **San Calogero**, about 8 km (5 miles) northeast, is the spa's origin, a thermal station hollowed out by Daedalus (legend has it). Before him Copper Age residents made human, animal, and grain sacrifices to placate the steaming gods below the ground.

High above Sciacca to the northeast is **Caltabellota**, a sun-bleached Medieval town where hermits and monks sought solitude in rock caves in the surrounding woods. The **Chiesa Madre** here was created in 1090 by Count Roger, who must have enjoyed the view across the "African Sea," as Pirandello called it, and eastward as far as Etna. But the city's most important date is 1299, when Charles of Valois, the Angevin, and King Frederick of Aragon signed the Treaty of Caltabellota, ending the war of the Sicilian Vespers.

Sambuca di Sicilia, to the west, is delightfully floodlit by night so that the Baroque palaces turn gold. Until 1921 the little town was called Sambuca Zabut, for the Emir Zabut's castle, now in ruins. Adjoining it is the tiny Arab quarter of seven streets and a merlon tower with an ancient clock. Sambuca has its own wax museum, complete with Chopin, Sand, Garibaldi, and other notables, in the **Palazzo Panitteri**. Have dinner at the **Barone di Salinas**, part of a baronial estate that is now the property of Tommaso di Prima, a local farmer who bought the estate—his lifelong fantasy—and who enjoys showing visitors about the premises.

AGRIGENTO

"Fairest of all mortal cities" was Pindar's tribute to Akragus, now Agrigento. Its site in the rolling valley and the grandeur of the long line of Doric temples drew high praise regularly from visiting Greeks, who found life there much as it was in Athens: a worldly blend of philosophers and scientists, sculptors and astronomers.

To enjoy the temples most fully, stay at the **Villa Athena**, located just across a tropical garden from the Tempio della Concordia. Seen from the hotel's terrace, dawn's brilliant pink light, the gold-red sunset, and the floodlit night view of the site rival one another in beauty. In Sicily's early spring the fields are covered with pink and white almond blossoms, heralding the festival that brings folk dancers from around the world in early February to dance at the temple.

The city was created when residents of Gela moved west along the coast in 582 B.C. to take advantage of this area's fine harbor (now the overbuilt Porto Empédocle) and immensely rich grain fields that would feed the Roman Legions a few hundred years later. The first ruler was Phalaris, whose tyrannical acts included roasting his enemies in a huge bronze bull, perhaps harking back to a Rhodian bull cult. That he was assassinated is hardly a surprise, even if not all tales of his treachery are true. Carthage, by then grown from Phoenician outpost to major power, was not happy to see another important city expanding across the sea and launched an invasion in 480 B.C. With the aid of Gelon, tyrant of Gela and Syracuse, Akragus triumphed, winning 70 years of peace for Sicily—her Grecian golden age.

In a time when Greek philosophers were examining the very basis of prescientific understanding, Empedocles of Akragus developed the theory of four elements: that all things are compounded of earth, air, fire, and water, with love and strife acting as alternating currents. Unlike the Eleatics (at Velia, across the Strait of Messina), he insisted that the senses, not just the mind, if properly used, were routes to knowledge. His *On Nature* covers subjects from astronomy to zoology, and his work in physics is basic to the field today. In later years he apparently believed himself a god, having already been a bush, a bird, and a fish. To die a death worthy of a god he is supposed to have leaped into the crater at Etna. (Some contend he died in Greece.) Of his native city he had said, "The Agrigentines enjoy luxury as if they would die tomorrow, but they build palaces as if to live forever."

Agrigento's wealth was so enormous as to be eccentric: Young girls had tombs built for their birds. Although a dictatorship, the city didn't maintain an army of highly disciplined warriors: One military directive limited soldiers to only two pillows per bed. During the Punic wars Rome attacked Carthage at Agrigento, which Carthage controlled by that time. Victorious in 241 B.C., Rome sold the people into slavery and used the grain to feed its armies, while the corrupt Roman governor Verres collected a crippling corn tax.

During the sixth century A.D. the Tempio della Concordia was converted into a church, escaping the vengeance of Christian iconoclasts. The city subsequently fell to the Saracens, who were routed by the Norman Count Roger in 1087.

From the entrance to the Vallata dei Templi, the road leads up to the temples of Hercules, Concord, and Jupiter and then on up to the Rupe Athena, the most ancient part of the settlement. The warm ocher temples were originally painted with white stucco and are Doric in construction, simple and sturdy—elegant in this setting of fields and, in the spring, wild flowers. The **Tempio di Ercole**, reached through a lovely garden, is the oldest. Built about 520 B.C., it is still marked by fires set by Carthaginian invaders. Once richly decorated and considered the most beautiful of the temples, it housed a splendid statue of Hercules, whose chin and lips, according to Cicero, were worn smooth by adoration of the faithful.

On high is the aforementioned **Tempio della Concordia**, focus of a dramatic approach along a road bordered with tropical plants and ancient tombs, making the route even more theatrical by night, when it's floodlit. Up close the tawny tones vary from pale yellows to rich ochers. One of the best-preserved Doric temples in the world, it exudes solidity and self-confidence. When the church was created the columns were walled in and the walls of the central Greek shrine, the *cella,* were removed. Beyond the temple to the east is the sacrificial altar. A sacred enclosure containing shrines and niches for ex-votos originally surrounded each temple.

If you continue to the top of the ridge, you'll see the **Tempio di Giunone** (460–440 B.C.) overlooking the valley. Still higher is the Norman **Church of San Biagio**, atop a road worn with ancient cart tracks.

You'll need a guide to climb to the Rupe Athena; they are posted throughout the area. At the top, down rickety steps, is a shrine to Demeter and Persephone around which hundreds of votive objects have been excavated. Beneath the shrine is an elaborate system of terra-cotta pipes, involved with a water cult's underground ritual.

In the section down the hill, on the far side of the road, stand ruins of part of the enormous **Tempio di Giove Olimpia**, the largest of Doric temples. The enormous stone sunbather on the ground, called the Sleeping Giant, is a copy of one of 38 *telamones*—figures used as columns—that decorated the temple. The original of this figure and a scale model of the temple are in the Museo Archeologico (see below).

Chthonic rituals took place on the round altars and around the three-column remnant of the **Tempio di Castore e Polluce**, which is a pastiche of several buildings. Some of the earth-goddess shrines were built during the seventh century B.C., when such cults were popular.

Although the modern urban sprawl in the distance is uninviting, it is fortunately only the outskirts of Agrigento, whose small, attractive Medieval center is preserved, despite such modern stores as Fendi. Notable among contemporary Agrigento's treasures is a sweet called *kuskusi,* made by the nuns at Santo Spirito. (Ring at the convent door off via Porcello, near the main via Atenea.) The Concordia pastry shop at the top of the hill, via Atenea 34, will do nicely as a substitute. Go inside the church of Santo Spirito to see the stuccos by Serpotta and statues by Gagini.

The Duomo, San Gerlando, is dedicated to the patron saint who not only persuaded his relative Count Roger to rout the Saracens but also caught a wicked dragon in his hat, or so we're told. A letter written by Satan to a nun of the Tomasi di Lampedusa family is in the Duomo's possession. Unfortunately, the text is not of this world, except for one word: *ohimè* ("alas").

Agrigento's **Museo Archeologico** is well organized, well lit, and a pleasure to visit. It houses an impressive collection of antiquities that includes a child's sarcophagus depicting his birth, death, and journey to the next world; and Phaedra's sarcophagus, Greek in design but probably Roman in workmanship, decorated with scenes of her tragic love affair.

Nearby in the town of **Caos** is Pirandello's house and a Pirandello museum by the tree where his ashes are buried: "One night in June I dropped down like a firefly beneath a huge pine tree standing all on its own in an olive grove on the edge of a blue clay plateau overlooking the African sea." He would scarcely recognize his Caos today, full of condominiums and second homes.

Apart from the Villa Athena, which has a good restaurant serving pumpkin sauces with pasta in the fall, try the **Taverna Mose** for dinner, where the beefsteak is seasoned with fresh herbs, and the falsomagro is delicious (*falsomagro* is a roast stuffed with meats, cheese, vegetables, and bread crumbs, thus "falsely thin," as the name says). **Del Vigneto** and **Le Caprice,** both near the temples, serve good grilled meat. Try a wonderful red Regaleali wine called Rosso del Conto.

Because of the highway system, Syracuse is reached most quickly from Agrigento by taking the highway to Catania on the eastern coast and then heading south past the industrial zone into Syracuse. However, a nicer route would meander through the southern and eastern coastal towns (see the section "Other Baroque Towns" below).

SYRACUSE

Once greater than even Athens and briefly capital of Byzantium when Muslims threatened the Eastern Empire, Syracuse (Siracusa in the Italian) now shows off its classical past in an archaeological zone just outside the modern city. But its greatest beauty today is Ortygia, an island of Baroque fantasy connected to the modern city by a bridge.

Before the Corinthian Greeks arrived in 734 B.C. and moved them out, Siculi inhabited this part of the island. The Greeks valued Syracuse's natural harbors for their beauty and defensibility, and so the harbors often saw violent battles, as Thucydides chronicles faithfully in *The Peloponnesian War.* Though tyrants dominated Greek Sicily, the court of Hieron attracted Pindar and Aeschylus, who probably wrote *Prometheus Bound* for its theater.

The tyrant Dionysius was a military genius and poet manqué. After years of hissing at him whenever he read his poetry in competitions, Athens finally awarded him a medal, but the honor prompted Dionysius to treat himself to an orgy so intense that he died of it. His son Dionysius II was once admired by Plato, who was always on the lookout for a philosopher king, but Plato left in dismay at his tyranny. Timoleon (343 B.C.–337 B.C.) gave Syracuse as close to good government as it would have—rebuilding, and concluding a treaty with perennial enemy Carthage. He died quietly, a rarity for the time.

When the Romans invaded Syracuse, they "failed to reckon with the ability of Archimedes," as Polybius put it, for Archimedes' genius had helped create the strategically brilliant fort of Euryalus as well as ingenious war machines. When the Greek forces were finally beaten, Rome sent Verres to govern Sicily. His habit of taking every Greek statue or frieze—no matter how large—was reported by Cicero in the *Verrine Orations*.

Syracuse would not flower again until the Spanish made it a Baroque fantasy, especially on the city's island of Ortygia, where women still carry decorated lacy fans in summer and cover their shoulders with embroidered shawls.

Ortygia

Ortygia's charm is seductive, especially when night highlights the Baroque shadows. By day, the delightful museum at the **Palazzo Bellomo** is open, displaying another version of the *Annunciata* by Antonello da Messina—a damaged masterpiece—and Caravaggio's *Burial of St. Lucy,* moved from the church of Santa Lucia, as well as a section on folklore with charming *presepi*.

At the nearby, spacious, windswept promenade, a freshwater fountain flows into the sea—although the **Fonte d'Aretusa** may be salted by now, owing to the earthquakes that have split the land around it. The last recorded taste was when Nelson took on freshwater provisions on his way to the Battle of the Nile. The fountain, legend says, is actually the nymph Arethusa, who, fleeing the river god Alpheus, jumped into the sea in Greece. Artemis changed her into a fountain, and she travelled undersea across the Mediterranean to emerge here, with Alpheus in pursuit. The Delphic Oracle confirmed the story: "An isle, Ortygia, lies on the misty ocean, over against Trinacria [as Greece

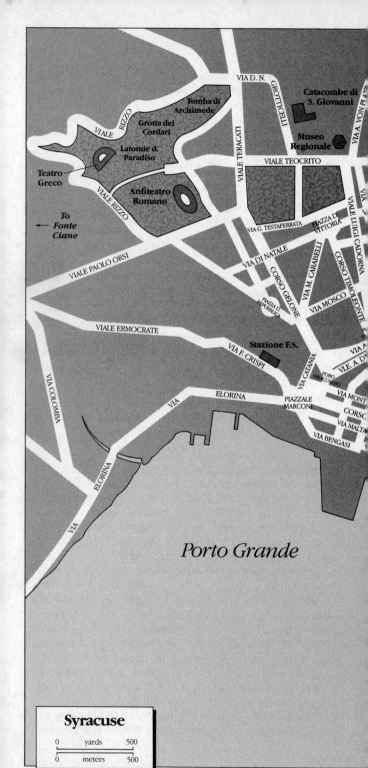

VIA D. N.

GROTTICELLI

Catacombe di
S. Giovanni

Tomba di
Archimede

Grotta dei
Cordari

VIALE   RIZZO

Museo
Regionale

Latomie d.
Paradiso

VIA VON P

VIALE TEOCRITO

Teatro
Greco

VIALE TERACATI

Anfiteatro
Romano

To
Fonte
Ciane

VIALE RIZZO

VIA G. TESTAFERRATA

PIAZZA D'
VITTORIA

VIALE LUIGI CADORNA

CORSO TIMOLEONTE

VIA

VIALE PAOLO ORSI

VIA DI NATALE

CORSO GELONE

VIA M. CARABELLI

VIA MOSCO

PIAZZA D.
REPUBBLICA

VIALE ERMOCRATE

Stazione F.S.

VIA F. CRISPI

VLE. A. D

VIA CATANIA

VIA COLOMBA

VIA

ELORINA

FORO
SIRACUSANO

VIA MONT

PIAZZALE
MARCONI

CORSO

VIA MALTA

ELORINA

VIA BENGASI

VIA

Porto Grande

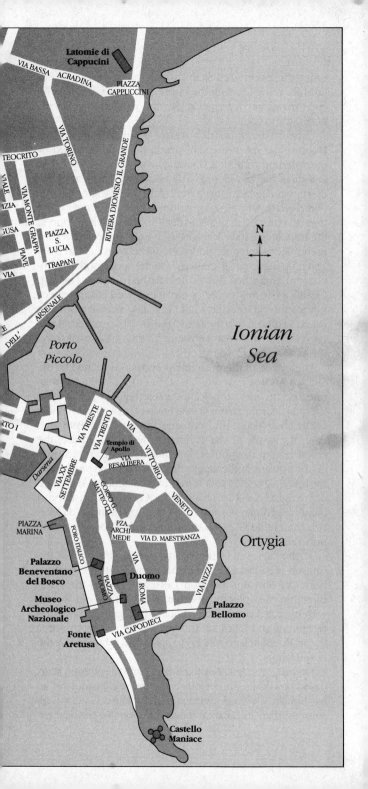

Latomie di Cappucini

VIA BASSA   ACRADINA

PIAZZA CAPPUCCINI

VIA TORINO

TEOCRITO

VIALE

VIA MONTE GRAPPA

ZIA

GUSA

PIAZZA S. LUCIA

PIAVE

VIA   TRAPANI

DELL'   ARSENALE

Porto Piccolo

RIVIERA DI ONISIO IL GRANDE

N

Ionian Sea

RTO I

Darsena

VIA TRIESTE

VIA TRENTO

VIA TRENTO

VIA VITTORIO

Tempio di Apollo

VIA RESALIBERA

VIA XX SETTEMBRE

CORSO G. MATTEOTTI

VENETO

PIAZZA MARINA

FORO ITALICO

PZA. ARCHI MEDE

VIA D. MAESTRANZA

Ortygia

Palazzo Beneventano del Bosco

PIAZZA DUOMO

Duomo

VIA ROMA

VIA NIZZA

Museo Archeologico Nazionale

Palazzo Bellomo

Fonte Aretusa

VIA CAPODIECI

Castello Maniace

called three-cornered Sicily], where the mouth of Alpheus bubbles mingling with the bubbles of broad Arethusa." A cup thrown into the river at Olympia in Greece reappears here, Strabo says.

Ortygia's most popular square by night is **piazza del Duomo**, the most beautiful piazza in Sicily, bounded by the splendid cathedral (Duomo) and grand palaces. The Duomo's site was sacred to the Siculi, who built a temple there, which was to have been followed by another one dedicated to Athena, some columns of which appear in the present church. Because the fleet-fingered Verres stripped the temple, we have a record of it only in Cicero's indictment: "More splendid doors, exquisitely wrought in ivory and gold, have never existed." On the roof stood a triumphant Athena whose gold shield flashed to sea as a beacon for sailors. Verres' booty had an unexpected positive effect: it introduced Greek art to the Romans, a turning point in Rome's cultural history. In 640 the Christian cathedral was moved here from San Giovanni on the outskirts of town, but an earthquake destroyed it.

The façade of the present **Duomo** was designed by the Sicilian Andrea Palma (1728–1751) to replace a Norman one that was the victim of another earthquake. The Duomo is praised for the brilliant execution of broken masses that create chiaroscuro. In front are statues of Saints Peter and Paul, the work of the Palermitan Marabitti. Inside, the centuries are harmoniously joined: Greek columns project from walls and chapels; fine wrought-iron work adds intricacy; a Norman font stands in the baptistry. At the end of the right aisle is the chapel of the Crucified Christ, with a painting of *Saint Zosimus* attributed to Antonello da Messina. Antonello Gagini's *Madonna of the Snow* graces the north aisle.

At the far end of the piazza del Duomo stands the Church of Santa Lucia alla Badia, dedicated to the Sicilian-born patron saint feted on December 13. In the other direction the splendid **Palazzo Beneventano del Bosco**, with its grand courtyard, maintains its dignity, despite the restaurant and disco on the ground floor. The palace is the work of Luciano Ali (1775) and is still inhabited by the noble family.

Ortygia's current pleasing mix of Baroque façades, staircases, balconies, and details is the indirect product of an earthquake in 1693. Baroque in Syracuse is more restrained than in Catania, more conscious of classical order and simple elegance—perhaps because of the city's strong Hellenic past.

Before returning to the mainland stop at the **Tempio di Apollo**, just to the right of the bridge. Here excavations continue around the oldest Doric temple in Sicily, built about 565 B.C. It had six columns at the front and 17 along the sides, placed unusually close together. The name of Apollo results from an inscription chiseled on the front of the temple, although Cicero attributed the temple to Artemis, which affirmed the co-worship of the two cults, here in the same location.

Mainland Syracuse

The **Catacombe di San Giovanni**, entered from the church of San Giovanni on via Teocrito back on the mainland, evokes the paleo-Christian past, a time when Saint Paul delivered a sermon at the altar of San Mariano in the catacomb on his way back from Malta. Frescoes, graffiti, and other remnants of the early Church lend the site a mystic aura (unless a school class arrives).

The **Museo Regionale**, newly reopened and expanded near the catacombs, is an invaluable resource featuring objects taken from the city's Zona Archeologica: metopes, statues, and such—a stone diary of Sicily from prehistory to the times of Greece and Rome.

Near the museum, at viale Teocrito 80, the **Galleria del Papiro** tells the story of papyrus—apparently given to Sicily by the Ptolemaic kings. The gallery owners demonstrate the Egyptian technique from stalk to finished painting.

The **Zona Archeologica** contains the major Classical sites that remain. The Roman amphitheater, off the corso Gelone's far (northeastern) end, is surpassed in size only by the arena in Verona, but much of its stone was carried away by the Spanish for construction, a familiar story in Sicily. The *cavea* (audience section), built into the hillside, is topped by a parapet engraved with the names of box holders. To the west is the largest sacrificial altar known to the Greek world, with ramps that held 450 oxen on their way to sacrifice. Once monumental in aspect, today it demands imagination. The structure called Archimedes' tomb is not, though Cicero did see the Greek mathematician's now-lost tomb somewhere in Syracuse.

The **Latomie** are deep limestone quarries where hapless slaves (often prisoners of war) cut away stone for building. The earlobe-shaped Latomie del Paradiso was dubbed by Caravaggio the Ear of Dionysius; legend has it that the acoustics are so good the tyrannical one listened at the opening on top to hear what the slaves were saying. In the **Grotto dei Cordari** (cave of the rope makers) the work is clearly evident, almost as if the site were just recently abandoned. Contrasting with the stone is luxuriant vegetation: lemon and orange trees, capers, palm, prickly pear, and particularly oleander—which lines the streets of Syracuse with dark rose and white flowers.

The **Greek theater**, among the most beautiful of its kind, originally enjoyed a view of the harbor and hills, but the Romans added a backdrop to facilitate their more elaborate productions—simplicity not being a Roman attribute. Syracuse was famous throughout the world for drama; Aeschylus and Euripides were performed regularly. When Hieron I founded a colony at nearby Mount Etna, Aeschylus wrote *Women of Etna* (lost) to be performed here; his Prometheus plays were also produced at Syracuse. All was not tragedy, however, for Epicharmus raised ancient comedy to artistic heights, and mime was a typical comic relief. Above the theater are the remains of a nymphaeum to which Hieron's guests could run during a downpour.

Lentini, near Syracuse, was the birthplace of the philosopher Gorgias (483 B.C.). His Sophist views led Cicero to say that doubt was born in Sicily. According to Gorgias nothing exists, for if it did it would have to come from something, and something can't come from nothing. And if something did exist, it could not be known, given the difference between thought and thing. Objective truth being thus impossible, there remained only the art of the Sophists: persuasion. Gorgias' challenge to speculative thought stimulated a more sophisticated approach to the problems of philosophy (and see the eponymous dialogue by Plato). He became known as the philosopher who introduced rhetoric to Greece, the art of persuasion that yields belief about things just and unjust.

Follow viale Teocrito east from the Zona Archeologica toward the sea and stop at the **Hotel Villa Politi** (where you may want to stay), whose gardens, part of the adjoining catacombs of the Cappuccini, are an organized jungle of palms and oaks, flowers and statues, and limestone quarries. Views from the front rooms are enchanting at night, when garden lights turn the outdoors into a Gothic mystery.

The adjoining Cappuccini catacombs are closed now, but they once held Athenian prisoners captive until they died—or could recite Euripides, a feat that would free them. The hilltop **Euryalus fortress**, which you can reach from here by bus, is a fascinating war machine engineered by Dionysius and Archimedes. Underground networks of trenches allowed soldiers on the deck of the boat-shaped structure to drag bodies away, along with whatever objects of warfare the enemy propelled in.

Far on the south side of town is the Fonte Ciane, the source of the river Ciane, named for Persephone's nymph, whose tears created the river when she learned her mistress had been carried away to Hades. Tall papyrus grows wild along the stream, which can be followed by boat (check the tourist office for the schedule).

If the Villa Politi's somewhat faded charms (Churchill was entranced) and faint cooling system aren't enticing, stay at the modern **Jolly**, centrally located on corso Gelone; its air-conditioning is often essential in the summer.

Everyone who visits Syracuse has a favorite restaurant. A common choice is **Ionico**, set on a beautiful quarry by the sea, just north of the center (near the Villa Politi) in a little garden filled with antiquity and kitsch. The family Giudice, led by master chef Pasqualino, has devised a superb Syracusan menu. Pasqualino is so impassioned about his native cooking that he travels the world giving demonstrations. Fish is, of course, at center stage here—swordfish, bass, tuna, mackerel—seasoned with capers, fresh anchovies (nothing like tinned), wild fennel, black olives, rich olive oil. Spaghetti may come topped with tuna eggs and herring. When the season is right you might request *spaghettata artistica d'Archestrato,* with shrimp, calamari, octopus, mussels, capers, garlic, olives, wine, and cheese. Or you could always have a plain grilled fish with lemon. The menu is in Sicilian, but the staff speaks English (even Italians look at the menu in bemusement).

Arlecchino's proprietor, Baldassare Ponza, comes from Palermo and serves his native dishes, as well as local ones, in a pretty trattoria decorated with masks of the commedia dell'arte. *Bass in cartuccio* (baked in a paper case) tastes of the sea, fresh and moist, and the vegetable pastas are excellent.

Acting students crowd **Archimede**, projecting over fresh fish and game and seductive desserts. In Ortygia the little **Minosse** is known for wonderful fish stew (*zuppa di* *pesce*), breaded swordfish, and tender calamari steamed in white wine. (King Minos, the restaurant's namesake, came to Sicily to find Daedalus, the master sculptor, and take him back to Greece; but Minos was murdered in his bath by daughters of Cocalus, the Siculi king.)

The pastries and ice cream in Syracuse are too good to ignore: almond pastry; super-rich *cassata* filled with pistachio cream and chocolate and candied fruit bits; the richest, lightest cannoli. Stop at **Marciante** in via Maestranza or the **Bar Viola** in corso Matteotti for ice cream.

THE BAROQUE SOUTHEAST

Almost every town in the Sicilian southeast, no matter how humble, boasts a Baroque church of distinction, and often a palace as well.

Noto

Noto, to the southwest about a half hour by bus from Syracuse, is the rarest gem of all. Designed as a golden urban unit, it was chosen by Antonioni as a symbol of past architectural triumph in his film *L'Avventura*. Much of the town is the work of architects Gagliardi and Landolina.

The central corso Vittorio Emanuele leads past three piazzas. The street to see, though, is **via Corrado Nicolaci**, so perfect as to seem trompe l'oeil (when cars aren't parked along it). Its balconies burst with griffins, mermaids, medusas, lions, and other oddities of decorative splendor.

Stop at the ultrasimple **Trattoria Carmine** on via Carmine for a pasta with vegetable sauce and grilled shrimp that make even Nettini (as Noto residents are called) crowd the popular spot. In back of the Municipio is the **Gelateria Costanzo**, where wonderful ice cream, sometimes even *gelsomino*—made from jasmine petals—is prepared. Noto has a music festival and an ice cream festival during the summer, caring for both body and soul.

Other Baroque Towns

Among towns to include on a Baroque itinerary are Ragusa Ibla, Modica, Scicli, Grammichele, Canicattì, and Palazzolo Acreide. Archaeological journeys, carefully outlined in a booklet available from the tourist office in Ortygia, will take you to the vast Siculi necropolis at Pantalica (13th to 8th centuries B.C.) and to other ancient towns.

To sustain yourself for the journey, have a meal at **Majore**, a family restaurant at Chiaramonte Gulfi, the ultimate pork establishment (with wild rabbit and partridge, too). Pork is prepared in sausages, roasted, jellied, in pasta sauces—always with a special taste, for the Majores' pork is given a very special diet. Ragusa (the province) is the center for *cacciacavallo* cheese, whose taste changes noticeably with the region. Tel: (0932) 92-30-19.

Just outside **Palazzolo Acreide** in the hills due west of Syracuse, in the Templi Ferali, are 12 rough figures called the Santoni, representing aspects of the goddess Cybele, who was worshiped here. (Ask the custodian to open the shrine.)

In Palazzolo Acreide a "house-museum" has been delightfully assembled to re-create the spirit of country life at the turn of the century. Stop also at the church of the Immacolata to see a lovely Laurana *Madonna*.

Caltagirone

Caltagirone, farther west from Palazzolo Acreide, is a paradise for ceramics fanciers, worthy of a detour inland. Not only is there a museum devoted to pottery and tiles through the ages, but the town's walls, railings, even the 142-step staircase—each step differently tiled—glow with multicolored ceramic designs. Small artisan shops continue the passion, most more modern than the traditional simple blue and white with an orange dab. The sophisticated town has a charming Art Nouveau park designed by Basile.

Stay at the modern **Villa San Mauro**, with its lovely view of the town and hills and a friendly bar and lounge for the travel weary.

Piazza Armerina

West of Caltagirone, picturesque Piazza Armerina is visited mainly en route to the Roman villa at nearby **Casale**. You may have to taxi from Piazza Armerina to Casale if you're not driving your own car. The luxurious villa at Casale was a Roman Imperial retreat during the third century B.C. Mosaics depicting chariot races, hunts, picnics, and bikini bathers cover a multiroomed villa. The children's section shows Imperial *bambini* at play.

CATANIA

The Baroque past of Catania, north up the coast from Syracuse, is impressive—and impressively in need of renovation. Palermo-born Giovanni Battista Vaccarini settled there in 1730 and brought about what Rudolph Wittkower calls "a Sicilian Rococo, by blending Borrominesque with the local tradition," admirably demonstrated by the cathedral façade. In the piazza in front is another of his designs, an elephant fountain similar to Bernini's in Rome.

Catania composer Vincenzo Bellini is buried inside the church (his house-museum on piazza San Francesco has memorabilia from *Norma* and *I Puritani*). To the right of the altar is the chapel of Saint Agatha, where the city's patron saint, whose veil stopped a lava flow from nearby Etna, is buried. Her martyrdom included having her breasts cut off, and they now reappear as pastries (*seni di vergine*) all over Sicily, an odd symbol of devotion. Catania frequently wins pastry design awards; Baroque didn't stop at stucco *putti* after all. The pastry shop left of the Duomo displays some amazing marzipan.

The Municipio in the same piazza demonstrates Vaccarini's flair; and the nearby market adds Baroque drama to fish selling. One of Frederick II's many castles, the **Castello Ursino**, can be visited, thanks to the eclectic museum housed there. It's worth going in, if only to see Frederick's interiors.

Catania Barocca is at its best on **via Crociferi**, whose scenographic allure derives partly from such lovely façades as that of the church of San Benedetto, and at night from the merry *putti* streetlamps. Via Etnea—looking north toward its namesake—is home to a university with a fine school of vulcanology, and for good reason. At the end is **Giardino Bellini**, a pleasant place to relax in a chaotic city and enjoy the flower clock, calendar, and busts of Bellini and other musicians. For an overview of Catania and for exercise, climb to the cupola of the church of San Nicolà on via Gesuiti, in the southwestern part of town.

A choice restaurant in Catania is **La Siciliana**, where *rigatoni alla Norma,* made with eggplant sometimes seared for added flavor, is a delicious tribute to Bellini. Stuffed fresh sardines, roast lamb, *involtini,* and such can be accompanied by wines from Mount Etna or selections from the La Rosa family's extensive cellars. A specialty you might try is *ripiddu nivicatu* (lava of snowy Etna), a plate of rice blackened with cuttlefish ink, snowy white with cooked ricotta and flaming with red pepper sauce. *Tiramisù* and *cassata* are sweet finishes.

Etna

"Etna, that wicked witch, resting her thick white snow under heaven, and slowly, slowly, rolling her orange-colored smoke," was D. H. Lawrence's response to the still-active volcano. Pindar and Plato talked of it, and Homer's Cyclops hurled rocks from its sides at Odysseus—rocks that now can be seen along the coast at Aci Castello where they fell (*I Ciclopi*).

To climb the volcano or drive up near the top is to pass through botanical zones of great beauty. Not only the site of a fine vineyard and citrus orchard, the volcanic earth in spring is a green wood with bright patches of saffron. Rare plants such as the Etna violet grow here, and chestnut trees from ancient forests are golden in autumn. In winter, broom lichen and wild flowers are dazzling against the dark slopes higher up. Pistachio—probably planted by Arabs—is cultivated under the volcano, and the white birches are as noble as Robert Frost's.

Daily excursions are arranged through CIT tours in Catania and Taormina to Mount Etna. If you have the time, take the Circumetnea railway around the volcano, stopping at some of the picturesque towns, such as Randazzo, that line the slopes. From Sapienza, reached by train or bus, a four-hour hike will take you to the crater or as close as you can get. You can also rent a Jeep there. Skiing on the slopes is permitted when the volcano has been quiet.

TAORMINA

North of Catania along the east coast, Taormina is at its most magical when approached gradually along the resort-flanked sea road. As you climb the tortuous, steep hill toward the summit, the sea, the castle-topped cliff, and Mount Etna take their places in an incomparable panorama.

The lure that has drawn the titled and the famous through the years is still strong, despite hotels and shops that threaten to overwhelm the Medieval charm of steep streets, flower-dripping balconies, Renaissance palaces, and tropical gardens. Avoid July and August, of course; but come in spring or fall, even at Christmas and New Year's, when the feasting board groans, and fireworks light up the sea.

Taormina is perched high above the water; you can reach the beaches at **Mazzarò**, directly below, or at **Naxos**, visible from the heights, by car or funicular. Naxos was the first Greek colony in Sicily (735 B.C.), though its ruins are few compared with the treasures of Agrigento. Those that do remain are found in the **Parco Archeologico**. Otherwise Naxos is a long line of hotels.

Taormina was established by Dionysius I in 403 B.C. after he had destroyed Naxos (they were Chalcideans and Ionians; he was Corinthian). The Arabs subsequently destroyed and rebuilt the city, and Count Roger rousted them in turn, as was his wont, in 1078. Its well-preserved Medieval look is due in part to the care of the House of Aragon and in part to the Allied bombers' unwillingness to do much damage when they attacked Marshal Kesselring's fine quarters here.

The view from the central seats of the **Teatro Greco**—of Etna, the sea, the coast, and the sky framed by the theater's open walls—is one of the most beautiful sights in the world. Returning in early morning and late afternoon to see the light change makes the experience even more rewarding.

The theater is carved out of the rock and was so extensively made over by the Romans that most of the present structure dates from the Empire. But the site itself is Greek—a location only they could choose. Its acoustics are still excellent, and the theater is used frequently for a variety of artistic productions.

Most churches here are attractively simple in construction, and palaces such as the **Corvaia** on the piazza Vittorio Emanuele are typical in their ornamentation of black lava and pumice inlaid in the limestone foundation. Its attractive courtyard, with panels depicting Adam and Eve and with an outside stair, as well as the grand hall and salons, are interesting to visit, a nice stop when you wander the maze of streets and alleys brightened by balconies of flowers.

The best hotels in Taormina are the **San Domenico Palace**, a 16th-century convent converted into a hotel that counts among its expensive charms spectacular panoramas from terraces, a pool, and, a dining room; the less expensive **Jolly Diodoro**—where you should try to take an end suite with panoramas north and south, and Etna in clear view, and with pool and garden; the stylish **Villa Belvedere**, still less expensive, nearby with the same panorama and flowery gardens and pool; the **Villa Paradiso**, inexpensive and in another perfect setting; and the small **Villa Fiorita**, with outdoor terraces, pool, and panorama.

At Mazzarò, on the beach just below Taormina, there is the luxury hotel **Mazzarò Sea Palace** and the charming **Villa Sant'Andrea**, which seems like an English seashore villa, merry with fabric prints. The front rooms with terraces facing the sea are the best, but the back faces Taormina's semitropical lushness. The price is moderate. One of its two restaurants is on the beach. Both hotels are reached by cable car from Taormina, but if you're athletically inclined you can make the ascent on the stairs, and if you are stuck in the town above late at night you can take a taxi back to the hotel.

For a day's excursion from Taormina you can easily go to Mount Etna and surrounding towns by train or tour. For a glimpse of Medieval Sicily (so typical that a wedding scene in *The Godfather* was filmed there), go to **Forza d'Agrò**, a clifftop town reached by car only; bus service requires spending hours there between buses. In the town's piazza only the click of embroidery needles breaks the silence, except for an occasional blast of Michael Jackson from a passing tape deck.

MESSINA

North of Taormina, Messina is the ferry entrance to Sicily from Réggio di Calàbria, worthy of a visit if only for its museum's two Caravaggios and a magnificent fragment of a polyptych by the town's famous native son Antonello da Messina. The city has seen destruction since its beginning—first by war, then by earthquake, tidal wave, cholera, and recently by World War II bombs; but it is now cheerful-looking and energetic, a busy port and university town. At the central piazza a noontime performance from the amazing clock tower features a crowing cock, a roaring lion, and Christ arising. Thus awakened, head for fashionable **Alberto's**, considered one of Sicily's best restaurants, and have fish carpaccio with herb sauce, scampi in crab sauce, and one of their superb lemon sorbets. Try the Sicilian favorite *neonata* (newborn fish) made up in croquettes flavored with fresh wild fennel. If you spend the night in Messina, try the **Jolly**, which has a fine view of the harbor. While in Messina you can cross the Strait in a few minutes by hydrofoil to see *I Bronzi*, the bronze warriors the sea gave up to a Calabrese fisherman, exhibited in Réggio di Calàbria's Museo Nazionale. You can see Messina on a day trip from Taormina or visit it en route while circling the island.

THE AEOLIAN ISLANDS

The Aeolians (also known as the Lipari Islands), off Sicily's northeast coast, were once ruled by the god of the winds, Aeolus, if we are to believe Homer and Virgil. They are volcanic mountains, stark and dramatic, with occasional bursts of bloom from the rich volcanic soil, excellent for growing grapes and vegetables, prickly pears, capers, carobs, and palms. Pumice stone, not surprisingly, is an export. During the Punic wars, Carthage used the islands as a base until Rome conquered all in 252 B.C. The Aeolians were inhabited well before that, as traces of Stentinello culture, especially pottery dating from the Neolithic period, have been found on Lipari. The Greeks were there later, but as early as 600 B.C.

Lipari is the largest of the islands and the one most adapted to tourism, with relics of its ancient past to marvel at in the **Museo Eoliano**. The views from Lipari, and from all the islands, are striking, dramatic in color and for sculpturesque rock carvings. A friendly island home is the **Villa Diana**, where terraces and private gardens overlook Lipari from on high; dinners of local dishes and wines are wholesome. More hotel-like is the **Meligunis**, with beach and garden, and the **Carasco**, with fine sea views and a pool. Dine at the **Filippino** on lobster, shrimp, and pasta flavored with Lipari's *pecorino* cheese; **E Pulera** serves good Aeolian food on a terrace bright with flowers and ceramics.

Salina, the greenest island of the archipelago, has a beautiful beach and a nature reserve to visit. An occasional puff of smoke will remind you of its volcanic origin. Salina is formed of two volcanic peaks, one rising more than 3,000 feet, and the sweep of land between them. Small hotels and some rooms in private homes have kept tourism manageable, and the island is still a wonderful getaway. Hotels on the island include the **Ariana** and **Punta Scario**.

Panarea is perhaps the most dramatically beautiful of the Aeolians, with its bizarre formations of volcanic rock and its clear water. Prehistoric villages dating from the 14th and 13th centuries B.C. can be seen on the volcanic slopes. Panarea is also a chic resort, attracting Italian celebrities who want to be alone—and without electricity, for the island has little. **Il Raya** is the place they are found; no children, please. **The Residence** and **La Piazza**, with many amenities, are also charming. Scuba diving is the sport of choice.

Stromboli frequently puts on a show at night, when its still-active volcano shoots firey pellets into the dark sapphire sky. Such dramatic spectacles send everyone to their boats to see the show from the sea, Pliny fashion. If the crater hasn't been too active, you can visit it with a guide. There are three villages: Piscità, Ficogrande, and San Vincenzo, all on the northeast coast; all are white towns surrounded by palms, olive trees, and orange groves. Rocky cliffs hide small beaches beneath and caves for spelunkers, or lovers—this is the island that Bergman and Rossellini made famous, after all. The most developed hotel is the pretty **Sciara Residence**, with a restaurant, a pool, tennis court, and a private beach. **La Sirenetta-Park Hotel** and the **Scari**—friendly, with a restaurant, bar, and only 11 rooms—are also good choices.

Vulcano is the island for mud baths; white steam and sulfur rise from the fumaroles, and you can walk along the rim of the dormant crater, which hasn't been heard from since 1890.

Elegantly alone and remote are **Filicudi** and **Alicudi**, where prehistoric dwellings are to be found. Take an excursion by boat to the Bue Marino cave, which is preferred by many to Capri's Grotta Azzurra, so dramatic are the displays of reflected light. Alicudi has a tiny hotel called the **Ericusa**, and local residents put up guests. You can travel around the island with a local boatman.

To visit the islands, leave your car at the car park at the pier in Milazzo, west of Messina. Daily sailings are available for Lipari, Vulcano, and Salina; less often (usually three times a week) to the others. A new helicopter service links Stromboli to Milazzo. During the summer there is daily hydrofoil service to all islands, and among them. Palermo also is connected to the islands by hydrofoil. The overnight ferry from Naples links them all, year round. Cars are allowed on Lipari and Salina but are not really needed. Small motor vehicles take care of luggage and local transport. Walking is the best means of touring, with an occasional boat ride.

If you travel back to Palermo along the scenic north coast, stop at **Tindari** to see the fourth-century B.C. Greek amphitheater, positioned with the infallible Greek sense of site. This theater opens onto a spectacular view of the Aeolian islands ahead and Mount Etna in back—a fitting end to this island journey.

GETTING AROUND
You can reach Sicily by plane, arriving in Palermo or Catania, or by train across the Strait of Messina from Réggio di Calàbria to Messina. The most beautiful approach, however, is from Naples on the overnight car ferry that arrives in Palermo in time for the deep pink African dawn over the city. First-class cabins are reasonably comfortable (reserve ahead) and there is a cafeteria on board.

A car is the thing if you want to see the smaller towns, because bus service is infrequent. Train and bus connections to all major cities, however, are quite good. Cars are not recommended in Palermo and Catania, where traffic and auto theft make them a headache. Nothing should ever be left in a car, even if it is locked. Outside these two cities there are fewer problems, and the local people will be happy to tell you where to park.

Tour operators such as Italtours, CIT, and Jolly Hotels offer very inexpensive independent packages, including hotel and car rental or sometimes a rail pass, which can be booked ahead through a travel agent. Culturally oriented tours are organized by Amelia Tours, 280 Old Country Road, Hicksville, NY 11081. Tel: (516) 433-0696.

ACCOMMODATIONS REFERENCE

(See also separate accommodations listings for Palermo, above in chapter.)

▶ **L'Ariana.** Via Rotabile 11, 98050 **Salina**. Tel: (090) 984-20-75.

▶ **Villa Athena.** Via dei Templi, 92100 **Agrigento**. Tel: (0922) 238-33.

▶ **Astoria Park Hotel.** Lungomare Dante Alighieri, 91100 **Trápani**. Tel: (0923) 624-00; Telex: 911228.

▶ **Villa Belvedere.** Via Bagnoli Croce 79, 98039 **Taormina**. Tel: (0942) 237-91.

▶ **Cala 'Mpiso.** Cala dell'Mpiso, 91010 **San Vito Lo Capo**. Tel: (0923) 97-22-86.

▶ **La Calette.** Località Caldura, 90015 **Cefalù**. Tel: (0921) 218-56.

▶ **Carasco.** Porto delle Genti, 98055. **Lipari**. Tel: (090) 981-16-05.

▶ **Cossyra.** Località Mursia, 91017 **Pantelleria**. Tel: (0923) 91-11-54.

▶ **Villa Diana.** Località Diana-Tufo, 98055 **Lipari**. Tel: (090) 981-14-03.

▶ **Ericusa.** Località Perciato, 98055 **Alicudi**. Tel: (090) 981-23-70.

▶ **Ermione.** Località Pineta, 91016 **Erice**. Tel: (0923) 86-91-38.

▶ **Villa Fiorita.** Via Pirandello 39, 98039 **Taormina**. Tel: (0942) 241-22.

▶ **Jolly.** Corso Gelone 43, 96100 **Syracuse**. Tel: (0931) 647-44; Telex: 970108.

▶ **Jolly dello Stretto.** Corso Garibaldi 126, 98100 **Messina**. Tel: (090) 434-01. Telex: 980074.

▶ **Jolly Diodoro.** Via Bagnoli Croce 75, 98039 **Taormina**. Tel: (0942) 233-12, Telex: 980028.

▶ **Kalura.** Località Caldura, 90015 **Cefalù**. Tel: (0921) 213-54.

▶ **Mazzarò Sea Palace.** Via Nazionale, 98030 **Mazzarò**. Tel: (0942) 240-04; Telex: 980041.

▶ **Meligunis.** Via Marte, 98055 **Lipari**. Tel: (090) 981-24-26.

▶ **Moderno.** Via Vittorio Emanuele 63, 91016 **Erice**. Tel: (0923) 86-93-00.

▶ **Mondello Palace.** Viale Principe di Scalea 2, 90151 **Mondello**. Tel: (091) 45-00-01; Telex: 911097.

▶ **Paradiso.** 91090 **Lévanzo**. Tel: (0923) 92-40-90.

▶ **Villa Paradiso.** Via Roma 2, 98039 **Taormina**. Tel: (0942) 239-22.

▸ **La Piazza.** Contrada San Pietro 98050 **Panarea.** Tel: (090) 981-11-90.

▸ **Villa Politi.** Via Politi 2, 96100 **Syracuse.** Tel: (0931) 321-00; Telex: 970205.

▸ **Del Porto.** Via Borgo Italia, 91017 **Pantelleria.** Tel: (0923) 91-12-57.

▸ **Punta Scario.** Via Scalo, 98050 **Salina.** Tel: (090) 984-41-39.

▸ **Il Raya.** Costa Galletta, 98050 **Panarea.** Tel: (090) 981-15-57.

▸ **Residence.** Contrada San Pietro, 98050 **Panarea.** Tel: (090) 981-11-90.

▸ **San Domenico Palace.** Piazza San Domenico 5, 98039 **Taormina.** Tel: (0942) 237-01; Telex: 980013.

▸ **Grand Hotel Villa San Mauro.** Via Portosalvo 18, 95041 **Caltagirone.** Tel: (0933) 265-00; Telex: 911420.

▸ **Villa Sant'Andrea.** Via Nazionale 137, 98030 **Mazzarò.** Tel: (0942) 231-25; Telex: 980077.

▸ **Scari.** Contrada Scari, 98050 **Stromboli.** Tel: (090) 98-60-06.

▸ **La Sciara Residence.** Piscità, via Cincotta, 98050 **Stromboli.** Tel: (090) 986-04.

▸ **La Sirenetta-Park Hotel.** Ficogrande, 98050 **Stromboli.** Tel: (090) 986-25.

▸ **Splendid la Torre.** Via Piano di Gallo 11, 90151 **Mondello.** Tel: (091) 45-02-22.

▸ **Grande Albergo del Terme.** Lungomare Nuove Terme, 92019 **Sciacca.** Tel: (0925) 231-33.

▸ **Torre Macauda.** Statale 115, 92019 **Sciacca.** Tel: (0925) 268-00.

SARDINIA

By Barbara Hults

If a poll was taken of the most beautiful beaches in the world, Sardinia's would be close to the top—and almost certainly in first place if the choices were limited to Europe alone.

Although the most famous beaches line the exquisite Costa Smeralda in the north, beach lovers could happily follow the island's entire perimeter, ducking down roads to find silvery-blue sea coves where wild rock formations and windswept pines frame the water. Even though the cement blocks of modern developments line many coastal areas, a private beach is still not hard to find.

The center of the island is mountainous: rugged and desolate as the moon in some places, or lush with tropical vegetation in almost uninhabited valleys. From this ancient mystical environment the *nuraghi* arose—conical stone towers used as fortress and home by the Sards before time was counted on the island. At Nuoro the settlement is especially vast, but *nuraghi* are in plentiful supply in all of Sardinia; some put the count at seven thousand.

Sardinian menus may specialize in stuffed snails, smoked tuna roe, wild boar ham, lobster, and fish of all the sea's sizes, shapes, and colors, and all sparkling fresh. Desserts of honey and bitter almonds and a good Vernaccia wine add the final note to dinner alfresco, overlooking the ever-near seacoast.

MAJOR INTEREST

The beaches
The *nuraghi*

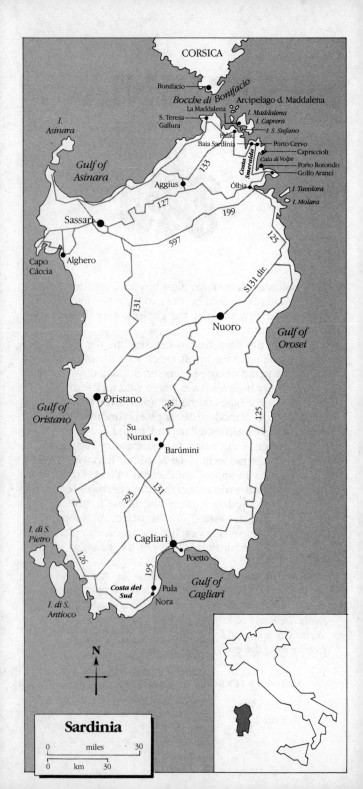

Porto Cervo and the Costa Smeralda, and the
    nearby islands of La Maddalena and Caprera
The grottoes, especially the Grotte di Nettuno
The cities: Alghero, Cagliari, and Sassari

Sardinia's past is dated from the *nuraghi* of the 15th
century B.C. The first settlers were Paleolithic people
about whom little is known. Later, Phoenicians and Carthaginians established bases, followed by Greeks, Etruscans,
and Romans. Settlers from Genoa and Pisa were much at
home here, and left their brightly striped churches as
evidence. In 1297 the pope made James of Aragon ruler of
Sardinia and Corsica, thus creating a new kingdom. During the 15th century Spain let viceroys run its colonies,
here, as in Sicily, for the most part without regard for
popular needs or requests. The War of Spanish Succession ended all that. In 1718 the Congress of London gave
the crown of Sicily and Sardinia to the dukes of Savoy,
who held Sardinia until 1861, when it joined the newly
formed kingdom of Italy. In 1948 Sardinia became an
autonomous region of the Repubblica Italiana.

One varied itinerary would begin at Cagliari and go to
Nuoro, Alghero, and Sassari, ending at the resorts of the
Costa Smeralda, having covered a bit of coast, of *nuraghi,*
of cities, and ending on a note of luxury, where warnings
about getting a suntan are as likely as warnings against
fresh air.

Cagliari

Cagliari, southern Sardinia's port, is part of a province
where sandy beaches and rocky cliffs, a sea jumping with
fish, and a usually mild climate set the tone. Here too are
the dwarf horses that run wild on the basalt plateau of the
Giara, near Tulli. In the city itself, the **Duomo** at the
center of town has been closed for repairs, but its museum contains works from its 14th-century past. The
Torre dell'Elefante nearby is a Pisan tower of 1307, and
from it the view of the city, the gulfs, and lakes is superb.
To the north is the **Museo Nazionale Archeologico**,
which has the most important collection of Sardinian
culture on the island. The first room looks at the prehistoric age, which seems not that long ago here. Tiny
bronze statuettes (more than five hundred have been
found) show the early people dressed in cloaks and caps,
tending sheep as the shepherds do today. Statues of

witches and earth goddesses provoke a sense of mystery, and the later rooms display Punic and Roman relics. The gold Punic jewelry splendidly evokes the era past.

Nearby, at the **piazza Arsenale**, modern museum rooms have been built in the fortress walls, overlooking the beach and salt marshes. A finer view is found from the old **Castello** not far off in the Old City. From the Orto Botanico (botanical gardens), to the north on viale Fra Ignazio da Laconi, the view of the sunset over the gulf is unforgettable.

It's time for a lobster, and for that you go to the beach of Poetto (bus service available), where **Ottagono** will present one in salad, Catalan style, or baked or au gratin. Try the sea urchins (*ricci*) too, best in months that contain an *r*. The beach beyond Poetto deserves an after-dinner walk. In Old Cagliari, **St. Remy**, in a former Medieval monastery's herbalist shop, is also prepared to keep your sea appetite satisfied or feed you cheese-stuffed veal, a specialty (*fagottini St. Remy*). Stay in town at the **Regina Margherita** or along the coast at the **Cormoran**, a 45-minute drive from Cagliari, on a beach where wind surfing is popular—and with a swimming pool and tennis courts—or at nearby **Capo Sant' Elia** on the sea.

Outside Cagliari

Near Cagliari is **Nora**, accessible by taking a bus to Pula, then walking two miles south. In 700 B.C. Nora was a Phoenician seaport and commercial center; then Carthage and later Rome intruded, and the Vandals finished it off. Now excavations have brought it back to the world. Roman temples and amphitheaters, Punic houses, a temple to the goddess Tanit, revered in the Mediterranean, and other evidence of its well-developed life are to be seen.

You can travel from Cagliari to Nuoro along interior roads for mountain scenery, or you may take the coastal route. The bus is faster than the train.

If beaches are your pleasure, head toward the southwest, where the **Costa del Sud**'s rocky promontory shelters some of the island's lovely shoreline, unspoiled by industry or dreary development.

Be sure to travel by way of Barumini, in the fertile countryside to the north, because less than a km (half a mile) to the east of it are the *nuraghi* of **Su Nuraxi**. These are the best preserved of Sardinia's stone houses, impressively set on a hilltop.

If you do stop at Barumini, don't then decide to omit the *nuraghe* of **Nuoro**, on the "if you've seen one *nuraghe* you've seen Nuoro" principle, for it isn't so. Nuoro has the additional fascination of traditional peasant dress, simple in town, and in greater variety in the **Museo della Vita e delle Tradizioni Popolari Sarde**, where costumes from all over the island are lovingly displayed. The wild spirit of Sardinia is to be found in mountain towns of less visitor appeal than Nuoro, and to see them requires a long, lovely time to spend exploring. You'll get a sense of this spirit in Nuoro's surrounding area, the *bargagla*, as the wilderness is called. The 1929 Nobel Prize–winning writer Grazia Deledda was a child of Nuoro. Stay at the rustic **Fratelli Sacchi**, 8 km (5 miles) to the east, where the garden is fragrant and the trout *alla Vernaccia* (Vernaccia is Sardinia's excellent dry wine) is a highlight of the country-style menu.

Alghero lies to the northwest on a wide, beautiful coastal plain, and is entirely charming. Stay at the comfortable **Villa Las Tronas**, on its own rocky peninsula, where the royal family of Italy once came to sun. It's comfortably palatial still, with elaborate furnishings and only 31 rooms, ensuring tranquillity.

Great sea ramparts constructed by the sea-blooded Genoese still protect Alghero from the sea, but no longer from the Spanish, who seem to have moved in comfortably, as the paella and the via Barcelonetta suggest. A fishing village is what Alghero still is, and proudly so. Wander the Old City and walk along the ramparts. The **church of San Francesco**, off via Carlo Alberto, opens to a lovely Gothic interior; on charmingly Medieval via Principe Umberto stands the Casa Doria, named for Genoa's seagoing noble clan. Down the street you can see the cathedral, gleaming from a majolica-tiled gable.

An excursion to **Grotte di Nettuno**—a world of stalactites—can be arranged by one of the two morning boats from Alghero. You can also take the bus—a dazzling coastline ride—to Capo Caccia and walk down the 671 hand-cut steps to the grotto, but then you have to walk back up, remember. The beaches are rather crowded in season near here, but if you go early you can avoid the crowds.

Sassari, an industrial city, can be visited easily from the Costa Smeralda. Its **Museo Sanna** covers centuries of Sardinian art, and the permanent exhibition of arts and crafts in the public garden near the city's center is a delight. The picturesque 13th-century **Duomo**, often renovated, has its own museum of treasures. Have lunch at **Il Senato** in the historic center of town: Lobster, crab, or other Sardinian specialties make a fine meal, and the risotto with artichokes is especially good.

The Costa Smeralda
and Other Resort Areas

The Costa Smeralda (Emerald Coast) was the dream of the Aga Khan, who is now also the head of CIGA hotels. It's as glamorous as a resort can be, at least when the right people are there. Yachts of the nouveau jostle the simpler vessels of the old guard; the light, the water, the beaches—all are like Impressionist watercolors. At the **Cala di Volpe** resort complex the look is a Moorish village (Moor as in oil-rich sheik, that is). It's beautifully and simply arranged and furnished, and the **Romazzino**, also at Cala di Volpe (the city's name too), has lawns that run down to the sea. Both are "villages" with individual bungalows. The **Sporting** at Porto Rotondo is elegantly simple and surrounded with sea views. If the sporting life is not what you had in mind, go to the **Capriccioli**, a small, rustic hotel that the Azara family has run for a quarter century. Its restaurant opens to grand views of the coast. The town (same name as hotel) lies along the eastern shore, next to Cala di Volpe.

Porto Cervo, on a northern cape, is home of the charming **Hotel Pitrizza**, elegant and simple, which is the style of the coast. Here that atmosphere is even more carefully fulfilled, indeed, it's downright clubby, with no discos, shops, or anything else to detract from its serenity. Each villa has four to six rooms and a private terrace, garden, or patio. There is no problem about space to moor a yacht, and the private beach will ensure repose. If you need to ask the price, go to the pretty **Balocco** here instead, or the **Smeralda Beach** at Baia Sardinia farther west.

Even farther west, off the gilded path but still stylish, is **Shardana** at Santa Teresa Gallura. Separate bungalows are set amid myrtle and juniper; beach, restaurant, piano bar, and water sports are available, at about a quarter the price of the northeastern coast. Dine at the **Canne al**

Vento on homemade ravioli Sardinian style, and on all things marine.

Elsewhere Around Sardinia

To the south of Santa Teresa Gallura, the town of **Aggius** is famous for the rough carpet weaves and wall hangings called *orbacce*.

Off the Costa Smeralda to the north lies the **Archipelago della Maddalena**, seven windswept islands. Napoléon landed on one (Santo Stefano) and fired on another (La Maddalena). The Sardinian captain Millelire made quick work of the little corporal, and now the islands know peace. Garibaldi is also at peace here, in a simple tomb near the house he bought on Caprera in 1855. The house is kept as he left it when he died on June 2, 1882. Stay at the **Nido d'Aquila** on Maddalena and dine there at the **Grotta da Setteotto**.

Ferries for the Maddalenas leave from Palau on the mainland or from Santa Teresa Gallura. If you want, you can continue north by ferry to Bonifacio, Bonaparte's Corsican home in exile. Or head along the east coast to Olbia, where ferries or aircraft will take you back to the mainland.

GETTING AROUND
Airplanes and ferries from the mainland service Sardinian cities. Tirrenia Line ferries are the most frequently used vessels for passengers and cars. Civitavecchia, north of Rome, is the port from which several ferries per day and an overnight boat leave for the 13-hour trip to Olbia (you can see the advantage of booking by night). The Italian railroad ferry service from Civitavecchia to Golfo Aranci near Olbia takes about eight hours. Flying has obvious advantages; airports are located in Alghero, Cagliari, and Olbia.

Ferry service is also available on the Tirrenia Line from Genoa to Cagliari (19 hours) and Olbia (12½ hours). Naples, Palermo, and Trápani also maintain ferry service (15-, 14-, and 10-hour trips respectively).

On the island rent a car if possible. Trains are slow, as are buses, often being the local variety, though that may be pleasant. If you are traveling without a car, expect to spend a few extra days in transit.

ACCOMMODATIONS REFERENCE

▶ **Cala di Volpe**. 07020 **Cala di Volpe**. Tel: (0789) 960-83.

▶ **Capo Sant'Elia**. Via Calamosca, 09100 **Cala Mosca**. Tel: (070) 37-02-52.

▶ **Capriccioli**. 07020 **Porto Cervo**. Tel: (0789) 960-04.

▶ **Cormoran**. 09049 **Capo Boi**. Tel: (070) 79-14-01.

▶ **Pitrizza**. Liscia di Vacca, 07020 **Porto Cervo**. Tel: (0789) 915-00.

▶ **Regina Margherita**. Viale Regina Margherita 44, 09100 **Cagliari**. Tel: (070) 670-03-42.

▶ **Romazzino**. Romazzino 07020 **Cala di Volpe**. Tel: (0789) 960-20.

▶ **Shardana**. Santa Reparata 07028 **Santa Teresa Gallura**. Tel: (0789) 75-40-31.

▶ **Smeralda Beach**. 07021 **Baia Sardinia**. Tel: (0789) 990-46.

▶ **Sporting Hotel**. 07026 **Porto Rotondo**. Tel: (0789) 340-05.

▶ **Villa Las Tronas**. Lungomare Valencia 1, 07041 **Alghero**. Tel: (079) 97-53-90.

CHRONOLOGY OF THE HISTORY OF ITALY

Prehistory

Italian prehistory extends at least to 700,000 B.C., when the earliest known relics of humanoids were left in Molise in central Italy. On the rugged hillsides of Sardinia, Stone Age inhabitants built towers called *nuraghi,* and archaeologists in Apulia and Sicily have uncovered Paleolithic cave drawings. After 3000 B.C. the peninsula was settled by migrating Indo-Europeans.

The sea-travelling Phoenicians established settlements in western Sicily and Sardinia during the eighth century B.C. from their base in Carthage; their influence spread across the sea to the shores of Latium.

Between the eighth and fifth centuries B.C., Italy was colonized in the north and south by Etruscans and Greeks respectively. The Etruscans, an advanced people probably from Asia Minor, are believed to have absorbed the culture of Greece without relinquishing their own cultural identity. Little is known about their architecture, but wall paintings and decorated sarcophagi in their burial grounds attest to a pronounced realism, a love for drama, and an attraction to the grotesque.

The Greeks

In the early eighth century B.C. Greeks from various centers founded more than 40 colonies on the coasts of Sicily and southern Italy, which in the aggregate were called Magna Graecia. A number of pre-Socratic philosophers, including Pythagoras and Parmenides, flourished here. Plato himself lived here for a time. The Greek Doric temples in Sicily are more numerous and better preserved than those in Greece.

The Foundations of
the Roman Empire

Some of the most fertile expressions of Roman artistic creativity are in the areas of architecture, engineering, and urban planning. Highly successful open spaces, such as the forum, continue to ensure the vitality of civic and commercial life today. As Jacob Burckhardt observed, the Romans set the seal of immortality on everything they did.

The major architectural contribution of Roman art was the refinement of vaulted construction (for the vast spatial advantages it allowed) employed in the building of baths, amphitheaters, palaces, aqueducts, and triumphal arches. During the republican period (510–30 B.C.) portrait sculpture became more realistic, departing from the ideal.

- **753 B.C.:** According to the Roman author Varro, Rome is founded by Romulus on April 21.
- **800–500 B.C.:** Sardinia is occupied by Phoenicians from Carthage, who war with the Greeks and eventually take over large sections of Sicily.
- **600–501 B.C.:** Greeks bring olive tree to Italy.
- **700–500 B.C.:** Etruscan political and cultural power at its highest in Italy. Tarquinius driven out.
- **510 B.C.:** Rome is transformed from a kingdom into a republic. After numerous victorious battles against the Etruscans, the Greeks, and the Carthaginians, Rome establishes its supremacy.
- **500 B.C.:** The Greeks begin their intermittent war with the Carthaginians.
- **500–451 B.C.:** Viticulture is started in Italy; wine stored in wooden barrels.
- **494 B.C.:** 30 Latium cities form Latin League, led by Rome.
- **450 B.C.:** Rome formulates Twelve Tables of Law, based on Greek models.
- **396 B.C.:** Rome captures Etruscan city of Veii, which marks decline of Etruscan rule.
- **390 B.C.:** Gauls invade Italy and occupy Rome, which pays a huge ransom to them to leave.
- **348 B.C.:** League of Latin Cities dissolved.
- **312 B.C.:** The Roman Censor Appius Claudius Caecus completes construction of Appian aqueduct and begins Appian Way.

- **264–241** B.C.: First Punic War. Rome wars with Carthage and drives them out of Sicily, and their former territories become a Roman province.
- **220** B.C.: Flaminian Way finished.
- **219–201** B.C.: Hannibal crosses Alps, invades Italy, and captures Turin; defeats Romans at Lake Trasimeno (217 B.C.). Romans, led by Scipio, carry war back to Spain and Carthage; Hannibal is defeated by Scipio at Zama (203–202 B.C.).
- **209** B.C.: Taranto, the last Greek city-state in Italy, is subjugated by Rome.
- **149–146** B.C.: Third Punic War—Carthage destroyed.
- **133–17** B.C.: Sicily becomes the "granary of Rome." Numerous slave revolts, including one led by Spartacus, result in protracted, bitter wars; reform movement of the Gracchi.
- **60** B.C.: The first Triumvirate is created by Pompey, Crassus, and Julius Caesar.
- **59** B.C.: Roman historian, Livy, born. Dies A.D. 17.
- **58–51** B.C.: Julius Caesar conquers Gaul.
- **49–45** B.C.: Caesar defeats Pompey and writes his history of the Gallic wars. In 45 B.C. he is elected dictator for life.
- **44** B.C.: At the height of the internal wars in Rome, Julius Caesar is assassinated. His great-nephew and ward Octavius ushers in a new form of government, the *principate,* which soon takes on the characteristics of a monarchy.
- **43** B.C.: The second Triumvirate is formed, including Mark Antony, Lepidus, and Octavius, Caesar's great-nephew.
- **40** B.C.: Herod, at Rome, is appointed King of Judea.

The Early Empire

In the early Roman Empire the equestrian statue is perfected, as evidenced in the bronze statue of Marcus Aurelius (165 A.D.) on the Capitoline in Rome. Painting reaches its highest achievement in the Roman cities of Pompeii and Herculaneum.

- **31** B.C.: Battle of Actium; Mark Antony and Cleopatra defeated by Octavius, and commit suicide; Egypt becomes a Roman province.

- **30 B.C.–A.D. 14**: Octavius, in A.D. 27 given the name Augustus by the Senate, establishes the Roman Empire and presides over a cultural awakening (Vergil, Horace, Livy, Seneca, and Ovid are among the writers and thinkers of the time); Pantheon in Rome is begun.
- **A.D.14**: Tiberius assumes *principate,* followed by Caligula in A.D. 37.
- **54–68**: Reign of Nero; has his mother, Agrippina, and wife, Octavia, killed; commits suicide.
- **79**: Pompeii and Herculaneum are demolished with the eruption of Mount Vesuvius.
- **98–117**: Under the emperor Trajan, the Roman Empire reaches its pinnacle. It extends from Scotland to the Sahara and from the Danube to Mesopotamia.
- **161–180**: Reign of philosophical emperor Marcus Aurelius; writes his *Meditations;* beginning of barbarian attacks.
- **200**: Bishops of Rome gain predominant position. First 12 bishops of Rome are Greek; Victor (189–198) is first Latin-speaking bishop of Rome. Period of neo-Platonism.
- **212**: "Civis Romanus Sum"—every freeborn subject in Empire is granted Roman citizenship; building of Baths of Caracalla.
- **220**: Arabs, Germans, and Persians, among others, begin attacking the frontiers of the Roman Empire.
- **249–269**: Persecution of Christians increases.
- **284–305**: The Illyrian emperor Diocletian initiates drastic reforms in government and the social order. He introduces a tetrarchy: Two emperors (*augusti*) rule over the western half of the Empire and two over the eastern half.

Constantine and the
Later Empire

- **313**: Emperor Constantine (306–337) formally recognizes Christianity with the Edict of Milan. In 330 he moves the capital to Byzantium and renames the city Constantinople. Rome is in decline.
- **349–397**: Saint Ambrose becomes bishop of Milan (374); refuses surrender of church to Arians; converts and baptizes Saint Augustine of Hippo.

- **391:** Theodosius determines Christianity to be the state religion; becomes last ruler of a united Empire.
- **395:** The Roman Empire is divided into a western empire, with its capital at Ravenna, and an eastern empire (Constantinople).
- **410:** Alaric, king of the Visigoths, invades Rome; Saint Augustine writes *The City of God* (411).
- **425:** Valentinian III is Western Roman Emperor under guardianship of his mother, Galla Placidia; in 446 she erects her famous mausoleum in Ravenna. During fourth and fifth centuries, Latin begins to replace Greek as formal language of Church.
- **455:** The Vandals, led by Gaiseric, sack Rome.
- **476:** The German general Odoacer deposes Emperor Romulus Augustulus and brings an end to the western Roman Empire, although a strip of coast around Ravenna remains under eastern Roman rule until 751.

The Founding of the Holy Roman Empire

From the fourth century, when Constantine moved the capital from Rome to Byzantium, until the 13th century, Byzantine art, mainly Christian in its themes, dominates the Italian peninsula. The most significant monuments of early Byzantine art are in the catacombs and basilicas (Ravenna, Venice, and Rome).

- **480–543:** Saint Benedict of Nursia, patriarch of Western monasticism, devises his "rule"; Benedictine monks throughout Italy and Europe contribute to the preservation of culture, including ancient and Christian thought.
- **493:** Odoacer is succeeded by Theodoric the Great and other Ostrogoth chieftains.
- **500:** First plans for Vatican palace drawn up.
- **524:** Boethius, Roman scholar and adviser to Emperor Theodoric, is accused of treason and executed; while imprisoned, he writes his *De consolatione philosophiae,* which becomes immensely popular in Middle Ages and provides a Latin perspective on the barbarians in Italy; introduces Greek musical letter notations to West; transmits

the logic of Aristotle and, through use of Aristotle's categories, begins process of development of Christian faith into a theological science that culminates in Scholasticism about 600 years later.

- **532–552**: Ostrogoth kingdom of Italy occupied by Belisarius; Totila ends Byzantine rule in Italy and becomes king; begins ravaging Italy.
- **553**: The Byzantine emperor Justinian succeeds in reimposing the rule of Constantinople on Italy.
- **568–572**: The Lombard king Alboin drives the Byzantines out of northern Italy, Tuscany, and Umbria. Lombards establish strong principalities in the areas. The rule of the eastern empire extends to Ravenna, Rome, parts of the Adriatic coast, and sections of southern Italy.
- **590–604**: Papacy of Gregory the Great, architect of Medieval papacy.
- **751**: After the Lombards conquer most of Italy, the last Byzantine stronghold—Ravenna—falls.
- **754–756**: The Carolingian king Pepin defeats the Lombards and forces them to recognize Frankish sovereignty.
- **773–774**: Charlemagne unites the Lombard kingdom with the Frankish kingdom.
- **777**: Fraudulent fourth-century "Donation of Constantine" first mentioned; written in the eighth century, it establishes the legal supremacy of the papal monarchy and is invoked in the 11th century during papal and imperial rivalries.
- **800**: Charlemagne is crowned emperor in Rome by Pope Leo III. Only Friuli remains independent, under Lombard control. In southern Italy, the sea republics of Amalfi and Naples and the duchy of Gaeta seek protection from Byzantium. Sicily and Sardinia are conquered by the Arabs as Islam expands in the Mediterranean; the city of Rivo Alto, today's Venice, is founded.
- **Ninth century**: Rival states are established and anarchy reigns with the demise of the Carolingian Empire.
- **828**: Founding of St. Mark's, Venice.
- **846**: Arabs sack Rome and damage Vatican; destroy Venetian fleets.
- **879**: The pope and patriarch of Constantinople excommunicate each other.
- **962**: The German king Otto I is crowned emperor

and founds the Holy Roman Empire of the German Nation. His attempts to conquer southern Italy fail.

The Papacy and the Empire

The Romanesque style developed from Early Christian architecture in the 11th century and embraced numerous regional variations. In architecture, the Romanesque style is characterized by round arches and by large, simple geometric masses. The Duomo at Pisa is one of the finest examples. The figurative sculpture and the painting that began to appear in the Romanesque churches of the 11th century showed considerable Byzantine influence.

- **1000–1200:** The Normans combine southern Italy and Sicily into a new kingdom. Byzantine and Arab cultural influences continue. Independent city-states emerge. The sea republics of Genoa, Pisa, and Venice emerge.
- **1022–1027:** Guido d'Arezzo improves musical notation and introduces solmization in music (do, re, mi . . .).
- **1041:** Important medical work is begun at medical school in Salerno.
- **1053:** Under the leadership of Robert Guiscard, the Normans conquer Pope Leo IX's forces in Apulia. In 1059 the pope invests him with southern Italy and Sicily.
- **1076–1122:** In the confrontation between the empire and the papacy, known as the Investiture Conflict, the pope distances himself from the emperor and focuses on the emerging states.
- **1077:** The excommunicated emperor Henry IV humbles himself before pope Gregory VII.
- **1095:** Pope Urban II declares First Crusade.
- **1119:** Establishment of the first university in Europe at Bologna.
- **1130:** Roger II founds the Norman kingdom in Italy and is crowned king of Naples and Sicily.
- **1152–1190:** Frederick Barbarossa of Hohenstaufen wars with Lombard cities and destroys Milan; in the Battle of Legnano (1176) Lombard cities defeat Barbarossa. Saint Francis of Assisi is born (1182); communes arise and northern and central cities in Italy experiment with self-government.

- **1194–1268**: Southern Italy and Sicily come under Hohenstaufen rule. Emperor Frederick II moves the palace from Palermo to Naples. Under the Hohenstaufen, magnificent fortresses are built all over southern Italy, from Sicily to Apulia.
- **1198–1216**: Papacy of Innocent III, great church reformer; Fourth Crusade; Venice leads in fighting Constantinople; introduction of Arabic numerals in Europe; Saint Francis issues first rules of brotherhood of Franciscans.
- **1224–1250**: University is founded at Naples; Inquisition under Dominicans commences; Pope Gregory IX excommunicates Frederick II; Frederick II's court establishes first school of Italian poetry; crusades and commerce enlarge intellectual boundaries of Italy, and Arab scholars translate the Greek classics; commercial and industrial boom in northern and central Italy.
- **1256**: Hundred Years War between Venice and Genoa begins.
- **1265**: Pope Clement IV gives Sicily and southern Italy to Count Charles I of Anjou as a fief. The French put an end to the rule of the Hohenstaufen. In 1268 the last of the Hohenstaufen, Conradin, is beheaded in Naples.

The Renaissance and the Emergence of the City-States

From 1250 to 1600 a politically fragmented Italy saw its city-states grow in both cultural and economic importance. During this same period humanists (Dante, Petrarch, Boccaccio) rediscovered ancient (so-called Classical) literature.

The Gothic style, represented most notably in church architecture by pointed arches, was introduced into Italy by the mendicant orders. The earliest Gothic church in Italy was completed in Assisi in 1253. The Duomo in Milan maintains true northern Gothic style; large public buildings and palaces, among them the Palazzo Vecchio in Florence and the Doges' Palace in Venice, also exemplify its lofty principles. Gothic painting was advanced by Giotto (1266–1337), who, breaking away from Byzantine iconography, imbued biblical scenes with naturalism and humanism.

With the patronage of wealthy ruling princes, and a theologically less restrictive approach to architecture, painting, and sculpture, the Renaissance evolved, its roots in Classical antiquity. In 15th-century Florence it reached its zenith. The architects of the Quattrocento (1400s), as the early Renaissance is known, adopted a new style modeled on Classical architectural forms. The subject matter of sculpture, heavily influenced by Classical art, now included secular, mythological, and historical themes. Portrait sculpture emphasized greater realism.

- **Late 13th–early 14th century**: Thomas Aquinas (1225–1274) writes *Summa contra Gentiles* and *Summa theologica;* teaches at Orvieto; Cimabue begins to soften the Byzantine look in art; Marco Polo (1254–1324) journeys to China, returns to Italy in 1295. Giotto (1266–1337) revolutionizes painting by cracking Byzantine mold; frescoes painted in Assisi and Padua. Dante Alighieri (1265–1321) writes *La vita nuova* (1290); *Divina commedia* (1307). Pisano family of sculptors works in major cities. Boccaccio (1230–1313) writes the *Decameron.* Petrarch crowned poet on the Capitol (1304); Pisa University founded; plague devastates Italy and rest of Europe.

- **1282**: The rule of the House of Anjou over Sicily comes to an end with the massacre in Palermo of the French, an event known as the "Sicilian Vespers." Charles of Anjou retains only the kingdom of Naples.

- **14th century**: Italian cities divide their allegiance between pope (Guelphs) and emperor (Ghibellines). The sea republic of Venice is at the height of its power. Florence establishes its reign over a large section of north and central Italy. In Milan the House of Visconti emerges as sole ruler (later replaced by the Sforzas).

- **Late 14th–early 15th century**: Flourishing artistic period—works of Botticelli, Titian, Bramante, Piero della Francesca, Perugino. Ascent of Medici in Italy; become bankers to papacy. Great Schism (1378–1417) begins after Pope Gregory XI dies; two popes elected. Papal exile in Avignon (1309–1377); Saint Catherine of Siena (1347–1380) helps bring back popes from Avignon. Brunelleschi (1377–1446) discovers perspective; Manuel Chrysolorus opens Greek classes in Florence

(1396); beginning of revival of Greek literature in Italy; Alberti (1404–1472), architect, writer, sculptor, poet—the Renaissance's Universal Man—publishes treatises on painting and architecture in which he systematizes the problems of perspective; Platonic academy founded in Florence (1440); Christoper Columbus discovers America (1492).

- **1442**: Alfonso IV, king of Aragon, conquers Naples and becomes "King of the Two Sicilies."
- **1453**: Fall of Constantinople.
- **1469**: Under Lorenzo il Magnifico, the Medici of Florence are at their supreme power.
- **1493**: Lodovico "Il Moro" Sforza is invested with the duchy of Milan.
- **1494**: Pope Alexander VI publishes bull dividing New World between Spain and Portugal.
- **1463–1498**: Giovanni Pico della Mirandola (1463–1494), humanist and wandering scholar writes *On the Dignity of Man*. Aldine Press in Venice publishes comedies of Aristophanes.

The High Renaissance

From the first half of the 16th century onward the High Renaissance spread to the great cities and courts of Europe. It was during this period that Donato Bramante (1444–1514) designed the new St. Peter's in Rome, and Michelangelo Buonarotti (1475–1564) executed the plan. Michelangelo's works in Florence included the famous statue *David* and the mausoleum of the Medici in San Lorenzo. In Rome he painted the magnificent ceiling frescoes in the Sistine Chapel. Leonardo da Vinci (1452–1519), sculptor, architect, painter, scientist, and builder, worked in Florence, Rome, France, and at the Sforza court in Milan. The Neoclassical architecture of Andrea Palladio (1508–1580) evoked the splendor of ancient Rome in San Giorgio in Venice and the Venetian villas, and provided a model for all of Europe. Titian's (1477–1576) paintings presaged the development of the Baroque style.

- **1494–1498**: Leonardo da Vinci paints *Last Supper* and develops his scientific studies.
- **1496**: Michelangelo's first stay in Rome; begins to paint Sistine Chapel (1508).
- **16th century**: The Austrian House of Habsburg and

the French kings begin their struggle for northern Italy, which is divided into numerous small states. Subsequently, almost all ruling houses of Italy are subjugated by either the Austrian or the Spanish line of the House of Habsburg. Palladio works on villas, theaters, and churches in the Veneto.

- **1507**: Martin Luther ordained; posts 95 theses in Wittenberg (1517); Diet of Worms (1521) marks beginning of Reformation.
- **1521**: Machiavelli writes *Dell'arte della guerra,* and *Il Principe* in 1532.
- **1527**: Castiglione writes *Il libro del cortegiano;* Rome sacked by Charles V's troops.
- **1545**: Council of Trent meets to discuss Reformation and establish principles of Counter-Reformation.
- **1550**: Vasari publishes *Lives of the Artists.*
- **1580**: Coffee from Turkey introduced in Italy.
- **1580–1581**: Montaigne travels in Italy.
- **1587**: Monteverdi's first madrigals composed.
- **1590**: Commedia dell'Arte company begins.
- **1596**: Shakespeare's *Merchant of Venice* performed.

The 16th Century to the Napoleonic Era

The art of the Counter-Reformation (mid-16th century to mid-17th century) became known as Mannerism because it emphasized the study of attitudes and expression. The Baroque style developed out of Mannerism in the 17th century and the early part of the 18th century. Painters of the Baroque style included Caravaggio (1573–1610), who delighted in the theatrical and emphasized the effects of lighting, movement, perspective, and trompe l'oeil.

No form of music is more Italian by nature than opera, and no country is more passionate about opera than Italy. Monteverdi (1567–1643) was the first composer to make opera available to a wider audience. The operatic music of Scarlatti (1660–1725) and Pergolesi (1710–1736) set the stage for the flowering of Italian opera in the next century.

- **1598–1680**: Life and works of Bernini, master spirit of Baroque, in architecture and sculpture; splendid colonnade of St. Peter's.

- **1600**: First opera, Florence.
- **1633**: Galileo is forced by the Roman Inquisition to recant his acceptance of the Copernican view of the universe.
- **1637**: First public opera house opened in Venice.
- **17th century**: The popes join the French in the battle against the Spanish-Austrian rulers. Savoy becomes the strongest state in northern Italy.
- **1706**: As a result of the victory of Prince Eugene near Turin, Austria controls all of Lombardy.
- **1706–1711**: Handel travels in Italy.
- **1713**: Following the Spanish War of Succession, Austria receives the kingdom of Naples and the island of Sardinia. Austria is now the major power in Italy.
- **1713–1714**: With the Treaty of Utrecht, Austria receives large sections of central Italy, but in return must yield Naples and Sicily to the Spanish Bourbons. With the demise of the Medici in Florence, the Grand Duchy of Tuscany also becomes part of Austria.
- **1769–1771**: Mozart works in Rome, writes three symphonies there: K. 81, 97, 95; string quartet K. 80.
- **1786–1788**: Goethe travels through Italy. His *Italian Journey,* based on the journals he kept during his two visits, is alive with vivid detail of 18th-century Italy.
- **1796**: Napoléon Bonaparte begins his Italian campaign.
- **1797**: The French defeat the Austrians at Marengo. With the Peace of Campoformio, Italy is ruled by France. Austria retains Venice and land south of the Adige. Eventually, Napoléon dissolves the papal states and incorporates them into Italy.
- **1805**: Napoléon crowns himself king of Italy.
- **1806**: Joseph Bonaparte, Napoléon's brother, becomes king of Naples.
- **1809**: The papal states are annexed to the French empire. Pope Pius VII is imprisoned in France in 1812.
- **1814**: The demise of the Napoleonic regime. Pope Pius VII returns to Rome.

The 19th-Century
Unification Movement

The ornate Baroque style of the 18th century gave way to the simpler lines of Classicism (or Neoclassicism), which was modeled after Greek and Roman art forms. The foremost Italian painter of the style was Antonio Canova (1757–1822). Verdi (1813–1901), whose works include *Rigoletto, Il Trovatore, Aida,* and *Otello,* escalated opera to an extraordinarily popular music form. Puccini (1858–1924) continued the development of the operatic form with *La Bohème, Tosca, Madama Butterfly, Gianni Schicchi,* and *Turandot.*

- **1814–15:** The Congress of Vienna reestablishes the former state structure. The supremacy of Austria in Italy is reaffirmed. Lombardy and Veneto become Austrian provinces. Tuscany is placed under Austrian rule, and Naples and Sicily are invaded. The papal states are reinstated.

- **1831:** Following several popular revolts against the Austrians, Giuseppe Mazzini founds the secret movement for independence, "Young Italy." The national resentment of the Italians against the Austrians (the *Risorgimento*) grows.

- **1848:** A general insurrection against Austria under the leadership of the king of Sardinia is crushed by the Austrians.

- **1849–1850:** Victor Emmanuel II of the House of Savoy becomes king of Sardinia. Cavour's government organizes the state of Piedmont.

- **1854:** Piedmont fights alongside Britain and France in the Crimean War.

- **1858:** Cavour and Napoléon III create an alliance at Plombières.

- **1859:** War is declared by Austria against France and Piedmont. Victor Emmanuel II places his army under the command of Garibaldi. Franco-Piedmont victories result in Piedmont obtaining Lombardy, and France obtaining Savoy and the county of Nice.

- **1860–1861:** Garibaldi frees the south from the Bourbons. The kingdom of Italy is proclaimed with Turin as its capital. Victor Emmanuel II is crowned.

- **1866:** Italy declares war on Austria but is defeated. The Austrian admiral Tefgthoff sinks the entire

Italian fleet. The Prussians join Italy and defeat the Austrians near Königgrätz, forcing them to retreat from Italy.

- **1866–1952**: Life and works of the Neapolitan philosopher, Benedetto Croce.
- **1869–1907**: Henry James makes frequent trips to Italy; his book *Italian Hours* recounts his impressions.
- **1870**: France withdraws its troops from the papal states and Rome becomes the capital of Italy. The Italian unification is complete. The pope retains sovereignty over Vatican City.
- **1882**: Italy makes peace with Austria. Under Umberto I, Italy forms the Triple Alliance with Germany and Austria-Hungary.

Italy in the 20th Century

- **1900**: King Umberto I is assassinated, and Victor Emmanuel III ascends to the throne.
- **1909**: Marconi receives Nobel prize in physics.
- **1913–1934**: Works of Luigi Pirandello; receives Nobel prize for literature (1934).
- **1915**: Although initially neutral, with territorial guarantees from Britain and France, Italy declares war on Germany and Austria, annexes Istria, Venezia-Giulia, and Trentino–Alto Adige.
- **1919**: With the peace treaty of St.-Germain-en-Laye, Italy receives South Tirol up to the Brenner Pass, Istria, and a number of Dalmatian Islands.
- **1922–1926**: After his march on Rome, Benito Mussolini is granted dictatorial powers by parliament and his Fascists take over the government.
- **1929**: The conflict between church and state is settled with the Lateran Pact. The Vatican is established.
- **1935–1936**: Italy invades and annexes Abyssinia in North Africa.
- **1936**: Germany and Italy enter into the "Rome-Berlin Axis." Italian troops fight for Franco in Spain.
- **1940**: Although at first remaining nonbelligerent, Italy sides with Nazi Germany and declares war on France and Britain.
- **1941**: Italy loses Abyssinia.
- **1942**: Enrico Fermi splits the atom.

- **1943**: Allied troops land in southern Italy and conquer Sicily. The Italian forces surrender; Mussolini is arrested and the Fascist government falls.
- **1945**: The German army surrenders. While fleeing, Mussolini is executed by partisans. The Christian Democrat Party forms a government led by de Gasperi.
- **1946**: King Victor Emmanuel III abdicates.
- **1947**: In the Treaty of Paris, Italy cedes Istria to Yugoslavia, and the Dodecanese to Greece. Italy renounces its colonies.
- **1953**: The Christian Democrat Party loses control; the frequent rise and fall of governments becomes the norm.
- **1954**: Trieste is divided between Yugoslavia and Italy.
- **1957**: The European Economic Community (EEC) is founded in Rome. The reconstruction of the country moves quickly.
- **1966**: North and central Italy are flooded; irreplaceable works of art in Florence and other cities are destroyed.
- **1970**: Following widespread strikes and unrest, the Statuto del Lavoratore (the statute of the worker) provides job security.
- **1976**: Earthquakes in Friuli and in the province of Udine cause severe damage.
- **1978**: Aldo Moro, chairman of the Christian Democrat Party, is kidnapped by the Red Brigade and found murdered 54 days later.
- **1980**: Severe earthquakes rock southern Italy.
- **1981**: Pope John Paul II is gravely injured in an attack.
- **1983**: Bettino Craxi is the first Social Democrat to become head of the Italian government.
- **1987**: Italy ranks fifth among Common Market countries as an economic power, nosing out Great Britain.

INDEX

WHEN TRAVELLING, PACK

All the Penguin Travel Guides offer you the selective and up-to-date information you need to plan and enjoy your vacations. Written by travel writers who really know the areas they cover, The Penguin Travel Guides are lively, reliable, and easy to use. So remember, when travelling, pack a Penguin.

☐ *The Penguin Guide to Australia 1989*
  0-14-019905-5 $11.95

☐ *The Penguin Guide to Canada 1989*
  0-14-019906-3 $12.95

☐ *The Penguin Guide to the Caribbean 1989*
  0-14-019900-4 $9.95

☐ *The Penguin Guide to England and Wales 1989*
  0-14-019901-2 $12.95

☐ *The Penguin Guide to France 1989*
  0-14-019902-0 $14.95

☐ *The Penguin Guide to Ireland 1989*
  0-14-019904-7 $10.95

☐ *The Penguin Guide to Italy 1989*
  0-14-019903-9 $14.95

☐ *The Penguin Guide to New York City 1989*
  0-14-019907-1 $11.95
  (available March 1989)